D1146068

DISTANT THUNDER

DISTANT THUNDER

T. D. Griggs

First published in Great Britain in 2012 by Orion Books,
an imprint of The Orion Publishing Group Ltd
Orion House, 5 Upper Saint Martin's Lane
London WC2H 9EA

An Hachette UK Company

1 3 5 7 9 10 8 6 4 2

A CIP catalogue record for this book is
available from the British Library.

ISBN (Hardback) 978 1 4091 0190 1
ISBN (Trade Paperback) 978 1 4091 0191 8

Typeset at The Spartan Press Ltd,
Lymington, Hants

Printed in Great Britain by Clays Ltd,
St Ives plc

The Orion Publishing Group's policy is to use papers that
are natural, renewable and recyclable products and
made from wood grown in sustainable forests. The logging
and manufacturing processes are expected to conform to
the environmental regulations of the country of origin.

www.orionbooks.co.uk

To Mr A. L. McTiffin, of the then Sutton County Grammar School . . .
because everyone needs a great teacher, and he was mine.

Acknowledgments

As ever my particular love and thanks go to my wife Jenny. No-one can do this sort of thing without a champion, and I could not ask for a doughtier one. My gratitude also goes to all the usual suspects, those long suffering friends and family who have followed *Distant Thunder*'s journey from conception to birth. They've never failed to sound encouraging – even when they have had to endure my tales of creative angst more than once . . . and sometimes more than twice.

The team at Orion have been keen supporters throughout this project, especially my publisher Bill Massey. The novel I originally discussed with him could hardly have been more different from the one you are holding in your hands, but if this gave him palpitations he hid them from me. If he had lost his nerve, I would certainly have lost mine, and I'm glad I didn't. And thanks finally to my agent, the inimitable Mark Lucas, without whom, as they say . . .

PART ONE

Bangalore, May 1893

1

She was singing. He could not see her, but somewhere in the dark and scented garden, his mother was singing.

The boy slipped in through the oleander bushes from the road and stopped among the flower beds to listen, struck by the beauty of her voice. He had heard nothing like it before. In church she cut a demure figure and trilled the hymns at a pitch painful in its purity, but tonight her voice was not pure, and nothing about it was demure. Nor was the song any kind of a hymn. He could hear sorrow in it, and yearning, and other passions he could not identify.

He stole forward across the moonlit lawn and through the bed of canna lilies under the veranda rail. A moth thrummed in the warm air close to his face. Her voice rose again and dipped, lifted once more. Now he could tell where she was, out by the stone tank at the side of the house where the servants drew their water. At last, from the corner of the veranda, he glimpsed her. She was all alone, swinging gently on the garden seat, her head thrown back and her long auburn hair loose across her shoulders. At her feet the moon rode like a silver plate among the lilies of the tank.

She stopped. He had made no sound, for he had learned to move like a cat, but just the same she turned her head and looked directly at him.

'Don't stand there like a startled faun, Frank. It doesn't suit you.' She patted the seat beside her. 'Come.'

He did not move. The moonlight had caught in her hair and her gown and transformed her into something from elfland. He was almost afraid of her.

She patted the seat again. 'Come along. It's all right, Father won't be home tonight. He sent word.' She rocked her head, mocking him. 'And no, I won't betray you.'

He crossed the dark lawn and climbed up onto the seat. She put her arm around his shoulders and he breathed in the warmth of her body.

'Did you think I didn't know about your little nocturnal adventures? You were with those native boys, I suppose. Javed, that Tamil boy from Cantonment Bazaar? And that silly braggart Ashok? You see, I am not so foolish as you imagine.'

'I never thought you foolish.'

3

'Well, I thank you for that. But I did not have to be so very clever either, to discover your secret. One need only keep one's eyes open and listen to the servants when they chatter. It is quite amusing when they don't know I have any Kanarese.'

Frank said nothing. He hadn't known it either.

'Not that I understand much. Not like you, Frank. I know you're as fluent as a bazaar urchin. But even I understand enough to have found you out.'

'You truly won't tell Papa?'

'Don't be silly. I'd come with you if I could. The bazaar at night! The temple ruins! The river! How wonderful it all must be when you're fourteen years old.' She paused. 'When you're any age.'

'It's dangerous,' he said stoutly. 'You wouldn't like it. It's dirty and there are thieves and wild animals where we go.'

'Really?' She squeezed his shoulders playfully. 'I shouldn't mind if I had you to protect me.'

'I will always protect you.'

'Is that what you want? To be my protector?' She laughed. 'You'd set yourself a task there.'

He looked down, embarrassed by her teasing, and she squeezed his shoulders again.

'You're a silly thing, Frank. But very well. You can be my knight in shining armour.' She made big eyes. 'Will you vow, sir knight, to take my part against all the world, to uphold my honour against all comers, and to avenge all wrongs against me?'

He raised his eyes to hers. 'Yes.'

She watched him in the darkness for a moment longer, her smile fading. Then she tilted her head back to look at the moon, where it hung like a lamp in the mango tree. Among the dry leaves something rustled, a long trickling sound: a python, probably, hunting mice. A frog fell like a dropped stone into the water of the tank, fragmenting the moon's image. Frank watched as the silver disc gradually re-formed itself and the water grew smooth once more. When she spoke again her voice was hardly more than a murmur.

'There was a time when I loved adventure, just like you,' she said. 'Can you credit that? You'd understand if you knew where I grew up. Huddersfield, a mean dark town in the north of England. And then one day your father came to give a magic-lantern talk at our church. I was just seventeen, and he was five-and-thirty. He wasn't rich but he had travelled and he seemed to know about everything. He was due to go back to India in a matter of weeks, to become a commercial agent in Peshawar. Can you imagine how that sounded to

4

me, Frank, who had never been further afield than Halifax? Peshawar! The Khyber Pass, the gateway to Kandahar and Kabul! The magic of it!'

From the servants' quarters behind one of the neighbouring bungalows a dog barked, and then set up a long hopeless howling until someone cursed at it and it fell silent again.

'So I found my adventure, Frank, in so far as a woman can find it. But I had not reckoned that there is also a journey of the spirit. And your father . . .' She seemed about to add something more, but then stopped herself. 'Your father is a good man. He has given me the journey I longed for, and unswerving loyalty, and he has given me you and Gifford. It is ungrateful in the extreme to ask for more.' Her voice caught.

He looked up at her. 'Do you ask for more, Mama?'

She gazed at him. Her eyes were bright and there was something like fear in them now. He touched her wrist, anxious to break the spell of that look, and she stared down at his hand.

'Frank,' she said, in a small and desperate voice. 'I'm just thirty-three years of age.'

2

Far ahead through the stormy night, Frank caught his first glimpse of the fires of Troy. Timbers groaned as the beaked prow plunged into luminous foam but when the ship lurched up once more towards the star-crowded sky he could see the pinpoint campfires of the Greeks encircling the city.

'Francis?'

Frank looked up quickly. 'Accusative plural, Father.'

'I shall not catch you out so easily, I see,' Mr Gray said. 'But I fear your thoughts were on the wine-dark sea once again, rather than on Greek grammar.'

Across the room, Frank's mother clicked her tongue. She was seated by the doors which stood open to the blue Indian night, fanning herself against the heat. That tiny click of irritation echoed in the room like the cocking of a revolver.

Frank kept his eyes on his book and hoped his mother would say nothing. His parents' tense little spats depressed him. Worse, they seemed always to be triggered by some niggling remark of his mother's. That made him angry with her and he hated himself when he was angry with her. Until just a few months ago, when they had moved south, she had always been his warmest friend, full of laughter and mischief. He stole a glance at her now. She sat in the wicker armchair by the open door to the veranda with her head thrown back and her auburn hair cascading almost to the floor. From time to time she would lift the mass of hair away from her damp neck and sigh at the heat. A few nights before in the scented garden she had not looked so very different, and this evening she was every bit as lovely. But the magic of that earlier scene had fled from her.

Mr Gray closed his tattered copy of Homer. 'I believe that's enough for this evening, Francis.'

'Oh, please,' his wife said, 'don't stop on my account.'

'My dear, we are evidently disturbing you.'

She turned sharply in her chair. 'Well, good Lord, Lewis. Latin? Greek? Poetry? *Tennyson*, for God's sake? Life's tedious enough without *Tennyson*. Do we all have to go through this ghastly routine every night?'

Mr Gray folded his hands quietly over the book. Frank kept very still. He felt hurt and confused: he liked the lessons his father gave; he was good at Latin and Greek and he especially enjoyed Tennyson – 'The Charge of the Light Brigade' was his favourite. He wondered if he was being disloyal to his mother by taking pleasure in these things and asked himself if in some obscure way these recurrent tensions were his fault.

'Francis,' his father said, 'you may leave the room.'

But it was Mrs Gray who got to her feet. 'No. Go on with your stupid studies if they amuse you. I'm glad somebody can find some entertainment in this place.' She swept out of the room and banged the door behind her.

Frank stared down at his hands, unsure where to look. Across the table he could hear his father putting books away in his leather case, and doing so with exaggerated care. Frank was sorry for him. He sensed that Mr Gray was out of his depth with these increasingly volatile scenes. He wanted to say something reassuring, but could not imagine how to begin.

Mr Gray ran out of small tasks to perform, and sat motionless on the other side of the table. The silence between them grew awkward. Frank decided then that he would slip away tonight. He rarely risked it unless his father was away from the house, but tonight he would go, and get away from this bewildering atmosphere of hostility.

A beetle the size of a walnut came blundering in through a gap in the screen and droned around the room until it collided with the dresser and clattered to the floor, its legs indignantly groping the air. Frank wondered if he dare go to the rescue of the struggling insect, and was grateful when his father did so, getting up and brushing the beetle into an empty water glass. Mr Gray walked over to the screen door and released the creature into the dark garden, then returned to the table.

'Your mother has been a little . . . unwell of late,' he said.

'Mama is ill?'

'No, not ill.' Mr Gray frowned, reconsidering his words. In the light of the oil lamp he suddenly looked elderly. 'No, that's not quite right. She is disappointed, Francis, to tell you the truth.'

His father was not given to confidences, and Frank did not want him to go on, but he seemed resolved to do so.

'She has not quite settled in Bangalore. She finds the city . . . oppressive.' Mr Gray cleared his throat. 'I wish you to understand this, Francis, so that you don't . . . think badly of her during this rather difficult time.'

Frank decided to risk the question that had been hovering at the back of his mind since he had heard his mother singing in the night-time garden.

'Does she want to return to England, Father?'

Mr Gray stared at him, caught off guard by the acuteness of the question.

'We did consider it, Francis. But my promotion, you see. One must take these opportunities in life.'

England? Frank had never been to England. He had seen pictures of cathedrals under grey skies, sluggish rivers with willows on the banks, stone castles and thatched cottages. He had heard a lot about drizzle and cold. But he knew too that England was the seat of raw power, and that its northern magic was every bit as potent as India's heat and mystery. He even knew that, somehow, one depended on the other. But to go there? To live? The thought was alien and terrifying, and yet his sense of adventure was stirred, and he felt a flicker of regret that so daring a scheme seemed to have died so meekly.

'Everything will be well, Francis,' Mr Gray said in a gentler voice, and in what was for him a gesture of some intimacy, he touched Frank's shoulder. 'You'll see.'

3

The locomotive's brakes shrieked like a fanfare of pagan trumpets, and in an instant steam and thunder filled the cavern of Bangalore City Station. With a final explosive exhalation the engine halted before them. Further down the train doors flew open and the wagons were engulfed in a flood of porters, food sellers, and third-class passengers climbing onto the carriage roofs with their bundles and sacks. Families clamoured to meet relatives and passengers threw down crates of live chickens, rolled sleeping mats, sacks of vegetables.

Gifford tugged at his father's hands and strained towards the locomotive.

'Steady on, old lad.' Mr Gray made a play of holding his straw hat on his head and let Gifford tow him along. 'Steady on, there.'

Gifford would be forgiven any excess of enthusiasm today, for it was his tenth birthday. As usual he'd shown no interest in party games with the neighbours' children nor ices on the bungalow lawn. All Gifford wanted – all he ever wanted – was to see the great engines, to be close to the massive intricacy of bolts, wheels, couplings. Gifford's fascination with how things worked was legendary. Items of household equipment had to be kept safe from him, or he would dismantle them to see how they functioned. The portable ice chest in the kitchen had fallen victim to his researches, and the aerated gas siphon. The ormolu mantel clock, a favourite of Mr Gray's, had run slow since Gifford had taken it apart while no one was watching him.

Mechanical mysteries didn't move Frank as they did his younger brother; but just the same he was happy to be at Bangalore City today. It lifted his spirit to see the Mysore State Railway locomotives thumping in from Tumku or the local trains from Cantonment Station just across the city. He liked to see the long distance cars of the South Indian Railway pulling in from as far away as Madras or Pondicherry on the other side of the subcontinent. He loved the romance of it, their liveries of royal blue, emerald and scarlet blazing in the sun. Their very names stirred him: Deccan Queen, Iron Duke, Southern Star.

His father had last brought him to the railway only two weeks ago. Then their visit had not been to the thronged passenger platforms but to the Dearborn & Company warehouse beside the dusty acres of marshalling yards nearly a mile away, where teams of sweating native labourers toiled among the freight cars. Here the brickwork was coal blackened and the stubby shunting engines far from magnificent. Nevertheless, Frank had loved the bustle of the place. He liked to eavesdrop on the labourers' bawdy chatter in the language of Karnataka, which his mother called Kanarese in the European fashion, but which he knew as Kannada. He liked to see the shunting engines chuff and clank as they nudged the wagons into order, making up the freight trains which would carry British manufactures up country, and haul Indian produce – raw cotton, rice, and tea – down to the distant ports.

8

He liked it because he could sense that it was here, amid the steam and the sweat, that the pulse of the Empire beat.

On that day they called in to the office above the warehouse, where Frank was introduced to the awesome Mr Furneaux, down from the company's city centre headquarters. Frank hadn't taken to Mr Furneaux, an austere man of fifty who wore a long dark coat despite the heat. Frank had recognised the need to be respectful to his father's new chief, but he didn't really see why his father should have a chief; he'd never had one in Peshawar. Mr Furneaux had insisted on putting a company driver and gig at their disposal, but this was not courtesy. It would never do, Mr Furneaux had said disapprovingly, for his deputy manager to be seen on foot. Frank was glad when he and his father could escape Mr Furneaux's gloomy office into the glaring heat of the day, and he guessed his father was as relieved as he was.

Mr Gray had shown him round the huge warehouses, cathedral spaces piled with sacks and smelling of spice and tea and hot dust. Then the repair shops where teams of workers laboured in a feverish clamour on trucks and locomotives and tenders, hammering, bolting, welding. They had spent an idle few minutes watching a new steam crane swinging merchandise off the flatcars.

'Do you know what's in those crates, Francis?' Mr Gray had asked. He stepped forward and thumped each crate in turn, an unusually extravagant gesture for him. 'Engine parts. Finished textiles. Jigs and tools. Everything from cutlery to canned fish. Yes! But more even than that. There's industry in these crates, Francis. There's prosperity. There's the future – our future.'

He was rarely so demonstrative, and it came to Frank that his father was an important man at last, and that being the son of an important man was not unpleasant. His father's promotion – late though it was – had dramatically raised the family's status, and now this huge and sprawling city was exploding Frank's own horizons. He sometimes missed the wildness of the north, but he could sense all around him a greater world opening.

Someone jostled him and Frank came back to the present. On the platform Gifford was still dragging Mr Gray towards the Bangalore Mail, a scarlet dragon crouching before him in wreaths of its own steam. A tall Sikh engineer in a blue turban was checking the locomotive's wheels as they approached, tapping each steel spoke with a hammer so that the metal sang. Steam escaped from the black recesses beneath the engine and engulfed the Sikh but he went about his work with the solemnity of a priest conducting a rite. Gifford broke free and ran so that the engineer had to drop his hammer and his dignity to catch him before he reached the wheels. The Sikh lifted the boy easily onto his hip.

'You like our engine, young sahib?'

'Yes! Yes!'

'We are also excessively fond of her. We call her the Maharani. Do you see the nameplate? She is an F Class 0-6-0 tank engine—'

'I know. Built by Dübs & Co. of Glasgow.'

'Correct!' The Sikh laughed in delight. 'A fine locomotive, and soon we will be building them here in India.'

Mr Gray came hurrying up. 'Gifford, let the gentleman get on with his business.'

But the engineer was enjoying his new role as guardian of the shrine. 'Perhaps the young sahib would like to blow the whistle?'

Mr Gray contrived to look awed. 'Is such a thing permitted?'

'Assuredly. I myself shall speak to the driver.'

'Gifford will be your friend for life.'

The engineer rocked his head. 'If only all friendship were as easy to win, sahib.' Gifford was already squirming in the Sikh's grip, straining towards the cab and the promised whistle. Laughing, the man carried him up onto the footplate. He spoke to a stout and sweating white man in braces and smut-blackened shirt. The man listened to the Sikh's explanation, glanced at Mr Gray through the steam and touched his cap. In a moment Gifford was borne high into the dim inner recesses of the cab, and Frank could see him pointing at gauges and dials and firing his endless questions at the two men.

Distracted, Frank did not at once notice that a tall young man had moved up to stand beside his father.

'Gray, is it?'

Frank looked up at the newcomer and saw his father do the same. The man was very tanned and wore a slouch hat with a leopard-skin band and a dusty khaki bush jacket. Behind him Frank glimpsed the porter who carried his luggage, a battered leather Gladstone bag, two hunting rifles in canvas cases, bandoliers of ammunition glinting like doubloons in the sun.

'I'm right, aren't I? You're Gray, the new Dearborns chap? I should have smoked you out long since.' The young man thrust out one lean brown hand. 'I'm Stokes. Assistant Collector. Sorry about the casual rig. Just got in from up-country.'

'Mr Stokes. Of course.' Frank's father took the offered hand and squared his shoulders a little.

Mr Stokes looked down at Frank and pulled a doleful face. His hazel eyes were alive with humour. 'You see how it is, young feller? Chaps like me are supposed to be here supporting your Papa's efforts, doing our bit, earning our keep, but we're so infernally lazy that we spend all our time hunting and take weeks even to introduce ourselves.'

He rested one hand on Frank's shoulder and turned his searchlight attention back to Mr Gray. Frank could tell that his father was flattered that Mr Stokes had recognised him. Frank felt flattered too, by the sheer fact of this man's attention, by the broad hand still resting on his shoulder. There was something both generous and imperious about young Mr Stokes, with his fine moustache and his big laughing voice, like some dashing medieval monarch jesting with his men-at-arms.

'Somebody said you were ten years up at Peshawar,' Stokes was saying. 'Could it really be that long?'

'Over twelve, in point of fact.'

'No! Twelve years! Still, they tell me the cricket's pretty good up there.'

'Yes,' Mr Gray agreed, 'and the jackal hunts.'

Frank could not decide if they were joking. His father was extremely bad at cricket and avoided it whenever he could. The Peshawar jackal hunts were the worst form of adolescent mounted mayhem and Mr Gray would never have dreamed of taking part. The two men seemed to be using some sort of recognition code to establish whether they were actually on the same side.

It seemed that they were, for suddenly Mr Stokes's laughter boomed out. 'All I can say is, Gray, you commercial chaps are worth your money! You'll be a breath of fresh air here, you and your fine young family. And, good heavens, we need it. You wouldn't believe the stuffiness! I won't be able to get you into the Bangalore Club just yet, I'm embarrassed to say. The usual nonsense about box wallahs.'

Frank glanced quickly at his father. Mr Gray hated to be called a box wallah, the derisory term for anyone in commerce: it referred to the native traders who went from house to house selling cloth or fake antiques from tin trunks strapped to their bicycles. But Mr Stokes voiced the phrase in such a way that it ridiculed only the people who used it.

'Fellows in commerce aren't good enough for the membership committee, apparently,' he said. 'As if commerce isn't what it's all about. One tries to change things, but progress here can be pretty glacial, despite the climate. Need to shift a few of the Old Guard out of the way. Meanwhile, we new boys need to stick together.'

'To be honest, Stokes, I'm not much of a club man.'

'Quite. Dreadful bore most of the time. However there is a rather good Saturday Club, and that is fun. Tennis, curry mornings, billiards, decent library. Best of all, a good bar. I'm a member myself, and I'd be happy to propose you.'

'That's kind of you.'

'Not a bit of it. The ladies always enjoy the Saturday Club, which is another advantage.' Stokes paused, dropped his voice a little. 'Moving's always worse for the memsahibs, I think. Takes a bit of adjustment.' He leaned forward and clapped Mr Gray companionably on the arm. 'You and Mrs Gray must come and join Patricia and me for a couple of pegs and a bite to eat. She'd love to see you both. Starved for civilised company, with only me to talk to.' Stokes made a fist, a gesture of solidarity. 'Stick together. That's the ticket.'

He ruffled Frank's hair and then he was gone, raising one hand over his shoulder in farewell, his straight back cruising through the throng, a foot above everyone else. Mr Gray stood watching him go, and Frank saw on his father's lined face an expression of profound relief, as if a burden had been lifted.

They both started as the locomotive's whistle blew with a shattering scream. Through the iron window of the cab Frank could see Gifford shrieking with silent delight against the din and tugging again and again on the valve release.

4

The servants had already cleared away the remains of dinner, and his mother had left to read Gifford a bedtime story. Frank was on the point of asking to be excused from the table, and, expecting his ritual request to be granted as it always was, he had started to rise.

'So, Francis, what did you think of our Mr Stokes?'

Frank sat down again.

'I liked him, Father.'

'I liked him, too.' Mr Gray sat back in his dining chair and, as if casually, drew an envelope from his jacket pocket. He placed it on the table beside his cheese plate and rested his hand on it. 'In point of fact, I asked a few questions about our Mr Stokes. It seems he is quite a celebrity in Bangalore.'

Frank could hear the distant murmur of his mother's voice drifting from the bedroom. Outside, beyond the opal rectangle of the French doors, zithering cicadas were fading in the deepening blue evening. It was time for his lesson, but it seemed that Mr Gray was in no hurry to fetch the leather bag in which he kept his books.

'The Heaven Born,' his father said, and his eyes twinkled. 'That's what they call the Indian Civil Service. They get a good deal of stick, but there's barely one thousand of them to run a continent of four hundred millions. Most of them are only young chaps like Stokes. Pretty impressive, I think you'd agree.'

Frank was embarrassed that his father had so clearly read his fascination. But it was true enough. He had not been able to get Mr Stokes out of his mind all day. He had even caught himself practising the young man's urgent but loose-limbed stride, and the louche way he wore his jacket so that it fell open across his body.

Mr Gray said, 'I'll tell you what I learned about that young gentleman, shall I, Francis? He took a First in Classics from Balliol. He's already had a number of postings in various places way out in the mofussil. In Bengal he apparently hunted down a gang of dacoits and personally shot their leader dead. They say he speaks three native languages fluently, and has explored parts of the mountain country near the border with Bhutan where they'd never seen a white man.' He gave Frank a solemn look. 'That was in his spare time, presumably.'

Despite the irony, Frank could believe all this and more of Mr Stokes. But he could not understand why his father was painting this picture for him. Perhaps he was being teased. Perhaps Mr Gray, in his measured way, was about to demonstrate that Frank's new idol had feet of clay. Frank hoped not.

'I can tell you something else about him, too,' Mr Gray went on. 'By the time he's forty our Mr Stokes will be Collector somewhere, or perhaps he'll be recruited into the Indian Political Service and become British Resident in one of the princely states. He'll be a big man, with the authority of a king. Power over life and death, the last word in law. Think of that, Francis: to bring education, public works, railways, trade, justice, to thousands of poor people. Millions. Don't you agree that would be a goal worth striving for?'

'Yes, Father,' Frank said, cautiously.

'It could be your goal, too.'

Frank stared at him.

'I don't like to blow my own trumpet,' Mr Gray said, 'but I think I have done tolerably well, given my lack of a proper education. I should like to see how far you could go if you had some.' He got up and crossed to the sideboard and, unusually at this time of the evening, poured himself a whisky. He filled up the glass with soda, brought the drink back to the table and sat down again. 'My family did not support me, Francis. They were quite humble people and felt that I had ideas above my station in life.' He gave Frank an oddly twisted smile. 'But they were right. I did seek something more from life. Not just for myself, do you see? For my children. For you and for Gifford. And now that we are on a rather firmer financial footing at last . . .'

Mr Gray picked up the letter beside his plate and tapped the stiff paper against his thumbnail. Frank saw that the envelope had already been opened, and that it bore a British stamp with the Queen's head and a wavy postmark over it.

Mr Gray spoke in something of a rush. 'Francis, I have arranged a place for you as a boarder at Napier College. Napier is a private academy in Warwickshire. In England.'

Frank said, 'We're going to England?'

'No. You will go alone. Dearborn & Company has no position for me in England. And without a position, I cannot afford . . .' He sounded suddenly testy, and took a sip of his whisky as if to put a stop to that line of talk. 'You will start at Napier in September.'

Frank was too stunned to work out exactly how long that was. All he could think of was that his birthday was in September. Was it three or four months away? That seemed suddenly very soon.

'Naturally, this will be strange for you at first. And your mother and I . . . will miss you very much.' Mr Gray lifted his whisky to his lips again, this time so abruptly that he spilled a few drops. He set the glass down again and made some play with his handkerchief, wiping up the spilled drops, before continuing in a curiously high voice. 'With your natural gifts, Francis, and such an education, there is nothing to which you may not aspire. Nothing. And it would make me proud indeed to see how far . . .'

Mr Gray turned away and stared into the corner of the room.

Frank said, 'Did Mr Stokes attend Napier College, Father?'

Mr Gray gave a little grunt of laughter and looked back at him, his eyes shining. 'I'm afraid I don't know where Mr Stokes attended school, Francis. But if you wished for a hero, that young man is perhaps the very type of Englishman you might choose to emulate.'

5

Moonlight fell in strips through the blinds and across the cone of Gifford's net-shrouded bed on the other side of the room. A rat scampered in the rafters above. Frank glimpsed it flitting like a shadow and in a second heard the tiny twitter of its young in the nest which he had found at the back of the wardrobe. He knew the rat, though he had not given it a name, and tonight he had left a fragment of biscuit for it on his bedside table. He waited a moment and the rat materialised there as if by magic, six inches from his face, and sat watching him with jet eyes while it ate, holding the biscuit between pale forepaws.

Frank wondered if they had rats in Napier College. From what he had heard, it didn't seem likely that such unorthodoxy would be tolerated there. In all probability Napier's own peculiarities would be nothing like as entertaining as half-tame rats. Frank had read about English schools with their discipline, their chill dormitories and rough blankets. He wasn't sure all of this was true, but in any case he wasn't worried by the prospect of physical hardship. In fact he relished it. He enjoyed the heady sensation that he had been selected for an elite, like some Spartan youth marked out as a future champion. If his training were rigorous, that was only as it should be, and he sensed he was equal to it.

In his mind's eye Frank saw athletic Mr Stokes again, easy and powerful in his dusty bush jacket, his rifles in their canvas sheaths and his ammunition winking in the sun. The Heaven Born. To wield authority, stern but righteous, from a vast cool office in Government House. Or to sit at the side of some venal native maharajah, and to champion British justice for the poor and the downtrodden. And, when duty permitted, to hunt and explore, to travel and learn, to sit down with holy men and speak to them in their own tongue, and to listen gravely to their counsels.

Yes, surely, this was his path.

Outside in the bushes he heard a night bird hoot. The rat, sensing Frank's sudden alertness, was gone in a blink. Frank rolled his head on his pillow and listened. The hoot came again. He had not expected Javed to come tonight, but what better night? He knew he would not sleep, and this news was too big to keep to himself.

He slid out from beneath the mosquito net and pulled on his clothes, stepped softly to the door and out into the corridor. The boards were warm against his bare feet.

A rattan screen separated the passage from the dining room. He realised that, despite the hour, his parents were still up, talking. Frank could see the gleam of light through the screen and caught the murmur of their voices. He could tell they were seated at the card table near the screened double doors; if he was careful they would never hear him. He placed his weight with exquisite care, keeping to the edge of the passage where the boards did not creak, and in a moment he was abreast of the doorway into the box room. Three short steps through that room to the window, and he would be over the veranda rail and away into the night. He shifted onto the balls of his feet, his toes gripping the wood.

'Why must you go?' his mother burst out.

It froze Frank where he stood, as if the question had been shouted at him.

'Why can't you stay with me, Lewis, the one time I ask it?'

Frank dropped his heels and moved a step closer to the rattan screen.

'Shall I explain it again, Marjorie?' his father said, and for once did not trouble to disguise his annoyance. 'The night train arrives in two hours. Half the cargo will be pilfered if I'm not there.'

'Let Barrett do it. What's the point of you being deputy manager—'

'Barrett has been taken ill. How many more times? Good Lord.'

'He's taken drink, you mean.'

'The man is ill, Marjorie.'

'And am I not ill?'

'Marjorie, you are as healthy as a young woman reasonably could be. Perhaps too healthy.'

At this, for some reason Frank did not understand, his mother began to sob openly. At the hopeless sound of it a wave of protectiveness washed through him. Had there been some secret hurt hidden in his father's words? He could not tell. Certainly he had never heard his father speak so sharply to her. He wondered suddenly if they always wrangled like this when he was not present.

He moved stealthily forward until he could see them, segmented by the chinks in the rattan. As he had guessed they were at the card table, his mother seated but his father on his feet, his case in his hand. An oil lamp stood on the green baize between them and, despite the screen, a swarm of insects swooped around the light. His father's whole attitude was one of a man at the end of his patience, his lips thinned and hard lines around his eyes and mouth. Frank's mother sat with her face in her hands, her shoulders shaking. Her hair had come undone and spilled over the graceful curve of her neck.

'Marjorie,' Mr Gray chided. 'The servants. The children.'

She blindly fumbled for a handkerchief but didn't lift her face.

Mr Gray sighed wearily, and stepped to the door.

'Lewis?' She groped out a hand to him and her voice was strangled. 'Lewis!'

Mr Gray took his linen jacket from the chair and slid open the screen. 'If we must, Marjorie, we can talk about this further in the morning, though in all conscience I believe we have said all there is to say.' He turned and went down the steps of the veranda with his back very straight, the screen door banging behind him.

Frank watched his mother as she sat at the table, her handkerchief crushed in her right hand. Her pale face shone with tears and sweat in the hot night but she sat like a statue, staring with despair in her eyes at the door through which her husband had passed.

For a long moment Frank stood undecided. He wanted to escape and he resented her for holding him back with her messy emotions. The box room door stood open beside him, and in a second he could be gone, and no one any the wiser. He pivoted silently towards the open window and the jasmine scented night. But then he remembered how he had found her singing to the moon, and he pushed aside the rattan screen and walked across the room to his mother.

She looked up, startled, and then turned her face quickly away and fussed with her handkerchief. 'Frank, go back to bed.'

'Why are you crying?'

'It doesn't matter. Go to bed.'

'I'll stay with you.' He pulled up the chair opposite her and sat down stiffly. 'Father couldn't. So I will.'

'I don't want you to.'

'We could play cards.'

'No. Please. Go to bed.'

'Are you angry with me?'

'No, Frank. No.' She started to cry again. 'Not with you.'

'With Father, then? Has Father done something wrong?'

She put her head in her hands. 'Oh, God, Frank. Not your father either. Your papa's too good a man by half. If he's done anything wrong it's only because he's too good. Too gentle. If he'd stood up for himself more, maybe he might have had a post in England and we could all have gone back together.'

Her voice collapsed into incoherence and for a few moments she sobbed helplessly. Frank stretched out one hand and touched her shoulder. The material of her dress was hot. She threw back her hair and lifted her streaked face to him.

'Dear Frank. You really are my protector.' She rested her hand over his; her skin was warm and moist.

'I promised,' he said.

'And you don't break your promises, do you?'

'No.'

'No, of course you don't.' She took a deep breath and sat up a little. 'Who was calling earlier? The owl that wasn't an owl?'

'Javed.' He knew there was no point in lying to her.

'Go with him then. I won't tell.'

'He'll be gone by now.'

'Then go after him.' She squeezed his hand. 'Go on. You can catch him.'

'I won't leave you.'

She gave him a mock imperious look. 'You promised to obey my every command.'

Frank wasn't sure he had promised any such thing, but he found that he could not contradict her. She leaned close to him, urgently.

'Frank, Frank. The best you can do for me tonight is to leave me. I have been . . . foolish, you see. And I need a little time alone to put right my own mistakes.'

'What mistakes?'

'You wouldn't understand.' She dropped his hand and patted it smartly. 'Now go. That's my command, Sir Knight. Do as I bid thee.' She gave him a lopsided smile.

He got reluctantly to his feet.

At the screen he stopped and looked back. She was sitting in the lamplight, her face pale and her hair disordered. She was, Frank thought, more beautiful than anyone he had ever seen. He let himself out through the screen door and ran into the velvet night, down the garden path and away into the black street.

He ran through the shadows of the jacaranda trees until he left the last of the bungalows behind him, and ran on through twisting alleys and backstreets towards the outskirts of the old city. As he ran he breathed the smells of orange blossom and jasmine and rotting refuse and the dank savour of the coming monsoon. And in his mind he saw his mother's face, pale as stone, glistening in the lamplight, with despair in her eyes.

6

Frank crouched beside Javed in the ruins of the old temple to Vishnu, squatting on his haunches native style, catching his breath. The fallen columns, their intricate and erotic carvings lit blue in the moonlight, lay half-smothered by scrub on the slope which led up to the railway embankment. Above them the struts of the water tower stood against the sky.

From here the vastness of the native town lay spread out below like an upturned jewel box, the small lights of stalls, workshops, and cooking fires mirroring the starred sky. Not a mile below them glittered Cantonment Station, and further to the west City Station where Frank, with his important father and with Gifford, had been a visitor just a day or two ago. North of the railway he could just see the lights of the British cavalry lines and of the infantry barracks, trembling in neat grids.

'I thought you were not coming,' Javed said.

'I'm here now.'

Javed turned his large grave eyes on him. 'Something is wrong?'

Frank waited, his breathing coming more slowly now. He could feel his friend's gaze upon him. 'I have news.'

Javed nodded solemnly. 'They are sending you to England.'

Frank said nothing. He had long ago learned not to be surprised at the wildfire spread of information here. Nothing could be kept from the servants, and Javed would have heard from a cousin or an aunt or a half-brother who had some connection with the Gray household. It was even possible that Javed had heard his news before he had.

'Now you are eager to leave us,' Javed said.

'No.'

'You want to leave,' Javed repeated, and nodded again. 'Of course. You will go to England and become a great lord, and forget about us.'

'I'll come back one day.'

'You will not want to know us then. You will be a master, and we will be your servants.'

'No,' Frank said, but he was ashamed.

Javed rose to his feet and put out a hand to pull Frank to his feet. 'Come, master. Your subjects are waiting for you.'

Frank climbed the dusty hillock behind his friend, confused and unhappy. He followed Javed as he ducked under the girders of the water tower, and looked around the circle of faces. In the starlight he saw half a dozen others he knew: two orphaned brothers who begged and sometimes stole from the visitors in Cubbon Park; a boy who worked as a sweeper outside the Bengaluru Palace; a mute urchin who lived on charity at the Dodda Ganesha temple in exchange for running errands for the monks. And Ashok, on his feet in the centre of the group. Frank didn't like Ashok, a light-skinned boy a year or two older than himself. Ashok's uncle was a steward in the officers' mess of the 4th Hussars. On the strength of this, and rumours that his natural father had been an English grenadier, Ashok carried himself with an insufferable air of superiority.

The iron skeleton which supported the water tower was lit by a liquid flash of lightning, and a second later came the crack of thunder. Ashok was in the middle of expounding one of his grandiose schemes. Javed looked at Frank again, and grinned. They had all heard the older boy sounding off before, and normally Frank and Javed teamed up to mock him. But Frank was not in the mood for mockery and kept his eyes averted.

'They bring up all kinds of stuff from Madras to Cantonment on their trains,' Ashok was saying. 'Food, wine, clothes – all the officers' things. Gold and silver and money.'

Frank began to pay attention. Perhaps this was the very train his father had spoken of, and thinking of this reminded him of his parents' argument and darkened his mood. It came to him that he should not have left the house. He did not know why, but he knew he should not have left home tonight.

Javed spat in the dust. 'You're an idiot, Ashok. Do you think the English leave their money lying around for street urchins to pick up? Besides, the rain's coming and we'll be washed off like spiders down a gutter.'

'Stay here then,' Ashok said with disdain, 'if you haven't got the balls.'

'At least I've got brains.'

Abruptly Frank came to a decision. He touched Javed's arm. 'I have to go home.'

'What?' Javed looked at him, distracted from his fencing with Ashok. Frank got to his feet. 'I should never have come.'

'What's the matter, English?' Ashok jeered. 'Running away already? Are you scared too?'

Frank stared silently at him. Did he know, too? Perhaps they all knew.

Ashok sensed some weakness in Frank's hesitation. He said, 'I saw your father tonight, English. He was walking like this.' Ashok paced around, head down, lugubriously long-faced, a clever and cruel caricature. Somebody laughed, then stopped abruptly. Ashok stood in front of Frank. 'He's such a great and important sahib now. Soon it will be your turn. Already you're too good for us *natives*.'

Frank stood in silence, knowing the whole group was watching to see how he would react. They could all hear the locomotive in the distance, beginning to thud its way up the incline towards them.

'Come, then,' Ashok said, grandly, knowing he had won.

7

Frank edged out onto the gantry. The iron, ridged with rust, was cold against his fingers. His inching hands dislodged dust and bird droppings from the girder above him. Through the lattice of struts he could see the purple sky and in the far distance the black humps of the Nandi Hills, lit silver every few seconds by flickering lightning. Sweat was running down his face and back and he could hear his own breathing, and that of Ashok ahead of him, and Javed behind. Three hundred yards away the locomotive's headlight threw a fan of yellow up the sides of the cutting and dark creatures skittered in the beam. The swaying carriages came on very slowly, each concussion of the pistons spurting white steam up into the night. Rain began to fall, a few fat drops at first, slapping warm as blood against Frank's back. In the long glare of lightning he caught an image of the three of them, clinging like monkeys.

The din swelled until it was enormous. It hurt Frank's ears but he could not take his hands from the iron to blot out the noise. The train came on faster than he could have imagined. In a single instant the rain fell in a hissing slab, and hot steam burst up from below and turned the world white and he tasted soot and smoke. He glimpsed the iron roof of the cab moving past his feet, and the driver in his blue cap and the fireman in his sweat-stained turban, and the half-empty coal truck, and then the sloping roofs of wooden carriages, as if he were seeing it all through storm clouds, from a balloon. He steeled himself and then let go and dropped into this white roaring chaos, dimly aware of the other two falling close to him. The roof of the wagon rushed up and hit him hard, and he lay winded. He rolled on the curved surface until he collided with a metal pot of some kind and clutched his arm convulsively around it. He smelled tobacco smoke over the reek of coal, which puzzled him. The car swayed beneath him and couplings clanked.

The rain hosed down on them and soot blew back from the engine as it gathered speed on the incline. The fringes of the town began to rattle past – low huts, overflowing gutters, a white cow in an alleyway hock deep in mud. Frank saw Ashok swing himself over the edge of the roof and when Frank looked down he saw him on the iron brake platform at the end of the car. Frank followed and Javed landed behind him and the three of them crowded onto the little platform, gripping the cold railing. Built into the end of the wagon was a wooden door on runners and Ashok was already rattling boldly at it.

The door slid open with a crash and a great gout of light splashed out over them. A sergeant in a kilt and khaki tunic filled the square of the doorway. He stared at them like a bewildered bull. Behind the hairy columns of his legs, Frank glimpsed rows of solid men in khaki, all of them kilted, swaying on wooden benches, sleeping, playing cards, smoking. Coils of smoke rose up towards the ventilator. Heads turned towards them down the length of the carriage.

'Thieving, are ye?' the sergeant bellowed. 'Thieving wee beggars, are ye?'

Javed dived like a fish over the rail and into the night.

'By the sahib's good grace,' Ashok pleaded in English, his voice cracking, 'they made me—'

Frank seized the older boy around the waist and thrust him out through the gap in the rail so that the two of them plunged out into the darkness. He had a confused impression of the soldier roaring with laughter behind him and then the gravel of the track bed ripped at his knees and elbows and he heard Ashok yelp, and they rolled down an embankment into sodden undergrowth and lay still. The train clattered on past them and away.

Frank got gingerly to his feet. His knees were numb. He ran his hands down his legs in the darkness and could feel shreds of skin and lumps of gravel embedded in his flesh. He saw the train rocking away towards the city, a python of lit windows. The warm rain sluiced over him. Javed slid down beside him in a clatter of stones, his torn clothes plastered to him. Ashok crawled out of the undergrowth, whimpering. The sight of him made Frank angry and he kicked the older boy in the ribs, not very gently. Ashok rolled over and sat, hugging his knees, rocking himself.

'*They made me?*' Frank mimicked and kicked him again.

Ashok blubbered for a while and then got unsteadily to his feet, smearing the back of his hand across his face. 'You all think you're God's chosen ones.' He pushed his slimy face at Frank. 'You speak our language and you copy our customs, and you think you're one of us. But it takes more than that, English.' A bubble of mucus grew from one of his nostrils.

Frank felt a great and malicious urge to drive his fist into the boy's face and kick him a couple more times, but instead he turned and walked away along the track. His knees were stinging now and he felt a little sick. He heard Javed come running up behind him.

'I know what you people are like under their fine uniforms!' Ashok shouted after them. 'I've seen them, coming out of the Officers' Mess, our imperial masters! Drunk and spewing and falling in the gutter! They're filth! Filth! You hear me? You're all filth!'

Frank stumped on, his head down.

Ashok screamed, 'Ask your mother if you don't believe me! Ask the Memsahib Gray, who's so fine and so pure!'

Frank stopped and slowly turned.

'I saw your father tonight, English!' Ashok jeered. 'But that wasn't all I saw!'

Frank took a couple of sprinting steps towards him, but Ashok vanished into the bushes like a deer and in a moment they heard him clattering away among the stones at the top of the embankment.

'We'll go to my grandmother's,' Javed said, taking Frank's arm. 'She'll feed us.'

Frank pulled away. 'I have to go.'

8

The horse shied as Frank limped around the corner of the alley at the back of his parents' bungalow. It was a fine horse, a big grey Waler, well cared for and glossy in the starlight. An elderly Indian groom was holding its head, standing under the shelter of the overhanging roofs. A cavalryman's horse. A hussar's horse. The animal stamped and turned his head and looked at Frank with his dark intelligent eye, and settled again as the groom clucked to it. The old man's face filled with alarm as he saw Frank and he glanced nervously towards the bungalow.

Frank ran past him, hearing the man call out after him. The mud of the street squeezed up through his bare toes. The house remained silent under the dripping black trees. He stopped. He could see the glow of the lamp through the screen door. The screen itself was slightly ajar. He took a few steps forward. For a second he thought he could hear voices, raised voices, but over the noise of trickling water in the drains he could not be sure. Then he saw the muddy prints on the veranda steps, and he began to run again, as fast as his grazed legs would let him, down the length of the path and up the steps, barging in through the screen.

The lamp was burning on the green baize as before, the halo of insects pinging against the glass chimney, but the room was empty. Frank stood there panting, with sweat and rainwater and blood running off him and pooling on the floor at his feet. A belt was slung over the back of the chair, a cross strap in dark polished leather, brass military buckles bearing regimental insignia which he did not recognise, and the butt of a gigantic revolver visible beneath a holster flap. Frank could read the maker's name and the weapon's model stamped in the steel: Webley Mk I. An officer's sidearm.

His mother screamed from the bedroom. There was a sharp crack and she screamed again, and a man's voice rose in the night.

'I've done this for you! Do you understand? For you! And you're coming with me, damn you!'

'Jack, you know I can't!' Her voice rose to a shriek. 'No! Please, please!'

Another slap and another cry and the man backed into the room where Frank stood. Frank caught a glimpse of a khaki tunic, pips on shoulder, yellow piping down a blue trouser leg. He saw his mother dragged by the hair and by shreds of a torn nightgown. He glimpsed her face, wet and bleeding from nose and mouth, saw the delicate bones of her bare shoulder as she struggled and the roll of one exposed breast and the shocking eye of a dark brown nipple, and he saw the man's hand raised for another blow.

Frank tore back the flap of the holster and wrenched at the pistol. The belt snagged and brought the flimsy table crashing down onto the floor, lamp and all, so that the room was suddenly plunged into darkness and in that darkness his mother screamed again. He could not free the cumbersome weapon but he got his hand under the leather flap and lifted pistol and holster towards the ceiling and dragged at the trigger. The detonation seemed to flatten the house. The recoil wrenched the pistol violently in his grip and Frank felt a blinding pain in his wrist and then a sick numbness. The leather holster whirled away from him, propelled by the blast, and as it spun the buckle cracked against the side of his head. Pieces of plaster and tile pattered down from the ceiling. As his ears cleared Frank heard his mother shrieking and he could see her pale shape crawling on all fours and the dark bulk of the man turned towards him, every movement fuddled and confused. Frank looked down and saw the pistol, free of its holster now, hanging uselessly from his right hand and his wrist was the wrong shape and he knew this meant it was broken. Lamp oil was burning on the floor behind him with a bluish light which sent shadows looming around the room. Frank could not see the officer's face: he had an impression of contortion, of bared teeth under a wide moustache. The man cursed, and took a lurching step across the room towards him.

'Jack!' Frank's mother clutched at the man's leg. 'Jack, please!'

The man swore again, turned, and drove his boot into her stomach. She grunted as the air went out of her, gargled a little, and fell silent. Her attacker took two steps towards Frank, who lifted the dangling revolver with his good hand, cocked it with his right forearm, and shot him.

The officer stood swaying in the flickering room, put his hand to his side and looked at it, bewildered. The hand glinted scarlet. He stepped forward, struck the pistol out of Frank's grip and hit him backhanded across the side of the head. His fist felt like a wooden club.

Frank felt the warm boards against his cheek and somewhere close was the blue flutter of burning lamp oil and he could smell the crackle and stink of the smouldering dhurrie rug. He tried to sit up and a bolt of pain shot up his arm from his broken wrist. He whimpered, curled on the floor, rocking himself, clutching his arm to him.

He opened his eyes and saw the revolver. It lay disregarded on the floor not three feet from him. He reached for it, felt the cold steel under his fingers. Something slipped in his mind then and he thought minutes had passed, but it must only have been seconds, for when he came to himself he found the gun was in his left hand and the officer was still in the room, lurching unsteadily towards the door.

The man was out onto the veranda now and moving down the steps. Frank got to his feet, the pistol heavy in his hand, and followed him. He knew clearly now what he was going to do, and struggled against the agony in his right wrist, fighting to drag the heavy hammer back. By the time he got to the top of the veranda steps the man had made a dozen paces and was near the gate, still on his feet but blundering from side to side against the wet bushes. Frank heard running steps and hoofbeats as the groom came hurrying up leading the grey horse, shouting. Here and there a light came on in the bungalows nearby and in the servants' quarters behind them.

The hammer came back and locked and Frank fired, the bullet clanging against the iron gatepost in a fountain of sparks. He walked down the steps onto the path, and this time the hammer clicked back easily. The old groom dodged in through the gate and grabbed the officer and bundled him towards the horse and turned to face Frank, flapping his hands.

'Young sahib, no. No!'

The officer fell to his knees in the mud beside the horse which nickered nervously. Frank stepped up to the gate and rested the pistol on the gatepost. The old groom made to block his line of fire but then his nerve broke and he moved aside. Raised voices now and lights and running feet. The officer clutched for the stirrup, and the horse jinked sideways, dragging him a few feet so that Frank's shot kicked up mud and water from the road. The man hauled himself up and into the saddle, groping for the reins. The horse pranced forward, threatening to unseat him, but he was away now, the Waler breaking into an untidy canter. Frank sighted along the barrel and pulled the trigger one last time. The recoil spun the weapon quite out of his numbed hands, but he saw the rider jolt upright in the saddle and slump forwards over the pommel as the horse carried him out of sight.

There was shouting, the banging of doors and shutters. Half-dressed servants came running past Frank towards the house, ignoring him. Their elderly neighbour Mr Pym appeared in a comical nightshirt, his slippered feet sinking in the mud. Frank thought Mr Pym would speak to him, but then one of the servants called from the house, and Mr Pym hurried past him up the path to the door. Frank followed, feeling sick and confused, cradling his injured arm. He wondered where the pistol had fallen. He thought perhaps he ought to go and find it; after all, it wasn't his. Inside the bungalow he could see yellow flames flickering, and the silhouettes of people stamping them out and red sparks gusting up around them. He supposed the dhurrie must have been burned beyond saving. That rug was a favourite of his father's and Frank wondered if he would get into trouble when he came home. Had he been responsible for the fire? He thought so. He had pulled the table over, hadn't he? He tried to remember what else he had done, but the pictures would not settle in his mind.

He reached the top of the steps. Two of the servants had put out the last of the fire, but the room was full of smoke and it was hard to see. He saw his mother, though, stretched on the floor. Someone must have thrown something over her, a red and white flag, apparently, although that didn't make any sense. Mr Pym was kneeling beside her and the red of the flag had somehow got onto his hands and his comical nightshirt. He turned his white moon face to Frank and his eyes and mouth were slack with horror for a moment before he regained control.

'Get the boy out!' Mr Pym bellowed in a voice of command of which Frank had never suspected him capable. 'Get him out of here at once!'

9

Dr Perry closed his leather bag with a snap and stood up. He washed his hands in the basin at the foot of the bed and then dried them and rolled his sleeves down again, slipping silver links through his cuffs with the dexterity of long practice.

'Right as rain in no time,' he said to Frank, and when the boy continued to gaze out of the window, the doctor nodded towards his bandaged wrist, where it lay on the counterpane. 'The hand. Right as rain.'

He waited for Frank to show some reaction, but Frank did not. Dr Perry pulled on his jacket and began clumsily to button it. The sound of his nervous breathing was loud in the room. 'Francis, your mother . . . you must not . . .'

Frank looked at him for the first time, and whatever the doctor saw in his eyes made him pick up his bag and let himself out of the room without another word. Frank heard him walk down the passage and call for his horse without even so much as a word of farewell to Mr Gray or the colonel.

Frank stared through the brilliant square of the window. The mango tree was loud with mynahs. The sun was already high and he could smell the hot dust and the tired scents of bougainvillea. The gardener was chopping listlessly at the weeds, and for a few moments it was almost like any other hot morning in Bangalore.

Except that it was not.

Since dawn people had been coming and going, hurrying, whispering in awed voices. Before that was confusion. He recalled waking in semi-darkness on the living room couch and trying to move his wrist and the shattering pain that caused. He remembered the servants carrying him into his own room and he could remember too his father's grey and stricken face above him. His father had asked him questions in a gentle voice which kept breaking, and though Frank was sorry for him and wanted to help, he could not seem to answer. He recalled his father patting him reassuringly on the shoulder and ushering people from the room, and then there were hushed conversations, and the wailing of one of the servant women, harshly silenced. He heard vehicles outside in the night, pulling up on the gravel, and men spoke softly and urgently, and he knew they didn't want him to hear, but he did hear. Bearers edged down the steps with a burden. The carriage's springs creaked as it took the weight, and then a whispered command and it drove away quickly. It was as if they were anxious to be gone before he could rouse himself and stop them taking her. In the silence that followed he thought he had heard his father weeping. White faced Dr Perry had come into his room then and given him something bitter to drink and the night closed around him like a curtain.

Dawn, and a new sound drifted into his mind. It was Mumtaz scrubbing at the boards of the veranda, sobbing as she did so. He slept fitfully, half-drugged, and came awake again. Now, just under the window, he could hear a horse tossing its head against the flies, making its harness jingle. He knew the horse belonged to Colonel James; in a dream he had heard the colonel introduce himself, and his father's subdued greeting. Then the colonel and his father had walked away through the house to the study.

Gifford appeared in the doorway. Mumtaz had scrubbed him pink and his fine blond hair shone like gold thread in the light. He clutched in one hand something made of wood and paper, a model bird perhaps. His eyes were wide and fearful.

'Is it true? About Mama? I didn't believe it, but—'

'It's true, Giff.'

'I thought it must be. Everyone's crying.' Gifford glanced down at his bird and up again. 'I don't feel like crying. Why don't I?'

'I don't know, Giff. But it doesn't matter.'

'I'm to be taken to the Reverend Talbot's for the day. They won't tell me what happened. Do you know?'

But Frank couldn't face that. 'Nobody really knows yet, Giff.'

The boy's sharp eyes flicked down to Frank's bandaged wrist. 'Did you do something bad?'

'Perhaps I did, Giff.'

'I thought so. I heard a bang. Lots of bangs. Are they going to hang you?'

'Maybe it would be better if they did.'

Gifford chewed his lip in silence for a few seconds as he considered his brother's execution. He said, 'I've made a glider. See? It flies.'

Gifford launched the paper craft into the air. It swooped, lifted as it met the draught from the open window, and swept down in a gentle curve to come to rest on the bed next to Frank. They both looked at it.

'So Mama's not ever coming back?' Gifford said.

Frank kept staring at the paper glider on the coverlet. Yes, she was coming back. To the scented garden at night, her hair tumbling over her white shoulder, singing. She would come back to every night-time garden for the rest of his life, wherever there were stars crowding the sky, or he smelled jasmine, or heard a frog drop like a stone into a pool and shiver the silver disc of the moon.

'Now *you're* going to cry.' Gifford retrieved his model and stroked it solemnly.

Mumtaz returned at that moment. Her eyes were red with weeping. She looked at Frank with a kind of terror, gathered Gifford up in the folds of her sari like a mother hen, and hurried away down the corridor towards the back veranda. Frank lay still, the hard light slicing in blades through the blinds. He felt like a plague victim, untouchable, isolated. His wrist throbbed.

Time passed vacantly, a few minutes or an hour, perhaps. He may have drifted off. At some time he was vaguely aware of a carriage drawing up, and of a brief bustle of activity as Gifford was ushered into it. Then it drew away. When Frank came fully to himself again the house had fallen quiet. For a while there were no new arrivals, until at length a two-horse tonga came clipping along the road at some speed and pulled up outside the gate. Frank heard the vehicle's springs as the occupant stepped down and spoke curtly to the driver. The newcomer strode quickly along the path and up the steps to the front veranda where Prakash the butler greeted him.

'Furneaux,' the man announced. 'Mr Gray. At once.'

Frank sat up in bed. He heard Mr Furneaux being conducted through the house to his father's study, his important boots knocking on the boards. Frank swung his feet to the floor. He felt light-headed and he had to hold his injured arm upright against his chest or it thumped like the devil, but soon his strength began to seep back. Down the corridor to the right, in the dining room behind the rattan screen, he could hear Mumtaz weeping again. Frank edged down the passage in the opposite direction. At the end he stepped into the empty guest bedroom, pulling the door to behind him. Glass doors opened onto a small balcony with steps down into the garden. Frank opened the screens and moved out into the blinding morning. He slipped along the side of the house behind a screen of oleanders. The eaves of the bungalow had kept the bushes from last night's rain and their paper dry leaves crackled beneath his feet.

An air vent opened from his father's study at just above floor level. Once, returning with Javed, Frank had seen the lights still burning in his father's room and the tiny grid of radiance which marked the vent. The two boys had crept into the bushes under his father's window and through the slats of the vent they had watched him working in a halo of lamplight.

Frank squatted in the dust. He hugged his strapped arm close to him. He was sweating and he felt faint, but it was easier now that he could sit still. His view of the room was segmented by the vent, but he could see all three men. His father sat behind his desk, his face colourless. Mr Furneaux occupied the armchair facing the desk, as stern and formal as ever in his dark coat. Colonel James was standing with his back to Frank, his hands clasped behind his blue uniform tunic.

The colonel was speaking, so thickly that his voice reached Frank as a half-understood rumble. '. . . in all my years of soldiering . . . unspeakable . . . not one of my officers, thank God . . .'

'A cavalry officer.' Mr Gray spoke vaguely, as if in a dream. 'My boy said it was a cavalry officer.'

'Not from the Fourth, sir. Seconded to us. It's bad enough that we took him on secondment, but I should hand in my papers at once if he were one of mine, I promise you that.'

'He is a murderer.' Mr Gray's voice still had that same unearthly quality. 'His regiment is of no concern to me.'

The colonel made a grunting sound in his throat, like a man lifting a heavy weight, but he said nothing. Frank saw his hands clench behind his back so that the tendons in his wrists stood out like wires. Across the room Mr Furneaux crossed his legs, ran his fingertip down the crease of his trousers, and said, 'Murdered,' as if mulling the word over.

Mr Gray looked at him.

Furneaux met his gaze. 'We don't know exactly what happened, Gray. I'm sure you agree that it's as well to be careful what we say. Your boy witnessed an assault. Disgraceful, of course. Unpardonable. But assault is not murder. And one has to remember the lad was injured, in pain, distressed. He told you he was knocked senseless, is that right?'

'Momentarily, but he—'

'We must think calmly, Gray. We must consider the questions which will be raised. By this man's defence, you understand.'

'What possible defence could he have?'

'My dear chap, in law there is always a defence. Innocent until proven guilty, and all the rest of it. To speak plainly, if this were to come to trial, certain arguments would be mounted by his lawyers.'

'*If* it were to come to trial?'

'There would be a well-funded defence, Gray, depend upon that, and a very public one. For an Army officer? Oh, yes. You need to consider what harm that could mean for you and yours.'

Frank's father pushed his hand across his face. 'Gentlemen, forgive me. I am all at sea . . . What more harm could befall us?'

Furneaux let a moment pass. Almost imperceptibly, the architecture of his posture hardened inside his dark clothes. 'Face facts, Gray. The scoundrel did not arrive at this house with murder in mind. If he had, he would hardly have left his revolver in your living room, buttoned into its holster, while he went to . . . call on your wife.'

There was a charged silence in the room which Frank did not understand.

Mr Gray uneasily took his eyes from Furneaux's face. To Colonel James he said, 'Has he yet been arrested? Charged? Whatever the formalities are?'

'Not as we speak, sir. Not . . . officially. Presently he is under guard in the military hospital.'

'I still can hardly believe that an officer in the British Army could do such a thing. Who is the wretched man?'

Colonel James started to speak and then stopped and cleared his throat noisily.

Mr Gray looked up at him. 'Well, Colonel?'

'The damnable thing of it is . . .' The colonel swallowed, then squared his shoulders and began again. 'The fact is, Gray, it would be better if I did not to reveal his identity to you.'

Mr Gray stared at him.

'It is in everyone's interests,' the colonel pushed on, 'in particular those of your family. Not even Furneaux here has been told the black-guard's name. Furneaux and I met early this morning, as soon as we heard of this unspeakable thing. And we've come to some conclusions.'

'What conclusions?'

'We might as well face it,' Furneaux cut in impatiently. 'This officer will never be prosecuted.'

'But . . . my wife is . . . *dead*. My Marjorie has been shot *dead*. In her own home . . .'

Furneaux got to his feet and placed his palms on the desk. 'I don't need you to remind me that this is a damnable mess, Gray, an appalling mess. For everyone's sake – and I mean everyone's – we need to keep our heads clear.' He stepped back, took out a pigskin cigar case and turned it over in his hands. 'All other considerations aside, the man has connections. As Colonel James says, even I don't know who he is and I don't care to be told. But I can tell you that some people in high places are making noises on his behalf.'

'Do I understand you?' Mr Gray looked from one of them to the other. 'You believe this man could actually escape prosecution? After this?'

'A prosecution of this officer will benefit no one,' Furneaux sat down again and crossed his legs, 'and therefore there will not be one. The matter will be dealt with quietly. No charges will be brought. It's better all round.'

'Is it?' Mr Gray said, his voice trembling. 'Is it indeed? Well, be very sure that I shall bring *charges*. For the murder of my wife? Oh, yes, I think I shall bring *charges* for that.'

Furneaux took a cheroot from the case and tapped it in an irritated fashion on the arm of his chair. 'Before you do, Gray, think about the position that will put you in. For one thing, think about your wife's reputation.'

He struck a match and lit his cheroot, blew a smoke cloud towards the ceiling, where the slowly beating punkah flattened it against the plaster. From where he crouched, Frank could see his father's face, an expression as if he had suddenly heard a gargoyle speak to him. Colonel James's polished cavalry boots shifted uncomfortably on the boards.

'Gray, believe me,' the colonel said, 'I'd have the scoundrel hanged, and be damned to his connections, but a prosecution won't do. There would be a scandal to end all scandals. You know India. Tongues would wag.'

'The truth could hardly hurt my wife, Colonel. Especially not now.'

'Your wife?' Furneaux laughed. Frank squinted at him through the slats of the vent, incredulous. But Mr Furneaux had actually laughed, cruelly and aloud.

The colonel said, 'Furneaux, damn it all.'

'If you can think of an easy way to do this,' Furneaux snapped at him, rising to his feet once more, 'you are welcome to take over. I would appreciate some help in getting across to Gray here just what the implications of this debacle could be. He seems unable to grasp the point.'

In answer Colonel James strode abruptly to the door and wrenched it open, and in a moment Frank heard his heavy footsteps clumping away through the house.

Mr Gray stared at the door until the sound dwindled to nothing. The colonel's departure seemed to drain the last of the spirit from him and he sagged in his chair.

Furneaux said, 'Your wife has been on the edge for months. If you didn't know that, everyone else did. God knows what her state of mind has led her to do.'

'Led *her* to do?'

'Do you imagine this bloody man just happened by last night? Simply saw a light burning and thought he'd take his chance? How likely is that, do you think?'

'Are you suggesting—'

'You know what I'm suggesting. I don't know what in heaven's name they were thinking of, sending you down here to Bangalore. Don't they think I have enough problems without a deputy who's over the hill, with a hysterical wife and a boy who's virtually gone native?'

Frank's father stood up, swaying slightly on his feet. 'I have served this company loyally for nearly thirty years, Mr Furneaux. I trust you to stand by us now.'

'Perhaps you should look to your own responsibility in all this before you ask Dearborn & Company to dig you out of the mess you're in. You should have got her out of the country long ago, instead of trying to buy that little savage of yours a place in the English middle classes. If he hadn't been there last night we wouldn't be in this position now! Thank God he didn't kill the man, that's all I can say.'

'My son knows right from wrong, at least,' Mr Gray said. 'It begins to look as if he's the only one who does.'

'Right and wrong?' Furneaux barked with contempt. 'And look where that's got us all. Right and wrong, indeed. God alive! Fourteen years old and he's waving a revolver around?'

'My son did his best to . . .' Mr Gray's face creased in disbelief. 'Are you seriously saying we should hide this crime? A white woman shot down in her own home?'

'Don't be a fool, Gray. Obviously there's no question of hiding it.' Furneaux paced almost up to the vent and then back again, smoking furiously. 'Atrocious tragedy. The whole community outraged. An unidentified intruder, no doubt some half-crazed native – a disaffected servant, perhaps. Your wife disturbed him and he attacked her. Yes, that should serve. We may even be able to hang someone for it.'

'But you can't . . .' The muscles jumped around Mr Gray's mouth. 'Francis saw everything.'

'He saw nothing. He wasn't even in the house. That way he won't be questioned.'

'You want us to lie? About a thing like this?'

Furneaux swung on his heel and pointed with his cheroot. 'I promise you, Gray, if you don't do as I say, they'll crucify you and your son in court. Are you ready for that? Perhaps you don't care about yourself, but the boy? He may act the tough young beggar now, but do you want to see him dismembered in public on the witness stand? That'll be a different story, I promise you. And you know what will come out.'

'The truth. That will come out.'

Furneaux snorted. 'Well, I hope you're prepared for *that*.'

For some reason Frank could not understand, Mr Gray's face changed. He sat down hard, as if his legs had just failed him, and stared at the wall, as if something ghastly had just appeared in the room.

Furneaux said, 'Make your travel plans quickly, that's my advice to you. We'll take care of the passage home, but after that you're on your own.'

Mr Gray swallowed. He seemed to have trouble tearing his eyes from whatever spectre it was that had arisen in front of him. 'You are telling us to leave?'

'Obviously. You can't stay in India. We have a position to maintain here. The Army, the company, all of us. The wogs hate us, naturally. There's nothing they like better than to see us fighting among ourselves.'

Mr Gray said nothing.

Furneaux's voice rose again. 'I am not about to see my work here jeopardised because some box wallah from up-country can't keep his wife and children in order.'

He strode from the room, flicking his still smouldering cheroot into the potted fern beside the door.

Frank slumped back against the wall. He didn't want to look at his father's face any more. He heard Furneaux march back through the house and summon his driver, and he heard the tonga clatter away. He felt nauseous, but he forced himself to his feet and began to push through the dry foliage back towards the glass doors of the guest room. He hauled himself up onto the small balcony there, but then could go no further and clung to the rail. His wrist throbbed, each throb an iron nail driven up his arm. The glaring day spun and he retched.

He hardly noticed the horse come jingling around the corner of the house, but when he looked up he found that Colonel James, resplendent in braid and blue, was a few feet from him. The colonel stared hard at Frank, his eyes travelling from his strapped wrist to his face. He reached inside his tunic, pulled out a small white visiting card and a pencil, and scribbled briefly.

'Take this,' he said, leaning forward from the saddle with a creak of leather. 'It's the address of my house in England. Lord knows when I'll be back there, but for what it's worth—'

'He should be punished for what he did!' Frank shouted. 'Why won't you punish him?'

The muscles tensed in the colonel's jaw. 'You don't want anything from me, boy, I understand that. But take it anyway.' He walked the horse forward, reached over the balcony rail and tucked the card into the pocket of Frank's shirt. 'Blame us, if it helps,' the colonel said. 'Blame anyone. But don't blame yourself. You did your best.' He touched his cap to Frank with his crop and trotted around the corner of the house and away down the drive.

Frank stayed where he was a few moments longer and then moved unsteadily through the guest bedroom, out into the cool corridor and down to his own room. He stripped off his clothes and got back into bed and lay there panting, his mind swimming with confusion and pain. He was sweating and he was angry and ill, but despite everything it was some comfort to be back between the cool sheets and not to have to move again. He lay very still, only half-conscious. Gradually his nausea retreated and the spiking pain in his wrist dulled.

Don't blame yourself. The colonel's words kept spinning through his mind. Every time his awareness drifted the phrase would ambush him and he would jolt into wakefulness again and the pain would return. *Don't blame yourself.* Had he not tried hard enough? But he *had* tried. Had they expected him to do more?

Frank heard the click of the study door and Mr Gray's slow footfalls came down the passage. The bedroom door opened and his father came to the side of the bed and sat down in the chair which stood there.

Frank kept his face turned to the wall. 'Will he die?'

'Thank God, Francis, the surgeon thinks not.'

'Why do we thank God for that?'

'Because between us we have enough to bear with.'

Frank rolled his head to look at his father. Mr Gray's face looked like that of a man ten years older and that hunted look was still in his eyes. On his lap lay Frank's discarded clothes. He could see the dried leaves which clung to them.

'You have a talent for subterfuge, Francis,' his father said, picking twigs from the clothes. 'I wonder where you got it from.'

And as if suddenly seeing something in these words which Frank himself missed, Mr Gray stood up quickly and stared out of the window, letting his son's clothes slip from his lap to the floor.

Without turning, he said, 'Francis, tell me exactly what happened last night.'

The question puzzled him. He had answered it already, surely. Or had he dreamed that? In any case, his father's tone forestalled argument, and Frank grappled with his memory. If he concentrated he could see the weapon in its leather holster, and could remember reaching for it. The ridged steel butt was cold against his palm, his fingers not large enough to grip it properly.

'I pulled the revolver out, Father. Out of the holster.'

'And?'

'I fired it into the ceiling. It hurt my wrist. But he wouldn't stop. He wouldn't stop hitting her. He wouldn't stop—'

'Go on, Francis,' Mr Gray said. 'Go on.'

'I meant to shoot him, Father. It wasn't an accident.' Frank sat up and his wrist spiked him but he didn't care. 'I meant to kill him.'

Mr Gray closed his eyes as if in pain. 'And then?'

'Then he knocked me down.'

Mr Gray's eyes sprang open. 'And took the weapon from you?'

Frank frowned. 'I don't remember how it happened. I just remember he hit me.' Frank saw his father's face sag. He wanted to help, to say whatever it was his father wished him to say, but his mind would only release to him the stink of the burning rug, the taste of smoke, the warm boards against his cheek. He could not bring anything further into focus and the effort hurt him. 'He hit me,' he repeated. 'I don't remember . . .'

Mr Gray breathed deeply. 'It's all right, my boy. We'll talk later.'

'I don't remember anything else until I was following him out onto the steps. I kept pulling the trigger until I couldn't hold the gun any more.' Frank stopped. 'I wish I had killed him.'

'Don't say that, Francis.'

'I wish I had,' Frank repeated fiercely, 'because nothing will happen to him now, will it? They've made a bargain, those men in your study. Haven't they? And you've agreed to it.'

Mr Gray gazed at him, his eyes filled with limitless weariness. 'Those men, Francis, are wrong about many things, but right about one. There would be a scandal. Do you understand what that means? We must think of your mother. We must consider how the world will regard her memory.'

'So is he to get off scot-free? I am not even to say that I saw him?'

'Listen to me!' his father roared, making him flinch back. 'I don't have a choice, do you hear me, Francis? I have to think of you.' Mr Gray felt behind him for the chair as an old man might and lowered himself into it. 'Of you . . . and Gifford.'

Frank realised he had gripped the bedclothes in his good hand and now he released them. 'I tried to help her, Father. Did I do wrong?'

'No, Francis. No one could have tried harder. You must not blame yourself.'

Those words again. And should he blame himself? Perhaps he should, after all. If he had not unclipped that holster, the pistol might never even have entered the equation. But what choice did he have? He heard again the screaming from the bedroom, saw his mother crawling. He realised that he had not been able to remember this before, but now all of a sudden it was clear to him. She was crawling and sobbing and screaming out.

'Jack,' Frank said abruptly.

Mr Gray lifted his head slowly.

'She called him Jack, Father. I heard her.'

'You can't be sure what you heard.'

'Yes. I'm sure. And he's with the Twenty-first Hussars.'

'You don't know that.'

'Yes, I do. I saw the insignia on the belt. I didn't recognise it at the time but I remember now. They're stationed in Secunderabad, the Twenty-first. They used to be stationed here, but they've been moved north—'

'No.' Mr Gray shook his head as if trying to clear it. 'You are not to say so, Francis.'

'But it's true.'

Mr Gray stood up and his chair rocked. 'We will not speak of this again. I have decided how this dreadful matter is to be handled, Francis. I have tortured myself over it these last few hours, but I have decided. And you will do as I say. Do you understand me?'

36

His father had never before spoken so forcefully to him and it scared him. 'Yes, Father.'

'We need to look to the future. We need to make a new life.'

Frank could find nothing to say.

'We are to leave India.' Mr Gray was speaking almost to himself now. 'All of us. All . . . three of us. I shall approach the company for a new position in England. It may not be easy at my age, but in view of my service, perhaps we may hope . . .' He did not finish the sentence but stopped and looked down at his son, as if he had forgotten his presence. 'I have made certain promises to you, Francis. No matter what I have to do, I shall see to it that those promises are kept. It is what I shall hold on to, if I can hold on to nothing else.'

He left the room and softly closed the door.

PART TWO

England, June 1893

10

Grace found her mother in the rose arbour behind the house. It was set around lily ponds, a place full of the trickle of water and the murmur of bees. Mrs Dearborn glanced up from her pruning and smiled at her daughter. She set down her basket on a stone bench and pulled off her gardening gloves and looked around her in the dreamy way so characteristic of her, as if she might or might not be planning to say something. This time she didn't.

'Mama,' Grace said, 'I wish to speak to you about Mrs Rossiter. She's been terribly unkind to—'

'Ah!' Mrs Dearborn cried. 'Now I remember what I was to tell you! I've been trying to think of it all morning.'

Her mother bent a stem bearing a closed rosebud close to her face and inspected it through her half-moon spectacles, but showed no inclination to say more. Grace waited, suppressing her familiar prickle of frustration. Her mother inhabited a peaceful universe all her own, and Grace was never quite sure how much of the real world filtered through to her.

'Mama?' she prompted. 'What was it you remembered?'

Her mother let the rose branch spring back. 'Your father is not coming today after all. He sent word that he will be travelling directly to town.'

Grace's world swooped into darkness. 'But he promised. It's my birthday.'

'Dear me, yes. Thirteen!'

'Fourteen, Mama.'

'Really? Well, don't worry. He said he would make it up to you. And the gifts are always so much finer when the gentlemen feel guilty.'

'How could he not come when he promised?'

'Because he's a man, my dear. I expect you'll get used to it.'

'I don't want to get used to it.'

A ladybird landed on Sarah Dearborn's finger and she watched it with delight, turning her hand to keep it in view. 'You've learned quickly enough how to handle your father. I've no doubt you'll manage.'

Grace wasn't sure if this was a compliment or not. 'Mama, about Mrs Rossiter.'

'Ah, yes. Our new dragon of a housekeeper.' Her mother puffed the ladybird off her hand and began to walk down the sanded path between the palisades of roses, regally signalling Grace to accompany her. 'What of her?'

'She was very unkind to Millie, who's so sweet tempered and has been with us for so many years. Poor Millie was in tears, and I spoke sharply to Mrs Rossiter about it.'

'You did? Good heavens, you're braver than I am, my dear. And one must admit that, despite her sweet temperament, Millie is – how shall I put it? – something of a lazy trollop.'

'Oh.' Grace was taken aback by this unexpectedly definite opinion. 'Was I wrong to express disapproval to Mrs Rossiter?'

'Who knows? Your father says she is terribly efficient. I confess I find her rather fearsome. But if she has spoken brusquely, I expect it's because of her loss.'

'Her loss?'

'No doubt it would harden any woman's heart to have her husband cut to pieces by savages. Even in a good cause.' Sarah Dearborn trimmed a stem. 'Oh, didn't you know? Poor Sergeant Rossiter *fell*, you know. Now that I call it to mind, I believe your father said not to mention it to you, for fear it might upset you. But no matter. You're not very much upset, are you, dear? That Sergeant Rossiter *fell*?'

Grace could not keep confused images of ladders and trees out of her head. It took her a moment to make the right connection. 'Do you mean he was killed, Mama?'

'Oh yes, some years ago now, whilst attempting to rescue gallant General Gordon – not all on his own, naturally. There were some others involved. Perhaps you've heard about General Gordon?'

'Everyone's heard about General Gordon, Mama.'

'The brave general was besieged in Cairo by savages. Or was it Carthage? Some such awful place. So of course Mr Gladstone had to try to rescue him. Anyway it was all perfectly useless. In the end, both General Gordon and Sergeant Rossiter were cut to pieces. And rather a large number of other people too, I seem to recall. Though not Mr Gladstone.' She smiled down at her daughter. 'I suppose they might all just as well have stayed at home. And then perhaps poor Mrs Rossiter wouldn't be quite so sharp of tongue, would she? But there, one must be forgiving. Oh! And what's the date, my dear, do you know?'

'It's the seventh of June, Mama,' Grace replied, darkly. 'My birth-day.'

'Of course, your birthday. Well, there you have it, you see. Today is the anniversary of the brave sergeant's death. Or some such anniversary.

I remember Mrs Rossiter told me that herself. In point of fact I planned to give her the morning off, but I confess it quite slipped my mind.' She frowned in irritation at her lapse but instantly brightened again. 'Still, never mind. Perhaps her daily round has helped keep the poor woman's thoughts from grief. And I do find it such a bore to manage the servants all on my own.'

She resumed her stroll, singing softly to herself. Grace stayed where she was, trying to decipher this astonishing information. She was thrilled by the image of the previously undreamed-of Sergeant Rossiter defying hordes of dervishes for Queen and Empire. She was disturbed to think that she had judged Mrs Rossiter so harshly, and was filled with a magnanimous urge to set matters straight. She could see herself making a grand and dignified apology, humbly setting aside her superior position in the face of Mrs Rossiter's Ultimate Sacrifice.

By the time Grace recalled herself from this generous vision, her mother was already far away, drifting like a lovely ghost down the green tunnel of roses, her face tilted to the summer sunshine as she walked.

11

It was not until the middle of the afternoon that Grace set out across the lawn and took the footpath to Mrs Rossiter's cottage.

The housekeeper's insistence on living alone and outside the household had caused some alarm among the servants, who saw it – accurately, as it turned out – as a portent of contrariness to come. Grace had thought it must be a drear life, alone in the cottage on the far side of the woods, and she had felt sorry for the woman. But now, as she followed the path through the trees and the little place came into view, she was struck by how pretty it was, set in a haze of wild anemones with the light filtering through the leaves onto a mossy slate roof. She stepped quietly forward until she stood in the patch of garden, hollyhocks and foxgloves, a pace or two from the front door. The door was ajar, and Grace realised that some part of her had hoped Mrs Rossiter would not be at home. There was something of the gingerbread house about that half-open door, an expectancy, a promise of things not altogether pleasant within. Grace's resolution wilted and she was in the act of turning away when the door was flung open, and Mrs Rossiter stood on the threshold facing her.

'Well, now! Young Miss Grace come calling, is it?'

'I'm . . . sorry to trouble you, Mrs Rossiter.' Grace braced herself. 'On a sad day like today.'

Mrs Rossiter stood there smiling, which Grace found unsettling. Her hair was down, which was inappropriate in an older woman, she thought. Mrs Rossiter's hair was grey, but very full and long, and it reached almost to her waist. Also, Mrs Rossiter had replaced her severe dark taffeta with a gingham print dress, open low at the neck. This and the cascade of long hair made Grace wonder if the housekeeper was younger than she had previously thought.

'So,' Mrs Rossiter said at last, 'someone's been talking to you.'

Grace had rehearsed quite a fine little speech, but now she could find no trace of it in her memory. She stood silently biting her lip and wishing very earnestly that she had never come.

'Cat got your tongue?' Mrs Rossiter said. 'Well then, you'd best come in and we'll try to loosen it for you.'

She ducked through the low door into her cottage, waving for Grace to follow. Mrs Rossiter's parlour was a small plain room made pleasant by broken sunlight falling through the front windows. A deal dresser stood against the far wall, with some pieces of blue and white crockery. Through a doorway into a lean-to Grace glimpsed a chipped china sink with an enamel jug on a draining board beside it, a zinc mesh meat safe, and shelves with jars and bottles on them. To her left Grace could see into a spare bedroom and she noted with some surprise that there were bookshelves in there crowded with pamphlets and papers and bound volumes.

Mrs Rossiter sat down at a scrubbed table just inside the door and gestured that Grace should sit opposite her. She did so, perching on the edge of her hardback chair. On the table in front of her she saw a square green bottle, two empty glasses and a fawn leather pouch worn soft with handling.

Mrs Rossiter filled one of the glasses and pulled it towards her. 'You're my first visitor here, miss, do you know that? No one else dares, I expect.' She leaned forward across the table and bared her teeth. 'In case I bite their 'eads off!'

She laughed as Grace started backwards. It was the first time Grace had ever heard Mrs Rossiter laugh, and it was a big laugh, almost a guffaw, which made her throw back her head and slap the table. Grace realised that Mrs Rossiter was a little drunk. She had seen her father drunk once or twice, and sometimes his friends when they dined at the house. The sight of men roaring and red in the face made her feel contemptuous, which seemed to be the appropriate female response, but she had never seen a woman drink to excess, least of all alone and in the middle of the day. The sight of it now was both disturbing and exciting.

Grace pointed at the leather satchel. 'Are those your husband's things?'

Mrs Rossiter stopped laughing. 'Well, now. You catch on quick.'

'I understand it is . . . his anniversary. I mean, of his . . .'

'Not his death, miss. Not quite. Eighteen years ago today I got sent this stuff.' Mrs Rossiter rested her hand on the satchel. 'He'd been dead and gone five months by then, but I only come to believe it when I see his kit.'

Grace avoided looking at the dead man's effects. 'You must be very proud of him.'

'Proud?'

'As a hero of the Empire.'

Mrs Rossiter thought about this. She poured half an inch of clear liquid into the glass which stood in front of her, and stared into it. 'Fancy that. Old Billy Rossiter, a hero of the Empire.' She drank, set her glass down. 'Silly bugger.'

Grace was shocked by such coarseness, and cast about for something to say which might move the conversation onto a loftier plane. 'At least Sergeant Rossiter died for a good cause,' she tried, hopefully.

Mrs Rossiter looked at her. 'Bringing light to the poor benighted heathen, miss?'

'Well, yes. That's what Papa says.'

Mrs Rossiter smiled thinly and leaned her elbows on the table. The glass in her right hand circled unsteadily. 'The Empire's not run for poor bloody heathens in Africa, miss. Don't you believe it. It's run for rich gentlemen in Manchester and Birmingham and London. Gentlemen like your papa.'

'Really, Mrs Rossiter, I—'

'Don't like the sound of that? Well, think of this, then. If there was no Empire, there'd be no trade, and so there'd be no ships. And that means no company, no money, no fine house. For the matter of that, no pretty Miss Grace Dearborn, with a French governess and a whole roomful of fine clothes she don't even remember she's got.' Mrs Rossiter sat back. 'See how it goes?'

Grace's colour rose. 'Papa works very hard. He built his business himself.'

'He didn't get chopped up in the Sudan while he was about it, though, did he? He left that to my Billy. And I'll tell you something else that everyone forgets. Sudan wasn't even *in* the Empire. That Godforsaken place was never anything to do with us. What's more, Egypt isn't ours either. It belongs to the Turks. So why were our lads

45

ever there, helping the Gyppos take old Fuzzy-Wuzzy's country? Answer me that.'

'But Mrs Rossiter, didn't they go to rescue General Gordon?'

'That psalm-singing lunatic?'

Grace was scandalised. There were times in her childhood when she had thought she was a little in love with the gallant General Charles Gordon, even though he was quite old. She could see him now as the paintings depicted him, standing at the top of the embassy steps, gazing down with contempt and pity at the maddened dervishes below, a revolver in one hand with which he did not even deign to defend himself.

'And what was Charlie Gordon doing there anyway?' Mrs Rossiter pushed on. 'Why was any of them there? Well, I'll tell you.' She tapped the table with her forefinger for emphasis. 'Because of the Suez bloody Canal, miss, and all the ships that go through it. British ships. Like the ships owned by your papa's company. That's why. Now don't tell me that's all about honour and glory and saving the 'eathen. That's all about money, that is.'

Grace stared at her, dumbfounded. She could not find her bearings in all this. Mrs Rossiter appeared to be talking not about the benevolent British Empire Grace knew, but about an entity as alien and dangerous as ancient Rome. Mrs Rossiter looked pretty alien and dangerous herself, Grace thought, with her long grey hair and the glass tilted in her hand, and that fierce combative light in her eyes.

The housekeeper drank some more and put her glass down heavily and her face hardened. 'The Empire can rot for all I care.'

'Mrs Rossiter!'

'Shocked, are you, miss? Well, there's another widow woman, sits on a throne up at Windsor, and I tell you this: if her old man had died under some Fuzzy-Wuzzy's knife instead of in a nice clean bed with his loved ones around, she might think the same way as me about her precious Empire and all it stands for.'

Grace stood up. 'You mustn't speak in this way! Papa says the Empire is the means by which we will all move forward in the world.'

'No, miss. It's just the way your papa will move forward in the world.' Mrs Rossiter levelled her forefinger. 'And you, too.'

'Me?'

'You're one of the chosen few, you are, miss. And don't you know it.'

Grace blushed violently. 'Mrs Rossiter, I think that most unfair. We don't in the least hold ourselves aloof.'

'No? Well, here's a thing: if you run back up to your big house and tell your nice papa what I've just said, he'll dismiss me without notice.

Think about that. A slip of a girl of fourteen years, who don't know nothing about nothing, and with a word you can get a woman like me put out on the streets. And you don't think you're a breed apart? Wake up, young Miss Grace. This whole bloody circus is run for your benefit. Billy and me and the likes of us are good enough to toil in it, to die for it. But it's you who gets the rewards.'

12

A brilliant panel of sky swung behind Mr Gray as he stepped into the stateroom and shut the steel door. He sat down opposite his son at the tiny desk under the porthole and set his well thumbed Homer between them, patting its calfskin cover.

Frank said, 'Are we to start lessons again, Father?'

'But of course. That is what we agreed.'

Frank did not argue, though this was the first he had heard of such a plan. It had become difficult to argue with Mr Gray on matters like this. There was a faraway light in his eyes these days. Quite often he did not seem to hear what was said to him, nor remember decisions he himself had announced with great firmness only hours before.

Mr Gray opened the Homer and flattened its pages. 'I shall read a little and then you render a translation.'

He did not wait for an answer but began at once to read. His manner was so natural that Frank wondered if after all they had agreed something like this. It would be good to believe that not everything was lost. And so he allowed himself to be drawn into the story, as familiar to him as breathing. He had always loved the ancient tale with its sirens and monsters, heroes and magic. The rhythm of the narrative flowed through him, and he took comfort in the slow roll of the ship and the thump of its engines, like the very chop of Odysseus's oars.

From where he sat he glimpsed the sea when the *Arbroath Castle* dipped far enough to lift a line of dark blue ocean across the porthole. The liner had to roll pretty far to do that − she was one of P&O's newest and largest − and Frank supposed this must be considered rough weather. From time to time the wind still dashed spray across the glass and the sky was white and strewn with torn rags of cloud as it had been ever since they had left Madras. He wondered if the clouds over the blue Aegean had looked that way to Odysseus.

The story soothed him and he wanted his father to keep reading, but presently Mr Gray stopped and pushed the open book across the desk.

'Now, Francis. Translate if you please.'

Frank did not trouble to look at the page. It had been a good dream, but now it was over. 'I don't need to translate, Father. I know it well enough.'

'Nonsense. Do as you are told.'

Frank held his father's gaze without defiance. He supposed he would be punished, but he was entirely indifferent, and Mr Gray must have sensed this for after a moment he reached across and closed the book with a soft thump.

'Very well, my boy. We will not argue. Perhaps we could spend a little time on Mr Tennyson instead. You might be surprised to hear that he wrote about more than military disasters. Indeed, he wrote about our old friend Ulysses once, whom we know as Odysseus. Do you know the poem? "My purpose holds to sail beyond the sunset . . ." '

Tennyson. They would sit here and discuss Tennyson, as if nothing had happened. Frank stared down at the closed Homer, suddenly close to tears.

His father saw his face and stopped in his recitation. 'You doubt the future, Francis. Well, I have suffered my moments of despair, too, you may depend upon that. But we will rebuild after disaster, my boy. We will come through.'

The optimism in his voice was as brittle as glass. Frank could not look at him for fear of shattering it. He was glad when his father stood up and went to one of the wooden cupboards in the corner of the room. He unlocked it with a key on his watch chain and took out his leather portmanteau and brought it back to the desk. He opened the case and took out a sheaf of six or seven cream envelopes, each addressed in his careful and precise hand.

'I have taken the expedient of writing individually to Dearborn & Company's major offices. Do you see? Bristol, Liverpool, Edinburgh. And so on. There are always openings for a man of my experience.'

Frank gazed at the letters and now he glanced up at his father's radiant and desperate face. He felt a hollow space open in him and dropped his eyes to the copy of Homer on the table between them.

Mr Gray's breath was coming fast and eager. He put the letters away in his portmanteau and after a moment's hesitation drew out another envelope, larger and fatter than the others. He set it on the surface between them. 'Open that, Francis. Then you'll see.'

Frank tore the seal. The envelope was packed with one-hundred-pound bank notes, a denomination he had never known existed, far less handled. He stared at the money.

'Do you know what that is?'

'No, Father.'

'It's your education, Francis. I have managed to put this money aside over the years, little by little, and it will pay for Napier College at least until we are settled once again.'

Frank lifted his head. 'I could still go to school?'

'It's what I've worked for all my life, Francis. I want you to know that, and thus be reassured that . . . that all will be well.'

'And Gifford?'

'Gifford is not yet eleven years old. By the time he is ready for a place like Napier College I will once again have a position and our fortunes will be restored. Yes, perhaps even more than restored.'

Mr Gray gathered up the envelope, made a clumsy attempt to seal it again, fumbled it back into the portmanteau. He was smiling as he did so, and making small sounds of eagerness.

Frank said, 'Where will we go when we reach England, Father?'

'I have written to your aunt Lily, my sister. Her husband is some sort of a superintendent on the canals in London. Respectable enough people, I gather. Oh, yes. We were never close, you know, Lily and I. But they'll give us a roof over our heads for a week or two while we find our feet.'

Frank could not imagine what manner of life these unheard-of relatives could possibly lead in London. A superintendent on the canals? He pictured black water and drear docksides. What could it be like, living with these strangers who had never been close? He thought of the large airy bungalow in Bangalore, and its tribe of servants, the warmth and the colour and the illicit thrill of the old city at night. All of it had melted away like some broken enchantment.

Mr Gray was watching him. Frank met his gaze at last, and as he did so the exultant light died away from his father's eyes and his smile fell from his lips and he was himself again. Stricken, grown old, but himself. Mr Gray reached into his case once more and held out a small framed photograph for Frank to take. It showed his mother at the age of perhaps eighteen, smiling, her head thrown back, radiant and lovely. Frank had never seen it before.

'That likeness was taken in Blackpool, in 1878,' Mr Gray said softly. 'We had been married just four months. It was a bright spring day, I remember how warm it was. A week later, my leave was over and we left for India.'

In the photograph his mother was bareheaded, her bright hair falling loose over the shoulders of her short-sleeved dress. The sun lay on her bare arms and her lips were slightly parted.

'Keep the picture.' Mr Gray got to his feet. 'Perhaps she was always more yours than mine.'

He reached forward as if to touch Frank's shoulder but at the last moment rested his hand on the closed Homer instead. He picked up the book, felt behind him and pushed open the door against the dazzle of sun and air. He stepped out and the door clanged shut behind him.

13

The fine weather broke that night and Grace spent the rest of the week mooching indoors while the rain fell. Her lessons helped. It was French and European history this week, given by a pretty governess from Toulouse. They met in one of the more airy upstairs rooms which looked out over early summer countryside under rolls of drizzle. Grace was quick at lessons, and Mademoiselle Taillard's praise soothed her feelings, but even so once or twice she had to be chided for gazing from the window, trying to glimpse Mrs Rossiter's cottage among the trees.

She never could catch sight of it, and sometimes she wondered if it really existed, and if that astonishing conversation had ever taken place. Over the last few days she had occasionally seen Mrs Rossiter bustling about her duties, a prim, upright, darkly dressed figure, barking at the housemaids in that peremptory way of hers. But this figure had nothing in common with the strangely wild woman Grace had met. Once they came face to face in the empty morning room, but the housekeeper gave not the slightest sign, not by so much as an ironic glance, that anything had passed between them.

Whenever she recalled Mrs Rossiter's words Grace found herself swinging between indignation and an obscure sense of shame, as if she had been personally accused of some wrongdoing of which, at heart, she knew she was guilty. There were times when she thought Mrs Rossiter was ungrateful – and foolish, to take such a risk with the daughter of the house, who could so easily pitch her back into poverty.

And yet she sensed that this was a trust which the housekeeper had deliberately placed in her, and that flattered her. No one had ever treated her so like an adult before, and she knew that whatever she felt about Mrs Rossiter, she would never betray her.

On the Friday evening of that week Grace was alone in the drawing room after dinner, practising her piano pieces. She normally enjoyed her exercises; it pleased her to fill a room with music, however imperfectly performed. But tonight her heart was not in it. The wet weather during the day had begun to get her down, and it depressed her now to hear the rain spatter against the tall black windows. She could have tolerated a driving storm, but the rain itself seemed to have lost spirit and had been falling with miserable steadiness all day long.

Grace sighed, sat back, and closed the piano lid. She gazed around the room without enthusiasm, at the ornaments under their glass domes and the stern portraits on the walls. The new electric light which her father had had installed was yellow and sickly, and the fire was unlit now that summer had nominally arrived, so that the room was uncomfortably cool.

'Miss?'

Grace looked up, startled. She could tell from the maid's expression that she had already spoken at least once.

'Your father, miss. He says, please to join him in his study.'

'Now, Millie?'

'He said I was to bring you directly, if you please, miss.'

Grace glanced at the clock. Nine thirty. The summons was surprising in the extreme. Whenever he was at home, her father's most treasured private hours were those he spent in his study after dinner. Grace had never been called there at this hour. She began to wonder whether she had done something wrong, and was tempted to ask Millie if she had any clues. But in the end she could not bring herself to betray her nervousness to a servant, and instead followed the girl down the corridor and across the hall to her father's study. Millie tapped on the door, bobbed her head and hurried away.

Grace heard her father's call and opened the door. He was evidently in expansive mood, she saw with relief, leaning back in his captain's chair behind his desk.

'Why, hello, Puss! Come in, and sit you down.'

She sat on the edge of one of the chairs. It struck Grace that her father was a dramatically handsome man. Still not much above forty, he was tall with thick hair just greying at the temples, and a habit of dressing immaculately. Grace had seen him in a rage several times, usually with incompetent servants, and then he could be frightening. But he never unleashed this other self on her, and tonight it was hard to imagine that it even existed. Dearborn locked his hands behind his head and swivelled in his chair, smiling. The scarlet dragons on his silk waistcoat shone in the lamplight and his diamond studs sparkled.

'Have you forgiven me, Puss, for not taking you to tea on your birthday, as I promised? Small consolation to you, I'm sure, but I was summoned by the Governor of the Bank of England. Damned cheek, eh?'

She lowered her eyes. 'I know you are very busy, Papa.'

'Oh, very demure!' he laughed. 'That's good. There was a time I thought you might stay a tomboy all your life. Hard to believe now. How old are you? Remind me.'

'Fourteen, Papa,' she said, although she knew he was quite well aware of how old she was.

'Fourteen! Well, well.' He tilted his head. 'My little girl is growing up fast, as anyone can see who takes the trouble to look. And I don't doubt some already do.'

She glanced up at him at this odd compliment, wondering where it was leading, where this whole conversation was leading. His teasing was always good humoured enough, but this time it was different. This time she felt strangely awkward, and she blushed.

He brought his chair forward so that his elbows came to rest on his blotter and he could look her in the eyes. 'We parents never notice our children growing up, Puss. They're always little ones to us, satisfied with toys and dolls and whatnot. But you're past that point, I think. Some way past it.' He opened a drawer in his desk, took out a small box of dark blue card and slid it across the polished surface towards her. 'Your birthday present. No more dolls or picture books for you. Open it.'

The cardboard was dry and firm under her fingers. She held her breath, lifted the lid. The pendant lay on a little cushion of royal blue satin, a black nacreous globe the size of a pea in a clasp of gold. She lifted it out gingerly, feeling the weight of it, the fine gold chain trickling like cool water between her fingers.

'It's lovely, Papa.'

'I believe it is. And I hope it's a gift worthy of a lovely young woman, Puss. Because that's what you've become.'

She gazed down at the jewel in her hands, her eyes filling. After a moment her father stood and came around the desk and took the pendant from her hands. He moved behind her and fastened the chain at the nape of her neck. He touched her elbow and raised her formally, as if leading her to a dance. In front of the mirror he rested one hand on her neck and gazed proudly at her in the glass. The pendant burned at her breast, black and gold.

'It's a black pearl,' he said. 'They come from the South Seas. Only one pearl in a thousand is black, some say one in ten thousand. Anyway, they're deucedly rare, and dangerous to come by, by all accounts.' He put his head on one side, inspecting her in the glass with a look Grace had never seen before, wondering and rueful in equal parts. 'My, my, Puss, we shall have to introduce you into society a little more, I can see that.'

He stepped back, letting his hand slide from her shoulder and giving it a little squeeze on the way, and she understood from this that the extraordinary interview was over. She knew she should thank him and leave, but she sensed that she had an opportunity to speak openly to him which might not quickly come again.

'Papa, are we very rich?'

He widened his eyes in amusement. 'Reasonably well-to-do, Puss. I'm doing my best to make us more so.'

'Are we rich because of the Empire?'

He leaned back against his desk, regarding her. 'The Empire has the capacity to make everyone rich, Puss. Or at least, richer.'

'Everyone?'

'I'd say so. In the end, everyone benefits.' He seemed to catch the train of her thought then. 'Take the niggers who dived for that pretty bauble of yours, for example. If it weren't for fond fathers in great houses in England, where would they sell their wares? Before we British came they would have been under the lash of some local tyrant, who'd have forced them to dive for his profit until they died.'

'Died?' She looked at him with alarm.

'Pearl diving's a risky venture. And they can be cruel to their own kind, these natives, if left to their own devices. They need direction, Puss, and we give it to them, at some cost to ourselves.' He paused. 'Dear me, but this is a grown-up conversation! What's sparked your interest in these affairs?'

'I read an article, Papa . . . In a periodical. I saw it in a shop in Guildford while I was waiting for Mama.' She held her breath, but the ground didn't open nor the heavens crash down. In fact the lie had been surprisingly easy.

'And what did this article say?'

'That not everyone benefits from the Empire. Not the Queen's subjects overseas, and sometimes not those here, either. Not always. That's what it said.'

'What's this?' he cried in mock horror. 'You take care, my girl, or we'll be seeing you in Regent's Park of a Sunday, with all the other savage revolutionaries. And was there more sedition in this article?'

She could feel her heart beating, but there seemed no point in stopping now. 'It said that we wage war for profit, not for glory.'

'Ah. I see.' He sat back, as if he had been half-expecting this. 'For instance?'

'Sudan, Father. The writer said we had only gone to war there to protect the Suez Canal. And that we might go to war there again for the same reason. I don't believe it, of course—'

'Well, you probably should believe it, Puss. In the Sudan, like

53

anywhere else, we'd go to war to protect our trade routes, and so much the better if we can keep the Frenchies out in the process. Would you not consider those to be good reasons?'

He was teasing her again, she was sure of that, but even allowing for that his answer was confusing. It had not occurred to her that there might be reasonable causes for war. If there were, she couldn't see how she might distinguish them from the unreasonable ones. It had all seemed much clearer when she was speaking to Mrs Rossiter.

'But surely it can't be right for us to take things from other nations?'

'We don't *take* them, Puss. We buy raw materials from the Empire – Indian cotton, Chinese tea, Australian wool – and make them into useful articles and sell them to the countries which can't manufacture for themselves. That's what free trade is all about. Does that not benefit everyone?'

'But then . . . we profit from the labour of poor people in other countries?'

'Well, you put it harshly, but when all's said and done, that's rather the idea.'

'But that means we buy fewer things made by British workers.'

'Our own workers cannot supply everything we need. And where they can, they need to be competitive. To pay people more just because they live in these islands would be a form of charity, wouldn't it? Demeaning for them, and unsustainable in the long term. No, no. Trade needs to be free and global. We must buy where we can obtain our goods most cheaply.'

'Can it be right that we should oppress people, Papa?'

He grew serious. 'We get the best of the bargain at present, I grant you. I would sooner be here at Cumver, warm and well fed, than cutting cane or toiling in a mine. And I won't pretend that many workers of that kind have an easy life of it. But that's an economic reality, Puss. It's not within my power to change it.'

'Not even a little?'

'You start tinkering with the cogs and wheels and pretty soon the entire mechanism grinds to a halt. It's regrettable, but there it is.'

'Just the same, Papa, you wouldn't . . . make slaves of people? Would you?'

'Slaves? I should hope not.'

'Do you promise?'

He looked at her thoughtfully. 'I see you want everything in black and white, Puss, signed, sealed and witnessed. Very well, if it will make you feel better, I promise. But remember this: without our investment, without trade, there would be no employment of any kind. If British

54

companies were to shut down their operations in India and Africa, for example, we would lose, certainly, but so would the world's poor workers, the very people you would like to help.'

Something about this argument troubled her, but before she could work out what it was he stepped forward and rested his hands on her shoulders. 'You've won the lottery of life, Grace. There's no denying that and it's well you should take note of it. I'm glad you do.'

'It's just that I wonder how I came to deserve it, Papa.'

'Life is unfair. Some creatures are stronger than others, and they rule by natural law. It can't be changed, not at least in the short term. The lion can't eat grass just to spare the poor zebra. One day, when you're a little older, you might read Mr Darwin. He has a good deal to say on the matter.' He stepped back, caught her hands and squeezed them. 'Now I have work to do, young miss.'

She walked to the door. By the time she reached it he was already behind his desk, rearranging his papers.

She said, 'Do men truly die diving for pearls?'

He glanced up as if surprised to find her still there. Once again she was struck by what a fine looking man he was, enthroned behind his huge desk the colour of port wine. The assurance that emanated from him was seductive, irresistible. Surely, she thought, he could not be wrong.

'Should you like to give back your beautiful necklace, Puss? We could sell it for the poor.'

Involuntarily she clutched the pendant in her palm and held it tightly to her.

'I thought not,' he said, and smiled.

14

The revolver is not yet in his hands. It is rocking on the boards just inches from his face. Flames from the burning lamp oil behind him wink on dull steel and the floor is warm against his cheek and there is a roaring in his head. He knows there is something very wrong, something which does not fit, but he cannot place what it is.

Frank jerked awake, sitting up so sharply in his chair that he had to catch the Homer before it slid to the floor.

But the image was still there before his eyes, the revolver rocking on the floor. He remembered he had been gripping it desperately hard, firing it – he recalled its vicious kick, a spike of pain and then sick numbness. He had changed hands and fired again. Yes, he remembered looking up to see the man swaying, his face in darkness.

And after that? The man had pressed the hand to his side and it had come away crimson, then he'd stepped forward, swung back his free fist. Frank remembered the knuckles clubbing him over the ear and he was on his knees and the room was tilting. The fist must have come back again, for something caught him like a mallet on the opposite side of the head and sent him sprawling. Now, for the first time, he heard the thud and clatter of the revolver against the boards as it was knocked from his hand. He knew this was important, but he could not understand why.

'Francis?'

He started. Matron Evans was standing beside him, her face full of concern.

'Are you all right, Francis? You were talking. Shouting.'

'I was not,' he said quickly and rubbed his cheek. Where he had slumped against the cabin wall the wooden panelling had printed his skin. He mumbled, 'I was reading. Reading aloud.'

'I see.' She stood watching him, unconvinced.

Frank moved his stool closer to the cot, settled the book open on his lap. Not long before he had indeed been reading aloud, about Achilles sulking in his tent, about the deadly duel between Patroclus and Hector, and Hector's bloody victory in that fight. He'd read about the passionate grief which goaded Achilles to revenge, when neither pride nor duty could move him. For a while Frank had been lost on the plain of the Scamander with the scent of thyme in the air and bronze blades flashing in the sunlight.

And then exhaustion had taken him, and carried him back to that dreadful room. How long had he been there, with the revolver rocking on the floor just out of his reach, while Matron Evans stood behind him, observing him? He had not heard her come in. Perhaps the ship's rumbling engines had masked the rustle of her starched dress. Now he wanted Matron Evans to leave him in peace so that he could ransack his memory before these new images faded. Perhaps she would leave if he read on, but the feeble electric light in the cabin seemed to have faded and his head ached with the strain of making out the print.

'Is that Latin?' Matron Evans asked.

'It's Greek.' He did not raise his head from the book. 'Ancient Greek.'

'Does he understand, do you think?'

Frank looked at the figure in the cot, the faded eyes. 'I don't know. I think he likes the sound of it.'

'The poor gentleman.'

She moved past him and tidied the bedclothes unnecessarily, murmuring to Mr Gray. She was a kindly middle-aged woman with iron hair. She was used to treating seasickness, malaria and a broken bone or two, but now she did not know how to help.

'You should go outside, young Frank,' she said as she worked. 'Get some fresh air. It's not every day a young man gets to see the Suez Canal.'

'I want to read some more to him first.'

She stood up. 'You've been reading for hours.'

'I want to try some Tennyson. He always loved Tennyson. "My purpose holds to sail beyond the sunset, and the baths of all the western stars . . ." '

He stopped. He didn't know why he had told her so much, perhaps to avoid seeing the dangerous sympathy in her eyes. Now he stood in silence, his head bowed, and refused to look at her.

'We'll be at Tilbury in two weeks,' Matron Evans said gently. 'Have you considered what you will do?'

'Father will be better by then.'

'But if he isn't?'

'We have family.' He fixed his gaze just above her head. 'Aunt Lily and Uncle Walter. In London.'

'I see.' She was quiet for a moment. 'Go outside, Frank. Gifford needs you, too. I'll sit here with your father for an hour or so.'

Frank hesitated a moment longer, and then placed the Homer on the table and left the cabin, stepping out into a velvet blue night. It was warm and still, only the steady motion of the ship generating a soft breeze. He walked to the rail. Beneath him was a stretch of black water and then a belt of palms and papyrus, silver under a dome of stars. Here and there along the bank stood mud-brick huts, and once an official looking square building with a tin roof and a flagpole. He saw no sign of human activity except for a single ox cart trundling in a plume of dust along the canal-side road. Beyond lay a vast and arid expanse of country, glimmering bone white in the starlight until it faded into the western darkness. Frank could smell scents which were new to him, and others which had become unfamiliar after weeks at sea – animal dung, rotting water weeds, the faint tang of an open fire. The liner's wash slapped against the banks, a phosphorescent ripple which followed them as they forged on through the night.

'It's one hundred and two miles long,' Gifford said happily from beside him. 'Did you know that, Frank?'

Somehow the boy was standing at the rail next to him. Plump Mrs

Grant in her dark dress and old fashioned bonnet was moving quickly away down the deck. Frank could hear her sniff back tears as she went.

'No, I didn't know that.'

'Well, it's true. It's twenty-six feet deep and it goes all the way from Port Tawfiq on the Red Sea – that's the port of Suez – to Port Said, and there isn't a single lock between the Mediterranean and the Red Sea. It took ten years to build and they say that at any one time thirty thousand men worked on it, lots of them forced labour. Those lights up ahead, that's the Ballah Bypass. Do you see them, Frank?'

Frank could see the lights clearly now, a distant glow fanning up into the sky from the desert. He could make out pinpricks of red and green, and even the black silhouettes of buildings and cranes.

'I see them, Giff.'

'Scores of ships pass through there every single week. Apart from the Great Bitter Lake, that's the only place they can get past one another. Most of them are ours. British ships, I mean. And all this is because of a French engineer. We opposed construction. Until we bought it, that is. We were keen enough then.' Gifford kept his eyes on the lights ahead. 'Papa's not going to get better, is he?'

'No, he isn't.'

'Poor Papa.'

Frank rested his hand on his brother's shoulder. He had never done this before. 'I'll take care of everything, Giff. I promise.'

'Oh, yes.' Gifford smiled up at him. 'I know you will, Frank.'

The cabin door behind them swung open and Matron Evans called, 'Frank? You'd better come.'

She sounded flustered and that frightened him. He stepped back in over the steel lintel, pushing past her starched skirts. She leaned past him out of the door and called urgently to Miss Grant, and he heard Gifford's querying voice as he was ushered away. The door clanged to.

'I turned my back for a moment,' she said, 'only for a moment . . .'

'It's all right,' Frank told her. He didn't know why he said this, because it was not all right, but the woman seemed to need to hear it from him.

Mr Gray had found his clothes somehow and had dressed in them in a haphazard fashion. Now he was seated on the cot pulling on his Oxford brogues.

'Father?'

'What is it?'

'Why are you out of bed?'

'Because I'm going to the club, of course. Overslept, dash it. Got to meet Mr Stokes. Splendid chap, Stokes.' Mr Gray stopped tugging at his laces and peered at him. 'Who are you?'

'I'm Frank, Father. I'm Francis.'

Frank reached out his hand but Mr Gray shrugged it away.

'Nonsense. A ragamuffin like you? My Francis is a fine upstanding boy. He'll be going to school, soon. An excellent school, too. Sends young chaps to Oxford and Cambridge . . . The Heaven Born! Hah!' He peered at Frank again. 'You? You'll never come to any good, whoever you are. That's plain for anyone to see.'

'I couldn't calm him,' Matron Evans whispered. 'He's been calling for things – shaving stuff, collar studs. Silly things.'

'Where's Marjorie?' Mr Gray demanded. He had managed to get his shoes on at last and now he stood up. Frank saw that his father's brogues were on the wrong feet. 'We'll make an entrance, Marjorie and I, won't we? Deputy Manager, Bangalore, and his lady wife. Hah!'

'Father—'

Mr Gray leaned forward, gripped Frank's shoulder, and peered earnestly into his eyes. 'I *don't* know you, do I?'

It took Frank a moment to find his voice. 'Perhaps you don't, Father.'

'As I thought.' Mr Gray stood up straight, pleased to have his judgment vindicated. 'Still, you can do me a service by fetching Marjorie for me. Mustn't be late for the club.'

'Father, she's—'

'Wonderful woman!' Mr Gray swung back to face him. 'I love her, you know. Always have. Bit of a dunce at showing it.' But then, with a suddenness that made him look clownish, his face fell. 'I've ruined everything. Haven't I?'

Frank took his arm. 'You should get back into bed now.'

Mr Gray looked into Frank's eyes. 'My son,' he said.

He died then, and Frank was not even quick enough to catch him as he fell.

15

The masts of the ships at Tilbury docks stood black against a brick-red night sky. The five of them left the Customs House in a small procession, Frank and Gifford in front, the porter trundling his trolley with their baggage just behind, and the two women following in their dark capes and bonnets.

On the quayside behind them families were embracing under the lights of the docked liner, but it was gloomy up ahead with only the gaslights around the iron gates making a hole in the night. Frank could smell the river. Rain slanted through lamplight onto tram tracks. Miss Grant was weeping again. Frank would have said something to comfort her, but he was too preoccupied to spare her any attention now, and he was glad when Matron Evans told her briskly to be quiet.

'There!' Gifford tugged Frank's hand. 'That's Uncle Walter!'

Frank peered through the rain. Outside the tall gates stood a cluster of cabs and carts, their waterproof hoods shining in the lamplight. Horses stood with their heads down in the drizzle and drivers clustered in what shelter they could find, black figures hunched into their coats. Frank had no idea why Gifford had decided the bulky form just inside the railings should be their uncle, but sure enough the man started towards them over the wet cobblestones.

'Frank Gray?' he called, before he was halfway to them. He had a big voice and a flat London accent. 'Is that you?'

'Uncle Walter?'

The man came up to them, his arms wide. He laughed, and then caught himself and let his arms fall. 'Not that there's much cheer in a meeting such as this, after what you've been through. But it's a sight to see family come home from so far away. Oh, yes, it's a sight indeed.'

He was a strong, stocky man in a heavy overcoat. He had a big moustache, but he was almost bald and the rain shone on his cannon-ball head. He was in his forties, and had a heavy face which arranged itself naturally into good humour, so that his efforts to keep his expression solemn were almost comical.

'You poor blokes,' he said, and put one meaty hand on Frank's shoulder. 'My word! What a bloody dreadful time you must have had! Begging your pardon, ladies, for my language.'

'You are Mr Bradshaw?' Matron Evans demanded, not altogether with approval. 'Mr Walter Bradshaw?'

'Miss Evans, is it? I had your telegram.' Uncle Walter put out his big hand and, somewhat reluctantly, she gave him her gloved one. 'And you sent it from Cairo?' he said. 'In Egypt? That's a first for us in our house, that is. A telegram from Egypt! Didn't know you could do such a thing.'

'That's of no consequence, Mr Bradshaw.' Matron Evans withdrew her hand. 'Only the boys' welfare is of concern at this moment. You are indeed their uncle?'

'I am, miss. My missus is their aunt Lily.'

'I should have preferred to have met the lady in person.'

'Someone has to cook the dinner, miss.' Uncle Walter grinned, then remembered again and put on his grave face.

Behind him, Frank heard Miss Grant start to sob.

Matron Evans glanced at the other woman with irritation. 'Very well. Miss Grant and I can't linger. Let us finish with the formalities.'

'Miss, if I may say, Lily and I will forever be grateful for your kindness in looking after the lads—'

'Yes, yes. Now if you'd be good enough to sign this document. It confirms that I have released the children into your care, as their next of kin.'

Matron Evans took a paper from her bag, spread it on one of the cases on the baggage trolley and tilted her umbrella over it. Uncle Walter signed clumsily with the fountain pen she gave him.

'There.' She took the letter back and folded it away. 'Now be a good boy, Frank, and you can rise above this tragedy, I am persuaded of it. And you, young Gifford, you remember to do what your older brother tells you. He has a wise head on his shoulders. Wiser than perhaps he knows.'

She put out her hand to Frank, but at the last moment bent down and caught both of them in a short and fierce embrace. Then she swung away, catching the sobbing Miss Grant's arm and hurrying her back through the rain towards the light and bustle of the dockside. Frank watched them go. He was cold and the rain was running down his face, but he didn't care.

'Kindly old dragon, ain't she?' Uncle Walter said gently. 'Always sad to part from people as have been good to you. But at least you're with family now, lads.' He pointed to the three battered suitcases on the trolley. 'Is that all you have?'

'There didn't seem to be much point in keeping things,' Frank said, still watching the dark silhouettes of the women as they dwindled away.

'Best start afresh, eh?' Uncle Walter felt in his pocket for coins and paid the porter and hefted the cases from the trolley. 'Well, let's be off. We have a bit of a ride, but your aunt Lily'll have something for us when we get in.'

Uncle Walter had brought a small delivery cart with a hood over the seat and the words *Camden Navigation* in fancy script on the side. He loaded the cases on the back and tied a tarpaulin over them, then lifted Gifford bodily up onto the box and pulled the hood over the seat as far as he could. Frank climbed up and sat between his brother and the big man.

'Right then,' Uncle Walter said, with an attempt at cheeriness. 'Off we go.'

But after that he did not speak again. Frank guessed that, now their meeting was a reality, his uncle was silenced by the very strangeness of it. He wondered what on earth the big man made of the pair of them, these new ready-made nephews suddenly catapulted into his life from a different world. Frank wasn't sure what he had expected of Uncle Walter either. He liked the man's rough warmth, and the solidity of him. But it was obvious to him already that Uncle Walter and Aunt Lily were not merely modestly situated, as his father had suggested, but were actually poor. That knowledge troubled him. He grew conscious of the fat cream envelope in his inside pocket. But he had no energy to think this through now. He closed his eyes and after a few minutes the swaying of the cart lulled him into an exhausted sleep.

'Is this London?' Gifford asked.

Frank came awake with a jerk. He didn't know how long they'd been going, but his brother was gazing out in wonder at a glittering vista of office buildings, at shop windows, and wet streets streaked yellow under the lamps.

'It's London all right, young Gifford,' Uncle Walter said, speaking for the first time since Tilbury. 'Old London Town.'

'It's big, isn't it?'

'You could say so, lad.' Walter glanced across at Frank. 'I know it's late, but I thought we'd make a bit of a detour, since the little lad was so keen. Show him some of the sights.'

Frank sat up and tugged his jacket around himself. He had expected the capital to be impressive, but he was unprepared for the vastness of the place and its chaotic energy even at this hour. Hurrying people bent against the wet wind, and roadways were crammed with omnibuses, horse trams, carriages, cabs. They were travelling down a broad embankment with the river to their left, the stippled water crowded even now with the black shapes of barges and tugs and lighters, their lights swaying with the tide. Ahead lay a great bridge, and over to Frank's left stood the Houses of Parliament, a block of lit windows and towers with that famous clock hanging above like a full moon. Yes, London was big, Frank thought. Big and cold and, beyond the reach of those trembling lights, its alleys and courts were as black as night itself. He could not imagine what kind of a future could be carved from this alien place.

He dozed again, and did not awake again until they were rattling down a wide thoroughfare flanked by commercial buildings, most of them closed and shuttered for the night. Through a gap in the buildings Frank glimpsed the roof of some huge railway terminus, the lights within glowing feebly through filthy glass. Uncle Walter slowed the horse and they entered a warren of streets, crossed a canal bridge with barges and narrow boats moored in ranks below, and after a few moments stopped outside a row of waterside terraces.

'Well, lads, here it is.' Walter leaned forward to haul on the brake. 'I doubt it's what you're used to, but it's 'ome.'

The door of the house stood open and in the lit doorway stood a middle-aged woman with her arms folded. She wore a sober dress and her hair was pulled back severely from her face. Frank climbed down and walked across the pavement to stand directly in front of her. He had meant to introduce himself, but something forbidding in her attitude stilled his tongue and he stood stupidly, staring at her.

'Your own nephews, Lil,' Uncle Walter called from behind him, and Frank could hear the false note in his cheeriness. 'Your own brother's kids. How about that, then, eh?'

The woman turned her small eyes to Frank, looked him up and down, and flicked her gaze on to Gifford as he came up beside him. 'Lord God Almighty,' she said, and walked away into the house.

16

Frank followed Uncle Walter up narrow stairs to a low room under the angle of the roof. The space was so cramped that Walter's bulk seemed to fill it, and he had to stand aside to let Frank and Gifford squeeze past. Boxes of dusty junk had been shoved against the walls. There was a single cot bed with a stained mattress, a pitcher and bowl and a candle set on the edge of the chimney breast. A pile of blankets lay on the floor.

'It's the best we can do for you, Frankie,' Uncle Walter said.

Frank shook out a couple of blankets from the pile and arranged them on the cot. He took Gifford's arm and steered the boy to the bed. He noticed the boy's jacket was wet through. He supposed his own must be, too. Meekly, half-asleep, Gifford climbed among the blankets.

Walter tilted his head down the stairs. 'Don't mind Lil. She barks fierce, but she knows blood's thicker than water. Come down when you're ready, Frankie. Eat a bite. Warm yourself. Things'll look better then.'

When he had gone Frank sat on the floor by the tiny window.

On the bed, Gifford yawned. He said, 'Will we be living here, Frank?'

Frank didn't answer at once. The wind leaned against the glass and pressed in through gaps in the frame. From this vantage point he looked out over a stretch of black water and some kind of inland dock forested with the masts of boats, and beyond that to wharves and warehouses. Rain drove through the gaslights and speckled the water. It was supposed to be summer. So this was what summer in England was like. To him the room was cold and damp. To the east the sky was just beginning to pale.

'Yes, Giff. For the moment.'

He walked over to his brother, but Gifford was already asleep, curled up in his nest of blankets. Frank eased the boy's wet jacket off and pulled the bedding up over him.

He went back to the window and ran his hands around the frame and down the brickwork to the floor. An old trunk stood half under the window and Frank pushed it aside and felt the uneven boards, poking at one or two, testing their solidity. Finally one gave a little under his touch. He opened his pocket knife and levered the board up, exposing the wattle of the ceiling below and a century of dust. He took the cream envelope from the inside pocket of his jacket, tucked the packet into the space and replaced the board, tapped it down again. He spent a couple of minutes disguising his work, brushing dust back into the cracks between the boards, pulling the trunk back into position to cover the spot.

He got to his feet and stood for a moment watching his sleeping brother before climbing down the stairs.

The little kitchen was raw with coke fumes from the stove, but Frank could smell food too, and his stomach grumbled. Aunt Lily was sitting very upright at the table, her mouth thin. Uncle Walter stood at the hob, lifting the lid off a saucepan, peering in and making comical smacking noises with his lips.

'There you are, Frankie,' he said. 'Sit you down. Young Gifford's hipped, is he? Poor little chap.'

Frank sat opposite his aunt.

'Two letters,' she said, without preamble

Frank looked up at her dully.

'That's what your father wrote to me,' she told him, her eyes narrow with anger. 'Ever since he went back to India with that woman all them years ago. Two letters. That's how much he thought of me.'

'Lil,' Walter chided. He put the lid back on the pot and came to the table. 'Poor Lewis was your brother, God rest his soul. Now get the boy something to eat, and stop your moaning.'

Aunt Lily shoved her chair back and went to the stove. 'And now I'm to look after his children, am I?' She ladled stew into a bowl, slopping it as she did so. 'He always had big dreams, Lewis did, but they never come to nothing.'

Uncle Walter slid the bowl over to Frank. 'Family's family, Lil. We'll make do.'

'I'll work,' Frank said. 'I'll pay.'

Aunt Lily banged the lid back on the saucepan and put her hands on her hips. 'You never done a day's work in your life. You've been waited on hand and foot by darkie servants since you was born.'

'I'll pay for us both,' Frank said, staring down into the bowl.

Walter regarded him thoughtfully. 'I will confess, Frankie,' he said, 'a few shillings wouldn't come amiss towards your keep, while we sort things out.'

'I'll do anything,' Frank said.

His uncle nodded. 'I'll take you down to the Lock first thing Monday. They'll find something. You know anything about horses?'

'A little. We had five.'

'Did you now?' Walter gave a rueful grunt. 'Well, I never had even a one, but there's hundreds of the brutes down at Camden Lock, and where there's horses there's always work for a willing lad. And then there's always stevedoring. Oh, it's hard, I won't deny it. And it pays a pittance, things on the canals not being what they were a few years back. But every little helps. How old are you now, Frank?'

'Almost fifteen.'

'Well, there's lads younger than that have had their start here. We'll see what can be done. Now eat.'

The stew was thin, but Frank was desperately hungry and he had to force himself to eat slowly. He was aware of the woman watching him with bitter eyes.

'And the child?' she demanded.

Frank said, 'Gifford will go to school.'

'School?' Aunt Lily looked in appeal at Walter. 'Do you hear the boy? How's that to be managed?'

'Gifford will go to school,' Frank repeated.

No one spoke after that. Frank went on with his sparse meal, very aware of the clink of his spoon against china. When he had finished he stood up and made to carry the bowl to the sink but Aunt Lily snatched it off him.

Uncle Walter got to his feet. 'I'd best take the cart back to the depot.' He reached across and thumped Frank's shoulder gently. 'Things'll look brighter after a bit of shut-eye, son.'

He walked down the short hall to the door and the front door closed behind him. Frank glanced back at his aunt but she was at the sink, keeping her face resolutely away from him, and so he climbed the narrow stairs back to the attic room. The candle was still flickering, and

Frank pulled another fold of blanket over his sleeping brother, and then began to unpack his case. He laid his things out with care: a spare shirt or two, some underwear, his father's old Homer, the photograph of his mother. He set the picture up on the ledge of the chimney breast and stood looking at it. The guttering of the candle flame seemed to make the image flicker into life.

'I never liked her,' Aunt Lily said.

When he turned she was standing at the top of the stairs.

'I know it's sinful to speak ill of the dead, but I won't lie.' She stepped into the room and leaned close to the photograph. 'I thought her flighty. The truth was, she was just younger and prettier than me. I wanted Lewis home again; I doted on him, my big brother. All she wanted was to go out to India with him and live like a grand lady. I knew she'd bring him to a bad end somehow.'

'It wasn't her fault.'

'No. Nothing was ever her fault. She was that type.'

Frank looked into the woman's drawn face. Just for a second he saw in her eyes something he had not glimpsed before, something weary and long suffering, and it reminded him of his father.

'It was the letters that did it,' he said. 'The mail came on board at Suez. Dearborns dismissed him. After thirty years' service.'

'Dismissed? What – with nothing?'

Frank hesitated, the image of the fat cream envelope beneath the floorboards floating into his mind. 'With nothing.'

Something about this almost seemed to amuse her. 'And you talk of paying?'

'I will make my way, Aunt Lily. I will work.'

She gave a snort of derision and stepped back to the stairs. 'You're a dreamer, Frank Gray, like your father.' She was about to descend, but then nodded at the photograph. 'How did she die? No one ever told me.'

'There was a man,' he said. 'There was a shooting.'

She opened her eyes, impressed despite herself. 'Someone done for her? Well, I never. And did he swing?'

'He's got away with it. So far.'

Aunt Lily stood on the top step, one hand on the newel post. He could tell she was on the point of saying something contemptuous, but whatever she saw in his eyes made her think better of it. She straightened her shoulders. 'This house is no place for you,' she said curtly. 'There's a workhouse at Hendon. I'm telling you, you'd be better off there.'

'We'll only stay here until I can find some way to keep us, Aunt Lily. I promise you.'

Her face hardened again. 'You're as bad as your father. You don't listen.' She gathered the material of her dress at her breast as if against a chill and started back down the stairs. 'If you had any sense you'd go now.'

17

The evening with her father settled the matter for Grace. She did not know how she came to the decision, but as she lay in her bed that night she knew that she would have to go back to see Mrs Rossiter again. The knowledge came to her ever more strongly as she rolled the black pearl between fingers in the moonlight falling from her window, feeling its silky opulence against her skin. She had no idea what she expected the housekeeper to tell her, but that she had something to tell her, and something which she must hear, Grace did not doubt. She slept.

The rain had stopped and the afternoon had bloomed into gauzy summer by the time Grace left the house the next day. The long wet grass drenched the hem of her skirt. When at length she came to the cottage in the woods she saw Mrs Rossiter in the little garden, pegging out washing on a line stretched between the trees. As on that earlier occasion, her grey hair hung loose. She stopped as Grace came up, and took from her mouth the couple of wooden clothes pegs she had been holding there.

'I thought you'd be back, miss.' She tossed the pegs into her basket. 'Come inside.'

Grace followed her into the house.

'Take off your coat, miss. It grows warm in here when the sun's out. And sit. We don't stand on ceremony here.'

Grace did as she was told, taking her former place at the scrubbed table. Now that she was here, she hadn't the least idea what to say, but Mrs Rossiter did not seem to expect her to say anything. Instead, the woman went into the little lean-to kitchen and came out with two thick glasses and the same squat bottle Grace had seen last time. Mrs Rossiter poured an inch of gin into each glass and nudged one of them across the table towards Grace.

'Last time you saw me,' Mrs Rossiter said, 'I was having a drink with Billy on his anniversary. But since he never turned up, I supped his drop too. It's my custom.'

'Mrs Rossiter—'

'But this ain't about Billy. This is about you and me, Miss Grace. Ain't it?' The housekeeper picked up her own glass and with the back of her hand she pushed the other one until it touched Grace's fingers.

Grace took a deep breath. She lifted the glass, tipped the drink back and swallowed it. The gin erupted in her mouth and swelled to a fireball in her throat. Tears started to her eyes and for a moment she could neither see nor breathe.

'Good girl.' Mrs Rossiter leaned over and patted her shoulder. 'Now we're sisters.'

She went into the lean-to and came out with a tin mug of water and set it on the table. Grace grabbed it and drank gratefully. Slowly, the fire in her throat cooled a little and she found she could breathe again. She blinked away tears. The gin was, she decided, the most repulsive potion she had ever tasted. It was inconceivable that people could swallow this stuff for pleasure, and yet Mrs Rossiter was swallowing hers. Grace could not quite believe what she had done. She took several deep breaths and blinked around the room. As she did so she saw that on the dresser lay the leather pouch which, on her last visit, had lain in the centre of the table. Sergeant Rossiter's mementos, not yet put away for another year.

'Mrs Rossiter, do you miss your husband terribly?'

'Billy? I hardly seen him from one year's end to the next. Not since we was courting, anyway. It wasn't like the old days, miss, when a soldier's wife could go with her man, like my ma done in the Crimea.'

Grace cleared her throat and wiped her eyes. 'Your mother went to the Crimea?'

'Oh, yes, and me too, miss. I wasn't much older than you are now, but I grew up quick over there. Pa was a gunner in the artillery. When he got the typhoid I went with him to the hospital down at Scutari, and after he died I stayed on and helped out as best I could. That's where I learned my doctoring. Stitching and cleaning. Holding them down while the surgeons were sawing.'

'You did such things?' Grace was awestruck. She had never seen a wound worse than a cut finger and she had fainted at that.

'They used to say it was easier if a girl held 'em. Pride of manhood stopped 'em thrashing about so much.' Mrs Rossiter snorted and drank a little more. 'Trust them to be thinking about their manhood at a time like that. You take a tip from me, miss. Don't you go falling in love with no soldier. They'll bring you nothing but grief. Not much on their minds, and what there is is precious little use to us.'

Grace tried to imagine the wards at Scutari, tried to bring to life the lithographs she had seen in history books and journals, and added embellishments of her own: the groaning of the wounded, the solitary lamp making its way down the wards as Miss Nightingale did her rounds. She suspected these visions didn't have much in common with the scenes of carnage and agony that Mrs Rossiter must have seen. Grace wondered what it was like to hold down a man's shoulders as one or other of his limbs was sawn off. Did they really use a saw? She imagined the sound of it, something like the noise Mr Callow made when he cut larch poles for the rose arbour. And that took so *long*! Did it take that long to cut through a bone? With the poor man awake the whole time? She shuddered. Manhood must be something powerful indeed if it prevented young men from shrieking while that was being done to them.

For some reason there was a warm glow inside her and she was aware of the last of her timidity slipping away. In fact she felt unusually confident and alert. She rather wished she had been at Scutari herself, with some affectingly vulnerable young dragoon gripping her hand for comfort while the surgeons went to work. She couldn't decide, though, which bit of him she would allow to be amputated in this fantasy. Perhaps they might just be probing for a bullet. In the shoulder. Being shot in the shoulder was rather romantic. Certainly it had to be somewhere that would leave him whole and handsome afterwards, though perhaps with some private pain, bravely borne, that only she would know about.

'How sad that you couldn't be with poor Sergeant Rossiter when he fell,' she said.

'When he fell off his 'orse?' Mrs Rossiter asked, momentarily nonplussed. 'Oh!' She laughed. 'When he *fell*! Well, there's not much I could have done for him, miss, by the time the Fuzzy-Wuzzies had finished with him. What there was left would've gone in his knapsack and still left space for his greatcoat, or so his mates told me.' She looked down into her gin. 'Silly bugger, getting hisself killed that way, at his age. A child he was, till his dying day. They all are, miss. Children. With their popguns and their pretty uniforms and their flags. They tell them to march, and off they march, our men-children, like they was lining up for a game of football in the park.' Grimly Mrs Rossiter took another drink. 'And down they go, like dumb oxen in a slaughterhouse, their brains blown out one way and their guts dragged out the other.'

The vulgarity repelled Grace, but she strove to keep this out of her face. She said, 'You told me some things the other day, Mrs Rossiter.'

'Did I? Told you too much, probably.'

'You spoke about the Empire. I had never heard anyone speak of it so.'

'Ah, the Empire.' The woman gave her a knowing look. 'Yes, well I've always got plenty to say about that.'

'You said—'

'I know what I said.' Mrs Rossiter cut across her sharply. 'I said it's us who do the dirty work, poor fools like me and Billy Rossiter. We do their cleaning and cooking and killing for them. We're not so much better off than the savages they sent Billy to butcher, when you get right down to it.'

Grace sat in awkward silence. She felt she should have been able to mount a better argument in defence of the natural order of which her father had spoken with such assurance. In some ways, she realised, she had come here hoping to find a way to do that, and she knew that later she would think of all the right and clever things to say. But she couldn't find them now. Mrs Rossiter spoke with such annihilating force that it was hard to imagine arguing with her. And besides, Grace was aware that for the first time in her life someone was taking her seriously enough to speak candidly to her, and she was flattered by that. More than flattered, she was filled with a heady sensation of new possibility.

'Mrs Rossiter,' she said in delicious horror, 'are you a . . . *socialist?*'

Mrs Rossiter laughed. 'Well, if I am, I don't have horns and a tail. You can look if you like.'

'But how does a woman come to think such things?'

Mrs Rossiter stopped smiling. She put down her glass and reached across to the dresser. She put the leather pouch between them, opened it, and upended it so that a litter of objects and papers fell out. Grace saw a couple of folded letters, a soldier's pocket book, half a dozen medals and clasps, and a piece of dark fabric perhaps six inches square. Something hard and heavy clattered onto the table, and Grace instinctively stopped it rolling with her hand. It was a live cartridge, still complete with dull lead bullet. She hefted it in her hand. It was remarkably heavy. The brass of the cartridge case was chewed and gouged around the base.

'That's what killed Billy,' Mrs Rossiter said. 'Jammed in the breech. Those bloody Martinis was always jamming when they got hot. Before he could clear it, they were on him. Abu Klea, it was. Seventeenth of January 1885. The only time savages ever broke a British square. Eighty-odd of our lads died there. They said it was a soldiers' battle. There's a monument there now, I hear tell: but it only has officers' names on it.'

She took the cartridge from Grace, and sorted the items into some rough order on the table top. Grace's attention was gripped by the patch of blackish material. She saw a shoulder flap, a brass button, and the three broad chevrons of a sergeant's stripes which had once been white. Mrs Rossiter held the cloth out to her.

'Take it, miss. Go on. Feel it.'

Grace took it nervously. It was heavy and stiff, as if it had been starched.

'This stuff here is all I got back from Billy,' Mrs Rossiter said. 'After twenty-six years of marriage, sixteen of them he was overseas on the Queen's service. And this is it. A bullet, a handful of campaign medals that ain't even silver. And a couple of letters he'd meant to send, but never got the chance.'

'Oh,' Grace said, awash with generous pity. 'They must have been so very hard for you to read.'

'They were, miss. They were to a tart in Gravesend.' Mrs Rossiter pointed at the cloth in Grace's hands. 'After the fight, one of his mates cut this off his uniform. He thought I'd like to have it.'

'I thought British soldiers had khaki uniforms, Mrs Rossiter.'

'So they do, miss. But blood tends to change the colour.'

Grace swallowed and put the material gently back on the table.

'Worthless rubbish, eh?' Mrs Rossiter picked up the fabric and ordered it neatly with the other items. 'But it started me thinking.'

PART THREE

England, December 1893

18

Frank kept working steadily despite the rain, his cloth cap pulled down over his eyes. As mechanical as a steam shovel, he thrust the blade into the gleaming coal on the quayside, and shot it ringing into the truck behind him. After months of this he knew better than to look at that daunting mountain of coal, constantly replenished from the barge by the thumping crane.

Frank had learned to labour without complaint, even when they set him to work in the holds of the big cargo barges which came up the Thames to offload at the Basin. That was the filthiest and most exhausting job, up to his knees in bilge water, but he did it, as he did everything, without complaint. The trade came the other way, too, barges bringing tallow, or bricks, or gypsum from the Midlands and from up north. Whatever it was, it had to be trans-shipped here, and Frank toiled to shift it.

In the first two weeks the heavy work had stripped the skin off his hands, and then flayed it off again just as it began to heal. But his body had – just – gained ground in this war of attrition, and his muscles and his skin had gradually hardened. He had grown whippet thin with the work and Aunt Lily's sparse feeding, but at least he could handle his shift now without weakening. And there was one part of his job which he enjoyed. Sometimes they would send him to work with the stable boys, mucking out the hundreds of boat horses in their dim canal-side stalls. It gave him pleasure to work with the big gentle animals which had plodded half the length of the country's towpaths, pulling the laden barges behind them. He liked their warmth and their large intelligent eyes, and even the stench of their urine, strong enough in the underground stalls to make his eyes sting.

The steam crane was swinging its bucket across now with another few hundredweight of Staffordshire coal. Frank and the others stood back to let it drop its load on the heap. He leaned on his shovel, breathing hard. His bare forearms steamed in the cold. It was drizzling, the thin rain falling through the gas lamps. The December sky beyond the lights was piled with clouds touched red by the lights of the capital. Rain and sweat, gritty with coal dust, trickled into his mouth.

'Frank?' Uncle Walter was trotting down the iron steps from the offices, buttoning his mackintosh over his belly as he came. 'Knock off. Shift's done ten minutes since.'

Frank hadn't noticed the time. He supposed that was a mark of his growing endurance, and he took some pride in that. He found his jacket, took the shovel back to the tool store. Walter was waiting for him at the top of the steps in Camden High Road, standing in the shelter of a shop's awning and smoking a cigarette, the rain beading on the brim of his felt hat. As Frank came up Walter reached into his pocket and counted out coins into his palm. Frank picked out a few coppers and handed the rest back to his uncle.

'Well, I can't say as it isn't needed.' Walter sighed and put the money back in his pocket. 'Come on, Frankie. It's Friday. I'll buy you a pint.'

'I'd best not, Uncle Walter.'

'We can run to a pint of beer. Besides, I want to talk to you.'

The King of Spain was green-tiled like a public lavatory. Yellow light spilled over the pavement through frosted glass doors. Frank walked through a raucous public bar to the yard at the back, washed coal dust and sweat from his face and arms in icy water from the rain butt and dried himself as best he could on his filthy jacket. He went back through to the saloon, a dim and comfortable room where quieter drinkers sat around polished wooden tables. A fire burned in a small iron grate. His uncle had already settled himself at a table with two pints of mild in front of him, and as Frank took his seat Walter pushed one of the beers towards him.

'Mud in your eye, Frankie.'

Walter drained a quarter of his pint and sat back, unbuttoning his jacket. Frank raised his own heavy glass. He disliked the warm and insipid English beer but he did not want to offend his uncle, so he drank a little.

'Tell me something,' Walter said, growing expansive in the warmth of the room. 'What did your dad tell you about me and your aunt Lily?'

'He said you were . . . respectable people.'

'Respectable?' Walter laughed. 'Well, I hope we're that, Frankie. But did he say we was, like, well-to-do at all?'

'He said you were a manager with the canal company.'

'Oh, a manager, did he say?' Walter pulled a face. 'Well, maybe that's what Lily told him. You want to know a secret, Frankie? She's a bit ashamed of me, your auntie Lil. Ashamed that I couldn't do better for her. What with her brother Lewis being such a smart chap, out there in India, playing the White Rajah, like.'

Frank said nothing. He didn't like to hear his father spoken of in this way.

'Well,' Walter said, picking up on his disapproval, 'that's the way it sounded to Lil, anyway. And there was me, just a clerk. Keep the ledgers straight, watch what comes in and goes out. Just a clerk and never will be nothing more. Oh, I had prospects once, Frank. When I started, working on the canals used to be good enough for any young chap. But that was before the railways strangled the business for good. I should've seen it coming, but I never did. Another twenty years and there won't be no canals and no barges neither. It's getting harder by the day.'

Frank felt sorry for him, for fat jolly Walter never quite able to live up to his wife's hopes. He felt sorry for Aunt Lily too, a pinched woman made sour by disappointment. And he couldn't deny that Walter was right: there had been no comparison between the Gray family's vivid life under the Indian sun and the mean workaday existence led by his aunt and uncle in this grim city.

'Maybe life out there in India wasn't all it was cracked up to be,' Uncle Walter conceded, 'but when all's said and done, old Lewis must have been doing pretty well compared to the likes of us. Servants, big house – five horses, was it?'

For the first time Frank sensed where this conversation was going. 'I know you and Aunt Lily can't afford to have us staying,' he said. 'I've saved a few shillings. You can have that. I'll see if I can scrape together a little more.'

'No, no, Frankie, bless you!' Walter looked wounded at the suggestion. 'Did you think we'd turn you out for the sake of a few bob? No, no. You pay what you can, I know that.' He made an airy gesture with his glass, then carefully replaced it on the table. 'Mind you, it's true we'll need to get your affairs sorted out, sooner or later.'

'My affairs?'

Walter grinned in a sly fashion. 'You're a smart boy, Frankie. I respect that. There's no one going to pull the wool over your eyes, eh? And you look after your own. Putting young Gifford into Miss Batts' school, the way you did. You've worked hard to pay for that. But then again, he's worth it. Oh, he's a sharp lad, that Gifford! I'm just saying that when the time's right, you and me, we need to have a look at what you're due from your poor dad's estate, and come to some arrangement. Man to man, like.'

Frank looked at him. 'I'm not due anything.'

'Yes, yes, I know, son.' Walter winked. 'It's good you've played your cards close to your chest. After all, you didn't know me and Lil from

Adam and Eve. But it's been months now and I'm your guardian, as you might say, or as near as makes no difference, you not being of age.' He made a solemn face. 'I have a responsibility for you, see, Frankie. To see you gets everything coming to you.'

'There's nothing coming to me,' Frank said. 'I had six pounds left when we landed at Tilbury. That was all that was in Father's wallet. I gave you that.'

'And so you did, Frankie. But then there's the matter of a pension. A big company like Dearborn's will be paying a pension, naturally, and when the paperwork's all sorted out—'

'There's no pension.'

'Oh, there'll be a pension, all right. They're a name, Dearborns are. Household name. We see plenty of their freight come through the Basin. I walked past their head offices in Leadenhall Street once – bloody great palace, it is. And that Stephen Dearborn's a big noise, with a damn great house out at Cumver Hill, down Farnham way. Now a company like that—'

'Uncle Walter, there is no pension coming to me. Father was dismissed. Dismissal cancels pension rights. It's a company rule.'

Walter blinked at him. 'That can't be right, son.'

'I had the captain and the purser look through the papers. It's there in black and white.'

Walter's face fell in heavy folds. 'I hope you're not pulling my leg, Frank, cos this ain't funny.'

'I thought you knew. If there'd been any money, I would have told you.'

Walter was quiet for a moment. 'Thing is, Frankie, I'm in a bit of a hole. I had some bad luck with the horses. Lil doesn't know. Well, she knows I have the odd flutter . . . See, I was banking on the fact that sooner or later your inheritance would come through, and we could . . .' Walter's eyes flickered away from Frank's and back again. 'There's some blokes I need to square. So this is no time for playing cute.'

'There's nothing coming to me, Uncle Walter. I'm sorry.'

Walter stared at him, the folds of his face sagging further. Frank could see the worm of a vein starting to beat beside his uncle's eye. The sight of the man's despair scared him and he said again, 'I'm sorry, Uncle Walter.'

But at that Walter recalled himself. He reached out and patted Frank's arm. 'Don't you worry, son. It ain't your fault how the bastards have treated you.' He made an attempt at a smile. 'We'll muddle through, Frankie. We always have. You get on home now. I've some coves to see.'

Frank waited a few seconds and then picked up his cap and backed to the door. When he opened it onto the wet street he glanced back and saw his uncle still sitting at the table, his shoulders slumped, gazing into his empty glass.

19

Frank walked the half-mile back to the house. Rain was pitting the canal. He let himself into the narrow hall. The downstairs was empty and chill, the stove not lit, Aunt Lily not yet home from the cleaning work she took on in one of the big houses on Camden Park. Frank could see the light of Gifford's candle shining under the door at the top of the stairs. He went through the kitchen to the lean-to at the back, stripped and scrubbed his body under the cold water tap. He came back into the kitchen, shirtless and with his braces hanging around his hips, found some bread and a little cheese and sat at the kitchen table to eat it in the dark, not troubling to light the lamp.

The memory of the odd exchange with Uncle Walter hung over him. It was still hanging over him when he rinsed his plate, put it away and climbed the stairs. It was cold enough for his breath to steam.

'Hello, Frank,' Gifford called.

The boy was kneeling on his bed under a tent of blankets, a book open in front of him. The candle was balanced in its dish on the bed-clothes.

'I've told you not to do that.' Frank moved the candle to a safer place.

'Now I can't read,' Gifford complained.

'At least you won't burn the place down.'

'No, but I'll be as stupid as all the others at Miss Batts'. Do you know they don't even know what fractions are? Let alone algebra! When I'm *that* stupid, it'll be your fault.'

Frank sat down heavily on the blankets which made up his own makeshift bed, and rested his back against the wall. 'Shut up a minute, Giff, will you? I'm thinking.'

Gifford closed his book with a snap. 'What about?'

'I'm thinking perhaps we should move out of here.'

Gifford laughed. 'What, tonight?'

Frank looked up sharply at his brother, and for a second a shadow flickered over his mind. He had not experienced this sensation since India, when he had haunted the dark alleys with Javed at his side. They

79

had been as alert as young foxes then, the two of them, alive to every danger, to every sound that could be heard and perhaps to some that could not. For no reason that he could have explained, Frank was tempted to do just what Gifford had jokingly suggested, bundle up their few things and head out this moment into the winter night.

'Well, I'm not going anywhere,' Gifford said with decision, reading his mind. 'It's cold outside and I'm sleepy.' He yawned and nestled down among the bedclothes, and almost at once he was indeed asleep.

Frank sat with his back against the wall for perhaps half an hour longer, wakeful and troubled. At some point he heard the front door open and Aunt Lily's steps on the hall floor. He heard her sigh tiredly, kick off her galoshes, walk to the kitchen. A plate rattled and water ran. The candle guttered out and Frank curled onto his side and pulled the rough blanket over him, and after a while he too slept.

He was jerked into wakefulness by Aunt Lily's shouting. Heavy footsteps were pounding up the wooden stairs. Frank sat up, but before he could get to his feet the door was hurled open and Uncle Walter barged into the room, a hurricane lamp swinging from his hand. He was purple in the face and his swaying bulk filled the low space.

'You've got something hidden, you young bastard, ain't you?'

Frank stood up. 'I don't have anything, Uncle Walter.'

The big man lurched towards him and stopped inches away. His breath stank of beer. 'Don't you *Uncle Walter* me! You think you're so fucking clever, but high and mighty Lewis Gray didn't leave you skint, so don't you try to swing that on me no more!'

He lunged forward, one hand extended in a claw. Frank dodged aside but he was not quick enough in the cramped space and the big hand shut over his shoulder and neck like a clamp. 'You've been hiding it away, ain't you? Smart, but not smart enough, Frankie. Where is it?'

'There isn't anything.' Frank could feel the man's thumb crushing the artery in his neck and his heart began to hammer.

'How d'you pay for the boy's schooling, eh?' Walter shook him like a rat. 'Not out of what you get paid at the depot, I know that much. You might have spun me a line for a while, but I ain't *that* fucking stupid!'

The room swam and Frank could hear the whistle of his own strangled breath. He was dimly aware of Aunt Lily appearing in the doorway, her mouth open and her hair wild. 'Leave him, Wally! You'll hurt him!' She stepped in and clutched at her husband but he swatted her away so that she cried out and stumbled against the wall. Walter gripped Frank with both hands around the throat and lifted him bodily.

'You'll fucking tell me where it is, boy, or you'll find out what hurting is.'

'Walter!' Lily screamed.

'It's under the window,' Gifford said. His voice was calm and clear. 'There's a loose board. That's where Frank hides the money.'

Frank felt himself dropped to the floor. He crouched there, dragging down air. He lifted his head and looked in disbelief at his brother, but the boy returned his gaze unabashed.

'It's no good to us if you're dead, Frank,' Gifford said.

Across the room Walter was already kneeling under the window. He tore up the broken floorboard, and in a second the fat cream envelope was in his broad hands.

'You young fucker.' Walter glared at Frank. 'You had money all along, but you kept it back. I knew you was up to something.' He belched and groped his way to his feet. 'After what we done for you. I as good as begged you!'

Frank rubbed his bruised throat. 'It's not mine.'

'Not yours? What's that supposed to mean?'

'It's Gifford's. It's for his schooling. I never touched a penny of it, only to send him to school.'

'Don't you give me that. You come here, talking so pretty, and acting like the Lord's Anointed. I have to stomach you making like the poor bloody orphan, after you've been living the life of Riley among the niggers. And all the time you was cheating us, holding out on us.' Walter shoved the envelope inside his coat. 'Well, finders fucking keepers.'

Frank got to his feet. 'Give it back.'

Walter's eyes found their focus and he began to smile. 'Come and get it, sonny.'

Frank took a step forward. 'Give it back, Uncle Walter. It's all we have.'

'Can't you see what he'll do to you?' Aunt Lily shrilled at him. 'He doesn't hardly know what he's doing!'

Frank hesitated. Walter was twice his size and strength, and ugly with rage. Frank knew he had no chance at all against him, and that in his present mood Walter would like the chance to prove that. Aunt Lily ran into the room and grabbed Frank's arm.

'I warned you,' she hissed into his face. 'But you wouldn't listen. Now get out! Take the boy and get out while you still can!'

Frank hung back a moment longer, breathing hard. Across the room Walter still stood, smiling that cruel smile, his eyes dead and black. But then Gifford was at Frank's side, tugging at his hand.

'Come along, Frank,' he said quite calmly. 'Come along. Let's go.'

20

Cumver Hill was jade green with frost in the winter morning. Grace sat back on the box of the gig as it bowled along between the bare hedges, the pony's hooves clipping cheerfully on the gravel and his breath chuffing in the cold. The day was bitter but she was snug in her grey coat. She loved this coat, cashmere trimmed with fox fur which ran like silk against her skin, and she loved mornings like this, with the December countryside still and silent under a white sky.

It was confusing to feel quite so joyously alive when she wanted to speak to her father about serious matters. It was as if her pleasure somehow took away her moral authority. Perhaps he guessed this – yes, certainly he did – for he kept glancing across at her as he drove, smiling in that maddening way of his.

He was slowing the gig now, turning through a farm gateway, and in a moment they were rolling up to a shabby brick cottage. Grace's spirit sank as she realised they had come to the Brashers' home. It occurred to her that her father had selected this as their last visit just to spite her. She pursed her lips in irritation. That would be just like him.

It was an unlovely place with a clutter of farm implements down the side and a scrap of garden behind. The Brashers had evidently spotted them as they turned in from the lane, for both were now standing outside waiting to greet them. Brasher, a thin-faced man of sixty, was already ducking his head while his sparrow of a wife stood at his side, nervously drying her hands on her apron, and then drying them again.

Stephen Dearborn brought the gig to a halt beside them, and touched the brim of his hat with his whip.

'A very good morning to you, Brasher, and your good lady. And compliments of the season.'

'And to you, sir, I'm sure.' Brasher snatched off his cap and bobbed his head to Grace. 'Miss Dearborn.'

She smiled wanly back.

Dearborn said, 'We'll be seeing you at the house on Christmas Day, I hope?'

'Oh, we'll be there, sir. Thanking you kindly.' Brasher ducked again. 'We wouldn't miss that, sir.'

'Excellent. And how's that boy of yours?'

Brasher's face fell. 'I doubt he'll be well enough for Christmas, sir.'

'I'm sorry to hear that.'

'But he's coming along, the doctor says. Back at work in no time, I shouldn't wonder.'

'Perhaps the New Year will treat him more kindly. Let us hope so.' Dearborn touched his hat again. 'Well, good day to you.'

'Sir. Miss.'

Dearborn clicked his tongue and the pony moved off. As they turned in the yard and trotted back past the couple, Grace looked back and Mrs Brasher dropped a stiff curtsey to her.

'Did you see that, Papa?' she whispered, scandalised. 'Does the poor woman think I'm the Queen?'

'Truth to tell, Puss, you're probably more important to Mrs Brasher than Her Majesty will ever be. After all, you'd like to get rid of them, and one day you'll have the power to do it, too.'

'Me? Why would I do that?'

'Oh, any number of reasons.' He seemed to weigh up the possibilities as he drove. 'For one thing, old Brasher smells a bit.'

'Papa!' She looked at him, appalled.

'Bone meal, I always think.' He grinned at her. 'I wonder if Mrs Brasher uses the same scent.'

She refused to smile. 'I shouldn't want anyone put out of their employment,' she said primly.

'Come now, Puss. You loathe old Brasher. Don't trouble to deny it, you make it pretty obvious.'

Grace stared ahead, blushing. It was true she disliked Brasher. He leered at her unpleasantly whenever he saw her, and all the more in recent months. She knew the girls on the estate told disagreeable stories about him, and took care to avoid him after he had taken drink. Mrs Brasher, by all accounts, had a hard time of it.

'Admit it, Puss. You'd dismiss him without a thought if you were mistress of Cumver.' Her father touched the pony with his whip and gave her an ironic look. 'But then what would the Brashers do? They're both too old for any other work. And of course he has no savings, the feckless old villain.'

She lifted her chin. 'What's the matter with their son?'

'He has consumption and he'll never recover. He's in a sanatorium down at Hastings.'

'Oh.' She glanced at him. 'Can they afford that?'

'It's taken care of.'

Dearborn turned the gig between mossy pillars and onto the drive which led to Cumver House, the pony trotting between flint walls smothered with ivy. The wheels crunched through icy puddles.

'I also pay to keep old Mrs Prall,' he went on, 'who doesn't know what day of the week it is. And to send the Bensons' boy to an apprenticeship. Oh, and I kept the Cusslers in their cottage after the idiot fell off the barn roof and couldn't work for six months. I don't say all this out of pride, Grace. I merely wish you to understand how things work. These bills are not paid by radical theories. Society must generate a surplus, and it must breed people who have some idea how that surplus is to be distributed.'

He slowed the gig to a walk. It was a fine prospect from here, at the foot of the long drive, with the distant house standing proudly against the sky and the fields rolling away to either side. Rose hips glowed like orange lamps in the hedges and a few crystals of snow drifted out of the whiteness and settled on her fox fur. She had never suspected this largesse of her father's. She knew she should be pleased about it, but she knew too that she had been outmanoeuvred.

'I'm sure it is very generous of you, Papa,' she said stiffly.

'It's an obligation I have, Puss, that's all,' he said. 'It doesn't make me a saint, I assure you, and I don't do it entirely out of the goodness of my heart.'

'Why then?'

'Because it's the natural order.' He made a mock pompous face. 'I'm the lord of the manor, and it's incumbent upon me.'

'And is that why you invite them all to Christmas dinner?' She made her tone sarcastic. 'Because you're lord of the manor?'

'Precisely so. It's what lords of the manor do.' He laughed. 'After all, only *noblesse oblige* would persuade anyone to invite smelly Mr and Mrs Brasher to dinner.'

He raised his whip and they bowled up the long drive between the bare lime trees, the little horse jingling his harness. The exchange had made Grace thoughtful and she said nothing. Off to her left her father's fallow deer were running through the frosty grass of their newly enclosed park, and she could see the white puffs of their breath.

They reached the carriage turn outside the house and Dearborn swung the gig through the brick archway into the stable yard. Lambert came up at once and took the pony's bridle, cursing at the animal when it shied. Grace could feel the stocky man's eyes on her as she climbed down. He had some sort of a tattoo on his right forearm; a bird of prey perhaps, ripping at something. It was the only tattoo she had ever seen and she thought it barbaric, but she couldn't keep her eyes from it even so.

'Morning, sir.' Lambert smiled. 'Miss Grace.'

She pretended not to hear and walked away to wait for her father by the archway. Dearborn spoke to the man for a few moments and then came strolling across the cobbles to join her.

'I suppose he's coming to Christmas dinner too?' she asked curtly.

'Lambert? Oh, yes.' He raised his eyebrows. 'Is he another one you don't care for?'

'Papa, do you see the way he treats the horses? I don't even like to ride when he's at the stables.'

'I must say, for a young woman of your liberal persuasions, you seem to have a healthy dislike for the lower orders. I agree he's a bit of a thug, but one can't pick and choose, especially not at Christmas. Spirit of good cheer and all that.' Dearborn took her arm and walked her round to the broad steps which led to the front door. But halfway up he stopped and faced her. 'It's just that I believe in discipline, Puss. You don't get anything done without it, and Lambert's rather good at discipline.'

'He's a bully.'

'That goes with the job, I'm afraid. One may use discretion in the exercise of authority, but in the end there does have to *be* authority.'

He trotted up the steps and into the hall, calling a cheerful greeting to Yelland as he went in.

Grace stayed where she was, staring out over the meadowland below the house which stretched away towards the beech woods. Smoke was curling up into the blank sky from chimneys in Leigh village. The houses were hidden behind the trees but she could see the spire of St Martin's with its weathercock rising above the bare branches. At the edge of the woods some workmen were loading a cart with sawn trunks. One of those would be this year's yule log and in a day or two they would all be gathered around while it blazed in the hall fireplace, workers, tenants and family together. There would be punch and presents and beer and too much to eat, and her father would talk with easy charm to everyone there. She supposed he was right, and that in one form or another it had always been like this. The natural order.

She looked up. Old Yelland was holding the front door open for her. It would be warm and bright in the house with the fires all lit. With the tree already up in the hall and most of the decorations in place, Cumver had taken on that thrilling sense of anticipation which she had always loved.

But something – the confusing conversation with her father, or Lambert and his repulsive tattoo – had put her in a bad temper. She turned her back on the bright doorway with its promise of warmth and welcome and walked away down the steps into the cold day.

21

The room stank of unwashed bodies and of coke from the iron stove. A knot of people had gathered around it, drying their rags of clothing, the men smoking. There was a hum of talk, a woman's cackling laugh, some coughing. A man spat and an attendant admonished him sharply. Frank edged a little further into the room, starved of warmth, with Gifford tight against his leg. He heard the sleet tapping against the window panes, and glancing out he could see ice spinning out of the night sky and drifting in the courtyard.

Gifford looked up at him, dull eyed. 'Where are we?'

'You're in the spike, son.' The man who had spoken sat at a table under the window. He was elderly with a long horse face, and a fat ledger lay open before him. 'Hendon Union Workhouse. It's not as you might call 'ome, but it's better than being out on a night like this. Names?'

Frank said, 'We just want something to eat, sir.'

'I said, what's your names?' When Frank didn't answer, the man sighed. 'Brothers, are you? All right. You're John Smith and the young 'un's Fred. That's what you told me, right? Where you from, son? From these parts?'

'We need something to eat and somewhere to sleep. We'll be no trouble.'

'Trouble? I should think not. But if you ain't from these parts, I can't let you in here. Not by rights.' The man peered at them. 'How did you get here?'

'We . . . walked here, sir. It took . . . two days, I think. I don't think it's far, but we got lost. We didn't have money for the omnibus.'

The man shook his head, made a note in his ledger with a stub of pencil. 'All right, you're from Willesden Parish. You must've told me that, cos it's writ here.'

Frank could feel the whole of Gifford's weight against his leg. The boy was asleep. Through his own exhaustion Frank recognised that the elderly man was an ally, and he said, 'Thank you, sir. We're very much obliged.'

'Well, well, manners, is it? Not heard them for a while.' The man lifted his pencil from the page. 'You got some learning, have you, boy? You come from a decent home?'

'We thought it was decent, sir.'

'How in the world d'you land in a place like this?'

'I don't know, sir.'

A darkly handsome young man behind Frank jostled him and spoke past him to the attendant. 'Come on, Mr Pawles. All I want is my meal ticket.'

'You again, Joe Tanner, you thieving didicoi?'

'I'm an honest wayfarer, me.' Tanner grinned.

'You're a gypsy, is what you are, Tanner. And that says it all.'

'Times is hard, Mr Pawles. I'm on my way to the Vale of Evesham to look for work at the racing stables – you wouldn't have me starve along the way, now would you?'

'Not a month goes by when you don't come in here, pleading poor-mouth. You just wait your turn.' Old Mr Pawles turned back to Frank. 'Well, however you got here, John Smith, you're here now. Strip off behind that wall. Washroom's at the end there.'

Frank followed his gesture and saw a whitewashed partition wall with a door. He could hear the slop of water and the clank of buckets, and the gasps of people washing in cold water.

'What about our things?'

'They get purified. Kills the lice.'

'We haven't got lice.'

'You soon will have. We give you a set of workhouse duds. They ain't yours but you wear them while you're here. If you're just a casual, you'll get a night shirt each.'

Frank hugged his bag close to him. 'I need to keep this.'

'You pick it up when you leave.'

'When will that be?'

The old man blew out his cheeks. 'Son, that depends on the master. I've known people who come in here for a night and they're still on the books ten years later.'

'We don't want to stay past tomorrow. All we want—'

'Rules is rules, son. It's not so bad. We'll give you some food and a bed of sorts, and you'll pay for it by breaking rocks for a few hours tomorrow, or picking oakum. Then the master will take a look at you. You might get out if you can find regular work, but my guess is they'll keep the boy till he's growed, unless there's family for him to go to.'

'I'm his family.'

'You're not of age. And aside of that, you're a pauper.' The man was beginning to lose patience. 'You're on the parish, son, you'd best get used to it. Now move along. The young 'un'll be taken to the children's dormitory by and by, and then they'll put him in the union school, just across the way. It's not much, but it's more than he'd get on the road. If the master agrees, you'll get to see the lad the odd Sunday afternoon for an hour.'

Frank stepped back, raising mutters of protest from the people behind him. 'We'll not be separated.' He gripped Gifford's shoulder and pushed through the crowd towards the door.

'Don't be a fool, boy!' Mr Pawles called after him. 'You'll freeze out there, the pair of you!'

But Frank was already through the door, holding Gifford at his side. He crept around the courtyard wall to the corner where the shadows fell. He didn't know where he was going but he hunted instinctively for the shadows, like a beaten animal. He let himself slide down the cold bricks until he sat on the ground, his arm around his brother. He could feel Gifford shivering. He supposed he must be shivering too. His mind spun like a broken compass needle, and while it whirled he sat paralysed, unable even to brush away the grains of ice gusting into his face.

He wasn't sure how long it was before he grew aware of the tall shape leaning against the wall a few feet away. The man was hunched into a jacket and the red dot of a cigarette glowed and shrank. Frank caught a whiff of tobacco.

'You'll die if you stay out here,' the stranger observed, in a matter-of-fact tone. 'Sure as eggs. Stone dead by morning, the pair of you. Stiff as boards.'

He moved and a shaft of light from the courtyard gas lamp fell across his face and Frank recognised the young gypsy who had stood behind him in the queue. Tanner reached into the pocket of his coat and held out a crushed slice of bread. Frank took it, broke off a piece for himself. He shook Gifford into half-wakefulness and watched while the boy gnawed on the crust.

'They let you out?' Frank asked.

'I'm a wayfarer, see?' Tanner grinned. 'I always liked that. *Wayfarer*. Romanies, travellers, tramps for the most part. That's what we are. You tell them where you're headed, they give you a meal ticket, and you can take it to some place along the route and exchange it for bread and cheese. You're too young to swing that one. They'd take you in, but you wouldn't get out again in a hurry.'

Frank got stiffly to his feet. He looked down at his brother, still gnawing like a rat at the crust. Tanner took a last drag of his cigarette, taking his time over it. He finally flicked the butt away and pushed himself upright from the wall.

'Come on, then, John Smith. Get the boy up and follow me.'

'Where to?'

The gypsy didn't reply, but led them out of the yard and around the brick perimeter walls which enclosed the workhouse exercise yards. The massive building loomed behind them, sleet settling on its roof. A wide area of bare allotments and gardens stretched away into the darkness behind the block. Tanner followed the line of the hedge, keeping to the shadows. The ground was knobbled with frost. They crossed a stream by a footbridge. Frank felt the blood come back into his legs as he walked. He gripped Gifford under the arm, half-carrying him now. After a few hundred yards Tanner stopped, and Frank heard the murmur of voices from the far side of a hedge. Between the leafless branches he glimpsed three gaily painted wagons in a field, men warming themselves around a fire, and, beyond, half a dozen carthorses in a clump against an ice-whitened fence.

'They don't take to outsiders, my lot,' Tanner said. 'But there's a shed further on where we keeps hay for the horses. You'll be all right in there, but be sure you're gone by first light.'

They walked on and entered the field through a gap in the hedge. In the far corner stood a wooden hut with a tin roof. Inside, out of the bitter wind, it felt almost warm. Frank moved a hay bale or two into the back of the shelter, picked Gifford up bodily and settled him, pulling loose hay over him and spreading his own jacket over that. When Frank came out, Tanner was seated on a bale just inside the shed entrance. Frank sat down beside him.

'So what'll you do now, John Smith?'

'I don't know. I've no money.'

'None? How come?'

Frank stared out into the night. 'Someone stole it.'

'Couldn't hang on to what's your own? You'd best learn to do that.'

Frank said nothing. His bag lay on the earth floor between them and the gypsy touched it with his toe, looked questioningly at him. Frank lifted the bag, opened it and took out the only two things it contained; his father's old copy of Homer, and the framed photograph of his mother. Tanner took the book, flicked through it.

'I never learned letters,' he said.

'It's a story. An old story.'

'What, like a love story?'

'Revenge,' Frank said at once. He had never thought about the *Iliad* this way, but now he did. 'Yes. Revenge.'

Tanner struck a match and peered at the pages, as if he might be able to decipher the Greek characters after all. In the flare of it Frank could see neat marginal notes in his father's handwriting, and his mind flew back to the perfumed Indian evenings, the cicadas sawing in the hot night, the chorus of bullfrogs from the tank, the lamplight, Mr Gray's voice as he sat reading aloud. His father had a different voice for every character, Frank remembered, a crafty rumble for Odysseus, a silky trill for Helen. It used to make him laugh when his father attempted Helen's voice. Of course it made him laugh, he realised now and for the first time; that was why his father did it. For an instant Frank saw again the lights of the Greek campfires around the walls of Troy and heard the clash of bronze as Achilles, mad for vengeance, strode from his tent towards the battle.

'Pity it's been wrote on,' Tanner said, still holding the match over the page. He saved the last of the guttering flame for a withered cigarette which he produced from nowhere, shook out the match and inhaled deeply. 'Still, I'll give you a couple of bob for it. Make it half a crown if you throw in the picture.'

Frank slowly picked up the picture frame and slit the backing paper with his thumbnail. He slid out the photograph of his mother.

'Two and thruppence,' the gypsy said, 'if you keep the picture of the pretty lady.'

Frank did not answer and Tanner stood up, felt in his pocket and tipped coins onto the hay bale between them. He picked up the Homer and the empty picture frame and stepped to the door of the shed. He looked down at Frank.

'They took more than your money, didn't they, John Smith?'

He walked away into the darkness, his boots crunching on the frozen turf. The sound dwindled to the merest rustle in the night, and finally vanished altogether, and even then – and for much longer – Frank stayed where he was. He could hear the small scrape of a branch in the icy wind and the cold kiss of snow on the tin roof above him. Flakes drifted in through the open doorway and settled on his eyebrows and in the folds of his shirt. Looking down at his bare arms he remembered that he had laid his jacket over Gifford, and he supposed he must be cold, but he felt nothing. Somewhere in the distance a church clock chimed eight. He had been here for two hours.

'Frank?'

'Go back to sleep, Giff.'

But the boy was beside him already, sitting on the bale, hugging himself into Frank's jacket. His teeth were chattering.

'What are you doing out here, Frank?'

'Thinking.'

'About Mother?'

Frank realised he still held her photograph in his hands. A little ice had gathered on the surface.

'Yes.'

'You look funny, Frank.'

Frank blew the crystals from the photograph and slipped it into his shirt pocket. He got to his feet.

Gifford slung the jacket from his thin shoulders and held it out. 'You'd better take this.'

Frank took the jacket and walked away into the night without a word.

22

For almost an hour he worked his way in the darkness across allotments and open snow-dusted ground until he could see the lights of the suburban villas along the high road. He cut through the backs of gardens with cucumber frames and toolsheds white in the frost, and emerged onto a major road. A signboard told him this was Edgware Road. Traffic was still brisk despite the snow and after he had trudged south for a while a two-horse omnibus stopped close to him to let off a passenger and he ran to it and swung himself aboard.

The houses and terraces were more closely packed now and the lights of London crowded the middle distance, painting the underside of the clouds. An underground train from Euston steamed past beside the road on a stretch of surface track, the lit carriages rocking and rattling. In less time than Frank had imagined possible the omnibus reached Kilburn. He began to recognise landmarks, and after a while he glimpsed the dingy glass dome of Paddington Station off to his right. It seemed incredible that it had taken him and Gifford so long to cover this distance on foot. He waited a little longer, and stepped down from the omnibus as it slowed for the corner. Head down, he walked on through the night for another hour, until Regent's Park appeared to his right. Almost without realising it he was among the familiar maze of streets around Camden Lock, its basin glinting in the night.

Opposite the King of Spain pub he slipped into an alleyway, crouching in the shadows behind a rubbish bin. Rats were foraging boldly for half-frozen scraps, but they ignored him, and he waited as the snow fell around him, watching the warm yellow windows of the pub throwing gouts of light over the street.

It took an hour for Uncle Walter to emerge. When he did he was laughing and rubicund, and wearing a smart plaid ulster that Frank had never seen before. Walter held the door open to shout some ribald comment into the bar. Even from across the street Frank heard the raucous laughter that followed. Then Walter let the pub door swing shut, and, still chortling to himself, crossed the road a little unsteadily and walked away down towards the canal.

Frank followed. When he reached the corner Walter was already halfway down the street, walking more or less straight now, his breath puffing in the cold. He was whistling. Frank ran about half the distance between them, the snow muffling his steps. His foot struck something in the gutter which rang against stone, and Walter stopped and turned to look back. Frank slipped into a ragged front garden. The pint beer bottle he had kicked was still rocking on the cobbles, but if Walter saw anything it did not apparently bother him. He walked on, and his whistled tune rang out cheerfully once more. By the time Frank slipped out of cover Walter had already turned the corner into his own street, the tar black canal on one side and the row of terraced cottages on the other. In a few paces he would be home. Frank scooped up the bottle he had kicked and moved fast, skidding a little as he sprinted around the corner.

He closed on Walter; if the man heard anything he had no time even to glance round before the bottle exploded against the side of his head. Glass tinkled on the stones, impossibly loud in the empty street.

It wasn't at all as Frank had expected. Walter did not cry out nor fall sprawling to the ground. He did not swing round like a goaded bull, as Frank had feared he might. Instead he merely staggered a little, and walked drunkenly on for three full paces. He rested his hand on the wall beside his own front door, breathed deeply once or twice, and sat down on the ground with his back to the bricks. He looked up at Frank with a puzzled expression, put his hand to his head and stared at it when it came away shining.

'Look what you done,' he said, reproachfully.

Frank tossed away the spike of bottle left in his hand, bent down and swung his fist into Uncle Walter's face, and then did it again, as hard as he could, feeling the man's skull bounce back against the bricks each time. Walter made no attempt to defend himself. He sat with blood streaming down over his new ulster, looking up at Frank with large child's eyes.

'I didn't mean no harm,' he said.

The fat man's helplessness infuriated Frank. He felt betrayed that his victim should have become harmless Uncle Walter again, when he wanted him to be the hard-eyed drunken bully of two nights before. Frank called to mind those mean black eyes with a conscious effort and pulled back for another swing. The front door opened. Aunt Lily looked calmly down at the injured man, and then at Frank. She crossed her arms.

'He can't give it you back,' she said. 'You know that.'

Frank hit Walter in the middle of the forehead with a force that bruised his knuckles. Walter's eyes rolled up and he slumped a little to one side.

'You're wasting your time,' Aunt Lily said, standing quietly with her arms still crossed. 'He's already spent it, gambled it, paid off them he owes money to for a week or a month. It's gone, anyways.'

'He's got to be punished!' Frank shouted. 'They can't all get away with what they do!'

'And you're the avenging angel, are you?' Her voice was full of pity. 'Look at you. You're crying like a baby.'

Frank stood back, panting. He put his hand to his face and found that it was wet. He let his arms fall to his side.

'It still has to be done,' he said.

Aunt Lily stepped over her husband's splayed legs and came to stand in front of Frank. She looked into his eyes with more tenderness than he had ever known from her.

'It's not this sad booby you want to kill,' she said. 'Is it?'

He pulled down a shuddering breath.

She nodded, as if this might be answer enough. 'Be off with you, now, before someone calls the law.'

23

Grace moved among the crowded tables, dispensing cider from a big earthenware jug. It was so heavy that her arm ached, but she was enjoying herself. She liked the noise and the laughter and the admiring looks she drew. She knew how fine she looked in her bottle-green silk with her dark hair shining and her black pearl glinting at her breast.

They had set up the trestles across the hall, with a space between the tables for dancing later, and the whole room was hung with holly and ivy and mistletoe. There were candles on the mantels and on the sills, and dozens more set in the two ancient chandeliers that old Yelland had the footman bring down from the attic every Christmas. The black windows reflected hundreds of tiny flames.

The party had been going for two hours, and the room was already growing so raucous that it was hard to hear the little orchestra in the gallery above. Grace made her way to the sideboard with her empty pitcher, stepping over the end of the yule log burning in the hearth. It was so long that it projected into the room and had to be supported on polished brass firedogs. Smoke curled around the trunk and escaped into the room, filling it with the scent of pine resin. That huge log was typical of her father, Grace thought. A real yule log which would burn for the whole twelve days of Christmas. That was the way things used to be done in baronial halls, he had assured her, smiling at his own extravagance, teasing her with it. She wanted to be disapproving, but she couldn't pretend she didn't love it, the tang of smoke and pine in the air, the crackling flames.

Grace poured herself a glass of punch from the silver bowl on the table. The footmen were bringing the pudding in now and the hall was rich with the savour of brandy and fruit. At the end of the room someone clambered onto a chair, produced a fiddle and began scratching out a tune to greet the pudding's arrival. The fiddler was met with whoops and claps, and in a second the whole room took up the applause. In the gallery the orchestra finally conceded defeat and began to pack their instruments away.

It was growing warm and Grace found it daunting to think of pushing between the boisterous tables with another heavy jug. She edged her way to the door and slipped unnoticed into the orangery. It was pleasantly cool in here, and a relief to be away from the noise. She paced the length of the tiled room, fanning herself, trailing one hand through the ferns, enjoying the smell of damp earth. It was quite dark outside now and the orangery's tall windows were panels of ebony. She made her way back down the room and stopped at the doors which gave out onto the lawn. It was so very dark out there. She cupped her hands against the glass and peered into the night.

Behind her there was a roar of laughter from the party and then a chorus of catcalls and jeers and she guessed the fiddler had fallen off his chair. She turned to listen. Somebody chimed a fork against a glass and shouted for silence and proposed a toast. She wondered if she ought to go back in, but then thought better of it and put her face to the window again.

The boy's face materialised in front of her, wild and white, the eyes staring directly into her own.

She shrieked and backed away. Her glass fell and shattered and the vision vanished. There was a clatter of chairs from the ballroom, a babble of confused questions, and in an instant a small crowd of people surged around her.

'Grace?' Her father took her arm. 'What is it?'

Her heart was tripping. 'Something outside, Papa. I saw it.'

'Something?'

'Someone. A man. A . . . boy.'

Dearborn wrenched the door open and the bitter wind gusted in.

'Bring a light,' he called over his shoulder, and stepped outside.

Grace followed her father out into the cold night, hugging herself. He had stopped a few yards away on the lawn, looking down at the ground. In the light thrown from the house Grace could see footprints in the frosted grass. The prints were doubled, as if someone had come to the orangery doors and then retreated again.

Mrs Rossiter came up, threw a shawl over Grace's shoulders and handed a lantern to Dearborn. Others were spilling noisily out onto the white lawn behind them, throwing questions at one another. Dearborn ignored the babble and strode off, following the line of footprints. Grace hurried after him. The tracks led across the corner of the lawn and through the back entrance to the stable yard. Dearborn ducked through the arch with Grace behind him. He stopped and lifted the lantern.

Grace saw the boy sitting on the old stone mounting block. He was thin, with unkempt dark hair, and his eyes were sunken and his clothes filthy. There was a crazed look about him which made her shiver and she hung back behind her father.

'What's the meaning of this?' Dearborn demanded. 'Who the devil are you, skulking around in the dark? What do you want here?'

At first the boy stared back dully, as if he hadn't heard. It seemed to cost him an effort to speak, and the voice when it came was hoarse and ghostly. 'We want what you owe us.'

Dearborn's eyes creased. 'What did you say?' Thin snow swirled around them in the light of the lantern. Dearborn moved close, raising the lantern. 'Am I supposed to know you, boy?'

Grace hugged herself more tightly. The sight of this unkempt young stranger twisted something in her, made her want to run. She caught her father's arm. 'Can't we give him something and send him away?'

Dearborn looked at her, surprised.

'Please, Papa. He frightens me.'

'My brother's sick,' the boy said. 'We can't go any further.'

Dearborn swung back to face him and lowered the lantern a little. 'Your brother? Where is this brother of yours?'

'In the stable.'

Over his shoulder Dearborn said, 'See to it, two of you.'

Two men hurried past him to the stable. In a second one of them called, 'It's true enough, sir. There's a child here. A little lad.'

'Take him into the house.' Dearborn stood back half a pace and patted Grace's hand where it lay on his sleeve. 'We can't see them starve, Puss. You wouldn't want that.'

Grace forced herself to look into the wild youth's eyes. She could read nothing there except exhaustion. But when the two men emerged from the stable carrying a fair haired child between them, a look of such pain and concern came over the older boy's face that Grace was ashamed. She glanced up to find Mrs Rossiter watching her.

'I've room at the cottage for this one,' the housekeeper said, indicating the older boy. 'He don't frighten me.'

Grace stared at the ground.

Dearborn said, 'How did you get here, boy?'

'From London.'

'I asked you how.'

'We walked.'

'Walked? Impossible.'

'We walked.'

Dearborn grunted as if to show that he was still unconvinced, although Grace instinctively knew the boy was telling the truth. Her father's bonhomie had somehow evaporated, and she sensed that this odd visitation had somehow shaken him as it had her. Dearborn turned towards the archway, taking her arm as he went. But when he had ushered her through onto the lawn he swung back.

'I shall want to speak to you again, boy,' he said. 'Be here at the stables tomorrow at noon. Do you understand?'

He gripped Grace's arm uncomfortably hard and hustled her back to the house without waiting to hear if he had been understood or not.

24

Frank lay still, watching the iron light touch the tops of the beech trees outside the window. He was in a small room with bare walls. A shelf below the window was stacked with books and pamphlets, and a bowl and a blue china pitcher stood on a washstand. As far as he knew he had not seen any of this before.

He remembered standing in a lean-to kitchen. The flagstones underfoot were stingingly cold and a fierce little woman was sluicing water over him from a bucket. He had been naked when this was going on, he recalled that, too, but he had been too spent to care. Certainly she hadn't. While he had stood there in a stupor of weariness she had taken the gritty block of soap and scoured him pink with it. She would not, she told him, have him getting into any bed in her house in *that* state.

He thought of Gifford's limp form carried out of the stable and he sat up quickly in the bed. But then all that came back to him as well. Gifford was all right. The woman had said that several times as she scrubbed him. Gifford was exhausted and hungry. Nothing more. She had seen to him herself. He was safe up at the big house. Did Frank understand? She kept saying it until he did.

He discovered that his feet were blistered, and they hurt him as they touched the boards, but he stood up anyway. There was no sign of his clothes, but others had been laid out on a chair; a linen shirt, workman's trousers and jacket. They had so evidently been left for him that he put them on. The shirt was patched and too big for him, but it was freshly laundered and the clean fabric felt good against his skin.

He opened the door and walked into the main room, buttoning the shirt as he went. The little house was vacant in the cold light. It reminded him of a scene in a fairy tale, a cottage in the woods, silent except for the noises from outside, the squeaking of branches against a window and the distant chatter of magpies in the trees. A faint warmth washed from the iron stove and Frank went to stand in front of it. A book lay open on the deal table. For some reason he had expected a romance, but it was a political treatise of some kind.

The door burst open without warning and the fierce woman from last night swept in, shedding her cape as she came.

'So,' she said. 'Young Lochinvar's up and about at last. Let the stove go out, did you? Don't you know how to riddle a grate?'

Without a word Frank got down on his knees and saw to the stove, shaking the ashes through, blowing up the embers and placing more coal on them from the brass scuttle once they were glowing. When he closed the stove door and got to his feet, smacking the dust from his hands, she was standing with her hands on her hips, observing him.

'So who are you, Lochinvar? Walking here all the way from London?'

'We did walk here from London.'

'I know. I saw your feet. So who are you?'

'My name's Frank Gray, ma'am.'

She waited, perhaps to let him say more. When he didn't she grunted in a derisory fashion, as if this were no more than she had expected, and put a small bundle wrapped in brown paper on the table.

'Mr Dearborn wants to see you in half an hour. Do you remember that?'

'I remember.'

'If you've a grain of sense you'll go and meet the gentleman, and be civil while you're at it. You need his good grace if you're to keep a roof over your brother's head for a day or two longer.' She paused. 'You can stay here till he's mended, if you mind your manners.'

'Thank you, ma'am.'

'Don't mention it, I'm sure.' She moved her shoulders in a brisk fashion. 'And I have a name. Mrs Rossiter to you.'

'Thank you, Mrs Rossiter. Where are my own clothes?'

'I burned them.'

'But I can't pay for these.'

'Oh, I know that, Frank Gray. I went through your pockets, and you haven't got a brass farthing. Just some bits and bobs.'

She pointed to the table, where a few scraps of paper lay beside a small penknife and a stub of a pencil. He reached urgently towards the little heap, but she had not finished.

'Oh, and there was this.' She reached inside her dress and pulled out the folded photograph and handed it to him.

The image was creased and faded, but still it was undeniably his mother. Perhaps she was waiting for an explanation, but he did not give one, and put the photograph away in his pocket.

She said, 'You can have the clothes. The servants passed them on, seeing it's Christmas, and the state you was in. Maybe Mr Dearborn'll be in a giving vein too.' She opened the door and held it. 'Follow the path. You'll see the house when you come out the woods.'

He walked to the door.

'Wait.' She picked up the brown paper packet from the table. 'A lad shouldn't go without his breakfast. Flapjacks, baked last evening. I got no proper food here, but these are better than nothing. Go on, take them.'

Frank took the packet and looked at it.

'Thank you,' he said again.

He stepped out into the clear cold morning. He had walked some distance down the woodland track before he heard her close the door behind him.

After a quarter of a mile the track ended in a stile set into a mossy stone wall. The weather had cleared and a wash of primrose sun lay over the rough pasture beyond. The grass was frosted blue in the shadow of the trees, sparkling wet where the thin sun had melted last night's last snow. To his right Frank could see the roofs of the village and white smoke climbing from chimneys. In the middle distance a man was leading a team of chestnut plough horses along a field edge, but up here at the fringe of the woods Nature did not seem to have woken up to his presence yet, and as he climbed the stile a hare came rocketing past, close enough for him to hear the soft tattoo of its feet.

A path led across the meadow to a ha-ha. Beyond that lay the lawns, the carriage turn, and the house itself, massive in red brick. Frank had little memory of it from the night before. He recalled a never-ending driveway leading up from the high road, the gravel locked by frost, and then the bulk of the house against the night sky with snow drifting across amber windows. He remembered feeling his way around the walls of the stable yard in a delirium of exhaustion, lugging Gifford with him, until he had found an iron latch, lifted it, and smelled the warm reek of horses. He'd settled the boy in the straw, and would have collapsed beside him, but it was then that he had glanced out through the back entrance to the yard. Through the orangery windows he had glimpsed hundreds of twinkling candles. He had heard laughter and music and smelled warm food, and this had drawn him like a hooked fish.

He leaned against the stile, gazing at the house in the thin light. He opened his paper bag and ate steadily. He had not eaten properly for days and he could feel the strength flowing back into his body as soon as the food hit his stomach. When he was ready he crumpled the paper into his pocket and climbed over the stile.

There was no movement from the house looming above him, but he felt strangely exposed, as if every blank window was observing him, and he was glad when he passed the corner of the building and walked through the archway into the yard.

It was very quiet and the windows in the house's flank were blank and empty, blinds and curtains drawn. A rat ambled along a gutter towards the stables, unconcerned at his presence. From the stables four horses looked over their half-doors at him, ears flicking. A roan mare nickered hopefully, and stamped in her stall. Frank walked over and stroked the soft muzzle and the horse huffed contented vapour.

Frank looked around him. Behind him stood a parked gig with its trace chains hanging onto the cobbles, and at the far end of the court was a horse trough and an old mounting block. It all looked very different in daylight but he vaguely remembered sitting on that mounting block last night while the small crowd gathered to gape at him. He'd hardly noticed their silly surprised faces. His focus had been entirely taken up by Dearborn, just a shade ridiculous out in the snow in his top coat and fine cravat, barking questions. There was one other face he remembered, now he thought about it: a girl, dark haired and pretty. She had looked very young and scared. He knew she was important but could not for the moment place why. Then he remembered. *Papa*, she had called Dearborn. *Papa*. Yes, he remembered her well enough now. And what she had said. He wouldn't likely forget that.

'What are you sneaking around here for, boy?' The man was short and blockish with very broad forearms, one of which bore a tattoo of an eagle with its talons hooked. He held a shovel across his chest like a quarterstaff. Frank did not recognise him, but before he could speak the man said, 'You again. I'd have dealt with you last night if Mr Dearborn had said the word.' He pivoted on the balls of his feet and knocked Frank hard on the upper arm with the shaft of the shovel. 'Bugger off.'

Frank stepped back, holding his arm. 'He wants to see me.'

'Well, you never turned up, did you? Now fuck off.'

Frank retreated further but the man moved after him and knocked his arm again, catching him on the elbow so that a bolt of pain shot down into his hand. Frank instinctively grabbed the shaft of the shovel, twisted it out of the man's grip and threw it clattering away across the cobbles. He was surprised at how easy it was. The stocky man opened his eyes wide, then grinned unpleasantly and rolled his shoulders to loosen them.

'Well, well,' he said. 'A young fighting cock, is it?'

'Lambert?' Dearborn came striding through the brick archway towards them, polished boots ringing on the cobbles. 'It's a little early for brawling.'

In an instant Lambert ceased to be the swaggering bully and became the loyal retainer, cruelly used in the discharge of his duty. 'I caught this young rascal poking around, Mr Dearborn, looking for something to steal, beyond doubt.'

'Well, you can relax. I told him to come.'

Lambert changed tack rapidly. 'Well, that's different, sir, of course. It's a fact I come upon him a bit sudden. Perhaps I startled the lad, like.'

Dearborn faced Frank. 'Do you hear that? Mr Lambert's prepared to be forgiving. To spare you the gallows, or transportation, or whatever fate awaits young miscreants. He's got a big heart, our Mr Lambert, hasn't he?'

Frank said nothing.

'Find something to do, Lambert, would you?'

'Sir.' The stocky man walked away across the cobbles and out through the arch.

'I know the man's an ignorant bruiser, but he has his uses. What's your name?'

'Gray. Frank Gray.'

'*Sir*,' Dearborn corrected, mildly. 'I'm not an unintelligent man, Gray, and I can read your resentment clearly enough. But I'd like us to observe the proper courtesies. All right?'

'Sir.'

Dearborn stepped forward to stand directly in front of Frank. He was, Frank thought, a remarkable figure of a man, at once imperious and elegant in his well-cut country tweeds with his yellow waistcoat and gold watch chain.

'Well, Gray. You look better than last night, I'm glad to see. Though I'm bound to add that that wouldn't be difficult. No doubt Mrs Rossiter has told you that your brother is recovering?'

'Yes, sir.' Frank met his eyes. 'Thank you, sir.'

'No need for thanks, Gray. I'm not a heartless brute. However, I don't encourage vagrants, far less those who come snooping around my house at night, terrifying my family. Why did you come here, all the way from London? And on foot, if you're to be believed? Let's have the truth, now.'

'I wanted to see what the future looked like, sir.'

Dearborn's brow furrowed. 'Come again?'

'My father told me once that Dearborn & Company was the future. I supposed that meant you. Sir.'

Dearborn shook his head. 'Upon my word, Gray, you're full of riddles. Did I know your father?'

'No, sir. But he knew of Dearborn & Company.'

'Well, everyone does. And where is he now, your father?'

'Dead, sir.'

'And you have no other family?'

'Only Gifford.'

Dearborn squinted up at the white sky. He said, 'You know, Gray, common humanity prompts me to see that you don't starve to death, not at Christmas, anyway. That would be awfully bad form. But once your brother is well enough you ought to be grateful if I gave you a couple of shillings and sent you both on your way. And yet something you said last night gnaws away at me.'

Frank looked steadily at him. 'What might that be, sir?'

'You said that I *owed* you. An oddly consequential turn of phrase for a young tramp of – how old are you?'

'Fifteen, sir.'

'Well, it's a mystery to me how I could be presumed to *owe* you anything. What did you mean by that?'

'Gifford and I were hungry. You weren't. That's all I meant.'

'I see.'

Over the other man's shoulder Frank caught a flicker of movement and saw the girl standing under the brick arch. She was wearing a blue and white dress with a fur-trimmed coat over it. She was taller than he remembered, and her hair was glossy black in the thin winter sunlight.

'Father?' she called, nervously.

'Go inside, Grace,' Dearborn said, raising his voice a little, but not taking his eyes off Frank's face.

She said, 'I should like to speak—'

'Go inside!' Dearborn commanded, still without turning. 'I shall call you when I'm ready.'

She hovered unhappily for another second, and then vanished in a flicker of blue and white.

'My daughter wanted me to send you away last night,' Dearborn said. 'That surprised me, since she has a tender heart for stray dogs. But I can see her point. There's something unsettling about you. I can't put my finger on it.' He let several seconds pass in silence. 'I'll tell you how things stand, Gray. You showed some grit, walking all this way just to present yourself here. My guess is you did that for your brother's sake, which is also why you're talking to me now, even though you'd like to spit in my eye. I respect that.' Dearborn thrust his hands into his pockets and jingled coins. 'So what do you want?'

Frank lifted his head. 'I want to work.'

'Indeed?'

'I want to earn enough to keep us, sir, so that Gifford can go to school.'

Dearborn raised his eyebrows. 'School for your brother, eh? Is that the limit of your ambition?'

'When I'm old enough I'll join the army. Then I'll have enough from my pay to support us both.'

'The army, is it now?'

'The cavalry, sir.'

'Well, well. You have commendably clear goals, I'll say that. Do you think any cavalry regiment will accept you? You don't appear to have too much to recommend you at present.'

'I shall see that they accept me, sir, when the time comes.'

'You're very confident. But then perhaps the cavalry owes you, too. Perhaps the whole world does. And meanwhile you expect some benign employer to support you?'

'I'll work for anything I get, sir.'

'And is there any work you're fitted for?'

'I'm good with horses.'

'Well, that may be a happy coincidence, because Lambert isn't good with horses at all. They can smell what a blackguard he is, I expect. My daughter won't even ride when he's here.' Dearborn stepped back a few paces, thoughtfully tugging at his moustache. He said, 'You'll saddle my daughter's mare. The roan, there. Do it every morning at eight, whatever the weather, whether she wants to ride or not. Beyond that you'll look after the stables and the horses. Lambert will be happy enough to leave you to it, I don't doubt, but you'll take your orders from him nevertheless. I'll tell him so. Ten shillings a week to start.'

'Thank you, sir.'

Dearborn levelled his finger at Frank like a duelling pistol. 'But if my daughter finds fault with you or your work, any kind of fault – if you speak out of turn in front of her or she continues not to like the way you look – there won't be a second chance.' He turned and strode away across the cobbles. At the arch he paused and looked back, smiling. 'Compliments of the season, Gray.'

Frank walked over and picked up the shovel and went into the stables. There were several horses stalled here: a hunter, an elderly mare, a cob, a pony for the gig. Frank fed the animals, talking to them, touching them, finding reassurance in the warmth of their bodies and the trust in their eyes. The dim interior was heavy with the smell of dung and foul straw and he could see that the place had not been mucked out for weeks. He stripped off his jacket and hung it on a tack peg and got to work. He was almost done when he glanced up to see Lambert lounging in the doorway.

'Well, you swung that one, Beggar Boy.' He hooked the toe of his boot into the filth of the floor and idly kicked clods of it in Frank's direction. 'See, what you got to understand is that Dearborn's just play-acting. He don't know milk comes from cows. But he wants to show this place off to his flash friends from London, so he play-acts the squire and I play-acts the bailiff. I touch me forelock and I make a big thing of looking after his fucking deer park and his fucking grouse shoot. And if you've got any sense, you'll play along too.' Lambert stepped forward and looked Frank in the face. 'These ignorant brutes hate me and I returns the compliment. You can have 'em for all I care. But you queer my pitch here, Beggar Boy, and I'll break you up.'

Frank watched the man walk away across the yard, whistling. The roan mare looked up at him sympathetically and he eased the halter over her head and started to brush out her mane.

25

Grace climbed over the stile and set off along the track. The afternoon was raw and the low light was failing, and she walked quickly. She had agonised about this visit for over a week, and now she was determined to get it over with.

Light glowed through the front window of Mrs Rossiter's cottage.

That made her nervous, but relieved at the same time. She was not sure she would have had the nerve to come again if the house had been empty. She walked to the door and knocked. Inside, a rocking chair squeaked and a moment later Mrs Rossiter opened to her.

'Well, miss. I thought you'd be along, sooner or later.'

Grace stepped into the low room. Mrs Rossiter's chair was still rocking beside the stove. An opened book and a pair of reading spectacles lay on the cushion. Grace shrugged off her coat and looked quickly around her.

'Young Lochinvar's not here,' the housekeeper said. 'I suppose it's him you've come to see?'

Grace opened her mouth to protest, but she knew it was no use. 'Mrs Rossiter, I wanted Father to send him away.'

'So you did, miss.'

'And on Christmas night.'

'Talking charity's one thing, ain't it, miss? Doing it's another. Let that be a lesson to you.'

Mrs Rossiter pulled out a chair for Grace at the table. She went to the sideboard and brought a bottle and two glasses and filled them.

'Mrs Rossiter, I don't think I should—'

The woman pushed Grace's glass towards her. 'Bottoms up.'

Grace stared at the oily spirit. She didn't want to drink, but it was clear to her what this was about. She had failed a test, and she was here asking for forgiveness. She knew that Mrs Rossiter had understood this from the beginning. Grace picked up her glass and drank half of the spirit down in a gulp.

'Good girl,' the housekeeper said and clinked her glass against Grace's. 'Still sisters.'

'He frightened me,' Grace said, when she could speak. 'I know that's no excuse.'

'He did look a sight, I'll grant you that.'

'I haven't been able to ride all week, because I would have to face him at the stables. I feel so badly about it.'

'Well, he ain't far away, miss. He's up there in the clearing, playing soldiers.' Mrs Rossiter snorted. 'They're all the bloody same, when it comes to it.'

Grace toyed with her glass. She knew Mrs Rossiter was inviting her to leave, to walk on through the woods to the clearing and make her peace with Frank Gray in person. But she wasn't ready to go yet. She drank the rest of her gin and waited while Mrs Rossiter refilled both glasses.

'He seems a strange boy,' Grace ventured.

'Don't know about strange. He's polite enough. Does his work. Reads my books.'

'He reads?'

'Did you think he was ignorant? He ain't that. He does his learning with that little brother of his. Smart as a whip, that young 'un. Frank too, if you ask me, though he won't let on.'

'Will they stay here with you, Mrs Rossiter?'

'I've got the room. I could use the few extra pennies. Tell you the truth I like the company.' Mrs Rossiter nodded at the window. 'It's getting dark.'

Grace had the peculiar sensation that the looming trees and the cold light falling in spokes between the trunks were part of some enormous stage set, not quite real, not quite solid. She stretched out her hand to touch a birch trunk as she walked, and misjudged the distance so that her fingers passed through empty air. Perhaps it wasn't the gin making her feel like this. Perhaps she really was floating effortlessly through the winter afternoon, not entirely present: she rather wished that might be so.

She heard hoofbeats drumming on soft ground quite close by. The sound came from her right, and she followed a slighter path through a tangle of hawthorn bushes. Even before she saw him she heard his voice from the clearing, talking to the horse, encouraging it, praising it. She moved forward breast deep through the hawthorns, the spiked branches scratching at her, until she could see him.

He wasn't at all prepossessing, now that she could see him in daylight, just a gangly youth with lank black hair. He did not see her and she experienced the powerful luxury of studying someone who does not know they are observed. She noticed the big joints of his elbows as he rode and his prominent Adam's apple. He was poorly shaved and there was a stippling of acne along the line of his jaw.

He was mounted on Bess, the elderly chestnut mare her mother occasionally rode, and he was taking the mare around the clearing, on each circuit hopping her over a fallen log. Grace saw with astonishment that he was riding bareback, and she wondered if perhaps he was a gypsy. He had that dark look about him, and everyone said that gypsies had an almost supernatural affinity with horses. Maybe that would account for this sense of the alien about him that she could not quite shake.

He brought the horse around again, speaking in a soft and caressing tone – *good girl, once more, that's the way* – and this time he sat up very straight and clasped his hands behind him. Grace had never seen anyone ride like this before, far less jump, and she caught herself holding her breath. He urged the mare on with his knees, leaned forward and straightened again as she landed, clearing the fallen log easily – *that's the way, well done, clever girl!*

Grace let her breath out in the smallest of gasps and the mare jinked nervously sideways. The boy slipped, clutched for her mane, missed his grip and hit the ground with a thud which Grace was sure she could feel through the soles of her shoes. She could hardly believe how swiftly this had happened. In the merest eyeblink the boy who had been riding so confidently was crumpled on the ground. She pushed through the screen of bushes, the thorny branches hooking her clothes. He lay curled up, his knees drawn to his chest, hugging himself.

At the edge of the clearing she stopped, unsure what to do next. The mare came ambling back and gazed curiously down at her fallen rider, as if wondering what he was doing in such an undignified position. The boy rolled over onto his knees, and reached up for the bridle. He still didn't see Grace, and she watched him as he blew out his cheeks and, catching his breath, stood up with his back to her, stroking the horse's nose and speaking gently. Grace had seen her father fly into a temper with a horse that had unseated him, laying into it with his riding crop until the animal bled. She rather thought that was what a man was supposed to do. Seeing this unknown boy when he was behaving so differently was as if she had caught him at some intimate moment. She cleared her throat loudly so that he spun round.

'I hope you have not hurt yourself,' she said, grandly.

He brushed twigs and leaves from his clothes. 'You startled her.'

'I most certainly did not!' She had no idea why she denied it.

'You startled her,' he repeated, in just the same level tone.

He led the horse away a few steps by the bridle and back again, and Grace felt as if she had been dismissed, and grew angry.

'You're very rude,' she said, and caught herself. This wasn't at all what she had come here for. She suspected it was the gin that was making her waspish, and she made an effort to soften her voice. 'What are you doing?'

He glanced at her as he led the horse around again. 'I'm practising. Training.'

'What for?'

'For the cavalry.' He halted the mare. 'Miss.'

'Are you to call me *Miss*?' She laughed uncertainly. 'I suppose you have to. But it sounds funny.'

He clucked his tongue to the mare and walked her round once more.

He didn't seem to have any intention of saying more, and that irritated her all over again.

'I think the army is a poor ambition,' she said, tossing her head. 'Killing natives who can't defend themselves, and then stealing their land.'

The boy still didn't answer. Frustrated, she stepped forward as he walked the horse round, and placed herself in his path so that he had to stop. She reached up and ruffled the coarse hair between Bess's ears. The animal snorted contentedly and nuzzled her hand.

'I came here to say I'm sorry,' she said.

She could see that this surprised him, though he struggled not to show it.

'For what?'

'I was uncharitable, on Christmas night. I told Father to send you away, back out into the cold. I don't deny it.' She lifted her chin. 'I should not have done that.'

Was he smiling? She could hardly credit it, but she felt sure that he was grinning at her. She blushed furiously.

'When someone apologises,' she said, 'you are supposed to accept it.'

He tilted his head. 'Well, then, miss, I accept it.'

They stood facing one another for a long moment, and then she held out her hand to him. She knew this was rather modern of her, and perhaps because of that the gesture seemed to catch him off guard. He rubbed his own palm down his breeches twice before taking her hand. His was warm and dry. She could tell that he would have liked to say something sarcastic but that her handshake had disarmed him, and this gave her a sense of triumph.

'So, Frank Gray,' she said, 'are we friends?'

But she knew it was wrong as soon as she said it. She could hear the condescension in her own voice. And he heard it, too, and let his hand fall from hers.

'Bonny will be ready for you tomorrow at eight, miss,' he said. 'Like every morning.'

He tugged the mare's head away, and swung himself up onto the horse's back. He kicked the animal lightly and was gone without another word, launching into an easy canter down the soft woodland path.

PART FOUR
England, September 1895

26

In the lecture theatre the blinds were down, and smoke coiled through the magic-lantern beam. These writhing blue serpents fascinated Grace. She knew that ladies were supposed to disapprove of men smoking in mixed company, but she liked the raw tang of tobacco and the sense it gave her of being in some secret place with a gathering of conspirators.

Which wasn't far from the truth, she reflected. Much though he loved her, it was hard to imagine what her father would think if he knew she was in this room, and this risk was precisely what made it so seductive to be here. She glanced at Mrs Rossiter on the folding chair beside her. She wanted to exchange a smile, to seal their complicity and to thank the older woman for introducing her to this new and passionate world. But Mrs Rossiter did not look at Grace. She sat gazing at the images flickering on the screen. The slide changed with a clack, and Grace heard shocked whispers in the darkened hall.

'Those are not piles of unfamiliar fruit, ladies and gentlemen.' At the podium Mr Abel Freedom Brindley hooked his hands into his waistcoat pockets. His voice, with its deep Southern American accent, was of extraordinary beauty. 'Those are human hands. Severed human hands. Hands hacked off by King Leopold's Force Publique as punishment for failure to meet rubber quotas.' Brindley paused. 'What is the Force Publique, you ask? It is King Leopold's private army, a body not accountable to any government, but to His Majesty personally. These atrocities are committed in his name. Do you doubt that, ladies and gentlemen? Well, and so did I. But I have seen these things for myself in my travels with the late lamented Colonel George Washington Williams. Oh, yes. I have seen this and more when I was in the company of that great man.'

Now the screen showed a group of young white men in pith helmets with bandoliers over their chests. They were standing under palm trees while a row of natives in tattered clothing knelt before them. The white men looked proud; the black men looked fearful.

'This force is officered by Europeans,' Brindley said, 'and yes, there are some British officers among them, men who were once soldiers of your queen. But the Force Publique's rank and file is manned by

Congolese natives, and this is perhaps the unkindest cut of all. Such is the rule of tyranny and terror in that benighted land that brother is set against brother, and son against father.'

The slide changed again. A white man with a hunting rifle across his lap sat in a wicker chair on a veranda, his booted legs crossed. At the foot of the veranda steps huddled three ragged black children. Their right arms ended in stumps. Two ladies at the end of Grace's row left the hall, one of them weeping. Before Brindley could speak again, a woman near the front fainted and there was a brief commotion while water was fetched, gentlemen made room, pamphlets were fanned.

Throughout this small commotion, Brindley stood patiently at the edge of the stage. While the emergency was dealt with Grace took advantage of the moment to observe him. She had never seen a black man in a position of authority before. The only other negroes she had ever seen had been servants. Abel Freedom Brindley was nobody's servant, that was very clear. A tall man, powerfully built, it was easy to imagine him in the uniform of the Union Army in which he had once served alongside his hero, the radical black campaigner Colonel Williams. That, at least, was what the leaflet circulated by the Aborigines' Protection Society said.

Grace had heard of Colonel Williams and his charismatic oratory. He must have been impressive indeed if he had been as powerful a speaker as his disciple. Brindley was still in his mid-thirties, with large bold eyes and a habit of authority which drew the attention of the room like a magnet. And there was that voice, a voice like honey. Grace's imagination started to play the game she so often caught it playing these days. But Abel Freedom Brindley? The fact that he was a black man made it all the more shocking. But after all it wasn't so very hard to picture. Mr Brindley would have no trouble making himself charming, she was sure.

Grace could see Mrs Brindley sitting at the rear of the stage, an attractive young white woman in a floral dress and hat, her face tilted up towards her husband, her eyes full of devotion. Grace wondered how Brindley had time for a wife, in between denouncing King Leopold's cruelties. He was married to his mission; indeed, she thought with a flash of insight, he was in love with it. Grace looked again at Mrs Brindley's radiant upturned face, and it came to her that the couple's shared cause might be more intimate and more passionate than any storybook romance.

The woman who had fainted was helped from the room and Brindley continued speaking as if there had been no interruption.

'Perhaps four hundred thousand souls have perished in the Congo in the last ten years. Whole native tribes eradicated, entire districts depopulated. The causes of such atrocious mortality? Enforced porterage, introduced European diseases, the search for rubber, and reprisals when quotas are not met.' He moved towards the centre of the stage. 'But the root cause is simpler. It is greed. The greed of Empire, of one nation's ruthless ambition to dominate and exploit another. For the fault is not that of King Leopold of Belgium alone – duplicitous and avaricious though he is – but of the iniquitous system of Empire which practises extortion and murder of Africa's sable sons in the name of enlightenment and progress.'

He stood with his head lifted after this declaration. Grace could see a sheen of sweat on his brow.

The September afternoon was still warm as the audience poured out onto Exhibition Road. Grace was struck by how quiet they all were, as if they had witnessed something shameful and recognised their own complicity. At that moment she felt the same. It seemed to her that the great city, throbbing and clattering around her like some vast engine, had been built entirely on the sweat and blood of unknown men and women brought to the condition of beasts.

The crowd moved off in knots of twos and threes, talking in hushed voices. Across the street, by the rear entrance to the Victoria and Albert Museum, Grace noticed two policemen standing and chatting, as if casually.

'You'll come to our next gathering, miss?' a woman demanded, placing herself directly in front of Grace. She was a small person of early middle age with a sharp nose and a hot light in her eyes, and her head moved forward in little pecking jerks.

Startled, Grace stepped back.

The woman advanced on her, *peck, peck, peck.* 'Mr Abel Freedom Brindley will be addressing a meeting of the Anti-Slavery Society and the Socialist League in Bermondsey in two weeks. You'll be there, of course?'

Grace looked around for Mrs Rossiter. 'I'm afraid we don't live close by—'

'Then you must at least subscribe.' The woman produced a printed bill and thrust it at Grace so that she had to take it. 'We must all fight the good fight, young lady. It is our duty. Nothing is more sacred.'

'Miss Grace!' Mrs Rossiter called. 'Hurry along, now!'

Grace pushed past the woman and fled to Mrs Rossiter, who had flagged down a hansom and was already giving instructions to the driver. She held the door until Grace climbed in. The small woman pecked her way up to the window, still talking even though she could no longer be heard, that weird light still blazing in her eyes. The cabbie clicked his tongue at the horse and at last the vehicle pulled out into the crush and din of the traffic. Grace gratefully breathed in the cab smell of leather and stale cigars.

Mrs Rossiter jerked her head back towards the receding figure on the pavement. 'Ladies who never wanted for nothing in their lives, and suddenly they're all for socialism and democracy and women's suffrage, all mixed together like a big fruit punch. They get drunk on it.' She sniffed. 'But where are pious little do-gooders like her when heads are getting broke?'

'Well, I'm sure it won't come to that, Mrs Rossiter.'

The housekeeper gave her a disdainful glance. 'What world do you live in, young miss? You never hear of Bloody Sunday? Trafalgar Square, November 1887. It wasn't just heads that got broke that day. Two men were killed by the police and the troopers and more than two hundred taken to hospital. The cavalry charged the crowd and cut them down with sabres. You didn't know that?'

'No, I . . . In London? What were they protesting about, these people?'

'Free trade. Unemployment. Privilege. They came back the next week, forty-odd thousand of them, and much the same happened. Another poor soul got killed that day. Alfred Linnell his name, not that anyone had ever heard of him before that, but they say 120,000 Londoners turned out to his funeral, so somebody noticed, even if you didn't. I know. I was there.' Mrs Rossiter adjusted the set of her shoulders. 'Ah, but then, that was eight years since, miss. You were only little, too busy playing with your dollies and prattling your French lessons.'

Grace said nothing.

'You ever heard of the Paris Commune, miss?' Mrs Rossiter asked suddenly.

'When the anarchists tried to take over Paris?'

'Oh, the anarchists!' Mrs Rossiter gave a knowing grunt of laughter. 'Was *that* who it was?'

'Is that not correct, Mrs Rossiter?'

She waited for a reply, but the housekeeper gazed wordlessly out through the blue square of the window. They were rattling into the forecourt of the station, a pillared area crowded with cabs and tumultuous with travellers and the traders who served them, flower-sellers, bootblacks, porters, old men hawking newspapers and boys shovelling up after the horses.

'Victoria Station,' the cabbie sang out.

They came to a halt but Mrs Rossiter remained seated.

'Thirty thousand, they say. That's how many *anarchists* they shot after the commune was crushed. That was in seventy-one, not much over twenty years back. Thirty thousand men, women and children. Most of them stood up against walls and shot down long after the trouble had stopped. Do you think there was ever thirty thousand *anarchists* in Paris, miss?'

'Victoria Station!' the cabbie bellowed again, and, so that there should be no mistake about it, he reached down to hook the door open with the handle of his whip.

'Ordinary folks,' Mrs Rossiter said, still not moving from her seat. 'That's who they were, Miss Grace. Ordinary working men and women who decided they'd had enough of the system. So the system taught them a lesson.'

'But surely that kind of thing couldn't happen here?'

Mrs Rossiter smiled coldly. 'That's what they said in Paris. They depend on you thinking that.' The cabbie, muttering, leaned down into the open doorway, but Mrs Rossiter rounded on him before he could speak. 'You shout at me again, Ben Hur, and I'll have your guts for garters.'

She stepped out of the cab and Grace followed her meekly.

27

They sat in silence on the train, the sole occupants of a Ladies Only compartment, as the train crawled over the river, and then rattled south-west through rank after rank of new suburbs of raw brick. The wild red evening arched over London.

Grace gazed out in silence. Mrs Rossiter's stories of street riots had cast a shadow over her mood. Visions of screaming mobs and broken windows depressed her. It all seemed so squalid and confused. Ordinary folk, Mrs Rossiter had said. And yet even in France the gendarmes and soldiers must have been ordinary folk too, presumably. Neighbours of the very people they oppressed, living in the same cramped homes, eating the same food, their children learning their alphabets side by side on the same school benches. It was all so complicated. How could anyone strike a clear moral balance in such circumstances?

Grace's mind veered away from the problem and fled back to the Africa of Mr Abel Brindley's magic-lantern show. Now *that* was the place for decisive action. In a place like that a bold reformer could fight against brutal injustice with head held high, in the clear knowledge of the difference between right and wrong. The very thought of it thrilled her. She thought of the black silhouettes of palm trees, and the chattering of creatures in the forest as night fell. Torrential rapids, rivers as wide as seas and steamers to ply them, trackless forests so huge they curved over an entire quadrant of the globe, hiding God knew what mysteries and wonders.

Grace shifted in her seat. It didn't seem quite proper that she should carry away from that lecture so vivid a sense of adventure. She should have felt nothing but outrage. Just the same she kept thinking of those smiling young Belgians in their solar topees with their rifles across their chests. They reminded her of the young men she had sometimes met at her parents' weekend parties, some of them destined for the world's wild places. Big, hearty, sporting types for the most part, one or two of whom flirted clumsily with her despite her youth. Surely, young Belgian men couldn't be so very different from their British counterparts. Were youths like this really capable of the cruelty Mr Brindley had described? The ones she had met had been at pains to impress her either by sounding earnest and high minded, or louche and cynical. She found it hard to believe these callow boys could mutate into monsters and hack off the hands of children. Such a process was beyond understanding.

But one thing she did understand, and that was what drew these overgrown schoolboys to the edges of the earth. It was a lust for space, for a vivid life and freedom from convention. Even for danger. She understood that well enough, and wasn't enough of a hypocrite to pretend otherwise to herself.

'The Royal Academy,' the housekeeper warned. 'We was at the National Gallery. We liked Mr Waterhouse's work specially, if anyone asks.'

'No one will ask, I assure you.'

'That's as may be, but I'd never have taken the risk had you not badgered me so, young miss, so just you take care who you talk to.'

Grace gazed out of the window. The train was rolling through open countryside now, farms and fields and fat cattle awash in a westering sun as yellow as butter. She saw a traction engine in a field at work on the harvest, chugging smoke, a cluster of workers busy around it like bees around a queen. So there was progress here, too, but still it seemed to her that the rhythm of the English countryside remained much as it had always been. How safe it was. How predictable. How utterly tedious. She leaned back in the seat and closed her eyes.

When she opened them again they were pulling into Alton Station, the steam flattening against the wooden roof to come billowing down around the carriage windows. As they walked from the platform, Grace saw to her annoyance that Frank Gray was waiting with the pony and trap. She had hoped she and Mrs Rossiter could make their own way home. That would have given them time to talk, to settle the lessons of the day in her mind. Now that wouldn't be possible, not with Frank Gray sitting up there on the box, and she felt as if a promised treat had been denied her.

She crossed the station forecourt at Mrs Rossiter's side. Frank was lounging on the seat in the evening sunshine, sharing a joke with the driver of a carter's wagon drawn up beside the trap. He threw back his head and laughed at something the carter said. When he heard their approach he turned, the smile and the sun lingering on his face, and jumped down onto the gravel beside them. It wouldn't be so bad, Grace thought, if the servant girls didn't keep gossiping about him. Personally, she couldn't see it. He'd filled out in the last eighteen months or so, added a couple of inches in height, and lost most of his coltish awkwardness – all that was true enough – but he was no more agreeable than he had been at the beginning.

'Well, young Lochinvar,' said Mrs Rossiter. 'Didn't know you'd started a cab service.'

'Cook said you might be on the London train. Naturally, I couldn't stay away.'

Grace had seen him play charming to Mrs Rossiter before, and seen the way she responded. After all Frank Gray did lodge with Mrs Rossiter, and some familiarity was to be expected. But it seemed so undignified of the housekeeper to play along in this way. Yet here she was, a stern woman of fifty or so, giving Frank Gray her hand in queenly fashion and allowing him to help her up into the trap.

Grace sighed, and Frank, hearing her, put out a hand to help her up too. She swept brusquely past him and climbed in unaided and sat with her back to the driver's seat. She could feel Mrs Rossiter looking curiously at her but she refused to meet her eyes, and in a moment they were bowling briskly through the darkening lanes. It was eight o'clock at night now, and the evening air was full of the scent of the cut meadows. Grace stared out over the hedges into fields where the long shadows of oaks and elms barred the turf. There were rabbits on the sweet grass by the roadside. She concentrated on the rabbits.

'You can drop me here,' Mrs Rossiter called out as they rounded the corner of the long drive. 'I'll walk home. That young brother of yours will be back from school long since, and if I don't watch him he'll burn the house down, or blow it up.'

Frank brought the trap to a halt, climbed off the box and helped Mrs Rossiter down. 'Best take care, going that way.'

'Oh? And why's that?'

'Lambert says there's poachers about. I don't know if it's true.'

Mrs Rossiter sniffed. 'Thanks for your advice, cabbie, but I hope you don't expect a tip for it. Besides, any poacher will get a tough old bird if he bags me.' The housekeeper brushed down her skirts. 'And now take this young lady straight up to the house before her coach-and-six turns into a pumpkin.' She waved one hand and set off down the path between the beeches.

Frank climbed back up on the box.

'Poachers?' Grace said with exaggerated scorn.

'It's likely all talk,' he said.

'Does my father know about this *talk*?'

She didn't know why she was speaking in this haughty fashion but he evidently registered it, for he turned to look at her, resting his arm along the back of the seat as he did so.

'How should I know?' he said. 'I'm not in your father's confidence.'

'Miss,' she snapped. 'You're to call me *Miss*.'

Frank gave her a long level look, and for a moment she thought he might answer back. She sat very upright with her eyes blazing, daring him to speak. But in the end he turned away and cracked the whip so smartly over the pony's haunch that the poor animal jumped. They rattled up the long drive between the elm trees, the ringing of the trace chains and the pony's hoofbeats filling the silence between them. She was furious with herself and with him.

'Drive to the stables,' she commanded.

She saw his back stiffen, but he clicked his tongue at the pony again, and swung around the carriage turn and back down the flank of the house and through the brick archway into the stable yard. He pulled up and jumped down beside the trap. Grace got out the opposite side and walked straight over to the stable door where the roan mare stood gazing at her. She kept her back to Frank and made a fuss of the animal while behind her she heard him unhitch the pony and lead him to the stone trough in the corner of the yard. Then she stalked away and into the house through the back door to the servants' hall and the kitchens.

28

Frank waited until he heard the door bang behind her. He unharnessed the pony and rubbed the animal down so hard that his coat gleamed in the twilight. Frank was sweating by the time he had finished, but the work calmed him. He led the pony into his stall, fed him, and closed the stable door, then cleaned the harness and hung it up on its hook. After that he wheeled the trap over near the coach house. There was a little dried mud from Mrs Rossiter's boots on the floor and Frank found a brush and swept it out. As he did so he noticed a flash of white from the crack between the leather upholstery and the door. A paper of some sort, printed in black type. He caught it between finger and thumb and drew it out.

'Still here, Beggar Boy? Seems like you don't never want to go home.' Lambert had one foot up on the mounting block, and there was an expansive air about him which meant that he'd been drinking, and was probably on his way down to the Rose and Crown to drink some more.

Frank slipped the paper into his back pocket. 'Horses don't feed themselves.'

'Dumb brutes. I never could take to 'em. But you? Now you're a natural. I'll say this much for you, young Frankie, for all your tight-arsed ways, you're more use than I thought you was going to be when you turned up here all them months ago.'

Frank watched him warily. In well over a year Lambert had barely spoken to him except to issue orders. He had never called him by his first name before.

'Mr Dearborn's having people down here Saturday and Sunday,' Lambert went on. 'A dozen of his flash friends. They'll likely want to ride Sunday morning.'

'The horses will be ready.'

'They'll need more than we've got here. You'd best get down to Dalby's stables tomorrow and hire a few nags.'

Frank looked at him in surprise. 'You want me to do that?'

'I don't know one horse's arse from another.' Lambert reached into his waistcoat and held out some folded banknotes. 'Mr Dearborn give me the money. Get half a dozen hacks and bring them up here Saturday, and make sure they're dozy buggers, mind. These city folks ain't never seen a horse, some of them, except pulling a cab up Threadneedle Street.' Lambert held on to the little wad a fraction longer than he needed to, then let Frank take it, and winked. 'Mr Dearborn don't count the change too careful.'

A bat flittered between them and suddenly the blue air of the courtyard was full of them, flicking like shadows in the twilight.

Lambert stepped back a pace and belched. 'He's having trouble with poachers, is Mr Dearborn. It's likely those dirty didicois camped down at Leigh Common. Nothing but trouble where gypsies is concerned.'

'So you said.'

'And it's true. A couple of does was taken last month, and just last week a stag. He gets real upset with me when that happens, does Mr Dearborn, though Lord knows, he only keeps the fucking beasts for looking at. What does he expect, I say, when venison fetches top money in fancy London restaurants?' Lambert spread his hands in appeal. 'I does me best, but I can't sleep with the bloody creatures day and night, can I, to keep them safe. A couple of likely lads could make off with the odd beast any time they chose, and no one the wiser.'

'Is that why you've been setting spring guns?'

Lambert's smile held but he grew still. 'Now, where did you hear such wicked nonsense?'

'There's talk.'

'Well, it can't be right, can it? Because spring guns have been agin the law these forty years or more. Even thieving poachers have rights, it seems. Spring guns, my arse! But you'd have to admit, Frankie, it don't do no harm for folks to believe it, eh?' Lambert got up and sauntered across to him. 'I know you don't think much of me, boy, but you could learn a bit if you wasn't too proud to listen. And maybe make a bit too. Think about that.'

Frank waited until Lambert's footsteps faded away down the drive. He unfolded the small wad of bank notes. It came to nine pounds, a big white five-pound note and four singles. Mr Dearborn could certainly hire riding horses for half this sum. Frank began to wish he had refused to take the money. He tucked the cash into his pocket, and as he did so his fingers touched the paper he had found in the trap. He drew it out and flattened it and held it up to the last of the light.

29

Grace swept through the servants' hall. Three or four of the footmen and some of the live-in maids were chatting over the remains of their meal. The men were relaxed, and Ralph, the handsome one, was lounging with his jacket open and one booted foot on the edge of the table. There was some startled commotion as Grace appeared, but she waved to them to stay seated and marched on down the basement steps into the pantry.

Two scullery maids were washing up the servants' dishes at the zinc basin and gossiping loudly. Polly Penfold was rinsing porcelain at the teak sink in the corner, and Grace saw that the girl was in tears over her work. The scullery maids stopped talking and, wiping their hands on their aprons, bobbed good evenings to Grace as she passed. Polly made a token curtsey, trying to hide her blubbered face. Grace might have stopped to ask the reason for her distress, but Polly was often tearful for one reason or another, and Grace felt so out of temper herself that she did not think she could manage to find much sympathy for the girl.

She walked through into the kitchen. The tall whitewashed room was striped with the last of the sunlight streaming through the basement windows. The atmosphere was quiet, almost reverent. Mrs Gillray was seated in some state at the end of the great kitchen table. She was wearing her white dress and apron, her spectacles on her nose and her kitchen ledger open before her. Mrs Gillray had been in the kitchens at Cumver for as long as Grace remembered, originally as a kitchen maid under old Mrs Mills. Now a stout woman in her forties, Mrs Gillray had risen to the rank of professed cook and was a formidable person indeed, with a staff of a dozen answering to her.

'Well, well.' The cook peered over the top of her spectacles at Grace. 'Here's a little visitor we haven't seen for some time. Too grown up for us nowadays, I expect?'

Moodily Grace pulled out a chair and sat down. There had been a time when she had come to the kitchen every day, often without her mother's knowledge. Mrs Gillray and the maids had always made a great fuss of her, letting her play on the warm flagstones, so long as she didn't get under their feet. Sometimes she was allowed to stir the cake mix and even to lick the wooden spoon. Grace had loved the bustle and order of the place, the bright copper pans gleaming on the walls, the blast of heat from the great range. In winter that range roared like a furnace and made the flags so hot they would burn through the stitching in the kitchen maids' boots. Grace vividly remembered all of this, but above all it was the smells which came to her mind: earth on vegetables, game hung long enough to drop maggots, frying onions, baked bread. This evening the kitchen was unusually calm. The mistress was away from home and the last meal of the day was finished. Even so, Grace could still smell her childhood in here.

Mrs Gillray patted papers into a neat square. Grace saw that the cook had been writing out orders for the poulterer and the butcher in Alton, long and expensive orders in her meticulous hand.

'It's for your parents' entertainment on Saturday,' Mrs Gillray said. 'Guests from London, I hear. Of course it's nice to have the dining room busy, miss. But there'll be a good deal of work for us. People have such fancy tastes these days.' She gave Grace a martyred look. 'Time was when a great estate might have supplied all the needful for its own entertaining. A plain cook might have prepared the most of it. But times change, don't they, Miss Grace?'

'I suppose they do, Mrs Gillray.'

'Amy?' The girl came hurrying to Mrs Gillray's call, drying her hands, smiling shyly at Grace.

'Mum?'

'Here's the list of spices for tomorrow. See that Mrs Rossiter gets it in good time. And stop by on your way down in the morning and wait while she unlocks her cupboard so you can pick it all up. Get Bella to give you a hand carrying it.'

The girl's face fell. 'Very good, mum.' She took the list and went back to her work.

Mrs Gillray adjusted her spectacles and added a few notes to her ledger. Grace knew what this piece of theatre was all about. The girls were frightened of Mrs Rossiter, and disliked having to go to her even for a simple errand like this. She had heard the maids' chatter, and knew they thought Mrs Rossiter proud, fierce and common – a fatal combination. What was worse, she was a sight too modern for their liking. It was unheard of for a housekeeper to live in a cottage in the grounds. All the other servants lived in, which was as it should be. Even Mrs Gillray, despite her exalted rank, had a room beside those of her maids at the very top of the house, like virtually every other cook in the country. The quarters of old Mr Yelland, the butler, were at the top of the servants' stairs, and nearby were the rooms normally occupied by the housekeeper. But Mrs Rossiter lived in her cottage and so the housekeeper's rooms stood empty, which was an offence against the divine order of things.

'I hear you've been up to London, miss?' Mrs Gillray asked innocently. 'With Mrs Rossiter again, was it?'

'To the National Gallery. Particularly to see Mr Waterhouse's latest work.'

'That Mrs Rossiter does have refined tastes.'

Grace looked down at her hands on the scrubbed pine of the table. Mrs Gillray could not suspect where she had really been, but just the same Grace knew she was being accused of betrayal, and in her heart she knew that she was guilty of it. Over the last few months she had turned her back on the comfortable hierarchy of the kitchen, and even on the modest dreams of the people who worked here. All at once the big warm room seemed as sad to her as a doll's house outgrown by the child who had once adored it. She could almost have wept, and that made her remember Polly Penfold, sobbing over the washing up in the scullery.

'What's the matter with Polly, Mrs Gillray? She was crying when I came in.'

The cook sniffed. 'Silly girl. She's always grizzling over something or other.'

'And this time?'

Mrs Gillray sighed and put down her pen. 'It's that Frank Gray, miss.'

'What?'

Grace spoke so sharply that Mrs Gillray raised her eyebrows.

'What I mean to say,' Grace said quickly, 'is that I had no idea Polly and Frank Gray were . . . that is . . .'

'Well, miss, I wouldn't know if they are anything or nothing. Frank walked her to the fair at Leigh Common last month, I know that. But as to anything further, it's hardly my business, now is it?'

Grace was aware that Mrs Gillray was watching her with growing amusement and this infuriated her.

'I keep my nose out of the girls' business,' the cook went on, 'so long as it doesn't interfere with their work. But it's true Polly does seem to have got some notion into her head.'

'I see.'

'It was that Ralph all last winter, though I don't doubt he encouraged her, the scamp.' The cook paused. 'And you'd have to own, miss, that young Frank would be a better catch than Ralph any day. A good looking lad, too, and not yet seventeen.'

'I hadn't noticed, I'm sure.' Grace got quickly to her feet.

'Won't you be having a bite of something? There's some damson pie.'

'I don't think so.'

'No? It would be like old times. I remember when my damson pie—'

'Thank you, Mrs Gillray. I'm not very hungry.'

Grace hurried out through the scullery the way she had come, hearing the girls' chatter die away as she passed, and then rise again behind her with new intensity, or so it seemed to her.

30

Frank had wheeled the trap out into the centre of the yard where the setting sun made the yellow bodywork shine. He had rolled his sleeves up and was sluicing dust and mud from the wheels. He gave no sign of having seen Grace as he carried his bucket to the pump and worked the handle, water ringing into the pail. He brought the bucket back across the yard and went on with his task, his back still to her, humming to himself as he worked a brush between the spokes. Grace was sure that he was deliberately ignoring her.

'I think it very ill of you, Frank Gray,' she announced loudly.

He stood up in surprise, the brush still in his hands. It was clear to her at once that he genuinely had not known she was there, and this made her feel foolish. Water sparkled in the hairs of his forearms.

He said, 'Miss?'

'I think it very ill indeed,' she repeated. His puzzlement was so galling she had to restrain herself from stamping her foot in vexation. 'To lead her on in such a way is unpardonable.'

Slowly he started to smile. 'Which horse would you be speaking of, miss?'

This time she really did stamp her foot. 'You know very well what I am talking about, Frank Gray. I'm talking about Polly Penfold.'

'What about her?'

'She's in there sobbing her heart out, poor girl.'

'I'm grieved to hear it.'

'That's all you have to say for yourself?'

'What would you like me to say, miss? Polly's crying fits are about as frequent as showers in October.'

'And I suppose you'll say you're not the cause of them?'

'Me?'

'You took her to the fair last month, did you not?'

'I did. Out of charity, because no one else would. They laugh at the poor girl in the servants' hall.'

'She believes there was more to it than that.'

'I'm sorry if that's so.' He bent back to his work again. 'But I'm not responsible if she gets ideas about me.'

Grace had the vertiginous feeling that she was tottering on the edge of a cliff but still she could not stop herself. 'You deny that you have encouraged her?'

He stood up again and dropped the brush so that it clattered on the cobbles. 'Yes, I deny that. Who says that I did? Does she?'

'No. That is—'

'Then who?'

Grace opened her mouth and closed it again. Had anyone actually said that, least of all Polly herself? Grace had not even thought of asking. Worse still, she realised that she didn't give tuppence for poor Polly's feelings one way or the other. She stared out through the archway over the evening fields, appalled at herself, wondering what had possessed her to start this conversation.

'There's something on your mind, miss,' Frank said. 'But I don't think it's Polly Penfold.'

She snapped round to face him, but mercifully he did not offer any answer to his own question. Instead he held up a paper, a printed pamphlet. She recognised it with a jolt.

'It was down the side of the seat,' he said.

'Give it to me.'

'Was it a good exhibition at the National Gallery, miss? That was where you went, wasn't it?' He held the paper within her reach and she snatched it from his hands. 'You should be more careful,' he said. 'Your father would be angry if he found out.'

She tossed her head. 'What do you mean by that remark?'

'Oh, you needn't worry, miss. I shan't tell him.'

'Am I supposed to thank you?'

'You can do as you please.' He bent down to pick up the brush.

'I'll have you know, Frank Gray, that what I do and what my father thinks of it are none of your concern. It's not against the law to take an interest in social issues.'

'No. After all, you can afford it.' He dipped the brush in the water and flicked suds off it.

'If you knew what was going on in the world,' she burst out, 'you might not be so glib. Even you might be shocked by some of the things that happen.'

'Might I now?'

'But you don't know about any of that, do you? You don't *want* to know. It's easier to go on believing the world is ordered just as it should be, that God is in his heaven and the sun will never set on the great British Empire. Because you're going to join the army and become part of it all! And it's all such a cruel farce.'

'You're going to change all that, are you, miss? By attending socialist meetings where you and all the other ladies with not enough to do can enjoy being outraged together?'

'Why do you always have to be so unpleasant? If you only had the eyes to see it, I'm on your side.'

'On the side of the world's downtrodden masses?'

'Yes, if you like.'

'Well, that's a relief, miss. Want to take a turn with the shovel?'

She swung on her heel and stalked away from him, the pamphlet crushed in her hand. But when she got to the archway she could still feel his eyes upon her back.

31

G race closed her bedroom door behind her and leaned on it. The bed with its bright patchwork counterpane had been hers since childhood and looked the same as it always had. Her dolls still grinned at her from the top of the wardrobe, and on the walls hung her clumsy paintings of flowers and birds and favourite dogs from long ago, daubed when she was nine or ten. Grace ran her fingers over the spines of her books: Walter Scott, Keats, Shelley, Jane Austen, Wordsworth. Next to them were the journals she had filled ever since she was a child. She had always loved to write, and now she took one of the diaries out and flipped it open at random. It told of a robin which had nested in the ivy behind the kitchen, of an organ grinder with a monkey she had seen at Farnham, of a sewing box she had received for her birthday. Inexpertly pressed between the pages were an elm leaf, a bluebell, a snowdrop.

She closed the journal and set it aside. These innocent things had been important to her once, and at that thought a well of melancholy opened inside her. In recent months the focus of her world had shifted, and in the process the hopefulness of her childhood had been eclipsed. She knew it would never shine again with the same unclouded brightness. This transformation must have been going on for some time, yet today it had become painfully final for her. She could not understand why.

It was Mr Abel Freedom Brindley's lecture, she decided. His talk had let darkness and doubt into her soul. That was why she was behaving so strangely, why she felt so ill at ease with herself. Surely that was it.

Night had fallen. The high rectangles of the windows framed for her the dark mass of trees, the lights of the village, and a luminous sky with a pale disc of moon. She stepped into the centre of the room and undressed, letting her clothes fall carelessly around her. She could see her nakedness reflected in the window, the long lines of her body painted by gaslight. From the stable yard below and out of sight she heard a horse clopping across cobbles and the clunk of the stable door being fastened. He had finished for the night. She could imagine him well enough, in his shirtsleeves and workman's cap, leading the pony into its stall, stroking the animal's warm flank. That impossible boy. Why did he dislike her so much? Why did every conversation between them go so dreadfully wrong? Was it just because of the way she had behaved on that first night, so long ago?

And now he – of all people – knew her secret. The crumpled pamphlet lay on her bed where she had tossed it. She gazed at it now. She didn't mind that he had found it. She was sure that, for all his prickliness, Frank Gray would be as good as his word and not betray her. No, she was glad that he knew. She regretted that he had learned her secret only because of the way that scene had played itself out. If she had handled things just a little differently she might have been able to talk to him about some of what she had learned. She would have liked to be able to do that. Perhaps there were things she might have told him. Instead, she had come out with that nonsense about Polly, and instantly he had shut her out, as firmly as if a portcullis had come rattling down. Well, and he was to blame too. He was touchy and obstinate and ungrateful.

Without realising it Grace had taken a couple of steps closer to the window, naked as she was. She crossed her hands over her breasts. For perhaps half a minute she stood gazing out over the dark woods and the distant lights of the village. Then she let her hands fall away.

It was quite dark now but the harvest moon was nearly full, and Frank followed the field path across the meadow below the house, his hands thrust into his pockets. He got to the edge of the woods and climbed the stile, and started to walk away down the woodland track, a patterned strip of moonlight and shadow.

He had gone no more than a dozen paces, enough for the canopy of the trees to close over him, when something stopped him. He couldn't place it: a sense that he was followed or watched. The hairs lifted on the back of his neck, and instinctively he stepped aside into the deepest shadow of the trees and stood motionless. He knew this feeling well enough. It was not fear, but a half-forgotten oneness with the trees around him and the earth beneath his feet. He had experienced it before in these woods at night, and in other secret places far away from here, and he was never wrong. If he kept still and waited, a fox would lope across his path, or perhaps a badger would come snuffling past his feet.

And yet this time the sensation was stronger than that. He looked back the way he had come. He could see nothing unusual along the dappled tunnel of the path right up to the stile. He retraced his steps to rest his hands on the top rail. Beyond, the meadow stretched out, bone white under the moon, fifty yards to the black bulk of the house. A light over the porch, a glow from the basement kitchens.

And on the second floor a single bright window shining, a tall rectangle of light. And in this rectangle a girl standing framed, so strange and potent in her nakedness that it took him a moment to recognise her. She couldn't possibly see him, he knew that, and yet she seemed to be looking straight at him and with such intent that he might have been the one laid bare. He could not turn away, and he stood as if commanded to attention until she stepped back from the window and out of his sight, and – for the moment – released him.

32

Frank brought the horses up to Cumver House on Friday afternoon. He rode the lead animal, an ancient hunter which would never clear a fence again, and led the other five hacks in a string behind him. He was glad to be alone. He wanted the warm afternoon to himself.

The horses were docile in the heat and he led them up the track to where it joined the lane from Leigh village, and then turned right through a farm gate to enter Buller's field. Sheep jogged away to gather under an oak tree in the far corner, bleating nervously. Frank rode on through the wet trample where the animals came to drink at the stream, hearing the suck and squelch of the horses' hooves behind him. He walked his little troop up the grassy slope beyond, and through the gap in the far hedge. The farm track led along the flank of a hill through stands of birch and after half a mile debouched onto the driveway to Cumver House. The horses shambled behind him, their hooves knocking now on the harder ground.

Frank turned his face up to the light and half-closed his eyes so that the glare shone dull red through the lids. And he saw it again as he had seen it every time he had closed his eyes these last three days: a lighted window, and her naked figure standing in it, as vulnerable as it was lovely. She had looked directly at him, though surely she could not have seen him standing there? He had tortured himself with that question ever since, even though every rational part of him knew that he had been invisible to her.

'Why don't you look where you're going?' she shouted. 'You nearly rode me into the hedge!'

Startled, he reined in the old hunter and walked him back a step, and the other animals shuffled to a halt around him. She was standing on the grassy verge at a bend in the track, almost under his horse's shoulder, her face open with fright and anger. The sunlight lay on her bare arms and on her hair. In the silence a horse grunted and stamped, and bees droned in a bank of bramble.

'Well?' she demanded. She was flustered and seemed to be growing more so. 'And are you going to sit there all day, staring?'

He wanted to speak, and yet he could feel the moment escaping from him even as he leaned forward in the saddle and opened his mouth. Before he could say a word she flung away, pulling her shawl around her shoulders, as if something more than the near accident had frightened her. In a second she had vanished through a gap in the hedge. He watched her helplessly as she strode away, stiff-backed, across the shining grassland.

Frank kicked the hunter hard and trotted his troop up the track towards the house.

He rode into the stable yard and dismounted, hitching the old hunter to the pump handle in the corner while he untied the hacks, fiercely tugging the knots free. The animals sensed his change of mood and grew restive, and he had to step back for a moment and calm himself before leading the first pair to the trough.

Lambert came striding in through the archway and stood with his hands on his hips, watching Frank as he worked.

He said, 'Didn't old Dalby have nothing else?'

Frank glanced up at him, his hand on the first horse's neck. 'What's wrong with these?'

'Nothing, by the looks. Which is my meaning. Dalby could have found you some broken-down old nags cheaper. Dearborn's fancy friends won't know no different.'

Frank didn't reply. He led the horses over to the stalls, shut the half-doors behind first one and then the other, and went back for the next two animals, leading them across the cobbles to the trough. When they were contentedly drinking he pulled out the money and handed it to Lambert.

'Here's the change. It's all there.'

'Oh, I don't doubt it is, Frankie.' Lambert sighed and took the money. 'I don't doubt every penny's there. More fool you. Just don't say I never give you a chance, that's all.'

'I don't want chances from you.'

'No. That's the truth, ain't it? You don't want nothing from nobody.' Lambert moved forward, his jaw jutting. 'And here's another thing,

Beggar Boy – you give me that holier-than-thou look again and I'll kick you into next week.'

Frank felt himself grow weightless. He was taller than Lambert now and stronger. He realised with a whiff of savage joy that he would like to do this. He would like to hit somebody very hard indeed, and he could think of no better candidate than Lambert. He swayed on the balls of his feet. For a moment an answering light flickered in Lambert's eyes, but then a doubt flitted across the man's face and he took a half-step back.

'Finish with these beasts and then fuck off,' he grunted, his eyes sliding away from Frank's. 'I don't want you around here after sunset.'

'Why?'

'I've been watching you, Gray. And I don't like what I see. So stay off Mr Dearborn's land until tomorrow, you hear me? Or I might have to speak to him about you.'

'And say what?'

Lambert did not answer, but grabbed his jacket and swung it over his shoulder. 'I'll be back here by seven tomorrow. See that you're not poking around here before that.'

He turned on his heel and stumped away through the brick arch.

33

Frank walked back to the cottage through the trees. The afternoon sunshine was warm and the woods loud with birds, but his mind was still dark.

The door was half-open, as Mrs Rossiter habitually left it when she was home. As he entered the cottage she was seated at the deal table with a newspaper and a china mug of tea in front of her. She glanced up as he came in, looking over the top of her reading glasses.

'They let you off early.' She tilted her head towards the kitchen door. 'Tea in the pot.'

He walked through and poured himself a mug of tea the colour of mahogany and brought it back to the table. He sat down and nursed it.

She said, 'Gifford's out in the shed. Gawd only knows what he's doing there. He's in another world, that boy.'

'He's just cleverer than the rest of us.'

'There's clever, and there's clever. But I'll grant you he's too bright for Mrs Parsons' school. I don't know what's to be done about that.'

'Neither do I.'

She folded the paper carefully and put her glasses on the neat square of it. 'Have you had words with someone?'

'Who would I have had words with?'

She crossed her arms high on her chest. 'Think I come in with yesterday's washing, Frank Gray? If her father catches you being insolent to her, you'll be out on your ear.'

'When was I insolent?'

'Perish the thought. Sweet talker like you? Coming back from the station the other day you were asking for a slapping, the way you spoke to her. I heard you, after I got down. So has that happened again?'

'What if it has?'

'Frank, she's Stephen Dearborn's daughter. Can you get that through your thick skull? You might think you can come over familiar and disrespectful, but the Dearborns don't work to the same rules as normal folk. Oh, Grace wouldn't say nothing, but sooner or later someone will notice the two of you are at daggers drawn. I thought you had more sense.'

'She's wanted me gone ever since the night I got here.'

'You bloody young fool. She could've had you out any time she chose.'

'Why didn't she, then?'

'Because she's got more heart than you have. Good Lord above, that I should have to listen to another man's nonsense! Can't you see where all this aggravation springs from? Can't you see what's happening to you?' She looked at him, shook her head. 'Well, I'll be damned, and p'raps you can't. I'll just say this, then. Young Grace is a fine girl, and a head on her shoulders, too—'

'And too good for me.'

He hadn't meant to say this, and didn't know why he had. It stopped her tirade, though. Mrs Rossiter settled back in her chair.

'Well, my lad. If the cap fits.'

He got up and walked to the door and stood there, glaring out. 'You'd know all about her,' he said. 'You and Grace Dearborn are great friends, after all. Do the two of you talk about me and how *insolent* I am?'

'Don't you flatter yourself.'

'But you go to *galleries* together.'

'If you know any different, Frank Gray, you'll do well to keep quiet about it. I won't have her get into trouble on my account, and not on yours neither. And it wouldn't just be her. You know what'd happen if Mr Dearborn took against us? We wouldn't see so much of the fine and generous country squire then.'

131

'I don't doubt that.'

'Well, then keep your wits about you, such as you've got, and your mouth shut. Especially around young Grace.'

He stood by the door, glowering out at the sunlit afternoon, furious with her for holding up this mirror for him, and with himself for what he saw there; and for what he had let her see.

'I saved you some stew,' she said at last, more quietly.

'I don't want any.'

She ignored him, got up and fetched a bowl from the range. 'There's some potatoes, too, and a few beans. If you're going to be a fool, there's no point in being a hungry one.'

Frank came to the table and sat down, avoiding her eyes. She set the plate before him and he ate in silence. She seemed reluctant to move away from the table.

'I knew as I shouldn't've let you through my door,' she said gently. 'I knew as you'd be trouble to me.'

He sat looking at his plate. He said, 'You know I won't stay for ever, Mrs Rossiter.'

'Oh, I know that. Young Lochinvar's going off to the wars, naturally. Well, that might be safer than ogling Grace Dearborn.' She reached past him to pick up the plate and let her arm cuff the side of his head as she did so. 'Go and see your clever brother. He wants to talk to you. Which I don't, no more.'

Frank left the kitchen and walked across the yard to the shed which had become Gifford's den. He pushed the door open. Gifford was seated on a stool with his chin in his hands, reading a book open on the bench under the window, a notebook beside him. Around him lay the usual jumble of tools, models and retorts. Frank stepped in, knocking askew a pile of bound journals so that they slithered and fell to the floor. Gifford gave no sign of having heard. Frank picked up a heavy textbook from the bench and dropped it with a smack. Gifford looked up at that, blinking like a mole.

'Hello, Frank,' he smiled. 'What's new?'

'Mrs Rossiter said you wanted to talk.'

'Oh, yes?'

Gifford glanced down at the book he had been reading and absently turned the page. Frank had the clear impression that if he said nothing more, his brother would go back to his reading and entirely forget that he was there. He reached across and flicked the book shut.

'What did you want to talk about, Giff?'

'Oh! I wondered if I could borrow a pound. Would that be all right?'

'A pound? Where do you think I'd get a pound? Every penny I earn goes into keeping us as it is.'

Gifford waved an airy hand. 'You'll find it somewhere, Frank. You always do.'

'You're a selfish little toad, Giff, aren't you?'

Gifford stared at him. 'Frank, I didn't mean to . . . It's not for me, exactly.'

'Who is it for, then?'

'Don't get in a bate, Frank. What I mean is, well, of course it's for me, but it's not as if I want it for . . . tuck, or something.'

Frank held himself back with an effort. He was filled with a fierce desire to grab his brother by the lapels and shake him until his teeth rattled.

'So what is it for?'

'The Science Museum is selling some of their old microscopes. I've sent off for one. It's beautiful, Frank. You'll understand when you see it. A bit old-fashioned, but it has a brass mount, and lenses with a magnification up to—'

'If Mrs Rossiter charged us full rent I wouldn't even be able to put food on the table. And you want to borrow money to buy a micro-scope?'

'Did I do something wrong, Frank?'

Frank looked at his brother's open and innocent face, his pale hair shining and his blue eyes wide. 'Nothing you'd understand,' he said at last.

He leaned against the doorframe and watched Gifford at his make-shift desk, surrounded by his treasures: a model steam engine he had built himself, engineering magazines, lengths of metal tubing, a battered tool box. The sun falling through the window shone on brass and copper.

'You really are going to be an engineer, Giff, aren't you?'

'Oh, yes. Or a scientist, or something. Do you know what advances men are making at the moment, Frank? For years now in Germany they've been putting Otto-cycle engines into horseless carriages, so that they can run on spirit – like lamp oil. They're starting to do it here, too. You talk about joining the cavalry, but in another ten years the horse will be a thing of the past.'

'Horses have been around a long time.'

'Not for much longer. Mark my words. And it won't end there. There are chaps in a dozen countries who are trying to fit an oil engine into a gliding machine, so you could drive it around the sky. Can you imagine that?'

'No.'

'But it's not a dream, Frank! It's going to happen. It *is* happening.'

Frank gazed out through the sunny square of the window. He supposed that the countryside beyond had looked much the same for hundreds of years. The England of oak trees and hedgerows and rolling fields. It looked eternal. But he was very much afraid that Gifford was right, and soon it would all be changed.

'You're too good for that school,' Frank said.

'Yes, I know.'

'We can't afford to get you into a good one, Giff.'

'That's all right. I'm going to work for Armstrong Mitchell, or maybe Babcock and Wilcox, or Vickers. One of the new engineering houses. That's where the future is.'

'Not without some proper education you're not.'

'Then I'll sweep the workshop, and when the time's right, I'll tell them my ideas.'

'It doesn't happen like that any more, Giff, no matter how clever you are. You need training, qualifications. The top engineers today are university men, and you won't get to be one of them unless you go to a decent school.'

Gifford was about to argue, but stopped himself as his brother's logic dawned on him. He sat frowning for a few seconds, puzzling through this, and then looked up brightly at his brother. 'So what's to be done, Frank?'

'I don't know. But you'll need more than a pound.'

Frank walked out into the warm evening. A few yards away Mrs Rossiter was hanging washing out on the clothes line at the back of the house. As he came over she shot one of her knowing looks at the shed behind him.

'It's your birthday on Sunday next,' she said. 'I see it on the calendar.'

'Yes.' He took a damp shirt from her basket and pegged it up.

'Maybe we could all do with cheering up. What say I cook something special?'

'Mrs Rossiter, I can't afford anything special and you can't keep giving us things.'

'Who said anything about giving? I make the best rabbit pie this side of London. You like rabbit pie? Course you do. Everyone likes my rabbit pie. And rabbits is something you don't need to buy, am I right? You seen that old rook rifle in the closet? Used to be Billy Rossiter's, and Gawd knows how old it is, but it still shoots. I've used it myself from time to time. Take it up to the top paddock this evening and pot two or three fat conies for us. Can you manage that, Frank Gray, without making a mess of it?'

'Yes, I can manage that, Mrs Rossiter.'

'Two fat ones. Three'd be better still.' She prodded him lightly in the chest. 'Go on with you. I've got to get back to the big house. The guests will be arriving in a few hours, and those useless trollops they call maids will have everything at sixes and sevens.'

She took the basket back into the cottage and after a few moments he heard her close the front door behind her and saw her walk away down the sunlit path.

Frank went back into the kitchen and sat at the table. It was strange to be here, idle and alone, in the afternoon. The late summer lay warm on the paddocks. Birds fussed in the bushes outside the door. Mrs Rossiter's food lumped warmly in his belly. He let his mind drift. The sun had fallen like beaten gold over the girl's bare arm, and her lips had parted in surprise.

He shook himself and got to his feet, found the old rook rifle in the broom cupboard where it lay wrapped in oil-stained cloth. He broke it, checked the breech and the bore, and set it on the kitchen table. The rifle hadn't been used for months, and there was a little rust on the barrel and trigger guard. At the back of the cupboard Frank found an oil can and a wire brush and started furiously to clean the gun.

34

'They owe it all to us, the ungrateful beggars,' Dr Matthews announced from the far end of the glittering table. 'Your nigger and your Chinee and your Hindoo.'

Sarah Dearborn adjusted the position of a yellow rose in a vase. 'One makes such pretty things from Indian cotton,' she said. 'It's curious, isn't it, that they don't undertake manufacture in India?'

'On the contrary, my dear,' Stephen Dearborn said, 'these days we manage quite a brisk trade in machinery to India. We moved a whole cotton mill out to Bombay just last month, Maudslay steam engine, spinning machines, the lot. Machine tools, too. They're setting up workshops to build locomotives and rolling stock at Jamalpur. That's what free trade can do.'

'But for a British company, I'll be bound,' Matthews said.

'I'll grant you that, Matthews. British company, Indian labour. Just as you'd expect.'

Dr Matthews, who had taken a good deal of wine, struck the table.

'There you have it! Incapable of managing any organisation, your Hindoo. He's a willing enough wallah when properly led, no doubt. But a factory? Hah! They need us for leadership, and yet they have the nerve to agitate.'

Grace bit her lip. It would be dreadfully rude to argue with one of her father's guests at his own table, but she hoped somebody would do it – perhaps old Major Bignall, who had spent his life in India. Bignall, though, had been drinking steadily all evening and sat now in a bovine stupor, his grey moustache wet with wine.

'Couldn't manage a thing for themselves,' Matthews concluded triumphantly. 'Like children! Need a firm hand.'

Grace heard herself say, 'How do we know what they could do and what they could not? They are never given the chance.'

Mrs Matthews leaned across the table and patted Grace's hand. 'Well spoken, my dear. I have a cousin in India, and she tells me that some of these people can be taught to do quite complicated things, with patience. Of course Henry won't hear of it.'

Dr Matthews glared at his wife. 'Your Indian will never learn to manage his own affairs.'

Mrs Matthews withdrew her hand from Grace's. 'As you say, Henry.'

Dr Matthews was, Grace decided, a fat, stupid little man. She said, 'I don't see why being Indian should make any difference. Surely it's only a matter of education.'

There was a moment of stillness around the table.

'My daughter seems to be developing into something of a radical,' Dearborn said lightly. 'You know, Matthews, there's little in this world as implacable as the awakening social conscience of a sixteen-year-old girl.'

There was some kindly laughter from the other guests. Grace looked sharply at her father, stung by his condescension. But to her surprise he winked at her, as if the whole exchange had amused him vastly.

Sarah Dearborn trilled, 'I think we're ready for the fish. I'm very partial to a little fish. Emily? Jane? You may clear away now. Tell me, Major Bignall, do they have fish in India?'

Bignall lifted his head and stared vaguely at her. 'Fish, ma'am?'

'Very large ones, perhaps? One thinks of elephants.'

'They have fish, ma'am.' Bignall lowered his eyes again and spoke in a distant voice. 'They have all manner of wonderful creatures in India.'

There was a pause while the table waited to see if he would go on, and when he did not the genteel clatter of dishes and cutlery flowed into the silence. A murmur of conversation rose up. Florence Mason leaned across the table to speak with Mrs Matthews and gave a peal of laughter at whatever reply she was given. Charles Horsfall, Member of Parliament and the grandest person present, began to lecture Dr Matthews about London's sewers - the envy of the civilised world, he insisted, as if daring the doctor to contradict him.

Grace was finding the whole evening confusing. She hadn't wanted any part of it at first. There seemed little amusement in a dinner party whose guests included a handful of her father's business associates, who would talk about money; the Tory MP, who would talk about power; and Dr and Mrs Matthews from the village, who would probably be grateful and obsequious. It wasn't that she disliked them all. She had always been fond of her father's partner, crumpled, shambling Uncle Welti – her godfather – with his floral silk waistcoats and his funny foreignness. And dashing Sidney Mason, who ran the Liverpool office, had a raffish charm that his wife was always mocking behind his back. But it infuriated Grace to hear them all bray on so about the favours they conferred on the world. She kept thinking of Mrs Rossiter, who was perhaps at this very moment drinking gin in her woodland cottage among books and pamphlets and relics of her butchered husband.

And yet the most confusing thing of all was that she was enjoying herself. She loved the glitter of candles on silver and glass, the garnet red of the wine as Yelland decanted it, the conviviality and the laughter. If Mrs Rossiter's gin was the spirit of dark dissent, red burgundy must be molten confidence. The sheer authority of these people was so very seductive. And the elegance! The men's dark jackets and pristine shirtfronts and their pearl and diamond studs and the gorgeous stuffs of the women's gowns. She couldn't help it; she loved the opulence of the house around her, and the sweep of the moonlit lawns beyond the windows and the late summer scent of mown grass drifting in from the night. But most of all she loved herself in her dark blue silk with her hair shining over her shoulder and her black pearl pendant glinting at her breast. Early on she had caught sight of her reflection in the window, and now she could not help glancing back at that ghostly figure, not quite able to believe how beautiful she was.

Her father was speaking to her, and she recalled herself from her own image with an effort.

'So, Puss,' he was speaking softly, leaning to her as the chatter around the table grew, 'you've got the measure of old Matthews right enough. He's clearly no match for any daughter of mine. What do you think of our Major Bignall?'

The question surprised and flattered her. She looked at the fuddled old soldier at the end of the table, anxious not to give the wrong answer.

'He seems rather . . . dull, Father.'

'Old Gerald? Damned good agent for us in Madras. He's ex-East India Company, and knows the ropes out there like no one else. But, yes, he must seem pretty dull. Anything else?'

Emboldened, Grace took a step further. 'The major seems to drink a lot, Father.'

Dearborn nodded, pondering this observation too. 'Gerald Bignall lost his wife in the Mutiny, you know.'

'Oh, I'm sure I didn't mean to—'

'No, you should know of such things. It's important. This was all forty years ago, but it's just like yesterday to Gerald. There was no warning of any trouble. He was out riding, and when he came back he found the sepoys had cut off his wife's head and left it on the piano for him.'

Grace bit her lip. 'That's horrible.'

'Yes, it is. But I suppose it serves to show that the progress of civilisation isn't always as smooth as we might wish.'

Grace sat in silence, shocked by the story and by the brutality of her father's telling. But just the same he had spoken to her as he would speak to an adult, and that was thrilling.

'We owe a lot to these bibulous old fools out on the edge of Empire,' he said. 'I try not to forget that. It's my one stab at humility.'

Grace looked down the length of the table. Yelland was filling Major Bignall's glass yet again while the major stared wordlessly at his own liver-spotted hands crossed on the tablecloth. Grace felt sorry for him now. Kindly Mrs Matthews probably felt the same way, for she was craning forward and trying hard to engage the old soldier in conversation.

As Grace watched, Bignall looked up sharply. 'I'm acquainted with the case, ma'am,' he told Mrs Matthews quite loudly, so that the buzz of table talk stilled. 'Too well acquainted, I'm bound to say. I never knew him, but the husband was an employee of ours.'

Mrs Matthews was flustered by his response. 'Oh. Perhaps I have misunderstood the matter, Major. But my cousin seemed very sure that there was a . . .' she became aware that the rest of the table was listening and lowered her voice, 'well, a whiff of scandal about the case.'

'Rumours,' Bignall growled. 'There are always rumours.'

'I beg your pardon. It's just that I had heard—'

'The poor lady was murdered by an intruder, ma'am. That's all I was told. I have no reason to believe ill of Mrs Gray.'

'No, of course not, Major.' Mrs Matthews fanned herself with her folded napkin. 'I didn't mean to suggest . . . I should not wish in any way to . . .'

'Should have done something for the family.' Bignall was speaking almost to himself now. 'Too damned late.'

'Oh, dear,' Mrs Matthews said, anguished. 'There were children, then?'

'A boy of fourteen or so. Another of perhaps ten.' Bignall stopped talking and gazed into his wine. 'God knows what became of them. Lewis Gray died on the passage home.'

Grace stared at Major Bignall. She became aware that beside her, her father's attention had sharpened as keenly as her own.

Frank stood up and broke the smoking rifle at the breech, and the reek of black powder made the night dangerous. He pushed through the screen of bushes to where the shot rabbit lay kicking. It was a fat doe and its terrified eyes shone in the darkness. He picked it up by its back legs, broke its neck swiftly and dropped the warm body into the sack with the first.

The moon washed over the rough pasture and lay in plates on the roofs of the village houses below. Lights glowed in the windows. It was getting late, too late for shooting. He had bagged two fat rabbits, just enough for Mrs Rossiter's Sunday pie, but all the same he felt a strange reluctance to go home. He loved the earthy smell of the night, the early autumn mist hanging over the grass, flowing into the hollows like milk. Behind him the beech woods of the Dearborn estate stood as dark and mysterious as a forest in a fable, the tracery of their leaves trembling in the moonlight. He threw his head back to look up at the wide sky, crowded with stars.

Perhaps it was the smell of gunpowder which did it, but all at once the revolver lay rocking on the boards before his eyes, glinting dully. For months he had not seen it, and now here it was again, like a warning, and with it the smell of the scorched rug and a singing in his head and that old nameless dread. And more, just a little more this time. He saw his good hand, like a small blind creature, grope towards the pistol. At the same moment a man's hand, glinting crimson in the half light, stretched down towards it.

An owl called almost over his head, and Frank's mind jumped back to the present. The bird ghosted away over the dark paddocks below him, and for a second he could not place where he was. He felt sweat cooling on his face, and his heart was thumping.

He shook his head, hooked the rifle into the crook of his arm and swung himself over the fence and into the trees.

'It's them, isn't it, Papa? It's Frank and Gifford Gray.'

Beside her Dearborn sat silent, his eyes still on Major Bignall. Around them the hum of talk rose again.

'And this Mr Gray worked for the company, Papa?' she persisted. 'For Dearborn & Company? And you didn't know?'

He pursed his lips thoughtfully. 'I know nothing of it, Grace. If it's true, the boy never said a word to me.'

'But how too utterly operatic!' Pretty Mrs Mason made shocked eyes at the other ladies around the table. 'And then for the father to die of – what? – a broken heart? It's delicious!' She leaned forward. 'But one would so like to know what these . . . *rumours* were all about.'

Grace suddenly loathed Mrs Mason.

'I don't concern myself with tittle-tattle, ma'am,' Bignall grunted. 'Besides, our man in Bangalore managed the whole business. I was not involved.'

'In my experience there's rarely smoke without fire.' Mr Horsfall glared around the other guests as if any one of them might be guilty of moral turpitude. 'Especially in the colonies.'

Grace decided she loathed him, too, a dry, thin man sitting in judgment. She wondered if he'd ever had an honest passion in his life. She loathed most of them, in fact, with their knowing headshakes and their righteous murmurings, and their barely concealed delight in this tragedy. And she loathed herself. The mother murdered, the father dead too, and in such a fashion. What would that do to a boy of that age, a boy hardly older than herself? And she had taken against him because he was rude?

She thought of Frank as she had seen him riding up the drive this afternoon, leading the saddle horses from the village. He had looked so easy with his string of charges trotting behind him, like an explorer setting out with his pack ponies for the dusty Karoo. He had seen her then, standing among the wildflowers beside the drive, and, caught off-guard, he had looked as if he might have spoken, but she had slapped him down. She had wanted to punish him for his insolence earlier in the week. And not just for that. No, not just for that. She thought: that dry stick of an MP isn't the only one here who sits in judgment.

She realised her father was still looking at her, and with growing curiosity. 'Does young Gray's story fascinate you so very much, Puss?'

Across the table, Sarah Dearborn said, 'Oh, Stephen, *really*!' and started to laugh.

35

Frank moved silently up the black path between the beeches. The vision was fading. He could still conjure it if he concentrated – two hands groping towards a fallen pistol, dreamlike, never quite reaching it – but other images were crowding into his mind now. Through the aisle of trees he could see the moonlit lawn of the house ahead, and in a moment the stile appeared, as emphatic as a Chinese character against the silvered grass beyond. He stepped up to it, rested one hand on the timber.

The dining room doors were open to the warm night and insects flared in the chute of light thrown out over the grass. He could hear the faint murmur of voices, the tinkle of glass. A cube of amber candlelight, three maids standing against the far wall in their aprons, old Yelland the butler in his tailcoat, eight men in sober evening dress, seven women shimmering in gold and crimson and royal blue.

It took him a moment to find her, because in that dress she looked so much more powerful than she had looked this afternoon, pouting by the side of the drive. Now she was regal and remote, as potent as when he had seen her from this very spot, framed by that lighted upstairs window. She was leaning forward, listening to a discussion at the far end of the table. He could see her dark hair shining in the candlelight, the flash of a jewel at her throat. Whatever she heard must have upset her, for a second later she swung away from the conversation and sat staring out of the window. Her gaze was so plainly directed at him that it was all he could do not to step back, even though, as on that other occasion, she could not possibly see him. Her father said something to her, and Frank saw Mrs Dearborn look up and start to laugh, and he saw the puzzlement on Dearborn's face, and he wondered what the exchange had been about.

Somewhere behind him in the woods a horse whinnied. Frank listened but the sound did not come again. Not one of the Dearborns' horses; he knew their voices like the voices of friends. It crossed his mind that one of the hired hacks might somehow have broken free and wandered off through the woods in search of its own stall. He took one last look up at the house. Maids were bearing dishes with shining silver covers, blocking his view. The horse nickered again, not far away. He picked up the rook rifle and moved away down the track towards the sound.

The path cut diagonally downhill through the trees towards the fenced parkland where the fallow deer were enclosed. It was very dark, though the moon scattered silver coins around him. Frank heard the horse whinny once more, surprisingly close. A new wooden fence ran along the boundary of the deer park, black rails against pale grass. From the paddock Frank heard low voices and the sound of chopping. He put the gun down and crept up to the fence. In the field ten yards ahead of him stood a packhorse with panniers over its saddlecloth. A little further on two men were at work cutting up a dead beast which lay on the ground between them. The nearest man hauled on one of the animal's legs as he slashed at stubborn tendons, grunting with the effort, and Frank saw the branches of antlers move in the moonlight.

The packhorse tramped around to face Frank, its ears pricked, and Lambert's voice said, 'Jimmy, will you shut that fucking animal up?'

'You hold him, then, Spike,' the other man protested, 'if you're so clever.'

Lambert cursed and threw aside his butchering knife. The horse sensed his aggression and jinked towards the fence. Lambert swore again, caught the animal, and then stopped with his hand on the halter, looking straight into Frank's face.

'Frank Gray? I thought I told you to stay clear, you stupid young bugger.'

'Spike!' the other man hissed. 'Let's go. Let's go now!'

Frank recognised the voice and the gangling form. Jimmy Bendelow, a day labourer who hired himself out around the village.

'No need for us to be running off nowhere, Jimmy,' Lambert told him, his voice softening. To Frank he said, 'Just don't you go getting the wrong end of the stick, Frankie. The beast was tangled in the fence. Broke its leg trying to get free, poor thing, so we put it out of its misery. Jimmy and me, we reckoned that it'd do no harm for us to take it.'

Frank said nothing.

'Listen now, Frankie. I'll own the beast wasn't ours to take, but then Mr Dearborn don't breed them up for the meat, so it's hardly a loss to him if we help ourselves, is it? We need it a sight more than he does.' Lambert paused. 'And since you're here, there'll be a bit in it for you, naturally.'

'I want nothing to do with it.'

'Suit yourself, Frankie. You always do. But don't you go telling no tales of poaching. That'd be unjust, because that's not what we were about. You don't believe me, you come over here and see for yourself. You'll find the poor beast's leg's broke, plain as day, and the wire tangled round it, just as we found it.'

Jimmy Bendelow hissed, 'Spike!'

Lambert waved the other man away, spread his arms wide and

backed away, leading the packhorse with him. 'Come see for yourself, Frankie. You go off telling tales about poaching and you'll have us in a ruck of trouble, so you best make sure you're right before you do that. Come and look, why don't you? Put your mind at rest.'

Frank eyed Lambert warily, but the man was unarmed and too far away now for any surprises. Frank put one foot on the middle bar of the fence and the other on the top rail, and paused there. Then he jumped lightly over, dropping towards the long grass on the far side. He caught the gleam of moonlight on steel as the ground came up to meet him, and his right foot touched the hard plate of the trap and the spring gun exploded under him with a monstrous bang. He was blinded and deafened and blown backwards in a cartwheel to come to rest with his back against the rails of the fence. He sat there, not quite in reality, smelling the hot reek of powder for the second time that night, aware of the peace and beauty of the land spread out before him, grateful for the absence of pain. It cost him an effort of will even to reach out his hands to see if his legs were still there. Halfway down his right thigh his fingers sank into pulpy flesh and touched something hard and jagged, like broken china. He could feel warm blood pulsing through his fingers. He became aware of Lambert standing over him.

'You stupid young fucker.'

Jimmy Bendelow came running up, panting, his eyes wild. 'Jesus Christ, Spike! What'll we do now?'

'We'll do nothing. They'll find him in the morning, him and the beast, one as dead as the other. And who do you think they'll blame?'

Jimmy began to back away, shaking his head. 'I won't have that on my conscience, Spike Lambert.'

'Conscience be buggered. He's done for. See for yourself.'

'I'm going to get help! I'm going to the house!'

'Don't be a fucking idiot, Jimmy.'

But abruptly Jimmy Bendelow broke and ran, pelting away across the field.

Lambert bellowed, 'Jimmy!' and took a few shambling steps after him.

Frank felt a great lassitude fill him. He was sweating and the air was sweet and cool on his face. There was no pain and no fear. But then the moon rode out from behind a bank of high cloud and the pure light of it reminded him of a lit window, and that stirred a regret in him, as if he had neglected to do something and had now left it too late. He shifted a little and a violent pain leapt up his leg and into his back, and he gasped and gripped the split flesh of his thigh with both hands.

Lambert came stumping back across the field, scared now. 'And I offered you fair and square, Frank Gray. I offered you.'

His shadow bulked large, and Frank could see his big hands opening and closing and could hear his laboured breathing. And then Lambert was gone, his blockish figure running head down towards the field boundary and the dark country beyond. Somewhere in the night, far away, Frank could hear Jimmy Bendelow shouting desperately for help.

36

The shot was hardly louder than the snapping of a twig, but afterwards Grace could always remember that she had heard it, and had seen the guests' faces arrested in the candlelight. It seemed only an instant later that Jimmy Bendelow came careering out of the night, frantic and dishevelled. He stopped at the open French doors, gasping, snatching off his cap so that his hair stood awry.

In a moment her father was outside on the lawn. She heard him demand, 'Where? Speak up, damn you!' And then, 'Matthews? Come out here, will you? You'll be needed, I think.'

Dr Matthews did as he was told. There was another volley of orders from Dearborn and someone brought the doctor's gig. In a moment both men climbed aboard and the gig bowled off fast down the dark drive with Dearborn at the reins, Matthews beside him and Bendelow hunched miserably in the back.

The party broke up in confusion. Guests offered hurried farewells, coats and shawls were fetched and drivers summoned. Unnoticed, Grace stayed behind as men and women bustled out of the dining room and into the hall. Very soon she was alone at the abandoned table, a battlefield of guttering candles and half-empty glasses and crumpled linen. A cold dread settled in her stomach, she didn't know why.

In an astonishingly short time Dr Matthews' gig returned and stopped on the gravel outside. Grace got to her feet, but could move no further. Old Yelland and two of the servants carried Frank in. Someone had strapped a jacket around his upper leg in lieu of a bandage and secured it there with a belt. She caught a glimpse of his white face, the eyes wide and vacant. One of the maids came to help, screamed and was sharply silenced. A chair went over in the confusion and a glass rolled from the table and smashed. Dearborn shepherded the group through the dining room, across the passage and into the library. Grace could hear him calling instructions – he wanted hot water, blankets, bandages – and she saw maids running in their evening aprons, one up to the bedrooms and two down the servants' stairs to the kitchen.

When the little crowd had swept past her Grace walked across the corridor to the library door. There was blood on the polished boards at her feet, a lot of it, smeared by hurrying footsteps. They had laid him on the couch in the library. Mrs Matthews was leaning over the back of the couch with an oil lamp which threw a pool of light for her husband, who knelt with his shirtsleeves rolled up. Grace could hear the doctor muttering and snorting to himself as he examined the wound. Frank's face was the colour of paper. She thought his eyes flickered as they met hers, as though he distantly recognised her. Matthews did something clumsy and the white face twisted.

The doctor hauled himself to his feet, pulled the blanket back over the boy's thigh and wiped his hands on a towel. 'The leg must come off.'

'Henry,' Mrs Matthews touched her husband's wrist, 'you haven't operated for ten years. And you've taken wine.'

'It must be done. There can be no argument.'

Grace realised that Dr Matthews wanted to cut off Frank's leg, that he relished the power this implied. She looked down at the boy on the couch. He lay like a broken thing, too weak to move, a slick stain the size of a tea plate already spreading through the blanket which covered him. She remembered once more how he had looked this afternoon, easy in the saddle with his packhorses behind him. Like an explorer, she had thought. Never again. Not with one leg. Never again. She realised that his wet white face was rolled towards her and that he was gazing at her steadily. This time she was sure that he knew her.

She stepped fully into the room. 'You mustn't.'

Dr Matthews glanced at her, displeased. 'This is no place for a child.' He turned away and finished drying his hands.

Grace moved to the end of the couch, standing between doctor and patient, and spoke across Dr Matthews to her father. 'Papa, we must fetch Mrs Rossiter.'

'The housekeeper?' Dr Matthews laughed. 'Good Lord!'

'She was in the Crimea,' Grace said very clearly. 'In the hospitals. She worked with Miss Nightingale. She did, Papa, it's true. She'll know what to do.'

'I know what to do, young lady,' Matthews said, opening his bag. 'Don't you worry your head about that.' He moved towards the couch in a purposeful manner.

Dearborn held Grace's gaze steadily for a moment. Then he said, 'Wait.'

Matthews stopped dead, staring at him.

'I'll fetch her,' Grace urged. 'I'll fetch her this instant. I'll take Bonny and bring Mrs Rossiter back here.'

Matthews drew himself up. 'Dearborn, I hope you don't intend to trust this boy's life to some washerwoman's folk remedies?'

Mrs Matthews touched her husband's arm. 'Surely, Henry, the boy will not die in ten minutes?'

Matthews gaped at his wife, appalled at such disloyalty. But it was all that was needed to collapse his confidence, and he sank into a chair. 'Well,' he said, in a small voice. 'I don't know.'

Mrs Matthews moved to stand behind him and put her hands on his shoulders. 'I think it's best, dear,' she said gently. 'I truly think it's best.'

Dearborn said, 'Fetch the woman.'

Grace turned on her heel and fled from the room, fleet-footed with mission, afraid that someone might yet call her back. As she ran down the corridor she could hear again her father's voice in her ear, the curiously harsh voice of command she had heard him use to his underlings. He had never used it to her before, but paradoxically that made her feel valued, as if it marked her acceptance as someone more considerable than merely his pretty daughter. She burst out of the French windows into the night, gathered up her skirts, and flew around the front of the house to the stables, the gravel spraying from her feet.

'Ah ha!' Mrs Rossiter made a deft movement with the forceps and dropped something into the basin with a musical clink. 'Five. And that's the last of them. The rest passed straight through, I fancy. Come here, girl.' She reached back with one bloody hand and beckoned to Grace. 'See that?'

Grace had always considered herself squeamish, but tonight she was unafraid. Mrs Rossiter pointed into the pulpy hole in Frank's leg, a hole the size of a coffee cup. The crater was livid and purple but the worst of the bleeding had stopped. Deep inside it Grace could see a flash of the purest white.

'That's his thighbone. The shot broke it clean through.'

Dearborn said, 'He'll keep the leg?'

'If he's lucky.' Mrs Rossiter got to her feet. Her hair had come loose in her hurry to reach the house and she had stuffed it roughly back into her cap, but despite her dishevelled appearance she carried more authority than portly Dr Matthews had done in his important evening dress. 'He'll need better care than I can give him in the cottage, though.'

'Well, of course he must stay here in the house,' Sarah Dearborn said at once. 'Mustn't he, Stephen?'

'You seem to have decided, my dear,' Dearborn said. He looked down thoughtfully at the injured boy.

37

They had set up a daybed for him in the bay of the library window. Grace didn't visit him for a full week, and when at last she entered the room she couldn't see his face properly against the dazzle from the window. The woods outside glittered in the windy light and through a sash left open a couple of inches the breeze moved tassels on the cloth which covered the bedside table.

She closed the door softly behind her, took two steps across the room, glanced at him and then quickly looked away. This gaunt, hollow-eyed, unshaven young man might be someone else altogether, someone older. She gathered to herself the bag of books she had brought.

'Good morning to you, Frank.'

'Miss Dearborn.'

His voice was hoarse. She came forward, moving a chair close to the bed and flicking her skirts aside to sit.

'Mrs Rossiter says you are recovering wonderfully well,' she said brightly. 'I'm glad of it.'

'Thank you.'

'I've brought you some books. I thought perhaps you might be bored. I remember when I had chickenpox . . .'

Chickenpox. She let her voice drift away to nothing. She could hardly believe she had mentioned chickenpox. She saw again the pulp of flesh and bone in which Mrs Rossiter had probed for shot, and quite suddenly felt sick, as she had not at the time. Chickenpox, indeed.

She fussed with her bag. 'These are all I have to hand. Poetry and silly stuff, but they seem to be the only books in the house.'

She saw him flick his gaze around the walls of the study, clad in volumes from floor to ceiling, calf-bound, gilt-embossed. There was an instant when they might have laughed together, but that felt dangerous to Grace and she kept her face stern.

'If there's something particular you'd like to read,' she said, 'I'll get it for you from the circulating library in Guildford this afternoon. I know you like to read, and I don't suppose you'll be able to do very much else for some time . . .'

She knew she was chattering but he said nothing to rescue her, and just lay looking at her with those unnaturally bright, hollow eyes.

'Well, then,' she said briskly, and got to her feet.

'Don't go yet, miss.'

'Mrs Rossiter says you need to rest. And after all, we all obey Mrs Rossiter, don't we?' She laughed. It sounded false and foolish even to her, but she couldn't help it; she was pleased that he'd asked her to stay but she was embarrassed that it showed. She took the books out of her bag and set them out on the bedside table, avoiding his gaze. 'You might as well have these now I've brought them. Keats. Shelley. Wordsworth. Lord Byron. Probably not your taste.'

' "She walks in beauty like the night," ' he said. ' "Of cloudless climes and starry skies." '

She sat down again abruptly and looked him in the face. 'Why didn't you say anything?'

'About what?'

'Frank, you know what I mean. Why didn't you tell us what happened to you in India?'

'I didn't come to this house looking for pity.'

'What did you come for? I've been wondering.'

'Gifford and I were starving. I could think of nowhere else.'

'That's not the only reason.'

'All right, then. For over thirty years my father worked for yours. I wanted to see what kind of a man he'd given his life to.'

She hesitated. 'It does seem . . . unjust that you were not provided for.'

'Unjust.'

'Father tells me there are regulations; I don't really understand.' She lifted her chin. 'But in any case I can't criticise. I was unjust too, that first night, and I know you've never forgiven me.'

'It's not a matter of forgiveness. But I am curious. Why did you try to turn us out? It's not your nature.'

'Can you judge my nature Frank Gray?'

'Perhaps not. But I'm still curious.'

Grace found she was breathing rapidly. 'If you must know, I was frightened of you.'

'And now?'

'Now I'm sad for you, because I know what happened to your poor mother and your father. I haven't been able to sleep for thinking about it. I've been wanting to say how sorry I am.'

'You have nothing to be sorry about,' he said. 'But there's someone who will be.'

She frowned. 'What do you mean by that? Who?'

'A man in India. A man who's never faced justice.'

'But I understood . . .' She cleared her throat. 'I thought justice had been done in the matter of . . . That is to say, I asked my father, and he has checked with his people. They say that the law . . .'

'He told you a man was hanged for killing her,' Frank said steadily. 'Is that what you mean?'

'Yes.'

'It's true. They hanged some poor wretch from the jail. An Indian, of course. He probably deserved the noose for a dozen other murders. But not for killing my mother.'

Her mouth had gone dry. 'I'm not sure I understand you. Are you saying . . . ?'

'I'm saying another man was guilty. Not an Indian. An Englishman. An officer and a gentleman.'

The threat in his voice was naked: it appalled her and, she was ashamed to discover, it excited her too. 'But how could such a miscarriage—'

'He was an officer. He had friends.'

'That could happen?'

'It did happen. They say they're covering up for the sake of her reputation, for the sake of the family, for any number of reasons. But really they're just looking after their own.'

'But that's unbelievable.'

He shrugged. 'Nevertheless.'

Grace stared at him. 'Have you ever told anyone this before?'

'No.'

'Then why are you telling me?'

'I'm not sure. Perhaps because I owe you, and this is all I have to pay you with.'

'Frank, if you mean to say that you're planning . . .'

She stopped. She knew quite clearly what he was planning, and it was foolish to pretend otherwise. An officer and a gentleman. In her mind she had a vivid glimpse of Frank riding Bess around the clearing all those months ago. Training, he'd said, for the cavalry. So he really had had plans all along, dangerous plans matured in secrecy and silence. She felt strangely responsible, as if she should have known earlier, as if knowing earlier might have made a difference.

She leaned forward urgently. 'Oh, Frank, why on earth didn't you tell us before?'

'What difference would it have made?'

'I don't know. Perhaps Papa might have done more for you.'

'That wouldn't have changed anything.'

'Well, then perhaps I would have understood you better.' She stopped, filled with an incoherent sadness, suddenly close to tears. She burst out. 'Perhaps we could have been friends.'

He shifted in the bed, winced. He said, 'I know I have you to thank that I still have my leg. Perhaps that I'm still alive.'

'It's Mrs Rossiter you should thank for that.'

'I will,' he said, 'but if it hadn't been for you—'

'And besides, that's not what I mean.'

'What do you mean, then, miss?'

All at once it seemed perfectly natural to her. She reached down, lifted his face between her hands and kissed him hard on the lips.

'There,' she said, releasing him and standing up. '*Now* we're friends.' She swept to the door, opened it and left without looking back.

38

Frank's steamer chair had been carried out into the yard and the high brick walls around him were warm with autumn sunlight. From where he lay he could see and smell the horses in their stalls. They had employed a couple of lads from the village to muck out and feed the animals, and from his couch Frank could watch the boys at work. He amused himself by shouting occasional instructions, or playing the tyrant when they larked about.

But he had not seen Grace since her visit to the library five days before. He had tried at first to convince himself that, like him, she was merely nervous about what was to happen next. But as the bright days had dragged on he had to face the fact that almost everyone but her had visited him. Mrs Rossiter came two or three times daily, and Mrs Gillray the cook, and several of the maids had put in an appearance, including tearful Polly Penfold. Once even Mrs Dearborn had drifted by for a few moments.

Only today had he come to accept the truth: that Grace didn't want to see him. He must have misinterpreted that impulsive kiss, and Grace had guessed that he had, and now regretted that she had given it. Perhaps even this was placing too much consequence on himself, and she had simply never given the incident another thought. Yes, that was certainly it.

He'd been a fool ever to think anything else. He grew steadily more surly with the stable lads as the day dragged on.

It was close to five o'clock. The sun was sinking and the yard had fallen into shadow. It was growing chill and in a moment Yelland would bring out a couple of the footmen and carry him back inside. But the firm footsteps which approached from behind him were not Yelland's.

'Hello, Frank,' Stephen Dearborn said easily. 'How goes the fight?'

Frank sat up. 'Improving, sir. Thank you.'

'Capital.' Dearborn took hold of the hardback chair placed there for visitors and turned it round, sitting with his arms crossed over the back. He rested his chin on his crossed wrists, looking at Frank. 'We're all very thankful you didn't lose your leg. If it wasn't for Grace that fool Matthews would have sawn it off. Now it seems you'll walk and ride again, good as new.'

'I'm obliged for your family's kindnesses, sir.'

Dearborn lifted his eyebrows. 'Very pretty. But do I detect a note of grievance?'

'Spring guns aren't lawful. Sir.'

'Well, you're right, Frank. Spring guns are not lawful. I need hardly say that scoundrel Lambert acted without my knowledge in setting one. In point of fact Sergeant Rogerson has already been up here from Guildford to see me about the matter. That's because Lambert was in my employ, and thus his actions could be seen as my responsibility. Now that he's on the run, of course, there's only me to question. This kind of thing is bad for me, Frank. I have hopes of being elevated to the House of Lords next year. It would be galling to have my chances spoiled because of a crime I had nothing to do with.'

'Yes, that would be very bad luck, sir. It was rather bad luck for me, too.'

Dearborn looked at him steadily, then got up and walked over to the yard's rear archway and stood there for a moment or two, gazing out over the rolling autumn farmlands. He turned and walked back.

'You don't much care for people like us, do you, Frank?'

'Sir?'

'Don't trouble to deny it. You have a good deal in common with my Grace, as far as that goes. I'm not sure where she's getting her ideas from, but she's decided we gentry are all something of a bad lot. Naturally her position's complicated by the fact that she's one of us.' Dearborn sat down again. 'In your case I understand why you should feel the way you do, now that I know your history. I also understand why you kept quiet about it for so long. In your place I might have behaved the same way. It's a matter of pride, I see that.'

Frank said nothing.

'But now that we both know what happened, Frank, let's put all our cards on the table, shall we? The fact is we – the company – have no legal obligation to you whatever.'

'I didn't say you had. Sir.'

'Good. Because I have had old Welti check all this. He handles our international operations. Your father was employed by our Madras subsidiary. It would have been different if he had been on the payroll of the parent company in London. Here, the laws are somewhat more indulgent to employees.'

'I know.'

'Well, and I make no apology for that, Frank. The company could not afford to support every employee's dependants, down all the generations, for evermore.' Dearborn paused. 'That aside, our man Furneaux in Bangalore might have used a little discretion in this case, in view of your father's length of service. I regret that something wasn't done.' He tilted his head. 'There. That's as close to an apology as you'll get. What more do you want?'

'I don't want anything.'

'Don't you, Frank? I rather doubt that. I've been looking into your affairs. Your brother is clever, they tell me. Is that true?'

'He's very clever, sir. Very clever indeed.'

'Then he'll need a good school, won't he?' Dearborn pushed his long legs out in front of him and leaned back, netting his fingers behind his neck. 'Here's what it is, Frank. I'm prepared to pay for him to go to St Dunstan's in Guildford, starting immediately.'

Frank looked sharply at him.

Dearborn laughed. 'Don't say thank you, Frank: you might choke on it.'

'I don't believe we need—'

'Don't be a bloody fool,' Dearborn snapped, sitting up. 'Of course you need it. If not for yourself, then for your brother. Good God alive, Frank Gray, you are the most difficult person to help.'

Frank looked down at the cobbles. 'Gifford will reward your confidence, Mr Dearborn.'

'I'm sure he will. And by the by, Frank, you must tell Sergeant Rogerson whatever you wish. Tell him it was a spring gun, or tell him Lambert wounded you with his own weapon and then fled. Whether you can bring your suspicious young mind to accept it or not, I shall make this settlement for Gifford no matter what you tell the good sergeant. What's more, you shall have Lambert's position and his salary, as soon as you're fit enough to work.'

Dearborn stood up. He flicked out the tails of his jacket, took a gold hunter from his waistcoat pocket, checked the time.

'Everyone tells me how clever young Gifford is,' he said. 'But you're no dullard yourself, are you? I've boned up on all that too. And you've worked hard here these past couple of years. Yet you still talk of joining the army. I wonder why that is?'

'It's what I want to do, sir.'

'The profession of arms is a noble one, naturally, but a future as a cavalry trooper seems rather beneath your capabilities. Whereas an enterprise like Dearborn & Company has openings for likely young men with your skills. I've known a number of them go far. Think about that.' Dearborn clicked the case of his watch emphatically shut. 'You'll find that some of us keep our bargains, Frank. Even when the deal proves expensive for us. Give my regards to the sergeant when you see him. Good day to you.' He walked to the archway, turned back. 'Oh, one other thing: Grace sends her best wishes for a speedy recovery. She was sorry not to have time to deliver them in person, and now she won't have the chance.'

'Sir?'

'I've sent her to a finishing school in Switzerland. Her mother tells me it's the proper thing for girls of her age to spend a year or two in such a place.' Dearborn kept his face blank. 'We'll all miss her, won't we?'

PART FIVE

England, March 1896

39

A wild spring wind furrowed the puddles on Leigh High Street. Frank had called into Tolley's ironmongers for saddle soap and brass polish and was emerging into the thin sunshine when he heard the hoofbeats come clipping down the street. He recognised the gig from Cumver House with the gelding Sam in the traces, driven fast. Unusually, Stephen Dearborn was on the seat, whip in hand. He wore a long tweed coat and leather gloves and to Frank he shone with elegance against the red brick of the village street. Dearborn caught sight of him and reined in at the side of the road.

'Good morning to you, Frank.'

'Sir.'

'And a fine morning it is!' Dearborn looked around him in high good humour. Fearing the whip, the pony snorted and tramped sideways. Dearborn swore and tugged at the reins. 'Damned animal's restive. He prefers you to drive him, I shouldn't wonder.'

'He's got a bruised forefoot, sir. He might be more biddable if you didn't push him quite so hard.'

'I can always buy another horse, Frank. I can't buy back a single moment with my daughter.'

Frank stood up straight. 'She's back?'

'Grace is arriving at Farnham in an hour. Home for a few weeks. There's been scarlet fever at the school and they've closed it down for a term.' Dearborn gave him a sunny smile. 'A surprise, eh?'

Frank kept his voice neutral. 'I could have driven down to fetch her, Mr Dearborn, if the coachman's not available.'

'Yes, I'm sure you'd have been happy to do that, Frank. But not a bit of it. I've spent the last three weeks locked in London boardrooms and I'm not going to miss the opportunity to take a spanking ride through the spring lanes to bring my little girl home.'

'Please give her my best, sir.'

'Depend upon it.'

He half-released the brake, and Frank thought he would drive off then, but Dearborn sat there holding the tension on the brake handle, observing him. 'How old are you now, Frank?'

'Seventeen, sir.'

'Still not old enough to enlist, I fancy. Or maybe you've had second thoughts about all that?'

'No, sir.'

'Pity. I happen to know that there'll be a couple of vacancies coming up in our Bristol office pretty soon. Could perhaps lead to an overseas posting, in time. That sort of thing might suit you, and it would be a step on the ladder.'

'I'll give it some thought, sir.'

'I wonder if you will.' Dearborn smiled and tugged at his gloves. 'Well, it's up to you. I keep my bargains, Frank, I told you that. You'll not be able to say that I didn't offer you a chance.'

He cracked his whip and the trap jerked forward. Frank watched as it bowled away through the puddles of the high street, the gelding now painfully lame.

40

'Frank?'

He lifted his head from the book with a jerk. She stood smiling in the doorway of the cottage wearing jodhpurs and corduroy shirt, her face rosy from the cool spring air. Her dark hair was cut very short and it revealed the swan curve of her neck.

'Well!' she laughed. 'Once more with feeling, if you please.'

He got up clumsily, the book still in his hands. 'Welcome back.'

'Where have you secreted yourself since I got home, Frank Gray?' She stepped into the room, her riding boots knocking on the boards. She was so emphatically present in the room that she intimidated him. 'I've been here for three days and haven't seen hide nor hair of you. Admit it, you've been hiding.' She walked up to him and without warning she hooked one arm around his neck and kissed him. 'There. That's better.'

She stepped back, took the book from his limp hands and moved a few steps away, leafing through the pages as she went. 'What's this?'

'It's Homer.'

'Is this your idea of entertainment on a sunny spring day?'

'I once had a copy like it. Father used to read it to us at bedtime. Or rather, we usually had to read it to him.'

'In Greek?' She looked archly at him. 'Did none of you ever consider English?'

'I liked the Greek. The Trojan Wars, Hector and Achilles, gods and goddesses. Gifford wasn't much interested, but I liked it.'

She set the book down on the mantel shelf and let her hand rest on the cover while she observed him.

'Are you alone here?' she asked.

'Giff's gone back to St Dunstan's. Mrs Rossiter's up at the house.' He swallowed, and added, 'Miss.'

She gave him a quizzical look. 'I think we're rather past the "miss" stage, don't you? Let me be Grace, from now on.'

Frank supposed she had learned this new assurance in Switzerland. Seven short months, and yet she stood more erect, held herself more open to the world. He could almost believe she had grown taller. He could still feel the warmth of that kiss on his mouth. And now he was to call her Grace. Presumably this was meant to put him at his ease. Grace.

She tilted her head. 'Bravo.'

'What?'

'You spoke my name.'

'I didn't mean to, I'm sorry.'

'Don't apologise. If you're Frank, I should be Grace. We should get over this ridiculous class nonsense which divides us.'

'You have to have class to think like that.'

She laughed aloud. 'Ah, now that's the Frank Gray I know.' She sat down in the chair opposite him and crossed her legs at the ankle, took a silver case from her shirt pocket and removed from it a cigarette with a gold ring around it. She tapped the cigarette smartly on the silver case and lit it, letting the smoke writhe around her face. She held the open case out to him. He shook his head.

She said, 'Papa hates it, too, when women smoke. God knows what he'd say if he saw me do it. He would definitely not approve.'

She held the cigarette languidly, her hand bent back at the wrist. Frank recognised the affectation in her manner. It made her human to him once more and some of his own assurance returned. He said, 'I doubt he'd approve of you visiting me, either.'

'Well, Papa's not here, is he? As a matter of fact, he's in Antwerp, of all places. He was called away on business this morning. Isn't that typical? I come home and he goes away for a week.' She blew smoke towards the door. 'And besides, I shall visit whomsoever I choose.'

'Did you learn this in Switzerland?'

She missed the irony and leaned forward eagerly. 'Oh, Frank, it was so exciting there! I always thought the Swiss were a bit – well, stuffy. But it's nothing like that at all. Do you know they really do have democracy there? The people can choose their own fate – not women yet, of course, but that will come. And there's turmoil everywhere, all over Europe. People are organising, protesting, changing the way things have been done for a thousand years. New thinking, Frank.' Her eyes were shining. 'New ideas. Thoughts that have never been thought before. Women are mobilising, trades' unions, workers' associations. Everywhere you look the world's being turned upside down. Can't you see it happening?'

'I see the rich getting rich and the poor getting poorer.'

'Frank, you're such a cynic! Don't you know how things have changed?'

'They'll never change. The strong rule the weak.' He pointed at the book on the mantel. 'It was like that in Homer's time and it's been like that ever since.'

'But it doesn't have to be that way! Nations are like people, they can use power well or badly as they choose. They can even give it up.'

'Nobody ever gives up power without a fight.'

'I don't believe that, Frank. People can choose between good and evil, and so can nations.' She paused. 'I've decided what I want to be. I'm going to be a writer.'

'Really?'

'You can smile, Frank Gray, but I will. I'll write novels like George Eliot, or even like Mr Dickens, or perhaps I'll write for a newspaper. Tell people what's really happening in this country we live in. Don't you believe me?'

'I believe you mean every word you say,' he said, 'miss.'

'Grace!' she cried. 'Call me Grace!'

Her fierceness took both of them by surprise. She took a deep breath and blew a plume of aromatic smoke towards the ceiling. She looked at the cigarette in her hand, got to her feet, and flicked the butt out through the door into the shining day. She stood with her hands on her hips while the cool air pressed in around her. She was breathing quickly. Brittle sunlight fell over her.

She said, 'Papa tells me he offered you a position.'

'In a manner of speaking.'

'Will you take it?'

He looked away. 'I have other plans. You know that.'

'Frank, he's trying to give you a chance to make something of yourself.'

'Oh? I thought I was already something.'

'Don't be obstinate, Frank. You could do anything, with Papa's support. Oh, I know he can be a bully when he chooses. I suppose people have to act in that way in business. But he's very honest after his fashion, and if he says—'

'Grace, I'm going to join the army.'

'But why?'

'Because I have no choice.'

'Of course you have a choice!' She was suddenly angry. 'I hate the idea that you'd go away and take up arms for something so unworthy. You'll be a soldier of this vile Empire, fighting for injustice. I can't bear it.'

'I don't give a damn about the Empire. You know that's not why I'm going.'

'So you're still plotting, are you? After all this time?'

'What's time got to do with it?'

'Frank, there's another road open to you now.' She didn't take her eyes from his. 'You can stay here. Father can help you. I'll see that he does.'

He shook his head.

'You think nobody cares about you? Is that it?' She stepped up to him and gripped his arms below the shoulders. 'It's not true, Frank. I promise you it isn't. Only don't go. Don't leave. Not for this.'

He looked down at her, drawn by her urgency. The warmth of her breath was on his face.

The footsteps were loud on the flagged path and an instant later Mrs Rossiter stood framed in the doorway. 'Oh,' the housekeeper said, and stopped. 'Begging your pardon, I'm sure.'

Grace let her hands drop away from Frank's shoulders. 'Why, Mrs Rossiter. I just had to call by and say hello to Frank.'

'So I see, miss. Well, don't let me interrupt you.'

'No, no. I'd best be going.' Grace brushed past the woman and stepped outside. 'Frank? I rode Bonny up here, but I think the poor dear has a stone in her hoof. Perhaps you'd take a look for me?'

'Very well, miss.'

He walked out past Mrs Rossiter, trying to ignore her pursed lips. Grace was striding away between the trees, and he followed and saw the mare tethered in the dappled shade a few yards ahead.

He caught up with her just as she reached the horse and at once she swung to face him. 'Your leg's all right now, is it?' She spoke briskly, as if nothing else had passed between them.

'Grace—'

'Can you walk far on it?'

The question brought him up short. 'As far as ever. Why?'

'There's a meeting in London next week. A rally. The Socialist League are leading it. With Father away, the opportunity seems too good to miss.'

'You're going with Mrs Rossiter?'

She looked at him with eyes very wide and innocent. 'In point of fact I had intended to go alone.'

'Is that wise?'

'Oh, Frank! It's just banners and marching and a little name-calling, that's all.' She paused as if a new idea had just that moment come to her. 'Why don't you come with me?'

'To a rally?'

'Don't look so shocked. You might even learn something. Mr William Morris will be speaking in Hyde Park, and Mr Keir Hardie, and Mrs Annie Besant. When you've heard them speak you can judge for yourself if they have anything useful to say.'

'I don't know, Grace.'

'I confess I am a little nervous,' she sighed. 'That great big crowd.'

'Don't go, then.'

She faced him calmly, dropping her stage manner. 'Oh, I shall go, Frank, whether you come or not. You may depend upon that.'

She didn't wait for an answer but mounted quickly, and he watched her ride away, cantering down the narrow track. He walked back to the cottage. Mrs Rossiter was in the lean-to kitchen, noisily rearranging pots and pans. She emerged as he stepped into the room, her sleeves rolled up to the elbow.

'How was the horse?' she said.

'What?'

'I thought the poor dear had a stone in her hoof?' Mrs Rossiter folded her bare arms over her bosom. 'I hope you know what you're doing, Frank Gray. Not that you ever did before.'

41

The tall man on the platform waited, his head up, one hand stroking his black beard, until the cheering fell away and the huge crowd grew still and expectant. He was an imposing figure in his late forties, broad shouldered and grim faced, wearing a tweed suit and deerstalker and a bright red tie. He paced a couple of steps to the left and then back again, one hand tucked inside his tweed jacket as if pensively, while ten thousand eyes followed him. A child wailed somewhere towards the back of the press and the smallness of the sound accentuated the silence.

'And what was my crime?' the speaker roared suddenly, shaking his forefinger at the clouds. 'That I spoke against the monarchy – a heinous crime indeed, but this is true, my friends. Yes, I confess it! Why would I do such a thing? I shall tell you.' His voice was powerful, with a strong Scottish accent; he dropped it now as if to address the crowd confidentially. 'My fellow Members of Parliament wished to make a statement congratulating Their Majesties the Duke and Duchess of York on the birth of a royal heir. I heartily concurred as any loyal subject would: but I requested that in the same statement these representatives of the people might express condolences for the nearly three hundred men lately killed in the pit disaster at Pontypridd. This my fellow members refused to do. It was, they said, inappropriate to introduce such a sombre note at such a moment. A sombre note, my friends!' His voice rose again. 'A sombre note? A tragedy which ripped the very heart from that honest and hard-working community. A sombre note, which tore husbands from wives, fathers from children, brothers from sisters – which plunged whole villages into penury and extinguished the future hopes of hundreds!' He paused. 'My friends, for years I myself hewed coal to earn my daily bread. I counted myself proud to be part of that noble breed of workers who keep our great empire fuelled. For *that's* why they need the coal, ladies and gentlemen: not for your hearths alone, but for our merchant fleets and our navies which are the sinews of empire. That is why this government resists change in the mining industry, why it refuses to heed the miners' demands for fair pay, for decent pensions, for improvements to safety in the pits. This is why 251 Welsh miners died an awful death in darkness and terror. And it is why more and yet more will die until this industry is reformed. Until the conditions of all our working people are reformed!' He stepped back, stroking his beard, while a patter of applause ran through the crowd. He raised his hand to silence it. 'Until that happens, my friends, we are all complicit in the great deception we call *Empire*. That huge swindle, by which we promise food to the hungry in our colonies, education to the ignorant, civilisation to the savage – and all the while export the labour which should be the right of our own people to undertake in dignity and security.'

In the far distance a man's voice shouted faintly. Frank thought he heard the ringing of shod hooves on cobbles, but there was nothing to be seen through the crowd which thronged the park, the sea of umbrellas and women's bonnets and working men's caps, the intent and rapturous faces upturned towards the stage. Grace nudged him, and Frank faced the front again.

'Look around this cruel world, my friends,' the man boomed, 'and you will see how empty are the promises of princes. Far from educating the earth's poor, we keep them in ignorance! Far from feeding them, we spare them slave's rations only that they can toil for our mills and factories! And not only do we steal the sweat of their brows – we steal their very birthright! Gold, gems, timber and rubber from Africa. Rights of passage for our ships from Egypt. Cotton from India. And everywhere – labour! labour! labour! And what do we send to them in exchange? Poverty and famine! Where they venture to protest, we shoot them down. Only see how we have acted against the Ashanti, the Zulu, the Sikh, the Maori. Against the black and the mulatto of the Caribbean, the Australian Aboriginal. Against the Sudanese and the Boer – and yes, the Irish. And is this different from the way we treat the coal miners of Pontypridd? Like the Romans with their legions, my friends, we British create a wasteland and we call it peace!'

Deafening applause erupted. Hats and bonnets and a blizzard of papers and pamphlets were thrown in the air. Somewhere in the middle of this cacophony rain began to fall, but for perhaps a full minute nothing dimmed the crowd's frenzy. Frank looked around him and could see only wild, ecstatic faces. Beside him, Grace was shouting, jumping to see the stage, waving. She wore a plain brown dress, which made her look like a serving girl, and a workman's cap, but in her excitement the cap had come askew.

'Isn't he wonderful?' she cried to Frank over the din. 'Imagine! Mr Keir Hardie himself!'

Frank said, 'Let's go.'

Grace cupped her hand over her ear. 'What?'

He took her arm and began to steer her through the crowd.

'But it's not over yet!' She tugged against his grip. 'Frank? Stop!'

But his arm was hooked through hers and she had to stumble in her long skirt and button-top boots to keep up with him. They were coming to the edge of the park. The crowd was thinning. People were streaming away under the blur of the strengthening rain, umbrellas held over their heads, a few of them running to escape the downpour. The turf was growing slick underfoot and the paper sellers and coffee vendors were hurriedly packing away their stalls. They reached the gates at Hyde Park Corner and had to slow down as the throng ahead of them funnelled through and poured out into Park Lane. Through the railings Frank could see hansoms and omnibuses jammed in the road, the horses nervous at the press of people surging out around them. A line of policemen in waterproofs stood nudging the marchers back to keep the road clear.

Grace pouted, pulling her arm free. She straightened her dress and then her cap. 'Mrs Annie Besant is going to speak next. I particularly wanted to hear her account of the Matchgirls' Strike.'

In the press ahead of them a woman with a placard slipped onto one knee in the mud. Someone helped her up but though she grabbed for her banner it fell from her hands and was trampled. As his own boots clumped over it Frank saw that it read 'Women's Suffrage will Bring Sunshine to the World'. The throng carried him and Grace out through the gates with such force that they were pushed over the kerb and into the road.

A hatless police sergeant stepped forward and prodded Frank in the side with his baton. 'Keep it clear, damn you! Can't you see where you're going?'

Grace bridled. 'You've no need to use such language, officer.'

The sergeant's eyes narrowed and his bald head shone like polished bronze in the rain. He tapped his baton threateningly into the palm of his hand. Frank bundled the girl across the road between two cabs, so that horses shied and a driver swore. On the far side of Park Lane they rejoined the crowd pouring into the small streets around St James's.

He said, 'Don't they teach you any sense in your fancy school in Switzerland?'

'They teach me to stand up for myself.' She rubbed her arm where he had gripped it. 'They teach me not to let bullies walk all over me.'

He wasn't sure whether she meant him or the policeman. 'That'll sound good,' he said, 'when you're in the gutter with a broken head.'

'Don't be absurd.'

He faced her. 'Grace, do you have any idea how this world works?'

Before she could speak a man cannoned into them from behind and hurried on up the street in the direction they were going, glancing back over his shoulder as he went. There was a gleam of fear in his eye. Frank looked back but saw only the ranks of rain-streaked faces pressing towards them, hats, bonnets, umbrellas, bedraggled banners. A woman screamed and three urchins dodged like ferrets through the legs of the crowd, one clutching a purse. There was something in the air that took Frank's attention, something volatile. He gripped the girl's resisting arm once more and moved her on. The street narrowed, bottling them as they approached a junction. As the crowd was forced to slow, so its urgency increased.

'I'm very angry with you, Frank,' Grace said grandly. 'Very angry indeed.'

'Something's going to happen,' he said.

'Oh, really,' she said, but then hesitated. 'Whatever do you mean?'

Now she did not resist, and let him hurry her through the press to the kerb and then back to the last crossroads. A laneway ran down the back of a row of tall buildings, dim in the lowering afternoon. They hurried down the laneway and after a few yards they were alone. Behind them the throng streamed past the mouth of the street.

They both heard the horses and the shouts of the officers and a moment later the wailing of the people. A police trooper on a bay horse came cantering past the end of the street, pushing into the fleeing crowd. The trooper swung his truncheon and cursed as he did so. A woman went down shrieking and people ran to help and a second trooper rode through and over them, scattering bodies to both sides. In a second there were more horses and more police and terrified people started to pour down the lane towards them and away from the mêlée, shouting, wide-eyed. Frank put his arm around Grace's waist and ran with her, though her long skirts slowed them, and frightened people in ones and twos were now overtaking them – a man with blood running down his face, a pair of sobbing shop girls. Grace pulled up her skirts and they were off again, fleeter now. He pushed her down an alley between dustbins and rotting garbage. People followed from the crowd, breathless and dishevelled.

Frank stopped to glance back and the others took his lead and stood with their hands on their hips, panting, staring back the way they had come. He thought they might have got clear, but then a mounted trooper came clattering past the end of the alley, saw them and reined in, dragging the horse's head round to follow them. Frank had time to see the iron shoes strike sparks off the paving before they were running again, pelting down the narrow passage with the anvil ringing of the hooves closing behind them. Frank heard the crack of leather on bone and someone behind him cried out and fell. The hooves faltered for an instant and then came on again, gaining now.

A few yards ahead a gate stood ajar in a wooden fence. Frank pulled the girl towards it but she lost her footing and fell full length into the angle between fence and pavement. The trooper overshot them at a canter, slashed backwards with his truncheon and missed, turned his horse. Frank dragged Grace to her feet but already the trooper was kicking forward at them again, grinning, swinging his truncheon high. Frank found himself stepping easily to one side as the cosh came down, and before the trooper could recover from the swing, Frank caught the horse's bridle and dragged it sharply down. The animal's front feet skidded and it came down onto its knees with a grunt. The trooper bounced yelling over the pommel, hit the cobbles face down and rolled until the opposite kerb stopped him.

Frank pushed Grace through the open gate, slammed it behind them. But somehow now she was ahead of him and leading him at a run across the stable yard of a pub which stank of hops and horse dung.

A footpath opened from the yard and she dragged him down it between dark buildings, gripping his hand. The path zigzagged a couple of times and brought them out into a cobbled mews at the rear of a terrace of handsome houses. It was suddenly quiet. Frank could see the roof ridges and chimneys of the houses silhouetted against a leaden London sky. The rain fell steadily, shimmering in the light of gas lamps. The mews was deserted, lined with the double doors of coach houses. Grace towed him along, shoving at one door after another until finally she found one that was unlocked. She pulled him in after her and hauled the door closed behind them.

Bars of light sliced in from dusty windows at each end of the building and illuminated an old-fashioned phaeton with high wheels. Glass and maroon varnish gleamed. Out of breath, Grace sat on the step of the vehicle so that it creaked on its springs. She looked up at Frank. It was only then that he realised she was laughing, throwing her head back and rocking herself in delight.

'Clever Frank! Something happened all right! How did you know?'

He didn't feel like laughing. He glanced towards the doors. 'I might have hurt him. That peeler.'

'Oh, you didn't hurt him.' She flicked a dismissive hand. 'I've had worse falls out hacking. I was more worried about the horse.'

'He might have broken something.'

'Well, if he did, it served him right. And anyway I haven't had so much fun in ages!' She patted her clothing. 'Oh, look, I even managed to save my gaspers.'

She snapped the silver case open and took out a gold-ringed cigarette, tapped it and lit up. She was less self-conscious than the last time he had seen her do this. She blew smoke into the darkness and glanced down at herself, her skirts still rucked around her waist and her white legs splashed with mud. Frank could see that her right knee was grazed and a drop of blood had run down her leg, twining around the swell of her calf. She saw him looking at it.

'God, what a sight I am! Like some little doxy!' She started to laugh again.

She had kept her workman's cap but it sat at an angle over her short dark hair. Frank touched the grazed knee with his fingertips. She stopped laughing. He brushed the small wound with the ball of his thumb and dislodged some fragments of grit. He did this again, stroking the raw skin so gently that she did not flinch, brushing away tiny flecks of gravel. She looked down at him for some seconds in silence, her face gradually softening.

'You don't have to go on this dark quest of yours, Frank,' she said quietly. 'There are other things to look for in life. Good things.'

He rested his cheek against her bare leg. Her skin was cold and smooth and it shivered to his touch. He cupped her calf in his hand and ran his palm down it and back again to the hollow behind her knee. She tossed away the cigarette and put her hands either side of her on the step of the phaeton and breathed deeply.

'Frank,' she said.

He kissed the swell of her thigh muscle. She rested one hand on his bowed head, tangled her fingers in his hair. But abruptly she stiffened, and held his head away from her, looking into his eyes.

'Not here,' she said firmly. She got to her feet with sudden decision, pulling him up with her. 'Come along.' She walked quickly to the doors of the coach house, and peered out through the crack between them. She beckoned him impatiently to her. 'Quickly, now.'

He came up behind her. 'The coppers will still be on the streets.'

But if she heard him she gave no sign. She slid the door open and stepped out into the dark cobbled mews, catching his hand and dragging him after her. She led them back the way they had come, down the dark alleyways and along the fence lines behind the looming buildings. Frank could still hear the sounds of disorder in the distant streets: shouted commands, the clatter of hoofbeats, once a man's scream of abuse. But her new authority left him no room for dissent, and he allowed himself to be led.

They reached the yard of the public house they had passed earlier and Grace walked in through the back door. Frank found himself following her up a dim passage between beer barrels and fruit boxes; the passage smelled of cat's piss and stale beer. Up ahead he could hear the buzz of conversation from the bar and smelled tobacco smoke hanging in the air. A stringy man in a barman's apron emerged from an open door to Frank's right and blocked their path.

'Oy! What are you two up to?'

Frank was about to speak, but Grace was too quick for him. 'You have rooms, don't you?'

'Yes, we have rooms, young miss,' he said, mocking her cultured accent. 'What of it?'

'We want one.'

The thin man looked from her to Frank, his eyes narrowing. 'This is a respectable house.'

'Of course it is,' Grace told him with majesty, and held out a half-crown.

The man looked at the money but didn't take it. He lifted his head back and looked down his nose at them. 'What's this in aid of, then?'

Grace said, 'My brother and I became caught up in a little trouble out there with the police. We just need somewhere to lie low for an hour or two. I'm sure you understand.' She reached into her shabby dress and produced another half-crown and smiled at the man. 'We'll be gone before you know it.'

Frank sensed that the second half-crown was a mistake. He knew the mean-faced barman was still thinking about her accent and that this had set off some calculation in his mind. But the man took the coins and pocketed them. 'Come on, then.'

He led them up the back stairs to a tiny attic room with a narrow bed, a washstand and a single low window. When the man had left Grace sat on the bed and pulled Frank down beside her. The bed was made up with coarse brown calico sheets and she bounced on it a little and laughed in delight.

'Do you suppose it has bugs?' she asked.

'I'd be surprised if it didn't.'

'Heavens!' She made round eyes at him. 'Real bedbugs! Does this make us bohemian?'

He kissed her hard and ran his hands over her short hair, feeling the curve of her skull beneath, the smooth stem of her neck. He realised that he had been longing to do that for days past. Her arms came up around him and she kissed him fiercely back. He fumbled for the hooks and eyes at the neck of her dress, but she rested her cool hands on either side of his face and stopped him.

'It's true, then, is it, Frank?'

'You know it is. You've always known it, and so have I.' He rolled his head to kiss her hands where they lay against his cheek. 'How does knowing help us?'

'The knowing's all that matters. Look at me.'

He did so at last.

'We have this chance, Frank, this one magical chance. We can start everything from this moment.'

He sat back a little to look at her. 'It isn't that easy. Your father—'

'Don't worry about my father.'

'He'd cut you off, Grace.'

'So what if he cuts me off? How could we be worse off than a million other couples?'

He took her hands from his face and held them between both of his. 'You don't know what that's like.'

'I know we'll survive somehow, if we have faith and courage. I have. Have you?'

He looked into her eyes, prepared to doubt. But what he saw there left no room for weakness. In that moment, for the first time, he allowed himself to believe that it was possible, that another way might be found. It broke on him like the light from a jammed shutter, suddenly thrown open on a closed room.

Her head went back as he kissed her and her arms locked fiercely round his neck and her mouth opened. She pulled her face away and breathed deeply and said 'Frank,' again, as if the sound of it pleased her, and she kept saying it, whenever he took his mouth from hers, and her hands slid inside his jacket and pushed it back from his shoulders and then unhooked the bodice of her dress.

The night wind leaned on the little window so that it creaked. Perhaps that was what woke her, for he felt her roll away from him. He couldn't tell how much time had passed – hours, perhaps. She sat up on the edge of the rough bed and got to her feet. When he opened his eyes she was standing naked by the window, her body very pale against the gloom. The room was chill, but she didn't seem to notice.

He got to his feet and stood there beside her in the cold starlight, put his arm around her marble shoulders. Outside, over the canted roofs of London, a cold dawn was breaking. She reached up, smiling, and put her arms around him and drew him down to her.

He didn't hear the footsteps outside, even though the men's boots must have made enough noise on the stairs. But he heard the door thrust open and crash back against the wall. He heard Grace cry out in alarm and he stood away from her and the light of their lanterns blinded him and before he could see again someone hit him across the side of the head and Grace cried out once more and then he was on the floor, trying to find a grip on the rough boards as they tilted under him and he slid off into darkness.

42

The groping hands reached the weapon at the same instant. He could feel the cold steel under his fingers and the man's strong grip, sticky with blood, crushing his hand against the butt. He felt himself dragged across the boards, and the man was swearing and clubbing at him, but he hung on, lurching in and out of awareness, as if in a dream from which he could not wake.

From some other reality the jingle of keys prised their way into his mind, then a clump of hobnails on flagstones. Frank started up. His head ached fiercely and the stone wall at his back had sucked all the warmth out of him. He must have slept, though he did not know how. In the grey light he saw that his cellmate, a ragged drunk he had twice fought off during the night, now lay crumpled in a pool of vomit on the floor. He wasn't sure the man was breathing, but he didn't care much one way or the other.

The lock rasped and the steel door groaned open on its hinges and the constable bulked in the doorway, his legs planted firmly apart. The man stroked his luxuriant moustache with one hand and tapped his truncheon against his leg with the other. Frank stood up. He realised only now that his left eye was swollen half-shut. He could feel the sagging weight of the bruise. He felt nauseous and put one hand against the damp wall.

'Gray?' The constable prodded him sharply in the ribs with his truncheon. 'That's you?'

Frank tugged his tattered jacket around himself, unable to find the energy for defiance. 'I'm Gray.'

'Well, young Gray, somebody out there must love you, though I'm bound to say you don't look lovable to me, and he don't hardly look the loving type.' The constable stood back from the open door. 'Come along with you, and look sharp about it.'

Frank followed the man down the narrow corridor, touching the walls on each side to steady himself. The passage stank of urine. The constable pushed open swing doors and they emerged into the front office. Frank saw a scarred wooden desk and a sergeant seated behind it, a handful of exhausted people, dirty walls in institutional green and cream. But the air was fresher in here and blessed daylight fell in through the windows, and there was a bustle of noise and traffic out there in the street.

The constable strode away, and Frank stood swaying in the middle of the room.

'You. Gray. Over here.'

Frank walked unsteadily to the desk. He saw only then that Stephen Dearborn was seated opposite the sergeant, charcoal cashmere overcoat swept around him against the morning chill and black leather gloves on the table top beside him. He was gazing at Frank with an expression of loathing so implacable that it felt like a physical force.

'Sign here, sir, if you please,' the sergeant told Dearborn, and looked at Frank with distaste. 'That is, if you're quite sure about this?'

Dearborn signed without a word in the marbled ledger. He rose to his feet, jerked his thumb at Frank and strode out through the swing doors into the street without looking back. When Frank emerged into the dazzling morning Dearborn was waiting on the pavement a few yards down, arms crossed, pedestrians parting around him as a stream parts around a black rock.

Frank said, 'Is Grace all right?'

Dearborn slapped him hard across the face with his gloves, and then again, backhanded. 'You dare to ask me that?' He swung the gloves back to do it a third time, but this time Frank lifted his forearm and blocked the blow. Dearborn swore and his face twisted.

Frank said again, 'Is Grace all right?'

'How should she be all right? She spent the night in a cell like a common criminal, with whores and beggars and madwomen. Do you understand what that means? My daughter?' Dearborn moved his face close to Frank's. 'And to think you . . . touched her! You? The thought of it makes me want to spew!'

Dearborn's mouth contorted. He turned away and for a moment Frank thought the man really would vomit in the street from sheer rage. Dearborn regained some composure and faced him again, pale and sweating.

'I was as good as my word, was I not? I gave you a position when you came begging. You'd be dead if it were not for what we did for you. I've kept your brother in school. And you treat us like this? What is this, Gray? Some vile species of revenge for what happened to your father? There was a time when I felt regret over that, but my God, I begin to see how such a thing came about, if everyone in your family was cut from the same cloth.'

'I didn't want this to happen.'

'No? And I suppose you'd have me believe it was all Grace's idea? Oh, yes – that's what she says, that it was her idea to come to London and join in with this ignorant rabble! I wondered where she was getting her seditious opinions from but I never guessed it was you!' Dearborn's spittle flecked Frank's face. 'And will you tell me it was her idea to take a room in some seedy public house? Don't you even dare suggest that! My God, what kind of a hold do you have on her, that she would lie barefaced to her own father who loves her?'

'I have no hold on Grace.'

'Well, from this moment on you don't, I can promise you that. I'm not often practised upon, Gray, but it won't happen twice. You'll find there are consequences for slighting me.'

'That was never my intention.'

'You have forty-eight hours. After that, don't let me see you or your brother again.'

Frank lifted his head sharply. 'My brother's still in school. This is nothing to do with him.'

'I told you there would be consequences. That's one of them.'

The constable had emerged from the police station, resplendent in his blue uniform, and stood watching them from a few yards up the street.

'Let me make it crystal clear to you,' Dearborn hissed, 'since your understanding seems to be failing you. I don't give a fuck what happens to you or yours. You can starve for all I care. I should have let you do that two years ago. If you know what's good for you you'll get a long way away from me and my family. And I promise you this – I'll help you on your way if you drag your feet. In fact I'd like that. I'd like that very much.'

'You can't order us to leave Cumver.'

'Can I not?' Dearborn's eyes glittered. 'Perhaps you think it's your right to live where you please, and act as you please, without fear of retribution? Do you, Gray? Well, shall we see how your liberal ideas stand up to a couple of bare-knuckle bruisers on a dark night?'

The constable sauntered over. 'Is this lad causing you trouble, sir?'

Dearborn stood back. 'Nothing I can't deal with, officer.'

'As you say, sir.' The constable eyed Frank coldly. 'I don't know what a wastrel like you has done to deserve this gentleman's generosity, but if I were you I'd count my blessings.' He hooked his thumbs in his belt and strolled away again.

Dearborn said, 'You mark this: if you have any contact with Grace again – *any* contact – I shall have you tracked down and dealt with. And I shall see that she is punished too, if you try to reach her in any way. Do you understand what I'm telling you?' Dearborn took out a pigskin wallet and flipped it open.

'I won't take your money,' Frank said.

'You've already taken my money, getting you out of there. I'd have left you to rot, but for Grace.' Dearborn held out the cash. 'Here – go to the devil with it.'

Frank didn't move.

Dearborn released the notes so that they fluttered in the wind across the street and under the churning hooves of the horses. 'Rot in hell, then.' He turned on his heel and strode away.

43

'Grace, I don't understand.' Dearborn stood behind his vast desk, leaning on his knuckles. 'What have I done wrong?'

Grace could tell that he had not slept, any more than she had herself, and her spirit slumped with guilt and weariness. His clothes were creased, his necktie askew and his hair uncombed. That was the worst of it, that he seemed so stripped of elegance, so abject. Part of her wanted to run over to him and straighten his tie, put her arms around him, find her papa again.

She said, 'You've done nothing wrong, Papa.'

'Then how is it we are in this position today? I don't understand.'

'I don't understand either, Papa.'

He breathed out hard and passed one hand across his face. 'I had such trust in you, Grace. Such hopes. You know, I've always felt that in so many ways you were like me, and I took pride in that. I thought that if I nurtured such qualities in you . . .'

'I had no thoughts of betraying your trust, Papa.'

'And yet you could not have done so more thoroughly.'

'What have you done with him, Father?' she burst out. 'What have you done with Frank?'

He looked her steadily in the eyes. 'I don't want to hear his name again.'

'I know you don't, Papa, but it can't be right that Frank—'

He did not speak but with his right hand he swept everything from his desk. She gasped and started back as an inkpot smashed in the fireplace and a crow-black blot leapt onto the marble surround. She kept her eyes down and tried to concentrate on the scarlet and gold whorls of the Turkish carpet. She had never seen her father so uncontrolled, so volatile, and this terrified her. But it was the dreadful hurt in his eyes that was so hard to bear. A vision of herself in the coach house came to her, smoking like a sophisticated woman, laughing gaily at her adventure. That young woman would have shown defiance, or at least nonchalance, but here and now, in the face of her father's agony, such a thing was unthinkable.

'It was not as you think, Father,' she managed to say. She could not keep her voice from quivering.

'Grace, please.'

'The police – they charged the crowd. They injured people. I had never thought the police would—'

'And what did you expect? You attended a gathering of undisciplined

174

troublemakers. If accounts are to be believed you even took part in the disorder. I suppose you thought it was fashionable to associate with such riff-raff?'

'I was foolish.' She dared not look up. 'I didn't expect it to be like that.'

'Foolish. Yes, indeed. We may agree on that much. Foolishness might be passed over in time, though God knows, I thought you had better judgment. It's not your absurd political posturing that distresses me, Grace, you know it isn't.' His voice began to climb again. 'But to carry on like a common street whore? And with . . . him?'

'It was my fault, Father,' she broke in, desperate to stop him. 'He warned me not to go. He tried to protect me. It was Frank who—'

Dearborn stepped out from behind the desk and struck her across the face with his open hand. She gave a disbelieving cry and stumbled back, one hand to her cheek, and stared at him, horrified. He had never raised a hand to her before. Nobody in her entire life had ever raised a hand to her. That it should be him was unbelievable.

'I warn you, Grace. I will not be responsible for my actions if you speak of him again.' Dearborn tugged down his cuff. 'Come, now. I know well enough what that sort of *protection* amounts to. But that my own daughter should seek it from a . . . a stable boy? With all the advantages you have had showered upon you? No, no. You must not seek to justify yourself.'

No, she thought, her hand still to her hot cheek. She would not seek to justify herself. Indeed, she could not. But with that realisation a spark of spirit came back to her.

'I never intended to hurt you, Father, but beyond that I have nothing to be ashamed of.'

A vein throbbed in his temple and for a moment she thought he would hit her again and she braced herself for it. This time she would take it without flinching. But he did not hit her.

'Do you think you can strike attitudes with me,' he said, 'like a heroine in some cheap romance? You are a child, Grace. You are not yet seventeen. Do you realise how utterly dependent on my goodwill you are?'

She said nothing and he walked back behind his desk and sat heavily in the chair, clenching and unclenching his fists. For a long moment all she could hear was his breathing and the hollow ticking of the ormolu clock on the mantel. The black crow of ink on the marble surround was running in streaks towards the floor. At length he slid open a drawer and took out paper.

'I should never have listened to your mother. It seems the woman does not exist who cannot be seduced out of her wits, not even my own daughter. You need discipline, Grace, and if you have none in your character it's clear you must be taught it.' His head was bowed as he wrote rapidly, his nib scratching on the thick paper. 'Well. You will be sent somewhere you will be more closely supervised than you have been to date. Far more closely supervised. Don't think for a moment this gives me pleasure.'

Grace moistened her lips. 'I am not to return to Switzerland, Father?'

'I have made other arrangements for you. Welti has a relation in Vienna who has agreed to take you in for a few months. She'll be keeping a close eye on you, depend upon that.'

Grace blinked. 'Vienna?'

'I want to see this wildness curbed, Grace. It's clear that won't happen if you stay in this house. I can't be on hand to supervise things every moment of the day, and with the kind of lax oversight your mother affords you it's little wonder things have gone so awry.'

'But Vienna?'

'Princess Wilhelmina has some considerable standing in society, Welti assures me. She's certainly in a position to teach you how a young woman of your standing ought to behave. You will stay with her, and you'll do as she says in all things.' He glanced up. 'Grace, I advise you not to try to deceive her as you have deceived me. Welti tells me the princess is a woman of considerable intelligence and wide experience of the world. Not much gets past her.'

He bent over his paper again. She looked at the top of his head as he wrote. It was some relief not to have his contorted face turned to her, so full of rage and pain, but even so she did not dare give voice to the question which rose to her lips. Perhaps he read her thought, because his pen stopped moving.

'Know this, Grace. I'm a powerful man. A word in the right ear, and I can destroy thankless wastrels like Frank Gray, and no questions asked. If I ever see him again, if I hear you have communication of any kind with him, believe me as I live and breathe, it will be the worse for him. Do you understand?'

'Yes, Father. I understand.'

He lifted his face at last and looked at her for a long time, the pen still poised over the paper. 'Grace,' he said, with such tenderness in his voice that she could hardly bear it. 'I've never wanted anything but the best for you.'

'I know, Father.'

'To think that by indulging you so freely I am somehow responsible for this . . . that is unendurable.' He took a deep breath. 'All I want is for things to be as they were. Perhaps, in time, they may yet be, and I shall have my daughter back. Shall we both hope for that?'

But her throat tightened painfully and she could not answer. Instead she stood there silently, her shoulders shaking and her tears dropping onto the blurred whorls of the carpet.

He lowered his head and started writing again. 'You may leave now.'

Grace walked blindly out of the room and into the hall, wiping her face with her hand. Two housemaids were coming down the stairs, laughing about some domestic mishap. They saw Grace and stopped talking in mid-sentence, then hurried quickly about their business, their heads down.

She stood disconsolate and alone in the centre of the marble hall, her breath still catching in her throat. Through her tears it took her some seconds to see old Uncle Welti, standing in the doorway to the drawing room. He was as untidy as ever, his waistcoat cross-buttoned and his spotted bow tie askew. He was checking his gold hunter, as if casually, but Grace knew there was nothing accidental about his presence.

'Grace, my dear child,' he said, tucking away the watch. 'You are upset.'

'Did you hear?' she demanded, growing angry now. 'I am to be sent away.'

'I did not need to hear.' Welti pulled a huge crimson handkerchief from his top pocket and handed it to her. 'Don't cry, my dear. It spoils the complexion.'

'I shan't go!' she said, wringing the silk handkerchief in her hands. 'He can't make me.'

'Ah, but he can. And he will. And you shall go.'

'I shan't—'

'Listen to me, Grace.' Welti leaned close to her and touched her elbow and she could smell cologne and tobacco. 'Remember that your father loves you. I also. And things may not be as bad as you fear. Vienna is a beautiful city, after all.'

'What does it matter how beautiful it is? I am to be held prisoner by this awful woman! And *you* suggested her!'

He stepped back and opened his eyes innocently. 'Did I?'

'Oh, Uncle Welti, you know you did! I shall never forgive you!'

'Well, and perhaps I did mention something to your father. I suppose I must have had my reasons.' He patted the back of her hand. 'If you keep open your mind, Grace my child, you may find Princess Willi not quite such a dragon. You may even learn some things from her.'

'Yes,' she said bitterly. 'I'll learn how to *behave* in polite society.'

He chuckled and patted her hand again. 'You are my goddaughter, my dear Grace. You know I have always your welfare at my heart. You know I would not suggest anything I did not think was for the best.'

'For the best? How can you—'

But he was already shambling away down the hall, rolling from side to side like an old bear. She watched him go, angry and confused, still twisting his handkerchief in her hands. At length she grew afraid that her father would come out of his study and find her hovering there, and she fled upstairs.

She opened the door of her room and walked to the window and stood there, breathing hard, staring out at the beech woods. They were dusted pale green with the first buds of spring. The day was fading, and beyond the belt of trees the lamps were just winking on in Cumver village. Somewhere among the trees Mrs Rossiter's cottage was hidden. A week ago she and Frank had met there in that bright, empty room. Now he would never return to that house. Less than twenty-four hours ago she had held him in her arms in that coarse London bed, held him in such a grip that surely he could never escape: yet already she had lost him, lost him utterly. She had no idea where he was now, nor where he might go. And now she was to go into exile in Vienna, of all places, with some dragon of a chaperone watching over her.

Grace heard footsteps on the landing. It was probably one of the maids, but for an instant she was fearful that her father might not have finished with her. All through her childhood, she had listened for his step on the stairs, willing him to turn left at the top towards her bedroom. And sometimes he did, even on those nights when he came home at all hours, smelling of cigars and brandy, when she should have been asleep and he should have left her that way. Then there would be a flower clumsily picked from the garden, or some trifle he had brought home from London – coloured pencils, or a picture book, once a linnet in a cage. She had always known that he could be overbearing to the servants, and that he didn't suffer fools gladly. But she had never been frightened of him before this evening.

A smart tap on the door made her jump.

'Leave me alone,' Grace called, without turning. 'Please.'

But the door was opened anyway. She swung round. Mrs Rossiter stood there, grim in her dark taffeta.

'So,' the housekeeper said. 'You went to London, anyhow. Have your fill of excitement, did you? Never mind I told you not to. Never mind I said there'd be trouble.'

Grace made a show of hauteur. 'Thank you, but I think I've had enough upbraiding for one day.'

'Don't you come the high lady with me. You've likely done for us all with your foolishness.'

'I don't know what you mean.'

'Your father thinks it was young Frank who gave you these ideas, don't he? And I don't suppose you disabused him, young miss, now did you?'

'Your position is safe, Mrs Rossiter, if that's what you mean.'

'I ain't talking about *my* position, you silly girl. What are you thinking of?' The housekeeper's lips set in a line. 'Very well, then. If you don't see what's needful, I do. I'll go to your father directly and tell him the truth of it.'

She turned to the door, but Grace stopped her. 'You mustn't do that.'

'He sent young Frank away, Grace, on account of what I got you into. And Frank didn't set him straight, bless him. Well, that can't be allowed to stand, and you know it as well as me. That boy's spent the last two years under my roof and he's as near family as I'm ever likely to have. This is my fault and your father has to know that. It's not right that the innocent should suffer for the guilty.'

'None of it's right,' Grace flung at her. 'But you can't make it so! Not like that. Telling Father won't help get Frank back for either of us. Not now. All you'd be doing, Mrs Rossiter, is getting yourself needlessly dismissed.'

'How's this?'

'It's not *politics* that made Father send Frank away. Don't you see?'

Grace sat on the bed and put her head in her hands. The housekeeper watched her for a little while, then walked over to the darkening window and stood where Grace had stood, staring out over the countryside.

'Contrary creatures, us women,' Mrs Rossiter said. 'One day we're demanding freedom from the menfolk, and the next we're throwing ourselves at their feet and offering them anything they bloody want.'

Behind her the girl sobbed, desolately.

44

Through the carriage window the fields lay cheerless in the afternoon light. Knotted willow trees stood along watercourses reflecting the tall sky. The very landscape seemed to speak of disappointment.

Frank touched the envelope in his inside pocket for reassurance but it no longer gave him any. The man in the ticket office at Liverpool Street had never heard of Barnes Wittering, and had taken his time looking it up in his greasy timetable book. He kept glancing at Frank's bruised face and at Gifford standing beside him, still in his St Dunstan's boater. Frank had pushed the few coins across the brass plate for the tickets. He regretted now not taking Dearborn's money, and the very fact that he regretted it brought his spirits lower.

'It'll be all right, Frank,' Gifford said cheerfully. 'You'll see. It'll all turn out.' The boy sat alert and bright faced on the bench seat opposite. He might have been going on an outing to the seaside.

'I'm sorry about St Dunstan's, Giff. I'd hoped you could stay longer.'

'Oh, that doesn't matter. I was getting bored there, anyway.' Gifford's eyes were sunny with optimism. 'By the way, where are we going?'

'Timbuctoo,' Frank said sourly.

'Is that near Lowestoft?'

If Gifford was joking it was impossible to tell from his face.

The train pulled in as the last light was failing. It was a tiny station, an unroofed platform and a clapboard stationmaster's office. An enamel sign announced that this was Barnes Wittering. The sign, in pale yellow letters, looked as foreign to Frank as if it had been in Eastern Europe rather than East Anglia. He and Gifford were the only passengers to get off. Frank walked ahead of his brother out into the gravel yard, empty except for a single unharnessed trap. On a patch of rough grass a few yards away an elderly grey horse was cropping the turf. Beyond, flat fields stretched away with hardly a tree breaking the horizon.

A man shouted something from the train and another man on the platform laughed in response. A whistle blew and the train gave a long exhalation and thumped steadily away. Frank watched the wooden carriages go, the lights of the train swaying and the engine's breath pluming up into the vast sky. He felt empty and lost. The bag on his shoulder contained little enough, but it suddenly seemed crushingly heavy and he set it down in the grit.

'Where to now?' Gifford looked at him hopefully.

Frank didn't reply. Behind them the gas light outside the station-master's office popped off and it was night. A fat man in uniform emerged carrying a lantern and locked the door behind him. Frank took the envelope out from his pocket, drew out the card it contained, and walked over to the man.

'Can you tell me how to get to this place?'

The stationmaster clipped his keys to his belt, pushed back his peaked cap and inspected first Frank and then Gifford. He took the card and peered at the address on it.

'Haill's Lodge, is it?' His accent was slow and full of round vowels.

'Is it far?'

The fat man sighed and handed the card back. 'You know, son, I made a big mistake when I joined the Great Eastern Railway. I should have set myself up in a little taxi-cab business. It's what I ends up doing anyways. Give me a hand hitching up the trap.'

It was a two-mile drive through the slate blue evening. Haill's Lodge was a large and ugly flint house behind laurel hedges on the outskirts of the village.

The stationmaster drew up to let them off at the end of the drive and gave Frank a sideways look. 'You say the old man's a friend of yours?'

'In a way.' Frank glanced at the grim house. Downstairs the blinds were drawn but he could see the lamps were lit. Even so, it did not look welcoming. 'Do you know if he's at home?'

'You'd best see for yourself. But I'll say this: I doubt you'll get much friendly conversation, from what I hear.' The man handed Frank down his bag. 'If you gets sent off with a flea in your ear come and find me at the Three Feathers. My missus wouldn't see you sleep in some hedgerow.'

'Thank you.'

The stationmaster released the brake. 'Taxi-cab business and a nice little boarding house. That would have done me proper, that would.' He clicked his tongue to the old grey horse, and drove away down the lane.

A plump maid in a starched apron answered the door. She was about Frank's own age and she looked at him with bold curiosity, her glance taking in his swollen face and the bag over his shoulder. She flicked her eyes down at Gifford and back to Frank and her expression hardened.

'Selling, are you?' She started to close the door. 'We don't buy from gypsies.'

'I've come to see Colonel James,' Frank said into the narrowing gap.

She opened the door again, inspected him with new interest. 'Have you, now?'

'He wrote the address for me himself. This address.'

The girl held out her hand. 'Show.'

'Is Colonel James here or not?'

'Well.' The girl lifted her chin.

A woman's voice from inside the house called, 'Janet? Who is it?'

'My name's Frank Gray,' Frank spoke, loudly enough for the invisible questioner to hear.

Before the girl could reply a tall woman in a grey silk afternoon dress came sweeping out of a lit doorway behind her.

'That'll be all, Janet.' The woman was of late middle age, with silver hair in a chignon, and she wore glasses on a cord around her neck. She lifted these without putting them on and looked at Frank through them. 'Do I know you, young man?'

'I'm Frank Gray, ma'am. Colonel James once said if I ever needed help, I was to come to see him. This is my brother Gifford.'

She inspected Gifford through her spectacles and turned her attention back to Frank. 'Did he, now?'

'Or is he still in India, ma'am, with the regiment?'

She hesitated. 'As a matter of fact, he is.'

'I see.' Frank felt the last of his spirit drain away.

'But then, in a way, so am I.'

Frank looked at her, unable to make anything of this. She saw the card he held and put out her hand. He gave it to her.

'Colonel James wrote this, ma'am. I've always kept it.'

She scanned the card with its scribbled note, handed it back. 'Well, young Mr Gray, this is from Cedric right enough. I don't know what you want of him, but I think you've had a wasted journey. Things have changed rather, of late.' She stood still, apparently undecided, but then made a small gesture of invitation. 'I suppose you had better come in for a moment.'

Frank followed her into the front room with Gifford behind him. In an instant he was swept back three years and more. The grim exterior of the house had led him to expect nothing like this; firelight blazed on Kashmiri rugs, paintings of the Mughal court, a screen of iridescent peacock feathers. The tusks of an elephant were crossed above the mantel, and carvings of Hindu gods stood on the bookshelves between photographs of white men in solar topees leaning on rifles, their boots on slaughtered game. The room glowed with warmth and colour and smelled of India: cardamom, saffron, cinnamon. It awoke such a heady yearning in him that he felt dizzy.

'Are you quite well, young man?'

'Yes, ma'am. Thank you.'

She looked at him doubtfully. 'I am Mrs James. The Colonel's wife.'

'Ma'am.' Frank stood with his cap in his hands. He didn't know whether he was supposed to shake hands. He hoped passionately that she wouldn't send them away, not at once. He felt drunk with the sensations of the room and the thought of leaving it was unbearable.

She said, 'And this is your brother, you say?'

'Gifford Gray, Mrs James.' Gifford stepped forward smartly, his hand outstretched. 'I'm very pleased to make your acquaintance.'

'I see. You are the charming one of the pair.' She took his hand and turned back to Frank. 'The older Mr Gray is perhaps only charming when he chooses to be. Where did you get that dramatic black eye?'

He thought about lying, but sensed that the time for that had past. 'A policeman hit me, ma'am.'

'Indeed?' She raised her eyebrows. 'Be that as it may, you came to see my husband. Well, here he is.'

She stepped aside. For the first time Frank saw the old man sitting in the armchair by the fire, utterly still, utterly vacant. His knees were covered by a tartan rug and he was staring into the flames, smiling slightly, china blue eyes in a sunburned face, his hair and moustache quite white. To Frank he looked as content and as mute as an old dog warming his bones.

Mrs James said, 'Over two years ago now. We hadn't been back here eight months. I told Cedric we should never have come, never left India, but . . . he would have it so. It was a stroke. He has no idea who he is, or was. As I said, I like to think that in some way he's still over there, with his regiment.'

Frank twisted his cap between his hands. 'I'm very sorry.'

'No doubt you are, if you expected something from Cedric.' She saw Frank's face and relented. 'Forgive me. I fear I am growing rather bitter, but I confess it does seem a cruel blow, after so many years of service.'

Frank put his hand on Gifford's shoulder. 'Come on, Giff. Let's go.'

'Do we have to?'

Frank turned the boy towards the door. 'We're sorry to have troubled you, ma'am.'

'It's just that it reminds me of home,' Gifford persisted. 'Doesn't it you?'

'Wait,' Mrs James said, and then, 'Janet? Take their coats, please.'

45

'It's late,' Mrs James said. 'I should let you go up. I'm sure your brother has been asleep for hours. Certainly Cedric has. He sleeps like a baby, poor dear. That's one blessing, I suppose. He never used to.'

'I've enjoyed talking, Mrs James.'

'You're kind to say so, but I'm afraid it must be a bore for you. Yet it's so long, Frank, since I have passed the time so pleasantly. It's almost like being back in Bangalore. I was born there, you know. I met Cedric when he was a mere subaltern, during the Mutiny. Officers couldn't marry until they'd reached the rank of captain, so it was quite a wait. And after that I stayed with him while he rose in seniority, all the way to colonel.' She smiled, remembering. 'The gentlemen with their *chota pegs* and cigars out on the veranda. Those splendid uniforms! The scent of the jasmine from the garden. The jacaranda. I'm afraid I was rather modern; I used to come out and join Cedric and the younger officers, just to listen to the darkness and see the stars. Those nights were like velvet, were they not?'

'Yes, ma'am, they were.'

Frank thought back to his father's bungalow, the rats scuttling in the rafters, the python trickling like liquid under the steps of the veranda. He was the only one who ever saw that python. He remembered too his expeditions with Javed. He liked Mrs James and he wouldn't have darkened her glittering memories, but his own were different. For him oil lamps trembled in earth-floored shanties, a pockmarked woman heated ghee over a fire of dung, and all around him was the smell of oil on the bodies of his urchin friends as they huddled under the water tower, planning some mischief. He too remembered at least one splendid uniform – glimpses of it – but not the way she did. And yet he felt no contradiction, no sense that she was gilding the past. Both realities existed, and many more besides. That was India.

The fire had died down. Mrs James was silent, staring at the embers. Frank waited, unsure if he should wish her goodnight and go up to bed in the spare room where the maid had left his things. But then Mrs James bent down and opened the brass scuttle and placed two more logs on the fire. They crackled into flame at once, sending flags of light around the room. She replaced the screen and sat back, brushing fibres of bark from her hands.

'In what way did you hope my husband might help you?'

'I want to join the army. The Hussars.'

'Cedric's regiment, I suppose? The Fourth?'

'The Twenty-first, ma'am.'

'The Dumpies? Why them?'

He hesitated. 'No special reason.'

'I see.' She sat observing him for a long time, so long that he began to feel uncomfortable. 'You're very young for the Hussars, Frank. They don't take just any lad with dreams of glory. Not nowadays. What are you, seventeen?'

'I could pass for older. I'm good with horses. And I was hoping Colonel James would put in a good word.'

'For a regiment not his own? I see. And what of your young brother? What's he supposed to do while you go gadding about as a bold hussar?'

'Gifford wants to be an engineer. If a place could be found for him, an apprenticeship, perhaps . . .'

'And you thought my husband would provide for the two of you in these schemes? That's rather a lot to ask.'

'I don't want charity, Mrs James. I plan to send money home for Gifford once I'm posted.'

'As a cavalry trooper?' She gave a short laugh. 'I believe you would make history indeed if you did that.' She paused and her voice changed. 'Let's not play games any more, Frank.'

'Ma'am?'

'I know about your poor mother's case. I didn't recall the name, not until you mentioned the Twenty-first. And no, before you ask, I don't know who the villain was. I never met him. All I know is that he came to Cedric looking for action – the Twenty-first was famous for missing it, you know. Cedric could have told you who the man was, obviously, but he would never have done so in any case, having once given his word.'

She got up and crossed to the sideboard and poured brandy into a squat glass, adding soda from a syphon. She poured a smaller glass of port and walked back across the room and gave the brandy to Frank. He had the impression that she had momentarily mistaken him for someone else, and he felt that this was an honour. She sat down.

'You know that Cedric resigned over that dreadful business? He could have had another two or three years, but it broke his heart, the way the matter of your mother was dealt with, the part he was forced to play in it.'

Her choice of words struck him as strange. 'In what way was he forced, Mrs James?'

Her eyes slid away from his. 'By circumstances, I mean.'

'By the circumstance that he was a brother officer?'

'Hardly that.' She sounded indignant. 'Loyalty would not go that far, I hope.'

He let a moment pass. 'Mrs James, they invented a story to cover my mother's murder. I was watching while they did it. Colonel James was there. He hated it, I could see that. But he went along with it.'

She looked into her drink. 'But I don't really know anything about it, Frank. Cedric told me that the less I knew . . .'

'Did the man really have such powerful friends?'

'I don't know. I told you. Cedric wouldn't discuss it.' She was growing agitated. 'I understood the intention was . . . forgive me . . .

185

to protect your mother's memory. There were rumours . . . It was to protect your family. Surely that was explained to you?'

'Yes. And I accepted that, Mrs James. For years I accepted that. But . . . to cover up a murder? It's hard to believe, isn't it?'

'I don't understand you.'

'I only ever told one person about this, Mrs James. A . . . a friend of mine. Someone I trusted. And that's what she said, when I told her. That it's hard to believe. I can't get that out of my mind. It's hard to believe. Were they really so concerned about my mother? Or was there something special about that man? It keeps coming back to me, the night it happened. Little bits of it that I couldn't remember before. I keep seeing him, reaching for the pistol, struggling with me. I can never see his face, but—'

'Stop!' She faced him. 'I don't have the information you want, Frank. I only know that vile man's sins drove us all out, Cedric and me, you and your family. He drove us out of Eden. And look now: your parents are dead, Cedric is lost, and I am in exile, while in all probability that repulsive man lives his life as if nothing had happened. The serpent is left in possession of the garden.'

'So you think he's still in India?'

'Who knows? He certainly survived his injuries, I know that much. He may have left the army years ago, but somehow I'm guessing that he did not.' She looked keenly at him. 'And I'm also guessing that he's the real reason you want to go back there.'

He didn't answer, and Mrs James got up and put her glass on the mantelshelf. She regarded herself in the small mirror there, adjusted her hair. 'I come from a long line of army wives, Frank.'

He kept quiet, wondering where this was leading.

'Oh, yes. My mother and grandmother before me married army officers. And so did my two sisters, and an aunt, and cousins and nieces too, out of number. All army wives. Officers' wives. My brother-in-law, for example, is a major at the Twenty-first Hussars' home depot in Canterbury. That's where they recruit.' She turned to face him. 'Now, isn't that a coincidence?'

Frank lay in the wash of moonlight from the casement window. Mrs James's spare room was built into the angle of the roof, furnished with an iron bedstead and a cheerfully painted chest of drawers. He could not sleep. Whenever he drifted off he was brought startlingly awake by the clash and colour of India. India seemed very close in this house, so close that he could not be sure that the perfume of herbs and incense were in his imagination or outside it.

He sat up among his tangled bedclothes and the springs groaned. Almost at once, through the partition wall, he heard the answering twang of the maid's mattress as she turned in her own bed. An hour ago, as he had climbed to his room, she had appeared at the top of the stairs in her nightdress, plump and tousled in the light of the candle she carried. She had giggled and retreated into her own tiny room with a show of coyness, but Frank was in little doubt what would have happened if he had followed her. Even now he knew he need only tap on those thin boards. For a moment, the ache of his loneliness brought him close to doing just that.

But he did not tap on the wall. He reached down for his bag and hefted it up onto his knees and pulled out notebook and pencil. He was gripped with the need to make contact of some kind across the gulf, and he scribbled Grace's name at the top of one of the ruled pages. But he knew no way of setting down what was in his heart, nor any means of getting it to her if he did. He tore the sheet out of the notebook and crumpled it in his fist.

He stared out over the fields, bone white under the spring moon. Cold light glinted on the drawn wire of a canal. He supposed that canal must lead to a river, and then ultimately to the sea. Soon enough he could be sailing that sea, heading east to a life that would be new and vivid, for all its hardships. That at least was something. He slipped out of bed and rested his forehead against the cool window. It was better this way. Better for him to be recalled to his purpose. Better for her to be cut free of him. She had said that all they needed was faith. She was wrong.

PART SIX

Vienna, Bangalore and Secunderabad,
April to December 1896

46

The train drew in under the arcades of Vienna's Südbahnhof. Grace, leaning from the window, watched the engine's last great sigh billow up towards the glass roof, so that pigeons went clapping away among the girders. The shouts of the porters and the cries of children made cathedral echoes.

A distinguished grey-haired man in dark blue opened the door for her and reached up to offer her his hand. 'Fräulein Dearborn? I am Berndt. Come, please. The princess awaits on you.'

'But Mr Berndt, my luggage—'

He inclined his head. 'Berndt, only. And your packs are already from the train taken. Come, if you please.'

Grace allowed him to hand her down, and followed his stately stride up the length of the platform, parting the crowds. They emerged through an archway into a cobbled courtyard with carriages drawn up and horses' breath steaming in the cold spring air. Berndt took her to a brougham with gleaming burgundy coachwork and, before she had quite realised what was happening, he was helping her up into it. The dim interior smelled of Turkish tobacco.

'And are you the English rose I must cultivate?'

She was about forty, her hair romantically long and her eyes huge and dark. She wore a Prussian blue overcoat trimmed with silver fur and, in the gloomy recesses of the vehicle, she was languidly smoking a cigarette.

Grace sat down stiffly on the edge of the seat. 'I suppose you must be Princess Wilhelmina. I might as well tell you, I don't want to be here.'

The woman looked at her through the smoke. 'Well, my dear, if you do, you are making a bad job of pretending.' She opened the window and tossed her cigarette out. 'What exactly did they tell you about me?'

'Only that you are a cousin of Uncle Welti.'

'A cousin? Is that what they said?' Princess Wilhelmina laughed aloud, a ringing, carefully modulated laugh which faded into a sigh. 'Well, young Grace, if I am to be your chaperone, I had better take you for a hot chocolate, and some vast and revolting confection. That seems to be *de rigueur* for the English in Vienna.' She closed her eyes as if against a headache.

'I loathe hot chocolate,' Grace snapped, 'so you can spare yourself the trouble.'

She stepped out of the brougham and into the chill daylight and stalked away across the forecourt, her face burning in the bitter air. She had no idea where she was going, nor what she would do next, only that it was simply insupportable that she should be expected to go through with this charade. The vehicle came rumbling over the cobbles to trundle along beside her while Princess Wilhelmina leaned through the open window.

'Grace, my dear, I'm supposed to be looking after you. Uncle Welti was most insistent. I'll get into dreadful trouble if I don't.'

'I don't need *looking after*,' Grace told her, not breaking her stride. 'As a matter of fact, I could do with a good deal less of it.'

'Well, that puts the case plainly enough,' the woman acknowledged from the window. 'But just out of interest, have you any idea where you'll go?'

'Paris. Madrid. Rome. Does it matter? I just can't go on with this farce any longer.'

'Quite. And you will be able to pay for this adventure?'

'I shall . . . stow away.' Grace stopped walking. 'I shall . . . work my passage.'

'On a train? How refreshing. What will you do, stoke the firebox, or whatever it's called?'

'If I have to.'

Princess Wilhelmina laughed in delight. 'Oh, my! I can see this is going to be much more fun than I thought. Call me Willi. And get in, do.'

It was like no place that Grace had ever been in before; a low cavern with smoke-blackened brick vaulting and tables set between pillars which extended back into darkness. It was bright day outside but in the interior of the café it was so dim that it had to be lit by candles burning in bottles entombed in wax. The walls and pillars were a patchwork of posters old and new, announcing rallies, meetings, public speeches, plays, political candidates. Smaller handwritten notices offered language lessons, tuition in piano and painting, cheap accommodation, and sex.

Many of the clients were students, ostentatiously bohemian in dress and manner. At a table in the depths of the room a young man with wild hair stood up and started to declaim a poem until his laughing companions pulled him down. A group of uniformed soldiers were getting drunk in a corner over a card game and shouting abuse at one another. A few feet away three women with hollow eyes were drinking something jade green from tall glasses.

'The green fairy,' Willi said, seeing Grace's interest. 'Absinthe. We'll try it one day, but perhaps not quite yet. For the moment we'll stick to cognac.' She put her shot glass back on the table between them. 'It was a man, I suppose?'

'I beg your pardon?'

'Come, come, Grace, my dear. Let's not fence with each other. Your father bundles you away to the continent to be watched over by an older woman of rank? There's a man behind this, beyond doubt. Was this paramour socially unsuitable? That's good. Quite the best kind, the unsuitable ones.'

Grace sipped her cognac. She could feel Willi watching her, as if waiting for a reaction, but after Mrs Rossiter's gin this spirit was child's play. She put her glass down. 'He was very unsuitable indeed, according to my father.'

Willi lit a cigarette and waved away the smoke. 'But my poor girl! And how long since you've seen this paragon of yours?'

'Five weeks. A little more.'

'And he's still on your mind?'

'So it seems.'

'Your constancy is remarkable. I could certainly never match it. Where is he now?'

'I don't know. Father sent him away.'

'How splendid! You've no idea where?'

'He wanted to become a soldier. To go to India. Perhaps he did something like that.'

'India? Good Lord, that is rather dramatic. And you've not heard from him since, naturally.' Willi sighed. 'Really, my dear, how could you expect to maintain a liaison at such a distance? Indeed, I wonder what the point of it would be.'

'I should have liked to hear that he was safe. I should have liked a letter I might have kept.'

Willi snorted. 'You wanted a great deal more than that. And you know it.'

Grace said nothing.

'Don't be so downhearted, my sweet. If it means so much to you, you can write to him from here. I promise I shan't tell. Good Lord, I'd be the last person! A little intrigue is good for the soul.'

'But I've no idea how to find him. I have no kind of an address.'

'Well, yes, I see the problem.' Willi thought for a moment and then waved a hand as if deciding that the whole thing was too difficult. 'But you'll survive, Grace, my rose. I shall see that you do. It's merely a question of finding suitable . . . distractions.'

'I don't wish for distractions.'

'You will. Trust me.' Willi drank a little. 'Old Welti didn't say anything about any thwarted romance. He gave me some tale about radical politics and unhealthy liberal influences. Is there anything in all of that?'

'A little.'

'How intriguing you are, Grace! One assumes they thought a princess of the blood would make the perfect antidote to adolescent socialism. The poor fools! I rather think your old Uncle Welti has done you a favour, having you sent to me.' She laughed gaily, and, as the waitress shambled past, she called, 'Two more cognacs, Renate, you fat slut.'

'Coming up, Princess *Schatzi*.'

As the liquor began to relax her Grace looked around the room once more. The group of soldiers had given up their card game and were howling with laughter at some joke, their arms linked. The student poet, in a pantomime of despair, was trying to rip up his manuscript while his friends struggled to restrain him. Grace's eye was drawn to a figure at the end of the poet's table, a fair haired young man in a linen jacket who looked on at this piece of theatre being played out in front of him. He was slim and quite tall, with round glasses which gave him a scholarly look. His friends subdued the despairing poet, who put his head on his arms and made his shoulders heave. The fair haired young man leaned forward, perhaps to offer some word of comfort, and as he did so his glance met Grace's across the room and he gave her an apologetic little smile.

Grace looked quickly back at Willi. 'Are you really a princess?'

'Oh, yes. We're from Russia, lineage back to the fifteenth century. Fortunately with lots of illegitimacy along the way, or we'd all have had six fingers and webbed feet, like cousin Louis.'

'How did you come to be in Vienna?'

'When Tsar Alexander was assassinated my grandfather took the hint. He sold up the estates and invested the money overseas. He's dead now, poor dull dear, but he saved enough to keep me. At least, I haven't reached the bottom of the barrel yet, try as I might.' Willi gazed out over the shabby crew packing the tables. 'It won't save us, of course. All this running away. We'll all be torn apart in the end. Princes and princesses. Dukes with comical titles. Doomed, all doomed. No doubt we deserve it.' She waved her glass at the room. 'These young ruffians are coming to rip us to pieces. Isn't that a thrilling thought?'

Grace looked around, startled.

'Well, not today, my dear,' Willi reassuringly patted her hand, 'but you catch my drift. Revolutionaries and dissidents. A few of them here are the real thing, in exile from Moscow and St Petersburg and Belgrade. Real plotters! Imagine! Gaunt fellows with mad eyes and bombs under their jackets. That sort of thing.'

The waitress arrived, wheezing, and set down two more cognacs.

Willi waved away cigarette smoke. 'They're an acquired taste, I admit. Revolutionaries, I mean. Naturally one doesn't give a damn about their idiotic politics, but some of them do have a certain passionate commitment which can be – let me put it this way – transferred to other activities.'

Grace studied Willi's face, wondering if just possibly she was joking, or striving for effect. But there was no sign of self-doubt in those fine eyes, only a species of honesty Grace had never seen before, at once fearless and predatory. She had expected to have to endure some stuffy chaperone of sixty watching her every move. It was very evident that living under Princess Wilhelmina's roof would be nothing like that at all.

47

The speckled shade of the neem trees gave some relief from the weight of the sun. Between the slender trunks the six horses blew and stamped, jingling their harnesses as they shook off the flies. Sergeant Clough, a sandy haired man sunburned to the colour of teak, walked his horse forward and stood in the stirrups, shading his eyes as he peered through the glare. His khaki tunic was caked with dust and dark with sweat under the cross-straps. Through the ochre haze which hung over the plain a distant point of light was winking, diamond sharp. The heliograph message was not coded, and Frank, fourth back in the line of mounted men, read it rapidly to himself.

'Corp' Gannon!' Clough shouted. 'What's that fucking thing saying now?'

Gannon, a tall Irishman of fifteen years' service, worked on a plug of tobacco and stared into the shimmering distance. The strap of his helmet bulged rhythmically as he chewed but his face remained expressionless.

'We're to stay put until one p.m., Sergeant,' Gannon said, after a decent delay. 'Then await further orders.'

Frank guessed Gannon had read the signal some seconds earlier, and as easily as he had himself, but had kept quiet about it. Everyone knew Sergeant Clough could barely read and write, but it wasn't wise to draw attention to the fact.

'Fucking manoeuvres,' Clough grunted, and walked his horse back into the trees. 'All right, stretch them out for five minutes. Not you, Tranter, nor you neither, Gray. You two take these poor brutes down to the village yonder and get them watered.' The sergeant swung himself to the ground with a creak of saddlery and the other troopers followed suit.

The village was no more than a straggle of mud-brick houses with palm thatch roofs around a single shade-tree. Frank rode with Tranter, a portly garrulous trooper approaching forty. They each led two horses down the dusty track and between the dwellings, their mounted height giving them a view into a walled courtyard where children were hulling grain and a woman in a yellow sari stretched dough. A flock of scrawny chickens fled away before their horses' hooves. An old man dozed in the shade of a wall. They reined in, the flies gathering instantly around the horses' heads.

'Hi!' Tranter shouted. '*Pani lao! Juldi! Juldi!*'

The old man started to his feet in confusion, bobbed his head a few times and doddered off among the houses, calling out piteously.

'You got to light a fire under 'em,' Tranter explained in his hacked East End accent. 'Best if you can do it in Hindoostani. See, what I done, I told him to bring water – that's *pani lao* – and *juldi*, that's like, move your arse.' He stretched contentedly in the saddle. 'You'll pick it up, son. Couple of years here and you'll be slinging the bat with the best of us.'

A boy of about thirteen ran up and beckoned to them, hooking his arm repeatedly to get them to follow.

'What're you on about, you little bleeder?' Tranter demanded, his Hindi already outpaced. 'We're not going nowhere. You can fucking bring the *pani* here!'

Frank started to walk his horse after the boy, leading the other mounts.

Tranter said, 'Oy! What're you about?'

But the fat man was forced to follow or be left behind. They filed down a narrow alley, ducking under the projecting ends of roof poles, and emerged into a dusty open space where the shade-tree stood, a covered stone tank beneath it. A noisy crowd of children had gathered around the cistern, excited by the fine horses and the gleaming nut-brown saddles and the two troopers with their sabres and carbines. A cover was slid aside and wooden buckets were filled and in a moment the horses were drinking contentedly, their ears flicking as the children rushed in squealing to try to touch them, and dashed away again when the animals raised their heads. A girl with a nose jewel and a peacock blue sari offered them a gourd of clear water. Frank took it and smiled his thanks.

'Don't touch that,' Tranter warned. 'No telling what's in it.'

Frank raised the gourd and drank. The water was shockingly cold and tasted of clean stone.

'Well, don't blame me if you're shitting through the eye of a needle by tomorrow,' the fat man huffed.

Tranter's fragile dignity had been compromised, and he was sullen and silent as they walked the horses back up the dust track to the neem grove. There had been some small drama in their absence, for a ragged boy stood in the centre of the dismounted patrol, terrified and furious in equal measure. Two of the troopers had drawn carbines from saddle holsters. A few feet from the boy, among paper-dry leaves, lay an ancient matchlock musket with a wooden stock. Sergeant Clough was standing over the urchin, his hands on his hips.

'What you caught there, Sarge?' Tranter called as they rode up, brightening at the prospect of some new entertainment.

'Little bastard was lying in wait with the gun, would you believe it?' Clough said. 'Causley went for a jimmy, bloody nearly pissed on him. We'd never have seen him else.' The sergeant grabbed the boy's arm, shook him and bellowed into his face, 'What were you up to, eh?'

The boy, twisting in his grip, shouted back in defiance and fright and Clough cursed and swung back his free hand.

'He says he was up here hunting,' Frank said.

Clough lowered his hand and turned slowly to look up at Frank. 'What?'

'He's speaking Urdu, Sergeant.'

'When I want you to stick your oar in, Gray, I'll ask.'

The boy, sensing an ally, loosed a desperate torrent of Urdu at Frank. Sergeant Clough hesitated for a second, then released the child's arm and stood back a step.

'All right, Gray,' he said with large dignity. 'Since you're so smart, *now* I'm asking you to stick your oar in. What's the little blighter talking about?'

'He says a leopard came into the village last night and killed some chickens, so he came up to hunt it.'

'Hunt a leopard? In broad daylight?' Clough scoffed. 'Tell me another.'

Frank put this to the boy, who answered fluently, gesticulating around the ring of troopers and their mounts, his eyes flashing.

'He says he might have had a chance,' Frank translated, 'if we hadn't come crashing along like a herd of elephants, scaring everything for miles around.'

There were some snorts of laughter, which made the boy bold, for he pointed at Clough and at the discarded musket and ranted for a few passionate moments more.

'What was all that?' Clough demanded, suspiciously.

'He says that a high ranking officer of your experience, Sergeant, could not possibly imagine that a boy of eleven would attack a squadron of British cavalry armed only with a musket made by his uncle.'

The men laughed openly at that. Sergeant Clough glared round at them, but he knew the joke was on him, and with good enough humour he picked up the boy's makeshift firearm and thrust it at him. 'Go on, then, bugger off.'

The urchin didn't wait to argue this time, but grabbed the weapon and sprinted away down the track with it, grinning up at Frank as he went. The fun over, the men collected their horses and walked them away to tether them in the shade. Frank had passed over the last set of reins and was about to dismount, but he found Clough standing at his stirrup.

'Where d'you learn to sling the bat so good, Gray? You ain't been here but a month.'

'I picked it up, Sarge. Here and there.'

The steady gaze didn't waver. 'Answer the question. And it's Sergeant to you.'

Frank shifted in his saddle. 'I was brought up here, Sergeant. In India. My father was an engineer with the railways.'

Clough nodded and stepped away. 'You want to be careful, son. You might be useful to somebody one day.'

48

Frank stretched out on the narrow cot as the evening wind prowled in through the high windows.

Trimulgherry Fort was a cool and massive two-storey building with white stone arches. It was as vast as a railway terminus. The wide space, dimly shaded against the sun, was divided into barrack rooms, the men's beds ranked at right angles to the walls, punkahs stirring the air above. The walls were crowded with shelves of personal belongings, hooks for kit, pinned notices and hunting trophies. Behind rattan screens at the far end of the long room Frank could hear laughter and the slap of playing cards. Around him men were dozing and smoking in the gathering darkness, a few reading in the light of candles. Across the aisle a trooper was sucking at a stub of pencil as he worked on a letter, perhaps to a wife or sweetheart whom he could not hope to see for three, or five, or ten years. Frank knew that some of the men had been here for decades, transferring from regiment to regiment rather than go back to a grimy terrace in Nottingham or a hovel in Belfast.

An old Indian man was dispensing coffee from an earthenware ewer which he carried on his head. Frank took a cup from him and paid him, giving him an extra anna or two. The man ducked his head and moved on. On the evening breeze Frank could smell horses, and cooling dust from the parade ground, and jasmine. He set aside his coffee and opened the kit locker beside the bed and removed his writing case. It was a handsome case of Kashmiri leather, the sole luxury he had afforded himself in his three months in India. He took out paper and pen and added another few sentences to the letter, trying to describe to Grace the hot bedlam of the markets, the weight of the sun at noon, the scent of the rains. He wrote to her of the ragged boy with his musket, of the mud-brick village and of water which tasted of stone. This had become his routine each evening when they were in barracks, and he knew it had earned him a reputation as solitary, even aloof. But he also knew that he was competent enough at soldiering to earn respect. He was good with the horses, learned quickly and never complained. The other men would have liked him better if he had been more sociable, but generally they left him alone, which was the way he wanted it.

Presently he stopped writing and put Grace's letter away. It was already a score of pages long, but he knew he would never send it. He gazed up into the cavernous vaulting of the room. Four months since he had last seen her standing by the pub window in the chill dawn. He tried to banish that image and to picture her instead in some less charged setting, moving quietly around the rooms of Cumver House, for example. Or maybe she would be back at her school in Switzerland. One way or the other she would be living her own life now, from which the very memory of him must surely have faded, a life which had been mapped out for her. And he had to live the one mapped out for him.

He drew three foolscap sheets from the writing case. He had drawn a chart on the top page, like a family tree, and the branches of this tree were dense with notes. He had been adding to his list of officers steadily for months as he discovered more names, or learned of others who had left the strength. But the task was dispiriting. He had discovered that the regiment was a living organism which renewed itself with bewildering speed. The middle-ranking officers in particular were an ever-changing group. They were forever departing on extended leave, taking secondments to other regiments, or obtaining discharges through sickness or injury. Several had died over the past few years, and keeping track of the living was almost impossible.

Several times already Frank had feigned some errand, and ridden the two miles down the tree-lined avenues of the immense cantonment to the white columned officers' mess. There he had stood in the violet evening for ten minutes each time, watching the officers as they left their horses with the syces and strode jingling up the steps in their spurs. He knew his ritual surveillance smacked of despair. The officer he sought could be almost any one of these confident, powerful, moustachioed men in their fine uniforms. Or none of them. He could be long gone, living or dead, discharged or retired or transferred.

Tranter and Gannon came walking up between the beds, Tranter talking as usual and the Irishman tamping a short briar pipe. Tranter swung his portly body up onto his cot, and balanced a bottle of Whitbread Pale Ale on his belly. Gannon leaned against the wall on the other side of Frank, next to the high window, toying with his pipe. As Frank glanced up at the tall corporal, Tranter leaned across the narrow aisle between the beds and picked up the list.

'What's this, then, Gray? Officers, is it? Bucking for promotion already, are you?'

Frank moved to take the paper back, but Tranter avoided him, holding the list up for Gannon to see.

'See here, Mick? The lad's got it all worked out. And he only got out here about five minutes ago. Sharp, ain't he?'

Gannon grinned around his pipe stem but said nothing.

'You're a dark horse, Gray, ain't you?' Tranter said. 'Like today in that village, chattering away like a bloody native. And now it's officers, is it?' Tranter waved the paper just out of reach. 'You've not got but half of them here. There's as many again away on leave, or sick, or about some devilment. Haven't got the sense they were fucking born with, officers. If no one's trying to kill them they get bored, and if there ain't no trouble they go and make some. Especially our blokes, being in the Twenty-first. You know what they say our motto ought to be? *Thou shalt not kill.* With a reputation like that, officers'll do anything for a shot at glory, the silly bastards.'

'Let me have it back,' Frank said quietly.

Tranter seemed on the point of continuing with the game, but before he could speak again Gannon took his pipe out of his mouth. 'Give it back to him, Tubs.'

The fat man shrugged, handed the paper back to Frank, and took a swig of his beer. 'What's all this about, anyway, Gray?'

'It passes the time.'

'A straight question owns a straight answer.'

High above Frank a bat was flickering against the shadows of the ceiling. He watched it swinging between the rattan sails of the punkah until it darted out again through the tall windows.

'I'm trying to find someone.'

'An officer? We'd know if he was here. What's his name?'

'I don't know his name.'

Tranter frowned. 'You don't know his bleeding name?'

'Jack. His first name's Jack.'

Tranter guffawed. 'Half the fucking regiment's called Jack! Half the fucking army!'

'Or John,' Gannon observed. 'Or James, maybe. They all get called Jack.' He spat a shred of tobacco from his lower lip. 'Fellers get called Jack when it ain't their name at all.'

'Jumping Jack,' Tranter suggested. 'Jack-o'-lantern. Jack Frost. Jack-knife.'

'This man was an officer on the strength a little over three years ago,' Frank said. 'Maybe he still is.'

'Three years back we was still at Bangalore.'

'That's right.'

'So what happened?'

'He was seconded to the Fourth, but there was trouble.'

'What kind of trouble?'

'With . . . a woman. He was injured. Shot.'

'Jealous hubbie, eh?' Tranter laughed. 'Well, that's what I *call* trouble. You must be able to find him from that.'

'It was hushed up. Maybe he was sent home, or posted on somewhere else. I don't know. I'm not sure he ever rejoined the Twenty-first, but my guess is that he did.'

'What rank?'

'I don't know that either.'

Tranter thought about this. 'All right, then. How old?'

'I doubt he's above fifty. Nor under thirty.'

'Christ. And that's all you have?'

'That's all.'

'What d'you want of him, Gray?' Gannon said. 'What's this mystery man of yours done to you?'

'That doesn't matter.'

Frank kept his eyes away from Gannon. He was afraid of what he might betray if he met the older man's gaze. Tranter, though, was warming to the riddle.

'Well, there's Lieutenant Piper. They call him Jack, don't they, Mick? And that Captain Redmond, is it? He's John, ain't he?'

'It ain't neither of them.' Gannon put his pipe back in his mouth. 'Piper's not one-and-twenty years of age, and Redmond only come out here two years back. Neither of them was even with the regiment back then.'

There was silence for a few moments after that. Frank slipped the sheets of paper into his writing case.

'I can't work you out, Gray,' Tranter said at length. 'You a gentleman ranker?'

'Me? No.'

'So why'd you sign up? Sharp young bloke like you.'

'Why not? You did.'

'That's different. The army's our mother and father, ain't that right, Mick? First new set of clothes I ever had was in the army. First time I was ever fed three times a day.'

'Ye made the most of that, Tubs,' Gannon observed. 'Ye're why they call us the Dumpies.'

'And where would the likes of us get housed in a grand fucking place like this,' Tranter continued, ignoring him, 'with grinning darkies running round after us, sweeping up and doing our dhobi and fetchin' and carryin'? Not that it'll be like this when they post us off to Timbuctoo or wherever it's to be.'

Frank looked up. 'We're to be posted?'

'Cape Town.' Tranter shrugged. 'Newfoundland. Who knows?'

Gannon knocked the dottle out of his pipe into one horny palm. 'Egypt,' he said. 'It'll be Egypt, mark my words.'

The old man with the coffee ewer slapped past on bare feet and, as if to prove his point, Tranter bellowed: 'Oy! *Harri bai!* Piss off quick and get me another beer. And one for our mate. *Juldi! Juldi karo!*' He tossed a coin to the old man, who showed a few yellow pegs of teeth, put his urn down and hurried off.

'But you, young Gray,' Tranter went on, 'you got learning. You talk proper. You don't go whoring or boozing or dicing with the other lads. And you speak wog lingo. Oh, you're a dark horse, you are, Gray.'

Gannon reamed out his pipe with a small knife. 'A dark grey horse, as ye might say.'

'Dark Gray!' Tranter crowed. 'That's good, Mick! That's what we should bleeding call you, seeing as you're so tight with the niggers. Darkie Gray!'

The old man came slip-slapping back, handed Tranter a bottle of Whitbread and gave another to Frank, but made no move to leave.

''Ere's to you, Darkie!' Tranter leaned over to clink his bottle against Frank's and cheerfully told the old man, 'You can fuck off, Leatherface. I already give you your money, so don't you go trying it on.'

In Urdu, Frank asked, 'What is it, Father?'

The old man stooped to take up his coffee urn and said softly, 'I have news of your Bengaluru friend, sahib.'

'Tell me.'

'He is a prosperous man now, my cousin tells me.' The old man rocked his head in admiration. 'His shop is in the market, behind the old temple of Vishnu in Cantonment Bazaar.'

'Thank you, Father.'

The old man took the coin Frank gave him, grinned his appreciation, and slapped away between the beds.

Tranter watched him go, looked across at Gannon. 'That's our boy, Mick. Dark by name and dark by fucking nature.'

49

Matilde bustled around her, hairpins in mouth, humming and tutting. Grace stared at the ceiling.

In England she had liked to be dressed, to have her hair brushed until it shone, to have it piled up in that *faux* casual way that only a truly expert maid could manage. To go through the sensuous ritual of preparation had always been a decadent delight. But tonight Matilde's fussing irritated her. She didn't much like Matilde at the best of times, a stout and smiling matron of forty, who always seemed to be on hand no matter what time she and Willi got home. Matilde was unfailingly cheerful, but just occasionally in the mirror Grace would surprise a watchfulness in the woman's eyes, a hardness in the lines around her mouth.

'That'll be all, Matilde,' she said shortly. 'Thank you.'

A flicker of surprise crossed the woman's face, but she gathered her pins and ribbons. 'Very good, miss. You look a picture, you do! Oh, you're going to have *such* a wonderful evening.'

When the maid had gone Grace walked over to the window. It was already nearly eight and she would have to go down soon. Outside, the late summer evening was still and warm. On the street below guests were arriving, the wheels of their cabs crunching on the cobbles. She heard greetings and laughter. From downstairs the murmur of conversation and the tinkle of glasses was already rising to her. She pictured them down there, the usual eclectic mix of Willi's past lovers and hopeful admirers. There would be a wealthy banker or two, a destitute artist, maybe a politician, a sprinkling of professionals and some minor aristocrats.

The lowering sun threw splashes of gold over the pavements. Through the windows of the grand houses opposite Grace glimpsed other lives, more settled lives. A butler was setting out a decanter for an old man in a smoking jacket. Two children in a nursery hugged their knees while their nanny read a story. A schoolgirl practised at her piano. The sight of these peaceful worlds filled her with an aching loneliness.

The doors burst open and Willi sailed in, rustling in ivory silk.

'Not ready yet? And everyone's here!' Willi took in the sight of Grace standing by the window in her royal blue gown. 'Though on second thoughts, goddesses are permitted to be late.'

'I'm sorry, but I really don't feel up to it.'

Willi swept up to her. 'What nonsense. It will be fun.'

'Willi, surely life can't just be one endless round of pleasure.'

'My sweet, you really must learn to suppress these Calvinist tendencies of yours. Come now. Let's go down.' She offered her hand, but Grace did not take it. Willi put her head on one side. 'That soldier-boy isn't still haunting your restless nights, is he? You have to stop this, my dear. It's been months now. You can't have an affair with a memory. That would be most unsatisfying. Now, come downstairs at once.' Willi cruised away towards the door.

'What am I to do, Willi?' Grace cried in despair.

The older woman halted, walked back across the room. She put her cool hand against Grace's cheek. 'What's this? Tears?'

'If only I had some way of reaching him.'

'Grace, face facts. If this boy of yours really wanted to get word to you, he would have found a way by now.'

'That's cruel of you.'

'No, it's the voice of experience, my sweet. He's forgotten you. He's a fool, obviously, but then they all are.'

'Even if you're right. It would be some comfort to know it is over between us.'

'It is, Grace, depend upon it. Come, come. Do you think you're the first woman this has happened to? Betrayal is our fate. It's how they treat us. And we have to be strong, and make our own way in the world, despite them.'

Grace straightened and took a deep breath.

'That's better.' Willi put an arm around her and squeezed her waist. 'We're going to make a bargain, you and I.'

'What kind of a bargain?'

'Well, let's see. It's already autumn. In just three months Christmas will be upon us again. Oh, Christmas is a wonderful time here, Grace! Skating, dancing, Glühwein, candlelight. All the men are more handsome at Christmas and all the women more beautiful. Everyone falls in love at Christmas. Now here's my bargain, and it's quite simple: if this impossible soldier of yours hasn't sent word by Christmas you are to put him out of your mind, and out of your heart.'

'But how can I do that?'

'Oh, you can do it, Grace. You have the strength inside you to put an end to this. And you should. You must know he's lost to you. A handsome soldier-boy? In one of those smart scarlet uniforms? Do you think other women haven't laid siege to him? I'm afraid there isn't a man born who can resist that kind of attention.'

There was something appalling in Willi's honesty, Grace decided, but it was impossible not to respond to her energy and resolve. And she was right: this pain could not go on. It simply could not.

'Until Christmas, Grace. Do we have a bargain?'

'I suppose we do.'

'That's settled, then. Now, let's go down.'

Willi crossed to the door and held it open, and in a moment they were gliding down the long staircase beneath the chandelier and the portraits of fierce bemedalled men and matriarchs in furs. Two uniformed footmen held open the double doors into the salon, bright with candlelight. The guests, perhaps twenty of them, had already been served champagne and a lively buzz of conversation and laughter filled the room. It fell away as the two women made their entrance.

Despite herself, Grace felt the unabashed admiration of these people lift her spirits. Only one guest seemed to be ignoring them, or perhaps was so deep in conversation that he hadn't noticed them. She was vain enough to resent that, and she stared haughtily across at him as he stood near the fireplace, his back half-turned to her. At last he became conscious of the silence, and looked around for the cause of it. He was a tall young man with untidy fair hair and large hazel eyes, and he was conspicuous in his collarless shirt and rough linen jacket among the fine gowns and evening suits. His gaze passed over Willi and rested on Grace, and he smiled apologetically at her and put on a pair of round glasses with wire rims. Through these he looked at her in an owlish and bashful fashion, but with recognition dawning in his eyes.

50

Frank pushed aside the curtain and stepped out of the clamour and stench of the night market. The workshop had a beaten-earth floor and a long bench facing the door with racks of silver jewellery along the walls behind. It was very dim inside. At the bench a young Tamil man and two boys sat working in pools of light thrown by oil lamps. Three young women sat at tables further back in the shop, their slender fingers busy in the lamplight. The place was fiendishly hot. Light caught the bars and twists of silver on the bench. Frank heard the musical ringing of a hammer, the whirring of a treadle drill, and from somewhere in the warren of dark and spice-scented rooms the lilt of a woman murmuring a lullaby.

The young man was working with intense concentration, using a large magnifying glass, and he did not at once hear Frank's entrance. Finally he looked up, set aside his tools and moved out from behind the bench. He was slight and bespectacled – not much more than a youth – and he was dressed in a loose-fitting blue salwar kameez and a skull cap. He took in Frank's uniform at a glance and arranged his features in an attitude of respect.

'The sahib graces us with his presence,' he said in English and ducked his head obsequiously. 'The sahib seeks perhaps some fine . . .' His voice drifted away as he looked into Frank's eyes, suddenly confused.

'Hello, Javed,' Frank said, and switched to Kannada. 'Robbed any trains lately?'

Javed turned to his little niece and snapped his fingers imperiously. 'Bring more rice!'

The girl grinned slyly at Frank to show what she thought of her young uncle's authority, but scampered off quickly enough to the kitchen space at the back where Javed's wife was at work, chopping and chattering with an aunt or two.

'I only had word of you a few days ago, Javed, or I would have come sooner.' Frank tore off a scrap of pitta bread and dipped it in the bowl. He looked around the low room. Oil lamps burned at the shrine to elephant-headed Ganesh and winked on brass and silver. 'Life has treated you well. You have become quite the prosperous merchant.'

'My uncle died of the cholera two years ago, soon after you left India, and the shop passed to me. I was not prepared for such an inheritance. I was only fifteen but my mother and my sisters needed to be fed and protected.' Javed smiled ruefully. 'So no more robbing of trains. And you, Frank!' He laughed in delight, gesturing at Frank's uniform, at his whole broad presence. 'And now you are back. And as a soldier! You are stationed here in Bengaluru?'

'Secunderabad. I have taken leave to come down to see you.'

'I am flattered. Such a journey to see an old friend.' Javed looked at him critically. 'You are twice as big, I think, as when we thieved and fought through the alleys of the city.'

'We were children then.'

'Ah, yes, children.' Javed rolled scented rice into a ball and tossed it into his mouth. 'Yet what you did at the end was not the act of a child.' He smiled, showing fine teeth. 'Sent home to England for shooting an English officer!'

'You knew that?'

'Of course! It's not what the British said, naturally. They said it was an Indian who attacked your poor mother. They even hanged a man for it, some vermin from Bengaluru jail who was guilty of a dozen murders, I don't doubt. But he wasn't guilty of that one. The servants in your father's house knew the truth. Come, Frank, you know India. How could such a story be kept from them? And it is a story indeed! Did they treat you as a great hero when you got home?'

'We weren't sent home for what I did, Javed, but for what he did.'

'But you did shoot him. You will not deny that. I should be most disappointed if you denied it.'

Frank ripped off a chicken leg and stripped it with his teeth and dropped the bone. He was sweating in the hot darkness and he felt too big for the space. 'He deserved it.'

'Undoubtedly. And yet he survived your anger, it seems.'

'You knew that too?'

'There was talk. There was a lot of talk about how important this man must have been, for the British to go to such trouble to protect him. Who was he?'

'I don't know. That's what I'm trying to find out.'

'Truly? You know nothing about him?'

'His name was Jack and his regiment was the Twenty-first Hussars. That's why I joined them.'

'Then assuredly he cannot be hard to find.'

'I didn't see him clearly that night, Javed. I was thinking only of killing him. Of nothing else.'

Javed dropped his own chicken bone into a dish. 'And still you think of nothing else. Is that not true?'

'The law will not help me.'

Javed rinsed his fingers. 'Frank, my friend, this is not a matter of law, which you British believe you have taught us, but of honour, of which perhaps we could teach you something.'

'Either way, it is a debt which must be paid.'

'You should be very careful. Settling such a debt might be an expensive business. It could cost you your soul.' Javed snapped his fingers and his niece dashed out of the shadows and collected dishes. 'And while you do not yet know this man, he knows himself. What would he do, I wonder, if he heard you were seeking him out?'

'I will find him first. But I have to find him quickly. We're to be redeployed soon. It will be twice as hard to trace him once we're out of India.'

'And this is why you come to me?'

'It's one reason.'

'I am just a silversmith.'

'The Indians know everything. You said so yourself. The mess orderlies, the dak-gharry drivers, the tailors, the grooms, the merchants. Even the washerwomen and the whores. They all work for the British. When the regiments go, they stay, most of them. I want to find someone who worked with the Fourth Hussars three years ago. Someone who knew of an officer seconded to the Fourth from the Twenty-first. Someone who noticed when that officer was suddenly sent back to his own regiment. Someone who heard talk.'

Javed was quiet for so long that Frank became aware again of the noises from the market outside, the lowing of a bullock, a shouted argument in Kannada, the rumble of cartwheels. He could feel the sweat running down the groove of his spine.

Javed said, 'We must find Ashok.'

51

Grace was holding a stilted conversation in German with an elderly lawyer when she sensed the tall young man begin to drift across the room towards her. She felt a flash of annoyance, but she couldn't pretend to be surprised. The moment she had seen that flicker of recognition in his eyes she had known that he would approach her at some time during the evening. He would attempt to be charming, and the thought wearied her.

So even when he was standing beside her she refused to allow herself to be distracted. She kept talking, although the lawyer was very dull and she had almost exhausted her German. The newcomer seemed not to feel her coldness. He waited patiently at her elbow until the lawyer, perhaps finding the conversation as tedious as Grace did, clicked his heels and left.

'I feel sure we have met before,' the young man said in accented English. 'Is this possible?'

'Anything is possible, I suppose.' Grace looked around her, as if there were someone else in the room with whom she simply had to speak. 'And by the way, that is not an original introduction.'

'Perhaps I have made a mistake. I beg your pardon.'

She felt guilty for her rudeness then and relented. 'You're not mistaken. I remember you now. You were at a table a little way from Willi and me. A café in a basement, some months ago. I don't know exactly where it was.'

His face lit up. 'Ah, yes, that place. Not a very respectable café, I'm afraid. I am almost ashamed you should remember seeing me there. I am Max, Max Krauss.' He bowed formally to her. 'You are Willi's English friend, I think?'

'I am Grace Dearborn.'

'Miss Grace. It is my honour.' He bowed again.

The old fashioned courtesy was engaging, if a little comical. He wasn't very impressive, she decided, but he had good hazel eyes behind those funny round glasses. And she liked the plainness of his clothing against the finery in the room. A small silence stretched between them.

'Your friend was reading poetry,' she said. 'It was my first day in Vienna. That is why I remember.'

'Ferdinand is from the Balkans. A very bad poet, but a good . . . what is your word . . . nurse? This not the right word, I think. I mean that Ferdinand assists in the hospital.' A waiter passed and Max Krauss took two glasses of champagne from his tray and gave one to Grace. 'When he is not writing bad poetry.'

'He is a doctor?'

'No, no. Ferdinand is a . . . helper, only. I am the doctor.'

Something fell into place for her when he said that. Yes, she could see him as a doctor. That fitted his quiet manner, his evident intelligence, and the hint of something stronger behind his diffidence, for she guessed he would not always be so self-effacing.

'Well,' she said, 'perhaps we would say Ferdinand was an orderly. Although that sounds rather military.'

'Ferdinand is not at all military.'

He laughed. He had an attractive laugh, a low warm chuckle. Grace caught herself smiling at him in response and had to make a conscious effort to look away. She felt an irrational urge to break off the conversation and walk away at once.

'You are not Austrian, I think, Dr Krauss?'

'No, I am from Berlin. But Berlin was rather too . . . Prussian for me.'

'So you came to Vienna for the music and the theatre?'

'I do not have the money or the time for such things,' he said, and she felt chastened. 'But perhaps you have a taste for them, Miss Grace?'

She sipped her champagne. She knew this was a test. She could answer him with a simple yes, and that would spell the end of the conversation. Yet she was unwilling to jeopardise the good opinion of this intense young man quite so soon.

'One can have too much of a good thing, Dr Krauss.' She put her glass aside, rather pointedly.

'This is an English expression?'

'I suppose it is.'

'It is a wise observation.' He glanced around the room at Willi's wealthy friends in their jewels and fine dresses. 'All of these elegant people here have too much of a good thing.'

'And yet you are drinking the same champagne.'

'Willi is a friend. She contributes to our work. It is necessary to observe some social conventions.'

Grace let a moment pass. 'Tell me about your work, Dr Krauss.'

'What should you like to know?'

'You are employed at the General Hospital, no doubt?'

'No, I am afraid mine is not a . . . fashionable practice. Our hospital, such as it is, treats only the poor.' He frowned. 'But this will not interest you.'

'On the contrary. It interests me a good deal.'

His gaze rested curiously on her for a long time, and she saw his eyes soften behind his large glasses.

'What is it, Dr Krauss?'

'Miss Grace, am I permitted to ask a personal question?'

'Very well.'

'What is it that causes such sadness in you?'

52

Frank worked the Martini-Henry's cocking lever and hugged the butt of the carbine hard into his shoulder, the strap tense across his left forearm. The ground under him crunched like dry biscuit and the weight of the afternoon sun lay full on his back. Two hundred yards away the target wobbled slightly in the heat. He took a deep breath, allowing the foresight to drop down towards the bull as he exhaled, and took the first pressure on the trigger.

Afterwards, he got to his feet and stood easy. His shoulder was numb from the recoil and his ears were still ringing from the explosions, but he was pleased with himself. He was a good shot and he knew his score would top the section once again. Behind him he heard the clatter of hoofbeats as a messenger rode up. The man reined in and spoke briefly to the instructor sergeant, then rode away again the way he had come. The sergeant walked down the line of standing men and stopped in front of Frank.

'Gray. Report to Captain Cavendish at the officers' mess. Now.'

Surprise made Frank dull witted. 'Captain Cavendish, Sergeant?'

The sergeant thrust forward his red and sweating face. 'If you have trouble with your 'earing, trooper, I shall give you a chit for an ear trumpet. Now move your arse.'

Frank mounted up and cantered back from the range towards the distant white buildings of the cantonment, puzzled and a little apprehensive. He vaguely knew of Cavendish, a silver haired intelligence officer, but he could not guess what such a man could want from a raw trooper. He reined in under the jacarandas beside the mess, gave his horse to a turbaned groom and walked around the corner of the building, conscious of the dust on his tunic and the smudges of black powder on his face. The white steps rose above him, dazzling in the sun and bustling with uniformed officers leaving after lunch, talking loudly in the way of self-assured men. Several of them gave Frank amused glances as he stood waiting. A smouldering resentment began to grow in him, and it took all his willpower not to glare from one arrogant face to another.

'Gray?' Somehow Captain Cavendish was standing right beside him. 'Sir.'

Frank started to come to attention but Cavendish was already walking away up the steps. When Frank hesitated Cavendish shouted over his shoulder, 'Come along, then, man!' and Frank followed, clumsy in his cavalry boots.

Before they reached the top the double doors swung open and Colonel Rowland Martin himself burst like Jove into the sunlight, a retinue of glittering minions around him. The colonel, a tall, precise man with an intellectual forehead, held a leather despatch case under his arm. He was in the act of passing some comment to the immaculate major next to him when he caught sight of Cavendish. A second later his gaze tracked over Frank and locked.

'Good God, Freddie! Is this the chap you wanted?'

'This is the one, sir.'

The colonel took a step down until he stood directly in front of Frank. He was about fifty, with a prominent Adam's apple and thoughtful lines around his eyes. His khaki uniform with its red staff officer's tabs was perfectly pressed. Frank breathed in the clean laundry scent of it, the colonel's light cologne, and the traces of his after-lunch cigar.

'Look at the state of you, man! Deuce d'you mean by it, presenting yourself like this?'

'We were at the range, sir—'

'Be quiet.'

'Sir.'

The colonel inspected him, not altogether without good humour. 'Well, you can have him if you want him, Freddie,' he said at last and swung away. 'Doesn't look as if he'll be much use to anyone else.'

'On paper he seems rather good, sir,' Cavendish suggested.

'Hasn't had time to mess anything up yet. Wet behind the ears.' The colonel stretched out one arm without looking and someone gave him his cap. He tapped it onto his head and trotted down the steps, but then turned back and barked at Frank, 'At the range, you say?'

'Yes, sir.'

'Any good?'

'Marksman, sir.'

Martin grunted and moved on, trailing his entourage like a comet. He waved his swagger stick over his shoulder. 'All yours, Freddie.'

Frank and Cavendish rode down the dusty avenues of the cantonment for some minutes, past store wagons and squads of marching men and mounted orderlies. Frank kept just behind the officer's left stirrup, hoping for some explanation, but not a word had been exchanged by the time they reined in outside a pretty ochre and white bungalow. The veranda and the garden were heady with jasmine and bougainvillea. A uniformed syce stepped forward and took both horses. Cavendish returned the man's greeting in good Urdu, stumped up the steps onto the veranda and into the house. Frank stopped in the doorway, not sure if he was supposed to enter. In the hall Cavendish stripped off his tunic and handed it to a butler and with a sigh of relief unhitched his braces so that they hung down over his hips. He glanced round at Frank.

'What are you waiting for? Want me to carry you over the threshold?' He pointed through a doorway. 'Go in there. Ali, get the young sahib a beer. You drink beer, Gray, I suppose?'

Cavendish shambled off down a corridor into the dim recesses of the bungalow without waiting for a reply. Ali, a sparrow of a man in white jacket and scarlet sash, ushered Frank through into a fine tall room giving out onto a back garden dazzling with white and yellow roses. It was cool and fragrant and a punkah swayed overhead. Rich carpets in crimson and peacock blue were spread over one another on the floor and a false ceiling of white painted muslin hung overhead. Two charpoys, with purple coverings and tasselled cushions, lay along opposing walls. Beside them stood low tables set with polished brass trays, and next to one of the charpoys was a low rosewood lectern with an illuminated Koran open on it. There were fresh flowers in vases in the corners of the room and in the centre a hookah on a brass stand.

Ali returned with a bottle of beer, set it on one of the low tables and put two glasses beside it, one empty and the other full of ice. He poured a little of the beer into the glass, and made a courtly gesture inviting Frank to take it. Frank did not. Ali busied himself on a practised ritual, plumping cushions, closing the latticed shutters against the glare of the afternoon, refilling the glass bowl of the hookah from a ewer. When he had gone Frank stood quite still in the filtered light, the sweat cooling on his body. Melting ice cracked loudly in the glass. The bottle on the tray had grown dewy and was unbearably tempting, but still he did not take it.

A man in white Arab robes swept past him into the room and stretched himself with a sigh on the charpoy against the far wall. It was Cavendish, Frank saw, and was no longer much surprised.

'What are you standing around for?' the older man demanded. 'Sit. And drink that, for God's sake.'

Frank perched on the edge of the opposite charpoy and picked up the glass and gulped down the beer in two swallows. By the time he had finished it, Cavendish was busy with the hookah, producing a small silver box and taking a pinch of some dry fibrous matter from it. He crumbled some of this into the hookah's dish, struck a match and lit the wick beneath it, then picked up one of the mouthpieces and drew deeply on it through his curled fist. The water in the hookah gurgled and smoke rose in the striped light. All at once the room was filled with a secret and musky aroma which sent Frank's spirit winging back down the years.

Cavendish took the pipe out of his mouth. 'You know what this is, lad?'

'It's hashish, sir.'

'Take some. Not sure how it goes with pale ale, but it might be an interesting experiment.'

Frank took up one of the pipes and drew in the sweet, pungent smoke.

'How is it?' Cavendish asked innocently.

'It's very good, sir.'

The strangeness of the situation and the warm rush of fumes in his lungs so distracted Frank that it took him a moment to realise that Cavendish's question had been put to him in Pushtu, and that he had answered in the same language. He found the captain smiling at him through the smoke.

'So,' Cavendish said in English. 'Urdu and Pushtu. Anything else?'

'Kannada, sir. Some Hindi. A little Arabic.'

Cavendish exhaled a plume of smoke. 'Your papers say your father was an engineer. One imagines he was posted from one end of India to the other, building railways for the Raj, while you picked up a new language in each place. Is that right?'

'I have an ear for them, sir,' Frank said carefully.

'You have an ear for Greek, too. And Latin, of course. Don't look so shocked, Gray. I've been through your locker and had a look at your books. I am an intelligence officer, after all, and even I know that railway engineers don't teach their sons classical Greek. Oh, don't worry. I really don't care. Plenty of young chaps give false information when they sign up. Sometimes they're running away from something. Sometimes they're running towards it – fame, fortune and adventure, and all that. Is that what you're doing here, Gray?' The perfume of hashish was filling the room. Cavendish drew down smoke and blew it out again. 'Come to that, what are any of us doing here, do you think?'

'Sir?'

'The British in India. How is it we've managed to maintain ourselves for so long over this vast and powerful subcontinent? Answer me that.'

'I'd say it was something to do with the breech-loading rifle, sir.'

'Ha! A cynic! But that's too glib, Gray, too glib by half. A few thousand soldiers can't subdue a land of four hundred millions by force alone. No, no. Such numbers can only be governed by acquiescence, if not consent. Oh, they had us on the run in the Mutiny, forty years back. But in the end that was put down because most of them didn't want any part of it and sided with us. And why do they tolerate us, Gray? After all, we rob them blind. I'll tell you why. Because they want things which at present only we can supply. A coherent system of government, education, the knowledge and skills to build modern industries, freedom from the superstitions of the past. When they have these things, they will expel us, Gray. And, when that time comes, we will go quietly, if we're sensible.'

Perhaps it was the drug freeing his mind, or some resonance struck by Cavendish's words, but a clear vision of Grace rose suddenly in Frank's memory. She was standing by the open doorway of Mrs Rossiter's cottage. Her colour was high from the fresh air and her head was lifted, and she had just fired anti-imperialism at him like a broadside.

'Do you think we'll be sensible, Gray?' Cavendish demanded. 'Do you think we'll go quietly when the time comes?'

'I haven't seen much evidence of it, sir.'

'No. Neither have I.' Cavendish took another pull on his pipe. 'I have to go to Peshawar quite soon. You know Peshawar? I assume so, since you speak Pushtu.'

'I was born there, sir. Lived there until I was nine years old.'

'And did you like the place?'

Did he like Peshawar? Frank couldn't answer at first, his mind was too crowded with images from a magical past – orchards of fig and lemon, fountains and courts and dark passageways, distant mountains, and, swaying down the dusty road from Afghanistan, the camel caravans with wild Pathan tribesmen riding guard, their long barrelled jezails inlaid with ivory and silver, glinting in the sunlight.

'Yes, sir. I liked Peshawar.'

Cavendish took the pipe out of his mouth. 'Me too. I studied to be an Arabist, you know, Gray, in another life. That was at Brasenose. I used to sit in Duke Humfrey's library in the Bodleian and stare at prints of places like Peshawar, Kandahar, Kabul – stuff brought back by chaps like Burton and Burnes and Doughty and a dozen other half-cracked adventurers. I used to wonder if such places really existed.'

Captain Cavendish's voice drifted into silence and he sat smoking in the dappled light, his eyes focused far away. Frank kept very still. The mouthpiece of his pipe was in his hand but he did not raise it to his lips.

'There are those who say we should leave them to it,' Cavendish said. 'The Pathans. Let them keep the Frontier if they want it so badly. It's nothing but rock and scrub in any case, and they've fought hard enough for it. Kicked our backsides between thirty-nine and forty-two, obviously, and we've never really been able to get control since. Funny thing, isn't it? We marked out the Frontier, along the Durand Line in ninety-three. But like idiots, we drew the border through the middle of the Suleiman Mountains, where it's impossible to police. So all that does is to set the southern edge of Afghanistan, not the northern edge of British India. The tribal Pathans own the border zone, and whenever they feel like it they come down onto the plains and cause havoc. Like a wolf on the fold, and so forth. A dozen uprisings in the last ten years –

if it's not the Mohmands, it's the Zakka Khels, or the Chitralis. When they get bored with killing one another, they start killing us. Dreadfully unsporting.' Cavendish looked up at Frank. 'Why do you think we bother with the place, Gray?'

'Because of the Khyber Pass, sir.'

'Oh, yes? And what about it?'

'It connects British India with Kabul, sir. It's the main trade route for the caravans from Central Asia.'

'Very good.' Cavendish raised his eyebrows. 'Why else is it important?'

'Because of the Russians, sir. They'd like to turn Afghanistan against us. But if we can keep the Khyber Pass open we can always put pressure on Kabul.'

'Excellent. Go to the top of the class.' Cavendish set his pipe aside and sat up on the charpoy. 'I'll tell you something that people don't often appreciate, Gray. We British exercise dominion over one-quarter of the world's surface, yet we have no hostile land borders, with just one exception: the North-West Frontier of India. Now the Russians cause us all sorts of trouble along that frontier, and that's par for the course. We do the same for them. But despite their efforts, in the past we've always managed to keep the lid on things up there, just barely. And how? A clever chap called Warburton came up with the answer to that. Heard of Warburton?'

'Yes, sir. Colonel Warburton. The Political Agent at Peshawar.'

'That's the fellow. You may know that his mother was an Afghan princess, so he speaks Pushtu like a native, like you. He *is* a native, to all intents and purposes, but fortunately he's one of us, too. Now clever Colonel Warburton realised that putting regular troops in the tribal lands only gives the Pathans something to shoot at. So he pulled the garrisons out of the Khyber, and bribed some of the Pathan clans to defend the pass against all the others. He gave them Martini-Henrys and bits and bobs of uniform and one or two British officers, and he called them the Khyber Rifles, but basically they're a bunch of brigands paid to guard against other brigands. Set a thief to catch a thief, d'you see? Risky, but it works. Saves British lives. Saves money. Keeps the Khyber open. It's rather elegant, don't you think?'

Cavendish got to his feet and paced over to the vase of roses in the corner and caressed one blossom with his fingertips.

'But things are changing up there, Gray. Over the past couple of years mullahs have appeared among the tribes, preaching Mahommedan fire and brimstone against all infidels. That changes the rules of the game, because about the one thing that the Pathan clans have in common is their religion. Persuade them to take up arms against the enemies of the Prophet and they'll unite against us. Remember the Mahdi in the Sudan a dozen years back? The tribes of Darfur and the Goz united against us, then murdered Gordon and threw us out. They had a point, I'll admit, but it's an awfully bad example to everyone else in the Empire, especially to other Mahommedans. Next thing you know we'll have a full-scale jihad on our hands, all the way from Khartoum to Kabul.' Cavendish lifted a bloom out of the vase and inhaled its perfume, keeping his back to Frank. 'You can say what you like against the Empire, Gray. But it does at least offer the hope of orderly progress. The North-West Frontier has become the border between the future and the Dark Ages. That's the theory, anyway.'

Cavendish replaced the rose and walked back to his seat.

'The regiment's being posted to Egypt soon,' he said abruptly. 'Sudan's brewing up again. Or did you know that already? How's the barrack room telegraph these days?'

'There's been some talk, sir. I didn't pay it much mind.'

Cavendish grunted. 'Well, it's true. But I won't be going. Not yet at least. They want me to take a look at things on the Frontier, I'll be leaving in a few days. I know those lands, and I know the people, and they know me. I'm Dost Khan, a merchant from Rawalpindi, travelling up to Kabul and back. I haven't been there for a while, but I used to go most years, sometimes twice or even three times. On the way out, I'd take indigo, cotton, tea, some manufactured goods – knives, tools, that kind of thing. Did rather well with sewing machines one year. Coming back I'd bring silks and silver, gold and spices. Somewhere in the middle of the outward trip I'd do a little private barter of my own with the Pathans: Remingtons and the odd Martini-Henry in exchange for information.' He paused. 'I'm getting too old to do this kind of thing alone.'

For the first time Frank saw where this bizarre interview was leading.

'There are British officers up on the Frontier whose Pushtu is passably good,' Cavendish went on. 'But of course they're all chinless wonders from Eton, and besides they're pretty well known to the locals. I need some new blood. I can get you a stripe, probably a couple of them—'

'I can't do it, sir,' Frank said abruptly.

Cavendish stopped in mid-sentence. 'What do you mean, you can't do it?'

'I'm sorry, sir. Truly.'

'Well, I'll be damned.'

'It's not that I wouldn't want to, sir. It's not that.'

217

Cavendish looked hard at him. 'No. I can see it isn't. So what is it, then?'

'I need to . . . stay here, sir.'

'In India? I told you, you'll all be shipped out anyway soon.'

'I need to stay with the regiment, sir. With the Twenty-first.'

'Your *esprit de corps* does you credit, Gray, I'm sure,' Cavendish said drily. 'But I could offer you a way ahead, do you realise that? Unless, of course, you'd prefer to remain a trooper all your life.'

'Sir.'

Cavendish settled back on the charpoy, took up his pipe again. 'I won't order you, Gray. But I confess, I'm disappointed. I don't often mistake my man.'

Frank said nothing.

'All right, Gray. You can go.'

Frank got up and walked back through the house to where Ali held the front door open for him. He stepped out of the subtle gloom and into the flat glare of the afternoon. He rode slowly back through the cantonment. He was a little dizzy from the hashish and his head ached. He could so easily have said yes. And if he had? Cavendish's offer might indeed have opened a future for him. For a second he glimpsed himself winning something beyond bitter revenge – he might even return to England one day a made man, a man with prospects. The sort of man for whom no prize was out of reach. He shook himself angrily.

He trotted the horse into the cool shade of the stable block. As he swung himself out of the saddle two native grooms came running up, followed at a more dignified pace by Darmindar, one of the older syces. Frank slid the carbine out of the saddle bucket and let the boys take the reins from him and lead the horse away.

'Clean rifle, sahib?' Darmindar asked.

'It's all right. I like to do it.'

Frank took the weapon outside, slid down on his haunches in the shade of the stable block wall. He worked the cocking lever to open the breech and tipped a little Rangoon oil into the mechanism, unclipped the cleaning rod, squinted along the barrel and blew down it. Looking up, he saw that Darmindar had followed him and was standing quietly over him.

'What?'

'I have news from Bengaluru,' Darmindar said, 'from Mr Javed.'

53

Mrs Desai poured weak tea for Frank and Javed from a floral china pot. She was a handsome woman in her thirties wearing a saffron sari. She bobbed her head and smiled at them as she filled their cups.

Ashok pushed the plate across the table to Frank. 'Dundee cake, old man?'

Frank took a fragment of the moist cake. On the plate was painted a thatched cottage in the snow with a coach-and-four rattling past. It was very hot in Ashok's room and the barking of dogs drifted in from the crowded night.

Ashok said, 'Major Briggs-Spicer is our catering officer, you know. An excellent chap. He is a very great friend, and it is Briggs-Spicer who is pressing these items upon me. In our mess we have abundance of such fine products from home. We have indeed . . .' he waved an airy hand, 'superfluity.'

On the table before them stood a pot of Cooper's Oxford Marmalade, a tin box of Yorkshire tea and a bottle of Sandeman's port. In pride of place on the wall hung a photograph of Queen Victoria, looking like a dour sphinx, and beneath it the crossed flags of the Union and of the Northamptonshire Regiment.

Ashok said, 'You know, Frank, old boy, I am now mess steward for this most excellent Northamptonshire regiment. One day soon I shall visit Northampton. A beautiful village in the old country, you know. You have been to Northampton?'

'No.'

'I have many good friends in the officer class there. I shall be made welcome.'

Frank toyed with the image of Ashok seeking out his friends of the officer class among the leafier suburbs of Northampton. He felt sorry for Ashok, playing the sahib in his neat Western trousers and his white shirt. Ashok's mixed parentage was clear now that he was older. His hair was reddish and the moustache which he had grown in imitation of the British officers he so admired was flaxen against his olive skin.

'Your Uncle Mohinda was a mess steward with the Fourth Hussars,' Javed interrupted in Kannada, not troubling to hide his impatience. 'Isn't that so?'

'Uncle Mohinda is sadly deceased,' Ashok told him, persisting in English. 'I am now the senior gentleman of the family.'

'But your uncle used to work with the Fourth?' Frank said. 'That's right, isn't it?'

'Oh, yes, indeed.'

'There's a man I want to trace, Ashok. An officer.'

'Really? Who is this man?'

'I don't know. That's my problem. I don't know his full name or his rank. About all I do know is that while your uncle was working in the Officers' Mess of the Fourth Hussars this man was seconded to the Fourth from the Twenty-first.'

'Seconded, you say?' Ashok made a show of interest.

'Seconded, or transferred, or he came on some assignment. I don't know why he was there. Perhaps he was looking for more action than he was getting in the Twenty-first. I need you to tell me if your uncle knew this man, or heard something about him.'

Ashok opened his hands helplessly. 'Naturally I should like very much to help. We English must stick together. But Uncle Mohinda did not discuss such matters with me. I was quite young, you understand.'

'Ashok, it's very important to me that—'

'We have enjoyed some japes in the past, isn't it, Frank?' Ashok laughed gaily, the subject already dismissed. 'Let us talk of those times.'

Javed said, 'We're wasting our time.'

'Listen to me, Ashok,' Frank persisted, 'a little over three years ago the officer I am looking for was with the Fourth Hussars, however briefly. Someone there must have known something about him. The Officers' Mess of a cavalry regiment isn't large.'

'But many officers came to the Fourth Hussars, Frank, old chap! A most splendid regiment.'

'This particular officer would have left the Officers' Mess suddenly. I can even tell you when. It would have been just after the night the three of us rode the train. Remember that? I know this man couldn't return to the mess of the Fourth Hussars because he was wounded in a shooting, and I know *that* because I shot him. Do you understand me?'

'Indeed, Frank, old boy, a most stirring tale, but—'

'And he never did come back to the Fourth. Now, perhaps your Uncle Mohinda heard some story about all this. Perhaps there were rumours. Rumours of a scandal, maybe. The mess stewards always know of these things. Think.'

Ashok rocked his head. 'It is a time long past.'

'He doesn't know anything,' Javed said in contempt.

Mrs Desai touched her son's shoulder and murmured to him.

'You are quite right, Mama. Time slips, isn't it?' Ashok got to his feet and held out his hand to Frank. 'But I shall rack the jolly memory, Frank. Now duty calls, as they say, and I must guard my loins, ha ha! Please, friends, finish your tea.'

He ducked out of the room. Mrs Desai smiled her vacant smile, moved the cups around, fussed with the teapot.

Javed said, 'I'm sorry, Frank. He told me he might have something useful for you. Idiot.'

'My son is consumed with the desire to please you,' Mrs Desai said in clear English, catching them both by surprise. She sat down facing them, no longer the smiling and subservient woman of the house. 'That is why he tells you that he has information when he does not.'

Frank said: 'Mrs Desai—'

'He wishes to please you so that you will like him, as you did not when he was a child,' she went on, as if he had not spoken. 'But you will never like him, because he is a foolish boy and a half-caste.' She folded her hands calmly in front of her. 'Is that not true?'

Frank looked into her eyes. The hostility he saw there shamed him.

'I do not have reason to love the British,' Mrs Desai went on in her musical English. 'I have seen others like you, Frank Gray, with your handsome faces and your fine uniforms and your empty promises. We are descended from kings, we Desais, and yet it was my profession to pleasure the British soldiers, as it had been my mother's profession before me.' She waited, as if daring Frank to express the merest flicker of disapproval. When he did not, she produced from the folds of her sari a tiny sepia photograph of a smiling man with a neatly trimmed moustache, his face shaded by a cork sun helmet. She held the picture out for him to see. 'But with this one, I made a mistake. I allowed myself to believe that I loved him. He only ever beat me when he had taken too much drink. Sometimes he made me laugh. Also, he was wealthy, or so I thought, and he made promises to me, which I wanted to believe. I had Ashok to support, you understand.' She paused. 'He was Captain John Herrick, then serving with the Fourth Hussars. He had come from another regiment. I don't know which. Possibly the Twenty-first.'

Frank felt a pulse start to tap in his throat. 'When was this?'

'Three years ago. A little more.' She made a weary gesture. 'Yes, yes, of course he's the one you seek. He disappeared the night that you two and Ashok took part in that foolery with the train. I recall because Ashok came home that night with many cuts and bruises, cursing you and all your kind. That same night Mohinda, my brother, brought news that one of the officers had been transferred suddenly. I remember that Mohinda thought this strange, even though officers were coming and going all the time. I did not realise until the next night, when John did not send for me as usual, that he was the officer concerned.'

'John Herrick.' Frank repeated the name softly to himself. 'Jack Herrick.'

'I have heard him called so.' She adjusted the folds of her sari. 'He said he was from a city called Grimsby. Is that truly a city in England?'

Frank stared at the photograph, the confident face with its dark wings of moustache. He reached out for the snapshot but she moved quickly to put it away in the folds of her sari.

'John told me that Grimsby was a place of golden domes with a castle of white marble,' she said. 'No doubt that also was a lie. In any case I never saw him again after that night, and he left no word. Mohinda told me he did not even return for his things. They were packed and sent on somewhere. I don't know where, perhaps back to his own regiment. I was merely a nautch girl, and no one discussed such things with me. But there was a story that Colonel James was very angry with him for something he had done.'

'There's no one by the name of Herrick with the Twenty-first now.'

Mrs Desai shrugged. 'With this, I cannot help you.' She rose to her feet. 'I am not sure why I help you at all. It is only that liars and deceivers should not go unpunished, and I have a sense that you understand this, Frank Gray. Perhaps you are the instrument of God.'

'Don't go. Please. What was he like, this man?'

'Does it matter? They are all the same under the uniform.' She gathered her saffron folds around her and swept from the room.

54

It was night when they left Ashok's house to walk in silence through the hot and crowded alleys. Old men squatted in doorways, sharing pipes and watching them, their attention drawn by Frank's uniform. Half-naked children ran after them in a gaggle before scampering off. Tethered oxen chewed dry stalks and a dead dog lay bloating in a ditch.

Javed pointed down a sinuous laneway. 'I go this way. My family will be wondering where I am.'

'I'm obliged to you, Javed.'

'It is too early for thanks. You have not yet found your man.'

'Now I know his name, at least.'

Javed looked thoughtfully at him. 'What will you do with this precious name, Frank, now that you have learned it?'

'I shall find the man who bears it.'

'And then what?'

Frank did not reply.

'You think your search is almost over,' Javed said, 'but to seek knowledge is one thing. To understand how to use it is another. We do not control fate, my friend. But to each of us sooner or later falls a choice: whether we will add to the world's pain or the world's joy.'

'You've become a philosopher, Javed.'

'Not long ago I was an urchin and a petty thief, slinking around alleys like these. But then came my inheritance. The friends I had then said I should gamble the cash, buy women with it, live in idleness as long as it lasted. But I turned my back on them and took over my uncle's business. Also his family. Now they look to me to provide for them. It was a good decision.'

'You're a lucky man, Javed. Your future was presented to you.'

'Perhaps yours would be also, if you did not blind yourself to it. What will you do now?'

'Get a train back to Secunderabad. My pass runs out tomorrow night.'

'And then?'

'I shall see if anyone in the regiment knows a man called John Herrick.'

Javed put out his hand and gripped Frank's arm. 'You want my advice? Go back to robbing trains.'

Frank waited until Javed's slender back had slipped away out of sight among the press of beggars and street vendors. Then he walked on until he struck a wider street, and swung himself onto the back of a passing ox cart. He gave the startled driver a few annas and brief directions. He settled himself between sacks of rice and the cart jolted him out of the stinking crush of the native town, past the civil lines with their neat bungalows where he had once lived, and on towards Cantonment Station. He lay back against the sacks and gazed up at the indigo sky.

55

The following day was closing before the endless jolting journey came to an end. Frank took a tonga from Secunderabad Station but told the driver to drop him by the roadside and walked the last mile back to the cavalry lines, and along the dusty roads to the barracks. It was still an hour before lights out, and Frank could see men lounging around the building, smoking and talking. He climbed onto the veranda by the side steps and made his way around until he found Tranter and Gannon near the corner taking the cool of the evening, their feet up and their chairs tilted back.

'Here's our boy,' Tranter said, pushing up the brim of his cap to look at him. 'Young Darkie Gray, sloping back from some shady business he won't tell us about. Eh, Darkie?'

Frank squatted with his back against the railings, facing the two of them. 'Herrick,' he said.

'Herrick, is it?' Gannon blew through the mouthpiece of his pipe, making it whistle. 'That was years since.'

Tranter said, 'Before my time.'

'Who was he?'

Gannon blew through the pipe again. 'Well, if it's the same cove you're talking of, he was a captain, with C Troop as I recall.'

'And did they call him Jack?'

'All Johns are Jacks, are they not? I heard him called Long John, on account of his being six foot high and more. And because he had an eye for the ladies, if you take my meaning.'

Tranter laughed, but something in the atmosphere on the dark veranda touched him and he stopped.

'You never mentioned him before,' Frank said.

'Like I said, it was years since. And you may believe it or not, young Darkie, but we don't spend our every waking moment concerned with your searchings. We might be more inclined, if you ever levelled with us about why you really want to find him.'

'Tell me about Herrick.'

Gannon shrugged. 'One of those characters who could charm the birds out of the trees if he was of a mind, but with a temper on him. Could be a stickler. Restless type, too.'

'And where is he now?'

'Got himself posted off.' Gannon got up and knocked the dottle from his pipe into the hibiscus. 'I heard he was serving with some native regiment up on the Khyber.'

Frank looked up sharply. 'He's on the Frontier?'

'If there's another Khyber Pass I've yet to hear of it.'

'Is he still there?'

'He never come back here.'

Frank got to his feet but Gannon shot out one hand and gripped his arm. 'You weren't thinking of going nowhere, were ye, young Darkie?'

'Let me be.'

'It'll be lights out in half an hour.'

'I'll be back before I'm missed. No one will even know I've gone.'

'You'll get your fucking self banged up in the corner shop and us on a charge, so you will. I waited a long time for these stripes and I don't plan on losing them.'

'I have to go, Mick.'

Gannon held Frank's arm a second or two longer, then released his grip and stood back from the rail. 'Go on, then. We didn't see ye.'

Frank dropped into the hot darkness below. He pulled off his boots, left them by the corner of the building and set off, running steadily. He kept to the back lanes of the cantonment and loped silently under the vast sky with its shoals of stars. Once he startled a jackal raiding rubbish behind some native huts; the animal glared at him with demon's eyes and slunk away into the night.

There was a light burning somewhere deep inside Cavendish's bungalow. Otherwise the place was shuttered and in darkness. Frank prowled around the perimeter, keeping to the shadow of the hedge. The dust was cool under his bare feet. The dark garden was filled with the perfume of roses and jasmine and the air hummed with moths. He slipped in through the gate and put his foot on the bottom tread of the veranda steps.

'So you've changed your mind,' Cavendish said.

He was seated in a wicker chair in the shadows at the end of the veranda. The blanket over his knees made him look like an invalid, but when he got to his feet Frank saw that he was in uniform, his leather cross-straps gleaming. Cavendish leaned over the rail to look down at him.

'You cut it fine enough. Do you want to tell me the reason for this Damascene conversion, Gray?'

'No, sir.'

'No, I didn't think you would.' Cavendish stretched, yawned, not much interested. 'Very well. If you can get back to your barracks without being shot, we'll see if this bird will fly. Report for sick parade tomorrow morning. I'll warn the MO. Then wait in barracks and you'll get word from me during the day.'

'Thank you, sir.'

'Don't thank me. We'll be away for months.' Cavendish opened the bungalow's back door and made to step through it but stopped with his hand on the jamb and looked back. 'Which reminds me. You should write to the girl.'

'Sir?'

'Grace, isn't it? You're in love with her, I suppose? Well, she may never get word from you again.'

Frank stared at him.

'Come, come, Gray,' Cavendish said, tiredly. 'You've scribbled about half a ream to her, you might as well post something. What's the problem? Is it a secret passion? Does the beloved not know?'

Frank was too surprised not to answer truthfully. 'I can't write to her directly, sir.'

'There must be someone who can get word to her, surely to God. You might be dead in a month. Either pledge your undying troth, or put the poor girl out of her misery.' When Frank said nothing Cavendish turned away, waving an impatient hand over his shoulder. 'I'm a romantic, Gray. Indulge me.'

He went into the bungalow and closed the door behind him.

56

The cab clattered across the Marienbrücke, the Danube Canal flashing below in the bleak afternoon light. Quite soon they left the gilded domes of the city centre behind and were rattling through commercial districts which were at first merely dreary, and then increasingly shabby as they moved further east. At length the cabbie turned left into a street overshadowed by boarding houses and cheap apartment blocks. He reined in the pony and leaned down from the box.

'You sure this is the church you want, miss?'

Even though she had taken care to dress simply, she could see the driver looking at her clothes, taking in their cut and quality.

'The Church of St Nicholas,' she said. 'I don't see it.'

'Down the alleyway.' He pointed with his whip. 'But there's more than one Church of St Nicholas in Vienna, miss. And pretty well all of them are in better districts than this.'

A chipped enamel street sign in Gothic script hung from the wall. On it Grace read the name *Polengasse*. 'This is the one I want.'

The driver tilted his head in a gesture which said that he had done all he could, and unhooked the door with the handle of his whip. She got out and paid him, and stepped across to the mouth of the alleyway. She refused to look back as the cab rattled away, leaving her alone on the cobbles.

It was cold and sleet had begun to fall from the white November sky. The narrow street was slick under a slurry of horse dung, and it was dark between the looming tenements. She could see nobody, but she had the uncomfortable feeling that she was being watched from the dim windows above. She set out briskly down the alley. It opened into a small square with an ancient fountain in the centre. Water leaked from the cracked basin and trickled away over the cobbles. There were few windows in the buildings and no lights that she could see in any of them. Two ragged men sat in a doorway, passing a bottle wrapped in sacking between them. Some barefoot children playing on a stairway stopped to stare at her.

The church with its squat tower bounded one side of the square. Grace walked up the steps into the porch and pushed on double wooden doors that hung a little open. It was dark inside, but she was glad to put the bleak and watchful square behind her, and she stood leaning on the rearmost pew for a moment, recovering her courage. It took her a moment to see the faint wash of light from beneath a door in the opposite wall. And now she could hear noises: a murmur of voices, wheezy coughing, and a sudden hoarse cry which shrank away at once. She walked to the door and thrust it open.

The hall was half-derelict, not much more than a huge wooden lean-to with a sheet-tin roof, propped against what would have been the outer wall of the church. She saw ranks of beds, perhaps forty of them, with humped shapes in each. Oil lamps were set at intervals, or hung from hooks in the rafters, and a glowing iron brazier stood at one end of the space. She smelled the acrid smoke from the coals, and the stink of unwashed bodies, and excrement. People were coughing, spitting, groaning.

A man and a girl were stooped over a bed not far from where she stood. The girl wore a nurse's uniform of blue and white. An old woman in the bed was struggling, crying out, and the others seemed to be trying to calm her. Grace glimpsed an open mouth and white eyes, a flailing arm quickly caught and held.

'Grace?'

Max Krauss appeared beside her. He was wearing a stained white coat, and he looked older than when she had last seen him at Willi's two weeks before. Now his face was set into hard lines, and his eyes were tired behind the round glasses.

'Good evening, Max.'

'What are you doing here, Grace?'

'A fine greeting!' She started to laugh, but his expression did not change and she stopped. 'I wanted to see your hospital, Max. To see your work. Every time we meet you speak so passionately about it.'

'I have no time to . . .' He pushed one hand through his hair. 'Grace, talking at Willi's elegant house is one thing. But this is not some exhibition.'

'Of course not.' Mentally she took a step back. 'Perhaps I should have sent word.'

'Yes, yes. That would be better.'

'Please don't misunderstand. I want to help, if I can.'

'A rich young society girl from England? What could you do? Read poetry to them?'

'That is disagreeable of you.'

'I have not the luxury of being agreeable at present. Even of being polite. There is an influenza epidemic, perhaps you have heard. People are dying.'

'There must be something I can do.'

He looked at her, the disbelief still in his eyes. 'You're serious?'

'Certainly.'

He hesitated. 'Very well. Come with me.'

He strode across the room, his white coat flapping. She followed, half-running to keep up. The man and the nurse still stood at the bedside, but the old woman in the bed was quiet now, her eyes half-open in vacant slits, her face the colour of whey. She was clothed in what looked like an ancient army greatcoat, her hands and wrists filthy where they protruded from the cuffs. Her hair was grey and she stank.

'She'll be quiet now, Max,' the man said. 'Rosa has given her morphine.'

Grace recognised him now; Ferdinand from the café, the bad Balkan poet. Here he looked much less romantic in a work apron over old clothes, his long hair stuffed up under a greasy woollen cap. Beside him the young woman called Rosa, severe in her nurse's dress, stood holding a basin of clean water and a towel. She was plain, with a pale, flat face. She stared at Max and then, with gathering hostility, at Grace.

'She has come to . . . help,' Max told them.

Grace detected the faltering in his voice, as if he were beginning to think better of this, like a man who recognises his point has been made and he needs go no further. She stepped past him and said firmly to the other two, 'Give me something to do, please.'

Rosa said, 'You have nursing experience?'

'None.'

The other girl's lips thinned. 'I suppose you know how to wash someone, at least.'

'I suppose I do.'

'So wash Lisl here.'

She thrust the basin and towel into Grace's arms and strode away between the beds, her heels clicking imperiously on the floor. Ferdinand gave Grace a weak smile, but he followed Rosa.

Grace sat on the edge of the old woman's bed. She could feel Max still standing behind her, but she ignored him and started to unbutton the greatcoat, concentrating fiercely on the task. The skin of the woman's chest was tea-brown with filth. Grace moistened the towel and began to wipe at it. She had no clear idea of what she was doing. She could hear the breath whistling in Lisl's congested lungs and could see the flutter of her heart between the sunken ribs. Lice ran glinting in the folds of her clothing and the exposed body gave off a stench of mingled urine, shit and alcohol. Grace stopped for a moment, swallowed hard.

'Lisl has tuberculosis,' Max said from behind her. His voice was no longer hard. 'She has syphilis too, being a prostitute. With the influenza she'll be dead in a day or two. But still, she needs to be washed.'

'I understand that, Max,' Grace snapped. She began again, dabbing uselessly at the foul skin. 'Why don't you go about your business? I'm sure other people need you.'

But he did not leave.

'We know Lisl quite well,' he said quietly. 'She is thirty-four years old.'

Grace bowed her head, squeezing her eyes shut. She clenched the cloth so tightly in her fist that water ran tinkling out of it into the bowl.

Max said, 'Grace—'

Lisl convulsed, upsetting the basin over the bed, and vomited over Grace's hands and arms.

Grace was dimly aware of people running, of the ringing of the fallen basin on the stone floor, and of her own flight between the beds, the hot stench of vomit running with her like some loathsome dog. She didn't remember bursting out into the bitter evening nor crossing the square, but when she came properly to herself she was standing at the broken fountain, scooping icy water over her hands and washing and washing again as if in a frantic religious ritual. It was very cold out here, and her breath plumed, but the clean astringent feel of it in her lungs was a relief to her. She splashed icy water over her face, and tilted her head up to the sharp stars.

Max came up behind her and draped a coat over her shoulders. 'I am sorry, Grace. I should not have . . . we are all very tired, you see.'

'I did not come here for these people,' she said. She did not look at him.

'You don't need to explain this.'

'I came for myself, Max. I came so that I could tell myself how virtuous I am. And to show you, I suppose.' She faced him, holding the lapels of the coat together at her throat. 'You knew that.'

'At least you came. Almost no one does.'

'How is she? How is Lisl?'

'She is dead. And there will be more tonight.' He breathed deeply. 'Come. I will have Ferdinand see you home.'

'I am not going home.' She swung the coat off her shoulders and handed it back to him.

57

Matilde bustled into the hall as the sleepy footman let Grace in and locked the door behind her.

'Goodness, Miss Grace! How late it is! The Princess left for the reception hours ago.'

'There was a reception? I had forgotten.'

'We wondered what had happened to you, miss.'

'I was detained.' Grace took off her jacket and saw the maid's face change as she took it from her. 'It stinks, rather, doesn't it? Have my clothes washed first thing tomorrow, Matilde, would you? I'll leave them outside my door.'

'Certainly, miss. And I shall have some warm water sent up.'

'Yes, I stink a little too, I shouldn't wonder. Oh, and Matilde, I shall need some working clothes. Maidservants' clothes, that sort of thing. Two or three changes.'

'You are going to a fancy dress party, perhaps, Miss Grace? Ah, I have always loved—'

'I shall be working at the hospital some evenings. Perhaps several evenings a week.'

Matilde blinked at her. 'At Dr Krauss's poor ward?'

'Precisely.'

Grace left the woman standing at the foot of the stairs and went smiling up to her room, pleased to have shocked her.

Once inside she stripped off her stained and crumpled clothes. She could still smell the ward on the garments – the smoke of the brazier, the tang of carbolic, traces of human filth. A few short hours ago this had revolted her to the point of nausea, but she knew that she had crossed a line when she had walked back into that pitiful ward tonight, and it was the line which marked the furthest boundary of her girlhood. She was a woman now, a complete woman. Every slopping bed pan she had emptied had confirmed it, and every soiled blanket she had changed. The others in the hospital all knew it, too. She had detected it even in Rosa's chilly stare. Once, late in the evening, she had caught Max looking at her thoughtfully across the room, and it was that one look which stayed with her now. Her instinct had been right; he was a strong young man under his modesty and shyness. A man with ideals. Yes, it was good to have the respect of a man like that.

She heard a footfall outside and someone knocked lightly. She slipped into a nightgown and opened the door to Matilde, who stood with a hastily roused maid behind her. The girl held a ewer of steaming water.

'I'm having some more water warmed, miss.' Matilde had recovered her authority. 'You'd probably like a proper bath, so I've brought Olga to help you.'

Grace took the jug. 'I shan't be needing Olga, so she may go back to bed. And this is quite enough water, thank you. Good night.'

Grace was in the act of closing the door when Matilde spoke again. 'Oh, one other thing, miss. A letter came for you earlier. From abroad? I thought perhaps you'd like to have it now.'

Grace straightened while Matilde patted her pockets, tut-tutting to herself.

'Well? Where is it?' Grace demanded.

'Yes, yes. Here it is.' Matilde produced a white envelope, holding it so that Grace could not see who had written the address. 'Good news, I hope, miss.'

Grace snatched the letter and closed the door hard. She leaned back against the wood and turned the envelope over, and her heart dropped. The letter was from her mother. The handwriting told her that at once. She ripped it open. News from the parish. Complaints about the servants. Gossip.

Grace released a breath she did not realise she had been holding and walked across the room to the window, tossing the letter onto the bed as she went. Outside, the canted rooftops lay paved with moonlight. She was suddenly wide awake, jagged feelings clashing in her mind: disappointment, anger, and most of all a sad species of guilt. She had been too busy tonight, she reasoned, and her experiences had been too vivid. That would be why she hadn't once thought of Frank Gray.

58

Under the blankets Grace could see only a little of the child's face. She was so very small, less than a week old, her skin as puckered now as it must have been at the moment of birth. Grace did not like to imagine that birth, on the cold cobblestones of a back alley, in mud and garbage. Someone had left the baby girl in the church porch, where Grace herself had found the mewling bundle on her way into the hospital four days earlier. That seemed to make the child her special charge, and as soon as she arrived each day Grace would hurry up to the crib in the warm space close to the iron brazier. When time allowed she took pleasure in changing the baby or feeding her, in watching her gain in strength day by day. Rosa had found a place for the child at a convent orphanage, and Grace knew she would miss her, and had prepared herself for that.

But not for this.

'They'll have to take her soon,' Rosa said, the effort of unaccustomed gentleness making her awkward. 'But we thought you'd want to see her first.'

'Thank you.'

'She started to convulse about an hour ago. She didn't suffer long. I've washed her.'

'Thank you,' Grace said again, as if this service had been performed for her benefit, as perhaps it had.

Rosa still hovered. 'It's all right to look at her, but it would be best if you didn't . . . Infection, and so on. Since we don't know what it was . . .' Her voice trailed off, and she marched away between the beds.

Grace sat down on the stool beside the crib, and folded the blanket back to look at the tiny blue face. She had hoped the child would look peaceful, but her expression was ugly and furious. As well it might be, Grace thought, and she began to weep, soundlessly, so that at first she was not aware of it herself. She didn't know how long this went on; longer, certainly, than she realised at the time. Finally she grew aware of a tall figure beside her, and Max rested his hand on her shoulder.

'I should have seen enough over the last few weeks,' she said, struggling to control her tears. 'I shouldn't be acting like this.'

'Everyone acts so, sometimes. If they do not, they should not be in this work.' Max took his glasses off and polished them. 'But perhaps you should not stay this evening.'

'If I could just stop crying.'

Ferdinand came past them, leading an elderly man in dark clothes whom Grace did not recognise. The man was holding his hat against his chest and carrying a large black leather bag. He set both hat and bag down on the floor, stooped over the dead child and inspected her briefly. Without ceremony he flipped the blanket back over the wrinkled face.

Grace said, 'Don't!' and started to rise.

Max gripped her elbow firmly and urged her away. She looked at him a little wildly, but his grip tightened.

'Come with me.' He was already steering her to the door and out into the chill porch of the church. 'Get your coat, please.'

She twisted her arm free of his. 'Max, I will not be sent home like a naughty child.'

'I have a little schnapps.'

'I hate schnapps.'

'You need some. Perhaps I also.' He took off his glasses and massaged the bridge of his nose. 'We will go to my room. It is just across the square. Drink a glass of schnapps. Come back to work. This will be best.'

He looked utterly spent. She realised that her own distress had blinded her to this and felt guilty. Probably he really did need a few minutes' rest as badly as she did, and probably he was past the point of considering how it would look to take her to his room, alone. Or perhaps he simply didn't care to pretend any more. In that case, she thought suddenly, neither did she. She pulled on her coat.

They pushed out of the church door into the cramped little square. On all sides the tenements rose like dark cliffs. It was bitterly cold and ice crusted the puddles. Max led her across the cobbles to a stairway in the angle of the wall opposite.

On the bottom step he hesitated. 'We do not have to go in, Grace, if you do not wish it.'

'You promised me a glass of schnapps.' She suspected that people often disappointed Max, and she was determined she was not going to be one of them. She pushed past him and started up the stairs. 'Come along.'

The stairwell was dark and smelled of mould and boiled vegetables. There were four doors on each landing, several of them boarded up, one or two standing open to reveal discarded clothing, litter, broken furniture. Grace heard babies crying, a woman singing in a cracked voice, and once a couple screaming at one another. On the top landing sat two old ragged women, rocking together. Max crouched to speak to them. She couldn't hear what he said, but his voice was gentle, and they smiled at him with rheumy eyes. He held his hand down to Grace and she stepped past the women, catching the sour stink of their unwashed bodies.

Max's room was small and utterly bare of comfort. Light from the night sky crept in from a roof window thick with dirt and pigeon droppings. In the dimness she saw bare boards, a mattress against one wall with blankets folded neatly on it, makeshift shelves loaded with books, and a desk of sorts. Max had rigged a rail across one corner of the room and from this hung his few clothes.

He pulled the hardback chair out from under the desk and she sat very straight upon it as he fussed with a small oil lamp. He lit it and their breath steamed in the shining disc of light. Max found a bottle and two glasses, polished one of the glasses on his sleeve, filled it and gave it to her. She nodded her thanks but did not drink at once. Instead, she got to her feet and moved around the little room, holding the glass between her palms.

There was a single picture tacked up above the bookshelves, a pen-and-ink sketch cut from an old issue of a German radical magazine, yellow with age. It showed a bearded man in an ornate uniform stretched out on the street beside the wreckage of a carriage, his mouth open, his suffering martyr's eyes lifted to heaven. He lay in a pool of blood, his booted right leg twisted impossibly under him and his left leg detached. Around him on the paving lay broken sabres and helmets, and in the background crippled horses and human bodies lay tangled. The caption read in German, *13 March 1881: the tyrant Tsar Alexander II pays for his crimes!*

She said, 'Why do you keep such a horrible picture?'

'To remind me of the price that must be paid.'

'But Alexander was the Tsar who freed the serfs. What was the point of murdering him?'

'The man was from a dynasty of monsters. He made concessions in the hope of retaining power for a few years more, that's all.'

She stood staring at the picture, confused and revolted by it. 'I don't believe anyone deserves this.'

'I take no joy in the tyrant's agony, Grace. But by killing him the assassins will have saved many more lives than they have taken. Capitalism will only be brought down by revolution. I wish it were otherwise, but those who hold power do not give it up voluntarily.'

The form of his words brought to mind another bare room, and in an instant she was in Mrs Rossiter's cottage again, the day she had ridden up to find Frank. She heard Frank making the same assertion Max had just made. No one gives up power without a fight. At the time she had cared less about his words than about the dusting of green leaves she had seen on the trees through the window behind him and the way the dappled light moved over his face.

She suddenly wondered what she was doing here in this tawdry apartment in Vienna, with this quiet, intense, unexpectedly attractive young man. No, she corrected herself; she suddenly understood exactly what she was doing here.

Max misread her silence. 'The picture upsets you, I believe. I am sorry to make more sorrow for you, Grace. This was not my meaning. I

234

do not wish pain or suffering for any people. But something must be done, do you see? While we sit talking our theories in our salons, people are starving and dying. You see it here at the hospital every day. The change is not made by talk, but by action. It distresses me much, but it is so. Yet it distresses me also if we disagree, you and I.'

She looked at him. It did distress him, and profoundly, she could see that. She had never been in doubt about his intelligence and his integrity: they were attributes plain to everyone. But she had never seen this vulnerability in him before. And yet she felt that she had been expecting it, like a hoped-for guest, the fondest friend of all who always arrives late.

'It distresses me, too,' she said. 'I should wish us to agree on many things.'

Her lungs felt large and the air which filled them was cold and thrilling. Out in the stairwell a woman shouted and something clattered down the steps and a door slammed. Anxious to do something with her hands, Grace sipped her schnapps. It burned her mouth and she grimaced and put the glass aside.

'I have learned a little, perhaps,' Max began again, and stopped.

She stepped closer to him. An odd tingling was spreading up from the roots of her spine. 'What have you learned, Max?'

He made a small, uncertain movement with his hands. 'I am twenty-seven years old and I have studied in universities. I have travelled. Yes, some things I have learned. But this, I have not learned. There never was the time, it seems.' He reached out to her and clumsily gripped her hands. 'This was not my intent in bringing you up here, Grace, and yet I have become to think of you so that my mind is not ever still. You must not let me speak when this is offending to you.'

'It is not offending to me, Max. It is not offending at all.'

'Then you know what I would wish for us, dear Grace.' There was wonder in his eyes, as if he could not quite believe she had not already rejected him. 'And perhaps you could wish it also?'

'Perhaps I could.' She gripped his hands hard. 'But I cannot, Max. Not yet.'

'There is, perhaps, someone else?'

'I have made a promise.'

'To a man?'

'To myself. To Willi, in a way. It's foolishness, but I wish to keep that promise.'

He gazed at her with those candid hazel eyes. 'Your promise will bind you for ever?'

'I shall know the answer to that question soon.'

'And am I permitted to ask how soon that may be?'

She lifted her chin, stepped away from him and released his hands. 'We should go to work.'

59

Grace reached home a little before midnight. To her annoyance it was Matilde herself who opened the front door and took her outdoor clothes, fussing around her with her false and implacable cheerfulness.

'My, my, miss. Out late again! Working at the hospital, were you?'

Grace ignored her. She would have gone straight upstairs to her room, but she noticed that the door of the library was open and that a light still shone in there.

'The Princess, miss,' Matilde said before Grace could ask. 'She came home early tonight, a little unwell. It's nothing, I believe. I've just fetched her a cognac. Would you care for one, perhaps? I can—'

'No. Thank you.'

Grace walked to the library door and looked in. Willi was sitting by the fire reading a magazine, spectacles on her nose. Grace did not think she had ever seen her look quite so domestic. Willi looked up and smiled.

'Grace, my rose. I wondered if I might see you. We keep such different hours these days. Come in and talk to me for a moment.'

Willi patted the cushions of the opposite chair, and Grace sat down. After the chill of the night the fire was a delight.

'Matilde said you were unwell.'

'It was only a headache, my dear, and mostly of the tactical variety. I was dining at the dreadful Geisslers – you know, those people who own half of South America? Or is it Africa? One forgets.' Willi waved one hand to dismiss the memory of the loathsome Geisslers. 'Shall I get Matilde to fetch you something?'

'She has already asked me.' Grace glanced towards the door. In the hall she could still hear Matilde occupied at some task which kept her within earshot, humming to herself. 'Does that woman never sleep?'

'You don't like our Matilde a great deal, I think.'

'I'm afraid I don't.'

'She can be . . . somewhat too familiar.' Willi took off her spectacles and closed her magazine. 'Probably she's been with me too long.'

Grace thought back to her first night at the hospital three weeks earlier, the pitcher of warm water, the sleepy maid summoned from

236

bed, and Matilde holding out her letter, smiling maliciously, knowing it was not the letter she longed for.

Grace said, 'She knows I've been hoping for news.'

'My dear, one can't keep such things from the servants. They know everything. Far more than we do, generally.' Willi tilted her head to look at Grace. 'Are you really still wishing for word from your soldier-boy? I thought perhaps you might have found something to take your mind off him.'

Grace said nothing.

'Well, of course, I realise your work at the hospital is entirely selfless,' Willi went on. 'You really do dress up like some gamine scullery maid solely in order to scrub floors and empty bedpans for the proletariat.'

'I try to help. That's all.'

'It's quite by chance that you look ravishing in that costume, then? And presumably the presence of the noble Doctor Krauss isn't of any interest to you one way or the other.' Willi laughed, reached across to touch her knee. 'Oh, please don't take offence, my dear. I'm teasing, and it's cruel of me. But I must say, I know where my own attentions would be tending if I were your age. Max is a fine young man. A fine young man.'

Grace stared into the fire. She said, 'If Frank hasn't sent word by now, he doesn't care for me. That's true, isn't it?'

'I'm afraid so.' Willi sighed. 'I have said so myself many times. On the other hand, a bargain is a bargain.'

Grace looked up at her, surprised. 'You mean I should wait?'

'Give your knight errant until Christmas. That's what we agreed. I confess, such scruples would have counted for little with me, but you? You'll never be able to live with yourself if you don't wait.'

'And then?'

'Then you must follow your heart, of course.'

60

Captain Cavendish dumped his valise and a small canvas grip in the overhead rack and pulled down the blinds against the din of Secunderabad Station. He settled into the window seat opposite Frank, took out a book, and at once began to read.

Frank had travelled through this terminus more than once recently but this time for some reason he found himself thinking back to that day at Bangalore City Station, years ago, before the world had changed. He remembered Gifford towing his father towards the engine, a blue-turbaned engineer, the dashing Mr Stokes with his easy elegance. That other platform, like this one, had been a chaos of hissing steam, shouting porters, food vendors crying their wares and selling water from different pitchers for Hindus or Moslems: *Hindi pani, Mussulman pani!* He rested his head back against the leather upholstery and closed his eyes.

In the corridor he could hear British officers cursing while servants manhandled their cases. The compartment was stiflingly hot, though the lowered blinds kept out the worst of the noon glare. A wheel of wet straw was mounted on a bracket on the ceiling and Frank hoped that would help cool things down once they got moving. 'Bring anything to read?' Cavendish asked abruptly.

'No, sir.'

'It'll take us days to get to where we're going. Bloody long way to go without reading.'

The older man held up his book to demonstrate how well prepared he was. Frank expected to see some solid tome on history or politics, but this was a booklet with tattered paper covers entitled *Slaughter at the OK Corral.* Under a line drawing of moustachioed gunslingers a caption screamed: *Storm of lead hurls three souls to eternity!* If Cavendish regarded this as anything less than serious reading, his face gave no sign of it.

'When we get to Rawalpindi,' he said, lowering the book, 'a chum of mine in the Dragoon Guards will have arranged some camels for us. Up until then, I'm Captain Cavendish, and you're Trooper Gray. After that, you're Daud Emin, and I'm Dost Khan, your uncle.' He gave Frank a level look. 'No doubt you find that as unlikely as I do, Gray, but we'll have to make the best of it.'

'It's a long way to Peshawar from Rawalpindi, sir.'

'Some weeks by camel, the way we'll do it – an opportunity for uncle and nephew to get their stories straight. Besides, we can't very well materialise out of nowhere in Peshawar bazaar one fine morning.' He went back to his cheap book.

'Sir?'

'Well?' Cavendish was evidently reluctant to be dragged away from Tombstone.

'I've heard there are some officers from the Twenty-first on the Frontier already.'

'Billy Fox-Moncrieff was there for a while. Charles Guest still is. And Herrick, I think. What of it?'

'Would that be Captain John Herrick, sir?'

'Major Herrick nowadays. He's been attached to the Khyber Rifles for years. What's your interest in Herrick? He left the Twenty-first long before your time.'

'I've heard of him, sir, that's all. Some of the lads mentioned him.'

'None too kindly, I don't doubt. Herrick could be a tartar with the men, as I recall, though quite a swell with the ladies. But see here, Gray, we are Punjabi traders. We do not take tea with British officers. We do not acknowledge them and they do not acknowledge us. If we do our job, they won't even know we're there.'

'I understand, sir.'

'I hope you do.' Cavendish grunted.

He flipped a page in his book, and then another, the rustle of the paper loud in the dim compartment. The train whistle blew and the couplings gave a clank and they were moving, the distant engine blowing like a horse. Cavendish looked up from his reading and moved the blind aside to watch the outskirts of the city jolting by. He let the blind fall again and glanced across at Frank.

' "Theirs not to make reply, Theirs not to reason why . . ." '

' ". . . Theirs but to do and die." '

Cavendish lifted one eyebrow. 'Let's hope it doesn't come to that. You're a storehouse of surprises, Gray. Tennyson another of your dark passions?'

'I always liked "Charge of the Light Brigade", sir. And "Ulysses". I don't know much else.'

'Why stop there?'

'My father died before he could teach me more.'

'I see.' Cavendish paused. 'Always been a lover of Tennyson myself. I'll look some out for you, if ever we get back.'

'I'd like that, sir.'

' "It is not too late to seek a newer world", Gray. Let's hope not, anyway.'

The train swayed and rattled on and the slatted light shifted across the compartment.

'Frontiers,' Cavendish said suddenly. 'Much the same anywhere. Arizona, Troy. Peshawar. Where there's no human law, men revert to the law of the jungle. And there's nothing very picturesque about Man's natural state. Remember that, if ever you're tempted to get romantic notions. Man's nature is savage and barbarous and cruel, and unless he's governed by law all he will get is petty tyranny or chaos.'

Frank said, 'Whose law would that be, sir?'

'Ah, now there's a question!' Cavendish's eyes gleamed, pleased to be challenged. 'Well, Gray, at present it's our writ that runs. And on the whole it runs pretty well, in places where they understand such concepts. That's why we get on tolerably in India, where parts of the place had civilisation while we were running around daubed with woad. They understand the idea. Cities, societies, institutions. Old hat to them. But it won't work everywhere. Do you think the Pathans will ever swallow it?'

'No.'

'Quite right. Neither do I. But we can't pick and choose, Gray, you and I. This is the job we've been given and we must try to do it. Ours not to reason why, and all that.' He paused. 'You admire the Pathans, don't you, Gray? I used to admire them too. Used to have a sneaking regard for all kinds of outlaws. Chaps who buck the system, carve their own path through life, knock down anyone who stands in their way. Yes, I used to like and admire the Pathans. These days I settle for being frightened to death of them.' Cavendish let a beat pass. 'See that canvas grip up there, Gray? Fetch it down.'

Frank lifted the bag out of the rack and set it on the bench seat. It was surprisingly heavy.

'Open it.'

Frank opened the bag. Inside he saw folded local robes, maps, a compass and a thick cardboard carton about the size of a shoebox. Cavendish leaned across and lifted out the carton and took off the lid. Inside was a squat revolver of dark steel with a soft leather holster and several packets of ammunition.

'It's a Bulldog,' Cavendish said with distaste. 'Strictly speaking it's a copy of the Webley. This one's made in Belgium, for some reason. Nine millimetre. Why they can't be like Christians and use inches is beyond me, but there it is. Not at all elegant, but anything you shoot with it will probably fall over.' He pushed the box across to Frank. 'Carry it under your clothes. It's no use to me. I can't hit the broad side of a barn with a shovel.'

Frank fastened the canvas grip again, leaving the cardboard box on the seat. Cavendish had opened the blind once more and was gazing out at the glaring countryside as it clattered by – thin oxen hauling carts, baked brown huts.

'Some believe in God, Gray, or duty, or England, or some such thing. But I believe in the Empire, for all its faults. Law and order. It has to be even-handed and incorruptible, and of course it never truly is. But just the same the world has to have law and order for anyone's aspirations to flourish. Strange how unfashionable it is to admit that, when you'd have thought it obvious to anyone who'd seen the alternative. But that's the trouble. People at home don't realise they live in

240

an oasis, hemmed in on every side by chaos and violence.' He looked up sharply. 'You believe in the Empire, Gray?'

'I don't give it much thought, sir.'

Cavendish snorted. 'You believe in something, though. I haven't quite worked out what, yet. It had best not be honour and chivalry and all that claptrap, because you'll find precious little in what we're going to do. We're spies, Gray. Miserable sneaking spies. We're going to creep into another fellow's country, seduce him into trusting us, and then betray him. That's our calling. Not so very noble, is it?' He lifted his tattered book and waved it. 'You won't be some kind of a paladin with a Buntline Special, calling on the outlaws to draw at high noon. You'll be skulking around with that nasty little Bulldog, and if you shoot anybody, it will be in the back.'

'Sir.'

'I'm prepared for that, Gray, because at heart I believe in the Empire. I made that decision a long time back. It's a compromise, but I've accepted it. In the end I think the Empire does more good than harm. That's why I'm on this train with you, for my sins, going north to the worst place on earth. Why are you on it?'

'To get to the Frontier, sir.'

Cavendish gave a bark of laughter, and closed the blind. In the sudden gloom he was holding something out to Frank. 'Here. Try this.'

'Sir?'

'*Jesse James Rides Again*. I left the Tennyson at home.'

61

The winter sun flooded into the breakfast room, and dazzled through the windows from the snow in Stephansplatz. Children were at play out there, skating, squealing, shouting, pulling one another along on sleds and pushing one another off them, inexhaustibly hurling snowballs. Every now and then one of these hit the window with a startling thud, leaving a white mound on the glass, so that Berndt the butler would open the door and bellow awful threats, not very seriously.

Christmas Day. And what a Christmas Day it was, Grace thought. Beyond the windows the sky was periwinkle blue and the bells from the Stephansdom were flinging joy across the streets and squares and to the white hills beyond. Grace's nerves quivered at the very surface of her skin, along the fine hairs of her forearms and the nape of her neck. Matilde poured more coffee and the dark perfume of it burst onto her senses with a dizzying richness. She became aware of Willi watching her across the table, smiling over her raised cup.

'I must say, Grace, my sweet, you are looking quite stunningly well this morning. Better than anyone deserves to look after one of my Christmas Eve parties. But Max did not attend, I notice. You couldn't tempt him away from his good works?'

'You know Max.' Grace made her voice as offhand as she could manage, but a cold thrill trickled somewhere near the pit of her belly.

Willi said, 'To think, he could spurn my Christmas party! I've a good mind to cast him into the outer darkness, only I'm not sure he'd notice.' She put her cup down carefully, and her brow furrowed. 'Matilde?'

'Princess?'

'Perhaps I'm mistaken, but didn't a letter arrive for Miss Grace?'

Grace looked up sharply.

'Yesterday, was it?' Willi went on. 'Or perhaps the day before? We didn't forget to pass it on, did we, in the excitement of my little get-together?'

Matilde set down the coffee pot. 'I shall go and look at once, Princess.'

Grace sat quite still. Like a violin string she felt the day and its unspoken promise stretch, creaking, towards snapping point. Willi sat opposite her, innocently sipping her coffee, until Matilde came back in with a silver salver bearing a single white envelope.

'Begging your pardon, Princess,' the woman said. 'There is indeed a letter for Miss Grace. It must have arrived while I was at church yesterday afternoon.'

'No matter, Matilde. What difference could a day make?' Smiling, Willi handed the envelope across the table to Grace. 'Here, my sweet.'

Grace found that she had held her breath and she released it now, not quite able to disguise the gasp of it, and tore open the envelope. A small card, a few florid lines of gossip. The note was from a merely casual acquaintance, inviting her to a New Year's party. Nothing more. She folded the card and put it back in the envelope, aware that her hands were shaking.

'Nothing of importance,' she said, keeping her face neutral.

Willi made a sympathetic moue. 'Well, to cheer you up let's go along to Arno's for a little lunch in an hour or two? Champagne does so restore the equilibrium.'

Grace sat staring out of the window at the glittering street. It was unendurable, this switchback of hope and disappointment. Unendurable.

'I can't come to Arno's, Willi,' she said.

'Oh, but what a pity. Why not?'

'I have an appointment to keep.'

Willi gave her that slow smile. 'I believe you do, my dear. Indeed I think you're running late for it already.'

The sky had grown heavy once more by the time she hurried through Stephansplatz with its stalls selling mulled wine and chocolate and its crowds milling in the sparkling cold. She walked the length of Rotenturmstrasse and crossed the Marienbrücke, the wind down the Danube Canal whipping her long coat around her. It began to snow afresh, the flakes driving horizontally down the waterway. She could take a cab, but she wanted to feel the icy spindrift stinging her cheeks, and the weight of the leaden sky above. She wanted whatever would make today monumental, final, never to be forgotten.

Beyond the bridge she walked down into the poorer byways of the city, where the revelry was less decorous and the children dirtier. Cobbled lanes, dark little squares piled with trampled snow, dim café doorways with red faced men peering out, vendors selling chestnuts from roadside braziers. Grace glimpsed the tower of St Nicholas's and hurried towards it, homing towards the pealing of its bells, knowing she was as conspicuous here as some exotic bird.

They had lit a bonfire of old timber in the little square. People were huddled around it, and the crackling of flame made the courtyard look like a medieval painting. She edged through the press, smelling un-washed bodies and the hot breath of the fire. He was in the very centre, behind a trestle table, ladling stew from a tureen. A line of ragged people had formed in front of him, and as their bowls were filled these people moved shuffling down past other tables piled with bread and boiled potatoes. Grace stopped for a moment and watched him work. Some strangers were helping him, and Rosa and Ferdinand were there as always. But Grace only saw Max, serious Max, exchanging a quiet word or the smallest of smiles with the people whose bowls he filled. The steam of the stew kept fogging his round glasses, and this seemed very funny to her. If there was one thing that finally decided her, it was those fogged glasses mocking his dignity, like pewter pennies over his eyes.

She pushed through the crowd and stood facing him across the table. 'Max?'

He rested the ladle in the pot of stew and took his glasses off and polished them, dumbstruck at the sight of her.

Rosa glanced across at them. 'Maximilian?' she called sharply. 'People are waiting.'

Grace stepped around the end of the table and took his hand, and without a word led him to the door to the stairwell and up the dingy stairs.

It was very cold in his room. The snow was mounding against the roof window and underwater light seeped in. Grace closed the door and wedged the single chair under the handle. She took off her coat and draped it over the desk and then with growing fluency she unhooked her dress and let it pool on the bare floor around her feet and stepped out of her undergarments. She was utterly unselfconscious; she hadn't expected that. She felt as if she were observing someone else, a tall and slender girl who balanced on tiptoe as she undressed in a cold room, poised like a heron on the margin of her life. She was filled with wonder at this girl's loveliness and courage.

She pulled back the blanket and lay down on the mattress, shivering a little at the rough kiss of the wool, and stretched her long arms up to him.

PART SEVEN

The North-West Frontier and England, February 1897

62

Frank tossed more brushwood onto the fire. It was light and dry and flared like pitch, but he was glad of that. The air had been molten all through the day's march, but the evening was already growing cool, and he pulled his loose tunic around him. He could hear the knocking of hammers on tent pegs in the dusk, and the cries of the food and tea vendors as they moved through the throng. A hundred fires twinkled across the blue valley and smoke drifted like incense. The tents were everywhere, and hobbled animals, and piles of trade goods – hides and furs from Bokhara, spices and fruits from Kabul, silks and bullion from further Asia. And, brought up from British India, tea, sugar, indigo, pots and pans, bolts of cotton from Lancashire, knives from Sheffield.

Frank had paid two jezailchis to stand guard over their own merchandise. The men squatted by the baggage a few yards distant, giggling in the high-pitched Afridi manner, their long-barrelled jezails propped beside them. Frank glanced up at the blockish silhouette of Landi Kotal fortress dominating the high point of the pass. The Khyber Rifles garrisoned Landi Kotal. Frank toyed with the idea that Herrick himself might be up there on those mud-brick ramparts, scanning the encampment below through field glasses, thinking of retiring to the mess for a brandy and soda, believing himself safe.

Cavendish materialised in the ring of firelight and sat down, resting his back against a packsaddle. He opened the bag he carried over his shoulder and handed Frank a fold of flat bread.

'There's mutton in it somewhere, rumour has it.' Cavendish sank his teeth into his own food. 'Not bad. Not bad at all.' He ate for a while, and jerked his head down at the thronged encampment. 'A touch more stimulating than Sevenoaks, you'd have to admit.'

Frank took a bite. 'I've never been to Sevenoaks.'

'Take my word for it, then.' Cavendish dusted crumbs from his hands, picked a sliver of meat from between his teeth with a thumbnail. 'God, what a relief it is to speak English.'

On the far side of the caravanserai there was a tiny flash and the pop of a gunshot. A packhorse screeched in the distance and another answered and a faint babble of shouting rose and died away. One of the jezailchis got to his feet, listened for a moment and sat down again, cracking a joke with his companion.

'Another debt settled,' Cavendish observed. 'And a new one incurred, no doubt. *Badal*. Blood feuds passed down for generations. You know the only things that interest these people? *Zar, zan, zamin*. Wealth, women, land. It's as if they're wild children who know no restraint.'

The remark seemed to carry some unexplained weight, but Frank could not make out the older man's face under the cowl of his cloak.

'You know, Gray,' Cavendish said, 'you're an enigma to me. A smart young chap, educated, personable. There must have been prospects in England for you.'

'I needed to come back to India, sir.'

'Oh, I know that. Not the girl, not even young Gifford could keep you away. Yes, yes, Gray, I know about your brother. You've been remitting pay to him ever since you got here. Very creditable. But it would have been easier to find yourself a respectable position in England and support him from there. Instead of which here you are, squatting by a campfire on the Khyber Pass, dressed like Aladdin and having to endure some old fool poking his nose into your private affairs. Was there a scandal, perhaps? Do you have a dream of restoring the family's fortunes? Something like that?'

'I was born here. This is my home.'

'Oh, that won't do, Gray. This place isn't home to any of us, as I think you know better than most.' Cavendish settled back. 'Ah well, I expect I could find out more if I made inquiries, but I rather enjoy the mystery of it. One thing I will say, though. It's good to have a dream. It's also good to know when to let it go.'

One of the guards spoke sharply and cocked his jezail. There was a frightened jabber of explanation and the guard waved a ragged old man into the firelight. He carried a yoke like a pair of scales over his thin shoulders with a pot suspended from one side and a tray of tiny brass cups from the other.

'Tea, masters?' The old man had buck teeth and a face like a walnut. He looked contemptuously back towards the guards. 'If your watchdogs do not shoot me for plying my trade.'

Cavendish accepted the small glinting cup. 'I'll take tea, Father, since you've risked so much to bring it.'

The old man stooped to pour. 'Gul Shah sends you greetings, Dost Khan,' he said softly.

Cavendish showed no flicker of surprise. 'Then carry mine to him. I am at his service, as always.'

'He hears you have some interesting merchandise.' The old man stood up. 'An hour into tomorrow's march, you will see two dead cedar trees in a nullah beside the track. They are white, and crossed, so.' He put one wrist across the other. 'Strike north along the nullah, up into the hills. You will be met. You alone, Dost Khan, and such beasts as you need to carry the goods.'

'I shall bring my nephew, Daud Emin.'

'That is not possible.'

'I don't much like the look of him either, but I no longer travel alone.'

The old man hesitated a second longer. 'Very well. But no other.' He took back the empty cup from Cavendish, caught the tossed coin, ducked his head and was gone, calling an insult to the guards as he went. Frank listened to his footsteps slapping away in the darkness.

He said, 'Who is Gul Shah?'

'He's malik of a sub clan of the Zakka Khels.' Cavendish leaned across to toss more fuel onto the fire. 'He is old, intelligent, and very unpleasant, and he smuggles rifles to the other Afridi clans in this sector. I sold him guns in ninety-three, mostly old Martinis. The Zakka Khels were making trouble then, and Lahore wanted to know where they were getting their weapons. The best way to find out was to sell him a few more. They should have listened to me last time, and had the old rogue shot.' Cavendish yawned and shifted his legs under him. 'Now we'll have to try to pull the same trick again.'

63

The two dead trees stood locked together beside a dry watercourse a few yards from the line of march. Frank turned his pony's head, leading the packhorse off the track and into the nullah, and heard Cavendish following him. Someone in the caravan called to them, a warning or perhaps a blessing, but within a few minutes the column was far below, a dun serpent of men and animals trailing dust in the rising heat.

The ponies' hooves slipped and clattered on scree as they climbed. After twenty minutes they reached a stony col, the sun like a weight on their backs. Frank reined in. Ahead lay a shallow valley, with patches of green among the ochre, and dark groves of deodar and walnut. He heard the faint shriek of a hawk. He leaned back in the saddle to search for the bird, but it was lost in an immense sky.

Cavendish came up with him. 'The Pathans say that when God

finished building the world he had some rubble left over. That's Afghanistan.'

Frank unslung his water skin and took a drink. When he looked out over the valley again, five riders were walking their horses towards them, rifles slung over their shoulders. There were four men and a boy of perhaps thirteen. Their clothing showed that they were local tribesmen, except for one: a wild figure with matted hair, dressed in a patched jibba. They were no more than three hundred yards away. It unsettled Frank to think they must have been watching from shelter, maybe sighting along the barrels of their jezails, while he and Cavendish sat on their horses and gawped around them like tourists.

'Just relax, Gray, would you?' Cavendish said. 'You're making me nervous. Say nothing unless you're spoken to, and do exactly as you're told.'

Cavendish urged his horse forward a few paces and called a greeting. The riders trotted up in a leisurely fashion on their shaggy Afghan ponies. The leader was a toothless old man with bright button eyes.

'Dost Khan!' he called, and his smile was a black crescent. 'Is it four years? We are honoured.'

'The honour is ours, Gul Shah.'

The old man chuckled and rocked his head modestly. He rested his hand on the shoulder of the boy who rode next to him, who, Frank saw, was a handsome child with wide dark eyes full of intelligence. The boy was doing his best to look grave, even fierce, but then he caught Frank looking at him and his serious mask slipped for an instant and he smiled.

'Do you remember Mohammed, my grandson?' Gul Shah was saying. 'He was a tadpole when you last visited us. Oh, and our friend here is Haddid Mullah, a most holy man and a guest in my house, bringing us instruction and enlightenment from over the seas.'

He made no attempt to introduce the other two men, who held back a few paces, with faces of stone.

Cavendish said, 'This is Daud Emin, my sister's child. I commend him to you.'

Gul Shah looked directly into Frank's eyes, his smile unwavering. Guiding the pony with his knees, he walked in a tight circle around him. Frank felt the hairs lift on the back of his neck as the old man passed behind him.

Gul Shah completed his circuit and nodded approvingly. 'A fine youth. I don't recall you mentioning him before?'

'We spoke only of business when last we met. And we must speak of it again.'

'Ah, business!' Gul Shah laughed knowingly. 'Business can come later. First you will both be guests in my house. Come, it is not too long a ride.'

But they rode for three hours through forests of fir and cedar, always climbing, one rocky defile after another, one stony and trackless mountainside after another. It was the middle of the day when they arrived at a huddle of ochre houses in a cleft between two hills. Shouting children and barking dogs ran out to greet them. A stream gushed like a fire-hose between the houses from the snows high above and bounded over the lip of a ravine so that the roar of it filled the air. At the far end of the village a substantial dwelling of mud-brick and stone stood in a patch of alpine meadow bright with wild flowers. A servant took the reins of Gul Shah's horse, ducking and bobbing.

Cavendish walked his pony up beside Frank's and pretended to adjust the bridle. 'The place is half-empty,' he said softly. 'D'you see? No men under fifty. Something's afoot.'

Frank looked around quickly and he saw that Cavendish was right. His pony danced a couple of steps to one side. For an instant he thought about whipping Cavendish's horse and setting the two of them bolting back down the mountain the way they had come. But then servants and children flocked around the party, and Gul Shah came striding through the crowd and caught the head of Frank's horse.

'Come, my friends! We must refresh ourselves and eat, and then you must spend the night with us.' The old man's smile grew fixed and his grip locked tightly on the bridle. 'First you will want to wash, and then a few moments for prayers. Haddid Mullah is very particular about such matters.'

In a low building at the end of the main house a runnel from the stream spouted water into a long stone basin. Frank washed with the others. On the prayer ground outside, looking out over the shimmering valley, Frank put his forehead to the ground and recited the shahada – *la ilaha illa'llah*, there is no god but God. He tried not to think of the pony which had stirred between his knees and the chance which had been lost.

Gul Shah's house was cool and low. Narrow embrasures threw wedges of brilliant light over carpets spread on a beaten mud floor. Veiled women hurried in and out through a low door in the end wall, setting out dishes of food. Gul Shah held court merrily as they ate. He passed food onto his guests' plates, shouted with laughter at his own jokes, and called repeatedly to the women in the shadows for water, bread, meat. Nobody else spoke.

'Perhaps we should take a look at what you have brought us, Dost

Khan,' Gul Shah said at last, wiping his hands. He lounged back and wagged a finger. 'Be sure you have something better to offer than those broken-down Martinis you sold me last time. They were of more danger to us than to our enemies!'

Cavendish got to his feet, knelt beside the long wooden case and threw back the lid. 'This is better than any Martini-Henry,' he said. 'Better even than a Lee-Metford. This is the best that the British have devised. Few of their own soldiers have it yet.'

He lifted the rifle from the box, unfolded the sacking which wrapped it, and held it out to Gul Shah in both hands like an oblation. The smile fled from Gul Shah's face. He got to his feet and took the weapon. Frank could see greed flash in his black eyes.

'A Lee-Enfield,' Cavendish said. 'It resembles the Lee-Metford, but they have changed the rifling of the barrel, so now it will last for years. And so accurate that at over five hundred yards it would cut an individual blade of grass, if any marksman had the eyes to see so small a target. It is like the Lee-Metford in that it does not jam, does not kick as hard as the Martini, and uses smokeless ammunition. A sniper never gives away his position. The bullets are of .303 calibre.' Cavendish dropped four glinting rounds into Gul Shah's hand. 'Feel, Gul Shah. A man can carry a hundred of these and not notice the weight.'

'We don't need such toys,' Haddid Mullah sneered, and got to his feet.

It was the first time Frank had heard him speak. His voice was harsh and impatient, and his Pushtu heavily accented.

'Rifles are always valuable,' Gul Shah said mildly, cradling the Lee-Enfield, caressing the polished stock. 'And to be on equal terms with the British . . .'

'The British are already finished,' Haddid said contemptuously. 'Everywhere they are beaten back. The port of Aden has been taken from them by the Turkish Sultan. Their great canal through Egypt has been closed and now it will take six months – six months! – for their reinforcements to reach India.' He jabbed his finger at Cavendish. 'You think we need a handful of stolen rifles? In every country the people are turning back to the Prophet and are rising up – here in Afghanistan, in Egypt, along the Red Sea, in the Sudan. Twelve years ago I myself saw Gordon cut to pieces in Khartoum. We beat down the armies the White Queen sent to save him – yes, even her greatest generals. They left their bones at Khartoum and in the forest of Shaykan – all along the road from Egypt. We did not need British weapons then.'

But if Gul Shah heard this diatribe, he gave no sign of it. He lifted

252

the rifle, squinted along the barrel, worked the bolt. 'How many of these can you get?'

'Perhaps fifty within the month,' Cavendish said. 'A consignment will come up by rail to Rawalpindi. It is possible to arrange for some to go missing—'

'Fifty?' Gul Shah laughed. 'You are out of touch, Dost Khan! There are twenty thousand of the faithful under arms at this moment, all along the Pass, waiting to strike at the British. Fifty will not go far. We get more from the Ghilzais every week.'

'Take care what you say, Gul Shah,' Haddid warned. 'Pedlars sell to both sides.'

The remark evidently struck home, for Gul Shah looked up thoughtfully at Cavendish. As if at a signal the other men and the boy Mohammed all got to their feet. Frank stood too, and moved back towards the wall, trying to keep all of them in sight.

'Forgive us, Dost Khan,' Gul Shah said, and seemed to relax. 'Haddid can be a little touchy. But I will not allow any unpleasantness today. Let's have some sport instead.' He took Cavendish's arm and led him to the embrasure and held out the Lee-Enfield. 'You say the weapon has amazing accuracy. We shall put it to the test. There, beyond the stream, on the furthest spur, that is Sinjab Sayad's house. See where his goats graze in the yard? Shoot me one of them.'

'Forgive me,' Cavendish said. 'I have no skill with weapons.'

'Ah, I understand,' Gul Shah sighed. 'We are neither of us growing younger, my friend, and our eyes are not as sharp as once they were. Your nephew, however: I'm sure his sight is as keen as an eagle's. Here, young Daud Emin. You try.'

Frank hesitated, then took the rifle and the four rounds from Gul Shah, avoiding Cavendish's eyes. From across the room he could see the boy Mohammed gazing at him with awe, his eyes shining, willing him to meet the challenge. Frank placed the rounds on the ledge of the window, fed one into the breech, closed the bolt. He braced himself against the edge of the embrasure, flicked up the vernier sight with his thumb and peered through the pinhole.

'Now we shall see if the youngster is up to the challenge!' Gul Shah cawed in delight. He gripped Frank's arm and pointed. His smell was feral and the claw of his hand was as hard as thornwood. 'Now, see, there? It's a tolerably long range, I admit, but then I'm sure with this fine weapon it will be possible. Come, I'll allow you three shots. That's generous.'

The view through the sight was blindingly sharp. The spur on which the house stood must have been three hundred yards away but Frank could see the goats clearly as tiny brown and white ants against grey rock. He felt the room grow quiet behind him. He hugged the rifle butt hard into his shoulder, and focused on one of the goats. The rifle kicked him hard in the shoulder and the crash of it filled the room and a whitish puff of dust spurted up two yards short of his target and a little to the left. Startled, the goat bounded up onto an outcrop of rock, where it stood silhouetted. Frank reloaded, adjusted the sights, settled himself again. He took the first pressure on the trigger. The tiny image of the goat filled his sight, and he knew he would not miss. He fired and the animal flew off the rocks and lay kicking in the dust.

'In two shots!' Gul Shah cackled, and slapped Frank on the back. 'We could use you against the English soldiers, Daud Emin! But wait – what's that moving?'

A tiny figure had come running out of the distant house towards the goat, and now crouched over the animal.

Gul Shah gripped Frank's arm again. 'Is it a dog, perhaps?'

'It's a child,' Frank said in a flat voice, though he knew that Gul Shah did not need to be told.

'Ah, yes,' Gul Shah said, fondly. 'That will be Akbar, Sayad's boy. His only surviving son. Sayad dotes on him, you know.' He smiled at Frank with his toothless gums. 'Kill him.'

'What?'

'Kill him. Shoot him.'

'Why?'

'Why?' Gul Shah laughed. 'Because I am your host and I wish it! Oh, don't worry, young man, my family has been feuding with Sayad's miserable clan for generations. Another death won't make much difference.'

Frank glanced up at Cavendish, who stood rigid and white-faced, his eyes giving nothing away.

'Never mind what your uncle thinks,' Gul Shah said, his voice growing hard. 'I request this of you, young Daud, and when you have done it I shall know that you are to be trusted. If you do not, of course . . .' He shrugged slightly.

Frank turned back to the window. He worked the bolt and the spent case jumped out of the breech and tinkled on the floor. He slipped in the third cartridge, closed the breech, raised the rifle. In the tiny cameo of the pinhole sight the child was still there, crouched over his dying goat, which kicked feebly. Frank wondered what the boy was doing: weeping, perhaps. He wedged himself against the window embrasure, hugged the rifle, let the sight drop down over the child, centred it. He took the first pressure on the trigger.

He stepped back from the window and shot Gul Shah through the face. He shut his mind to the rest of the room, snapped back the bolt, reached for the last round, clicked it into the chamber. By the time he lifted his eyes Gul Shah's body was still sliding down the far wall, daubing it crimson. Cavendish was grappling with a man on the floor, another man was hurling himself out through the door, and Haddid Mullah was almost on him, roaring like a madman. Frank lifted the barrel and the man ran onto it and Frank pulled the trigger. He did not hear the explosion, but the mullah whirled away, patched jibba flying. No time to scrabble for more ammunition now. Frank tossed the rifle aside, pulled the Bulldog revolver out of its holster, put the barrel against the turban of Cavendish's assailant and blew the man's brains over the carpet. He reached for Cavendish and dragged him to his feet.

Then they were outside in the evening sun and Frank had a confused impression of women screaming and chickens running. He saw the horses a few yards away, nervously tugging at their tethers. Cavendish reached the ponies first, leaped up onto one with what seemed to Frank astonishing agility, and held the other while Frank mounted. Cavendish kicked away down the stony track. As Frank made to follow, a figure darted up on his blind side, and slashed at his arm. He felt the nettle sting of a blade and swung the Bulldog and pulled the trigger in one movement and only then saw that it was the boy Mohammed who had run at him. His dark eyes were wide with innocent surprise and there was a keyhole in his forehead where the bullet had entered. Frank's pony capered, nudging the child's body, which fell like a doll. Frank kicked the horse and was gone.

The track fell steeply between rocks, the lengthening shadows striping the path. They went down it helter-skelter. A clump of cedars stood at the foot of the slope and Frank knew that once they had rounded it they would be out of sight of the village and would have a chance. Cavendish was a few yards ahead, riding easily, his pony bounding like a cat down the stony slope. Frank saw him plunge into the shadow of the trees and momentarily present side-on as he rounded the bend. A flat bang from above and something cracked past Frank's ear and he distinctly saw the material of Cavendish's robes jump when the bullet struck above his left knee. But the older man kept his seat and in another instant they were past the trees and away.

64

Grace waited at the door while Max's steps receded down the dim stairs. She was always lonely without him, but over the last few weeks she had learned to endure her solitude during the long winter days. She thought of it as a sacrifice she made for their work.

She came back into the room, tidied away a glass, folded the blankets neatly on their bed. The morning was very cold, and she lit the oil heater in the corner. It stank of paraffin, but she liked the squat little stove, with its bow legs and black enamel. It was the one luxury she had so far persuaded him to accept. She loved to make comfort in his life and she was pleased with this new softness in herself.

The February sleet fell against the roof window. Grace stood with her hands on her hips and surveyed the bare room. Self sacrifice and commitment were all very well, but there was only so much political theory she could read, sitting alone here with the stove ticking and the sleet rattling on the roof. Today she would go out and buy him something special, a proper desk, perhaps, instead of the makeshift arrangement he used now, which was no more than a board between two tea chests full of his books. Maybe she would even buy a print for the wall. She hated that morbid drawing of the Tsar's assassination. She would prepare the room and then pay a couple of lads a schilling or two to carry her purchases up here, and it would be done, a surprise for him.

She got to work at once, removing the board from the two tea chests and emptying them, stacking his books on the floor, volumes in German, French and Russian. Night after night she had watched him writing here, his glasses flashing in the light of the oil lamp. She had often enough resented the way his studies kept him from their bed, and dismantling the desk felt a little like revenge. She would buy him something elegant to replace it, something that would remind him of her while he worked.

She emptied the first chest, moved it aside, and came back for the second one. It was heavier than she had expected. She gripped the edge and hauled hard at it. The side tore off with a splintering of wood and she stumbled back while papers, stationery and a rosewood writing box all tumbled out over the floor. The box made a crack as it hit the boards and flew open. She looked down at it like a guilty child, and knelt to pick it up. She had never seen it before. It was handsome, with mother-of-pearl inlay, and it was more precious than any object she knew Max to own. Perhaps it was an heirloom. The brass lock had sprung as it hit the floor and she was distressed enough to wonder if she could get it repaired without him knowing. She put the box gently to one side and gathered up the papers which had spilled from it.

Mrs Rossiter's clumsy handwriting was so out of place here that it took her a moment to recognise it. But there was no doubt: an envelope with a British stamp, addressed to her in Mrs Rossiter's hand. There were two sheets inside, the smaller one a stilted note to her from the housekeeper, explaining only that she was forwarding the enclosed letter. Grace unfolded the second sheet.

12 September 1896

Dear Mrs Rossiter,

Perhaps you have wondered what has become of me. I am in India, and I should say at once that I have no prospect of early return. I have wanted very much to write to Grace, but I know her father would punish her.

However, someone whose opinion I respect has persuaded me that it is only right Grace should know how things stand. I don't like to ask anything more of you, Mrs Rossiter, after all you have done for me, but if you can find it in yourself to pass word to Grace, I should be grateful indeed. I wish only that she should know I love her, that I always have loved her, and that I believe I always shall. She should also know that I understand there can be no future for us. My purpose in coming to India remains fixed – she will understand that – and the outcome is uncertain in the extreme. For that reason I do not look for any answer to this letter.

I expect she has long ago put me out of her mind, and indeed that is the only possible course for her. Just the same Grace deserves to have the truth of things laid out plainly. With your help I trust that has now been achieved, and I release her from any lingering sense of obligation she may feel. But I shall take leave to hope that from time to time she may think of me, not entirely without affection. For my part I shall always remember her with love.

FRANK GRAY

65

Berndt opened the door as she came up the steps. He smiled nervously as he saw her face.

'Miss Grace! We were not expecting you. I shall inform the Princess—'

She swept past him – through him – and up the long marble stairs. A maid carrying linen stepped quickly aside, bobbing respectfully, keeping her eyes averted. Grace shoved open the door of Willi's room. Willi was reclining in bed, her long dark hair spread over a snowy hillock of pillows. Matilde was bending over her, collecting a tray of breakfast things. For a second both women froze into a startled cameo.

'Why, Grace, my dear! We haven't seen you for days! But isn't this a little early in the morning for a social call?'

Grace walked to the end of the bed. She drew the letter from her dress and held it up.

'You kept this from me.'

'Now, now, my sweet. Let's not be melodramatic.' Willi set her cup delicately on Matilde's tray. 'It's my duty to consider your welfare.'

'You deceived me. That is considering my welfare?'

'You were, as I recall, attracting the attentions of Max Krauss at the time that letter arrived from your ridiculous soldier. You should thank me that Max did not throw you over at once. It was I who persuaded him not to.'

'And should I thank you that Frank Gray now thinks I care nothing for him?'

'Indeed you should.'

'You kept my letter from me, and then passed it to Max. Why? So that you and he could gloat?'

Willi's face hardened. 'Don't be foolish, Grace. Think what I have done for you! Left to yourself you would never have found a shred of pleasure in life. I put that right for you, that's all.'

'Are you saying you procured Max for me?'

'Oh, please!' Willi laughed scornfully. 'Don't trouble me with your frigid little conscience. Who would not have Max if they could? No, no. If you are to throw accusations, throw the right ones. I procured *you* for Max.'

Grace felt the room sway and gripped the post of Willi's bed.

'You should think yourself lucky,' Willi pushed on. 'Can you seriously pretend to prefer some moonstruck trooper, stinking of horses, to Max Krauss? You want this glorified farm boy, because he fumbled you in a haystack? My dear, you only ever fucked him once. At least with Max, you seem to have learned how to do *that*.' She flipped a hand. 'Go away now. You're giving me a headache.'

Matilde, still standing beside the bed, set down the tray on the dressing table and touched Grace's arm. 'Come, *Schatzi*.'

'Get your hands off me.' Grace spun to face the woman. 'Did you read my letter on Christmas morning, and giggle over it with the fine princess here? And then pass it to Max so that he could snigger over it too?'

Matilde's smiling face fell into sullen folds. 'You will go out now,' she said, and reached out for Grace's arm again.

Grace struck Matilde backhanded across the face and at the smack of the blow the woman shouted in shock and the dressing room door opened and Max was there, wrapped in a blue silk dressing gown, owlish without his glasses. He opened his mouth to speak, and saw Grace, and his eyes widened and his mouth stayed open.

The joyful release of it, the shattering of precious porcelain – cups, plates, cream jug – the splintering of the Louis XV mirror and of the little gilt chairs and the smash and tumble of vases, cosmetic pots and pictures in their frames – and best of all, Max's yelp as the hurled coffee scalded him and crockery and glass exploded against the wall around him until at last Matilde bundled him out of the room and away.

Grace wasn't aware that she had been screaming, only that her throat was raw and that now she was breathing noisily. Somehow she had cut her right hand and blood was dripping onto the carpet. Willi was crouched on the bed, shaking. She had kicked aside the coffee-stained sheets and she looked impossibly small, curled naked against the pillows, her hands over her face and her hair tangled.

'How long?' Grace asked, quite calm now. 'You and Max. How long?'

'From the beginning. Before.'

Grace flicked blood from her fingertips. 'How could you do this to me?'

'I am growing old, don't you see?' Willi squirmed onto her knees on the bed, and pointed with both hands at her blotched face and then down at her body. 'Soon I will be nothing. I will have nothing. The world I know will be nothing!'

'Don't talk nonsense, Willi. You're rich.'

'There is no more money. I shall end in a mean room without servants, without love, without beauty, old and alone. Me! It's unthinkable. Obscene.'

'So you sold me to Max? I was the price?'

'You have everything, Grace. You are young and beautiful. You are a child of this new world. But he wanted you and so I gave you to him. It was the only way I could keep him. And what did it cost you? Oh, don't say you didn't enjoy it. Spare me that, at least. But you are so besotted that if you had read this pathetic note from your soldier, you would have turned your back on Max. Is that not so?'

Grace looked down at Frank's letter. She had crumpled it in her rage and it was smeared with blood from her hand.

She said, 'Yes. It is so.'

She walked out of the room and started down the stairs. Before she reached the hall, Max appeared on the landing above her.

'Grace? Grace, stop.'

She did not turn. Below her in the hallway, Berndt the butler placed his hand on the front door latch, as if to block her path, but then thought better of it and moved away. Grace crossed to the door and made to open it but she heard Max's steps behind her. He stepped past and placed his hand flat on the wood.

'Grace, this is ridiculous.'

'No,' she rounded on him, 'I am ridiculous, Max. You have made me so. But you shall not have the opportunity again.'

He stood back a little in the face of her now glacial fury. He was dishevelled and out of breath. He dabbed at his face with a hand-kerchief and the front of his dressing gown was sodden with the coffee she had hurled at him. He put the handkerchief away. His cheek and brow were reddened where the hot liquid had caught him.

'There is more than one kind of sacrifice, Grace. Perhaps you will come to learn that.'

'I have learned all I wish to learn from you.'

'Do you think I would have chosen her over you?' He jerked his head in contempt towards the bedroom. 'I needed her, that's all. The hospital needed her. Her money, at least, while she had some.'

'For God's sake, Max. Don't make this any worse than it is.'

'I have never hidden from you that this is a hard road we must travel.'

'Oh, how you must have suffered!'

'Grace, sooner or later we all must choose whether we are truly prepared to give up what we most love for our cause.'

She looked at him in disbelief. Misunderstanding her hesitation he reached for her hand but she snatched it sharply away. Blood was still running down her fingers and she saw that she had left a trail of dark stars across the marble floor.

'You should let me look at that,' he said.

'I shall never let you look at me again. Depend upon it.'

She clenched her fist and held it against her dress, and with her good hand she reached for the latch and clicked it back. The door swung open and the winter wind hissed into the hallway, carrying the sounds of the street. Dried flowers rustled in an ormolu vase beneath the stairs.

'Grace,' he said from the doorway.

Something in his voice tugged at her and she saw that there were tears in his eyes. She walked down the steps and into the winter street.

66

It was almost dark at last, and growing chill. From somewhere up among the rocks came the coughing bark of a jackal. Frank took a final turn on the makeshift bandage and heard Cavendish gasp. He tore the cloth and knotted the ends.

'A fine idea of intelligence work you have, Gray,' Cavendish said. 'Our best source in the Khyber, and you blow his brains all over the wall. What d'you mean by it? Eh?'

Frank struck a match and crouched forward, shielding the sudden yellow flame and shaking it out almost at once. The rough binding on Cavendish's leg might stop the bleeding until they set off again. That wouldn't be pleasant. By then the wound would have stiffened and it would be agony to move it.

'Have you any idea the trouble I went to getting hold of that Lee-Enfield?' Cavendish was complaining now. 'And you just leave it there? Should have your pay docked, young Gray, by rights.'

Frank sat back on his haunches. Blood was sticky on his hands and he rubbed his fingers in the dust in an effort to clean them. He said, 'The bullet's not in deep, but you'll need a surgeon.'

'Government property, that weapon. You do realise that?'

'Or I could cut it out myself in the morning.'

Cavendish fell silent. Frank could not read the expression on the older man's face. He looked up at the magenta sky, willing it to fade, and settled himself against a rock, stretching his right arm out carefully as he did so.

'You have an injury?' Cavendish asked.

'It could use a couple of stitches, that's all. It's nothing.'

'Let's have a pact, then. I won't play seamstress if you don't play surgeon.'

Frank knew this was a joke, but he didn't reply. He was jumpy and he felt nauseous. Somewhere back among the rocks the horses shifted. He jerked around, feeling for the revolver in his waistband.

'It's like eating olives,' Cavendish said quietly. 'Killing men. The first one's difficult. All the rest are easy. Though I have to say, four is extravagant for a first attempt.' He tilted his head in the darkness. 'Or maybe this wasn't your first time?'

Frank opened the revolver, examined the cylinder with more concentration than necessary. 'I did not intend . . .' He spun the cylinder. He found it strangely hard to speak. 'The boy came for me, but I did not see . . .'

'He would have killed you without a second thought.'

'I know that.'

'Frank, it's done, and cannot be undone. This kind of thing happens in our profession.'

Frank spun the cylinder of the Bulldog sharply, hoping the metallic whirr of it would put an end to the exchange. 'They'll come after us tomorrow,' he said.

'They're already after us. But not even the Afridis can track us at night. We'll be away at first light.'

'With that leg?'

'Can't very well leave it behind.'

Frank thought of Cavendish's clothes, and the flank of his horse, sodden with blood. How much of a trail had that left? Cavendish produced a leather-cased compass and opened it, so that Frank glimpsed the luminous numerals, as bright as fireflies in the gloom.

'We'll head back to the fort at Landi Kotal,' Cavendish said. 'It's a couple of points off due south, and at a rough guess, not much more than twenty miles. The Khyber Rifles are at Landi Kotal. We should be safe enough if we can get there.'

The Khyber Rifles were at Landi Kotal. Frank took empty cartridge cases from the Bulldog's cylinder and pocketed them. He clicked fresh rounds into the chamber, loading by feel, and thought about the Khyber Rifles.

Cavendish shifted on the stony ground, wincing with the pain. He drew a breath and, though he tried to disguise it, the chattering of his teeth was clearly audible.

'I can light a fire,' Frank said. 'In this hollow they'll see nothing.'

'No fire.'

'If you get a fever you won't be able to ride.'

'No fire, Gray, dammit.'

Cavendish settled himself, sighed in pain, and they were quiet for a while. The last of the light hung in the western sky but overhead the stars thronged. The ancients, Frank knew, had believed the earth was surrounded by a shell, and that the unbearable brilliance of the heavens blazed through chinks in this carapace, as through crannies in a door. That was what we saw, not stars but radiance shining through pinpricks in a vast black mantle. If that were so, Frank thought, tonight the pinholes were myriad and very close, for the sky was exploding with light.

'There's going to be a full scale uprising,' Cavendish said, just when Frank thought he had drifted off to sleep. 'A *jihad*, if not now, then very soon. I always said we'd be in trouble if the mullahs started rallying the tribes. Religion's the one thing they agree on. Where do you think that cove Haddid was from?'

'Maybe Zanzibar. He looked dark enough.'

'Too far east. I'd take a guess he's a Nilotic Arab. A Mahdist Sudanese. We don't want those madmen up here, spreading tall tales about us losing the Suez Canal and the Empire crumbling about our ears. Gives these chaps ideas.' Cavendish paused. 'You did kill him, I suppose? Haddid?'

In his mind Frank saw the mullah blown from the muzzle of the rifle, spinning like a child's top in a flail of limbs and robes. 'I didn't stop to take his pulse.'

'Don't be impertinent, Gray, there's a good chap,' Cavendish said easily. 'And while I have the strength to insist upon it, you'll give me my rank.'

Frank looked down at the revolver which still lay in his hands. 'Sir.'

Cavendish let a moment pass, and then went on, 'Funny thing, but I'll miss Gul Shah, the old rogue. Known him on and off for twenty years and more. There wasn't much to choose between us, when all's said and done. He wanted weapons so that his people could kill ours; I wanted information so that ours could do the same to them. It was like a dance we engaged in. I think he guessed years ago where my real loyalties lay. Sometimes I think he was more sure of that than I was. Of course he'd have murdered us in an instant, and if his people catch us tomorrow they'll do a great deal worse than that. But still, I'll miss him.'

Frank closed the revolver with a snap. 'Maybe I should have shot the child instead. Sir.'

'Oh, I assure you, Gray, I'd have supported you in whatever you'd done.' Cavendish rolled his head to look at him in the starlight. 'Which is rather disgraceful, when you think about it.'

Frank turned away quickly and curled up in his robes with his cheek on the cold shale. He did not expect to sleep, but even trying to sleep – even pretending to – was better than talking. After a moment he heard Cavendish ease himself down among the stones, hissing through his teeth as he moved his injured leg. But in quite a short time the older man's breathing steadied and deepened.

Frank slid his hand inside his robes and gripped the cold butt of the revolver for comfort. The stars soared above him; a nightbird hooted. Gradually, warmth gathered in the folds of his clothing and he felt his eyelids close and his hold on the revolver loosen.

Two hands, groping for the weapon, clutching it at almost the same instant, hoarse breath in his ear, the bruising crush of the man's grip over his. And then he was being dragged, his knees skinned on the boards and the dark room pinwheeling around him. He would not let go. He *would* not. And then at last the glimpse of her his memory had denied him until now, her breast bare and blood on her face, propping herself on one elbow and stretching out her hand, imploring, begging. 'Jack! *Jack!*'

A hand over his mouth. He fought it, clawed at it. He remembered the gun and clutched for it with new strength and then a weight fell across his chest, trapping his hand.

'For God's sake, Gray,' Cavendish hissed in his ear. 'Be still, will you?'

The older man's body lay half across him, locking his hand inside his clothing. Frank released his grip on the Bulldog and Cavendish moved back.

'I don't know how a chap's supposed to get any sleep around here,' Cavendish grumbled, relaxing a little, 'with you having the midnight horrors.'

He waited, as if to give Frank a chance to talk. When he did not, Cavendish pulled himself back to his blanket, dragging his injured leg.

Frank lay on his back on the stones, his heart thudding. He could feel sweat running down the sides of his neck despite the night's chill. He had been granted one last glimpse of her. He had longed for that. So why did it terrify him?

Above him, the cold stars trembled.

67

Frank crested the slope a few yards in the lead. He let the horse pick his way a short distance down the far side before reining in. The broken country lay stretched out before him, ochre and grey in the hard light. The horse was breathing hard after the climb. Frank unhooked his water bag from the saddle and allowed himself a single swallow. Cavendish came clattering over the hill behind him, riding clumsily, and looked up at him vaguely, as if surprised to find him there. His face was white and he swayed in the saddle. Frank glanced down at the wounded leg. The bandage was still in place, but it was dark with blood, and below it the horse's flank was once again streaked and glistening.

'Did I give you permission to halt?' Cavendish demanded.

Frank ignored him and peered ahead down the barren valley, shielding his eyes. A distant thread of grey wormed around the shoulder of a mountain: the road through the Khyber Pass. And, glimpsed in the sharp light, a squat fortification dominating the high ground beyond.

'Landi Kotal.' Frank gripped Cavendish's wrist, feeling the heat of the man's skin. 'Do you see it? Maybe four miles.'

Cavendish gazed at him with bloodshot eyes. 'What d'you mean by it, Gray? That's what I should like to know.'

Frank pushed the water bag into Cavendish's hands. 'Here. Drink it. All of it.' He folded Cavendish's hand around the bag and lifted it to his mouth and held it there so that Cavendish had to gulp it down.

'Superior officer,' Cavendish protested, choking a little. 'Bad form.'

'You're right, sir,' Frank said soothingly. 'Dashed bad form.' He hooked the empty water bag onto his saddle again. 'Now stay here and don't move.'

He rode up to the crest and looked back the way they had come. Beyond lay the harsh country they had crossed, a moonscape of scree slopes and jagged peaks, here and there a mulberry tree or a clump of cedars, shadows ink black in the sun. Frank saw the riders almost at once. He had sensed they were there somewhere ever since dawn, and he felt better now that he could see them, half a dozen dark dots angling down a bare hillside perhaps a mile away, a faint smudge of dust rising above them. He walked the pony back below the crest, but he knew they would have seen him and Cavendish as they came over the hill, and probably long before that. They would have seen Cavendish's blood on the pale stones, too. They knew their quarry was weakening, and that they were closing. It was a matter of time.

Frank rode back to Cavendish, who had allowed his horse to amble away a few yards. 'We have to get moving.'

'I believe I'm in command here,' Cavendish said loftily. 'Do I make myself clear?'

Frank looked into his eyes; they were strangely vacant. He said, 'There's not much time.'

'You will address me as *sir*!' Cavendish roared. 'Do you hear?'

Frank walked his horse closer, leaned across and bunched Cavendish's robes in his fist and shook him until his teeth clacked together.

'Very well, *sir*.' He shook him again. 'Now if you'd be so good as to stay on the fucking horse, *sir*, just for the next little while, I'd very much rather not die out here. If it's all the same to you, *sir*.'

Cavendish's eyes focused and he seemed to come back from somewhere far away. He tugged at his crumpled clothing and straightened in the saddle. 'Since you put it like that, Gray, perhaps you'd better lead on.'

Frank kicked the pony and the animal took off down the hill, hooves slithering through loose rock. He let it find its feet, jinking past boulders and trees in a zigzag descent so steep that in places Frank had to lean back over the horse's rump. He didn't dare to look back at Cavendish – if he were unhorsed they would be finished – but he could hear his pony not far behind, and in a few moments they emerged through a screen of brush onto flat land above a dry nullah. Frank set the horse into a steady canter along the edge of the dry watercourse's bank and kept going until the animal began to blow. He halted and let Cavendish come up with him. The older man's face was twisted with pain but he was still in the saddle.

Frank stood in the stirrups and saw their pursuers crest the rise behind them, perhaps eight hundred yards away. He saw them halt, saw three dismount. A brief pause, and then three tiny black puffs of smoke rose up, and a moment later two spurts of dust jumped out of the ground yards to his right. Something cracked against a rock on the far side of the nullah and triggered a small runnel of sand and pebbles. The popping of the shots reached him a second after that. He recognised the characteristic cough of the jezails and that gave him some hope. At ranges not much less than this the Pathan jezail was fiendishly accurate but it was a clumsy muzzle loader. Their pursuers would have to lose at least a few moments reloading. But they were wasting no time about it. In a few seconds the faint and characteristic clang of a ramrod being pushed home reached him on the clear air. Frank put his horse over the lip of the earth bluff and down into the dry riverbed, where the banks would afford some protection. Cavendish reached the bottom a moment later, reeling in the saddle like a drunken man.

Frank let him ride on ahead and followed his swaying back as they twisted between the sandy banks and clumps of dry reeds, the tough little horses running hard. After a few minutes Frank heard his mount's breathing grow ragged and he reined in. He stood in the stirrups and listened. Over the horse's chuffing breath he could now hear the men behind, still distant but gaining, an occasional shout, the clatter of hooves on shale. It was very hot in the nullah and the sun was a weight on Frank's shoulders and he could hear his own breath rasping with that of the horse. Frank kicked the animal and urged it on. Some distance ahead of him now, Cavendish was bent low over the pommel. He had tangled his hands in the pony's mane and had given the creature his head, no longer pretending to any control of his own.

A double bang from behind, surprisingly close, and a branch exploded from a dry tree over to Frank's left. The nullah wound to the right and they plunged down it, hemmed in now by banks of reddish earth six feet high. Frank risked looking up – he had not realised how low he had been crouching – and between the banks glimpsed the square fortress of Landi Kotal on the high ground ahead. Another shot from behind, this one smacking into the pebbles almost at the pony's feet so that the animal shied sideways and all but unseated him. Then the road was suddenly ahead, crossing the nullah on a low stone bridge. Frank kicked forward and grabbed Cavendish's bridle and put his horse up the side of the watercourse where the banks had crumbled, dragging Cavendish's mount with him through the soft earth.

They burst up onto the track. Somehow a group of dismounted Pathan riflemen blocked the way just ahead. Frank could hardly believe they had been outflanked now, at the last moment, but he hadn't time to worry about it. He lashed the rump of Cavendish's horse and it leapt forward, scattering the men on both sides, almost carrying its rider clear before a Pathan lunged forward and caught at the reins. Then two more shots cracked from behind him and Frank's horse screamed and slid on its knees and he was hurled over its head and came down on his back and rolled over and over into the thistles at the side of the track, winded and dazed. At once a ragged burst of firing erupted just above him and he looked up in time to see a knot of horsemen on the road a hundred yards back. One of them was knocked from the saddle as he watched and when the rider hit the ground his companions broke and fled.

Frank got to his knees, unable to understand what had happened, or how he was still alive. He had trouble breathing and pain stabbed him in the lower ribs when he tried. He groped inside his clothes and felt the revolver in its holster and guessed it had broken one of his ribs as he fell. Two yards away his pony was thrashing in the dust, shrieking, blowing bubbles of blood. Turning the other way Frank saw two Pathans pulling Cavendish from his horse. He closed his hand over the pistol's grip under his clothes, but before he could stand and draw it someone kicked him in the back. A man was standing over him, a tall handsome man in a khaki tunic and a turban with a puggaree of red cloth wound around it, the mark of the Khyber Rifles.

'Who the devil are you?' the man demanded.

Impossibly, he was speaking accentless English. Frank stared up at him, trying to make sense of this. He felt sure he had seen the man somewhere, but his brain would not function and as he was struggling with this riddle the man kicked him again.

'Answer me!' This time he spoke in bad Pushtu. 'Or have you lost your tongue?'

Past the man's shoulder Frank could see Cavendish seated by the roadside a few yards away, his injured leg stretched out in front of him.

One soldier was examining his wound while another was holding a goatskin of water to his lips. Cavendish pushed the goatskin away.

'The boy is with me,' he called, his voice weak but clear enough. 'He's one of us.'

The tall man put his hand on his hips and looked from Frank to Cavendish and back again. 'Looks like a dirty little wog to me.'

'He's as English as you or me,' Cavendish said, wearily. 'So don't shoot him just yet, Herrick, there's a good chap.'

Frank got slowly to his feet, easing the Bulldog out of its holster but keeping it under his clothing. Herrick faced him, watching him curiously. He was a big, sunburned man, with a finely trimmed moustache, and despite his dusty uniform he had a hint of the dandy about him. Frank recognised the face in Mrs Desai's creased photograph, a few years older, but undeniably the same man. Herrick held Frank's eyes for a long moment, puzzled by the intensity he saw there.

'Name?'

'Gray, sir. Trooper. Twenty-first Hussars.'

Herrick frowned: 'Do I know you, Gray?'

'Not yet.'

'What was that?' Herrick slitted his eyes and prepared to say more, changed his mind. 'Whoever you are, you've got a damned impudent manner about you.'

He turned his back and began to walk away. Frank pulled out the revolver and cocked it. There was an instant ripple of attention from the other men and one of them lifted the muzzle of his Martini-Henry. Sensing the tension, Herrick stopped in his tracks, his back still to Frank.

Frank stretched out his arm and shot the maimed horse through the head.

68

Yelland handed Grace down from the carriage. The old man opened an umbrella for her and, unable to keep up the proper reserve, he beamed at her as she stepped onto the gravel.

'It's good to see you home, miss. Very good indeed.'

Grace was on the point of making some cool remark concerning her homecoming, but then she saw that there were tears in the old butler's eyes and she felt ashamed. She smiled at him, and waited on the steps as the bags were carried up past her, looking around her. Well, it was good to see the rolling beech woods again, she could say that much, and even the silver winter rain was comforting and familiar. On the first floor the lamps were already glowing through the windows of her childhood bedroom, and Grace could not help taking pleasure in that too.

'Grace, dear? Why are you dawdling there in the rain?'

Her mother, standing under shelter at the top of the steps, asked the question as if there might be a literal answer to it which for the moment escaped her. That, Grace thought with a rush of affection, hadn't changed either.

'Hello, Mama.'

She ran up the steps and kissed her mother.

'Back from banishment,' Mrs Dearborn said, holding her at arm's length. 'No doubt you've properly repented of all your sins, whatever they were.'

Grace said nothing.

'Of course you have, my dear,' her mother supplied, and led her through into the hall. 'I shall have some tea sent in and we can chat in the drawing room. There's a lovely fire in there. You can tell me all about Venice.'

'Vienna, Mama.'

'Was it? I'm afraid all these French cities sound the same to me.' She started to guide Grace towards the door of the drawing room and then rested her hand on her daughter's arm. 'I nearly forgot. Your father wants to see you. At once, he said.' She raised an ironic eyebrow. 'Terribly masterly.'

Grace stopped. 'Mama, it's not going to start already, is it?'

'Oh, I expect so.' Her mother laughed gaily. 'Just let him have his head for a while and everything will be fine. They're like horses, my dear. Haven't you learned that yet?'

'Horses?'

'Men. You cannot win a trial of strength against them, but if you're a skilful rider you can manage them quite well. Then you can try to steer them away from harm and, if you're lucky, occasionally get taken to where you want to go.'

'Mama, how can you bear such compromises?'

'Life is compromise, my dear. That's what it's about.' Her bantering manner fell away. 'I had to learn that a long while ago. Perhaps it's time you did.'

Across the hall, the study door opened, and her father called, 'Grace?'

His voice was firm, neutral, betraying nothing. Grace met her mother's eyes for an instant, then swept across the hall to meet her father.

'Papa.'

'Grace, my dear. I'm pleased to see you home.' He hesitated, and added, 'So very pleased.'

He inclined his head stiffly and allowed her to kiss his cheek. She felt the familiar roughness of his jaw and smelled his cologne and for a moment her heart swooped and she longed to forget everything and throw her arms around him. She might have done just that, but he seemed anxious to keep his face averted from her and turned away too quickly, and the moment was lost.

She followed him through the door into the study. He waved her to sit by the fire which glowed in the grate, but she remained standing, her hands resting on the back of one of his red leather chairs. She saw that a faded inkblot still stained the marble fire surround, a shape like the ghost of a Habsburg eagle. It seemed decades ago that she had stood in this room and watched with horror as that stain was created. In fact it was barely twelve months, but she felt much more than a year older. Her father had aged too, she saw. He was greyer, heavier, less fluid in his movements. He fiddled with his watch chain. She realised with surprise that he was nervous. And – with still more surprise – that she was not.

A letter lay on the desk just behind him. He pointed at it without looking. 'This is unfortunate news about Princess Wilhelmina.' His voice was a shade too loud.

'Indeed, Papa?' She wondered what he had been told.

'Ruined, or so Welti informs me. Extraordinary.' He picked up the letter. 'I suppose this explains your unexpected return.' He slapped the letter against the back of his free hand, perhaps waiting for her to confirm this or deny it. When she did neither he said, 'At any rate I can't pretend that it isn't good to see you home. Where you belong.'

'Thank you, Papa. I'm glad to see you, too.' And she had to add, because it was true, 'Very glad.'

'I hope your stay in Vienna was . . .' He cleared his throat, but could not seem to decide how to go on.

'I learned a lot in Vienna, Papa.'

'Good. Good.' He stared past her at the wall. 'I hope we can . . .' Once again he stumbled, as if he had rehearsed a speech but now found that he could not deliver it. At last he looked directly at her, and when he spoke his voice had lost its formal timbre. 'Do you know, Puss, what my fondest wish is?'

'Papa?'

'That everything in this house might once again be as it was. That's all.'

For a moment she thought her heart would break. Was it so much to ask, after all? He looked so very worn and tired. She wondered if he was unwell, if perhaps she was responsible for that: she knew that if there was anyone who could get beneath his armour and wound him, it was she. Was much more demanded of her now than one of her mother's harmless compromises, a form of words only, a gesture of obedience, something that would allow him to keep his dignity? Then everything might be as it once was.

'Things will change here, Grace,' he said, and his eyes were bright. 'I shall see to it that they do. The mistakes have not been entirely on your side, I am bound to say. I have neglected to take account of your . . . of your needs, as a young and spirited—'

'Father, this isn't necessary.'

'No, Grace, let me speak. There has been little company for you here at Cumver, suitable company. I have been very taken up with business, you see . . . Well, well, that shall change. We shall introduce some new faces here, new, young faces. Weekend parties. Dances. What do you say to that? And perhaps we might take a town house in London for the season, introduce you to some new society.'

'Father—'

'And travel. Your mother's been telling me for years that we should see more of Europe. Monte Carlo, Biarritz, Switzerland . . . I could do with taking some time away from the company, and there's very little that old Welti can't handle on my behalf. As a matter of fact I have taken some steps. The moment we got word that you were coming home . . .'

He opened his desk drawer and took out a handsome cardboard wallet printed with the colours of the Pacific and Orient steamship company. He put the wallet on the blotter and patted it, smiling desperately at her.

'A cruise. It was all rather short notice, but I have managed to secure some excellent berths. The Mediterranean countries are chilly at this time of year, I grant you, but at least the weather will be brighter than here. Now this will take us to Malta, and then Alexandria, and through the Aegean to—'

'Father,' she said, more loudly.

'My dear?'

She stared down at the little packet of tickets. She would so have liked to have accepted his offer, but she knew it wouldn't do. And looking at his eyes, so uncharacteristically eager and supplicant, she guessed that he, too, knew that it wouldn't do. She took a deep breath.

'Father, you should know that I won't be staying at home for long.'

She saw him wince as at a jab of pain, furrow his brow to disguise it. 'Not staying? I don't quite understand.'

'I'll be here for just a couple of weeks. I intend to move out after that.'

He forced a laugh of sorts. 'Grace, you've just this moment got back.'

'I'm sorry, Father. I wish to move to London, and I think perhaps it will be less painful for all of us if I did so sooner rather than later.'

'Come, Grace. There's no need for this.'

'I am of an age to make such decisions for myself. I'm going to move to London.'

She could see him struggle to master his reaction, but he managed it, made his tone gentle. 'My dear, things were difficult when you left. No one's denying that. And I understand too that, coming back after all this time, you might find life here at Cumver somewhat provincial—'

'Those are not the reasons.'

'You fancy yourself a young woman of the world. You're restless—'

'Father, it's nothing to do with all that, at least not in the way you imagine.'

'What, then?' He shook his head helplessly. 'I'm trying to understand, Grace, believe me.'

'I have seen certain things in Vienna, experienced certain things. I now know the world is not as I always believed it to be. I know that there are aspects of it which need to change.'

'And this is your responsibility?' He laughed in a brittle fashion. 'To change the world?'

'I suppose it is everyone's responsibility. I have no inflated ambitions, Father, but I shall try to do what I can.'

'But how?'

'I've found employment. I shall be earning my own income.'

'You have no need to earn your own income. You never will have such a need.' He looked bewildered. 'Come along, Grace. I'm overjoyed to see you. Your mother is, too. Can we not celebrate that? Must we start one of these destructive arguments within the first ten minutes?'

'There's no need at all for argument, Father. That's the last thing I want. But I've found a position, and there it is.'

He straightened his spine and she could see the tenderness drain from him. 'What *position* is this?'

'It's on a newspaper. I contacted them on my way back from Vienna.'

'What newspaper?'

'*The Free Briton*. In the Strand. It's not large, but it has quite a respectable pedigree. Mr William Morris, Mr Ruskin, Mr Keir Hardie – they have all contributed to it.'

'You call that respectable?'

'Of course it would be a very humble position to start with, merely an extra hand in the office, for a few shillings a week.'

'Do you think I would permit my own daughter to work as an office menial for some subversive scandal sheet?' He moved to stand close to her. 'To be an employee anywhere?'

'I would like your blessing, Father. But if I can't have it, I shall manage without. And I shall support myself.'

'You've no idea what that means.'

'Then I shall find out. After all, I only wish to do as you have done, and make my own way in the world.'

'Neatly turned, Grace, but not good enough. You're a rich young woman. A very rich young woman. The destiny I have in mind for you does not involve *employment*.'

'What about the destiny I have in mind for myself?'

'You'll permit me to be the better judge of that. I have plans for you.'

'I have my own plans, Father. I'm sorry if they cause you distress.' She looked at him levelly. 'You might as well know. One of my plans is to find Frank Gray.'

His face suffused. 'If you dare so much as mention—'

Her patience snapped. 'Father, this is all perfectly useless. I'm not the frightened and posturing girl who stood in this room a year ago. I've seen rather too much of life to be susceptible to browbeating. I've grown up, don't you understand that?'

He stepped back from her as if struck and the hurt and puzzlement flooded back into his face and made her pity him again.

'I'm sorry, Father. I know this is difficult for you. I would so much rather have your support. So much rather.' She left a pause, but he did not fill it, and so she walked past him to the door. 'I won't stay long. It would cause constant friction between us, and I should hate that.'

'Then leave this house now.'

That caught her by surprise. 'Now?'

'Now. Today. I never thought you would treat me in this way, Grace. I'm unaware of what I am supposed to have done to deserve it. I would have done anything for you. I would still . . .'

Unbelievably, his voice trembled. She stepped towards him.

'Father, please—'

He turned away sharply. 'Grace, I thought you might at least have learned that there are consequences to actions. Since you have not, you had best start learning that lesson right away. I shall not support you, Grace, if you leave. Not now and not in the future. If you're going to leave, you will leave without a penny.'

'If that's what you wish.'

'It's not what I wish, Grace. It's what you force upon me. If you are leaving, you have an hour to pack. One hour. That's my last word.'

She stood with her hand on the door jamb, looking back at him. 'You know I have always loved you, Father. I don't quite know how things have come to this between us, but I should not wish that to go unsaid.'

He snatched up a paper at random from his desk and frowned fiercely at it. 'An hour. Do you hear?'

She stepped out into the hallway and quietly closed the door behind her.

A little dazed, she walked down the hallway and found herself at the front door. A footman opened it for her and she emerged into the rain and stood under the portico, listening to the chuckling of the down-pipes and gratefully drinking the cool air. Under the wide sky she felt foolish and exultant and frightened by turns. She was glad she was alone.

But at that moment she saw that she was not alone at all. At the bottom of the steps stood a curious bright red contraption with a hood like an over-sized perambulator, leather seats, and large shiny-spoked wheels. A horseless carriage. She had seen a few in London, but as far as she knew no one had ever brought one here. A man was crouched on the wet gravel beside one of the front wheels, adjusting something with a spanner, and as Grace spotted him he looked up and smiled. He was a sandy haired man of about thirty with a tweed jacket, ridiculous goggles and a white scarf. His breath steamed in the raw air and he was very wet, his fair hair pasted to his skull by the rain. He had a smear of grease on his cheek.

'Hello,' he said brightly.

'Who are you? And what's that . . . *thing* doing here?'

He opened his mild blue eyes. 'As to the first question, miss, my name is Alec Strathair. I had some business with your father, though my timing seems unpropitious. As to the second, this *thing* is a Panhard-Levassor automobile which is doing very little at present, to my chagrin. I think its timing needs adjustment, like my own.'

'Really.' She tossed her head. 'So what are you staring at?'

He grinned and flicked raindrops off his moustache. 'A third question! Well, if I were staring, I think I'd be forgiven for it.'

But his attempt at charm merely annoyed her. He had a soft Scottish accent and that annoyed her too. She couldn't be bothered to find a civil reply, or any reply, and after a moment she turned on her heel and stalked back into the house and ran up the stairs to her room.

69

Her trunk and her few bags had already been carried up and Millie and one of the other maids were busy unpacking them. The floor and the bed were littered with books, papers and clothing. Both girls bobbed to Grace as she came in.

'Ever so happy you're back, miss,' Millie said. 'Cumver's been empty without you.'

The girl's sincerity was so clear, and the bright room so familiar, that Grace felt her throat tighten. 'Thank you, Millie. But I'm afraid Cumver will have to get used to being empty again. This will all have to be repacked.'

Millie looked at the other girl in consternation, and then at the strewn clothes. 'But we was just finishing, miss.'

'I'm sorry, Millie. I want all these clothes put back in my bags.'

'Miss—'

'You can do it in a moment. I shall send word. Now I'd like to be alone.'

'Yes, miss.'

The maids left, exchanging significant looks. Grace stood for a moment after they had gone, glancing around her. Her childish paintings still hung on the walls, and the psalter she had embroidered as an exercise when she was ten; even her old girlhood toys ranged in their habitual places on the top of the wardrobe. She wished her father had given her just a few days. It seemed cruel that she should rediscover these old familiar comforts now, only to be forced to leave them again at once. She stepped between the opened bags to stand by the window, her old vantage point over woods and downs. Outside, crows were calling from the bare woods as the evening drew in. It came to Grace that she had stood in this spot and listened to those birds from her earliest days, knowing herself safe, knowing herself loved, if sometimes clumsily. Now she would never stand here again.

There was a sharp tap on the door and Mrs Rossiter swept in, her dark taffeta rustling. She closed the door behind her and stood with her back to it.

Grace said, 'I'm glad to see you, Mrs Rossiter.'

'What's this about?' the housekeeper demanded. 'You just got back, and already the servants are at sixes and sevens and your mother's in floods, which I never seen before.'

'I'm not staying.'

'You're just going to walk out?'

Grace gave a short laugh. 'I think I'll have to.'

'And do what?'

'I shall work. In London. I have a job, of sorts. On a newspaper. I suppose that's what I always wanted.'

'You don't have the least idea what you're letting yourself in for.'

'I'll survive.' Grace selected one of the emptied cases, put it on the bed. She stuffed clothes into the case, found there was no room for them and dragged them out again.

'For Gawd's sake, give that here.' Mrs Rossiter snatched the case out of Grace's hands, tipped the clothes onto the bed, and began savagely to fold and pack them. 'You think you'd be able to live for a week without your father's money?'

'Yes.'

Mrs Rossiter flung the suitcase lid down. 'And could you wheel and deal, miss, and lie when you need to, and trade for your daily bread? Sell a bit of your soul every day, just to eat, just to live?'

'I'd be selling my soul if I stayed here. That much I do know.'

Mrs Rossiter seemed about to snap back a retort, but then changed her mind. She busied herself closing the catches on the suitcase and spent a moment or two running her hands over the leather. 'Lord, miss,' she said in a smaller voice. 'You won't even be able to lift this.'

Grace reached past her and hefted the suitcase. It was monstrously heavy. She tried to pretend it was not, but it was hopeless. She let the case thud onto the floor and stood looking at it.

The housekeeper got up, walked around the bed and suddenly caught Grace in her arms. 'Give it up, miss, I'm begging you. Swallow your pride, go and speak to your father. Apologise. Promise him anything. Do what you have to do. He's not a bad man, but he's proud, and he won't relent, not once you walk out that door.'

Grace patted the woman's back but pulled away from the embrace, not trusting herself to speak.

'Where will you go?' Mrs Rossiter said finally.

'I'll find somewhere. A little hotel at first. I have enough put by for that. Then I shall find a room of my own.'

'In London? Miss, you don't even know how you're going to get there.'

'I'll take the train.'

'Your father won't so much as let the coachman drive you to the station.'

'Then I shall walk.'

'Two miles? You? In this weather? With that case?' Mrs Rossiter shook her head. 'I'll have Jimmy Jervis take you down on the farm cart. He owes me a favour. I'll tell him to meet you at the bottom of the drive, but you be sure you're not seen, or we'll all be in trouble.'

They both fell silent. Outside, the evening birds were still calling from the woods.

'I should have burned that letter,' Mrs Rossiter said. 'It's brought you no good.'

'It brought me to my senses.'

'And are you in your senses now?'

Grace said nothing.

'I don't know where Frank is,' the housekeeper said. 'I'd tell you if I knew. He just vanished, and young Gifford likewise. No one has word.'

'Well. I shall find him, somehow. How did the letter reach you, Mrs Rossiter?'

'From Madras, sent through the Base Post Office there. But that's no help. I asked around some of Billy Rossiter's old muckers, such of them as are still drawing breath. They say you'd never trace a man through Madras, not a private soldier.'

'But the Army must keep records.'

'D'you have any idea how many men pass through that place every year? Thousands upon thousands. Men serving their time, signing up again, new drafts, men going on leave and coming back again, being posted off to God knows where. Plenty of them don't even use the names they was born with.'

'He would have joined the cavalry, Mrs Rossiter. I'm sure of that much.'

'In India, a good part of the Army's cavalry. Maybe if you checked every recruiting depot in England for new signings over the last year or so . . . But I wouldn't know how you'd start to do that.'

Grace stared out over the grey woods. They were fading like a fogged negative in the sinking light. More rain was gathering in the eastern sky and as she stood there she caught a distant rumble of thunder.

'It ain't my business, miss,' the older woman said at last, 'but Frank Gray could have told you where he was, if he'd wanted you to know. He told you to forget him, and I don't doubt it cost him something to say so. Maybe you should respect that.'

'I believe he was trying to protect me. To leave me free.'

The housekeeper sniffed. Grace turned to her.

'What do you believe, Mrs Rossiter?'

'I believe he's a soldier. There's no future in pining for a soldier, not on the strength of one pretty letter. He's after something out there in India. After someone, maybe. P'raps you know what that's about. I don't. But I do know it won't come to no good. That sort of business never does. He said as much himself.'

'He also said he loved me.'

'And that's enough for you, miss, is it?'

'Yes.'

The housekeeper sniffed again, and moved her shoulders inside her dress. 'Well, I suppose it was always enough for me, too.'

70

The office was cool after the heat of the late afternoon. Frank could feel sweat drying on his back, cold as alcohol. He stood to attention in front of the desk while the officer seated at it finished writing. The man was an imposing Afghan of middle age with a white turban, a khaki tunic, and a double row of campaign medals glinting beneath his magnificent beard. Through the single glaring window came the sound of men tramping on the parade ground, a distant order shouted in Pushtu. Frank found it soothing to listen to this distant activity, and to the small scratch of steel nib on white paper, and he hoped this would go on. But after a few moments the officer set his pen aside and looked up at him.

'Gray, is it?'

'Sir.'

'Do you know who I am, Gray?'

'Yes, sir. Colonel Aslam Khan, sir. Commandant of the Khyber Rifles.'

The colonel tilted his head approvingly. 'Very good. How is it my fame has spread so far?'

'I grew up in Peshawar, sir. Everyone in Peshawar knows you.'

It was true. When he had been a boy Aslam Khan's name had already been spoken of, scion of the Afghan royal house and closest collaborator of Colonel Warburton, Political Officer Khyber and founder of the Khyber Rifles.

From behind him, Herrick snapped, 'Stand to attention, Gray,' and Frank realised he had been swaying on his feet.

The colonel peered at him. 'The man's done in, Jack.' His English was accented but immaculate. 'Get Feroz to bring him a chair. And ask

Subahdar Mursil Khan to join us, would you? I should like him to hear this.'

Jack. Jack. Every time the name was repeated Frank could hear his mother screaming in the night, could see that broad-shouldered figure looming above him in the shadows.

'Sir.' Herrick made no attempt to disguise the distaste in his voice, but he strode to the door.

Frank hated the feeling of this man moving behind him. In the anteroom Herrick barked orders in his bad Pushtu and then came back into the office and stopped on the edge of Frank's peripheral vision. It appalled Frank to think how close he had come out there today, the revolver in his fist, his blood up, the first sight of the man he had dreamed about for so long. If he had pulled the trigger Herrick would have died without even knowing the cause, and within moments, Frank knew, he himself would have been shot down. What shocked him was that he had never thought of this. He had plotted his meeting with this man for so long, and he had always known the outcome, but he had never once considered how it was to be accomplished.

'Sit down, Gray,' Aslam Khan told him.

It was possible the colonel had already said this once. Frank felt behind him for the chair and sat clumsily. There was a third man in the room now, a magnificent subahdar with scarlet cummerbund and royal blue turban. He was standing by the side of the colonel's desk, legs planted apart, regarding Frank with coal black eyes. He had ferocious whiskers and scars on his face and hands. He was, Frank thought, the most fearsome man he had ever seen.

'I have visited Captain Cavendish in the infirmary,' the colonel said. 'This gallant officer is in a serious condition. I pray things may improve for him, but that is in God's hands.' He sat back so that his chair creaked. 'He spoke to me of the situation in the tribal lands bordering the pass. He also urged me to speak to you, Gray.'

'To me, sir?'

'That surprised me somewhat, also. Yet Captain Cavendish seems to value your opinion. What do you make of that?'

Frank stared over the colonel's head at the photograph of the ageing Queen Victoria that hung on the wall. A trapped fly buzzed against the window. 'I couldn't say, sir.'

'Captain Cavendish believes there is to be an imminent uprising among the Afridis. Why would he think that?'

'Captain Cavendish offered to sell them Lee-Enfields, sir. Gul Shah would have taken the bait, but he had a mullah with him who spoke against us. He said they already had enough weapons.'

The room grew quiet.

'What mullah?'

'Mullah Haddid, sir. That's what Gul Shah called him.'

'And what exactly did he say, this mullah?'

'That they could already arm twenty thousand Pathan warriors.'

'Twenty thousand of the beggars?' Herrick said with scorn. 'This is balderdash. The Pathans are always short of rifles. They'd sell their own mothers for a Martini-Henry, never mind a Lee-Enfield.'

Aslam Khan raised his hand to silence him. 'You believed this mullah, Gray?'

'More or less, sir.'

'And yet, as Major Herrick points out, they're always short of rifles.'

'Then I suppose they've got them from somewhere else, sir.'

'The Pathans make their own,' Herrick said. 'Every fool knows that. At Darra Adam Khel they've been copying our breech-loaders for years. But they couldn't possibly have enough for twenty thousand men. It's preposterous.'

Aslam Khan tilted his head at Frank. 'What do you say to that, Gray?'

'That's true, sir. If they have the number of rifles Haddid bragged about, they must have come from further afield.'

'Where?'

'I don't know, sir. Perhaps Sudan.'

'Why do you say that?'

'This mullah was a foreigner. Captain Cavendish was fairly sure he was from the Sudan. Also, Haddid let slip they've been dealing with the Ghilzai clan, sir. They specialise in smuggling rifles over from the African side.'

Herrick snorted in derision, but the colonel held his hand up again.

'Let him speak, Jack. Go on.'

'As I understand it, sir, the Ghilzai buy or steal rifles mostly from the Egyptian police and army. Remingtons and Martini-Henrys. Then they have them shipped across the Red Sea in dhows, and over the desert to Afghanistan. I'd guess the Pathans have recently taken delivery of a lot more, sir.'

Frank sensed the three men looking at one another.

'So you think we should take this Mullah Haddid seriously?' Aslam Khan said.

'Not any more, sir.'

'Why not?'

'Because I shot him. But I expect there are others like him, sir.'

'I expect so, too.' The colonel leaned back in his chair. 'Mullah

Sadullah in Swat, for instance. Or Mullah Powindah in Waziristan. You have heard of these men?'

'No, sir.'

'Well, we are hearing a good deal about them. They seem to be of the same stripe as your Mullah Haddid, but locally grown. There are others, too. Mystics, fanatics, Wahhabists, *ghazis* of one sort or another. There are rumours that men like these are inciting the Pathan tribes, uniting them under a false banner of the Prophet, convincing them that the British can be beaten, that in fact the Empire is already crumbling. The tribesmen have no way of knowing the truth of these stories, but are anxious to believe them all the same. They would like an excuse to fight the British instead of one another.' Aslam Khan pursed his lips. 'You are British, Gray. Do you think your armies can be beaten?'

'Yes, sir.'

'You do?'

'Anyone can be beaten. And after all, they've done it to us before.'

'Impertinence!' Herrick hissed from behind him.

But Frank saw a flicker of amusement in Aslam Khan's eyes.

'Very well, Gray. You are dismissed.'

Frank stood, saluted, and marched out of the office. As he passed, Herrick said, 'Wait outside, Gray. I want a word with you.'

Frank waited outside in the ink shadow of the buildings, half-asleep where he stood. A hundred yards away a fierce havildar in shiny boots and immaculate puttees was drilling a squad of Khyber Rifles recruits on the parade ground, their bare feet kicking up yellow dust. They were a savage-looking band, with their scraps of uniform and their bandoliers of cartridges and their wild hair. Half of them were grinning, as if performing these ridiculous movements were the most amusing thing in the world to them. The more they grinned, the more furious the havildar grew. Above them the Union flag drooped from its staff, colours gaudy against the pale sky. Frank wondered what any of them were doing here, he and Cavendish, Pathan recruits and British soldiers alike, going through movements nobody understood, pretending to wield some sort of authority over this utterly alien place.

'You think I don't know what you're about, Gray?' Herrick said, moving up behind him. His voice was easy and musical. 'You might convince the colonel you're God's gift to military intelligence, but not me. I'm afraid swanning about with poor old Cavendish has given you ideas above your station.'

Frank stood rigidly to attention as Herrick stalked around him.

'A little sniping and brigandage is one thing, but a revolt? I don't think so. They're savages, these people. If you want to make a name for yourself, Gray, you'll have to do better than cook up some Pathan conspiracy. Do you understand?' When Frank didn't answer Herrick prodded him in the breastbone with his swagger stick and repeated with exaggerated clarity, '*Do you understand me?*'

Frank kept his eyes on the squad of shambling recruits. His silence was insubordination, and Herrick could punish him for it, they both knew that, but for some reason Herrick seemed reluctant to do so. He lowered his voice again.

'You're a strange one, Gray. I'm bound to say there's something about you that puts me on edge. What might that be, do you think?'

'I don't know, sir,' Frank said, meeting his eyes for the first time.

Herrick stood looking at him, his mouth pursed. Frank wondered if there was any glimmer of recognition in the man's mind, or had he been too wild with drink or pain or fury to remember anything of that night? Or had Frank himself changed too much? Well, Herrick would remember soon enough. That thought must have shown in Frank's eyes.

'You're an insolent young swine, Gray, aren't you?' Herrick snapped. 'I shall be rejoining the Twenty-first very soon. I shall look forward to seeing you then, I give you fair warning.'

He rammed his swagger stick under his arm, turned on his heel and strode away.

Frank waited until the man was out of sight and then made his way around the parade ground and between the clutter of low buildings until he found the infirmary. A civilian orderly was on duty, an elderly Afridi with a face like pickled leather. The man was dozing in the shadow of the doorway. Frank stepped past him into a long room which had plastered walls and a pitched corrugated iron roof with cobwebs hanging between the beams. He glimpsed a dozen wooden beds, all apparently empty. He walked between them and heard the orderly scramble to his feet and hurry after him, his bare feet slapping on the floor. The room was hot and dim. Sacking had been tacked over the windows to cut down the glare but a few spokes of sunlight found their way in as if a battery of searchlights had been mounted outside. A punkah, operated by a boy out of sight on the veranda, moved sluggishly in the afternoon heat. Frank could hear distant shouted orders, the snort of a horse, the drone of flies.

He found Cavendish on the last cot at the far end of the room, shrouded by a mosquito net. Frank gently pulled the net aside. Cavendish's eyes were closed and he was paler than Frank had ever seen a living man. His right knee was swathed in fresh bandages, but thin fluid had already leaked through and a couple of flies were circling lazily around the wet stains. Frank waved them away.

'I have done what I can for the officer,' the orderly said in Pushtu. 'The colonel sahib commanded it himself. But he is very sick, very sick. The wound is burning. I have cut out the bullet, but we have no doctor, you understand. I am not—'

'What's your name?'

'I am Tariq, sahib.'

'Show me where I can wash, Tariq.'

'Through there, sahib. I shall bring water.'

'And then I'll sleep in here for a while.'

'But sahib, it is not permitted—'

Frank ignored him and stepped through to a lean-to at the rear of the building and gingerly stripped off his rags of native clothing. A purple bruise spread from under his left arm, where the revolver had been holstered, and round to his breastbone. He fingered the bruise, probing for the raised edge of a broken rib. A stab of pain told him he had found it, and he felt faint, and leaned against the wall until Tariq came slapping in with a bucket. Frank washed as well as he could, the cold water reviving him, then went back into the main room of the infirmary and sat on the cot in the corner, opposite Cavendish's bed. The cot was no more than a stained mattress on a wooden base but it felt like luxury and Frank's head swam with the urge to stretch out on the rough ticking and sleep and sleep.

Tariq reappeared with a roll of wide bandage. 'The rib is broken, sahib. It must be strapped, or it will pierce your lung.'

He gestured to Frank to lift his arms and Frank did as he was told, too weary to resist. With surprising dexterity the old man wound the bandage under his arms and around his chest. It hurt damnably, but when Tariq had finished, the firm support of the binding was comforting. Frank looked past the man's grizzled head as he worked, and out through the torn sacking of the window above the bed. A horseman was riding around the perimeter of the dusty parade ground towards the gate. The man reined in, there was an exchange of orders and salutes, and the great gates were swung open. It was only as the rider urged his horse out into the wide evening beyond the walls that Frank recognised him as Herrick.

'Now, there's a man with hot blood,' Tariq observed, following Frank's gaze, and rocked his head admiringly. 'A fierce officer, that Herrick sahib. A fierce drinker, too.'

As the gates swung closed Frank glimpsed Herrick once more,

spurring his horse down the track in a cloud of grit, an impatient man on a mission.

'Where does he go?'

'To the caravanserai, young sahib. He rides down there often.'

'How often?'

'Every night, almost, except when the officer sahibs dine off silver here in the fort, with the colonel.'

'What does he do there, in the caravanserai?'

'He says that he goes to check on the latest *kafila* in from Kabul or Peshawar.' Tariq grinned, tied the loose ends of the bandage and tugged the knot so tight that Frank gasped. 'But we all know the truth, sahib. He has a woman at the caravanserai.'

'What time does he return?'

'Late. Always after the guard has changed.'

Frank sat staring out of the window at the gates. After the guard changed. After midnight.

'Tariq, I'm going to sleep now. I want you to watch over Captain Cavendish.'

'As the sahib wishes.'

'Keep him cool. Give him water. Keep those damned flies away from him.'

Frank rolled himself carefully down onto the mattress and closed his eyes. In a little while he heard Tariq shuffle away on the bare floor, muttering. His ribs ached like the devil, but it wasn't the pain which kept him awake, despite his weariness. It was the image of Herrick, unsuspecting, half-naked in some whore's arms, or later, fumbling for his horse in the dark behind the caravanserai, fuddled with drink. Not too fuddled. Frank didn't want that. He wanted him to know what was about to happen, and why. Frank reached for the Bulldog and slid it under his pillow. He let his hand rest over the butt and fell asleep.

71

He came awake, sharply awake, to the bugler sounding Sunset. He waited, unmoving, for perhaps another hour. The infirmary was cooler now, and washed with light from an enormous moon which hung above the fort walls like a great lantern. Outside, crickets were sawing in the mulberry trees around the parade ground. Frank sat up, caught his breath as his injured rib stabbed him. He moved more carefully after that, dropping his feet onto the cold floor and standing up slowly. He pulled on his clothes, slipped the Bulldog into his

Khyber Rifles here and I expect we'll manage without you.' The colonel paused. 'And as a matter of fact, after England, you won't be coming back to India at all. I hear your regiment's being redeployed to Egypt. Some trouble in the Sudan. So if you are spoiling for a fight, you might get one. But not here.'

Frank stood in silence. Outside in the early cool he could hear a parade forming up, the tramp of boots, bellowed orders. Tonight, probably, Herrick would be down at the caravanserai again. But by then Frank would be on the way to Peshawar. On the way to England.

'You're a remarkable young man, Gray,' Aslam Khan was saying. 'I've recommended your promotion to corporal. If I'm any judge and fortune smiles on you, I should be surprised if you did not rise a good deal higher in the Empire's service.' He paused. 'I expect you meant to thank me for that, Gray.'

'Yes, sir. Thank you, sir.'

'Very well. The *kafila* is leaving from the caravanserai before midday. Be sure that you and Cavendish are with it. And good luck.'

72

Jimmy Jervis avoided her eyes as he whipped the old horse hard along the familiar lane to the station. It was full evening now. The rain was falling heavily and dark trees were shifting in the rising wind. Jimmy pulled into the station yard.

'Here we are, miss.' He glanced behind him as if afraid of pursuit. 'Quick sticks, now. Jump down.'

His tone brought Grace back to herself. She climbed down, biting back a sharp answer. *Quick sticks* indeed. Just a few hours ago such informality would have been unthinkable. He did not even get down to help her with her suitcase. Indeed he pulled away before she had quite got it off the back, so that the heavy case knocked against her leg. Before she could protest the cart clattered out of the station yard and back down the lane. Jimmy didn't even look round.

She stood watching the vehicle dwindle out of sight between the wet trees. So this was the new world she had entered, a world where ignorant working lads felt they did not even owe her courtesy. Well then, she had best get used to it. She began to lug her case across the yard. As she reached the ticket window the stationmaster emerged from his office.

She drew herself up. 'Good evening, Mr Manners.'

'Miss Dearborn.' He looked at her in surprise. 'I heard you were back, miss. Welcome indeed.'

'Thank you.'

He glanced down at the suitcase. 'Off on another trip so soon?'

'Evidently.'

'I see. Well, I hope you haven't come for the 6.27, miss. 'Tis cancelled. A problem with the track near Farnham. I just put it up on the board there, see?'

She put her case down. Of all the setbacks she might have expected, she was unprepared for this one. 'But I have to get to London.'

'Sorry, miss, but cancelled it is. Was it that Jimmy Jervis who brought you down? I'll get someone to fetch him back if you like.'

'No. There must be another train, surely?'

'In the normal course of things there'd be the 9.03, miss. But that'll only run if the line's clear, and even so you'd not make a London connection at Guildford.' Mr Manners pushed back his peaked cap. 'Is everything all right, miss?'

'Please don't concern yourself, Mr Manners.'

He sucked his teeth. 'Thing is, I'm locking up now, miss.'

'You'll not be back?'

'I'll come back down if the 9.03's running. But you wouldn't intend waiting for that. It's close on three hours and it's going to be a cold night.'

'Certainly I shall wait.'

'But I can get one of my boys to run you back up to Cumver.'

'No.' She realised she had spoken sharply, and made an effort to soften her voice. 'No, thank you, Mr Manners.'

He sighed, bent down and picked up her case. 'Well, you're welcome to use the waiting room, miss. I'll leave it open for you. I lit the stove in there earlier, and it's still warm.'

The waiting room floor was littered with cigarette butts and the iron stove gave off fumes which caught in her throat. She supposed that was what was making her feel sick. But after a few minutes the stove burned itself out and it began to grow chill. Grace got up and paced around, but the dry hiss of the gas lamp oppressed her, and the reek of coke from the dead fire. She opened the door and stepped out onto the platform. The night air was sharp and clean, but it was still raining and she was surprised at how cold it was. The church clock in the village struck seven.

She put on her coat and pulled her hood over her face and walked across the yard and up onto the bridge where the road crossed the track. There was still some light in the sky to the west, and the wet rails shone. If the train did run, she would eventually see the engine from here, and it made her feel less helpless to watch for it. Besides, from this vantage point she could scan the lane from Cumver. She was almost sure her father would not come after her; such a capitulation was not in his nature. But she began to torture herself with fears of what she would do if he did, and if she were indeed to see the lamps of his gig come winking between the trees. She wondered if she could find the courage to face him down again. Yet it was impossible even to contemplate an ignominious return to Cumver now.

And then her heart jumped, because there they were already, two yellow pinpricks of light in the distance, blurred by the rain. But there was something odd about them. They did not move with the bouncing rhythm of the carriage lamps on the gig, and they seemed to be approaching unusually fast. She caught a sound then, a low sputtering growl which grew louder.

The machine rushed the last few yards, roaring and smoking, and she glimpsed a man in a leather coat in the driving seat, white scarf flowing in the wind. He must have seen her at the same moment, for the vehicle squealed to a halt on the opposite side of the road and stood there clattering. He pushed up his goggles and leaned out of the car, gazing at her in astonishment.

'Miss Dearborn, is it?' He switched off the clamouring engine. The hissing of the rain seemed suddenly very loud as the din shrank away. He climbed out, peeled off his gauntlets and walked across to her. 'Miss Dearborn, whatever are you doing here? Is something wrong?'

'There's nothing at all wrong. I merely missed my train, that's all.' She knew how absurd she must look, standing by the side of the road, cold and wet.

'Well, you can't stand here. You're soaked.' He took her arm and tried to guide her to the car.

She pulled her arm away. 'Thank you, but I don't need assistance.'

He stepped back. 'Forgive me, but you're shivering. Please, just sit inside the car a moment. The hood leaks a bit, but it's better than standing in the rain.'

His concern was so unaffected that this time she let him usher her across the road to the car and into the leather passenger seat. Before she noticed what he was doing he had found a travelling rug and draped it around her. He climbed in beside her and sat with his hands on the steering tiller as if he wasn't quite sure what to do with them.

'I suppose you know what happened,' she said tersely. 'At Cumver, I mean.'

'It would be hard not to know something had happened. Your

father's very upset. He's not the sort of man to show it, but it was plain nevertheless. I was invited to stay, but I don't mind telling you, the atmosphere in the house was such that I cut short our business meeting and left early.'

'I see.' She looked quickly at him, and then away again. 'I've forgotten your name.'

'Alec Strathair. I'm pleased to make your acquaintance.'

He held out his hand, but she pretended not to see it and stared out through the shimmering windscreen. He put his hand in his lap.

'Mr Strathair, can you drive me to Guildford?'

'Can I? Well, yes, for the matter of that, I can.'

'All right, all right. Will you?'

'That's a different question.'

'It's a perfectly simple request.'

'If I may say so, Grace – may I call you Grace? – it is not at all a simple request. Because I know what I ought to do. I ought to drive you back to Cumver, and urge you to make amends with your father. But' – he raised a finger before she could move – 'if I so much as suggest such a thing you will get out of the car. So I will not suggest it, because I don't wish you to catch your death of cold, if you haven't already. On the other hand, if I drive you to Guildford, I become complicit.'

'There's no complicity involved, I assure you, Mr Strathair. Complicity implies something underhand. My train's been cancelled and I want to go to Guildford. It's as simple as that.'

'Aye.' The bantering tone left his voice. 'That's very fine. But in fact, you're a young girl who's run away from her home, and who isn't even aware of the vulnerable position she has put herself in, out alone on a deserted road at night. I should be complicit indeed if I went along with that.'

'I assure you I've been in more threatening situations than this.' Grace threw off the rug. 'But thank you for the lecture.'

'There again, Grace,' he continued, in a steady voice which stopped her as she was about to step out of the car, 'I understand something of your position, having had experience myself of, shall we say, heavy handed parents.'

It was silent in the car except for the soft roar of the rain on the hood.

'Where are you really going?' he asked.

'To London.'

'And where in London?'

'I shall stay a night or two in an hotel. I don't have a particular one in mind.'

'I see. And then?'

'I have . . . an offer of employment. Tomorrow or the next day I shall find a room.' She stared stonily ahead. 'Is that sufficient information?'

He drummed his fingers on the tiller. 'Well, Grace, no man could call himself a gentleman if he motored past a damsel in distress on a night like this, leaving her to fend for herself. Yet, at the same time, no one who ever wished to have dealings with Mr Stephen Dearborn would advance his case very much if he helped the said Mr Dearborn's errant daughter on her foolish flight from duty and obedience. So it seems clear to me that this meeting never took place. Did it, now?'

She looked at him directly for the first time. He was gazing innocently at her with his blue eyes.

She said, 'No.'

'Good. Well, as it happens, I'm not driving to Guildford. But I am going up to London. Shall I tell you how we'll do this, Grace? I know a respectable family hotel not far from Tottenham Court Road. I am prepared to take you there, on one condition.'

'I don't believe I am subject to conditions.'

'No? Well, that's a shame, because I shall insist on this one before I drive a non-existent young woman to London. Otherwise I think she might be better off taking her bedraggled plumage back home.'

Grace stared out at the road, where the rain was now thrashing the puddles. 'Very well. What is this condition?'

'That I give you my address and you promise to contact me tomorrow.'

'Why?'

'Because I wish to be assured that when you leave the hotel you find respectable rooms, or if you don't, that at the very least you have someone to turn to for help. I need hardly say, I have no other motive. That's my condition. If you don't accept it, you can step down now.'

Strathair didn't wait for her to answer but got out, walked round to the front of the vehicle, inserted a long metal handle in the front and swung it easily. The engine burst into life. He came back to the window and leaned in to drop the handle ringing behind his seat.

'I have a suitcase in the station waiting room,' she said, keeping her eyes straight ahead.

'Very good. I shall fetch it.'

'And Mr Strathair?'

'Yes?'

'Thank you.'

He laughed and, hooding his jacket over his head, ran away through the rain to the station.

Three hours later Grace sat by the window in her hotel room, sipping tea Mrs Ashe the landlady had brought her. It was lukewarm now, but it was better than nothing. She was chilled; the journey here had been a blur of rain and noise, and the vibration of the awful vehicle had shaken her to her very bones.

Outside a horse-drawn tram went clattering by, ringing its bell at the corner of Gower Street. A couple of hackney carriages followed it, their lighter wheels hissing along the wet tarmac. Grace could hear the drivers exchanging grim jokes about the weather. Unfamiliar chimes struck eleven from a church somewhere in Bloomsbury. Eleven o'clock. It was preposterous to think that so short a time had passed since she had stood in her father's study. But it was so. The world, which had seemed jammed like a gear against a cog, had suddenly slipped and delivered her with a jolt into her new life.

The room was plain but pleasant enough, with pale blue walls and paintings of wildflowers hanging above the mantel. The streetlamp outside winked on the brass of the bedstead and threw long shadows across the ceiling. The noises from that strange sprawling city beyond the windows made her feel cocooned, but she knew she wouldn't be able to enjoy that sensation for long. She could afford perhaps three days here, and by then she would need to find a place of her own. She doubted it would be as comfortable as this.

Grace sighed and got to her feet and stripped off the last of her damp clothes, hanging them over the end of the bedstead. Her morocco writing case lay on the bed where she had put it, and she could see the corner of Frank's letter peeping out. Somewhere, presumably, Frank was inhabiting a new life of his own, a life even more alien than this. She had hoped that the thought of him would make her feel better, but as she sat on the bed she felt as alone as at any moment in her life.

Alec Strathair's card lay on the bedside table. He had pressed it into her hand downstairs in the hall, then ordered the tea for her from Mrs Ashe, and left. Just like that. He had not even taken his stupid goggles off. She remembered the clatter and roar of his bizarre machine as he drove away down Gower Street.

Grace lay back on the bed and pulled the sheets over herself. She reached over for Strathair's card, screwed it up without looking at it, and shied it across the room towards the grate. Then she rolled onto her side and closed her eyes.

PART EIGHT

England, June to September 1897

73

Grace could hardly see Mr Calloway through the filthy glass of his office partition and the fug of cigarette smoke within. But she heard his summons well enough. Mr Calloway wanted his tea.

Grace sighed and stood up. She made her way through the cramped tobacco-reeking reporters' room, between the battered tables and desks, each one of them piled with copy slips and newspapers, crammed ashtrays and stained cups. A couple of the reporters had been genial enough to Grace when she had arrived, and one or two openly lustful. She found them an odd crew, intense young men with university accents, tough characters from the labour movement, and a sprinkling of hard drinking hacks who could no longer find work on better paying publications. Today only four or five of them were at their desks. One of the subeditors, a bald man with bags under his eyes and rubber bands holding back filthy cuffs, leered at her as she passed. The others ignored her as they usually did, smoking furiously, hammering at their ancient typewriters.

She went out through the glass doors onto the stairwell and into the closet that passed for a kitchen, and put the kettle on the gas hob. The room was squalid, with half-eaten sandwiches curling on the draining board and tea leaves clogging the sink. It smelled of cat's piss, a stench that reminded her depressingly of Max's building in Vienna. It was the meanness that upset her most. The place lacked any touch of dignity. As did Mr Calloway himself, with his black nails and mottled skin. She hadn't expected that when she had corresponded with him. She'd imagined someone out of the ordinary, certainly – someone even slightly bohemian – but someone with at least a whiff of crusading zeal about him. If such passion still lurked somewhere under the cynicism and the foul language, Grace had never been allowed to see it.

She poured the tea, spooned in four sugars, stirred it, grimaced. She couldn't imagine drinking tea like this, dark as mahogany in its chipped pint pot, but that's how Mr Calloway liked it. And if that wasn't how it was presented to him he'd been known to throw it across the room. That hadn't happened to Grace yet, but just the same she hated making his tea. She supposed this was what Mrs Rossiter had meant by compromise.

She carried the mug back across the editorial room. She tapped on Mr Calloway's door and walked in at his shouted command. The room's windows were grimy and he was reading by the light of the gas sconces on the wall behind his desk. He stubbed out one cigarette and lit another and did not look up as she set the tea down beside his blotter. She retreated to the door, took a breath of the blue air, and swung to face him.

'Mr Calloway?'

He squinted at her. 'What is it?'

'I wondered how one would go about . . . finding someone. Someone who was lost.'

'What are you talking about, girl? Who?'

'A soldier, for instance. How would one go about finding a soldier?'

He screwed up his eyes. 'You want to find a soldier? That shouldn't be difficult, pretty face like yours. Try Chelsea Barracks.'

'Mr Calloway—'

'Come to think of it London's full of smart uniforms, what with the jubilee. You could have your pick. What about one of those colonial types in a turban? Might suit you.'

'What I mean is . . .' She looked at him, a mean-spirited old man with inky fingers, and walked over to stand in front of his battlefield of a desk. 'Mr Calloway, I have an idea for a newspaper article.'

'An *article*?'

'About soldiers' wives. About the women left behind. They have so little support, you know, and if their husbands don't come back, the government does almost nothing for them. I thought I might ask—'

'You're not suggesting you should write such an article? You?'

Grace squared her shoulders. 'It's what I came here to do. To write, I mean.'

'How long have you been here, girl?'

'Four months.'

'Four months? And you want to be a journalist? Have you any idea how many women journalists there are in London? Well, I can tell you. Next to none.'

'Flora Shaw has done very well on *The Times*.'

He let his pen fall onto the blotter. 'Oh? You want to be the next Flora Shaw, is that it?'

'Mr Calloway, I understood that in coming here—'

'From tea-girl to foreign correspondent?' He began to laugh his wheezy laugh, which became a volcanic cough as it always did, so that he grew purple in the face and his eyes bulged. He produced a wrinkled handkerchief and spat into it, waved the handkerchief at her. 'In four months?' He choked with mirth. 'You come in here with your manners and your accent, and you think that's all there is to it?'

'I do not—' she retorted, so sharply that he stopped laughing. She moderated her tone. 'I do not think any such thing, Mr Calloway.'

He looked at her with narrowed eyes. 'What do you know, girl?'

'What do I know?' Grace frowned. 'I don't understand.'

'You don't know anything. You don't know what a working man earns in this city. You've no idea what it costs to support a family of ten. I'll bet you hardly even know what a loaf of bread costs.'

Grace said nothing. This was all true, or as true as made no difference, and she knew he could see it in her face.

'You're a little rich girl, that's all.' Calloway stabbed his long forefinger at her. 'You're playing at it, that's what *you're* doing. Playing at this job, playing at life. Think I haven't seen rich young ladies like you before, desperate to get a bit of grit under their manicured nails? You think it's romantic, you girls, the smell of sweat and toil. And now you come in here with some cock-and-bull story about soldiers' wives?' He drew again on his cigarette. 'Who's this Johnny you're trying to find, then?'

'I beg your pardon?'

'This soldier-boy? Think I was born yesterday? Run off and left you, has he? Well, you're not the first. But you're not going to use my newspaper to find him.' He ground the cigarette out and pulled down his eyeshade. 'Now run along. I've got work to do.'

Grace walked to the door. Her mind swam. She opened the door, but then closed it quietly again and faced him.

'I'll tell you what I do know, Mr Calloway.' Her voice had dropped an octave but she did not seem able to control it. 'I know what it's like to have a baby die of hunger in my arms. I know what it's like to see prostitutes freeze to death on street corners while rich people in fur coats step around them. I know what it's like to watch a man open the veins of his wrists out of sheer despair.' She had reached the desk and she leaned across it. 'I came here to write about these things, Mr Calloway. Not to make your filthy tea.'

She turned and walked away from the desk. On the other side of the glass partition wall the news room had fallen silent. She felt light-headed, free, appalled. She wondered where she would get another job.

Calloway said, 'Wait,' and she stopped. He had pushed back his chair onto two legs and put his hands behind his head. 'So, the pretty cat has claws.' He let the chair come forward with a bump and put his elbows on the desk. 'It's our illustrious Queen's Diamond Jubilee this month. Maybe you noticed that?'

She said nothing.

'Well, I'll tell you something, Miss Cat. I'm sick to the back teeth of old Vicky's pomp and bloody circumstance. You find me something about the real London, the one the crowds don't see. You might even learn something. And I might look at it.' He picked up his tea and turned his attention back to his papers. 'And next time, more sugar.'

74

Frank leaned against the rail, while the Indian Ocean and the sky swung in a burnished disc around him. The door of the cabin opened and a middle-aged nurse in starched white emerged. She had a long face that reminded him of a horse. Holding her hat onto her head against the wind, she spotted Frank and beckoned him over.

'Captain Cavendish is reasonably comfortable now. I have changed his dressing. How long ago did he receive this wound?'

'Four months ago, ma'am.'

'And who has been treating him up to now?'

'I have, most of the time.'

'I must say, that seems irregular. Was he not attended to in the military hospital at Madras?'

'It's a hellhole. I moved him out.'

She looked at him with disapproval but with a grudging flicker of respect. 'Well, young man, you seem to have done an adequate job. He's still in danger from any recurrence of fever, but the wound alone will not kill him. I doubt he'll ever ride again, however.'

'He'll ride again.'

He could see that his contradiction displeased her, but she decided to let it pass. 'I have administered quinine. That should keep the fever at bay. And now that he's in a decent cabin, that will help. I shall check on him twice daily. You will stay in attendance in case he needs anything.'

'Yes, ma'am.'

'Very well, then. He's asking for you now, but see that you don't keep him talking too long. Good day to you, Corporal.'

She strode away down the deck, her long skirts swirling in the wind.

Frank stepped into the cabin. The suite boasted a small carpeted lounge, with a divan, chairs and a marquetry table set beneath a louvred window – a genuine rectangular window, rather than a porthole. Through the louvres the rocking of the ship sent striped sunlight swaying across varnished cabinet work.

'Bloody disgrace,' Cavendish snorted, and slapped his newspaper on the edge of the bed. He was in the sleeping space to the right of the main room, half-hidden by a curtain. 'What do they expect? Tell me that.'

Frank pulled up a chair. 'What's happened?'

'Warburton's to retire as Political Agent in Peshawar, and the Punjab government plans to let him go. Aslam Khan's tipped to take over from him. Who will they put in as commandant of the Khyber Rifles if Aslam Khan goes?'

'I don't know, sir.'

'No, neither do they, I'll guarantee you that. Some British middle ranker, I suppose, wet behind the ears. What do you think that will do for our prestige among the tribes, eh? I kept telling them, the Afridis never gave their loyalty to the government. They gave it to Warburton personally. With him gone, God knows what will happen.'

'There'll be an uprising?'

'Sure as fate. We saw the preparations for it.' Cavendish slapped the paper against the bed again and fumed for a few moments, before adding, unexpectedly, 'Oh, and by the by, we're lancers now.'

'Sir?'

'The regiment. We're no longer the Twenty-first Hussars, it seems. Someone in their wisdom has redesignated us the Twenty-first Lancers. The men are already training in Egypt.' Cavendish folded the paper roughly and tossed it aside. 'Lancers, eh? Does that sound suitably dashing?'

Frank had hardly thought about the regiment for the past few weeks but now he felt an unexpected pang of nostalgia. In his mind he saw Tranter and Gannon and heard again the coarse banter of the barrack room. He wondered what Mick Gannon would say about his newly won stripes. And Herrick would be rejoining the regiment in Egypt. He had said as much. Perhaps he had already rejoined.

'Are you listening to me, Gray?'

'Sir.'

Cavendish was looking at him closely. 'I said, Gray, that we'll be in England in two or three weeks.' Cavendish seemed about to say more, but then changed his mind. 'How did you manage to get us into a first class cabin?'

'A Mr Hiram Burdock II gave it up for you. An American gentleman, sir. Very generous.'

'He gave up a first class cabin? For me? I've never even heard of the man.' Cavendish narrowed his eyes. 'What did you say to him?'

'I explained the situation, sir. Mr Hiram Burdock II thought it was disgraceful that a wounded officer of the Queen had to take second class accommodation. He thought that was an insult to Her Majesty, sir, especially in the year of her diamond jubilee, so he moved down to second class himself and vacated the cabin.'

Frank stared out of the window. He had indeed had such a conversation with Mr Hiram Burdock II. He had met the gentleman on the dark companionway the night before, when the American was returning from the saloon somewhat the worse for drink. He had explained Captain Cavendish's situation to Mr Burdock, and pointed out how very unhealthy it was for a sick man like Cavendish to be confined to the stifling second class cabin on the wrong side of the ship for all this long voyage. Then he had helped the befuddled Mr Burdock back to his own cabin, and in passing had pointed out how easy it was to meet with an accident while climbing all the way up to first class at night.

Cavendish kept his eyes on Frank for some moments. He said, 'One of these fine days, Frank Gray, you'll go too far.'

75

Mr Fawcett descended the sweep of the stairs, immaculate in pinstripe, his patent leather shoes clicking on the steps. A loop of gold watch chain swung from his waistcoat pocket. Grace knew at once it was Mr Fawcett, even though she had never seen him before. She had heard the severe woman at the reception desk speak his name, and now she caught the woman glancing up at the descending figure with something like awe.

Mr Fawcett paused at a turn in the staircase. He took his watch out and glanced at it but Grace knew that this was a pretence and that he was using the movement to camouflage a rapid survey of the reception hall, and of her in particular.

There were a dozen people with her on the bench. They were petitioners of one sort and another, she guessed, just as she was. Four or five of them were certainly retired military men, grizzled veterans, one missing a leg, another blind. Two well dressed young men who avoided one another's eyes had probably come for employment interviews. A portly man who held a bowler hat on his knees might have been a contractor, and the three elderly women at the end were here to pursue pension claims. Grace knew none of this for sure, for she had not spoken to any of them, but she had had plenty of time to speculate as the day wore on into late afternoon and the rumble of traffic outside rose and fell.

Mr Fawcett continued down the steps and came tapping across the floor to stop at the bench.

'Miss Dearborn, is it?'

'That's right.'

'My name is Fawcett, assistant private secretary. Perhaps you'd come with me.'

He led her back up the handsome stairs to a landing at the top, flanked by stone caryatids and Ionic columns with bronzed capitals. Whiskered men in uniform glowered down from ornate frames.

'In here, if you'd be so good.'

She stepped past his outstretched arm and into a reception room with a sofa in plush red velvet, two gilt chairs and a low table.

'Do please sit, Miss Dearborn.'

She did so, taking one of the chairs. Mr Fawcett sat on the sofa with his long legs stretched out before him. He allowed his jacket to fall open over his silk waistcoat, and let his hand rest near his watch, allowing the silence between them to lengthen. Outside Grace could hear hammering and the shouts of workmen as stands and barriers were erected in Pall Mall ready for the jubilee crowds.

Mr Fawcett said, 'You've been very patient, Miss Dearborn. One might almost say persistent.' He widened his eyes in schoolmasterly fashion so that his spectacles flashed. 'I am told you have been down there for some hours.'

'I managed to get the day off.'

'Very determined of you. And yet I believe you were told at the outset that the War Office would be unlikely to be able to help.'

'I was told that. I didn't believe it.'

'I see.' Mr Fawcett looked faintly amused. 'Sadly, it is true nonetheless.' He took a small notebook from an inside pocket. It was black leather with gold reinforcing around the corners. 'You are searching for a private soldier by the name of . . . Francis Gray. Your reason for wanting to find this young man is unspecified.'

He looked at her over his spectacles, but she kept her face blank.

'You believe he has enlisted in the cavalry, and is currently in India.'

'I believe so, Mr Fawcett.'

'And that's all the information you have? You don't know his regiment, nor where he may be stationed?'

'No, sir. That's exactly what I'd like to find out.'

He sighed and flipped his notebook closed. 'I'm afraid this is quite hopeless, Miss Dearborn. You have endured a long wait for nothing.'

'You must be able to find this information, Mr Fawcett. I don't believe you can't.'

'What makes you think so?'

'We are talking about a soldier. This is the War Office.'

'My dear young woman, let me explain. There are thousands upon thousands of British troops in India. Fifty-four regiments at the last count I made, seven of them cavalry.'

'Only seven? That's not too many.'

'That still makes close to five thousand men, Miss Dearborn, even if we stick to the strictest definition of cavalry. And I am speaking here only of the British Army. There is also the Indian Army, which is a quite separate command under the aegis of the India Office, not us. The Indian Army does not recruit British private soldiers, but such men may be seconded from time to time from one or other of our own regiments. India is a vast possession, Miss Dearborn, stretching from Burma to the Frontier, and down to Ceylon. An individual soldier might be anywhere. Anywhere at all.'

'He must have joined here in England.'

'I imagine so.' Mr Fawcett pulled out his watch.

'The recruiting depots must keep records.'

'Possibly,' he acknowledged. 'But checking them would involve a huge amount of detective work.'

'Which you are not prepared to undertake.'

'Correct. Such a search would be expensive, time consuming, and to no good purpose that I can see. Now, if you'll forgive me—'

'The man is serving his country, Mr Fawcett. And you are not able even to find out where he is?'

Mr Fawcett took off his already gleaming spectacles and polished them. 'Young lady, if you are so concerned with this soldier's where-abouts, may I ask why it is that you don't know them already?'

'What do you mean by that?'

'Only that I'd be intrigued to know his reasons for − how shall I put it? − covering his tracks so thoroughly. He does seem quite as con-cerned to hide from you as you are to find him. Or presumably he would have told you how to reach him.' He smiled faintly at her. 'I wonder what the reason for that might be?'

She glared at him.

'I'm impressed by your determination, Miss Dearborn,' Fawcett spoke in a harder voice now, 'but I don't know where your young man is, and I doubt it is among the responsibilities of Her Majesty's War Office to find him for you.' He got to his feet, crossed to the door and held it open for her. 'If you'll forgive an observation of a personal nature from a man old enough to be your grandfather, I'm sure you could do a great deal better than a common cavalry trooper.'

76

It was after eight o'clock before Grace crossed Waterloo Bridge and made her way through the maze of red-brick terraces south of the river. The streets were busy and festive and she could taste something like hysteria on the air. In some places the roadways had been blocked to traffic for diamond jubilee street parties and people were setting up trestles, stringing banners between the buildings. There were flags everywhere, Union flags draped from windows, strung across the street as bunting. On doorsteps and benches and outside the pubs groups of men had already started their own jubilee celebrations in the summer evening, drinking beer from dark bottles and calling out to her as she passed. Most of the comments were good natured, inviting her for a drink, mock gallant. A few were ribald. She ignored them all.

She had burned off the fury and frustration that Fawcett had sparked in her, but she was bleak in spirit. The jubilee preparations depressed her, the naked jingoism of the flags, and the soldiers – soldiers everywhere – black and brown men in exotic uniforms, sunburned white men in khaki, strutting the West End streets, gawping at the sights, eyeing the women. She hated them all, with their glittering buttons and polished leather, hated the admiring glances they drew, their self-conscious arrogance, their air of possession. Soldiers of the Empire.

Grace let herself into her apartment. Outside the evening sun was still bright but her building lay in the shadow of a gasometer and, as always, the room was dim. She struck a match and lit the gas lamp, and sat at the small table listening to the hiss of it, and to the rumble of the trains from the railway terminus at London Bridge a few hundred yards away. She often sat here as the day faded, and over the weeks the noises of the city had grown comforting to her in their familiarity – the iron shoes of cab horses ringing on cobbles, a steam whistle from a factory, the laughter of people leaving the pub. She liked to think of the men in their cloth caps streaming home from work, of ladies and gentlemen in hansoms hurrying towards the theatre or to a party. But tonight the noises of jubilee preparations had taken over, and with it they had taken over her peace.

Still, as she sat there, she grew aware of a new noise, something she could not place. It was a distant rhythmic thump, like that of some heavy machine. The sound was so faint that sometimes she was not sure she could hear it at all, but then it would touch the edge of her hearing again and she would listen hard for a few seconds. It might have been a locomotive getting up steam, but she was used to that, and in any case this pulse was slower, even and steady, and neither rose nor fell in regularity. It puzzled her, but she did not have the energy at this moment to bother much about what it might be. A traction engine, perhaps, set up to power a children's carousel in some park; part of yet more jubilee foolishness.

Grace got up from her chair and paced around the tiny apartment, restless and dissatisfied. She supposed she ought to eat, and remembered that she had kept part of last night's loaf, and three penn'orth of pease pudding she had bought last evening from a stall on the Embankment. She had always thought of pease pudding as working man's food, and the first time she had bought any she had done so as a joke, but then, to her surprise, she had discovered that she liked it. Not tonight, though. Tonight the thought of the cold green slurry nauseated her.

Dinah Jowett, the blonde waitress who lived in the flat below, shouted up the stairs that the bathroom was free. Grace sighed and for a moment considered not answering. Bathing here was never a particularly pleasant experience. The other girls always left the floor slopping with water, with hair and crescent nails in the chipped old bathtub. But she mustn't miss her turn in the bathroom, whether she felt like it or not, or it might be tomorrow or even the next day before she could wash properly. She opened her door and called down to Dinah that she would be there directly.

She quickly unfastened her hooks and eyes, stepped out of her dress and folded it on the bed, wrapped herself in a dressing gown and hurried down the stairs. The bathroom door was open, billowing steam into the stairwell. Dinah put her broad smiling face around her door and called a greeting. She looked so comical with her hair turbaned after her bath that Grace could not help smiling back, and she felt better at once. In the bathroom she removed a hank of fair hair from the plug hole, as she did every time she followed Dinah in here. She didn't know why this task always fell to her, but it was impossible to be annoyed with Dinah.

Grace liked living here, she decided as the bath filled. She liked it despite everything. She liked the bustle and camaraderie of the place, its energy, even its occasional sluttishness. All the occupants were female, which Grace found a relief after her days at the newspaper office. The two girls in the ground floor flat were dancers at the Gaiety, and sometimes came home tipsy at all hours of the night and woke the whole house. A pair of middle-aged and genially eccentric sisters occupied the middle apartment with a tribe of cats. There was a portrait painter living upstairs – also a woman, astonishingly – though the male clients who visited her studio never seemed to leave with any paintings.

Yes, Grace liked it here, she decided, stepping into the bath. It was a home she paid for herself, and it was something to have a warm home, and warm-hearted neighbours, especially on days like this.

She lay in the bath at full length, keeping her feet away from the scalding water still trickling from the Geyser. She would get an early night, she decided. She would treat herself. She had borrowed a novel from the circulating library, a three-decker romance which would get her to sleep, and then tomorrow she would think about Mr Calloway and his challenge. Something about the real London. He was sick of the jubilee, he had said; well, that was a start, a rare point of agreement between them. She would think of something. She didn't know what it might be, but when she had utterly banished Fawcett and all his kind from her mind she would think of something. She reached up and turned off the tap and the tinkling of hot water shrank away.

She noticed it again then, that soft and rhythmic thumping. It was clearer from here. So clear, in fact, that as she lay in the water she could see the surface tremble slightly with every concussion. Grace climbed out of the cooling bath and opened the small window. On the fresh evening air she could hear it quite distinctly, the chuff and clank of some huge engine – not a traction engine, but a pile driver, perhaps – not so very distant after all. She could hear other sounds now that the window was open, the clink of workmen's tools, the rattle of chains, and once, confusingly, a sudden outburst of angry shouting. At one point she thought she even heard a woman's scream.

Grace drained the bath and wrapped her dressing gown around her. On the landing she almost collided with Dinah, plump and glowing in a new yellow dress, and evidently on her way out.

'Staying in, Gracie, love? It's ever so much fun out there.'

'Is it?'

'Everyone's so friendly! It's the diamond jubilee that does it. Gawd bless Her Maj, I say.' She winked. 'Po-faced old baggage.'

Grace laughed. 'Just the same, I think I need an early night.'

'Well, I hope you can sleep with that going on.' Dinah jerked her thumb towards the landing window. 'That bloody engine. After a while you get so's you can't shut it out of your mind. Couldn't get hardly a wink myself last night.'

'What is it?'

'They're pulling down some old houses by London Bridge for the railway works. You'd have thought the station was big enough already. My auntie lives out that way, and she says all the goings-on fair knocks her eardrums out.'

Grace remembered the shouting she had heard, and at the same moment noticed that the stairwell was cool. She hugged the gown around herself.

'What happens to the people who live there?'

'They chuck 'em out, poor sods.' Dinah started down the stairs. 'Whole families, kiddies an' all, lived there for years. My auntie's seen them, put out on the street with nowhere to go. A jubilee present, I suppose that is.'

Grace moved to the banister rail. 'Can they do that?'

'They can do what they like, love.' Dinah clattered down the last few steps to the front door and waved to her. 'Ta-ra.'

77

It was dark now but workmen had built bonfires of broken timbers from the demolished houses. Grace could see men labouring in the light of the flames, emptying the iron buckets of the rattling steam hoist as they rose up from the pit, lowering gear on ropes into the black gulf beneath street level. The pile driver, half-hidden by smoke and steam, detonated like a cannon within its tower of scaffolding every half-minute or so, and startled her every time.

The gardens of the vanished houses were churned to mire, with just here and there some pathetic relic of the lives that had been lived here – a tool shed, a sagging fence, a vegetable patch with beanpoles poking crazily at the sky. The flames lit the naked backs of the adjacent buildings, some of the walls still with patterned paper on them, even a framed picture or two. The houses, or what was left of them, were narrow half-timbered affairs which might have formed a warren of alleys and courts since the Middle Ages, a living community swept away overnight.

Across the street from where she stood on the edge of the cutting she glimpsed huddled figures in the darkness, women with babies, sullen men in caps, silent children. Around them were the pathetic piles of their possessions. She saw a chamber pot, a roll of oilcloth, a chair. Through a gap in the buildings the fairy-tale spires of the new Tower Bridge were proudly lit against the night sky. Even from here she could see the flags fluttering from the towers to mark the jubilee of the Queen Empress.

Grace crossed the street towards the huddle of people. There were more of them than she had thought at first, perhaps twenty or thirty, staring blankly at the destruction. A tall man in a ragged jacket was leaning against a wall to one side.

'What's going on?' she asked him.

He looked at her respectable clothes with undisguised contempt. 'What does it look like? They're building the new London, that's what.'

She turned her gaze from him to the crowd. One or two women stared back at her in open hostility, others turned away.

'They give us notice.' The ragged man spat in the gutter. 'They say that makes it all right. Only they don't say where we're supposed to go now.'

He pushed himself away from the wall and shambled away. She would have gone after him and spoken to him again, but at that point someone caught her elbow from behind.

'You'd best move along, miss.' He was a policeman, a sergeant, a bulky man with glittering buttons. Even as he spoke he was already steering her back the way she had come.

She wrenched her arm free. 'What's happening here?'

'It's the new railway, miss,' he said patiently. 'The contractors are clearing the old slums. That's progress, that is.'

She could not tell if the irony was deliberate. 'And these people?'

'They're being moved away for their own safety. They had good warning.'

'They're to be put out on the street?'

'That's not my affair, miss. I'm just here to see that things go off orderly. Now if you'd be so good—'

He reached for her arm again but she twisted away and they stood facing one another while the trip hammer thumped and the flames from the bonfire gusted up into the night sky. From behind the sergeant, down a side street, Grace heard a splintering of glass and people shouting. A door opened not forty yards from where she stood and a man was suddenly flung out onto the cobbles. He rolled over, hugging his arm and cursing, while from inside the house a woman screamed. A young police constable stepped out of the front door and swung his truncheon at the fallen man, who scrabbled away out of reach.

Grace moved towards the alley but the sergeant put his arm out like a beam of oak. 'I wouldn't advise that, miss. These things are best left to themselves. They generally get sorted out without too much trouble.'

Grace ducked under his arm, pulled up the hem of her dress and ran down the street towards the scene, closing her ears to the sergeant's bellow from behind her. A crowd was gathering on the far side of the street now, and the crawling man was pulled to safety among them. There was a lot of shouting. She glimpsed the tall ragged man she had spoken to earlier, now bawling curses and swinging a beer bottle in his hand. The constable was still standing on the doorstep, tapping his truncheon against his open palm and grinning at the crowd as if he enjoyed their impotent anger.

Grace walked up to him, pulling her notebook from her bag as she came. Behind her the din quietened a little.

'What d'you want, then, darling?' the constable asked. 'Come to see the fun?'

From behind his broad back the woman was still screaming inside the house. Grace caught a glimpse of shadowy figures within and heard the shattering of china and the thud and crack as furniture was systematically broken. Again and again the woman screamed and the sound lanced into Grace's mind, goading her.

'What's happening in there? What are you people doing to that poor woman?'

'It's the contractors. She won't come out, see.'

'Can't you help her?'

'I just helped her old man,' the constable grinned. 'She might be better off without my help.' He prodded Grace gently in the breast with the end of the truncheon. 'And you might be better off running along.'

She drew herself up. 'I want to speak to her.'

He smiled broadly. 'Fuck off. Miss.'

She held her notebook up. 'I work for a newspaper, officer. I caution you that I shall report—'

He reached forward and took the notebook and pencil from her hand, snapped the pencil, tore the book in two and threw the pieces up into the night air. Before she could protest she heard the sergeant come puffing up behind her. He seized her arm in a brutal grip which made her cry out, but just at that moment something like a bombshell broke against the brickwork above the doorway. Both policemen cursed as brown glass sprayed over them and there was sudden mayhem. Grace found herself on the cobbles with a crush of people all around her, stamping boots and confused shouting. She heard the thump of a fist and then another and a grunt of pain. Inside the house the woman was screaming on and on and on.

An arm hooked around her chest and pulled her up and she was dragged out of the scrimmage and hustled away. She was manhandled around the corner into an alleyway and she started to fight, kicking, scratching at the one hand she could reach. Its owner gasped with pain.

'Grace, Grace! Calm down, will you?'

She pulled away and stood staring at him in astonishment. 'Mr Strathair?'

'Under the circumstances, we might be permitted Christian names.

Mine's Alec, remember? Come along, we can't linger here. Are you hurt at all?'

'No, but—'

He took her arm and began to walk her quickly down the alley. At the end a street lamp made a yellow rectangle of the gap between the buildings. They emerged into the wash of light and he paused here, looking her over rapidly.

'You seem to be in one piece. A minor miracle, I must say.'

Without giving her time to reply he walked her quickly on to the junction with a main road. She recognised Borough High Street. It was gone eleven and the street was shuttered and deserted under its gas lamps. Strathair flagged down a horse-drawn tram and they stepped inside and settled on the slatted wooden bench. He brushed down the knees of his suit. In formal clothes he looked rather less outlandish than in goggles and silk scarf, she thought. She saw that her nails had put a lattice of red scratches over the back of his left hand.

He caught her looking and smiled. 'Lucky for you I wasn't that police sergeant.'

'Lucky for him,' she said. 'How on earth did you get here?'

'Oh, I attend a lot of these events. Some of them can be quite entertaining, as you've discovered. More to the point, what are you doing here?'

'I'm writing an article about all this.' The intention became reality as she voiced it. 'At least, I am now.'

'About the evictions? So you really did find employment on a newspaper.'

'I told you I would.'

'I wasn't sure I believed you. I wasn't sure what to believe when you didn't contact me as you promised.' He flicked dust from his jacket. 'Why was that?'

'I was grateful for your help, Alec. But I didn't need any more of it.'

He nodded but didn't say anything. The creaking tram was almost empty and they sat in silence while the horses pulled them past Southwark Street's darkened warehouses and workshops. The conductor came through the car and Strathair paid him. Grace sat looking out of the swaying window at the lights of the West End across the river.

'Where are we going?' He had taken charge so completely that it had not occurred to her to ask.

'Almost anywhere would be an improvement, I'd say. Do you live near here?'

'Not far.'

'There's a coffee stall outside Waterloo Station which is passable on a good night. I shall buy you a cup there, we'll have a brief chat, and I will put you in a cab back to your home.'

'I can walk. Thank you.'

'No doubt. But I want to talk to you.'

The stall was in the forecourt of the station, a few yards from the tram stop. Strathair bought two mugs, chatting easily to the stallholder as if he knew the man, and then led Grace to the embankment overlooking the river.

'Since you've been rolling around on the cobbles,' he said, 'I don't suppose you'll mind if we sit on the wall.'

She stared out over the black river, wondering quite how she came to be here with this enigmatic young man. A paddle steamer, ablaze with lights and noisy with music, was thrashing upstream, the passengers waving miniature Union flags from the rail. A few yards from where they sat a train in its tunnel under the roadway exhaled a sudden gust of smoke and steam up through the grated blowhole in the street so that pedestrians veered aside, covering their mouths or flapping their handkerchiefs. The hot gust twirled the bunting strung between the streetlamps.

Grace sipped her coffee and was instantly grateful for it. She thought back to the brawling scene they had just fled and felt less courageous now than she had at the time. From the ripples in her coffee she could see that she was trembling and, anxious that Alec Strathair did not see this, she gripped her mug with both hands.

She said, 'That was outrageous. What was happening at London Bridge.'

'The city hires contractors to pull down homes to make way for the new railways, either for tracks or for generating plants for the new electric lines which run underground. The contractors hire bully boys to throw the tenants out, and the police arrest them if they try to resist. Those houses were bad enough, in all conscience, but the rents were low. They'll not find anything so cheap, not without moving miles away from the city.'

'And the government doesn't have to find new homes for them?'

'Not at all. They have no compensation. Oh, but it's not all bad news. They get cheap tickets once the railway's built.'

She let a few moments pass. 'Why were you there, Alec? You haven't told me.'

'I'm a barrister.' He reached into his jacket and handed her a card. 'Tonight was what you might describe as a watching brief. They send me along to see what's going on.'

She took the card. Until now she had assumed he was a business associate of her father's, and that had dictated in some part how she had felt about him. This new information was confusing.

'Who sends you?'

'A number of radical and reforming interests. Tonight it was Sir Charles Dilke and some liberal-minded colleagues of his. You've heard of Dilke, I suppose?'

'Of course. He almost became prime minister.'

'Yes, until they sabotaged him. He's still a political force, though, and he has a mind to put a stop to the evictions if he can find a legal way of doing it.'

She looked down at the card. It read, *Alec, Lord Strathair, Barrister at Law.*

'*Lord* Strathair?'

He smiled. 'A crumbling and extremely ugly castle in the Highlands, but thankfully some quite profitable copper interests in South America, too. That's why I can afford to choose my clients so incautiously.'

She made to hand the card back.

'Keep it,' he said. 'I expect you threw the last one away. And if you're to be writing an article about what we've seen tonight – who knows? I might be able to introduce you to some useful people.'

'Why would you do that?'

'The law is a magnificent machine, but its gears grind dreadfully slowly. By the time we put a case together and it reaches the courts, the railways will all have been long built. A single pithy article can achieve results that years of litigation cannot. Now if I could put you in touch with, shall we say, Lady Octavia Hill, or Sir Charles Dilke himself, they might have interesting things to say.'

'You could do that?'

'Certainly. I'm quite disgracefully well connected. You tell me what you need, Grace, and I can find almost anyone for you. Think about that.' He got to his feet. 'Shall we go? The breeze is freshening.'

He took her empty mug and they walked over the road and back to the stall. He shared a final joke with the stallholder, and then called over a hansom from the line parked below the station steps.

'Take the lady where she wants to go,' he told the driver, and gave the man some coins. He opened the door and handed her up into the cab. 'Goodnight to you, Grace. It's been a pleasure.'

She looked down from the open window at him. 'Anyone?'

'I beg your pardon?'

'Could you really find *anyone*?'

78

The cab clattered between gateposts half-choked in ivy and onto a drive striped with the shadows of poplars. In a few moments the roof of the house rose into view above beech hedges in full leaf.

'Don't say I didn't warn you,' Cavendish muttered.

He had been growing steadily more tetchy since the *Cape Matapan* had docked at Southampton two days earlier, and once they had stepped down at Sevenoaks Station an hour ago his mood had become still more prickly. Cavendish had spoken so disparagingly of Faldonside that Frank had come to expect something ugly, but this was a fine three-storeyed Georgian house of yellow brick set among trees, with the Kentish downland rolling away green and gold beyond it.

The driver reined in his horse at the foot of the front steps. Frank heard an excited cry as one of the maids spotted them, then other voices echoed inside the house and people came running over the gravel. Cavendish caught Frank's eye.

'Faldonside,' he said darkly. 'Where Cousin Harriet holds dreadful sway.'

The door of the cab was tugged open and an imposing woman in a maroon-striped dress filled the space.

'Cousin Freddie!' she cried in a strong voice. 'Seven years away and you're complaining already, I'll take a wager on it. Come and give me a kiss this instant.'

Cavendish shrank back. 'Harriet, my dear, I really think—'

But she leaned bodily into the cab, kissed Cavendish heartily, and held him back at arm's length. 'There you are, Freddie, now that's all over. My God, how old you've grown! And thin as a rail. Still, I suppose we can remedy that, given time.' She called over her shoulder. 'Alan? Bring the chair.'

'Missus.'

'I don't need a chair, dammit.'

'Of course you do. And you'll like this one. It's got wheels – your very own chariot. Remember how we used to play Romans and Britons around the lawn?' She turned to Frank. 'He used to be the Roman general, and I could never understand how they won.'

'They wouldn't have, if you'd been Boadicea,' Cavendish grunted. 'Now let me get out of the damned cab.'

She stood back and Cavendish, muttering crossly, was helped down by the gardener, and settled into a wicker wheelchair. Frank started to step down himself and saw her clearly for the first time, a handsome woman in early middle-age with a full figure and heavy dark hair, slightly greying, neatly pinned up. Despite her evident self-assurance she looked to Frank quite unlike the gorgon Cavendish had described.

'And you're the formidable Corporal Gray.' She offered her hand. 'You know who I am, of course.'

He took her hand. 'I'm pleased to meet you, Mrs Freeman.'

'Freddie's told me what you've done for him, Corporal, and it won't be forgotten.' She looked him up and down appraisingly, taking in the uniform and the shining stripes on his arm. 'My, what a young Achilles it is. They could have made an exhibit of you at the jubilee a couple of months ago, along with all the other strapping young turkeycocks.' She clicked her tongue. 'Well, come along, Corporal.'

She led him towards the steps, where Cavendish in his wheelchair was already being pushed up a ramp, grumbling as he went. What looked like the whole of the house staff – a butler, the gardener, half a dozen house maids, an elderly cook in her apron, and two girls from the kitchen – all crowded around Cavendish to welcome him, the women and girls curtseying, the butler and the gardener helping to manhandle his wheelchair in through the door.

'And now you've all greeted the wounded hero,' Mrs Freeman told the little crowd, 'you can say hello to Corporal Gray, who a dozen times over has prevented my cousin from arriving in a box instead of a chair.'

She didn't wait for anyone to answer, but took Frank's arm and ushered him through the door into the cool polished hall beyond. A couple of the younger maids smiled and bobbed their heads at him as he passed.

'And you can keep your eyes off *them*, Corporal, if you wouldn't mind,' Mrs Freeman said, prompting giggles from behind them. 'They take an age to train up, and I don't want any of them suddenly disappearing to South Africa or Singapore or somewhere. Besides, if you're the paragon Freddie tells me you are, I might very well have to marry you myself.' She walked on a few steps, her head held high, entirely the mistress of her own house. 'Mrs Pugh? Dinner at seven thirty, if you please.'

79

Frank finished his pigeon pie and put aside his knife and fork. 'Thank you, ma'am. I haven't eaten so well in months.'

'My, my. The young Achilles has manners. Whatever next?' Mrs Freeman gave Frank a courtly twirl of her hand. 'You're entirely welcome, I'm sure, Corporal. And I must say you look as if you need it. You're as thin as gypsy dogs, the pair of you.'

'Get used to it, Gray,' Cavendish growled across the dining table. 'Harriet's answer to the world's problems is to feed people.'

'That sounds a good policy.'

Mrs Freeman rolled her eyes. 'Wit, too.'

Frank wasn't sure he felt quite at ease with Mrs Freeman, with her mockery and her bossiness. But it was pleasant here in the lamp-lit dining room, the cutlery glinting, and the light fading outside the French windows, and an English blackbird singing in the early autumn dusk. He found himself filled with a soft melancholy. He shook himself and banished it.

'Something on your mind, Gray?' Cavendish barked across the gleaming table.

'No disrespect to Mrs Freeman's hospitality, sir, but I was thinking about the regiment.'

'What about it?'

'I should like to rejoin it, sir.'

Cavendish put down his napkin. 'You're my orderly until further notice. And we'll be here a little while. That prospect doesn't please you?'

'I thought, sir, now that you're safely home—'

'I'm touched, Gray. But you'll rejoin when I do.'

'Heavens, Freddie,' Mrs Freeman snorted, 'what an old curmudgeon you've become! Take no notice of him, Corporal. I'm sure you don't. And if I were you, Freddie, I'd wait and see if you're capable of rejoining anything more ambitious than the Chelsea Pensioners, before you get your hopes up. Besides, you've only been here three hours. Take some burgundy, for goodness' sake.'

'No wine, thank you.'

She stopped, the decanter poised in her hand, apparently noticing for the first time that his glass was untouched. 'Well, well! Have you become an abstemious Mahommedan in your travels, on top of everything else?'

'I haven't touched alcohol for years.'

'That may take a little getting used to, for those of us who knew the old Freddie Cavendish. Here, Corporal, I'm sure you have a young man's appetite for the good things of life.'

Frank let her fill his glass again, but he did not take his eyes off Cavendish, who sat looking at him across the table with gimlet eyes. Cavendish's left hand rested on a pile of letters, newspapers and telegrams beside his plate. He had been scanning them during the meal, despite Mrs Freeman's scolding. Cavendish seemed on the point of speaking again, but then his shoulders sagged and he pushed away his plate.

'The journey seems to have left me rather hipped,' he said. 'I should like to spend a few moments in the study, and then retire.'

'You're going straight to bed, Freddie, and make no mistake.'

'The study, Harriet,' he said, firmly. 'I need a word with Corporal Gray.'

Mrs Freeman pursed her lips. 'Ten minutes, mind, Freddie. No more.'

She was in action at once, summoning the butler, calling orders to the maids. There was a bustle of activity as Cavendish's wheelchair was brought and he was helped into it. Frank followed the little entourage down the dark hallway and into the study. Firelight was reflected in glass-fronted cases around three walls. Boxes of books, half-unpacked, were stacked on an oak table, beside a globe, notebooks, writing materials. An easel had been erected near the window, and on it a map of Egypt, Upper and Lower, had already been pinned up. Frank stood back against the table as Cavendish was wheeled in. He flipped open a book at random. It was a fine hide-bound edition of Sir Richard Burton's *The Book of the Thousand Nights and a Night*. In the flyleaf the great Arabist had scrawled a dedication in his own hand: *To my friend Capt Fred'k J. Cavendish – I too nursed in my breast dreams of Araby!* It was dated 1887.

'If you'd only wait until tomorrow morning, Freddie,' Mrs Freeman complained, 'the room would be properly prepared for you.'

'Leave us, would you, Harriet?'

Frank thought she would argue, but she merely gave a sniff of disapproval and stalked out of the room.

'Damned contraption.' Cavendish smacked the arm of the chair. 'Push me over near the fire, Gray.'

Frank did so.

Cavendish stirred the embers with a brass poker and placed more coals in the grate. Frank thought about helping him, but instinctively knew this would not be welcome.

'The Frontier's in revolt,' Cavendish said. 'There's been a full scale Afridi uprising. Landi Kotal's fallen. Half of the Khyber Rifles driven back and the other half deserted. I suppose you heard.'

'Something about it, sir. I saw a newspaper at Southampton.'

'It seems they replaced Warburton with a Captain Barton as commandant of the Rifles. A mere captain, put in a position like that! And then they withdrew Barton too, and left Mursil Khan in command. Now Mursil Khan's dead and maybe two or three hundred of the Rifles, and the rest scattered.'

Frank thought of the fortress of Landi Kotal, looming like a battle-ship above the Pass. He recalled too his meeting with the fearsome Subahdar Mursil Khan in Aslam Khan's office. It seemed unthinkable that the fortress could have fallen, even to Pathans, with such a man leading the defence.

'What will happen now?' he asked.

'They've recalled Warburton, I gather. Pulled him out of retirement. That will help. Then there'll be the usual rigmarole. A field force or two to teach them a lesson, and maybe a campaign into the Tirah. So we'll lose a few hundred and they'll lose a few thousand and in a couple of months we'll all be back where we started.'

Cavendish stirred the coals moodily, and then replaced the poker with the other brass fire irons.

'Tomorrow or the next day,' he said, 'I shall cable the War Office, and Colonel Rowland Martin, and anyone else I can think of. Tell them I'm back. Tell them I'll soon be fit for duty. Arrange a medical. Then the wheels will start to turn.'

'You can barely walk yet.'

'Cavalrymen don't need to walk. That's what the horse is for. Didn't anyone tell you? Besides, I could ride before I could stand. Time was I could hang upside down from a beam, just by gripping it with my knees.' The fire flared up and lit Cavendish's face. 'In my wilder days I used to do that trick for a wager in the Officers' Mess, but that was a long time ago.'

Frank thought it must indeed have been a long time ago. He tried to picture grey-haired and bookish Cavendish, bold with wine, hanging head down like a bat above the regimental silver while puce officers roared encouragement. The image was ludicrous.

In a different voice Cavendish said, 'I know you're anxious to get back to the regiment, Frank, but it will happen soon enough, mark my words.'

Frank said nothing.

'Kitchener's already building up his forces to close with the Khalifa in Khartoum. See the line there?' Cavendish gestured at the map. 'The Sudan Military Railway, he calls it. Wadi Halfa to Abu Hamed. Finally it will reach Berber, which is four hundred miles from the Egyptian border, or two-thirds of the way to Khartoum. That will cut out most of the Dongola Loop – the Nile bend between the Fourth and Fifth Cataracts. And *that* saves our boys taking a 900-mile river trip to get to the same point, dismantling the steamers at the cataracts and making portages across the rapids, being fired at from the banks the whole way. Can you imagine it? Men going to war by railway, in the middle of

Africa? There are those who say even now that it can't be done, but it will be. A brilliant man, Kitchener, never mind what you hear about him. Knows the Sudan like the back of his hand, speaks better Arabic than the Arabs, and an organisational genius to boot. And remember this: the Twenty-first Lancers are the only British cavalry he's got in Egypt. Sooner or later he'll have to call them down south to join him.'

Cavendish reached for the poker and stirred the fire again. Coal hissed and spat in the hearth.

'But you don't give a damn about all that, do you, Frank? You want to rejoin the regiment for an altogether different reason.'

'Sir?'

'That last night in Landi Kotal you told me some things.' Cavendish put down the poker. 'You thought I was dying, or you wouldn't have spoken. Ah, but I didn't die, and I remember. Something you had to do. Something that shuts everyone out. What is it, Frank, this obligation of yours? A debt you have to collect? A score you have to settle?'

'You were delirious. You don't know what you heard.'

'Don't I?' Cavendish looked hard at him. 'I was a young fool once, Frank. Perhaps you don't credit that. Came close to throwing it all away, and in a sense I did, or I'd not be a mere captain at my age, having to be pulled out of trouble by young whelps like you. Don't you make the same mistakes I did.'

The door burst open and Mrs Freeman marched in. She looked rapidly from Cavendish to Frank and back again. 'Time's up, Freddie. Bed.'

Before Cavendish could find his voice again the butler had taken hold of the handles of the wheelchair and was propelling him out of the room and away down the corridor. Mrs Freeman marched beside the chair to Cavendish's room and Frank could hear her in there, supervising the servants and fussing over the invalid.

Frank got to his feet and walked to the door of the study, glad that Mrs Freeman had interrupted when she had. He savoured his few moments alone in the dim heart of the house, with its smells of polish and cut flowers. He heard a door slam and Mrs Freeman came back up the corridor, shaking her head.

'It's so good to have Freddie back,' she said. 'But no one is ever likely to mistake him for a little ray of sunshine.'

'I'd best say goodnight too, Mrs Freeman.'

'Nonsense. You'll take a cigar first.'

Mrs Freeman waved away his objection and led him back into the dining room. She brought an inlaid ebony box from the sideboard and offered it to him. 'It's been a little while since I've entertained gentlemen at my table, and the evening won't feel complete without a whiff of Cuba in the air.'

He took one of the fat cigars and turned it uncertainly in his hands. She struck a match and only then saw his awkwardness. She shook the match out.

'Here. Let me.' She took the cigar from his fingers, produced a silver cutter from the box and deftly clipped off the end.

He allowed her to light it for him, and drew in the aromatic smoke.

'It's not quite dark yet,' she said. 'Let's take a turn around the garden before I show you to your room. Your quarters, I suppose you soldiers would say.'

She led him through the house to the front door, where she threw a woollen stole over her shoulders and gathered up her hem in a skirt lift. She took his arm formally and led him across the dark lawn. The windows of the house were pale with gaslight, the trees around it black against the sky.

'You were expected last month,' she said. 'What happened at Genoa?'

'Captain Cavendish fell ill again, ma'am. Fever. We had to take a villa above the town and wait for four weeks until he recovered.'

'Presumably the Army helped with these arrangements?'

'The Army's rather lost track of us, ma'am.'

'So you handled all that yourself? And stayed with Freddie?'

He didn't answer. Mrs Freeman tore off a sprig of lavender and touched her face with it. 'You're fond of him, aren't you, Corporal?'

'Captain Cavendish was ordered home. I was ordered to get him here.'

She nodded in a knowing fashion. 'I see.'

They walked on through an orchard of ancient apple trees, one or two hung with globes of fruit, and around the edge of a large pond spread with lily pads. The evening air was growing cool, and bats were out, swooping against the slate blue sky and down to ruffle the water which mirrored it.

'Well, you did get him here,' she said, in a new and matter-of-fact voice, 'but he looks like death. I thought I'd weep when I saw him in the cab, and I don't often do that. Will the Army ever want him back? In that state?'

'He's an Arab expert, Mrs Freeman. My guess is they'll recall him as soon as he can convince them he's halfway fit.'

'And you hope that's very soon indeed. Isn't that true, Corporal? You'd go tonight, only you have to stay because you're Freddie's orderly.' She made much of the word, teasing him with it.

He drew silently on the cigar.

'Most young men would be glad of a spell at home,' she said. 'Don't you have family or friends you'd like to see? An apple-cheeked grandmother? A sweetheart?'

He hesitated. 'I have a brother.'

'Oh, yes?'

'Gifford. He's very clever. He's . . . fourteen now, I suppose. He's an apprentice at an engine works in Deptford.'

'Deptford's no distance from here. You must go and see him. Of course you must.'

He studied the tip of his cigar.

She said, 'Don't you want to see your brother?'

'He doesn't know I'm in England. No one does.'

'And you'd rather it stayed that way?' Mrs Freeman cocked her head to one side. 'What an enigma it is, this young Achilles.'

They had emerged on the drive again, at the side of the house. In the light from the kitchen windows Frank could see a square coach house set back among the trees. Stone steps led up the outside wall to an upper level. Oil lamps glowed in two windows and light spilled through a half-open door at the top of the stairs. Mrs Freeman led him up the steps, pushed open the door and walked in. She inspected the space within, her busy shoes knocking on bare boards. It was a tiny room built into part of the hayloft, spartan in the extreme. An iron stove stood against one wall, and a wooden table and a chair against the other. The bed was a narrow cot and on it Frank's valise lay unpacked, with his few belongings spread out on the blanket; a spare shirt, a couple of books, his washing and shaving kit. He was glad he had kept the Bulldog revolver hidden under his tunic. He tried to imagine the maid's reaction if she'd found it in his valise.

Mrs Freeman trimmed the wick on one of the lamps, which was guttering a little, checked the table top for dust and rubbed her fingertips together afterwards. He had the impression that she was embarrassed about offering him this accommodation, but could not quite bring herself to say so.

'I expect you've seen worse,' she said finally, in what he judged was an apology.

'Indeed, ma'am. Much worse.'

'Indeed, ma'am,' she mimicked. 'How precisely you put things. Perhaps that's why they call you an orderly?' She snapped open her purse and took out a wad of banknotes. 'Here is fifty pounds. First thing tomorrow morning, go away for a week and spend it.'

He looked at the money. 'I can't take this.'

'Oh, please don't be proud, Corporal. It's such a bore.' She tossed the notes onto the table and swept to the door. 'I want you away from Freddie, do you see? That's why I put you in here. If you're near him he'll not relax. It will be endless chatter about the Sudan and dervishes and God knows what. So I'm granting you some leave from your duties as his *orderly*. Go and see your clever brother. Spend the money in public houses or music halls or dens of ill repute, or wherever you young men go. Do as you please. But stay away for a week so that I can make sure my cousin gets some rest.' She opened the door and stepped out into the night, dismissing him with one hand raised languidly over her shoulder. 'Goodnight to you, Corporal. We breakfast at eight. See that you're gone before then.'

80

Calloway scanned rapidly through the copy slips, marking here and there with blue crayon, slapping each slip over with the flat of his hand as if killing a wasp. The ash from his cigarette fell on the pages and he breathed stertorously in his concentration. He smacked down the last page and looked up at Grace.

'How d'you get to Dilke? He's kept his head down since that Virginia Crawford affair. And Lady Octavia Hill, no less?' Calloway dropped the cigarette butt into his tea mug where it died with a hiss. 'No, don't tell me. It might damage my faith in human nature.' Calloway sat back with his arms crossed. 'You must have some useful friends, that's all. I didn't think you had it in you, I'll own that much.'

It was absurd to be so pleased by a compliment from this odious little man, but she was pleased nevertheless.

'Starving kids in the street, heartless property barons, working men deprived of employ.' Calloway tapped the stack of copy slips. 'Any more like this coming along?'

'I'm . . . looking at one or two possibilities.'

'Keep looking, then.' He waved his hand. 'Go on, that's all. And get me another tea.'

'Yes, Mr Calloway.'

She had reached the door when he added, 'On second thoughts, get that useless bloody copy boy to make it.'

Grace returned to her desk in a daze. She passed Mr Calloway's instruction on to the terrified copy boy and sat down. Vaguely, she heard the double swing door from the stairwell creak open, but did not trouble to look up. It was only when she became aware of a small stir of interest in the room that she raised her head. Alec Strathair was standing just inside the doors. He was smiling, chatting easily to one of the younger reporters. He looked impossibly well-groomed in his dark suit, with his silk necktie and his gold watch chain. The reporter pointed her out, and as Alec caught sight of her he raised his hand in greeting.

Grace hastily grabbed her coat, hurried across the room.

He said, 'I'm sorry to drop in unannounced—'

'Come along.' She took his arm and bundled him unceremoniously out through the doors and onto the stairs.

'Is there something wrong?'

'I'm just surprised to see you here, Alec, that's all.'

'Oh, dear,' he laughed, as she hurried him down the steps. 'Have I compromised your socialist credentials? I do apologise. Perhaps I should have worn clogs. Let me see if I can put things right with the aid of a cup of tea and a cream bun.'

'Alec, I'm at work. I can't be away long. What is it?'

'Twenty minutes.' He was already hailing a cab. 'Just twenty minutes.'

He found them a table by the window in the restaurant of Morley's Hotel, not five minutes' walk away on Trafalgar Square. She didn't know how he managed to do that, because the place was packed with people, but Alec could always manage this kind of thing. They were served almost at once too, a silver pot of tea and two extravagant cream confections. He made some theatre with the teapot and the milk and she saw that he was deliberately teasing her. She began to grow impatient, but she was determined not to show this and looked out through the wide windows and across Trafalgar Square. There had been a few days of Indian summer, and the day was so warm that a group of barefoot children were splashing in the fountains under the supercilious gaze of Landseer's lions. The windows of the restaurant were open and the high room was exotic with the smells of coffee and vanilla and almond. Grace forced herself to relax, cut a piece of her cake and lifted it to her mouth.

He said, 'The Twenty-first Hussars.'

She raised her eyes slowly to his. 'What did you say?'

'Francis Gray joined the Twenty-first Hussars at their home depot at Canterbury in March of last year. The Twenty-first Lancers, as they are now, apparently. He seems to have gone out to India to join the regiment quite soon after that. They were stationed in Secunderabad at the time, but within a few weeks of him joining they were redeployed to Egypt.'

The cake collapsed through her fork and fell back onto the plate.

'Forgive me for springing this on you, Grace.' He was pleased with himself, she could see that. 'I'd have given you some warning, but my people had a lot of trouble getting the information. Even now it's not—'

'He's in Egypt?'

'His regiment is.'

'I must contact him.' Her tone was peremptory. 'I must contact him at once.'

'No, Grace, wait. It seems he's not actually with the regiment at present.'

'I don't understand you, Alec. If he's not with his regiment, where is he?'

'I don't know that yet. I'm not sure anyone knows at this moment. I've had a chap wire the adjutant of the Twenty-first. He wasn't very helpful. Apparently men come and go all the time, and there's a good deal of confusion, what with the regiment leaving India after so many years. Anyway, the long and the short of it is that your Frank Gray seems to have been detached for months now, on some kind of an assignment. You can write to him via the regiment, of course, but I've no idea how long it would take—'

'What *assignment*? Where?'

'I don't know that either, I'm afraid. My man had the impression that he was still in India, and had been seconded as some sort of an interpreter. Would that sound likely?'

'He does speak some Indian languages.'

'Does he, indeed? Well, perhaps that explains it. But this is just guesswork. My chap rather thought the adjutant himself did not know where your Mr Gray is, or perhaps wasn't willing to say.'

'Frank's not in any trouble, is he?' she asked, suddenly anxious.

'Trouble?'

'I mean, he hasn't . . . done anything wrong?'

'On the contrary, I gathered he was something of a model recruit. Unless I misunderstood, he appears already to have won some form of promotion. It's just that no one can tell us at present precisely where he is.'

'I see.' She swallowed. 'Yes, I see.' She looked past his shoulder into the crammed room, glittering mirrors and tables with shining cutlery, young men and women close together, laughing in the sunlit room.

Alec said gently, 'Perhaps you'd like to drink some of your tea?'

'Lancers are cavalry, aren't they?' Grace said. 'He always said he'd join the cavalry.'

'Grace, the last thing I wished to do was to distress you. I thought you'd be pleased.'

'How long do they sign up for?'

'A private soldier? Six years with the Colours and another six with the Reserves, I believe.'

She took a moment to digest this. 'And leave? When do they have leave?'

'Only officers get home leave. Not troopers.'

'Nonsense,' she said shortly, as if he might just have invented the rule to spite her. 'You can't tell me that they'll keep him overseas in the army for five more years?'

'I suppose the regiment might be redeployed to England, but that doesn't seem likely. You must have seen the reports.'

Of course she had seen the reports, Mahdist uprisings in the Sudan and Kitchener's build-up in Upper Egypt. She could hardly have missed them. The British public was displaying all of its gross appetite for imperial warmongering, she reflected, especially when it could be camouflaged as righteous retribution. The papers had reprinted again and again the famous painting of General Gordon standing defiantly on the steps of the Khartoum residency back in 1885. Every time she saw it Grace had a vision of Mrs Rossiter, sitting in her cottage with the relics of her dead husband spread on the table in front of her.

Alec reached out and touched her hand. 'Grace, I don't quite know what more we can do to track down your Mr Gray.'

She stared down at his hand on hers. He had not touched her in this way before, but she did not mind. The gesture was comforting, brotherly. Brotherly. A connection snapped shut in her mind.

She looked up at him, her eyes widening. 'Gifford,' she said.

'What?'

'Frank has a brother. I don't know where he is, but he has a brother.'

81

Frank stood in the mouth of an alleyway and gazed through the drizzle at the wrought iron gates. The words *Gooch & Sons, Engine Makers* were picked out in fresh blue and red paint, but those flashes of colour were the only lively thing about the works. Frank had hoped for more from the place where he knew his brother would have to toil through the long years of his apprenticeship, but Gooch's looked as gloomy as a prison, a clutter of grimy red-brick buildings and workshops, cranes and chimneys. The yard was littered with iron wheels and lengths of rail, rusting on the wet cobbles. Men and boys in overalls and caps, their heads bowed against the weather, hurried between the buildings.

A whistle blew shrilly, and in a few moments the yard filled with workers, men in coats and caps, many wheeling bicycles, tradesmen with toolbags over their shoulders. A group of young lads kicked a greasy football between them. The gates swung open, screeching on iron wheels, and the crowd flooded out across the tram tracks and began to surge away down the streets and alleys of the town, men shouting to one another as they parted, collars up, hunched against the rain.

Frank kept his eyes on the group of lads with the football. There were a dozen of them, dodging between the carts and trams, larking as they came. It occurred to him that he might not even recognise his own brother after the eighteen months that had passed. Perhaps Giff had grown into a boisterous lad like these. Perhaps he had learned to make friends. Could Gifford have changed that much?

The boys came past him, one or two of them glancing up at his uniform, trying not to show they were impressed. One mock-saluted and stuck out his tongue. Frank scanned the little group for a flash of pale hair beneath the caps, watched for some trace of Giff's dreamy expression on one of those eager grinning faces.

'Frank?' Gifford said.

He had been walking alone, excluded from the group or careless of it, a sheaf of papers clutched under his jacket to protect them from the drizzle.

'Giff. So you haven't changed.'

Gifford put his head on one side. 'You have, Frank. You have.'

In the high street café, Gifford shovelled down his mashed potato as if he had not eaten for a week.

'You've been getting the money I sent?' Frank asked.

'Oh yes.'

'You never wrote.'

'Neither did you. Still I guessed you were still alive because the money kept coming. So you're a Lancer now, are you, Frank? I thought you were a Hussar, or something. Capital grub, by the way.'

Frank wondered how the old St Dunstan's argot was greeted in this milieu, but he could see that Gifford didn't care one way or the other what others thought. The outside world was a puzzle which Gifford had never been much interested in solving.

Gifford said, 'So you'll have to use a *lance*? I mean, a long thing you stick into people?'

'I suppose that's the general idea, Giff.'

'Will you use a sword, too?'

'A sabre, yes.'

'Well, that's a sword, isn't it?' Gifford laughed at the absurdity of it. 'God, Frank! We have Maxim guns which fire at six hundred rounds a minute. We can talk to people down a wire and send messages across the world. We have camera apparatus which can look inside you and take pictures of your bones. And you still have to ride around on a horse with a spear, like Sir Lancelot? Why do they make you do that?'

'Now you mention it, Giff, I'm not entirely sure.'

'Maybe they think it wouldn't be fair on the Fuzzy-Wuzzies. Though you'd have thought they'd be just as dead if you dropped a bombshell on them from a dozen miles away, then it wouldn't much matter if it was fair or not.'

Frank decided there was no sensible answer to Gifford's logic, and so didn't make one, and instead let his brother get on with his meal. He had grown out of practice at dealing with Gifford's tangential thinking. Or maybe Gifford was the only one who had things right.

'How is it for you at Gooch's?' he asked at length.

'Awful. They're dolts. Numbskulls.' Gifford spoke through a mouthful of food, but even as he did so he spooned more onto his plate. 'Do you know, they still think the future is in horizontal steam engines? Like Maudslay's engines? Half of the managers trained at Maudslay's forty years ago, so I suppose it's not surprising. Of course, that was all very well in its day, but they have no vision for the future, these people.' Gifford shook his head mournfully.

'Do they make it hard for you? The gaffers? The other lads?'

'I'm no fun to them. I just ignore them and after a while they go away.' Gifford took up a chop bone, tore at it with his teeth, and gestured with it. 'It's just that they're so stupid. So old-fashioned. Horizontal steam engines, I ask you! Meanwhile, there's a chap called Parsons just beginning to get famous – now, he's a fellow who can see the future. Studied mathematics at Cambridge, then did an apprenticeship, just to prove he knew how to get his hands dirty. He's developed a steam turbine. Axial flow. Of course, he started off with radial flow, which didn't really work – you know the difference, I suppose, Frank?'

'No, Giff, but—'

'Well, the axial flow system uses high pressure steam.' Gifford began to draw on the tablecloth with his chop bone. 'It's injected so that it flows along the axis of the turbine and turns a central rotor. That develops something like two thousand revolutions per minute, which, you know, is between thirty and forty times as high as a conventional steam engine. Well, you can imagine the power potential. They're already installing Parsons' machines to generate electricity on Tyneside, and pretty soon they'll have them all over the country. For ships, too. Perfect for ships. Any big industrial operation, really.'

'Yes, Giff, I see. But we ought to—'

'You'd think an engine maker would catch on to that pretty quickly, wouldn't you? Or invest in one of the other coming technologies. Internal combustion, for example. Good Lord, people are already driving around in their own horseless carriages. It must be pretty clear the streets will be packed with them within a decade. But not at Gooch's, oh, no. They've had me working on Corliss valves, would you believe it? Equipment that was designed fifty years ago, and they think it's modern. I swear some of the engines they build were designed by James Watt himself. Gooch's export these things to places like India and South America where their customers don't know any better, and they think their market is safe for ever.' Gifford filled his mouth again and announced breezily, 'You'll have to get me out, Frank.'

'Out? Where to?'

'Oh, college full-time. It's the only way. Cambridge, perhaps, like Parsons.' Gifford waved his fork. 'I'm doing evening classes, naturally, at the Mechanics' Institute, but they're all so backward. It'll take for ever to get anyone to notice my ideas unless I get out.'

'Giff, I can't pay for you to go to college. I can barely afford to keep you in the apprenticeship.'

'But it's all happening *now*, Frank,' Gifford cut across him urgently. 'You've heard of Otto Lilienthal?'

'No, I haven't. Giff, listen to me—'

'Yes, yes you have, Frank! I've told you about him, I'm sure I have. The German experimenter who was building a soaring machine? He's dead now. Killed last year in a flying accident. But he *was* flying, Frank. No, really, he was. He'd built a flying machine big enough to carry him – it glided, like a kite, up in the air. Well, of course, that's been done before. George Cayley did it forty years ago and sent his coachman up. But Lilienthal *controlled* his soaring machine, that's the difference.'

'It doesn't sound as if he controlled it too well.'

Gifford waved a hand. 'Oh, the details need work, I'll grant you. But Lilienthal had a machine which would go where he wanted through the air. Do you see how important that is? In Berlin last year he *flew* it. It didn't just carry him up.' He paused. 'I say, Frank, you couldn't let me have five pounds, could you?'

'Don't tell me you want to go to Berlin, Giff. Please don't tell me that.'

'Of course not!' Gifford laughed. 'There wouldn't be any point in that, now Lilienthal's dead. But there's a man in Scotland who's working on the same sort of thing, and even using some of Lilienthal's designs. His name's Pilcher, Percy Pilcher. He's a lecturer at Glasgow University.'

'So you want to go to Glasgow now, is that it?'

'Oh, no. I've already been. But it cost a bit to get there, so I borrowed a few pounds from a chap . . . and you see, I have to pay it back. He's getting rather rude about it. Oh, I know I shouldn't borrow money, Frank. Neither lender nor a borrower be, and all that.' Gifford's eyes were shining. 'But to meet a man like that! A man who's going to fly like a bird!'

Frank struggled to take this in. 'You turned up on this man's doorstep?'

'Yes, well, more or less. I went to the university and met him there. And he was awfully nice. Quite a young chap. Used to be in the Navy. He let me sit in on one of his lectures, and afterwards he took me to a hotel near the station and bought me cream tea.' Gifford smiled at the memory in a self-satisfied manner. 'I believe we exchanged a number of useful notions, Mr Pilcher and I. As between fellow enthusiasts. It was he who insisted that I have to go to college.'

'Gifford,' Frank said despairingly, 'you're fourteen. You're an apprentice. If it weren't for the few pounds I send you, you couldn't even afford to be that. And you borrow money to travel to Glasgow and meet some . . . some moonstruck engineer who thinks he can fly?'

'I went second class,' Gifford protested in an injured tone. He frowned in puzzlement. 'Did I do something wrong again, Frank?'

Frank looked at his brother's open and innocent face, his fair hair shining and his blue eyes wide. He opened his wallet and gave Gifford a sheaf of Mrs Freeman's crisp pound notes. 'Pay the man back. But you should have written to me when you got the urge to flit off to see some birdman.'

'Thanks, Frank. You're a brick.' Gifford pocketed the money. 'But I couldn't very well write to you, could I? You vanished ages ago. It's as I said, if the Army hadn't kept remitting the money I'd have thought you were dead. As a matter of fact, I'd pretty well decided you were anyway.' He frowned. 'What *are* you doing here, out of interest?'

'Waiting to be sent to Egypt.'

'Oh? Why?'

'So I can stick spears in people, I expect. Meanwhile I've got a room at the Green Dragon, down by the river. I told them I'd stay till the end of the week.'

'Capital! Then you could buy me dinner in the evenings and I could tell you all about college.'

Frank held himself back with an effort. He was seized by that old desire to grab his brother by the lapels and shake him. But at the same time the very familiarity of that feeling filled him with nostalgia. Gifford was so reliably what he always had been, what he always would be.

'Oh, I almost forgot.' Gifford's hand was still in the inside pocket of his jacket where he had slipped his money. He felt through each of his pockets in turn, turning them out onto the table: a screwdriver, stubs of pencil, tram tickets. He drew out a buff envelope, crumpled from his pocket, and set it on the table top in front of Frank. 'Open it.'

Frank opened the envelope and withdrew a front page torn from a newspaper. The masthead said *The Free Briton*. Frank looked at it. It meant nothing to him.

'There,' Gifford said, pointing. 'That article there.'

The column was headlined: *Fresh Outrage as More Families Thrown onto London Streets*. Even then it took Frank a moment or two to see the words printed beneath: *by Grace Dearborn*.

'It has to be her, Frank, doesn't it?' Gifford was saying. 'How many Grace Dearborns could there be? And she was always a bit of a radical. The article's only a few weeks old. It should be simple enough to find her from that.'

Frank took the cutting and smoothed it on his knee.

'I liked Miss Grace,' Gifford said. 'She was a corker. You should—'

'Just shut up, Giff, would you?'

Gifford sat up straight, all injured innocence. 'What's the matter now? Don't you want to see her?'

Frank said nothing, staring at the sheet of newsprint on his knee.

'Well, you're a chump, Frank! The two of you went together like duck and peas. You simply must get in touch with her.'

'Things have gone too far.'

'What things?'

'Gifford, you don't understand. I'm a corporal in the Lancers, and in a couple of weeks I'll be recalled. There'll be a war, and even if I come through it I probably won't be back in England for years. Grace is Stephen Dearborn's daughter. Are you following this? Now apparently she's making her own name, too. What could I possibly offer a girl like that?'

'You think you're not good enough for her?'

'Well, what do you think?'

'I think you're a chump, that's what I think. She wouldn't care about any of that. Even I know she wouldn't.'

'I wrote to her months ago and released her. So there's an end to it.'

'And what about you?'

328

'What do you mean?'

'Are you released?'

Frank did not answer. He tucked the article away inside his tunic and made to stand.

Gifford said, 'What's this really about, Frank?'

Frank sat down again. He opened his wallet and held out for Gifford the photograph of their mother, creased now and soft with folding. 'Have you forgotten?'

'Of course not, but after all this time?'

'What's time got to do with it? Giff, every last thing that has ever gone wrong for us has sprung from that night, from what that bastard did.'

'I know, but—'

'And now I know who he is and where he is. I've seen him, even spoken to him. I couldn't get to him then, but I know where he's going to be – with the regiment in the Sudan – and I'm going to be there, too.'

'And then what will you do?'

'Is that a serious question?'

'It's serious, all right. I don't see how you could shoot him down like a dog, or challenge him to sabres at dawn, or whatever nonsense you've got planned, without getting into the most awful hot water yourself.'

'I'll take my chances.'

'I don't think you'd have much chance at all, Frank, would you? This chap's obviously got some pretty powerful friends.' Gifford reached out one fingertip and thoughtfully touched his mother's photograph. 'In fact, I've often wondered about that.'

'About what?'

'To get them to cover up a murder? How important a chap would you have to be for people to hush up a thing like that? I mean, maybe they'd do it for the Prince of Wales . . .' Gifford laughed at the thought, caught himself. 'Did he look like that sort of a cove to you when you met him, Frank? Terribly rich and powerful?'

Frank put the photograph away, snapped his wallet closed and put it away. Strangely his heart had begun to thump. Herrick? Had he indeed looked like *that sort of a cove*? Hardly. He had looked like an Army major on the frontier, a career soldier, no different from a thousand others, a man of no special wealth or influence. That's what he'd looked like.

Gifford was speaking again. 'Because that dry old stick Furneaux must have lied about things, and Colonel James, too. And Papa, of course. They all hushed it up. All for this man. Doesn't that seem strange to you?'

Frank's mouth was dry. 'It wasn't just for him. It was to protect Mother. Her . . . reputation. You know that.'

Gifford tilted his head doubtfully. 'That's what they said. I suppose it must be so. But it's a bit odd they went to such lengths to cover for this chap – a murderer, after all – when he was so clearly guilty. Don't you think that's strange? It's not as if there was any doubt about the facts. You caught him red-handed.'

'Of course there wasn't any doubt.' Frank spoke with such force that the people at a neighbouring table fell momentarily quiet. 'How could anyone be in doubt? I was there, Giff. Remember?'

'I know, that's what I said—'

'I tried to stop it. I know what happened.'

'All right, old boy.' Gifford blinked at him. 'Keep your jolly shirt on.'

'I saw the gun and I picked it up.' Frank lowered his voice with an effort. 'He put his hand over mine and tried to get it from me, but I wouldn't let him have it.'

'Yes, yes, I know.' Gifford reached across and patted his brother's arm, spoke very softly. 'I'm sorry, Frank. I was forgetting. You saw it. You saw the swine shoot poor Mama.' Gifford looked up at Frank's face and stopped. 'You did, didn't you?'

Frank moistened his lips. 'I can't seem to focus on him doing it, Giff. On that moment. I keep trying, but it slips away. Why is that, do you think?'

'He hit you. You were knocked silly.'

'For a few moments. But still, I get glimpses. I just can't seem to get the whole picture.'

'If I were you, Frank, I wouldn't wish a clear memory of that on yourself. It would have been horrible, seeing him do that. You know how when people have bad accidents they can't recall the moment it happened? Sometimes it comes back later, but not always. I've read in a journal . . .' Gifford let his voice trail away. 'I bet that's what it is.'

Frank stood up and tossed some coins on the saucer with the bill. 'I'll be at the Green Dragon. Come over when you're ready.'

He walked out through the café door and into the grey and rainswept street.

PART NINE

England, November and December 1897

82

The Savoy Grill was crowded with men in evening dress and women in flowing gowns of silk and satin. Three army officers in scarlet uniforms sat at the next table, and in an alcove opposite, two bishops in full fig and gaiters were already guffawing over their second bottle. A string quartet was playing Bizet from a stage almost smothered by potted palms.

Alec tut-tutted. 'Capitalism in action, eh? Dreadful.'

'My glass is empty,' she said. 'That's what's dreadful.'

He laughed and signalled the waiter. He had not taken her to such a place before. She had made an effort to look the part, and was glad that she had, for she felt good in her dark green velvet, with her father's black pearl at her throat. It occurred to her that she had not worn the jewel since leaving Cumver, nor attempted to dress so well, and she found that she missed that. She looked around the room again, at the glittering chandeliers, the trolleys and side tables set with crystal and china. Yes, she had been part of this world once, and not so long ago. Alec, she supposed, still was, and for an instant she was envious of him.

Alec leaned back on the maroon plush bench and swirled the last of the wine in his glass. 'We make a good team, Grace, don't we? We both believe in the same things. We are . . . kindred spirits in many ways. And there is so much more that I feel we can achieve together.'

She said nothing. He seemed to be taking his time composing his next sentence, and for a moment she was wary. But when he spoke his words surprised her.

'Grace, have you heard of a man called Morel? E.D. Morel?'

'I don't believe so.'

'Remarkable chap. I met him just a few days ago. In a way he's a journalist like yourself: he writes for, among other papers, the *Shipping Telegraph* and the *Liverpool Journal of Commerce*. But that's a part-time employment to supplement his salary as a clerk with Elder Dempster, the shipping line. Well, Mr Morel seems to have discovered something rather singular while working for them.'

The waiter arrived and Alec tasted the wine. He said no more until they were alone again.

'Morel is half-French, and bilingual. He became involved in

supervising Elder Dempster shipments through Antwerp. The important point here is that virtually all Belgium's trade with the Congo passes through Antwerp. Know anything about the Congo?'

Her mind winged back to a smoky hall, a magic-lantern show, Mrs Rossiter at her side and a fine-looking black man with a beautiful voice. And the slides, those visions seen through serpents of tobacco smoke writhing in the lantern beam: white men wearing pith helmets and cradling rifles, stacked elephant tusks, a garden ringed by skulls and a mound of severed human hands looking like piled yams.

'Grace?'

'I'm sorry. Go on.'

'As he tells it to me, Morel noticed two things while checking cargo manifests. Firstly, that the value of the rubber and ivory being shipped out of the Congo into Antwerp is a great deal higher than is being declared. Someone has been skimming off a lot of money for personal profit. King Leopold, obviously.'

'That's hardly a surprise.'

'No. But secondly, that the cargo being sent in the other direction – *to* the Congo – includes almost no trade goods at all. No manufactures, no finished cloth, no tools. Nothing you might expect. In short, goods worth vast sums are coming out, and almost nothing is going back. Well, not nothing, exactly. Guns. Ball cartridge ammunition. Percussion cap muskets. Military stores for Leopold's private army. That's what's going into the Congo. Morel's conclusion is that the rubber and ivory and gems and all the rest of the Congo's riches are being taken by force. It's the systematic rape of an entire country.' Alec sipped his wine. 'He's a persuasive chap, Morel, and he has a neat turn of phrase. As he puts it to me, it would be bad enough to stumble upon one killing, but he says he has uncovered an international secret society dedicated to mass murder and theft, and with a king as its mastermind.'

Grace found she had been leaning forward as he spoke and she forced herself to sit back. 'And you want me to write about this?'

'It's a far cry from rapacious landlords and hungry children on the streets of London, I'll grant you. But if the British public were to hear from some enterprising journalist that British firms were involved in such practices, there would certainly be an international outcry.'

'Yes.' She poured herself some water and drank a little. 'Yes, of course there would.'

'Now, Grace, you have to think carefully. There will be powerful interests who would much prefer to keep this quiet. I don't know how they will react, but I'd be lying if I said that writing about this did not involve an element of danger, at the very least to your professional career. On the other side of the ledger there are a number of eminent people who would support such a campaign. Miss Mary Kingsley for one. She's travelled extensively in the Congo and what she's seen there supports everything Morel has said.'

'You could introduce me to Mary Kingsley?'

'Certainly. Then there's our old friend Sir Charles Dilke: he has strong views on Empire, as you know. Not quite yours and mine, but he is a deeply honourable man.' He sat back. 'You don't have to agree to anything now, Grace. I know it's a lot to think about.'

'Do you imagine I need to think about it? Of course I shall write it!'

But to her surprise he didn't say anything to that, and instead sat watching her thoughtfully.

'There's more,' he said.

'Tell me.'

'I've been interested in the Congo for some years, Grace. Long before I heard of Morel.'

'Well?'

'Did you never ask yourself why I was talking to your father the afternoon we first met?'

'My father?' She sat up straight.

'I wanted to ask him about the involvement of Dearborn & Company in the Congo trade.'

'No,' she said. 'Not if it involves underhand dealing. That's not his style.'

'Grace, listen—'

'No, Alec. I shan't believe that.' She shook her head firmly. 'Absolutely not. General trade, certainly. That's his business. But what you're saying goes far beyond that. My father would never taint himself with involvement in such activities. He believes in Empire and Free Trade precisely because he thinks they will bring prosperity to everyone. No. He would have nothing to do with this.'

She picked up her wine glass, drank, set the glass down again. The wine had tasted good before, now it seemed acid to her.

'That's exactly what he told me,' Alec said. 'And I won't pretend to you that I have been able to uncover a shred of proof against him.'

'Well, then.'

'But I have to tell you that Morel believes otherwise. He claims to have seen papers which show that Dearborn & Company—'

'Then he's wrong,' she snapped. 'Perhaps you should be careful of whatever else he tells you.'

'Let me finish, Grace. This isn't simply a matter of shipping a few military stores and keeping quiet about it. Morel believes that Dearborn

& Company is among several trading houses which not only handle cargo between the Congo and Antwerp, but have taken concessions on rubber production there.'

'What does that mean?'

'If it's true, it means these firms effectively have their own estates in the Congo, that they are moving from transport into production. That they issue their own contracts for gathering rubber, that they have their own workforce, their own supply lines, their own production facilities. It means that effectively they have their own fiefdoms in the Congo. And that means that they are responsible for the atrocities in those territories.'

'Not my father.' She could not control her rising anger.

He leaned forward with his elbows on the table. 'Grace, this is not to be so easily shrugged aside. If it is true that these crimes are being committed, we cannot pick and choose whom we would wish to be the guilty parties.'

'*If* it is true,' she countered. '*If* it is.'

But she had not seen him quite so determined before and the more those calm blue eyes rested on her the more agitated she became.

'Morel says he can prove his claims,' he said. 'He has promised to send documents to my chambers early next week. Meanwhile I'm having some people of my own look into his assertions. I had hoped you might be interested in helping.'

'Alec, you're not suggesting . . .' An awful suspicion dawned in her mind. 'Have you been building up to this all these months? Was this all just a roundabout way of inducing me to spy on my own father?'

'Come now, Grace, you can't believe that.'

She got noisily to her feet, attracting glances from the tables around. 'I'm not sure what I believe.'

'Grace, no one is asking you to do anything against your conscience. But of all the journalists in the country well placed to ask the proper questions—'

'That's why you've been favouring me with your contacts and your introductions?'

'Please sit down, Grace.'

'Shame on you, Alec Strathair.' She flung down her napkin and stalked away between the tables.

It was after ten o'clock before Grace climbed the stairs to her room. Her anger had leached out of her, but it had left her heavy with an unexpected sadness. Her great adventure was over. What had seemed so heady and promising, a noble pursuit of justice which might

336

conceivably have shaped her whole career, was extinguished, just like that. A little plain speaking, a sudden awakening to what should have been obvious, and it was gone. She had been naive, no doubt. Perhaps she had even been a fool, and had so wanted his introduction to the world of power that it had blinded her to everything else. All the same, she knew that it was not just self-reproach which afflicted her. She wouldn't see Alec again, and the thought ached like a bruise.

She stopped with her key in the lock. The white envelope protruded from beneath the door. She stooped to pick it up and knew at once it was from him, although he had written nothing on the envelope. She supposed it contained some sort of apology, and for a second her indignation flared afresh and she considered tearing it up unread. But in the end she could not deny that she was relieved to hear from him. She opened the envelope where she stood on the stairs.

It contained a single sheet of paper. On it was typed an address in Deptford, and the name Gifford Gray.

83

The lane was ankle deep in mud chopped by the hooves of cows. Frank let Cavendish stump on ahead up the steepening slope. The older man was panting with the effort but he refused to use his stick or to slow down, throwing quick-fire questions in Arabic over his shoulder as he walked. Frank answered fluently and without thinking, closing his mind to the English rosehips glowing in the winter hedges, and the English larks tinkling in the white sky. He was used to Cavendish's routine of instruction. It had been repeated every morning for weeks.

They climbed out of the woods and took a chalky path across rising downland. At the top of the hill Cavendish stopped, leaning against a gate, blowing hard in the keen air.

'Well, no one will ever take either of us for Nilotic Arabs,' he said, 'but if it comes to it, we might pass as volunteers from Aden, or somewhere.'

In thin November sunlight the Kent countryside lay spread before them, a quilt of russet and green. Not far below them lay Faldonside. Frank saw a maid airing bedding from an upstairs window and Mrs Pugh at work in the kitchen garden among the rows of winter greens. Cavendish flexed his leg, grimaced, flexed it again.

'Damn nearly whole again.' He slapped his thigh. 'Do you know, Gray, I used to be able to hang from the rafters by my knees? Party trick.' He glanced at Frank. 'Told you that already, did I?'

'You did, sir.'

Cavendish grunted, put his right foot on the bar of the gate and pulled himself over. As his left boot came down on the far side he slipped. Frank moved forward and caught his elbow.

'You shouldn't go back,' Frank said.

Cavendish straightened, embarrassed by his stumble. 'What are you talking about?'

'They haven't sent any orders yet. If you put in for it now they'd give you a medical discharge.'

'Indeed? And then?'

'You could stay here. You've earned it. Mrs Freeman would like nothing better.' Frank found he had not released his grip on the older man's arm, and he did so now, awkwardly.

Cavendish said, 'Finished?'

Frank stepped back. 'Sir.'

The east wind silvered the grass around them. In the small silence which followed, something about the house below caught Frank's attention and, glad of the distraction, he glanced down the hill. Mrs Pugh was no longer in the kitchen garden, but had walked around to the front of the house carrying her trug of greens and was talking to someone, a mounted man in a peaked cap.

'Telegram,' Cavendish said, ominously. 'We'd best go down.'

By the time they had reached the foot of the hill the rider had gone. They stopped at the front steps of the house, knocking the mud from their boots. Mrs Freeman appeared above them.

'It's not your marching orders after all,' she said, her lips pursed. 'As a matter of fact, it's for you, Corporal Gray.'

Frank took the flimsy envelope from her and tore it open. He read the telegram twice before he could make sense of it.

VITAL MEETING CAMBRIDGE UNIVERSITY TOMOR-
ROW STOP MEET YOU GREEN DRAGON TONIGHT STOP
BRING FUNDS STOP GIFFORD

84

Frank stepped down from the train and hefted his bag onto his shoulder. A cadaverous inspector in railway uniform stood at the barrier, clipping tickets. He glanced up at Frank's khaki.

'Back from the wars, Tommy?' The man tapped the side of his nose. 'Make the most of your leave, lad. The lead'll start to fly again any day now. I was at Majuba Hill, and I can smell trouble.'

Frank walked down Deptford High Street through the evening crowds flowing from shops and factories and dockyards. The pavements were packed with men in cloth caps, shopgirls in flowered hats, clerks in cheap suits. He supposed that somewhere in that mass of men and boys would be Gifford, with his head full of crazy dreams of flight and of his important meeting in Cambridge tomorrow. He would have liked to be angry with Gifford, but the boy's sheer buoyancy made it impossible to nurture resentment against him for long.

Frank turned down the side street towards the river, and at the end pushed through the swing doors of the Green Dragon. There were a few drinkers in the public bar, men who had stopped for a pint after work. On his right the frosted glass door of the saloon stood open. The room was half-empty and flooded by low wintry sunlight with cigarette smoke curling through it. Mrs Peters was behind the counter, polishing glasses.

'Young Mr Gray! Good to see you again so soon.'

Frank dumped his bag on the floor. 'I was hoping for a room, Mrs Peters.'

'Oh, yes, it's all arranged. That nice brother of yours called in, said you'd be along. Such a polite young man.'

'You've seen Gifford already?'

'An hour or more back. Said I should give you the best room, under the circumstances.'

Mrs Peters smiled at him in an oddly knowing fashion, reached under the counter and dropped a key into his hand. She pulled out a fat ledger and took an envelope from between the pages.

'And he left you this, did your brother. Said he'd see you when he got back from — where was it he was off to? — Cambridge, was it?'

Frank took the envelope from her. Gifford had printed his name on it and nothing more. 'He's already gone? I thought he needed . . .'

But Mrs Peters was bustling off into the other bar, calling 'Coming! Coming!' in answer to some call for service Frank did not hear. He tore open the envelope. There was a postcard in it, and on this Gifford had written: *Honestly, Frank, you really are a chump!* He stared at it, nonplussed, vaguely aware of someone moving up behind him.

'Hello, Frank,' Grace said.

85

He ran his hand down the curve of her neck, feeling the small buzz of her short hair. She came awake slowly and nuzzled against him like a cat. Her eyes opened lazily and she smiled. He cradled her against him and she arched her back to kiss him, her breasts rolling against his chest.

'Mrs Rossiter warned me not to fall in love with a soldier.' She reached up one hand and sank her fingers into his hair.

'She told me you were too good for me,' he said.

Grace gripped his hair and tugged it. 'You see? What a wise woman she is!' She rested there for a moment, gazing up at him. But gradually her smile faded. 'Frank, we have to talk.'

He bent to pull her up against him, suddenly afraid of what she might say next, but she placed her hand flat on his breastbone, rolled away from him and sat on the edge of the bed. Outside the window the first light of dawn was turning the Thames to mercury. A flurry of rain speckled the glass. The halyards of moored vessels tinkled as they rocked on the tide. Grace lifted his khaki tunic from the chair beside the bed and pulled it around her. She stood up and walked across the room to sit by the window. The tunic sagged on one side and knocked against her thigh.

'Leave that,' he said, sitting up quickly.

But she was already pulling the squat Bulldog revolver from the pocket, dangling it from the trigger guard. She looked at it with disgust.

'It's not loaded,' he said.

'It's horrible. You carry this around with you?'

'I can't leave it at the house.' He got to his feet, took the pistol from her hand and put it on the bedside table. He sat on the bed, obscurely ashamed that she should have seen the weapon, as if he were a secret drinker and she had stumbled upon his hidden bottle.

She seemed unable to take her eyes off the gun, as if it exerted some awful fascination for her. 'Have you ever used it?'

'Don't ask me that.'

She shuddered and wrapped the tunic around her. 'I hate to think of it. The things they make you do.'

'I'm a soldier, Grace.'

'A soldier of the Queen. My God.' She got up and gazed out of the window at the shining river. 'How soon can you get out?'

'Out?'

'Out of the army. Get your . . . discharge or whatever they call it.'

He sat looking at the cello curve of her back, touched by the early light, and at the river slipping past behind her. He experienced a strange illusion that she was receding from him, as if she were being carried out of his reach by that sliding water.

'How soon?' she repeated.

'I can't get out, Grace.'

'Of course you can. You must be able to resign, or hand in your papers, or whatever soldiers do.'

'Troopers can't *resign* from the army.'

'Frank, the bloody Empire will survive with one less soldier.'

'I've signed on, Grace. I belong to them for six years.'

She snorted in disbelief. 'Frank, you don't imagine I'm going to let them keep you? Not now?'

'It's not a matter of choice.'

'Of course it is. Just refuse. Stay here with me.'

'That's desertion.'

'So it's desertion. Pay their stupid fine.'

'You don't understand. They won't slap my wrist or lock me up for thirty days. They can shoot people for desertion.'

She blinked, shook her head hard. 'No, no. This isn't right.'

'We need to face facts, Grace.'

'No. There's another way. There's always another way.' She was speaking rapidly, as if to shut out anything else he might say. 'Yes, I have it. This is what we'll do. We'll go away. We'll give ourselves new names, start a new life – abroad, perhaps. America or Australia. Thousands of people migrate every year, it's easy to get lost among them. I have a little money put away, enough for our passage . . .'

'I can't do that.'

'What do you mean, you can't do it?' she burst out.

'I'm a serving soldier, Grace. I have to go where I'm sent.'

'Do you? Well, I'll tell you this much: you won't be going to the Sudan, nor anywhere else. I won't have it.'

'What either of us will or won't have is not important.'

'This man Cavendish you speak of with such respect. You saved his life. He'd do anything for you.'

'Captain Cavendish is an officer. He isn't going to help me desert. And the army won't just look the other way if I don't report for duty when they call me.'

Suddenly she was shouting. 'I won't be robbed of my future for such a cause! I will not, Frank! Do you hear me?'

The self-assured young woman had vanished, and she seemed to him at that moment like a lost little girl. He went to her and took her in his arms and held her against him. 'The army won't listen, Grace. We have to find a way through this without talking about desertions or discharges.'

She flung away from him and stood facing him. 'You're not telling me the truth.'

'What?'

'This isn't just about that evil old woman at Windsor and her damned Empire, is it? You're still planning to settle your own feud.'

He said nothing.

'Answer me!'

'I want justice. That's all.'

'Oh, yes. Justice. And you're God, I was forgetting.'

'Grace, listen to me.' He gripped her shoulders. 'I know who he is. I know he will be in Egypt when I'm sent there. If there is some way I can expose him, bring him to the law – perhaps with Cavendish's help—'

'That's not what you want. Not that kind of justice.' She pointed to the ugly revolver on the bedside table. '*That's* what you want.'

He realised that he was gripping her arms with painful force and he released her. 'He will not go unpunished, Grace. I made a promise, and I shall keep it.'

'A promise to whom?'

'To my mother.'

'She's dead, Frank. Your promise is to a dead woman.'

'That's why I can't break it.'

'And what about the living?' Her eyes were hot. She grabbed his hand and held it between her breasts. '*I'm* living. Feel that? And I'm to wait until the man I love can get some vile revenge, and then, if he isn't hanged for it, he might return to me in a few years, when the army lets him go. Is that approximately the situation?'

'If I could set this burden down, do you think I wouldn't do it? Until I settle accounts with this man, however it is to be done, I will never be free. Never.'

'Frank, that's nonsense. The truth is you won't be free until you've turned your back on the past. There will always be evil men. You cannot pay them back for all their sins, least of all by committing sins of your own. You'd be destroying us, not him. I told you once before you needed to have faith. In me, in us. In the future. But you've lost that faith, haven't you?'

'I've lost faith in things turning out well for us just because we wish them to.' He turned to gaze out of the window. Dawn had broken. A steam barge was thumping eastward against the incoming tide, puffing white vapour against grey water. 'There isn't any way out for me until I settle this.'

'You'd have come with me once, Frank.' She was weeping now, the tears running straight down her face and falling to the floor. 'The last time, the night after the rally. If those policemen hadn't found us, you'd have given everything up for me, for us.'

'I wasn't a soldier then. I hadn't found Jack Herrick then.'

She leaned across and picked up the revolver from the bedside table, dangling it from the trigger guard as she had before. 'You hadn't found this then.'

He moved to her, but she stepped back out of his reach, flinging the pistol away from her as if in disgust. The weapon clattered over the floor almost to his feet, where it lay rocking on the boards. Grace let the tunic slip from her shoulders and fall, gathered her clothes from the chair, pulled her dress up around herself. Her face was crumpled and wet with tears.

'How could you do this to me, Frank?'

'I thought you understood.'

'And perhaps I do, at last.' She bowed her head, fastening her clothes, fumbling with hooks and eyes.

'Grace, what are you doing?'

'I have to get away. I have to think.'

He stepped towards her again and as he did so his bare foot struck the revolver and automatically he bent to pick it up. And froze there, with his hand on the weapon, his fingers closing around the cold butt. It was monstrously heavy, immovable, as if rooted into the core of the earth. He could not lift it, but nor could he release his grip on it. The room grew dark and hot around him and the stench of burning lamp oil was in his throat and a man was crushing his hand around the pistol butt and a woman was shrieking his name, again and again.

'Frank?' Grace had stopped crying and now her voice was clear and calm. 'Frank?'

He looked up at her dumbly.

She said, 'Will you not even ask me to stay?'

He crouched on the floor with the revolver under his hand and stared at her. Sweat was running down the sides of his face. He struggled to speak but no sound came. She shook her head and turned away, and in a moment the door slammed and her quick steps were on the wooden stairs.

The room had grown light. A watered sun fell through the window and lay in ripples over the boards and over his back, but he did not feel its pale warmth. He did not hear the steamships thudding out on the tide nor the gulls crying like lost souls. He barely heard the chambermaid knock, call out, and rattle at the door handle.

But he could hear his mother screaming. He need only heft the revolver in his hand to hear that again, to be back in that dark room, the air acrid with smoke and flame shadows dancing across the rattan blinds. He could see it all now, see and hear it all, as if it were played out on a magic-lantern show before his eyes, the images flickering, over and over again.

She lay sprawled on the boards in her white nightgown, her face bleeding and her bare breasts rolling, groping out to him with one hand. Frank had no time to meet her eyes, for he was fighting, grappling desperately while the man's bruising grip crushed his fingers around the gun butt. Rank breath stinking of wine was in his face, and his cheek was jammed against the coarse material and hard buttons of a tunic. The tunic was warm with blood in a patch above the waistline. Frank could feel himself weakening, but he would not let go: he had reached the revolver first and he would not give it up. He would find the strength to force it round just far enough, push the muzzle against the man's chest and finish this.

He almost managed it. Rage and fear made him invincible and the injured man was gasping as his own strength ebbed. With both their hands locked around the butt Frank wrenched the pistol back an inch, another half-inch, yet another. He had a wild surge of hope: he might succeed. He *would* succeed.

His mother shrieked, 'Jack!' and lurched up onto her knees, reaching for them, and as Frank made one last desperate lunge to inch the barrel around the man twisted towards the woman's voice. The action swung the revolver out and away from his body, the muzzle wavering in the darkness.

Frank did not hear the shot. He felt the trigger give under his jammed fingers, and felt the kick of the weapon, and knew that his mother had abruptly stopped screaming. And all at once the weary struggle was over and the man was standing, swaying above him in the darkness, and the revolver fell clattering to the boards as Frank released his hold on it. The last of his strength left him and he sagged over onto his right side. His broken wrist folded under him and in the resulting blast of agony he slipped out of the present.

When he came back to himself the man was at the top of the veranda steps, starting to stumble down them, one hand clutched to his side. The revolver was on the floor inches from Frank's face, still rocking gently. He reached out to it with his left hand, got to his knees and then to his feet, cocking the pistol with his right forearm. He lifted the pistol and walked after the man.

He did not look round at his mother. He could feel her still presence behind him, but he did not look round.

He knew now why he had not.

Don't blame yourself, they had said. *Don't blame yourself.*

86

Three hours later Grace walked through the booming vault of Waterloo Station and out into the thin morning. She crossed between hansom cabs and steaming horses and set off down the narrow streets towards Southwark.

It was odd to be here in the middle of the working day. The red-brick terraces lay quiet under a white winter sky and only a few women were out scrubbing doorsteps or hanging washing in tiny front yards. Children were playing hopscotch on the paving stones. No one paid Grace any attention, and she was glad. She let herself into her building and mounted the stairs to her flat. The gasometer across the street was low and steely light fell across her little room. It was chilly and she lit the oil stove, and sat in the chair with the burst horsehair cushion. She felt dull and sick. She dared not think of Deptford, of the wild look in his eyes as he had crouched on the floor. She waited for the warmth of the stove to reach her, grateful for the silence.

She was not sure how long she sat there. Hours, perhaps. When she first grew aware of the clattering engine it came to her as if in a dream. But by the time the vehicle turned into the street she was alert, and anxious too, for she knew at once who it was.

She reached the window just as the red motor car pulled up outside. It popped and banged once or twice and then fell silent while Alec pushed back his absurd goggles and climbed out. Grace stepped back quickly from the window in confusion. She did not want to see him; she did not want to see anyone. But already she could hear him on the stairs, and in a moment he was knocking at her door. When she did not answer at once he knocked again, harder, and this time she opened. He stood on the landing in his long leather coat and gauntlets, a black portmanteau under his arm.

'Grace, forgive me for coming unannounced. Rather bad form, after our parting, I know. But I simply couldn't leave matters as they were.' He looked closely at her. 'Is this a bad moment?'

She knew that if she offered him a single cold word he would be on his way, and that was what she had earnestly intended when she opened the door. But now she found she couldn't speak.

His brow furrowed in concern. 'Are you unwell, Grace? You look pale.'

'I'm well enough, Alec.' She touched her hair distractedly. Another few seconds passed. She stood back from the door. 'Come in.'

He seemed suddenly reticent. 'I don't mean to . . .'

'Come in, Alec.'

He walked past her into the flat. In his big coat he seemed to fill the room. He set his portmanteau on the floor at his feet and began to pull off his gloves, looking around him as he did so, and she remembered that he had never been in her shabby little rooms before, and she wondered what he must think of the place.

'You received Gifford Gray's address?' he said. 'I wanted at least to be sure you had.'

'I received it, thank you.'

'I felt such a fool, leaving it without so much as a note of explanation, but after our words at the Savoy I didn't quite know . . .' He let his voice drift away. He glanced at her overnight bag on the bed, and again at her white and strained face, and understanding filled his eyes. 'Perhaps I can guess what has happened.'

'Perhaps you can.' She waved him to a chair but she remained standing. 'Tell me, Alec, did you contact Gifford before you sent me his address?'

'I took that liberty.'

'Why?'

'I wished to be sure that he actually knew where his brother was. I wanted to spare you the pain of disappointment. I had no notion, until young Gifford told me, that Frank Gray was actually in England. Grace, if I have somehow brought you distress—'

'It's not your fault.'

She realised she was weeping for the first time since she had left Deptford. She pushed the heels of her hands across her face.

'Perhaps you'd rather not talk about it,' he suggested.

His tone was hopeful and she knew her distress tortured him, but she couldn't help that. She needed to talk about it.

'Frank's a soldier,' she said. 'Apparently that means he has to go and kill for the Empire whenever they tell him to.'

'I see. And I suppose they will . . . tell him to?'

'Quite soon, probably.'

'I see,' he said again. He stared down at his hands.

'He wants me to wait for him,' she said.

346

He looked up at her slowly.

She said, 'He must go to the Sudan and fight for this atrocious Empire, and settle God knows what barbaric vendetta of his own, and he wants me to wait while he does all this.'

'And will you, Grace? Will you wait?'

The directness of his question startled her. 'How can I?' She walked away a couple of paces, and stopped. 'Surely you don't think I should?'

'My dear, it's hardly my place—'

'For God's sake, Alec! Don't be so mealy-mouthed. Tell me what you think.'

'Very well.' He straightened a little in his chair. 'You love him. That's patently obvious. And certainly he's a fool if he doesn't love you back.'

'And so what? What difference is all that supposed to make?'

'It makes whatever difference you allow it to make, I suppose. But I do know this much: it's not every day that we love and are loved in return.'

'You only say that because you are a man.'

'Hardly.' He gave a sharp little laugh. 'If that were my thinking, I'd be more likely to advise the opposite.'

His laughter seemed to her strangely bitter, and she looked at him, realising that she had not properly seen him since he had first stepped into the room. He sat facing her, solid in his buff leather, resolute and calm, but there was something hidden behind his eyes.

'What do you mean by that?' she asked.

He stood up and took her hands in his. 'Grace, you know I only wish you well. I have no right to suggest what you ought to do. But after so long an absence, your reunion was bound to be difficult. Perhaps it would be a mistake to rush to judgment. That's all I mean.'

She wanted to throw back at him that, no, he had no right at all to suggest anything, and that he could mind his business and leave her to hers, but in the face of his calm blue gaze that was quite impossible.

She pulled her hands away from his. 'I'll give it some thought.'

He stood back. 'I should be going. You look as if you need some rest.'

'Yes. Yes, I'm rather tired.'

He stooped to pick up his portmanteau. 'If there's anything I can do, Grace, you know . . .'

He didn't bother to finish the sentence, but walked past her to the door and reached for the handle.

She fought against the impulse and lost. 'What's in it?'

'I beg your pardon?'

'In your briefcase.'

'Put it out of your mind, Grace.' He opened the door. 'You've done enough. Let someone else worry about it.'

'Are they the documents from Morel?'

He hesitated. 'They are.'

'Why did you bring them in here? To show me?'

'Not at all. I could hardly leave them in the motor. No, I'm taking them to a man I know on the *Daily Telegraph*.'

'The *Telegraph*? Good God!'

'I believe he may be interested.'

'And I would not be?'

'Grace, you made it clear—'

'What do the documents say, Alec? Is Morel telling the truth?'

He tightened his lips. 'Yes,' he said finally, 'the documents confirm everything that Morel says.'

'And my father? Do they say anything about him?'

He faced her and closed the door again, leaning with his back against it. 'Nothing you'll want to hear, Grace.'

87

Grace thought she had never seen Cumver Hill look as beautiful as it did on that fading winter afternoon, with the last of the light falling across the bare beech woods and lamps gilding the tall windows. She remembered the last time she had seen this view, long months ago. She had twisted around on the seat of Jimmy Jervis's cart for one last look as it rattled down this driveway, carrying her away like a refugee.

Now, as the cab from the station drew away, she walked in through the ivy-clad gateposts and stopped to look at her old home. The air was chill and tasted of woodsmoke and crows were calling from leafless trees. In a few weeks it would be Christmas. She remembered a Christmas not so long ago when her father had stopped his gig at just this point and they had talked about *noblesse oblige* and the natural order, and the funny way Mr Brasher smelled. There had been ice on the puddles then, she recalled, and rosehips glowing in the hedgerows, just as they were now. Did her father still have the workmen cut a yule log? Would he and her mother host their party as they had always done, the two of them lording it like Oberon and Titania, the hall decked with holly and shimmering with candles? Would they pretend nothing had changed? She wondered if the servants or the tenants ever dared to ask about her. She wondered who was looking after Bonny in the stables now.

In Leigh Village, hidden behind the grey woods, the church clock struck four. Grace gathered herself and walked quickly on. A few minutes later she was hurrying up the broad stone steps, reaching for the bell pull. But the doors swung open before she could touch the rope.

'Lord, miss,' Mrs Rossiter said, staring at her. 'Is it really you? Back here in this house?'

'Good afternoon, Mrs Rossiter.' Grace swung off her coat and gave it to the housekeeper. 'Is my father in his study?'

The housekeeper folded the coat over her arm. 'You look thinner, miss. Are you well?'

'I am quite well, thank you.' Grace brushed down her dress, but Mrs Rossiter still gave no sign of answering her question. Grace said, 'Where is my father? There is a matter I need to discuss with him.'

Mrs Rossiter stood searching Grace's face. 'Something's happened to you, miss. I can see it.'

'I . . . I'm not sure what you mean.'

'Yes, you are. You've found him, haven't you? Young Frank. You've found him. Is that why you're here?'

'No.' Grace felt her eyes fill and looked away. 'But I have seen him, Mrs Rossiter. He's well, you need have no concerns on that score. He's well enough.'

'When? When did you see him?'

'Just . . . this morning. But—'

'He's in England, then?'

'For the moment. But there is to be war, you know, and—'

'So what are you doing here? Why ain't you with him?'

Grace tossed her head. 'Mrs Rossiter, things are far from resolved between Frank Gray and myself. Now if you would kindly—'

'Don't you *if you would kindly* me.' Mrs Rossiter gripped Grace's arm, as if she might be about to shake her. 'Do you think you have time to waste here on some quarrel with your father? Go to Frank now. This minute.'

Grace tugged her arm free. 'There's something I must settle first.'

'And don't that sound familiar? Go now, you foolish girl. How long do you think life will wait?'

Grace hesitated at that, but then the door of her father's study swung open, and Mrs Rossiter strode away across the marble hall, and Dearborn was standing in the study doorway with the firelight behind him. She saw with a shock how altered he was, and at once lost all the cool words she had rehearsed.

He said, 'Grace?' and his voice was filled with joy.

'Father.'

'Grace, I have prayed—'

'I am glad to see you, Father.'

She swept past him into the study before he could stop her or say more. Nothing seemed to be working out as it should. The exchange with Mrs Rossiter had thrown her, and now it was all happening too quickly. The very familiarity of the study, with its heavy furniture and its smells of tobacco and her father's cologne, threatened to throw her back into a time when her certainties counted for nothing against his. She stood by the fireplace, waiting until he closed the door and followed her in. She found that she was trembling and was glad of the hearth's warmth.

She heard her father move into the centre of the room behind her. At length she risked looking back at him. He seemed years older than she remembered, grey and a little stooped, and there was such pain in his eyes that she could not look into them.

'I shouldn't have come,' she said at last. 'Alec said I shouldn't.'

'Alec?'

She shook her head. 'I have to go. I have to.'

She wanted to walk out but although he did not move to stop her she found she could not take a step.

'You can't leave now, Grace,' he said. 'That would be too cruel. I have so longed for you to come home.'

'Father, please.'

'I've been unwell, you see. Quite unwell. Illness concentrates the mind most wonderfully. I have given a great deal of thought to the way we parted.'

'I am not coming home, Father. That's not why I came.'

He winced. She was furious with him for showing weakness now, and with herself for the way it touched her.

He said, 'Some hard words were spoken, Grace. On both sides, I'm sure, but I take my share – more than my share . . .'

She bowed her head. 'Please don't, Father.'

'All I ask,' he said, 'is that we might from time to time talk once again as we used to do, that I might once again be your father and you my daughter, and that we might relive some of the happier times we spent together as a family. We did spend happy times together, Grace, did we not?'

'Of course we did, Father. But things have changed since those days.'

'Then we will change them back. Please, Grace. I have had no joy since you've been gone. There is no point in my denying that, though I've tried hard enough to do so.'

'Father, it's too late for this.'

'And since I have been so unwell . . .'

'I am sorry you've been ill, Father.' She almost shouted the words. 'But I did not come to offer sympathy.'

He leaned back against his desk, as if he needed the support. 'What did you come to offer, Grace?'

'Something quite different. But that's not important now.'

'I fear it is important, nevertheless. I can see it in your eyes, that old crusading zeal.' He smiled sadly. 'That usually bodes ill for me.'

She sank into one of the fireside chairs and gazed desolately at him. 'Oh, Father. How did we come to this?'

'I don't know, my dear.' He sat down opposite her and leaned across to take her hand in his. 'I'm sure I don't know.'

He had always had such powerful hands, but now she could feel the cylinders of bone roll beneath his skin.

'I wish . . .' she began.

'Nothing between us is so broken that it cannot be mended,' he said, patting her hand. 'And I should very much like to mend it. I did not think the Good Lord would grant me another chance, and yet He has done so.' He cocked his head. 'Will *you*, Grace? Will *you* grant me a chance?'

Grace put his hand aside and stood up. 'You'd best let me go, Father.'

He rose to face her. 'Do I stand accused of something? Is that why you came?'

'Yes.'

'Am I not even permitted to know what I have done? Surely that's unjust.'

She hesitated a moment longer, opened her bag and held the paper out to him. 'What does this mean?'

He took it, frowned at it. 'It is a contract. What of it?'

'A contract for what?'

'For the supply of rubber from certain territories in the Equatorial province of the Congo Free State. Technically, it's a concession.'

'That's not your signature on it.'

'No. It is Andreas Welti's.'

'And Uncle Welti works for you.'

'You say it as if I might deny it. But of course he does. As you know, he is director of several of our overseas subsidiaries. This is a contract with one of them. A company incorporated in . . . Antwerp, I believe. You see, here? Why are we discussing it?'

'You know how rubber is collected in the Congo?'

'I suppose I am tolerably well informed.'

'So you know about the Force Publique, and the quotas, the deaths from porterage, the punishments by cutting off of hands—'

'Such dreadful things do go on, yes. I have no doubt of it. What is this to do with me?'

'Years ago, I stood in this room and you promised me that you would never involve yourself in oppression.'

He opened his hands. 'I am not involved in any such thing.'

'But this document directly implicates Dearborn & Company.'

'This is a contract with an overseas subsidiary. Welti is director of that overseas subsidiary. He manages and directs it, I do not. Do you follow?'

'But that's the merest sophistry!'

'Grace, they are the legal facts.'

'How can you sit there and say this to me, hide behind legalities in this way? You know what is happening in that country.'

'I have no influence over how the colonial administration of the Congo Free State goes about its work. I'm sure it's less than perfect, but I have no power over it. Neither does Welti, for that matter. This is King Leopold's responsibility, not ours.'

'You wash your hands of it?'

'It is not a question of that. I wish no harm to the people in that country, but we have to deal with the government which is in place.'

'Even when you know it is corrupt?'

'All governments are corrupt to some degree.'

'And yet you knowingly profit from that corruption.'

'Yes, I profit from it. I could wish for Leopold's people to be less venal than they are, but I certainly profit from my contracts with them. So does every company which has dealings there. For that matter, Grace, so do you.'

'Me? I want nothing to do with it. I never have wanted anything to do with it.'

'You don't have a choice.' His voice was gathering strength. 'You may turn your back on it all now, but you cannot give back your education, your privileges, the very habit of confidence you carry around and which opens so many doors for you. Those things had to be paid for. Like the village school which I fund, the hospital in Farnham I endow, the tenants I support. Where do you think the money has come from for all this? Where do you think the money comes from for the way half the British nation lives? Violence and oppression were routine in Africa long before we arrived, Grace. For centuries those people have lived in abject poverty and under the heel of local tribal chiefs who were every bit as brutal as the Belgian colonists, and more.'

'But to exploit their situation is shameful!'

He screwed up his eyes as if in pain. 'You have things the wrong way around, Grace. These natives had nothing. Now they have at least something. And do you think that if we went away they would suddenly become free, upstanding citizens? The truth is that these people are in the Stone Age. Do you seriously expect them to run their own affairs? Of course we exercise dominion over them, we or the Belgians or some other advanced people, and yes, I expect that such dominion is necessarily sometimes harsh.'

'We steal their birthright from them, and give them bullets and tyranny in exchange.'

'And what is their birthright? Rubber? And what good is rubber to them? They have no use for it. They have no roads, no vehicles, they haven't even invented the wheel. What if we do take rubber from their forests, and profit in the process? They get at least something from the exchange. They never even knew the stuff was valuable before we came along.'

'But the way they are treated . . .'

'It's hard labour, certainly. I would not deny it. But we didn't invent this system, Grace. The African tribes were trading in human beings for centuries before any of us came along. The Romans engaged in it, too, as I recall, and the Greeks. We generally consider them pretty enlightened.'

'It's a sin, what's happening in the Congo. It's slavery by another name, and it's the nature of Empire to prolong it. How could it be otherwise? There's no incentive to stop.'

'Nonsense, Grace. You talk of slavery. But it was this Empire, which you so despise, which abolished slavery and fought wars to put it down.'

'Not in the Congo, evidently.'

'The Congo is not British. What King Leopold does in his own country is his own concern. I am a businessman, Grace. Not a judge. Not a charity. Trade is what will set these people free. Commerce. With each exchange a little trickles down to them, a little money, a little education, a little training. They see the way we manage things and they emulate us, just as the natives are now doing in India. And gradually they build up. That's how progress is achieved.'

'You should make a stand against this. You should pull out.'

'You know very well that if we did so our place would be taken in an instant by a French or a German or an American company. What would be gained?'

She snatched back the paper from him. 'I so hoped you'd deny all this, Father. Even if I'd doubted what you told me, I would have accepted a denial from you, rather than believe this.'

He placed one hand behind him on the desk, as if the exchange had exhausted him. 'Grace, perhaps we shall never agree about these matters. But I know this: you will always be my daughter, and against that, our political differences are of no weight.'

'Our differences are not political, Father. They're moral.'

'Grace, my dear . . .' He reached out to take her hand, but she avoided him.

'Don't.'

He let his hand fall to his side. 'I know I've been unreasonable in the past,' he said, 'even unjust at times. I've been pig headed. When I see what a fine young woman you've grown into I realise just what I have denied myself. But Grace, we're very alike. I suppose that's why we clash. That shouldn't be a surprise. After all, I helped make you into the person you are.'

'Father, I have to go.'

'But go where?'

She had not decided until that instant, but now it was suddenly clear to her. 'To London. There's someone I must see . . . before he leaves for overseas. If I haven't already left it too late.'

'Stay a while, Grace.' He was breathing rapidly, and she saw, with wonder, that he was frightened. 'As you love me, stay. All I want in the world is for us to close this rift between us.'

Once again she felt that treacherous stab of pity for him. This time she fought it down. She reached for the black pearl at her throat, closed her fist over it. 'I'm sorry, Father. Truly.' She twisted until the gold chain stretched and parted, held the jewel out and poured it into his hand.

Mrs Rossiter was standing in the hall with her coat. 'The gig's waiting to take you to the station, miss. Jimmy'll drive you. Go and don't stop.'

Grace let Mrs Rossiter settle the coat over her shoulders and usher her towards the tall doors. She heard footsteps on the stairs behind her and her mother called, 'Grace?'

Grace kept walking. Mrs Rossiter pulled the doors open for her and she saw the gig standing on the carriage turn at the foot of the steps, its lamps throwing yellow bars across the gravel.

'Grace?' her mother called again.

This time Grace turned and as she did so the study door banged open and Dearborn stood framed by the light of the fire behind him. His face was bone white and glistening and his blue lips were working and spittle hung from them and with one hand he clawed at his chest.

Grace ran back towards him. 'Papa!'

His body arced as if caught by a hook, and he twisted and fell full length across the marble floor. Grace knelt beside him, her mind filled by his ghastly choking and the slapping of his limbs against marble and her mother's shrieks echoing up the stairwell.

88

Dearborn's face was the colour of linen, with a faint smudge of blue around the mouth. His breathing was laboured, a grotesque sound in the quiet room. He made a faint movement of his hand, and Grace leaned forward to hold a glass of water to his lips. She put the glass aside and sat back at the bedside and took his hand. His skin felt cool and waxy under her touch.

'It cannot be long,' he whispered.

'I know.' Grace patted his hand under her own. 'I know, Father.'

Sarah Dearborn said, 'Stephen, we will consult the best doctors, the best specialists . . .'

She talked on urgently about experts and surgeons, rest cures and drugs. Dearborn did not look at his wife as she spoke, but lay with his eyes half-closed. It took her a few moments to notice that he was not listening to her. She stopped talking and her lips thinned. She looked at Grace.

'You tell him, then. It seems he only listens to you.'

Grace did not take her eyes from her father's face. 'Mama, the doctors said as much.'

Sarah Dearborn gave a cat's hiss of exasperation, but her husband's eyes creased a little. He might have been smiling. He signalled so that Grace bent low to hear him.

'Is Welti here?'

He seemed unable to see the rumpled little man no more than arm's length away.

Welti leaned forward. 'I am here, old friend.'

To Grace her Uncle Welti looked even more dishevelled than ever, with his grey hair awry and his floral waistcoat cross-buttoned. She saw with a twist of her heart that his face was shining with tears.

'Take note of this, Welti,' Dearborn whispered. 'Write.'

Welti went to the bureau and returned with writing paper. He produced a gold fountain pen and uncapped it, and sat like a prim secretary waiting for dictation. He was still weeping soundlessly.

Dearborn waited, gathering his strength. 'Everything,' he said at last, 'is to go to Grace.'

Grace sat up. 'But you said—'

'Everything. Company. House. Everything.'

Appalled, Grace looked at her mother, but Sarah Dearborn's pinched face betrayed no emotion. It was as if she had not heard.

'It will be in trust until you are of age,' Dearborn went on, so softly that Grace had to strain to catch the words. 'But you are to have control over all my affairs, and access to the income, effective at once.' He swallowed, and spoke more firmly. 'Mark that, Welti. Effective at once. Do you understand what I'm saying, Grace?'

'I don't want this, Father. I never wished for it.'

'You don't get everything you wish for in this life, my dear.' His hand stirred under hers and he gave a wheeze of laughter. 'But sometimes you get a good deal more.'

She shook her head. 'Mama should have it. Mama, tell him.'

Sarah Dearborn got to her feet and with a rustle of skirts swept from the room, shutting the door behind her. For a few seconds all Grace could hear was Dearborn's harsh breathing and the scratching of Welti's gold nib.

'I won't accept it, Father.'

'You will accept it.' He moistened his lips. 'You are the blood of my blood, and you cannot refuse.'

Grace stared at him, helpless with pity. It was as if his life energy were streaming out of him as she watched, as if he were fading before her eyes. But still, she had a baffling sense that now, in his hour of weakness, he had beaten her as he had never been able to beat her when he was strong.

'Welti will do anything you tell him,' Dearborn was saying. 'Anything. Isn't that so, Welti?'

The little man tilted his head in acknowledgment. Grace could hear his tears tapping onto the paper as he wrote.

'Make sure that's legible when you've done with it, you old fool,' Dearborn told him with a hint of his old briskness. 'Write up a fair copy and bring it back for me to sign. And do it quickly.'

Welti nodded dumbly, got to his feet and left the room.

Grace turned her father's cool hand in hers. 'You ought to rest,' she said.

'Soon enough.' He tried to shift in the bed, but a sudden pain made him catch his breath.

'Corporal Gray?' Mrs Freeman's voice rang clear in the night. 'What on earth do you think you're about?'

'I'm getting drunk, ma'am.'

He thought this a reasonable response, but through the fog in his mind he sensed that her imperious presence boded trouble. He tried to focus on her without success as she hovered in the gloom below like a vengeful ghost. Then she was mounting the steps, rapidly and with menace.

'Do you think this is some sort of regimental bawdy house, Corporal?' she demanded, standing over him. 'Somewhere you can roll back to, drunk and disgusting, just whenever the mood takes you? Well, let me inform you that it is not. It is my home, and you are a guest here —'

'Do you put all your guests in the barn?' He swung wide one arm and declaimed grandly to the moon, 'Raise high the roof beams, carpenters! For the young heroes return over the wine-dark sea, shining in glory from the fields of Troy! Oh,' – he raised a wavering finger – 'but stick that awkward Corporal Gray in the shed.'

He awaited her counterblast, but she said nothing, which confused him.

'That's the Odyssey,' he mumbled. 'More or less. I made up the bit about me. I can do it in Greek, too.'

Still she stood there, her arms crossed over her breasts, staring down at him with an expression he could not read – dumb fury, he assumed, although somehow it did not look like it. He could see her more clearly now. She wore a shift embroidered with blue flowers, and a nightgown thrown over it. She had not stopped to gather up her hair, and it fell in tresses to her waist, shining in the moonlight.

She shook her head. 'Oh, Corporal Achilles, I very much fear that somebody has found your heel.'

Unaccountably, her tone sobered him in an instant. 'Perhaps you're right, ma'am,' he said. 'But it's not as you think.'

'Then what's this about, Corporal? Why have you got yourself into this state?'

'I learned something today, Mrs Freeman. When a man makes a contract with the gods, it cannot be broken just because it suits him. The vow must be honoured, or he will never be free, and the more he struggles, the more entangled he becomes. That was true for Hector and Agamemnon. And it's true for me.'

'What nonsense is this?'

Frank gazed past her and out over the fields, bone white under the moon. 'All the time I thought it was to protect him. But it was for me.

It was all so that I would not be judged. That was why my father agreed to it. That's what destroyed him. And now that I know the truth, it will destroy me too.' He glanced back at her. 'The man who caused this is going to pay.'

She hugged herself as if against a chill. 'I don't know what this means, Corporal, but I'm sure you shouldn't talk in this way.'

'I shall make him pay, Mrs Freeman. It doesn't matter what happens to me now, and I shall make him pay.'

Cavendish's figure appeared in the lamplight below. 'Harriet? The Devil's going on?'

Mrs Freeman gave Frank a significant look, as if to show that for her part the exchange would remain their secret. 'It's your *orderly*, Freddie,' she called back, in her old bantering tone. 'Though he's distinctly disorderly just at present.'

Cavendish stumped across to the foot of the steps, leaning on a cane, and stood looking up, peering hard at Frank. 'Harriet, get one of the girls to put on some coffee. Have it brought to the study.'

Without a word Mrs Freeman went down the steps and into the house.

Cavendish clacked his stick against the cobbles. 'And as for you, Corporal Gray, get yourself down here now, if you can do that without breaking your bloody stupid neck.'

90

Frank sat on one of the hardback chairs with a cup of Mrs Freeman's coffee in his hands while Cavendish lit a lamp. As the soft light blossomed Frank could feel the last of his drunkenness drain away. He was sitting in his belt and braces, his stained tunic hung over a chair. Cavendish trimmed the lamp's wick, walked over to put a log on the fire. When it was blazing he stood back and surveyed Frank, arms akimbo.

'No damage done, apparently. I must say it would be pretty foolish to escape the Pathans, and then kill yourself stumbling home from the Eight Bells.'

'I hired a horse, sir. From the inn. I'm not sure . . . quite where I left him.'

'A horse?' Cavendish looked around the room in a stagey fashion. 'Well, he doesn't seem to be in here, does he?'

'I'm afraid I fell off him, somewhere on the lane.'

'You *fell off*? You call yourself a Lancer and you *fell off*?'

Frank said nothing.

'The horse will find his way home,' Cavendish said gently. 'Frank, I'm not in a position to lecture a young man about drink. However, I do know this much: there are not many questions to which it's more than a temporary answer. Here endeth the first and last lesson.' He sat down opposite Frank in the firelight. 'How's the coffee?'

'Very good, sir. Thank you, sir.'

Cavendish stroked his moustache. 'Speaking of thanks, I've never thanked you for getting me back here. You know, Frank, in the last days since you've been away I've come to appreciate all that I might have lost. One more sight of England in the autumn was worth all the pain. And Faldonside, and Harriet. Yes! Even Harriet. And none of this would have been granted me, if it had not been for you.'

Frank looked down. 'I was ordered to bring you home, sir.'

Cavendish snorted. 'Please don't insult my intelligence. You could have left me to Gul Shah's men. Probably you should have. You could have left me to die at the hands of some army sawbones at Peshawar or Madras or Genoa, and nobody would have blamed you. Nobody would even have known.'

Frank set his coffee cup aside. He felt entirely sober now, but a hammer was tripping in his head, and the other pain – the worse pain – was flooding back. 'I was tempted to leave you, sir. Several times I nearly did.'

'Oh, I know you were tempted, Frank. Sorely tempted. You wanted to get back to the regiment, and whatever unfinished business you have there. But you didn't do that. You brought me back home. You gave me a chance, and perhaps in doing that, you gave yourself one, too.' Cavendish leaned forward urgently in his chair. 'Listen to me, Frank. I can help you. I can see to it that you carve out some sort of a career for yourself in the Army. They don't promote many from the ranks, but with a little money and the right support it can be done.'

'I know you want to help, sir—'

'I never had a son, Frank, but you remind me of myself when I was young. And look at me, a captain at close to fifty. There was a time when they thought I was a coming man, but I'll never go any further now. I've no family of my own, besides Harriet. I'll die a lonely old bachelor, if the good Lord doesn't have something nastier lined up for me before that. But it doesn't have to be that way for you.'

'Sir, something has happened that makes it—'

'This girl,' Cavendish cut across him. 'This Grace. You went to see her, didn't you? Oh, come now, Frank, give me a little credit. Do you think I can't guess why you're in this condition? So what's happened?

361

Did she get tired of waiting? Did she find someone else? Or did you just bungle things?' He paused. 'Don't know much about women. Not my strong suit. But if you wanted a few days extra leave . . .'

'There's no point, sir.'

'How's that?'

'She wouldn't want me now, in any case.'

'Why not now?'

Frank said nothing.

Cavendish cleared his throat. 'Well, it's none of my business. What would I know? But I do know this: you can move up in the world, Frank. You can become someone. The face of society is changing, just as Kitchener's damned railway is changing the face of war. But you must look to the future and not to the past.'

'I believe I've heard that before.'

'Then perhaps you should have listened. Whatever's happened between you and this girl, you can't build your life on – what is it? Vengeance? An old feud? If it's not that, it's something like it.'

'May I go now, sir?'

'No. Listen to me, Frank. You won't credit it, but I know what I'm talking about. There's a beast inside all of us. It's always lurking there. It wants blood, and if you give in to it, it will drink yours. It will devour you, heart, brain and spirit. I know, believe me. You have to slay that beast before it slays you. The man you're going to become will need a bigger calling than some petty vendetta. He'll need a greater dream altogether. An Imperial dream, perhaps. Something with scope for great deeds.'

Frank got clumsily to his feet. 'If you'll excuse me, sir.'

'There's a lot wrong with the Empire, Frank,' Cavendish went on. 'Sometimes not a lot right with it. Even so it's the best and biggest idea we've got. And pretty well everywhere in the world today, it's better than the alternative. But it's changing. Don't you see what an opportunity that gives you? Just to be young, to be British, at this moment in history? In a little over two years we'll be in the twentieth century. Already the old ways of power are crumbling, as if a great tide has come surging in to sweep them away. The kings and queens. The Church. The Empire itself. What are we to do, Frank, if the good isn't to be swept away with the bad? Think of the things you could achieve, the causes you could serve, the wrongs you could right. And I can help you take that opportunity, if you'll let me.'

Frank took his tunic from the back of the chair. He stood running the collar through his fingers. 'I don't believe I need the Empire, sir.'

'Maybe not. But the Empire needs you.'

Frank folded the tunic over his arm and walked to the door.

'We British aren't the only power in the world any more,' Cavendish said, 'and some say just as well. The peoples over whom we've exercised dominion won't permit it for much longer. Who do you imagine is to manage that transition? Do you think worn-out romantics like me, or red-faced old colonels from Bath, are to be entrusted with such a task? Least of all slick politicians or proselytising priests. Good God! No wonder the Arabs rise up against us in Holy War. No, no. The challenge ahead calls for new men. Men fit for a new world. Men like you, Frank.'

'I'm very grateful, sir, for your . . .' Frank looked down at his own hand on the doorknob. He could feel Cavendish's eyes on him, but could not meet them.

'I'll protect you as long as I can, Frank. But in the end, it's you who must slay this beast in you. Only when that's done can you move on to greater things.'

Frank forced himself to look up. 'Goodnight, sir.'

Cavendish sat with the flames painting the planes of his face. 'Goodnight, my boy.'

91

At last, Grace heard the pony and trap come clopping through the fog into Sevenoaks station yard. She hurried out of the waiting room into the raw air. By the time she reached the yard a young man in a business suit had already put his bag into the back. She pulled the bag out and dumped it at his feet.

'I'm sorry.' She looked up at the startled driver. 'You must take me. It's very urgent.'

'You can't do that!' the young man protested. 'I have clients to see. I absolutely insist—'

'I'm sorry,' Grace said again, and pushed past him to climb up onto the seat, 'but if you want to get me down you'll have to drag me. And I shall scream, believe me.' To the driver she said, 'Go, please.'

'Now, miss, I don't know—'

She grabbed the whip out of his hand and cracked it over the horse's rump and the animal leapt forward. She handed the whip back to him and he fumbled with the reins, but in a second the station yard and the outraged young man were swallowed in the mist.

'Thank you,' she said.

The driver glanced at her nervously. 'Where was it you wanted?'

'Faldonside. A house called Faldonside. And as fast as you can. The train was delayed.'

'It's this fog, miss. Can't see your hand in front of your face, hardly.'

'Just drive.'

Grace stood at the end of the lane and listened as the clopping of the horse retreated into the thick air. It wasn't like London, where the acrid murk had been yellow and choking, but even here in the country this December fog made a blanket over the countryside, deadening every sound. Even the birds were silent in the dripping hedgerows. She walked on and in a few yards found cast iron gateposts set into the hedge. Beyond them a drive wound away between dark poplars, blurred like images on an inexpertly exposed photograph. She started to walk down the drive.

Quite soon she saw the house. Lamps were burning in the windows downstairs, quilts of warmth against the grey. She stopped. A figure passed across a window and in a moment the front door opened and a stately woman of early middle age stepped out and started up the drive towards her.

'Good afternoon. Can I help you?'

'I am Grace Dearborn.'

'Forgive me. Should I know the name?'

'I have a friend . . .'

The woman looked at her and her aloofness seemed to slip away. She said: 'Ah.'

'Gray is his name. My friend's name. Frank Gray. He's . . . he's a soldier.'

'Oh, my dear.' The woman's face fell. 'They're gone. My cousin and your friend. A few hours ago now.'

'Gone?'

'Off to the wars, or wherever men go. Their orders came through this morning.'

Grace looked wildly around her. 'I'll go after them.'

'It's no use. They left before the fog came down. You'll find no one to take you. In all probability they're halfway across the Channel by now.'

Grace looked past her down the cobbled yard to the bulk of a building which stood there, a coach house or barn.

Gently, the woman said, 'Are you in mourning, my dear? Your clothes . . .'

'It was my father . . . I could not leave . . .'

'I'm very sorry.'

'The funeral is tomorrow. I suppose it was dreadful of me to come away at such a time, but I thought I could steal a single day for myself . . .'

'It's not dreadful. I should have done the same.'

'And yet it seems so unfair. It is just a single day . . .'

The words caught in her throat. The woman stood quite still, watching her. There was pity in her eyes, and something else, too. Grief. Her own grief.

Grace said, 'Did Frank leave anything for me?'

'No, my dear. He did not.'

'A note, perhaps?'

'I'm sorry.'

Grace took a deep breath. 'Thank you.'

She turned and walked away up the gravel drive. The first poplar tree grew at the bend three or four yards ahead and she thought she could probably get that far, so long as the woman did not speak to her. Perhaps by the time she got there she would have gone back inside her house, back to her own sadness, and would leave Grace to hers. Grace took what felt like the right number of paces and groped blindly until she found the trunk and leaned her cheek against the rough bark.

The steps stopped just behind her.

Grace lifted her head but did not look round. 'Did he never mention me?'

'Come into the house for a moment.'

'Never once?'

She stood motionless, staring at the fibrous map of bark an inch or two from her face. The woman rested her hand on Grace's shoulder.

'They don't know how to love,' she said, softly. 'It's not their fault, poor lambs. But they don't know how.'

'Perhaps they're not the only ones,' Grace said.

PART TEN

England and the Sudan, January to July 1898

92

Frank awoke to a change in the harsh rhythm of the wheels. He shifted his legs on the floor and stretched. The sun sliced through the slatted sides of the goods wagon and the heat was stifling. Cavendish lay slumped opposite him, asleep in a throne he had constructed for himself from ammunition boxes. Sweat blotched his khaki uniform and he looked old.

Frank got to his feet and put his eye to the gap in the door and saw a blinding wedge of desert and acacia scrub. A plume of yellow dust churned up by the train's bogeys hung over the wagons. Shadows cast by the thorn scrub told him that evening was approaching. That meant they should be nearing Berber, and he was glad. After close to four hundred miles on the Sudan Military Railway he wanted a wash, relief from the endless jolting clatter, and some food.

Already the engine's pulse was slowing. At the far end of the truck a dozen Sudanese railway labourers in striped jibbas sat among the sacks and crates. One of them caught Frank's eye and grinned at him in a strangely joyful manner. Frank wondered what the man had to be happy about. He had seen the grave mounds of Sudanese labourers dotting the stony desert all along the track, men who had died in their scores from heat, sickness and overwork in the service of an imperial adventure that could mean nothing to them.

The locomotive snorted and couplings clashed as it slowed. Through the crack in the door Frank saw earthworks and dark soldiers in tarbooshes, clusters of mud-brick buildings with sheet-iron roofs glaring in the sun. The brakes screeched and the train came shuddering to a halt.

Cavendish moved up beside him. 'Think yourself lucky. Fourteen years ago we had to walk here, with Fuzzy-Wuzzy cutting us up all the way.'

The doors were dragged open and they stepped down, blinking in the hard light. They had come to rest in a vast marshalling yard, jostling with labourers and troops and piled with pyramids of goods and stores. Within seconds the train was engulfed by shouting men swarming in through the truck doors to offload boxes of food and arms and ammunition, field guns, building materials, crates of shells. A steam crane

369

thumped into life and started swinging sections of rail from a flatcar. Squads of Sudanese and Egyptian soldiers trotted through the mêlée, their sweating British NCOs bawling for order and cursing when they didn't get it.

A smart Sudanese private, enormously tall and very black, materialised in front of them and saluted. 'Captain Cavendish? Major Pembleton says you come now, sir.'

'Does he indeed? Well, lead on.'

The soldier gestured to a couple of bearers who took their bags, then led them away from the crowds and chaos of the railhead.

Some hundreds of yards on, and outside the ochre clutter of Berber town, the Union flag hung listless in the heat above a vast encampment. Bronze dust hung over the scene, thrown up by squads of marching men, teams of horses, trundling wagons. The private guided them down an avenue of tents until they reached one with a makeshift canvas windbreak erected outside it. In the shelter of this a naked portly man, his back to them, was soaping himself in a canvas bath while two Sudanese orderlies were taking turns to sluice water over him. The little man turned his head as they approached.

'Freddie Cavendish!' He jumped out of the water, unabashed by his nakedness, and gripped Cavendish's hand with his own soapy one. 'Fourteen years and here we are again! From the world's great snare uncaught, as they say, if a bit nibbled around the edges.'

'Major Pembleton, sir.' Cavendish snapped an ironic salute.

'Oh, the devil with all that.' Pembleton stretched out one arm and an orderly draped a towel over it. '*Pinkie* will do very nicely from you, Freddie, thank you. Besides, you should have been a major long before me. You'd be a colonel by now if you'd played your cards right and hadn't been such a damn fool.' He nodded at Frank. 'Who's this chap?'

'Gray. My right hand.'

Pembleton looked Frank up and down, his eyes resting on the two stripes on his sleeve. 'Couldn't you find some eager young subaltern? Some terribly bright chap out of Eton with a First in Classics and a weak chin? Plenty of them about.'

'Thought I'd grow my own.'

Pembleton's bright little eyes scanned Frank's uniform, picked up the insignia on his shoulder. He began to towel himself so vigorously that his round belly wobbled and his voice shook. 'So, Freddie, how are the Dumpies these days?'

'We haven't seen much of the regiment for the last few months, Pinkie.'

'Well, you won't find them here. They're still up in Cairo, at

Abbassia.' As he towelled himself, Pembleton continued to regard Frank with professional interest, as he might have examined a horse, a potentially useful creature but incapable of speaking for itself. 'The Sirdar hasn't decided yet whether he needs any British cavalry.'

'The Sirdar?' Cavendish raised his eyebrows. 'How very Asiatic.'

'General Herbert Kitchener. Our lord and master. Hero of the people. Shadow of our sovereign on earth, and Sirdar to the Khedive of Egypt.' Pembleton tossed his towel aside and began to pull on clothes as they were handed to him. 'Though down here we just call him the Sudan Machine. The perfect engineering officer. Drives the trains himself when he gets the chance. You'd like a snifter, I suppose?'

'What I'd really like is a cup of tea and about two days' sleep. Oh, and to know what you're going to expect us to do. I'm mildly curious about that.'

'Reggie Wingate is Kitchener's Director of Intelligence, and that Austrian chap Slatin is advising him. I suppose you heard about Slatin Pasha? A prisoner of the dervishes for God knows how many years, but escaped to come over to us. Remarkable insights. But that's by-the-by. I work for Wingate. You'll get the full briefing from him.'

'But you're going to tell me, anyway, Pinkie, aren't you?'

'Of course.' Pembleton turned to Frank, buttoning his tunic. 'Bugger off for a beer at the NCOs mess, there's a good chap. Emin will show you where it is.'

'Let him stay. A man ought to know what it is he's risking his life for.'

Pembleton snorted. 'Don't let that idea get about, Freddie. All these chaps might start asking the same question. Good God, *we* might. But very well. Look here.' He took his swagger stick and drew a long curving line in the dust. 'The Nile. Kitchener's cut off a great loop of it by building the railway this far. Now he wants to push the steel further south still, down *here* to the confluence of the Nile and the Atbara. He's already set up Fort Atbara down there. He'd go on extending the line all the way to Khartoum if he had his way, and then we could all go to war in comfort. Unfortunately, the Khalifa Abdallahi might object. He's still in Khartoum with maybe eighty thousand men, and more joining every week from all over the Arab world.'

'Kitchener wants to lure him out, obviously.'

'Hence the railway. If the Khalifa doesn't make a move soon, Kitchener will be building a station at the Mahdi's tomb in Omdurman, complete with buffet and waiting rooms. However, that strategy hasn't worked yet. Here's why.' Pembleton made an emphatic dot in the sand with his stick. 'The Khalifa's blue-eyed boy and senior lieutenant, Sharif Mahmoud, has moved to Metemma, *here* on the Nile, between us and Khartoum, with an entire army of about twelve thousand Baggara tribesmen. We'll have to deal with him first. Now Mahmoud's a young chap and spoiling for a fight, and he has a couple of options open to him. He could advance up the Nile to meet us head on at Fort Atbara, which is what Kitchener would like. A march like that would expose him to our gunboats all the way up, and at the end he'd have to attack a heavily fortified position, which naturally favours us. Or he could avoid the gunboats by striking east across the desert *here* to the Atbara river, which is pretty well dry at this time of year. Then he could follow the watercourse up to close with us, or possibly bypass Fort Atbara altogether, and head straight for us here in Berber, or for our lines of communication. Which would be rather clever of him.'

'But you don't know which alternative he's planning to take.'

'Unhelpfully, no. We think there's tension between him and Osman Digna, who's waiting in the wings with five thousand of his Beja rascals. Remember that old fox from eighty-four? Mahmoud wants them to join forces, but Osman isn't having any of that. The Beja and the Baggara don't mix well, you'll be aware. The Beja don't even speak Arabic. Besides all that, my guess is that Osman favours the clever plan, and young Mahmoud the bull-at-a-gate option. But we're not sure.'

'You want us to drop in and ask him?'

'I knew you'd think of something original. Wingate has a network of spies all over the Sudan, but they're almost all natives. There aren't many of our own people who might pull it off.' Pembleton waved them to camp chairs. Violet light flooded the sky, and the air was suddenly cool. 'I'm sure you won't underestimate these chaps, Freddie. We both recall how we misjudged them fourteen years ago. And they're better now. Some decent weapons, better organisation, larger numbers – and just as bloody fearsome. What's more, God's on their side.'

'Really? I thought he was on ours. The old turncoat.'

Pembleton turned abruptly to Frank. 'You're up for this sort of shenanigans, are you, young man?'

'Sir.'

'You'd be a damned sight more comfortable with the rest of the Dumpies up at Abbassia Barracks. Fleshpots of Cairo an electric tram ride away, and all that sort of thing.'

'May I ask a question, sir?'

Frank had kept his voice flat but just the same he saw Cavendish glance up sharply at his words.

Pembleton said, 'Fire away.'

'Would you know when the Twenty-first might be deployed down here, sir?'

'Missing your old muckers, Gray? Well, I couldn't say for sure, but my guess is you'll get to see them again soon enough, if Freddie doesn't get you killed first. The Twenty-first is the only British cavalry the Sirdar's got. He may not need them for the showdown with Mahmoud, but he's sure to bring them down here before we meet Abdallahi.'

'Thank you, sir.' Frank stared out into the gathering dusk, avoiding Cavendish's eyes.

An hour later, a Sudanese orderly led Frank and Cavendish through the cool dust between the lines of tents. They walked in silence. The orderly stopped after a few minutes and ducked into an empty tent, lit a hurricane lamp, and unrolled Cavendish's Wolseley valise on the camp bed within. He held the flap open for Cavendish, who stepped in. The orderly saluted and vanished into the darkness. When he had gone Cavendish's face reappeared, framed in the lamp-lit vee of the tent opening. He looked narrowly at Frank.

'We're at war now, Gray. And hard though it may be to believe, General Kitchener's Sudan campaign was not designed solely as a stage for your personal dramas. Don't you forget that.'

He let the tent flap fall.

93

The felucca heeled in the last cat's-paw of wind from the open river. Forty yards offshore the craft slid beneath the stern of a battered gunboat moored in deeper water, rust streaking the hull and the upper plates scarred and pitted from earlier fights. It wasn't much bigger than a Thames pleasure steamer, but it was a gunboat just the same, with the barrel of a Nordenfeldt cannon jutting over the railings and the Prophet's green flag hanging at the masthead. They glided towards the crowded shore between clumps of papyrus. Smaller boats swarmed around them, heavy with men and stores. Others, lightened of their loads, paddled back out into the open reaches of the Nile.

Frank, jammed in the bow with Cavendish and a dozen recruits to the Khalifa's cause, could already hear the wasps' nest buzz of Metemma as they moved closer to the shore. He shifted onto his haunches and peered over the gunwale. The town, a sprawling clutter of mud buildings, slumped in the fierce sun under a dun haze of dust. The narrow beach below was jammed with craft, drawn up on the sand or lashed to makeshift wooden landing stages which stood out into the shallows. Their cargoes were piled on the bank in great heaps, sacks of rice and meal, boxes of ammunition, live fowl in wicker cages. Men stripped to their loincloths toiled up the dusty slope to the town, burdened with stores themselves and driving pack mules laden with more.

The felucca touched with a soft thump. Frank grabbed Cavendish by the arm as the boat tilted, elbowed the others aside and helped the older man over the side and into the shallow water. He held both their rifles above his head, and together they waded to dry land. The beach was a jostling mass of men, labouring, shouting, laughing, cursing.

He and Cavendish joined a ragged crowd of new arrivals gathering on a patch of ground above the shore. They made an exotic crew, men of all ages and conditions: elderly patriarchs, tribesmen with spears, herdsboys still in their teens. Some were fearsome enough, big bearded men with wild eyes and rifles or home-made jezails on their shoulders, but most looked to Frank like simple villagers, ignorant and bewildered. He remembered the ranks of artillery at the British railhead, the clank and beat of engines, the railroad shimmering southward into the desert. The Sudan Machine. He doubted any of these men had the least idea what faced them.

An emir, a tall black man in a stylistically patched jibba, was moving among the lines of newcomers. He carried only a cane, but half a dozen armed guards followed in his wake. The emir glanced at each of the new arrivals, stopping now and then to murmur a question at one man or another. Frank saw that he was singling out the stronger and younger men, touching some on the shoulder with his cane. When he did this the guards would usher the man to one side, so that a little group of selected recruits was gathering a few yards away.

Frank kept looking straight ahead. It had not occurred to him until this moment that he and Cavendish might be separated, and he was surprised at how afraid he suddenly was. Out of the corner of his eye he watched the emir as he made his quiet progress, his face unmoving. There was a good deal of talk among the newcomers, and several spoke directly to the emir as he passed, but he never replied. One of the bolder men reached out to touch the emir's arm, but instantly a guard clubbed him back with his rifle butt. After that the inspection went on in silence.

The emir reached Frank, stopped. His eyes were very dark, the whites yellowish, and his gaze was so penetrating that Frank could not meet it. The touch of the cane came as he knew it would, tapping his arm, and at once a guard gripped his shoulder and started to hustle him out of the crowd.

Cavendish stepped between them. 'Find someone else. I need this one.'

'You don't choose, old man. Move aside.'

The guard renewed his grip on Frank's shoulder but Cavendish put his hand on the man's chest and pushed him back. 'My nephew is a halfwit. Understand? He's no use to you, but I'm lame and he's my legs. I need him if I'm to fight.'

The guard cursed and moved forward again but the emir raised a hand to stop him.

'You are foreigners.' The voice was very soft. 'Where are you from?'

'We came from Aden to fight for the Khalifa,' Cavendish said loftily, 'not to be ordered around by baboons like this.'

'The Khalifa is not here. The Sharif Mahmoud commands here.'

Cavendish shrugged. 'I don't care who commands. So long as there's to be fighting here, it's a good enough place for me.'

'Perhaps you are too old to fight as hard as you talk.'

'An old man can pull a trigger as well as a young one. Just put us somewhere we can kill *Feringhees*. You don't even need to find us weapons.'

'So I see.' The emir reached out one hand and touched Cavendish's rifle with a fingertip, and opened his hand. Cavendish passed the old carbine to him. The emir took it, worked the action a couple of times, hefted it in his hands.

'The British use Lee-Metfords now,' he said. 'Better than this.'

'The Remington shoots as straight as ever.'

'True. And we could use more rifles like it. Where did you come by these?'

'The Egyptian Army would sell their own children, if anybody would buy them, the way they've sold their souls to the *Feringhees*.'

The emir nodded thoughtfully. 'You are old, he is an idiot. We could take the rifles and not trouble with you.'

'You need all the men you can get if you're to stop the *Feringhees* before they reach Omdurman. They've already moved south of Berber, and they will be on the march again soon.'

'Perhaps they are not fated to meet us. The prophecy says they are to be destroyed on Kerreri plain outside Omdurman.'

'Kitchener doesn't know the prophecy. All he knows is that he can't leave Sharif Mahmoud and thousands of men behind his route of advance. They will close with us, sooner or later.'

'In that case we might all travel to Paradise together.'

'Good,' Cavendish said. 'I'd rather die serving the Khalifa in this rat hole than lying in my bed. But whatever happens, the youth stays with me.'

Frank stood very still. He could feel the emir's black eyes travel over him again and then over Cavendish. Sweat broke out down the sides of his neck. The emir handed the rifle back to Cavendish and spoke to the guard.

'Whenever the fight comes, see they are stationed in the trenches out by the zariba.' He smiled for the first time. 'There he'll get plenty of chance to kill *Feringhees*. And if he is lame he can't run away.'

94

Grace concentrated on the crows. There were at least a dozen of them, blundering through the naked branches of the churchyard elms.

'I didn't know your father well,' the elderly man was saying as he clasped both her hands, 'but he was a prince among merchants. A prince.'

Grace did not recognise him. She did not recognise most of the mourners. This one had an astrakhan coat with a velvet collar, she noticed absently, and he looked wealthy. But then most of them did. She gave him the sad smile he seemed to want and in a moment he moved on. The crows were so clumsy that they snapped off dead twigs as they hopped about in the branches. She could hear the twigs clattering onto the roofs of the carriages parked beyond the churchyard wall. Or were they rooks? She had never been sure of the difference.

'Such a loss, Grace.'

This time at least she knew the mourner who stood before her. It was Sydney Mason from the Liverpool office, his long handsome face almost a caricature of misery. She had not seen him since that fateful dinner party, years before.

'Your father was a towering figure,' he said. 'And to lose him so young! Lord knows who we will find to replace him.'

Andreas Welti was standing at the grave a few paces away, his head bowed, but at the words he glanced up and caught Grace's eye. The little man's face was haggard, but she did not miss the glint of irony in his expression, and she wondered what Sydney Mason would say when he learned that she was now his employer. She had to fight down an hysterical desire to laugh at the absurdity of the thing. Instead she patted Mason's hand so that he moved on.

She thought that the crows looked rather like mourners themselves in their windblown black plumage, but still she preferred them to these dismal people. She liked the birds' raucous and irreverent squawking, their utter lack of hypocrisy.

'A fine man,' another stranger said, taking her hand and trying to look directly into her face, in that intrusive fashion so many of them had adopted today. 'He was a fine, fine man.'

She smiled fixedly and pulled her hand free.

Past the man's shoulder she saw her mother at Welti's side, her face startling white against her black coat. Sarah Dearborn did not return her gaze. Beyond, on the far side of the churchyard wall, the household servants stood in a respectful crowd, heads bowed, several in tears.

Grace wondered how long she could stand this. But now yet another black-clad figure had moved up to stand in front of her. Automatically she put out her hand, but she did not look at the newcomer. Her attention was taken by a crow which had flapped down to the lychgate roof, and, with a fine show of indifference for human solemnities, had started turfing dead leaves out of the gutter, cackling gleefully.

'Hello, Grace.'

She looked up sharply.

'I didn't know whether I should come.'

'Alec, thank God you did.'

'Are you all right?'

'No.' She gripped his arm. 'Walk me back to the house, would you?'

'I have the motor here.'

'Spare me that, at least. Besides, I want to walk.'

There were other mourners waiting to pay their respects but she ignored them and let him guide her between the tombstones and out through the back gate through the churchyard wall. Someone called after her, but she pretended not to hear. The path led up into the beech woods, and very soon the church was out of sight. She felt calmer as soon as they were among the great trees, last year's dead leaves rattling in the chill wind. She took pleasure in the cold air on her face, and felt some of the tension slip away from her. She hooked her arm through Alec's.

'There'll be no article,' she said. 'I expect you realise that.'

'Of course not.'

'If you choose to pass on the information to another journalist, then you must do so. I won't blame you. But they'll find no evidence of wrongdoing by my father. I have seen to that. I can do nothing else for him, but I owe him that much.'

'Grace, I wouldn't dream of it.'

She looked up at him. 'Just the same, I'd like you to know that

Dearborn & Company is no longer involved with the Congo. When I have had a chance to go through everything with Welti, we will no longer be involved in anything of the kind, anywhere. Even if it ruins us.'

'I understand, Grace. And I expected no less. But I didn't come to discuss the article.'

'No. I didn't think you had.'

They had come to a clearing among the trees and he stopped and faced her. 'What will you do now, Grace? You're a very wealthy young woman, if the rumours are true.'

'They're all true, I'm afraid.'

'Then you are free to do anything you want.'

'Yes.'

She moved a few steps away from him and gazed around her, at the looming moss-green trunks and the patch of open ground at her feet. She remembered another bitter winter day when she had walked through these woods, and suddenly she remembered standing here, just here in this very clearing, with Mrs Rossiter's gin singing in her blood. He had been no more than a boy then, a thin boy with acne on his jaw, riding Bess bareback, hopping the old horse over a fallen log. The log was still here, she saw, furred with lichen and half-collapsed into the soil. And there was the place he had fallen when she startled the horse. He had curled himself on the ground almost at her feet, unaware of her presence as she stood over him. She stirred the damp soil with the toe of her boot.

'Alec,' she said, 'do you know Lord Cromer?'

'Of course. He's the British Agent in Egypt. I should think everyone knows of Cromer.'

'Yes, everyone knows *of* him. I'm trying to establish if you know him personally.'

He narrowed his eyes. 'Now, Grace . . .'

'It's a simple question.' She looked innocently at him.

'I know a good few lords and earls, Grace, but I don't count many proconsuls of Empire among my intimates.'

'General Kitchener answers to him, I believe,' she continued.

'At least technically, yes.'

'And General Kitchener, as Sirdar of Egypt, commands all the soldiers of the Queen now serving in the Sudan. Isn't that so?'

'Grace, listen to me. If you think Lord Cromer would prevail upon Kitchener to release—'

'I don't imagine anything, Alec. But I should very much like to meet

Lord Cromer, just the same. Do you think you could arrange an interview? You're so good at that.'

He folded his arms across his chest. 'Grace, you're relentless.'

'No. I'm a wealthy young woman. You said so yourself. And I can do anything I want.'

95

The streams of exhausted men and animals engulfed Nukheila as the army dragged its way into the village. It was a miserable enough place to make a stand, Frank thought, shifting the weight of Cavendish's rifle and his own across his shoulders. A huddle of huts on a hummock of land above the floodplain of the Atbara. The river was now no more than a swampy trough in the land, half a mile wide and studded with reed-choked pools. A few miles north, on the banks of this same riverbed, Kitchener was encamped, perhaps no more than a day's march away. That's what the rumours said. Frank thought of the railhead at Berber, the ranks of artillery and rocket batteries, the neat lines of tents, the railway and the heliograph and the armouries; he wondered what this valiant rabble was supposed to do against such efficiency. The Sudan Machine.

And yet the dervish army was already digging in for defence. The fittest men, who had come in a day or two earlier from the march, had already started building the camel-thorn zariba which would protect the position from the desert, and teams of workers were already digging a network of trenches and gunpits. Closer at hand as he trudged on Frank could see the strong inner palisade which was half-built around the centre of the village. Presumably, Mahmoud would have his headquarters here. Despite everything, the sense of activity and purpose was a relief. Held back by the older man's lame leg Frank and Cavendish were among the last to come in from this last stage of the march from Metemma. Frank did not like to think back on the last few days. Men, women and children racked by dysentery and dying beside the track, begging pitifully for water; bloating carcases of camels and horses; captured tribesmen harnessed to the few artillery pieces, their backs whipped bloody as they struggled to haul the guns out of sand holes. He guessed that there had been hundreds of desertions every night, and had several times seen groups of men drifting off into the desert with no organised attempt to stop them. For all Nukheila's filth and misery, and whatever was to befall them, Frank was glad they would stop here.

A market of sorts had been set up at what had been the village's central crossing and the narrow ways were congested by traders selling whatever they had been able to scrape together – hacked gobbets of meat, ammunition, scraps of vegetables, *dom* palm fruits. The crowds jostled in their hundreds to buy from them, lean Baggara tribesmen and a few Beja, their shocks of hair stiffened with animal fat, stocky peasants from the Nile Valley, men half-naked and men robed, women and children. It was fiendishly hot and the din cacophonous, the bellowing of animals, the tramp of feet, men shouting in Arabic and Tu-Bedawi. Dust and dried dung and smoke hung in the air between the mud walls.

A pair of Baggara guards took charge of them as they straggled in and almost at once moved them around the edge of the throng, clubbing a path with their rifle butts. Beyond the edge of the village lay stands of palms and a patchwork of what had been scrubby irrigated fields. Perhaps five hundred yards ahead Frank could see the zariba clearly now, five feet high and as broad, extending for over half a mile in an arc between a low stony outcrop to the south and dense acacia forest which bordered the town to the north. Teams of men were dragging fresh thorn branches to add to the barrier, pegging and pinning them into place. The open ground within the zariba was cross-hatched by trenches and earth ramparts, dugouts and rifle pits. All were occupied by armed men, digging, resting, eating, cleaning weapons.

The leading guard halted at a stretch of trench almost in the shadow of the zariba. A big man with broken teeth was digging with a wooden spade into the back of the trench, while a boy of twelve or thirteen dragged away loose spoil in a basket. The boy had an iron shackle on his leg, though no chain was attached. The man stood up from his labour and looked sourly at Frank and Cavendish and then at the guard.

'What's this trash you've brought me?'

'The younger one's an idiot but he looks strong enough. The old one says he can shoot.'

'An old man and an imbecile. Why does he always send me the dregs?'

The guard laughed. 'He sent you young Yussuf, didn't he?'

'This Ja'alin runt?' The big man kicked out at the boy. 'All he can do is grin.'

'Be grateful, Hamid. At least these two have rifles. Besides, it doesn't much matter in this position. You'll all get to Paradise in the first ten minutes if the *Feringhees* come.'

The guard walked away with his companions, chuckling. Hamid swore under his breath and spat, but before he could speak again Cavendish stepped down into the trench and pushed roughly past him. While Hamid watched, astounded, Cavendish made some theatre of measuring the depth of the trench, kicking at the earthen walls, sighting over the rough parapet.

'This is no good,' Cavendish told him peremptorily. 'This won't do at all.'

Hamid stared at him. 'What?'

'That yokel was right. This pit will be our grave if you don't make it deeper. And put in a firestep, too.' He pointed at the spade in Hamid's hands. 'Get to work.'

Hamid threw the spade aside. 'Who do you think you are, old man, to give orders?'

Cavendish stepped up to him. 'See if you can grasp this, peasant. If you want to beat the *Feringhees*, you have to learn how they do things. I know how they do things. If I have to die it won't be from your stupidity. Is that understood?' He walked away to sit on the edge of the trench. 'My nephew's simple-minded, but he is strong. He'll help. But if you give me any trouble, he'll shoot you like a dog.'

Frank dropped the muzzle of his rifle and moved his right hand to rest over the trigger guard. He saw Hamid register the movement and glance over to where his own weapon, an old Snider, stood propped against the lip of the trench, out of reach. Even so the big man stood balanced for a dangerous moment between violence and submission.

It was the boy who broke the tension. He grinned around at them with very white teeth, picked up the fallen spade and starting to dig furiously at the loose soil. Hamid glared up at Frank, who stood looming above him, then turned away sullenly and snatched the spade from the child.

96

The sun was a ball of molten iron hanging over the desert to the west. Frank kept his head down and picked his way through the maze of trenches and away from the swarming warren that was the centre of the encampment. The goatskin water bags rolled against his shoulder and in the sullen heat they felt shockingly cold.

Here and there in the flat ground within the zariba labourers were still digging new trenches or whipping mule teams to drag palm trunks for more fortifications. But most men seemed resigned to making do with the scant cover they already had. They squatted silently in trenches and dugouts, wherever they could find shade, cradling their mismatched collection of weapons – rifles, jezails, leaf-bladed spears.

Tension was rising in Nukheila as the days passed, and fear of what was to come drove men in upon themselves.

It was a long trek out towards the zariba, but Frank was glad to leave the worst of Nukheila's stench behind. Over twelve thousand men were crammed into the village with little organisation, almost no shelter, and no sanitary arrangements of any kind. Men used the riverbed, when they could reach it, or dug their own pits, or simply squatted on the ground. The earth was dotted with the results. Disease was spreading and every day when he fetched water Frank saw the bodies of the dead laid out for prompt burial in the Moslem fashion. They bloated in the heat just the same.

Frank shielded his eyes to gaze out across the glaring plain. To his right dense thorn scrub blocked the approach to the camp. Away to his left, beyond the zariba, the flat land stretched out to low red bluffs, wobbling in the heat. That was the way they would come, sweeping south from Kitchener's base, now only a few miles north. The Anglo-Egyptian infantry would brush the zariba aside and roll over these trenches like some great traction engine. Frank imagined Hamid banging away with his ancient Snider, the boy Yussuf handing him cartridges as the front ranks came storming over. It would take more than courage, more than a few thousand Hamids and Yussufs, to stop the Sudan Machine. Frank looked around at the sullen men in their holes and trenches, weary, underfed, ill-armed. He had shared enough of their hardships, and it gave him no sense of triumph to picture what was going to happen to them.

Frank reached the trench and found Cavendish staring over the earth parapet towards the horizon. He stepped down beside the older man.

'It's safe,' Cavendish said. 'We're alone for the moment.'

Frank was surprised to hear him using English; for weeks they had spoken nothing but Arabic to one another. He took a long drink of the foul tasting water and passed the goatskin to Cavendish.

'They're digging in another Krupp on the south-east corner,' Frank said. 'Or trying to. That makes seven.'

Cavendish was still staring out over the desert. 'Kitchener will come soon.'

'They've not been maintained in years, the Krupps.'

'Mahmoud should have moved out, kept mobile,' Cavendish said finally. 'Should have had his dervishes to harry us every step of the route, the way they did in eighty-four. Use Osman Digna's cavalry. Blow up the railway. Wait for their moment to overwhelm us piece-meal. They'd make us pay then.'

'Maybe this is a trap. Maybe he wants to tempt Kitchener out into the open.'

'He'll get his wish, then. Kitchener won't let this opportunity pass. But it's no trap. Mahmoud's underestimated his enemy, that's all. Underestimated the nineteenth century. My God, chaps dressed in chain mail against Maxim guns.' Cavendish drank from the water bag, grimaced. 'It'll be a massacre. A good old fashioned imperial bloodbath. I suppose the politicians will like it.'

Frank took the goatskin back and squatted in the shade beside the older man. 'We should get out now. Any longer and we'll be trapped here ourselves.'

Cavendish looked at him. 'One of your instincts, Gray?'

Frank stretched his legs out in front of him and drank again. 'They've started chaining men into their trenches at night. We could be next.'

Cavendish thought about it. 'It will be risky.'

'When it gets dark we should be safe enough, and once in the forest they'd never find us.'

There was a sudden scuffle above their heads and the boy Yussuf jumped down into the trench, staggering under the weight of an ammunition sack. Hamid followed him with another sack over one shoulder and his Snider slung over the other. Yussuf dumped his own burden among the few stores in the dugout at the rear of the trench, took Hamid's sack and stowed that too and at once began to gather slivers of palm leaf to start a fire, placing them carefully between the stones of their makeshift hearth. He hunkered down to strike sparks from a flint, and when Hamid wasn't looking he glanced at Frank and smiled. Hamid caught him at it and pushed the boy onto his backside, passing the chain through his leg irons as he lay there. When it was done Yussuf bounced back up onto his haunches as if nothing had happened and carried on with his work at the fire. Once again he caught Frank's eye and grinned.

Hamid took his rifle from his shoulder and thrust it at Cavendish. 'The block's jammed.'

Cavendish raised his eyebrows. 'A misfortune.'

'You know how to fix these things.'

Cavendish took the weapon and handed it on to Frank without comment.

'What would he know?' Hamid protested. 'He's an idiot.'

'An idiot who knows more than you do, evidently,' Cavendish said.

Frank turned the weapon in his hands, took out his knife to ease out the jammed breech plug, blew hard into the breech.

'It is a fine rifle, is it not?' the boy Yussuf asked eagerly. He had coaxed a tongue of flame from the kindling. The fire popped and blue smoke hung in the hot air.

Frank said nothing, inverting the weapon and knocking loose powder and grit out of the chamber. He gave Hamid a contemptuous look as he worked.

'It's the cartridges.' Hamid was resentful at the implied criticism, and kicked the bag of ammunition. 'The Khalifa's armourers make this stuff. They cheat him on the powder. Mix it with dust.'

'Not good like *Feringhee* powder,' Yussuf said, fanning his flame and placing lumps of dried dung around it. '*Feringhee* powder for a *Feringhee* rifle.'

Hamid cuffed the boy. 'Shut your mouth about the damned *Feringhees*. You'll be chained to me when they come, so you'll get a good look. Then you can see if they're as clever as you think.'

Frank flipped open the breech, lifted the flange of the breech plug and worked the extractor back and forth. He squinted as far as he could see down the barrel, which was half-choked with burned powder, unclipped the ram rod and cleaned the barrel, upending the weapon and tipping more loosened grime out onto the ground. He opened and closed the breech once or twice to free it. It would clog again within a few shots, but the action at least felt smoother.

'Where did you learn to repair the *Feringhees'* rifles?' Yussuf asked, wide-eyed.

Again, Frank did not answer, but worked the extractor a few more times, blew hard down the barrel again. The lack of any reply did not seem to put Yussuf off. When Frank glanced up he found the boy was watching him, still grinning in that impish way of his.

'He learned from me,' Cavendish said. 'In Aden we had many British soldiers. That's where I learned about their weapons, and much else besides.'

'You have seen the *Feringhees'* works, then?' Yussuf asked. 'Is it so that they have iron houses which breathe fire and move on an iron road?'

Something about the boy reminded Frank of Gifford. He was only a little younger, and carried with him the same air of wide-eyed optimism.

'Yes,' Frank said, keeping his eyes on his work. 'It is so.'

'Truly, then,' Yussuf laughed at the wonder of the idea, 'how are we to defeat such people, who can create these marvels?'

'Oil,' Frank said, and held out his hand.

Yussuf handed him an earthenware pot of cooking fat and Frank trickled a little into the lock, closed the breech, worked the breech plug in and out a few times more and handed the Snider back to Hamid, who took it and tested the action for himself, suspiciously.

The man's eyes settled on Frank. 'Perhaps you're not as stupid as you seem.'

Frank stared back blankly at him.

'He can do simple things,' Cavendish said, airily. 'But his mind is far away.'

But Hamid kept his eyes on Frank for a long moment. He said, 'My cousin's Remington misfires one time out of three. Come. I'll take you to him.'

'No,' Cavendish said. 'My nephew is to stay here. But you may bring the weapon. He will repair it for the Khalifa's sake.'

Hamid hesitated, but knew he could not force the issue. He adjusted the bandoliers which crossed his belly, climbed out of the trench and began to walk quickly back towards the huddle of huts in the centre of the camp. They watched him go. Cavendish looked at Frank, a question in his eyes. It was growing dark quickly now, with cooking fires springing on all over the camp and the smell of burned wood hanging in the evening. Frank waited silently for Cavendish to make the move. It seemed an age before he did, rising stiffly to his feet.

'I'm going to the forest,' Cavendish said for Yussuf to hear, and stepped up onto the trench lip. 'The camp middens are unspeakable. These damned *dom* nuts. They churn a man's belly into butter.'

Frank stood up too.

Yussuf looked from one of them to the other. 'What should I do, brothers, if the *Feringhees* come while you are all away?'

At the top of the ladder Frank glanced back down. The boy was gazing up at him from behind the crackling fire, his dark eyes wide, his face open and bright.

'If the *Feringhees* come,' Frank said, dropping all pretence of stupidity, 'climb behind the stores in the dugout and keep very still. Do you understand that?'

Yussuf looked solemn for once. 'But Hamid will whip me if I hide from the *Feringhees*.'

'Dead men are not good with a whip. And dead boys are not worth the whipping.'

Frank vaulted out of the trench and walked after Cavendish into the deepening dusk.

They followed the rough perimeter track along the inside of the zariba. After some minutes the track led them to the acacia forest which protected the flank of the encampment. Scores of men had set up camp between the trees and their fires daubed crooked branches with light.

They walked on, threading between rifle pits and rough fortifications erected between the trunks.

They worked their way towards the edge of the forest, where the trees thinned and opened onto the empty desert beyond. Frank could see the plain beyond the woods and began to wonder if they might actually reach it without once facing a challenge. All around them groups of men were sitting in the scrub, gathered around fires, eating what food they had, talking in low voices. No one seemed to notice two more men, looking for somewhere to sleep.

They gained the edge of the wood. A few yards out someone had built a campfire on the stony ground beyond the protection of the trees. Frank could see two men in the light of the flames. One, hunkered over the fire, was roasting something on a long knife. His companion was stretched out on a saddle blanket on the opposite side of the fire. Two rifles were propped together just outside the ring of firelight. The crouching man looked up as Frank and Cavendish walked out of the shadows.

'You seek something, brothers?'

'Only sleep.' Cavendish made a play of drinking in the clean night air. 'We'll settle over there, out of the way.' He gestured vaguely into the desert.

'It is not permitted,' the man said.

'We shall not trouble you, my friend,' Cavendish said mildly. 'We just want some peace, away from the rabble.'

'It is not permitted,' the man repeated. 'You must stay within the forest.'

He turned his knife over the flames. Frank couldn't make out what creature was spitted upon it; perhaps a rat. Meat juices spat in the fire.

'And yet you are here,' Cavendish observed. 'That seems to be permitted.'

'There have been deserters. Our orders are to watch.'

The man looked at them more closely as he said this. He arranged a couple of rocks beside the fire and balanced the makeshift spit upon them. Frank saw that in another moment he would rise to face them, and the stacked rifles would be almost within his reach. The second man, on the far side of the fire, propped himself onto one elbow.

'Come, my friends,' Cavendish said, spreading his arms expansively, 'I'm sure we can—'

Frank stepped forward while Cavendish was still speaking and cracked the barrel of his rifle against the side of the crouching man's head, hooked his foot into the heart of the fire and booted the whole blazing mass over the other man on the ground. He grabbed the two rifles and hurled them away into the night, turned to shove Cavendish towards the encircling darkness. But Cavendish was already running, his robes flying, and Frank followed, keeping low. He heard shouting behind him and a man cursing in pain, but no one fired. He ran on, out over the flat land, the darkness closing around him, hearing Cavendish still pounding along somewhere ahead. A dry nullah opened in front of him and he half-fell into it and at the bottom slid into cool sand, listening for pursuit. There was none, but he could hear Cavendish panting a yard or two to his right. Frank crawled over to him.

'I thought you were supposed to be lame.'

'That was subterfuge, Gray,' Cavendish said with dignity. 'Whereas your lunacy is now proven beyond question.'

97

Frank could hear the distant roar and clatter of the camp outside, but in the tent it was so quiet that he could make out the small dry hiss as the Sirdar's fingertip tracked across the map. It was a large scale chart of the confluence of the Nile and the Atbara, spread out over two campaign tables, and it had gripped Kitchener's complete attention, for he had not once taken his eyes off it since Pembleton had brought Frank and Cavendish in. That was a full minute ago now. Frank thought they must make an absurd little cameo – portly Pembleton as smart as a chocolate soldier, and he and Cavendish in filthy jibbas and head clouts. He tried to ignore a louse which he could feel creeping across his inner thigh, and wondered if Kitchener could smell their unwashed bodies across the ten feet or so which separated them.

Still without looking up, the Sirdar said, 'What have you got for me, Pinkie?'

'Captain Cavendish, sir, and Corporal Gray. Just in from Mahmoud's camp.'

The leonine head lifted at last. Frank kept his gaze fixed straight ahead, into the recesses of the Sirdar's tent, but he felt the cold grey eyes track over him and on to Cavendish.

'Cavendish? Have we met? Name's familiar.'

'Briefly, sir, in eighty-four, when we were both here with General Wolseley.'

'I do seem to recall.' Kitchener straightened. He was a powerfully built man in his forties, awesome in immaculate khaki. 'So you've been with Mahmoud. How long?'

'Since January, sir. We got in among the dervish army at Metemma,

387

then marched across the desert with them to the Atbara. They were dug in at Nukheila when we left them last night.'

If Kitchener was impressed he disdained to say so. He stroked his sandy moustache. Frank noticed that one of his eyes had a slight cast, so that it was hard to tell exactly where he was looking. The effect was disturbing.

'How many has Mahmoud got now?'

'About twelve thousand, sir, mostly Baggara, and maybe two thousand horse. Osman Digna and his five thousand Beja are in the wings, too, but they haven't joined forces yet. It looks as if they may not.'

'And morale in the army?'

'There've been a lot of desertions, sir, especially on the way across the desert to the Atbara. And there's a good deal of disease in Nukheila. Dysentery, mostly. The conditions are foul and getting worse. Also, they're short of modern weapons.'

'But you think they'll fight?'

'They will fight, sir. It's what they want most, to get to grips with us. It's the sitting still that drives them wild.'

'And yet they won't come out to meet us. What do you make of that, Cavendish?'

'Mahmoud thinks he can do us more damage from a defensive position, sir.'

'Does he, indeed? Well, he's probably right.' Kitchener put his hands behind his back and locked them there. 'Artillery?'

'Gray saw more of that than I did, sir.'

The heavy head swung towards Frank. 'Well?'

'I counted seven artillery pieces, sir,' Frank said. 'Krupps and Nordenfeldts, and at least three Maxims. They're all in bad condition, and the crews aren't trained. Also, the powder is poor quality. They make it themselves.'

Kitchener let a beat pass in silence. 'Tell me about the zariba.'

Cavendish began, 'From what I saw, sir—'

'Gray can tell me.'

Frank kept his eyes straight ahead. 'Thorn branches, sir, piled five feet high and lashed together. About a thousand yards internal diameter. The zariba touches the bluffs along the Atbara River on one side, and the acacia forest on the other. There's an inner palisade around the centre of the encampment, but that wouldn't be much of an obstacle once you were through the zariba.'

The Sirdar beckoned Frank to the map table. 'Show me.'

Frank was acutely aware of the filth under his nails as he pointed the features out on the map. 'Only the frontal stretch of the zariba is open to direct assault, sir. That's four hundred yards long, and there's a network of trenches inside it, with rifle pits every few yards.'

'And in the centre of the camp?'

'Dugouts, food stockpiles, tents, and the livestock, sir. Mahmoud's top men have taken over the houses of the original town, what there is left of it. His own quarters are there somewhere, too. There isn't much visible organisation, sir. Men, women and children crammed together.'

Frank took two paces back from the table, glad to escape from the clean laundered scent of the Sirdar's pristine uniform, which mocked his own feral smell.

Kitchener stroked his moustache again. 'Have you actually examined the zariba for yourself, Corporal? At close quarters?'

'I have, sir. Captain Cavendish and I were posted right behind it.'

'In your opinion, how much of an obstacle would it be to infantry?'

'Determined men could pull it apart, sir, with covering fire.'

Kitchener stepped out from behind the map table and placed himself directly in front of Frank. 'Lieutenant Colonel Hunter, one of my most aggressive and experienced officers, rode up to within sight of that zariba just yesterday. Were you aware of that?'

'We saw a patrol approach, sir, yes.'

'Hunter believes the zariba to be virtually impregnable. That we could lose hundreds getting through it. What do you say to that, Gray? Do you maintain your opinion, when an officer of such seniority says otherwise?'

Frank stared at the far wall of the tent. 'I do, sir.'

'Good.' Kitchener swung away. 'Gentlemen, give your full report to Major Pembleton in the morning. And Pinkie? Bring it straight to me when it's done. That will be all.'

They saluted and ducked out into the blazing afternoon.

98

'That bloody zariba,' Pembleton grumbled, as soon as they were out of earshot of Kitchener's tent. 'Nukheila's only a dozen miles away, but the Sirdar's hesitating because of that damned thorn hedge. He's even checked with London.'

'It's not like him to hold back,' Cavendish said.

'He's afraid a big butcher's bill will give Whitehall the jitters.' Pembleton looked up at Frank. 'So you'd better be bloody well right, my lad.'

They walked on in silence for perhaps half a mile between row upon row of tents, horse lines, store wagons. Sudanese, British and Egyptian soldiers sat in what shade they could find, cleaning kit and weapons, washing, sleeping. Pembleton led them to a pair of tents on a bluff above the valley of the Atbara River. A grove of *dom* palms shaded the canvas and the hot wind down the valley rattled the fronds and snapped the canvas in and out.

'All to yourself, Freddie,' Pembleton said. 'Best site in the camp. I thought you'd earned a little civilisation. But you'd best make the most of it – when things happen around here, they tend to happen quickly. You'll find fresh kit in the tents.' With his stick Pembleton pointed down at the Atbara, shrunk to a chain of brown lagoons and stands of papyrus in a sandy bed. 'Note the extensive washing facilities. And my God, you could do with a wash and shave, the pair of you. You look like Moses and Aaron, and smell about as bad. Oh, there's been some mail for you. It came down to the railhead and I took the liberty of collecting it, or they'd have sent it back around the world again. I'll have it brought over.'

'Much appreciated, Pinkie.'

'By the way, there's so far no word on when the Twenty-first Lancers will get here, but they'll be along before the final show. The Sirdar's already brought in every other British unit from Cairo.'

Pembleton raised his swagger stick in farewell and strode off towards the main camp. Cavendish flipped open the tent fly and glanced inside. He let the flap fall again and stood up to face Frank.

'Do I look as bad as you do, Gray?'

'Possibly worse, sir.'

'Hmm.' Cavendish jerked his head towards the Atbara. 'Do you think there are crocodiles in there?'

'They wouldn't touch us, sir. Not in this state.'

'Quite right. You can go first, then.'

Frank stripped off where he stood, ran down the bluff and plunged into the nearest lagoon. The water was as warm and brown as tea; it was delicious to feel it slide over his skin. He thought of Mahmoud's camp at Nukheila, just a few miles away along this same watercourse. There had never been enough water there, certainly not enough to waste on washing. There hadn't been enough of anything, except filth and fear. He rolled onto his back in the water and watched the palms swaying against the polished blue sky. He felt clean for the first time in weeks, and for once neither hungry nor thirsty. All this was a novelty. He seemed to have been constantly hungry for the last four weeks, and looking down at his body he could see all of his ribs and the horns of his pelvis.

Violet dusk was advancing over the desert. Frank saw that Cavendish had come down to the lagoon's edge and was standing primly in the shallows, throwing water over himself. All along the bank groups of black, brown and white men were washing in the river pools, some of them splashing one another like children at play. From behind the bluffs smoke from cooking fires rose into the burnished blue. How many men were here now? Twelve thousand, Egyptians, Sudanese and British? More? A muezzin started to call from the Sudanese lines and men came to their knees on the sand, naked as they were, facing east.

The cooking fires would be lit at Nukheila, too, and men would be fetching water, and a muezzin would be calling. Yussuf would be making the fire, grinning in the face of Hamid's brutishness. Frank shook out his long hair so that the water lifted it. The curtain was about to go up on the last act of a fourteen-year drama which had started with Gordon and the Mahdi, and nothing now would stop it unfolding to its inevitable conclusion. Mahmoud and his courageous host would be swept away with their swords and spears and antiquated firearms, and after that Kitchener's road lay open to Khartoum and the Khalifa's adjacent capital of Omdurman. And before that happened, the 21st Lancers would be here. All of them, men and officers alike.

He rolled over in the water and stroked slowly back to the shore.

Dripping and naked, he waded past Cavendish and climbed back up the bluff to the tents. A Sudanese orderly had arrived with canvas buckets and warm water and a shaving kit. It was almost dark. Frank squatted in the cool dust and the man held the mirror for him. He shaved off his full beard with a cut-throat razor while the orderly grinned his appreciation at the lean brown face which emerged. After that Frank went into the tent and dressed.

By the time he came out Cavendish was already seated in a folding chair under the palms. His own grey beard had gone. A leather satchel was on the ground beside him and he was leafing through papers in the light of a hurricane lamp. Insects pinged off the glass chimney.

'I told the orderly chappie to make us some tea,' Cavendish said. 'I expect he could find you something more stimulating, if you prefer.'

'Tea will do very well, sir.'

Cavendish held up a letter in a white envelope. 'Here.' When Frank did not react, he added, 'It's a letter, Gray. Perhaps you've seen one before. Not everyone of your acquaintance is illiterate, I suppose? Take the damned thing, will you? My arm's getting tired.'

Frank took the envelope, ripped it open.

My dear Frank,

I have tried so hard to find you, and written so many times. And yet I still don't know if I can even allow myself to hope that this will ever reach you. You have no idea how hard it is, writing into a vacuum. And yet I find I cannot give up. I am haunted by our parting last December. I wanted so much for us to speak again; I tried to come to you, but sad events intervened, and then it was too late.

And what would I have said if I had been in time? I have asked myself that question again and again. Perhaps I would have told you that, after all, I would wait for you like a good soldier's wife. But that doesn't sound like me, does it? All I know for certain is that I would have begged you once again to put aside this awful duty you have imposed upon yourself. I know you refused before. But Frank, you should know that things have changed now. My father is dead. I have a great inheritance. I did not want it, but it at least leaves me free to act as I choose. I have spoken to lawyers in London, and I can free you from the army, Frank, if you allow yourself to be freed.

However, no lawyer, and no riches, can free you from your self-imposed burden. Only you can do that. I cannot dictate what you must do, Frank, but only implore you to make a choice for life, and not one for violence and death, which can only bring you and those who love you unutterable pain. I hesitate to invoke your poor mother's memory, but you know she would not have wished this for you, and neither do I wish it for you, dear Frank.

If you can only put vengeance aside, if you can free yourself, then I shall indeed wait for you for as long as it takes for us to be together.

Your own Grace

Frank folded the paper. He walked a few paces to the edge of the bluff and leaned against a palm trunk there. Below him night birds were calling from the reed beds and the lagoons shone like enamel in the last of the light. He was aware of soft footsteps close to him, and Cavendish moved up to stand a few paces away, staring out over the shadowy river bed.

'It's from the girl, I suppose?' He tilted his head towards the white letter in Frank's hands. 'There's time to reply, you know.'

Frank did not face him. 'I can't reply, sir. I have released her.'

'She doesn't want to be released, Frank.'

Frank looked at him now. Before he could speak a sudden tattoo of hoofbeats sounded on the soft track behind them. They both turned as Pembleton trotted a black polo pony into the circle of lamplight and stopped just beyond the guy ropes. He did not dismount.

'I told you to make the most of it, Freddie.' Pembleton grinned, the pony dancing under him. 'Kitchener will march on Mahmoud's camp tomorrow night. You can watch the fun from the rear.'

Frank crumpled the letter in his hand and tossed it into the dark gulf below, then walked back into the firelight.

<h1 style="text-align:center">99</h1>

The zariba was in ruins, the palisade of branches dragged apart into tangled heaps by the Cameron Highlanders and the Royal Warwicks in their assault. Here and there the thorn branches were in flames, and the crackling of the dry wood parodied the popping of gunshots further ahead. Blue woodsmoke drifted across the desert and mixed with the reek of burned powder.

By the time Frank reached the zariba, moving forward with the rear rank of the Seaforth Highlanders, the enormous din of the firing had moved on. It had already swept like a great surf over the trenches and rifle pits and had engulfed what remained of Nukheila itself. So far as Frank could tell, fighting was now concentrated on the redoubt in the centre of the village. He couldn't see much; the scene was obscured by smoke from the dervishes' black powder and from burning huts set afire by British artillery and rockets. Even the palms on the riverbank were ablaze.

Ahead of him, the Seaforths burst through the remains of the zariba, hurling themselves forwards with savage exultation, and in a second they were in among the rifle pits and trenches, howling, shooting and bayoneting. There wasn't much left for them to kill, Frank could already see that much. He slowed to a walk and let the Scots surge past him. The stony ground outside the perimeter had been bad enough, strewn with dead – British, Egyptian and Sudanese soldiers, lying in their ranks from the only organised volley the defending dervishes had been able to get off. But here inside the zariba the carnage was infinitely worse. The remains of Mahmoud's army lay everywhere, an obscene litter of corpses, bloody clothing, smashed weapons, animals writhing and screaming: the effects of Kitchener's twenty-four guns, of shrapnel and explosive bullets. A dervish Krupp cannon lay dismounted and smoking behind its emplacement, its crew in shreds around it. A dead dervish in helmet and chain mail, like a medieval knight, lay under his decapitated horse.

A corporal of the Lincolns lay sprawled dead at Frank's feet. He turned the body over with his boot, picked up the man's Lee-Metford rifle and began to walk the length of the outermost entrenchments, keeping the muzzle low. The trench at his feet was collapsed by artillery fire and choked with dervish dead. A few wounded still lay moaning. Here and there a dead British or Sudanese attacker lay among the bodies, identifiable by khaki tunic or tarboosh or kilt.

The top of Hamid's head was missing, but Frank recognised the glossy beard and crossed bandoliers. The corpse was seated against the rear of the trench as if taking a rest, the Snider rifle which Frank had cleaned less than two days earlier cradled comfortably across its chest. Frank took the weapon from the dead hands and checked it. Hamid had not fired a single shot. He nudged the corpse with his rifle barrel and it toppled sideways, pulling down with it a small barricade of boxes and sacks in the mouth of the dugout behind.

From the darkness, the boy stared out with large eyes.

'Hello, Yussuf,' Frank said. 'Are you hurt?'

The boy gaped at his uniform.

'You are a *Feringhee*,' he said, and understanding dawned in his eyes. He pulled a crude knife from under his clothes and looked at it. 'I should stab you with this.'

'You could try,' Frank agreed. 'But I'd shoot you dead.'

Yussuf nodded gravely and put the knife away. 'Then I won't.'

A Scottish soldier lurched into view above the lip of the trench, his hair wild and his face powder-blackened. He shrieked something, his voice cracking like a maniac's, and lunged at the boy with rifle and fixed bayonet. Frank knocked the thrust aside with his own weapon, but the impetus carried the man sliding onto his knees into the trench. There were two or three more of his comrades nearby, Frank saw now, men who had drifted back from the main fight. They were moving down the lines of the trenches, cackling with bloodlust and firing at anything that moved and at much that did not.

Frank said, 'The boy is my prisoner.'

'He's a dead fucking prisoner, then!'

The soldier wrenched back the bolt of his weapon and lifted it and Frank hit him across the side of the head with his rifle. As the Scot fell to his knees on the floor of the trench Frank put his boot on his rifle, trapping his hand beneath it. The man cursed and struggled to rise and Frank heard his companions come running up.

'Step back, you men,' Cavendish called from above. 'That's an order.'

He was on horseback, and his revolver was drawn and resting on the pommel of his saddle, as if casually. This, and the surreal smartness of his appearance in this chaos, commanded obedience. Madness faded from the young Scot's eyes and he blinked a couple of times as if wondering where he was. Frank moved back and the man retrieved his rifle, climbed out of the trench and walked off with his comrades without a word, his head down.

'You were told to stay at the rear, Corporal Gray,' Cavendish said sternly. 'I could have you shot for insubordination. Now there's a thought.'

Frank unclipped the sword bayonet from his rifle, worked it under the staple which secured Yussuf's chain, and prised it free. 'Run to the edge of the forest,' he told the boy, 'and after that keep running.'

Yussuf bounced up onto the lip of the trench, darted a glance to left and right, and was off like a deer. In a few seconds he was inside the line of trees and lost to sight.

'Very touching,' Cavendish observed. 'Let's hope he doesn't come back and bite us at Khartoum.' He swivelled in the saddle, surveying the scene of smoke, fire and death. 'The word is they've captured Mahmoud. Imagine that. Twenty minutes ago he was a sharif with an army behind him. All over for him now. Hear that firing? That's our brave lads slaughtering what's left of his people as they cross the Atbara. Not much of an end for men who hunted lions with spears, is it? Shot down in the mud at half a mile by some lout from Liverpool. Makes you proud to be British.'

Frank climbed out of the trench. 'Aren't you always telling me there has to be order?'

'Ah, yes. Order.' Cavendish smiled without humour. 'When the Nile rises in a couple of months, and Kitchener can get his gunboats upriver, we'll be off to Khartoum. Khalifa Abdallahi has sixty thousand men waiting for us. Some say more. Imposing order on them might be more difficult.'

From a hut not far away a woman was shrieking. Frank shut his mind to it. A Baggara in a blood-drenched jibba, his face blank and both hands loose at his sides, rose from a trench and wandered past them as if sleepwalking. Frank lifted his rifle on reflex, but the man was so utterly devoid of threat that he lowered the weapon again and let him walk blindly away.

'Funny things, letters,' Cavendish remarked, as if this were the most natural thing to say on a battlefield. 'They can change everything.'

'If you say so, sir.'

'Oh, I do.' Cavendish holstered his revolver. 'I still think you should write, Frank. A note from you would reach her in a few days. Kitchener's efficiency even extends to the postal service. You might as well try: after Khartoum, we could all be as dead as these poor devils.'

'Why are you always so concerned with my private affairs?'

'It's because I still harbour just a faint hope of talking some sense into you, Frank, before you ruin everything for yourself. I told you in England I can help you. That offer still holds. Our stock's pretty high now with Kitchener's staff. I can put in a word in the right quarters.' Cavendish sat up in the saddle. 'But you won't have that, will you? All that matters to you is settling this score of yours, whatever it is.'

'I request permission to rejoin the regiment in Cairo. Sir.'

'Denied. Once again.'

'Why?'

'Because I say so. Yours not to reason why, remember? Besides, you're needed here. We both are.'

Frank stepped forward and rested one hand on the older man's stirrup. 'You can't keep me away from the Twenty-first for ever. Sooner or later Kitchener will bring them down here.'

Cavendish met his gaze steadily. 'And just what are you going to do when he does, Frank?'

'I shall rejoin them.'

'Not without my permission you won't.'

'Am I dismissed? Sir?'

'No.' Cavendish leaned forward with his arms crossed over the pommel so that the leather creaked. 'You're determined to throw it all away, Frank, aren't you? And for what? To satisfy some private blood-lust? How does that make you any different from these poor brave savages lying slaughtered here, with their pride and their ignorance and their violence? Follow that path and you'll come to the same end. You're worth more than that. You *owe* more than that.'

'I don't owe anybody anything.'

'Oh, yes. I told you before, Frank, you have a destiny, and if I can I shall see to it that you don't destroy yourself before you fulfil it.'

Frank stepped back from the horse. 'Leave me alone.' He drew himself up, saluted crisply, and walked away.

'I did not dismiss you, Corporal!' Cavendish bellowed after him, with such force that his horse capered under him.

But Frank kept on walking, picking his way between the burst bodies and the wounded men who were now straggling back across the littered ground, arms looped over their comrades' shoulders, shocked, bloody, white-eyed.

100

Grace paced the length of the pillared hall, fanning herself. At the far end, near the great staircase, she stood in front of one of the tall windows which gave out onto the Agency's immaculate gardens, and let the moving air cool her neck and face.

After the deafening chaos of the streets the orderly calm in here was delicious. Immaculate sentries from some Indian regiment, in turbans and puttees, stood motionless by the archway, their rifles grounded. A British military police sergeant sat at a reception desk just inside; he had checked Grace's details minutely against a visitors' book and issued her with a pass. On the marble benches nearby sat a variety of petitioners: Egyptian businessmen in red fezzes and Western suits, a very old man in magnificent Arab robes, four army officers, and a handful of British men she assumed to be officials.

She amused herself by wondering what they were all doing here. She had no trouble imagining roles for the soldiers and the Egyptians, but it was the group of officials who struck her most forcibly. They might have been middle-ranking civil servants on London Bridge Station, having just stepped off the suburban train from Sydenham on their way to work. Administrators, she supposed, or engineers, teachers, contractors, doctors. They puzzled her. In her mind the Empire was peopled by arrogant military men and rapacious merchants, but she glimpsed for the first time in these modest functionaries something of the complexity and the reach of the imperial machine.

'Miss Dearborn?'

A very tall man stood at her elbow, gorgeous in full military dress uniform. He was about forty, prematurely white haired and quite unreasonably handsome. The light dazzled from his buttons and shone on the polished leather of his Sam Browne.

'Since you're the only lady present, I take it you must indeed be Miss Dearborn,' he supplied, when she didn't immediately answer. 'I'm Colin Macallan, Lord Cromer's aide. One of them.'

She recovered. 'I'm pleased to meet you, Mr Macallan.'

'It's Major, actually, but let's not stand on ceremony.' He inclined his head to her in invitation. 'Lord Cromer is rather pressed for time, so shall we go up?'

Grace followed Macallan up the wide stairs. He walked with a slight limp, she noticed, and she stilled her gathering nervousness by concentrating on the uneven jingle of his spurs.

'Have you met his Lordship before?' he asked over his shoulder.

'Never.'

'I thought not. You'll find him a remarkable man. No doubt you know he's been British Agent here for twenty-five years? He was plain Sir Evelyn Baring at the start. Since then he's rebuilt the country's finances and administration virtually from scratch. And now, of course, with this business brewing in the Sudan, he has even more on his plate.'

'Well, I shan't ask the Empire to spare him for long.'

He glanced down at her. 'As a matter of fact it's quite unusual for him to give interviews to the press. I gather it was a certain Lord Strathair who put in a good word? Useful to have influential friends in your line of work, I should imagine.'

Grace didn't trouble to answer. They emerged onto the broad landing at the top of the stairs. An Egyptian messenger in uniform hurried past with buff files piled on a tray. She could hear typewriters and low voices in the other rooms, and a bad tempered English voice demanding tea. Macallan surprised her by smiling in a sympathetic fashion, then tapped lightly on double doors and swung them open. He stood back to let her into a large light office with a fan circling overhead, the morning sun falling in bars through the shutters. A map of Egypt was unrolled against one wall, shaded in pink, and she saw a cabinet of antique curios, potted palms, and framed photographs of the pyramids.

Macallan followed them in and closed the doors behind them. 'Miss Grace Dearborn, sir.'

In the centre of the room Lord Cromer rose from behind his ornate desk. He was in his sixties, and even more massive a presence than she had heard, heavily built and with broad shoulders. She could see now why Cairo society called him 'the bear'. But it was his eyes she noticed, keen light eyes under a high intelligent forehead. He was dressed in a grey frock coat of somewhat old-fashioned cut which Grace knew was a trademark of his, and which he wore everywhere, despite the climate. She took a deep breath and advanced boldly across the rich carpet.

'Lord Cromer, I'm delighted to meet you.'

'Miss Dearborn.' Cromer took her hand in his large one. His voice was sonorous. 'The pleasure is mine, though I fear the meeting will be somewhat rushed. Unexpectedly I have to meet his Excellency the Khedive in less than an hour.'

'I'm sure we'll have time, my Lord. I have only one request.'

The choice of words evidently puzzled him, but he waved her to a chair. 'Do please sit, my dear young lady.' He sat down himself, flicking out the tails of his coat in a swirl of grey. 'A request? I understood that you were to conduct an interview.' He took a paper from his desk and adjusted his monocle to read from it. 'On the prospects for investment in the Sudan following its pacification. For the . . . *Free Briton* news-paper? That seems to be what Lord Strathair indicated in his letter to me.'

Grace folded her hands in her lap. 'I'm afraid the letter does not tell the truth, Lord Cromer.'

He took out his monocle to look at her. 'It does not?'

'No. I bullied Lord Strathair into writing it. I have very little interest in imperial economics. I have a much simpler request for you.'

Lord Cromer lay the monocle on his desktop with great precision. 'And what is that?'

'I need your help to track down a soldier, my Lord.'

Behind her, Grace heard Macallan give a cough of surprise, quickly suppressed.

Cromer blinked at her. 'A soldier?'

'His name is Frank Gray, Lord Cromer, and he's with the Twenty-first Lancers.' Grace felt a reckless exhilaration now that it was said. 'I need to see him, you understand. It's very important that I see him.'

Cromer looked uncomprehendingly at Macallan and then back at her.

'I'm quite aware,' she pushed on, 'that General Kitchener is in military command, but he is in the Sudan most of the time, and I have been unable to make any headway with his staff. However, if you were to—'

Cromer raised a heavy hand to silence her. 'Am I to understand, Miss Dearborn, that you have gained entry to my office under false pretences?'

'Yes. You would never have consented to see me otherwise. Now what I need to ask—'

Again the hand came up. 'Let me see if I understand you correctly. You come to me in the hope that I can take time away from running the government of Egypt to establish the whereabouts of a single officer?'

'A corporal, actually.'

'Good God.' Cromer looked at Macallan in appeal. 'Can you believe this, Colin?'

'Hardly, sir. I'm very sorry. I'm not sure how . . .' Macallan stepped smartly forward to stand beside Grace. 'You'd better come with me, Miss Dearborn. His Lordship has matters of state to attend to.'

Grace stayed seated. 'Gentlemen, this isn't complicated. All I ask is for permission to travel south and look for him. I have my own funds. I do not intend to use any of your resources. I merely need your permission.'

Macallan leaned closer, but Cromer gestured for him to stand back.

'You wish to travel to the seat of war? My dear young lady, I'm afraid you have no idea what you are asking. General Kitchener's troops are engaged in operations against a ruthless and barbaric enemy, even as we speak. At a place called Nukheila only last week he fought a most bloody action, at the cost of several hundred lives, British, Sudanese and Egyptian. And you wish to pay the troops a social visit as if they were in barracks at Aldershot?'

'I need to find him, Lord Cromer, that's all there is to it. I have spent three months sending letters and telegrams, to his regiment, to General Kitchener's staff, to the War Office. You are my last hope.'

Cromer fixed his monocle back into his eye and turned his attention to a file on his desk. 'Colin, see the lady out.'

Grace lifted her chin. 'I am a wealthy woman, Lord Cromer. Perhaps you've heard of Dearborn & Company? I own it. I can pay for everything, even protection for myself, if that's what concerns you. But I need—'

Macallan placed the lightest of hands on her elbow. 'Come along, Miss Dearborn.'

She jumped to her feet and shook off his hand like a wasp. 'I will not come along!' She put her fists on Cromer's desk and leaned towards him. 'Sir, all you need do is sign a travel warrant. That's all. One stroke of the pen. I'll deal with all the rest myself.'

'This way, Miss Dearborn.'

Macallan took her arm firmly this time but once more she flung away from him. 'Oh, but you're all too busy fighting wars, aren't you? All too busy showing how powerful and important you are, and waving that shameful flag, to care about anything that really matters.'

At that, Cromer lifted his head slowly. 'Men are dying for that *shameful* flag down in the Sudan, Miss Dearborn,' he said, his voice very low. 'Perhaps they are misguided. Perhaps we all are. There are times when I am not confident about that. But I'm confident of this: now that it's started, whatever is happening in the Sudan is more important than you, or me, or anything we might wish for ourselves. Good day to you.'

Macallan followed her as she strode to the door, somehow getting there ahead of her and opening it for her. She ignored him and half-ran down the broad steps into the cool lobby, so that he had to struggle to catch up.

'Miss Dearborn? Miss Dearborn, please.'

She stopped in the middle of the hall, breathing hard, aware that she was attracting the attention of guards and visitors, and not caring. Macallan came limping up to her. It gave her unkind pleasure to see the effort this cost him.

'I admire your spirit, Miss Dearborn.'

'I don't care what you admire.'

'I'm aware of that, but, for what it's worth, Lord Cromer really does have to see the Khedive of Egypt. He might have been a little more patient otherwise. He's a decent man.'

She faced him. 'Major Macallan, I don't give a fiddler's fuck about the Khedive of Egypt, or about Lord Cromer.'

'Oh, I know.' He smiled at her. 'You only care about Frank Gray.'

She looked at him coolly. 'Was there anything else you wanted to say?'

'Only that the Twenty-first Lancers are here in Cairo, Miss Dearborn. At Abbassia Barracks.'

'I know. I've already been to Abbassia, spoken to the commandant. Frank isn't there. He's never been there.'

'And you're convinced he's with Kitchener in the Sudan? Even though his regiment isn't?'

'Frank often spoke of an officer called Cavendish. I think the two of them are working together down there. On some assignment. They have done this sort of thing before.'

Macallan had produced a small leather-bound notepad. 'Cavendish, you say?' He noted the name with a gold propelling pencil.

It took Grace a moment to realise she had found an ally. 'Major Macallan, if I could just get a travel warrant—'

'Please believe me, young lady, there's not a chance of that. No one will let you anywhere near the theatre of operations, and you would be able to achieve nothing if they did.' Macallan pocketed his notebook and drew himself up. 'Where are you staying?'

'At Shepheard's.'

'For how long?'

'For as long as it takes.'

He regarded her thoughtfully. 'Well, perhaps I could make some inquiries.' He raised a warning finger. 'I make no promises, Miss Dearborn. There are over twenty-five thousand troops in the Sudan and more coming and going all the time. No promises at all.'

'I understand that.'

'But?'

'But I don't understand why you'd help.'

'Miss Dearborn, I know something about the dangers of a soldier's life. I survived twenty-three years of front-line service. Untold numbers of people tried quite hard to kill me, and I escaped with nothing worse than a gammy leg. And then my wife died of diphtheria fever in Harrogate two weeks before I was due to hand in my papers. Life's a risky business. I'm rather on the side of anyone who tries to beat the odds.'

He clicked his heels to her with mock formality, and then walked back up the wide marble steps, his spurs ringing in that disconcertingly off-beat rhythm.

PART ELEVEN

Egypt and The Sudan, August and September 1898

101

The troops were already off the train by the time Frank got to the railhead. All around sweating men in khaki bawled at Sudanese bearers, argued over piles of kit, bartered with the local food vendors who swarmed around them. Crates and sacks were offloaded by lines of soldiers in shirtsleeves and piled by the trackside. Troopers struggled to coax dull-eyed horses from the wagons.

Frank made his way through the press. He was sorry for the horses; they looked in desperate condition. Most were small Syrian ponies – quick and sure-footed, he had heard, but without the stamina, or the stoic spirit, to withstand two weeks on the jolting Sudan Military Railway. Once off the train they stood in dispirited groups beside the track, their heads down. A subaltern was already picking out the worst of them and having them led away, and desultory gunshots sounded from behind a line of railcars. Further down the train teams of men were hauling out arms and ammunition, tents and stores. A crane was swinging off the massive steel sections of a steamer, ready to be assembled.

In the crowd Frank saw the uniforms of the Grenadier Guards, the Rifle Brigade, the Northumberland Fusiliers. He searched for the shoulder flashes of the 21st Lancers. As he worked his way forward through the throng he collided with a thickset trooper rummaging through a pile of personal gear. The man, bad tempered and purple in the face, swung round and swore at him.

Frank made to push past, but the man gripped his arm.

'Darkie? Darkie Gray?'

Frank looked down into the shiny round face, and the man grinned and punched his arm, his evil humour evaporating at once.

'You remember me, Darkie! It's Tubs Tranter. Well, fuck me! What's it been, two years? We thought you was dead, up on the Frontier somewhere. But here you are, large as life. What're you doing in this dump, Darkie?'

'That's a good question, Tubs.'

Tranter looked at Frank's sleeve and pantomimed awe. 'Two bloody stripes in two years, is it? Mick? Mick! Come and see what the cat's dragged in. But you better talk respectful. He's got rank, now.'

Gannon appeared from the crowd, the stub of his pipe sticking out of the corner of his mouth. He gripped Frank's hand, nodded at the stripes on his arm. 'Ye couldn't have come by them honest.'

'I knew what I was about when I named you,' Tranter said, shaking his head sagely. 'Dark by name and dark by nature. He's been sunning hisself down here, Mick, while we've been sweating our arses off up at Abbassia.' He looked around him. 'And by the way, where is *here*?'

'Fort Atbara,' Frank told him. 'The end of the line.'

'Looks like a standard issue shithole to me.' Tranter surveyed the dun hills beyond the railyards, shimmering in the heat. 'We had a bloke die of the heat on the train, and Christ knows how many horses. How long we going to be stuck here, Darkie?'

'Kitchener's waiting for the Nile to rise before he moves, so he can get the gunboats down.'

'And how long will that take?'

'Two or three weeks. You can look forward to a decent ride after that.' Frank turned to Gannon. 'Did the officers come down with you, Mick?'

'A few. Most didn't fancy sitting in that sweat box of a train for days on end. Took a nice leisurely Nile cruise instead.' Gannon took the pipe out of his mouth and spat. 'Ye wouldn't still be looking for your old mate John Herrick, by any chance?'

'Is he with you?'

'He will be. What's your beef with that bastard, anyway?'

'When does he get here, Mick?'

'He'll arrive just in time for the showdown, if I'm any judge. Too busy whoring in Cairo for the present.'

102

Cavendish sat back and stretched his booted legs. It was dim in the tent, lit only by the last dregs of the evening light seeping through the open flap. On the camp table lay maps, reading spectacles, compass. Cavendish's swordbelt and helmet hung from the back of a camp chair. A shower had burst over the camp, an echo of the thunderstorms of the previous night, and rain slapped against the canvas and dripped musically from a leak in the corner. It was chilly and the dank smell of thirsty soil filled the air.

'Can't read this damned weather,' Cavendish observed. 'Hotter than the hinges of hell during the day, but as soon as the sun's gone, we're in an English April. Can't even have a light to read by. Sirdar's orders. Pity the poor devils out there, eh?'

Frank supposed Cavendish was talking about Kitchener's twenty-eight thousand British, Egyptian and Sudanese troops now huddled within the thorn-hedge zariba which encircled the village of Egeiga, their backs to the Nile. Or perhaps he meant the Khalifa's hosts, hunkered down less than two miles away on the Kerreri plain outside Omdurman, where the prophecy had foretold that Sudan's enemies would leave their bones. Whatever the truth of that, the positions were reversed since Nukheila four months earlier. This time the dervish army was massing to attack, while Kitchener crouched in wait, dug in behind his own zariba of cut thorn branches.

Frank kept his eyes on the tent pole behind the older man's head, watching the raindrops slide down the smooth surface. The silence yawned between them.

Cavendish brought his chair forward with a bump. 'For the love of God, Frank, how long are we going to keep this up? You've been sulking like a child for weeks.'

'I wish to be returned to the Twenty-first, sir. To normal duties.'

'Why?'

'It's my regiment. Sir.'

'That's not the reason.'

Frank kept his eyes on the tent pole, but his own voice was rising. 'You've kept me away from the Twenty-first for four months, running errands, carrying messages, interrogating prisoners—'

'Important work. You ought to be flattered.'

'Flattered be damned!'

'Mind your tongue, Corporal.'

'And the Twenty-first are here now, down at the southern end of the zariba. I saw them come in. I want to rejoin them.'

'Do you, indeed?' A nerve jumped in Cavendish's cheek. 'Well, Gray, for your information we'll both be riding with them tomorrow, so you'll get your wish soon enough. Meanwhile, you'll follow orders, like every other miserable soldier in this army. I could have you charged for insolence, do you know that? Have those two stripes off you before you're out of this tent.' Cavendish stopped himself with an effort, pushed a hand through his grey hair. 'Frank, you know I kept you here because I've been trying to save you from making the worst mistake of your life. Who is it you're looking for? Who is it who's supposed to have done you such wrong?'

'With respect, sir, that's my affair.'

'Get off your high horse, will you? Sit down and talk to me.'

For the first time, Frank looked directly at him. 'I'd rather stand, sir.'

Their eyes locked for a long moment.

Cavendish said, 'Dammit, Frank, this is absurd. We've been through a lot together. We could all be carrion this time tomorrow, and we can't even talk?'

Frank looked at the lined face, the thinning hair and pepper and salt moustache. At that moment Cavendish seemed to him an exhausted old man, and he felt sorry. He stood listening to the calls of men from the camp, the barking of a dog answered by another, the dropping of the rain from the flap of the tent. In his mind he saw Grace silhouetted against a dark window, somewhere in another world. The rain had been falling that night, too. He saw again the despairing lines of her letter, the letter he had crumpled and tossed away, along with the last of his hope. Almost the last of his hope. He stepped forward and sat down in the canvas chair opposite Cavendish.

He said, 'It's Herrick, sir.'

Cavendish sat up very straight. 'What?'

'Major Herrick. Jack Herrick. I want him brought to justice.'

'What for?'

'He assaulted my mother five years ago. He raped her.'

'Frank, that's a serious accusation.'

'Of course it's a serious accusation.'

'And are you sure of it?'

'He might as well have killed her. Killed all of us. It was his fault, all of it.'

Cavendish stared at him for a long moment. 'You mean to say it's Herrick you've been pursuing all this time? He's the reason you joined the Twenty-first? The reason you're here?'

'He was never punished for what he did. I want him punished.'

'So you've been planning to punish him yourself.'

'I always thought that would be necessary. But I've been thinking. Perhaps, if you stood by me, sir, there might be another way. A decent way. A legal way. Then I might be . . . free. Do you see?'

'Jack Herrick.' Cavendish shook his head incredulously. 'My God.'

Frank sat back a little. 'You promised to help.'

'Indeed I did promise, Frank. So I did. I'm glad you've told me. Very glad. Of course I am.' Cavendish picked up his spectacles from the table, put them down again. He seemed to want to stand, to pace around, but the tent did not afford him the space and he looked momentarily trapped. 'What would you like me to do?'

'Well, have him arrested, of course. Sir.'

'You think it's that simple?'

'For years I've been planning an even simpler solution. But perhaps, with your help . . . Don't worry, I can prove he did it.'

'There were witnesses?'

'I was a witness. And if they won't believe me, he'll have scars on his side where I shot him.'

'You *shot* him? Good Lord.'

'We could go to Colonel Martin and make a statement. It wouldn't carry any weight coming from a mere corporal, but with you—'

'Am I to understand that you mean we should do this *now*?'

'Yes, now. Why not now?'

'Damn it all, Frank! We'll be fighting a battle tomorrow, maybe even tonight.'

'What's that got to do with it?'

'Would you like me to stop the war, so that you can pursue your rights?'

Frank sat still for a long moment. 'You're not going to do anything, are you?'

'Be reasonable, Frank, for God's sake. If we get through tomorrow, we'll go to see Colonel Martin. I promise you that. But you don't seriously expect to deal with a matter like this *tonight*? We might all be dead in a few hours.'

'That's precisely why it has to be dealt with tonight.'

'No, no, no.' Cavendish shook his head sharply. 'That's out of the question. I won't hear of it. We have certain duties . . . we are soldiers . . .'

Frank got slowly to his feet. 'I never expected this from you.'

Cavendish raised his head sharply. 'Don't take that tone with me.'

'You're just like the others after all. You all look out for one another, no matter what.'

'You watch your words, Corporal! I warn you!'

Cavendish half-rose, but Frank was already pushing through the flap of the tent and stepping out into the wet night.

103

Frank moved through the seething village in the darkness, his fury making him clumsy in the thronged streets.

Until a few days before, Egeiga had been no more than a mud-brick hamlet clinging to the banks of the Nile. Now thousands upon thousands of British troops and their allies crammed every conceivable corner of it, men sheltering in the mud houses, stores piled in the streets, horses and camels and donkeys tethered in noisy corrals. The stench of horse dung and rotting garbage hung in the night.

The rain eased as Frank moved on, but water stood in puddles and the alleyways were slick underfoot. He stopped, breathing hard, and tried to think. But as he stood there he suddenly sensed danger, and pressed himself into a doorway. It seemed ironic to him that his old instinct should still operate here. In this place, danger was everywhere and yet nowhere in particular. He glanced back the way he had come, but the scene behind him was innocent enough. In the unlit alley he saw two Sudanese soldiers sat crouched on their haunches against the wall trying to shelter from the last of the rain, their rifles propped beside them. A British sergeant strode across from a passage on the left to one on the right. A village boy hawked tea from a tray through the window of a hut.

Frank moved on, keeping to the shadows. At least the delay had calmed him, brought him focus, and now he knew what he would do.

He found the 21st bivouacked beyond the village proper on sloping land that bordered the Nile. Their horse lines, several hundred mounts, stretched between the tents and the river. Troopers in shirts and braces moved between the animals with feed and water, and two farriers were at work with hammer and anvil. In the camp itself men were clustered in small groups, some cleaning weapons and equipment by rising starlight, some talking quietly. Others sat alone and silent with their thoughts.

Frank skirted the encampment, moving to his left, towards the river. Two Lancer officers came striding past him, talking in braying voices. He saluted, received a languid lift of a swagger stick in response, moved on. A captain and two lieutenants, all of them unknown to him, sat outside a tent with their feet up and a bottle of wine on a table between them. They were laughing over their drinks in the over-loud way of men trying to bolster one another's courage. Frank began to circle back around the horse lines, watchful and alert. Presently he saw a young lieutenant strolling alone, perhaps taking in the sounds and sights of the camp. Frank stepped into the subaltern's path and saluted crisply.

'Begging your pardon, sir.'

'What is it, Corporal?'

'I've a message for Major Herrick, sir. Can't seem to find him, sir.'

'Herrick, is it? Well, I'm a new boy myself, Corporal. But let me see. Herrick. Big officer? Fine moustaches?' He gave Frank a look of amused complicity. 'Rather a fierce type of chap, if I don't miss my guess?'

'That's Major Herrick, sir.'

Frank kept his eyes straight ahead. He didn't recognise this helpful officer, a tall, fleshy man with humorous eyes. He could feel the sweat gathering between his shoulder blades: please God this pleasant young man wasn't going to start a conversation. Not now.

'I saw him down on the riverbank a few minutes ago,' the lieutenant said. 'Smoking a cigar, I think. Good notion. Wish I had some myself. See those two palms, close together? Just about there. And—'

'Thank you, sir. Thank you very much.'

Frank saluted and walked quickly on, wondering if the lieutenant would call him back and upbraid him for his rudeness. He did not.

The bank beneath his feet sloped down to a belt of reeds. The Nile beyond lay extended like sheet steel under a vaulted sky. Frank could hear the river chuckling over mudflats in the darkness. A short distance upstream lay the bulk of an anchored steamer, and beyond it another, and others beyond that, ghostly shapes in the mist which rose off the water. Downstream, another spectral flotilla rode at anchor. As he watched, searchlights sprang on from the decks of the steamers and threw blinding spokes of light high over the village and into the black desert where the dervish army waited. By the river's edge the reflected glare turned the water to silver and blazed in the upper fronds of the *dom* palms.

Not far from where Frank stood, troopers were watering a string of horses at a muddy beach. If they noticed him, no one called a challenge. Frank moved on towards the pair of palms trees pointed out by the lieutenant. They stood like black paper silhouettes against the opalescent water. As he moved closer he could see they formed part of a grove on a small promontory where the shore bulged out into the river. He slipped in among the black trunks. Stopped. Listened.

The river murmured as if in secret conversation with itself. The vast camp behind him buzzed softly. Quiet words of command floated to him from the moored gunboats, carrying with extraordinary clarity over the water. A horse snorted as it drank. From the papyrus reeds a waterbird chimed in alarm, a sharp metallic note, repeated three times.

It was the smoke he detected first. Tobacco smoke. And then, a few yards ahead, the red dot of a cigar. The rest of the figure gradually took shape as Frank focused on it, a big man lounging back against a palm trunk. The man's face glowed crimson as he drew on the cigar. Frank recognised the bold moustache, the strong brows. He waited for the glow to bloom again. When it did, and he was sure, he slid his right hand into his tunic and eased the butt of the Bulldog revolver out a little. He moved silently forward a few paces and checked around him. A small knot of men stood on the bank fifty yards downstream, washing, filling billy cans. Upstream, the troopers he had first seen were leading a fresh string of horses down to the water's edge. He could hear their hooves clop and suck in the trample.

The steel butt was slick with sweat. It came to Frank that he could do this thing by stealth and escape. He could step a little closer, fire twice at point-blank, then toss the revolver into the Nile and slip away as he had come. For a second he grew light-headed at the prospect of it. He slid the Bulldog into the open, saw light glint on the short barrel, held it down by his side. But he knew he could not shoot the man down like that. Herrick had to know why he was to die. Just a word or two, that was all. Then he could fire and be gone. Frank cocked the pistol, hefted it in his hand, shifted his weight onto his forward foot.

A shocking blur of action swept over him and his hand was wrenched up and the weapon twisted out of it. Before he could react Cavendish had grabbed him by the lapels and was ramming him up against a palm trunk.

'You damned young fool! I knew you were up to something like this.'

'Leave me—'

'Shut up.' Cavendish hit him hard across the face, and with his other hand eased down the hammer of the revolver and slipped the pistol into his own pocket.

Ten yards away Herrick pushed himself upright and flicked away his cigar in a starshell parabola.

'The devil's going on?'

'It's a personal matter, Herrick. Don't worry about it.'

'Cavendish? Is that you?' Herrick stepped forward, peered at Frank in the darkness and then at Cavendish. 'A personal matter? There was a weapon.'

'There was no weapon,' Cavendish said coolly. 'You're imagining things.'

'No weapon be damned! I saw it, I tell you! I saw the light glint on it.'

'Be quiet, Herrick, there's a good chap. There was no weapon, and no harm done. Let's forget it, shall we? Then we can all go and get ourselves properly killed tomorrow.'

'Damn you, Cavendish. Who is this man?' The searchlight swung from left to right above them and momentarily washed them in glare and Herrick leaned forward into Frank's face. 'I thought I recognised you. You were at Landi Kotal.'

'Quite right,' Cavendish said. 'Corporal Gray, my orderly. Of course you recognise him.'

Herrick moved forward. 'I never did like the look of you, Gray.' And to Cavendish, 'You stand up for him? I'll have the swine broken.'

'As you please, Herrick. But just run along for now. If you've still got the stomach for it by then, we can settle this after tomorrow. That is, if any of us are left alive.'

Herrick still stood, breathing hard, but before he could say more Cavendish gripped Frank's arm and forced him away through the trees towards the water's edge. Even when he reached it he pushed on a yard or two further, out onto a spit of mud and sand which jutted into the river. He stopped and they stood facing one another under the stars. Frank could feel the soft mud give under his boots. The Nile lapped at his very feet. He had the weird impression that they were standing on water, far out in the ancient river, and that the dark shapes of the village and the ghostly gunboats were floating somewhere very distant. The murmur of the current was loud in his ears.

'You bloody fool, Frank,' Cavendish said. 'You blind, bloody young fool.'

'Why did you stop me? You know I'll only try again.'

'To kill Herrick? *Herrick?*'

'What choice did I have? You didn't leave me a choice. I thought you'd understand.'

'Frank, it's you who doesn't understand. Do you seriously think your mother would have looked twice at a puffed-up dandy like Herrick?'

'What are you talking about? What would you know about it?'

'I know this much.' Cavendish tore aside his tunic and the pale skin of his belly shone in the starlight. 'Do you want to see the scar? Want to feel it? The scar that Herrick is supposed to have? You missed my liver by a fraction, Frank. It was me. It was me you shot that night. *Me*. Not Herrick.'

Frank stared at the bare flesh, at the puckered scar. He felt himself swaying, caught himself. 'Jack. She said *Jack*.'

'Frederick John Cavendish. Marjorie always called me Jack. You saw the dedications in my books at Faldonside? *To Frederick J. Cavendish.* I thought you'd guessed then. Part of me kept hoping you would. I wanted to tell you. But first I wanted to find a way to make some kind of restitution.' Cavendish fastened his tunic. 'At least, that's what I told myself.'

'But in Bangalore—'

'In Bangalore you were told that Herrick left the Fourth Hussars after a scandal. Did you think he was unique in that?'

'The woman . . . Mrs Desai . . . She knew it was Herrick.'

'Then she had her own scores to settle, and hoped you'd settle them for her. Frank, Frank. You so badly wanted it to be him that you couldn't see the truth in front of your own eyes. I'm still a captain at my age. Did you never ask why? I knew it was you almost from the moment you signed. Good God, you didn't even think to change your name. I wanted you with me. I thought there might be some chance.'

'Chance for what?'

'For you. And some chance of redemption for me. Fooling myself, obviously.' Cavendish took a long breath, put his hand into the pocket of his tunic. He reached for Frank's hand and slapped the small revolver into it. 'Here. Finish it. You'll probably get clean away. At least I won't tell.'

Frank looked at the weapon.

'You can't hold back now.' Cavendish nodded down at the pistol. 'Go on. Show some backbone. Put us both out of our misery. But before you do, know this, Frank: I loved your mother.'

The gun came up as quick as a snake and in an instant was levelled six inches from Cavendish's forehead. 'You *loved* her? You dare tell me that?'

'She wouldn't come away with me because of your father and you two boys. She'd promised me, faithfully promised me, but when it came to the point she refused. I behaved worse than an animal, and I shall never be cleansed of that sin. But it doesn't change the fact that I loved her, and she loved me.'

'Liar.'

Frank thumbed back the hammer. They both heard the chamber revolve.

'It's the truth. It was love for your mother that blinded me. Drink. Lust. Jealousy. All these things. But it was love that sent me mad. I've been paying for that ever since.' Cavendish held Frank's eyes. 'I no longer care about myself. But if you pull the trigger, you'll pay too. And go on paying until the end of your life.'

Frank held his stance, rigid, the muscles of his arms and shoulders locked. 'Tell me what happened.'

'Frank, even now you'd like me to tell you that somehow it wasn't the way you remember it. Do you think I don't know that? But there have been enough lies, and I won't add another. You may kill me for it, but that won't change things for either of us.'

The muzzle of the pistol quivered. The searchlight swung back and in its glare Frank saw the weary face and the dark eyes full of pain.

He whispered, 'Tell me.'

'We struggled, you and I. We both had hold of the revolver and it discharged. Yes, your finger was on the trigger, but my hand was over yours. What does it matter, Frank? The guilt remains mine. Of course it does. But I did not want her harmed, any more than you did, and I won't stand here and claim otherwise. I can offer her nothing else now. Afterwards I told Colonel James that I had shot her down in a moment of passion. I knew that's what you believed, and I wouldn't have cared if they'd hanged me for it. But James was too shrewd for me. He could see I didn't have it in me. If it had come to trial, Frank, I would have been disgraced, cashiered. But it's not a crime to fall in love with another man's wife and matters would have ended there for me. But you? They knew you'd seized the gun, that you'd tried to kill me and nearly succeeded. Whatever I'd told them, they'd always have believed that it was you who'd pulled the trigger in panic and fear. They'd have proved it to you and the world. I agreed to keep my mouth shut so that you didn't have to face that.'

Someone quite close must have seen them then, for a voice from the darkness called a question. Called again. Footfalls approached, squelching through the weeds of the bank.

'Make your decision,' Cavendish said. 'Make it quickly. If they find you with the gun you're finished.'

Frank took a deep breath. The footsteps drew nearer. Someone called, 'Who's there?'

Frank drew back his arm and threw the Bulldog far out over the sliding waters. He followed it with his eyes as it turned, blazing briefly in the searchlight beam, to burst through the surface far, far out.

'I shall never be free,' he said.

'My boy, this is the only way you will be.'

Cavendish reached out to him but Frank struck his hand away. 'Don't ever touch me.'

He made to shove past but Cavendish gripped his arm with extraordinary force and swung him back.

'Tomorrow, Frank, if we survive, we'll go to see Colonel Martin. We'll bring all this into the open at last. You won't have an argument from me. But I'll tell you this: until then I still hold the Queen's commission and you're still Corporal Gray. And that means that when the time comes we'll ride out with the rest of the Twenty-first and behave like soldiers.'

'Do you think I give a damn what happens tomorrow?'

'That's not good enough, Frank. We're in this together with all these other poor souls. And whatever happens afterwards, until then we'll play our part the way it's written for us. I promise you that.'

Frank tore himself free and walked blindly away into the darkness. Behind him he could hear other men come up and Cavendish's voice reassuring them cheerfully that all was well.

104

The horses picked their way over the sun-baked ground in the silky light. The sand ridge rose gently before them, blocking their view towards Omdurman, and the rocky slopes of the hill called Jebel Surgham climbed to their right. Glancing back, Frank could see the rest of A Squadron gathered a few hundred yards behind them, with Major Finn at their head. The dawn light was as clear as a lens. It was eerily quiet, with not so much as the cry of a bird, only the clatter and ring of shod hooves on shale.

Ahead of him, Lt. Smyth had almost reached the shoulder of the ridge with Gannon almost at his stirrup. Frank glanced back. Behind him rode Tranter, already sweating through his khaki, then a score of troopers he knew only by sight, and at the rear another lieutenant, riding with his helmet pulled down over his eyes so that his face was shadowed. Behind this man's shoulder and beyond the distant clustered horses of A Squadron stretched a mile and a half of dun plain and then the dark line of the zariba, within it the formations of the allied force in and around Egeiga village. And beyond that the polished snake of the Nile, dazzling in the low sun behind its fringe of *dom* palms, and the steel-grey shapes of the gunboats riding on it.

Frank could still taste the bully beef he had eaten in the pre-dawn dark just an hour before. It had been greasy and unappetising but he knew he would remember that taste as long as he lived. He would remember other things too; the men's mumbled curses as they rolled out of tents damp from the dew, the jingle of equipment, the snorting of the horses as they were fed.

The British camp, impregnable as it had seemed when he was part of it, looked tiny now in the vastness of the Nile floodplain, lost under a dome of African sky. Frank's old instincts began to prickle in him. What were they doing in this alien and savage place, little squares of toy soldiers, standing against the tide? How had Tranter got here from his Hackney tenement, or Gannon from his soft Limerick farm? And himself, most of all himself. He could not shake off the sense of unreality which had settled over him the night before. He no longer had any reason to be here. But Cavendish was right about this much: the curtain was about to lift on this dusty plain, and none of them could leave the stage now.

'Wakey, wakey, Darkie my son!' Tranter grinned, coming up beside him. 'Off with the fucking fairies, was you?'

Lt. Smyth, stationary now a few yards ahead, threw up a hand. 'Quiet there.'

He beckoned the second officer forward and the two of them conferred for a moment. Then Smyth waved the right-hand file of lancers to follow him and moved off cautiously to the north-west, further up the line of the sand ridge, keeping below the summit.

Frank, staying back with the remaining group, grew aware of a weird sound, deep and rushing, like a distant surf. A few paces ahead the other lieutenant dismounted and called over two of the troopers.

'You two men, take the horses to the foot of the slope and hold them ready, in case we need to absent ourselves in a hurry. Any of the rest of you who'd like to see history can dismount and come up to the crest with me. Bring your carbines. But keep your heads down.'

Frank dismounted and set aside the awkward lance. He slid his carbine from its saddle boot and walked after the officer up to the crest of the sand ridge, hearing several others of the patrol come forward too. Dropping onto their stomachs they squirmed to the top. From here the wide ochre country opened out before them, a great sweep of plain between low hills to the north and the dun huddle of Omdurman just five miles to the south-west, mud walls, minarets, and the onion dome of the Mahdi's tomb, a jagged hole blown in it the day before by the new British lyddite shells. A low cloud of dust hung over the land, and under this haze the whole scene, from a mile ahead of the lancers' position, was crammed with men: a vast lake of white and blue and black robes, horsemen, swordsmen and riflemen, the shimmer of light on their steel rippling as if on a numberless shoal of turning fish. Banners of every colour drifted on the morning air above them.

Beside Frank, the officer quoted, ' "Silent, upon a peak in Darien",' and gave a grunt of laughter, as if at his own pretentiousness. 'A fine time for Shelley, eh?'

'Keats,' Frank said, automatically. 'Sir.' He glanced at the officer and saw that it was the young lieutenant from whom he had asked directions last night.

'I stand corrected, Corporal.' The lieutenant gave him an ironic smile. If he recognised Frank, he gave no sign of it.

'Bugger me,' Tranter said, awestruck. 'Thousands of the bastards. 'Undreds of thousands.'

The lieutenant produced field glasses. 'And on the move, too. What would you say, a thousand yards?' He seemed to be speaking to Frank.

'About that, sir.'

'It will take them a little while to get here to the sand ridge. But once over that, they'll be within range of our artillery. And all over us, incidentally.' The lieutenant rolled onto his hip and took a leather-bound notebook from his pocket, scribbled in it, tore out a page. He beckoned forward one of the troopers. 'Take this down to Major Finn, there's a good chap. Have a good look while you're up here, and tell the major what you see.'

The man saluted, took the note, glanced uneasily over the ridge at the sea of hostile humanity below, and jogged down the sandy slope to his horse. In a moment he was gone.

The officer adjusted his field glasses and spoke without taking his eyes from them. 'Any of you fellows want to go back to the horses, please feel free. Personally, I'd like a closer look.'

He put away his binoculars, got up on all fours and scuttled forward for several yards. Frank followed him automatically, and found Tranter and Gannon and a couple of the others had done the same. The dervish host was in full view now, and that low surf-like booming was moving closer. Frank glanced round and caught an anxious lift of the eyebrows from Tranter as the fat man wriggled up beside him. He knew what Tranter was worried about: getting too far from the horses could be suicidal. The lancers were slow and vulnerable on foot, and any one of these lean tribesmen could run them down in less than a minute if they did not remount in time.

The lieutenant had thrown himself flat now at the very top of the sand ridge and, helmet off, was already peering over the lip. Without his helmet he looked boyish, a youth having a lark. Frank scrambled up beside him. They were directly in the path of the advancing army, a solid mass of men no more than six hundred yards away. The hum of chanting was like the noise from a gigantic hornets' nest, a soft thunder which grew in strength by the moment, crested, and broke into a roar. Drums were beating now, a harsh and urgent tattoo, and trumpets shrieking.

A corporal came cantering up from the direction of the British lines behind them, reined in and scrambled up to join them.

'Colonel Martin's compliments, sir, but you are to return to the zariba immediately. The others are already in.'

The lieutenant had his field glasses out again, and did not take his eyes off the advancing enemy to reply. 'Thank you, Corporal. My compliments to the Colonel. Tell him that I am watching the enemy's front and will return to the zariba shortly.'

The corporal hesitated, as if reluctant to take back such a breathtakingly insubordinate reply, but after a moment he muttered, 'Sir,' and slithered back down to his horse.

When he had gone, the lieutenant turned to Frank. 'You're Gray, aren't you?'

'Yes, sir.'

'You don't know me. Churchill, Fourth Hussars. Got myself attached to the Twenty-first so I could see a bit of this. Going to get more than I bargained for.' The lieutenant grinned, as if the presence of the dervish army beyond the ridge was the purest fun. 'We met last night, Gray, when you were looking for Major Herrick. I'd have liked a chat, but you seemed in a hurry.'

'Sorry, sir.'

'No matter. You and Cavendish were up on the Frontier, I hear. I was there myself, briefly, with the Malakand Field Force – punishing the natives, you know, for failing to recognise the benefits of Empire. Didn't do an ounce of good, obviously. You can't shoot down an entire way of life.'

Frank cleared his throat. He tried not to look at the advancing army. 'No, sir.'

Lt. Churchill turned his attention back to the host of men, closer now, their shields of rhinoceros- and elephant-hide clearly visible. Some carried double-edged swords, helmets and armour flashing in the sun. A great smear of dust rose against the azure sky above them. Four hundred yards.

'Magnificent, isn't it?' Churchill said. 'As splendid and barbaric as the Crusades. Where else could you see the past, rushing to its ruin against the future?'

Mick Gannon said, 'They're coming on fast, sir.'

'Then I suppose we should do our bit to stop them, shouldn't we? Independent fire, gentlemen, when you're ready.'

It was there again, that sense of otherworldliness. Frank brought the carbine to his shoulder and fired steadily, again and again, scarcely conscious of the banging of the other rifles around him and the tinkling of spent cartridge cases among the stones. Somewhere in that press of warriors men were falling, presumably, dead and dying and maimed, the tide of their fellows engulfing them as they went down. It was impossible to see any effect of their puny fire against such a multitude, unthinkable that such an engagement could make the slightest difference. And everyone knew it; Frank knew it, and Gannon, and Tranter, and even this odd lieutenant with his poetic turn of mind. Certainly the dervishes knew it. And yet it was inevitable that the two worlds would clash today, and one of them would be utterly destroyed, and this was the start of it.

There was a smacking and a buzzing in the air now, and puffs of smoke from black powder jetted from the massed ranks ahead of them. The stony soil on the forward slope of the ridge began to kick and flick up. A ricochet moaned. Three hundred yards.

'I think honour is satisfied, gentlemen. Shall we retire?' Churchill got to his feet in a leisurely fashion and walked back to his horse.

They cantered in a loose group back across the plain towards the safety of the zariba they had left only an hour or so before. Frank wondered if it had really grown hot in so short a time. As they came up to the thorn hedge he dropped back a little, reined in, looked back.

The first packed waves of dervishes breasted the sand ridge along a two mile front. For a second they seemed to pause there on the crest, bellowing defiance and brandishing their spears and swords, their trumpets braying and the roll of their drums shaking the air. Then the first shells came howling over, some of them clearly visible in the stark light, to burst in scything sprays of shrapnel.

105

Frank lost track of how long it went on after he got back inside the zariba. To him the impossible din was endless, deafening, flattening. Officers bellowed themselves hoarse calling the rifle volleys of the British Brigade: *ready . . . present . . . fire . . . ready . . .* until the weapons grew too hot to handle and were exchanged with the rifles of the reserves. Maxims chattered in typewriter rhythm. The naval guns on the steamers in the river hurled shells over the village and out into the packed masses until their advance was simply shredded to a halt. By the time the firing thinned at last, not one warrior had come closer than three hundred yards to the defences. Most had died so far out on the plain that they had never seen their enemy.

Frank found himself drawn towards the perimeter as the gunfire faded away. He could see little at first beyond the masses of infantry and the thorn hedge zariba. He focused on Jebel Surgham, the stony hill up which they had ridden just a couple of hours earlier. At its foot, and for thousands of yards across the front of the British position, he saw a swathe of untidy bundles of clothing, half-obscured by dust and smoke. Here and there something moved, a fallen horse reared its head or a shattered figure jerked. Now and then a marksman fired from within the zariba, careful shots finishing the last pitiful survivors. A barking of orders, a clatter of equipment, the rattle of hoofbeats and limbers as fresh ammunition was run up. But beneath these noises, a stunned silence flowed between the men, as if they were amazed and appalled at the slaughter they had made. To Frank too it seemed impossible that death on so biblical a scale could be so swiftly meted out.

'Darkie?' It was Gannon, striding after him between the tents. 'Shift yer arse back here, Darkie, will ye? We're moving.'

They rode out in lines of troops, four hundred and forty troopers and officers, the first time Frank had ever ridden with the whole regiment except on parade. He supposed he should be reassured they were in such strength, but instead he felt clumsy and awkward, boxed in by the formation they kept. He disliked the encumbrance of the bamboo lance as much as he had during this morning's patrol on Jebel Surgham. He couldn't settle. The battle was supposed to be all but over, with most of the surviving dervishes in retreat to the west, but he couldn't shake his nagging sense of unease.

They rode out towards Jebel Surgham once again. From here the carnage was all too visible, bodies and parts of bodies and discarded weapons scattered across acres of stained sand. The hot wind fluttered a bloody robe here, a tattered banner there. Carrion birds were already gathering in the sky and among the rocks. Beyond, straggling out for miles over the stony ground, ragged columns of injured and dazed survivors, stumbling south towards Omdurman. Frank wondered what they thought awaited them there. Through the wavering heat haze he could make out the ruined dome of the Mahdi's tomb in the distance. A dust pall still hung over the shattered shrine.

Someone shouted an order and the regiment halted.

'Why don't we charge?' a young trooper near Frank kept asking nervously, gesticulating at the retreating rabble. 'Isn't that what we're for? Lancers charge, don't they?'

Nobody answered him. Frank suspected that the thought of hacking into those broken stragglers sickened all the men, and that, like him, they hoped the order would not be given. It was not, and in a moment they were dismounted, the troopers using the halt to drink, adjust harnesses, check weapons. After a while a rider came in from the zariba behind them. Frank saw Colonel Martin speak to the messenger. He caught a glimpse of Cavendish in the knot of officers around the colonel, and perhaps Cavendish saw him, but Frank looked quickly away. In a few moments they were mounted again, and heading south-east, towards the Nile and the main route to Omdurman.

'Ye'll spike one of us with that fucking bargepole if ye're not careful.' Gannon rode up beside him and leaned from the saddle to adjust Frank's grip on the unfamiliar lance. 'For the love of God, take hold of it like this.'

Frank said, 'What's going on, Mick?'

'Kitchener'll march straight to Omdurman,' the Irishman grunted, still fiddling with Frank's lance. 'He'll want us to see the road's clear.'

'It won't be,' Frank said, looking ahead at the ochre ground trembling in the heat.

Gannon raised his head. 'Ye've that feeling too, have ye?'

They rode two or three miles south of the zariba before they halted again. A patrol set off, heading further south, and presently returned, trailing dust. To his right front Frank could see Colonel Martin conferring once again with his staff and with the patrol. The regiment moved off, riding for another twenty minutes or so. At length Gannon tapped Frank's arm and pointed ahead. A crowd of robed figures blocked their way, not three hundred yards distant. They halted.

A rider trotted up on Frank's other side and reined in.

'Corporal Gray, once again.' Churchill gave Frank an amused look. 'Oh, please don't salute, you might drop your lance, and then we'd all look foolish.' He nodded towards the clustered tribesmen. 'We missed the county hunt, but it seems we might have a bit of sport after all. What do you think?'

'They're Haddendowa, sir.'

'Which speaks for itself, yes.' The lieutenant squinted against the hard light. 'Cut Hicks to pieces, fourteen years ago, as I recall, and came close to doing the same to Wolseley. After today, they'd love to do it to us. Can't blame them.' He smiled suddenly. 'Funny thing, Corporal. Chatting away like chaps at a polo match, and we could leave our bones here. Makes you think of all the things you've left undone in life, doesn't it?'

Frank stared ahead. The dark figures were silent, watching them. It grew quiet, except for the jingling of harness as the horses tossed their heads, smelling danger. It was very hot.

Frank turned sharply to the officer. 'Could I beg a favour, sir?'

The young man tilted his head curiously. 'Ask away.'

'Would you have a notebook on you, sir?'

Churchill raised his eyebrows in surprise, but unbuttoned the flap of his tunic pocket and took out a leather-bound notebook and held it out to Frank. 'Please. Feel free.'

There was a silver propelling pencil in a loop at the back and Frank slid it out and scribbled on a blank page, tore it out and folded it over. He slipped the note into his pocket and handed the book back to the lieutenant.

'I'm very much obliged, sir.' He looked ahead at the dark line of the tribesmen. 'I just needed to write it.'

The young officer looked at him quizzically. 'I'm sure you'll be able to deliver your message in person, Corporal,' he said, quite gently. He drew himself up in the saddle. 'Let's talk again, if we get through this. Good luck to you, Gray.' He put out his hand and Frank took it. Churchill touched his horse and cantered off.

The troops wheeled left in response to a new command, and in a moment they were moving off, trotting east, across the front of the tribesmen. That seemed to galvanise them, for all at once a score of rifles exploded from their ranks. Frank saw a trooper a hundred yards ahead knocked from his mount, and then a horse went down screaming quite close, and another, still closer, was shot through the lungs and folded under its rider. An officer was galloping up the line, shouting. Frank heard someone – perhaps the galloping officer – bellow out, 'Why the blazes don't we charge the buggers?'

At that moment the bugle sounded *right wheel into line*. As Frank brought his horse round something cracked past and beside him he heard Gannon gasp.

'Mick?'

'Some cheeky fucker's winged me,' Gannon protested indignantly, and held up his left arm. His sleeve was torn and a red stain was spreading on the material.

Lt. Smyth, on his other side, called, 'Fall out, Corporal Gannon.'

'Be buggered if I will, sir!' Gannon cried, outraged.

'Gannon—'

'But it's a scratch, sir. Look, left hand. Nothing broken.'

'Do as you're told, man,' Smyth snapped. 'Go to the rear.'

'D'you think I'd miss this, for such a pinprick? The regiment's first charge?'

Frank grabbed Gannon's right arm and silenced him. Fury dark in his face, the Irishman gave way at last. He started to back his horse out of the line. Frank thrust the folded note at him. 'If I don't get back, Mick, see this gets sent.'

Gannon took the folded note, frowned at it. He might have spoken, but then there was no longer time to talk, for the entire line was bounding forward and away with a roar, lance points dipping, and Frank was with them, his horse grunting and stretching out, Gannon's forlorn figure dwindling behind them and the dark-robed tribesmen looming closer.

Frank could see almost at once that they had been tricked, and he knew every man in the line could see it too: behind the screen of warriors was a gulley three or four feet deep, massed with armed men. In this dead ground the warriors had been invisible. There was no possibility of stopping now, and the troopers surged over the lip of the depression at a wild gallop, and into a mêlée of steel and gunfire and grinning, contorted faces.

Frank angled the nine-foot lance toward a bearded tribesman with a rhino-hide shield, missed him by a yard, but accidentally hit another warrior through the eye with an impact which tore the lance out of his hands. He struggled to draw his sabre, his horse dancing in frenzy. Beside him a trooper was dragged down and vanished screaming beneath a flashing of blades. He caught a glimpse of Lt Churchill far to his right where the press was thinner, coolly firing a blockish Mauser pistol down at a man trying to hamstring his horse. Closer, Major Herrick, roaring like a bull, was fighting from horseback with naked sabre.

Frank swung his own sabre at the face of a man in a blue robe who sprang up at his knee, saw the man go down. Two yards away Tranter was struggling to disengage his lance from a screaming warrior who was impaled on it. A riderless horse trailing intestines cannoned into Frank, almost unseating him. He regained his balance, struck back at someone who poked at him with a spear, hearing the blade chop into either wood or bone. A press of men all around, shrieking, hacking, swinging blades. Spurts of black smoke. A young subaltern riding with his right hand flapping, almost severed, jetting blood. Crole-Wyndham, the regiment's second-in-command, bare headed, fighting on foot with pistol and sword.

A figure rode up fast behind Frank and he made to cut back at it, but at the last minute saw that it was Cavendish, revolver drawn. 'Frank—'

'Leave me be!'

'Frank, you young fool, listen to me! Haddid's here! I've seen him!'

'What?'

'Mullah Haddid, for God's sake! From Gul Shah's house. He's alive!' Cavendish fired his revolver across Frank's saddle at a tribesman swinging a two-handed sword and the man sat down on the ground and folded sideways.

'He's there, Frank!' Cavendish gestured wildly with the revolver. 'Do you see?'

Frank looked. Under the far bank of the nullah a small group of dervishes was gathered around a figure with matted hair. Mullah Haddid seemed shrunken, twisted, one arm bent into a claw, but it was the same man. Frank remembered the rifle bucking in his hands, its muzzle pressed into the man's body. He remembered the mullah whirling away as the shot hit him. His survival seemed so incredible that for a moment Frank simply stared.

A thrown spear clipped the pommel of his saddle and his horse capered in fright and he heard Cavendish shouting at him. 'Frank, we have to get out of here!'

A sergeant with his face hanging from the front of his skull blundered blindly across in front of them. A trooper, his body split open, lay flapping and shrieking on the earth a few feet away. But a few men – bloody, helmetless, swordless – had reached the far side of the nullah and were urging their horses desperately up the bank and to relative safety. A Haddendowa warrior with frizzed hair appeared at Frank's hip, swung his empty rifle as a club. Frank jabbed the point of his sword into the man's face but the swinging rifle came down across his chest and drove the breath out of him, knocking him out of the present.

Cavendish gripped his arm and steadied him. 'Follow me, Corporal. That's an order.'

Half dazed, Frank shook him off. 'Fuck your orders.'

He wheeled his frightened horse and spurred forward towards the knot of tribesmen around the mullah, raising the sword. He had no clear idea what he planned to do, but the sight of Haddid maddened him. Cavendish swore but followed him, firing as he rode. Frank saw a man throw up his hands and fall, then beside him a warrior grabbed Cavendish's bridle and Cavendish shot him through the body, and then the revolver was empty. Fat Tranter reappeared from somewhere, his lance free at last. He rode past Frank, bawling curses, and a man rolled under his horse, slashed upward, and the animal screamed and reared and Tranter went down. Frank kicked his own horse forward in time to see Cavendish dragged from the saddle and men hacking at him, and then he was directly in front of the mullah and for a second caught a gleam of recognition in the man's eyes. Frank cut at him with the sabre but a warrior blocked the blow and another rose with an ancient flintlock and exploded it directly into the chest of Frank's horse, and he was out of the saddle and he tasted hot dust and blood and as he rolled he saw their white eyes and the sun on their blades.

106

Outside Shepheard's Hotel a passing horse-drawn omnibus had clipped a fruitseller's stand and bright oranges rolled in the street. The fruitseller was berating the omnibus driver while urchins scuttled in the dust retrieving fruit and stashing it in folds of their robes. Traffic had backed up around the square and an Egyptian policeman was advancing with massive dignity to the scene.

Grace watched it all from her first floor window. She was sorry for the fruit vendor, whom she knew slightly; she passed him every morning on her walks into the old city. But still the little drama was a distraction, and she was grateful for that. She didn't want to look at the *Times of Egypt* again. It had arrived with her breakfast as always at seven thirty, freshly ironed, carrying the scent of her warm bread rolls, but now it lay on her writing desk beside her correspondence from Welti, soft and crumpled from repeated reading. She knew that if her glance fell on the newspaper she would pick it up and read it through yet again, as though the information she wanted might only need more careful study to be discovered. So she kept staring out of the window, as the Egyptian policemen was joined by a British sergeant shouting as he tried to clear a way through the chaos for his officer's cab.

At last Grace heard the sound outside. She wondered afterwards if part of her had been trying to ignore it, for when she turned she could hear it quite clearly over the shouting from the street. It was the uneven jingle of a man's cavalry spurs as he limped down the passage towards her door. Without waiting for him to knock she walked to the door and pulled it open.

'Good morning, Major Macallan.'

He stood in the doorway in his splendid uniform, curiously rigid. Something cold touched the base of her spine and trickled into her belly.

'Perhaps I'd better come in, Grace.'

He walked past her across the room to the window, and stood where she had stood, staring out, his peaked cap tucked under his arm. She closed the door and leaned on it. The room seemed suddenly stifling to her and she found it difficult to breathe. The noise from outside shrank away. The ceiling fan hummed and clicked.

He flicked a hand towards the newspaper. 'I see you know about Omdurman.'

'Light casualties,' she said, with desperate brightness. 'That's what it says. Very light casualties.'

'Among our chaps, yes. Awful carnage on the other side, I'm afraid.'

'I don't care about the other side.'

'No. I imagine not.' He faced her. He looked ten years older than when she had last seen him. He was holding something out to her, a scrap of paper. 'Grace, I don't know any other way to do this.'

She lost a minute or two, and was never afterwards able to find those moments in her memory. When she came to herself again, she was sitting in an armchair close to the window, her eyes fixed on the scrap of paper held in her hand. A leaf torn from a notebook, folded, and with

426

her name scribbled on the outside. She wondered irrelevantly what sort of a notebook it was; expensive cream laid paper, by the look of it. Had it been bound in calf skin, that notebook? Frank wouldn't have an expensive book like that, she was quite sure, and yet this was his handwriting. She wondered from whom he had borrowed the notebook, and whether the owner was upset that Frank had torn out a page. She would have been, if it had been hers.

Macallan was standing in front of her. He was in the act of pouring a glass of water for her. 'Corporal Gray rejoined the Twenty-first in the zariba the night before the battle. That's two days ago now. I got word of him only then, but didn't want to tell you until it was confirmed.' He stood with the glass of water in his hand. He seemed to have forgotten he had poured it for her.

She touched the paper with her fingertip. Dried blood formed a dark map in one corner of the note and glued it together. She disliked that. It wasn't the sensation itself; it was a distant memory of sitting at a table on a sunlit afternoon, with a scrap of fabric between her fingers. That had also been stiff with English blood from the Sudan, she recalled. Billy Rossiter's blood. Mrs Rossiter had sat watching her, just as Major Macallan was watching her now, she remembered that too. *Don't you go falling in love with no soldier, my girl. They'll bring you nothing but grief.*

Macallan was speaking again. She supposed she ought to pay attention.

'I can't tell you how sorry I am, my dear girl.' He put the glass of water down on the desk and knotted and released his fists. 'We don't seem to have lost above one hundred men out of all that number, and that he should be one of them . . .' He stopped talking.

She glanced up at him. 'Tell me, please.'

'Tell you what?'

'Well, everything you know, of course.' She smiled at his slowness. 'You will have made enquiries, Major. I know how thorough you are.'

He looked down at his hands. 'The details are somewhat distressing.'

'But I should like to know how it happened, you see.'

'I . . . I'm sure you don't want to hear—'

'Tell me what happened!' shrieked a madwoman in the room. Startled, Grace looked around before she realised that the madwoman was herself.

Major Macallan drew himself up, in the manner of a soldier delivering a report. 'The body was found the evening of the battle. The second of September. They weren't sure at first who it was. A corporal, but . . .'

'Mutilated.'

Her directness made him flinch. 'Savages, you see . . .'

'Go on.'

'The note was on his . . . body. But nothing more of importance. Everything else had been lost, or carried away. It was the letter that identified him.' He paused. 'It was quite a sharp engagement. Twenty or so lancers lost their lives, I gather. Many more wounded. Some bodies have still not been recovered. Never will be, I suppose. The desert. Jackals, and so forth. Vultures.'

His voice trailed away into silence. She picked up the note again, folded it fully open and stared at it again.

'Would you like to know what it says?' she asked, brightly. 'I know you won't have looked.'

'That's not necessary.'

'I shall tell you all the same. It says: "*Grace, I shall love you till the last moment of my life.*"'

He closed his eyes for a moment and opened them again. 'Whatever will you do now, Grace?'

She folded the note. 'Does it matter?'

107

'Like Christ and the two fucking thieves.' Tranter coughed, a harsh, wet cough, and spat. 'All we need now's a bleeding centurion.'

Drifting in and out of the world, Frank couldn't make sense of this. It irritated him that he didn't understand, and his irritation brought him back a little. His head was forced forward by the stake which was bound like a yoke across his shoulders. He tried to move and a sharp pain shot up into his skull from the back of his neck. His hands were bound numbingly tight to the stake. Pictures began to form in his mind, fragmented pictures of himself stumbling over a stony plain, with a thousand feet slapping the dust all around him, silent men dragging injured comrades, or letting them down at last and shambling on.

Somewhere in this nightmare he had seen Gifford. He remembered that now. Of all people, Gifford, darting in and out of his delirium. His brother was altered in some way, but those wide eyes were unmistakable, curious and alert as they gazed at him. Gifford, for God's sake. At least he had regained enough clarity to know this was insane.

And just as insane was this talk of thieves, Christ, a centurion. It nagged at him, and yet he knew he ought to recognise the reference. He rolled his head a fraction and could just see Tranter, bound to his own yoke. The fat man caught his eye and jerked his head towards Cavendish, tied between them.

'See, Darkie? He's on the big cross, and we're on the little ones.' Tranter coughed and spat again, viscous blood hanging from his mouth. 'You can tell he's the fucking officer. Beggin' your pardon, sir.'

Frank tried to answer, but his dry lips cracked and he gave up. He wondered where the fat man found his spirit. A spear wound between Tranter's ribs on the right side had punctured his lung. His tunic was crusted with blood, and how he had survived the march was a mystery to Frank. He wasn't sure how he had survived it himself. But at least now he got the joke.

'Do you read your Bible, Tranter?' Cavendish whispered, his voice hoarse.

'Me mother read it to me, sir. Now I hear it in me head. Heard a good bit of it today.'

'That's good, Tranter. Very good. But best not talk.'

Frank glanced over to the guards at the edge of the grove, two of them, their rifles propped between their knees. They had pulled the loose folds of their robes over their heads and the evening sun threw their faces into deep shadow. They had not stirred since the ragged band had stopped here an hour or so ago. Frank guessed they were sunk in a coma of shock and weariness not much less profound than his own. He could understand that, if these men had been out on the Kerreri Plain. He could still hear the awful rolling fire of the British and Sudanese infantry within the zariba, on and on like a gigantic surf. He could still see the shells hurled up into the clear sky to fall and burst and sweep away whole families, clans, communities which had survived unchanged since Abraham. *You can't shoot down an entire way of life.* That's what the young subaltern, Churchill, had said only that morning. Frank wondered if he'd say the same if he had stumbled through the searing day among proud tribesmen reduced to a broken rabble, maimed men with numbed minds, lacking the energy even for hatred.

'Frank?' Cavendish whispered. 'Frank? Can you talk?'

Frank licked his cracked lips. 'Leave me in peace, for Christ's sake. We're all going to die anyway.'

'I want you to know—'

'If you want forgiveness, ask God. You'll get to see him soon enough, if you're lucky.'

'Now, now, my lads,' Tranter chided. 'None of that talk. Ransom. That'll be it. They don't take prisoners else, the Fuzzy-Wuzzies. It's ransom. You'll see.'

Frank didn't speak. He knew Tranter didn't believe they would be ransomed. He lifted his head as far as he could. It was growing dark. The dervishes were camped a hundred yards away in a hollow of land beyond a screen of acacia scrub. Frank could see the flicker of a dozen campfires through the bushes, though he doubted these broken survivors had anything to cook. They had lit the fires as warmth against the chill of the desert night, or perhaps to ward off a greater darkness. How many of them? A thousand? Fewer? There must be bands like this scattered all over Sudan, stumbling back to the *goz* country in the east, to the women without husbands, to the herds with no one to tend them. Frank could hear the murmur of voices, the moan and babble of injured men among them.

He twisted his head against the rough wooden yoke, but he could not move far enough to see the sky. He regretted that. To gaze just once more on the sweep of the desert stars, to sense one last time the measure of his own insignificance: that would have made losing everything more endurable. At least he had written to Grace. God knew what she would make of his note, but he had sent it, and there it was. Perhaps it would bring some finality for her. He could do no more.

'Only thing I'm sorry about,' Tranter breathed, his voice a whisper in the gathering dusk, 'I didn't go down fighting back to back with Mick. Been through hell and high water, Mick Gannon and me. But when we got in amongst it with them savages, I couldn't find him nowhere. I suppose he went down with the others.'

'Gannon's safe,' Frank said, glad he could offer the man some comfort. 'He wasn't in the charge.'

'What's that you say?'

'He was wounded before it started. Just a graze. Smyth sent him to the rear. He didn't want to go, but he went.'

'Mick's safe, Darkie? You wouldn't be lying to me, now?'

'It's true. I was next to him in the line. Smyth sent him back.'

'Well, that wouldn't please old Mick,' Tranter said with a wheeze of laughter. 'Oh, no. Our Mick'd be spitting chips at that one!'

And quite suddenly Tranter began to cry, a small, desolate, animal sound in the darkness.

108

Frank drifted back into the world. Perhaps he had not been out of it for long, but long enough for him to have the most vivid dream. He had seen Gifford again, moving around him, Gifford with his wide inquisitive eyes and his maddening questions, and yet – and even in the dream this had puzzled him – it was a Gifford transformed somehow into a skinny young dervish, complete with patched jibba.

Frank came fully awake with a jerk. It was full night, but the grove was washed with starlight strong enough for the palms to throw crooked claws of shadow. The clearing was very quiet. He knew something had changed, but it took him a moment to register that the guards were gone, and that this was strange. He twisted his neck urgently and could see himself, Cavendish and Tranter silhouetted by starlight looking just as Tranter had described: Christ and the two thieves. And another shadow, a smaller one, moving, just behind him. Something touched his arms, crawled towards his wrists, something living, and a spurt of cold terror flooded his stomach. He wrenched his head around, but could not turn far enough to see.

Then, impossibly, his arms fell free of their bonds and swung down to his side, numb and nerveless dead weights. He stared at them stupidly, at the rawhide strips which had bound him to the stake, hanging loose now from his wrists, their cut ends unravelling and dropping to the ground. He straightened his spine a little, tentatively, his back and shoulders screaming at him, and the yoke fell away, and as it did so Gifford moved in front of him, his finger to his lips.

'Quiet, *Feringhee.*'

'Yussuf?'

'We must move quickly. I have told the guards they are called to eat in the camp, but they will soon discover that I lied.' Yussuf stooped and sawed at the bonds at Frank's feet. 'I have found a horse, *Feringhee.* A fine horse, wandering in the desert. There are many such, lost, their masters dead.'

'Good, Yussuf.' Frank frantically worked his hands and wrists, forcing the circulation back into them, ignoring the agony of it. 'That's good.'

'It is yonder, in the bushes, my fine horse.'

Frank kicked his feet loose. 'Good, good.' He tried to stand. He was as weak as a kitten. 'Cut these men free.'

'No time, *Feringhee.* Come.' Yussuf raised his head like an animal scenting the air. 'They are here already. Quickly.'

Frank hesitated. Yussuf grabbed his arm and dragged at him.

Above him, Cavendish hissed, 'Run, Frank. Don't be a fool.'

Frank took the knife from Yussuf, fumbling it in his numbed hands, and slashed at the bonds around Cavendish's feet, the only ones he could reach. But he could hear them now, and see them too, two or three men, coming through the bushes, a burning torch held aloft. Frank took Yussuf by the shoulders and shoved him bodily into the dense shadow of the scrub. He found his fallen yoke and fumbled it

431

back over his shoulders, leaned back against the palm trunk in his former position, his head hanging. They came into the clearing, the two guards with Remington rifles held ready across their bodies. They stood respectfully aside for the third man. The fluttering light from the torch fell over the shrivelled right arm, the matted hair and wild eyes.

Haddid limped up to Cavendish, holding the burning torch high in his left hand. 'Dost Khan,' he murmured, lovingly. 'That was the name, was it not? How you fooled us! The respectable merchant from Peshawar. I didn't think that God would grant me the good fortune of this meeting. We should both give him thanks. Come, thank him, Dost Khan.'

He touched the flame to Cavendish's face and Cavendish screamed. Frank breathed hard, gripping the stake across his shoulders. Haddid smiled, lowered the torch and turned to him.

'And Daud Emin. What a memory I have, you see? But then I would not be likely to forget you. Such a marksman! I have proof of that, have I not? There is still a hole under my shoulder you could get your fist into.' He held up the claw of his right arm, gnarled like a thorn branch. 'You need good eyes to be a marksman, Daud Emin, do you not?'

Haddid moved his face closer, so that Frank could smell the grease on his body, and then edged the torch towards Frank's eyes. The heat shrivelled his eyebrows and hair. Frank smelled the stench of it.

Tranter roared suddenly, 'I told you we'd get a fucking centurion! Got your vinegar and your sponge, you filthy savage?'

Haddid took half a pace back. He signalled curtly to the guards. One of them walked over to Tranter, drawing a knife as he went.

'Ain't you got a lance, wog?' Tranter bellowed at the man, cackling with crazy laughter. 'It says in the Good Book you're supposed to—'

The guard slung his rifle across his back to free his hands, reached up and cut Tranter's throat. Frank swung the stake like a quarterstaff against Haddid's body, and the mullah lurched backwards towards Cavendish. Cavendish twisted convulsively against his bindings, flung out his freed legs and locked them around Haddid's head and neck. The guard nearest to Frank lifted his rifle but Frank knocked the barrel up and then drove the end of the stake into the man's face. He wrenched the Remington out of his hands, reversed it, fired into the man's chest. The explosion was blinding in the little grove and in the light of it Frank saw Tranter's body still jerking and the guard who had killed him struggling to unsling his rifle. Frank knelt, scrabbled open the leather pouches of the dead man's bandolier, scooped up brass-cased cartridges, thumbed one into the breech. The second guard fired and something like a bullwhip slashed Frank across the left side, knocking him sideways and onto his hip. But he had fired too, almost without realising it, and the guard was already flailing back against Tranter's legs and sliding to the ground.

Frank stood up, surprised to find he could do so, automatically re-loading, pivoting back to face Haddid. He was in time to see Cavendish give one last desperate heave with his locked legs, and to hear the mullah's neck snap like a stick. Cavendish let the body slump to the ground.

'Used to be able to hang from a beam by my knees,' Cavendish said weakly. 'Ever tell you that?'

Frank stepped to him, groping for Yussuf's knife in his belt. 'Yes, you told me that.' He reached up for Cavendish's wrists.

'Leave it,' Cavendish breathed, his mouth almost at Frank's ear as he stretched up. 'No time. I'm done, anyway.'

Frank closed his mind and hacked through the bindings on Cavendish's right hand, felt them part, started on the left.

But there were other sounds behind him now, shouting from the camp, the slap of running feet. He risked a glance over his shoulder. The fallen torch lit the clearing in a weird dancing light. He sawed frantically at the bindings.

Yussuf burst through the bushes astride a white Arab mare. 'Come, *Feringhee*! Come now!'

'Get out of here, for God's sake!' Cavendish pushed Frank away hard with his boot so that he stumbled back, dropping the knife.

Frank stared up at him as he hung from the yoke, one hand still lashed to it. The running feet were very close now. Frank gathered up the rifle, stepped back, tangled his hand in the horse's rough mane, his eyes locked on Cavendish's eyes. He pulled himself up behind the boy, aware for the first time of the pain in his side, sharp and growing sharper. He cocked the rifle. Cavendish used his free hand to rip aside what was left of his tunic and bare his pale belly in the torchlight. He lifted his chin defiantly and with his forefinger he touched the old bullet scar below his ribs.

'Just a little higher than last time, Corporal,' Cavendish commanded in a clear voice, 'if you'd be so good.'

Frank levelled the rifle, hugged the cool butt to his cheek. He took the pressure on the trigger, let his breath out in a long sigh. Fired.

109

Grace leaned on the ship's rail, feeling the engines thrum through the steelwork under her hands. Above her the red and white *Messageries Maritimes* flag snapped in the freshening breeze. Alexandria was slipping astern, a clutter of grey naval shipping and russet sails in the harbour, and beyond these the ramparts and white minarets. For the moment the wake's long arc still tethered her to Egypt.

'Isn't that a dolphin?' Alec pointed. 'Yes, I'm sure it is. Do you see?'

Reluctantly she took her gaze from the receding shore and followed his outstretched arm. Directly below them, fleet black shadows wove at impossible speed through blue water.

'I don't believe I've ever seen one before,' he said. 'Do you know, they can be trained, like dogs? It's true. I've heard of dolphins guiding ships through dangerous channels. Why do you think they should do that?'

She watched the dolphins. Each time she thought they had gone they would magically reappear on the edge of her vision – a triangle of black fin, a sleek flank flashing in sunlight – and each time her spirit would lift. It confused her, this small stab of joy. Everything confused her: the loveliness of the sunlit sea in the evening, the blue wind flapping in her face and the prickle of spray on her skin. She should not be able to take pleasure in these things, but she couldn't seem to help it.

'Would you like me to prattle on indefinitely about marine mammals?' Alec asked. 'I'm quite capable of it. In fact I have an endless store of inanities about cetaceans. Or shall I just shut up and leave you in peace, which is probably what any sensible chap would have done ages ago?'

She smiled and rested her hand on his sleeve. 'You can talk as long as you like, Alec.'

She was glad he was here, which was also confusing, because she had not expected to be. She had spent the last two weeks in her room at Shepheard's, or so they had told her, while the meal trays and the unread newspapers piled up. Most days she had not even troubled to get out of bed, though she had no clear recollection of deciding to stay there. Of deciding anything. When she had first heard that Alec was coming she had been indifferent, apathetic. But now she was grateful that he was here, taking charge, talking nonsense about dolphins, quietly organising everything.

She became aware that he had dropped his cheerful manner and was looking critically at her.

'You know, Grace, you look bloody awful.'

'Why, thank you.'

'I know one thing, there'll be a case of Dom Perignon on the way to that Major Macallan for cabling me the way he did.'

'He was very kind.'

'Of course he was. He was in love with you, poor chap, not that I blame him. Pretty well everyone in Cairo must have been, I imagine. The pale and pining lady at Shepheard's Hotel.'

'I couldn't seem to get out.' She stared down at the churning sea. The dolphins were still following, darting through the foam. 'I couldn't seem to decide what to do next.'

'You don't have to decide anything for a while yet.' He braced himself against the rail, the wind in his face. 'We'll be in Marseille in a couple of days, and Paris a day or two after that. Within a week you'll be back home at Cumver, and perhaps things will begin to look . . . well, different, anyway.'

She glanced up at him. He had caught some Egyptian sun across the bridge of his nose, bringing out the freckles on his fair skin, and this made him look for a moment like an earnest schoolboy.

'You're very kind, Alec,' she said firmly, anxious to make a statement of it and not merely a conventional compliment. 'You are a very kind man.'

He peered at the horizon, narrowing his eyes as if he had suddenly spotted something there. 'It's just that we've got work to do, Grace, that's all. You have to be strong so we can tackle it.'

'Do I?'

'I don't imagine you're going to stop writing. Not you.'

'I'm not sure I've given it a thought.'

'You will. And remember, Grace, you don't have to be poor to fight for justice. Think what you could achieve from your new position. Good Lord, you could set up your own newspaper, if you wanted. It would do you good to pick up the cudgels again.'

She gazed out to sea. Had she really not thought about it? She didn't believe she had. She thought about it now, about filthy Mr Calloway, the smell of newsprint and the rumble of the presses in the basement, about clandestine meetings in hotel lobbies where Alec would introduce her to the great, and to the good, and to the downright subversive. In particular she thought about the thrill of seeing the result in print under her own name, and the storms of protest it always provoked. That had all meant so much to her such a short time ago. Was she really so changed that it could never mean anything again?

She said, 'They say there were fewer than a hundred British dead at Omdurman, and something like twelve thousand of theirs. Not to mention fifteen or sixteen thousand injured, crippled and maimed.'

He stiffened, and she knew that her change of tack made him uncomfortable. 'It's damnably bad luck, Grace . . . what happened. Worse than bad luck.'

'That's what Major Macallan said. Bad luck. One hundred dead, and Frank has to be one of them. But I think of those twelve thousand dervishes sometimes, too.'

He looked at her warily, uncertain where this was going.

'There must be twelve thousand women out there somewhere,' she said, 'cooking at campfires or giving orphaned children the breast, or trying to herd cattle and build huts and cut crops with no men to help. Twelve thousand women whose men will never come home to them.' She turned to face him. 'Just think of that, Alec. All those thousands of women who all feel the pain I'm feeling. You'd not think there was room for such desolation in the world, and for it still to go on turning. And yet it does, doesn't it?'

He cleared his throat. 'Yes, Grace, it does.'

'How do those women manage, do you think?'

'I imagine they get on with it, Grace, the poor devils.' He kept his eyes on the horizon and spoke with unusual firmness, almost harshly. 'I imagine they make what they can of life. Just as we do.'

She gazed astern. Through the darkening air she could see lights springing on in distant Alexandria. The coastline was no more than a mauve smudge on the horizon now, fading as she watched.

PART TWELVE
Egypt and England, December 1898

110

Cairo's December rains had turned the streets into a slurry of mud. A thin man made his way slowly between the dripping stalls of the market which had sprung up outside the barracks gate, past carts selling rugs, spices, curios, curved daggers in red leather sheaths. The stranger was feeling his way with a stick which did not look much more solid than he was himself, and he took care, like an old man to whom a fall might be a serious matter.

But he was not old. A few of the stallholders noticed this, and saw too the rags of uniform he wore beneath the filthy blanket thrown over his shoulders. From beneath their sodden awnings they watched him tap his way up the alley towards the gateway arch.

Inside the guardhouse a sergeant with a brick-red face was seated behind a table, talking to a sentry who stood, contrary to orders, just inside the door. The sentry leaned on his rifle, nodding as he listened. The rain had darkened his waterproof cape. It was dim in the hut, and an old oil stove struggled to warm the air, but succeeded only in filling the small space with paraffin fumes. The flashes of the 21st Lancers shone on the sergeant's shoulder and his solar topee with its padded neck flap sat on the desk before him.

'So I told her,' he was saying, 'that if she wants to marry a bloke as has no prospects, then it's her lookout, see?'

The sentry was not much interested in the fortunes of the sergeant's distant daughter. He had heard the story more than once – more than twice, in fact – but it was marginally less uncomfortable in here than out in the rain, and so he nodded again, sympathetically.

'I told her she'd best not come running to me when it all goes belly-up,' the sergeant continued. Then he stopped, as beyond the sentry's shoulder he saw a thin man with a stick tap his way past the door. The sergeant stood up with a clatter. 'Oy! Mohammed! Where the fuck d'you think you're going? Froggett, stop that man.'

But the thin man did not need to be stopped. He had halted as soon as he heard the voices. Trooper Froggett grabbed his rifle and came bustling out of the guard hut. He made to shove the newcomer back out into the alleyway, but then his jaw dropped and he stared wide-eyed at the man before him.

'Well, I'll be damned.'

'What's the matter with you, Froggett?' The sergeant shoved back his chair and came striding out into the rain. He gripped the thin stranger's shoulder and turned him roughly so that the blanket slipped down into the mud. The sergeant stepped back so abruptly that he collided with the doorframe. 'Fuck me.'

'Hello, Sergeant Clough,' Frank said. 'Still having trouble reading the heliograph?'

Colonel Crole-Wyndham paced across to the wall map, and stood pretending to look at it with his hands crossed behind his back. Frank stayed seated in the hardback chair he had been given. He knew Crole-Wyndham was trying to cover his astonishment, as if to betray the scale of his surprise might lessen his dignity.

'Three months?' He swung back to Frank. 'More than three months! It's bloody miraculous, Gray, that's what it is.'

'Yes, sir.'

'I thought I was lucky enough. They shot my horse under me in the charge, but I got through without a scratch. But your story is something else altogether. Ever hear of anything like that, Teddy?'

'No, sir,' the adjutant replied from his desk. 'It's quite extraordinary, sir.'

'Tell me again how it happened.'

'The boy Yussuf took me to his village, sir,' Frank repeated. 'When the wound became infected, his people took care of me.'

'Incredible. And after the drubbing we gave them at Omdurman.'

'Yussuf was Ja'alin, sir. The Ja'alin didn't have any sympathy with the Khalifa. He was forced labour, with a dozen others from the village. Most of them didn't come back.'

'You almost didn't come back yourself, judging by the state of you. You must have been pretty far gone.'

'I was half-dead most of the time, sir, and after that too weak to do anything about it. I tried to get them to send a message, but they would never do it. I think they wanted to be sure I'd live. They were afraid of reprisals if I turned up dead in their village.'

'Well, they did the right thing by you, Gray. This boy especially. Where is he now?'

'He's in lodgings, not far from here.'

'I'll see he's rewarded.'

'He doesn't want a reward, sir. Not money.'

'What then?'

'He wants to work on the railway, sir.'

'The railway, by Jove!'

'It's his one dream. Give him a chance, sir, and he'll probably be running the Sudan Military in five years.'

'Make a note of that, Teddy, would you? Oh, and go and find yourself a cup of tea for half an hour. I'd like a quiet word with Gray here.'

'Sir.' The adjutant gathered his papers and withdrew.

When he had gone, Crole-Wyndham said, 'We might do better than tea, I think.' He took a bottle of Glenmorangie from his desk drawer, poured two glasses. 'I've got the MO's report here, Gray. He says you could make a full recovery in time, but he recommends a discharge. You should take it, of course. You've earned it, and you'll be no more use to us for a while.'

Frank swallowed. 'Thank you, sir.'

'That's settled, then.' Crole-Wyndham gave one of the whiskies to Frank and lifted his own. 'Here's to returning from the dead.'

Frank had not touched alcohol for months and the spirit was raw in his mouth, but it gave him strength.

The colonel wiped his moustache with a flick of his forefinger, a brisk and practised habit. 'You were captured with Cavendish?'

'Yes, sir.'

'How did he meet his end?'

'He was shot, sir.' Frank looked into his glass. 'I'm satisfied he did not suffer.'

'That's something, I suppose. Brilliant chap, Cavendish.' Crole-Wyndham moved his mouth to one side. 'Brilliant, but flawed, or so I'm given to understand.'

'I wouldn't know about that, sir.'

'You were fond of him?'

Frank looked at the Colonel. 'He was like a father to me, sir.'

'Quite, quite. I see.' Awkwardly, Crole-Wyndham refilled their glasses. 'And Tranter was the third man, poor chap. Cavendish, Tranter, and you. We thought Gannon was the third one taken, but obviously it was his body they found in the *khor*. Mistook it for yours.'

'That's the only part I don't understand, sir. I thought Corporal Gannon had gone to the rear.'

'Disobeyed Lt. Smyth's order, it seems. Couldn't bear to be left out of the charge. I don't blame him; I might have done the same in his place. The first charge ever made by the Twenty-first, and it'll probably be the last. But that insubordination cost Corporal Gannon his life. He was dreadfully cut about, which was why they thought his body was yours.' The colonel sipped his drink. 'Also, there was the matter of your letter, found on him.'

'I gave it to him, sir. I thought he had more chance than I did.'

Colonel Crole-Wyndham gazed out of the window. Out on the parade ground, Frank could hear a sergeant-major bawling at a squad, his voice made small by distance.

'Your note was passed on to Miss Dearborn, Gray. Don't know whether that was a kind thing to do, but we felt she should have it. Having met her, I thought she could . . . handle it.'

'You met her?' Frank frowned. 'You met Grace?'

'Yes, I suppose you wouldn't know that. She came here.'

'To Cairo?'

'To this very office on one occasion. Looking for you. Remarkable young woman. Remarkable.'

It came to Frank then that something was troubling Colonel Crole-Wyndham. He could not guess what it was, so he said nothing and waited.

The colonel pushed out his lips thoughtfully. 'I felt bad about it, having to see to it that she was informed of your death. Your . . . supposed death. She was so very determined to find you.' He let a few moments pass, and then came to a decision. He put his whisky down firmly, slid a newspaper from a tray on his desk and held it out to Frank. 'Damn it all, Gray, you can't blame her. The poor girl thought you were dead. We all thought you were dead.'

Frank took the paper. It was a month-old copy of *The Times* of London, folded open at the Engagements column. He read it in silence. Read it again, and then again, until finally the words became understandable.

He said, 'I need to send a telegram, sir.'

'Look at the date, man. They were to be married yesterday. I cabled London this morning to check that it had actually happened, but I'm afraid it's true. I'm sorry.'

'But I have to—'

'Gray, a cable from you couldn't do you any good now, but it could do a great deal of harm. Think about that.'

Frank thought about it. He put the paper aside and got unsteadily to his feet. 'I want to go home, sir.'

'You're not fit enough for that.'

'I want my discharge, sir, and I want to go home.'

Colonel Crole-Wyndham sighed. 'Very well. I suppose it's the least we can do for you.' He paused. 'I'm most dreadfully sorry, Gray. But if it's any kind of consolation . . .'

'It isn't. Sir.'

'Face facts, man.' The colonel's shoulders went back. 'You're a corporal in the cavalry. She's a very rich young lady. And she's married a lord. Sometimes these things turn out for the best.'

'This hasn't.' Frank gripped the back of the chair so that his knuckles whitened. 'Not yet, it hasn't.'

111

Frank begged a lift from a builder's van, and sat in the back among sawn timber and drums of nails. He had the man drop him off at the bend in the lane, and waited until the cart had clattered away out of sight, the driver waving cheerfully over his shoulder. Then he slipped through a gap in the estate wall and into the leafless beech woods on the flanks of Cumver Hill.

He made his way slowly up through the aisles of trees, stopping every few minutes to lean on the stick and recover his strength. The pain had come back with the strain of travel, a sharp, jabbing pain in his side, but the leaf mould was soft underfoot and the damp winter air was like a wet cloth on his face. It took him a long time, but at last the cottage was in sight. Smoke rose from the chimney through the trees, and light burned in the front room. A few more steps and he was standing by the door. He raised his hand to knock, but Mrs Rossiter must have heard his stick clacking on the flagstones, for she pulled the door sharply open.

'What's your business?' she demanded. 'I don't give to beggars . . .' She backed away from the door, her face working. 'Oh, Christ.'

'I'm not a ghost,' Frank told her. 'Not quite.'

But she kept moving backwards, her hand to her mouth, until she collided with the edge of the table, where she stopped. She stared at him for long moments, and then her control seemed to come back all at once. She stepped past him and shut the door, went to the lean-to kitchen and came back with the gin bottle and a glass.

'Sit down, Frank Gray,' she said, 'sit down before you fall down.'

He did so, lowering himself into her easy chair next to the stove. She poured him a gin and gave it to him and stood over him while he drank it and refilled his glass.

'What in the name of God's happened to you?' she said.

'It was a mistake.' He drank again, gratefully. 'As you see.'

She gave an incredulous laugh, which jumped for an instant to the edge of hysteria. 'Well, thank God for the stupid bloody military and their stupid bloody mistakes.' Her voice caught and she turned away.

'I have to see her.'

She swung back, aghast. 'Oh, my God, Frank, didn't you know? She's married.'

He held out the glass for her to refill. 'That's why I have to see her.'

'You don't know what you're asking. They only come down from Scotland two days back, from the wedding. They're leaving tomorrow for the honeymoon. You can't—'

'Yes, I can. I want you to go to the house and send her here to me. Now.'

She chewed her lip. 'I don't know if I can do that, Frank.'

'Then I'll go myself.' He swallowed more gin, grimaced. 'I could make quite an entrance, couldn't I? How would the happy home be after that?'

'You wouldn't be that spiteful.'

'Would I not? I've nothing to lose.'

'They're just married, for God's sake. This isn't their fault. No one thought you were even alive. And he's a good man, Frank. Truly he is.'

'I don't give a fuck how good he is.' He shifted in the chair, winced again. 'I'm tired of playing second fiddle, Mrs Rossiter. Tired of waiting, being denied and of denying myself. Not this time, no matter what it costs.'

'You don't hardly know what you're saying, Frank. You're not right. It's your pain making you talk this way, and all you'll do is make more of it, for everyone.'

'Let her choose, then,' he said bitterly. 'Tell her I'm here, and see if she doesn't come to me, no matter that she's wed to such a good man.'

Mrs Rossiter hesitated a moment longer, and then went to the door. She unhooked her coat from the rack and pulled it around her, never taking her eyes off him. She shook her head. 'What's become of you, Frank Gray? Whatever's become of you?'

She stepped outside and closed the door behind her.

112

The gin helped. He sat drinking it while the dying fire in the stove clicked and rustled beside him, and at length the pain slackened. Rain began to fall. It was afternoon, and the daylight was already beginning to dim. He heard the lonely call of a thrush in the wet woods outside, and water slapping through the branches and trickling in culverts.

Finally the hoofbeats came, as he had known they would. She was riding Bonny hard up the track. He heard her rein in directly outside, the horse blowing from the run. Wet leather creaked as she dismounted.

The door was flung open and Grace stood in the light. She kicked the door closed behind her and without a word crossed the room, tossing aside her crop, and knelt beside him, taking him in her arms and kissing his face and neck. Afterwards she leant against him for a long time, breathing deeply, not looking at him and not speaking, her hair against his cheek, her weight against his body. It hurt him but he didn't care.

At last she sat back, holding both his hands in hers. 'Frank,' she said, and her voice was desolate. 'Frank.'

'I wasn't sure I'd find you here, Grace.'

'We only came back to settle things. We leave for Monte Carlo tomorrow.'

'Honeymoon in Monte Carlo.' He heard the acid in his own voice.

She stood up, released his hands. 'Don't sit in judgment on me, Frank. You were dead. Everyone thought so.'

'You didn't wait long, just the same.'

'What was I to wait for? They'd found your body. They'd even found your letter.'

'How long have you known him?'

'A long time. He's a good friend. Oh, Frank, what does all that matter now? The fact is I'm married.' She paused. 'Alec's a fine man.'

'I'd be happier if no one else told me how fine a man he is.'

She shook her head. 'You're angry. I don't blame you.' She pulled up a chair and sat beside him and rested her cool hand against his cheek. 'My God, Frank, you look so bad. What happened to you?'

He caught her hand and kissed it, and she leaned against him and began quietly to weep. 'What are we going to do?' Her voice was broken against his neck. 'Frank, what are we going to do?'

'There's a train,' he said. 'A London train from Alton Station at seven tonight.'

She pulled back and stared at him. Her face was wet and wild. 'How could we do that?'

'How could we not?'

'Frank, I stood before a priest and swore.'

'I don't care about priests.'

'I swore to Alec, too. It will break his heart.'

'I don't care about that, either. I'm free, Grace. Don't you understand? At last, I'm free. Free of the army, and of my own beast – that's what Cavendish used to call it, a beast in the blood that I had to kill before it killed me. Well, I've done that. It's what you always wanted of me, that I should make myself free. You can't tell me now that you're not.'

'Oh, I shall never be free of you, Frank Gray,' she said, in a hollow voice, 'it doesn't matter what I say or what I swear. We'll never be free of one another. But to do this . . .'

'Tonight, Grace. At the station. Seven o'clock.' He reached up for her hands. 'It's right, Grace. Trust me. After all we've been through, would anyone say we don't deserve it?'

She moistened her lips. Her eyes were wide, fearful, appalled. 'Tell me what to do.'

He got to his feet and the pain stabbed him so hard that he had to fight not to gasp aloud with the force of it. He took her shoulders in his hands and looked into her face. 'Where is he now?'

'Alec has business in Guildford. He won't be back until late.'

'All right. Go back to the house now. Pack whatever you need, no more than you can carry. Leave Bonny saddled in the stable yard. At six thirty ride her down to Alton Station. Don't tell anyone you're going out, not even Mrs Rossiter. Do you understand?'

She nodded dumbly.

'Go on, then,' he said.

He stood leaning on the table until he heard Bonny's hoofs thudding and splashing down the wet track. The stove had gone out, and it was chill in the room, but his breath was coming fast and he was sweating. He poured the last of Mrs Rossiter's gin into the glass and tossed it down.

113

He picked his way down the path, leaning heavily on his stick. It was raining hard now, and by the time he arrived at the road it was a silver sheet of water, the roadside ditches brimming and turbid. His wet clothes clung to his back.

He rested by the wall for a long time, then climbed through and began to plod steadily along the shining gravel in the direction of Alton. It was two miles to the station, and he supposed he would have to walk the whole way. He felt faint and nauseous. But it was only four o'clock and if he could just keep going he would make it.

With his head down against the rain he did not see the motor car until he was almost upon it, a bright red contraption with big wheels, pulled half up onto the verge. A man in a long leather coat lay stretched out on the road on his back, heedless of the rain, his head and shoulders under the vehicle. Frank almost tripped over his legs before he saw them. The man was muttering to himself, but he stopped as he saw Frank's boots, and rolled out from beneath the car. His leather coat was sodden, he had grease on his face and his fair hair was pasted against his head, but he was grinning.

'Well, good afternoon to you, sir!' He got to his feet, tossing a couple of spanners jingling behind the seat. 'My, my, you look even wetter than I am, my dear chap, and that's saying something, after an hour under this infernal contraption.'

Frank stood silently in the rain. He didn't want to talk to this cheerful stranger, but could find no way of walking past.

'I say,' the man said, and looked more closely at him, 'you don't look so good, old fellow. Are you unwell?'

'I'm all right.'

'You're pretty wet and cold, I can see that much. Hop in for a minute. At least it's under cover. Perhaps the rain will slacken off.'

'That's kind of you, but—'

'Come along, don't be bashful.' The man took his arm and guided him like an invalid to the passenger side of the car and helped him in. He walked around the car and got in the driver's side. 'Where are you off to on a filthy afternoon like this? And on foot?'

Frank hesitated. 'Alton.'

'Well, that's only a couple of hundred yards around that bend, but I can give you a lift, for what it's worth. I'll give the old girl a quick swing in a minute and I'm fairly sure she'll start. Temperamental old buses, these Levassors. Time I changed her for something more up-to-date, really. Something British.' His light blue eyes registered Frank's khaki tunic beneath his coat. 'Military man?'

'Discharged.'

'In that case, I'm proud to be able to give you a ride. It doesn't look to me as if you should be walking at all, if you don't mind my saying so. Did you come from Cumver direction?'

Frank looked at him, suddenly alert. 'I came past there, yes.'

'Pity I didn't see you earlier. That's where I'm from. I could have picked you up. Mind you, if I had, you'd have been sitting here waiting for me to fix the old girl.'

The man laughed, but then quite suddenly stopped, and looked at Frank again, his eyes narrowing.

Frank said, 'Do you work at Cumver?'

'Yes, that's it.' The man glanced out of the silver windscreen as if nervously, and then looked back again. 'I work there, yes. Chauffeur, you see.'

'You'd know Lord Strathair, then.'

'Pretty well.' The tension was plain in the other man's voice now. 'Yes, pretty well.'

Frank stared ahead down the road. 'I hear he's a good man.'

'Did you hear that?' The man smiled, as if sadly. 'That's gratifying. I only hear that he tries to be.'

'And recently married. Is that right, too?'

'It is. To the most . . . wonderful girl.'

Frank nodded. 'And does Lord Strathair love his new bride, do you think?'

The man turned in his seat to face him. 'He loves her to distraction, old chap. He'd die for her. He'd do anything to make her happy, anything at all. She's not always been happy, I know; but Lord Strathair would see to it that she never has another day of sadness. He'd want you to know that. He'd want everyone to know that.'

The rain drummed on the roof. They both became aware at the same moment that the driver had placed his hand on Frank's arm as he spoke, and now he gently withdrew it.

'I'll walk,' Frank said.

He stepped out of the car. The other man did not call him back. Frank trudged on in the rain. After a moment he heard a crank handle being swung, and behind him an engine coughed and died, coughed and died.

114

Frank plodded around the last bend of the road and saw the railway bridge ahead, and beyond it the station yard. The pain was lancing him now, forcing him to limp, and he was at the limits of his strength when he dragged himself up the steps and under the shelter of the station roof. The stationmaster emerged from the waiting room as he sank onto a bench.

'There's a fire going inside, sir. You look as if you need it.'

'Thank you.'

But Frank stayed where he was, too weak to move, trying to catch his breath. The stationmaster hovered nearby, curious or concerned. Frank recognised him vaguely: Manners, he thought. Some such name. Well, Mr Manners would not recognise him. Not now. And soon it wouldn't matter anyway.

'Where would you be off to, then, sir?'

'London.'

'I'll fetch your ticket out to you.'

'I shall need two. First Class.'

'Very good, sir.'

'Is the train on time?'

'Seven o'clock to the minute, sir, I've just checked. You've an hour or more to wait, though. You might be more comfortable in the waiting room.'

When Frank still didn't move Mr Manners disappeared into his office. In a few moments he returned with the tickets. Frank paid him for them.

'Don't I know you, sir?' Mr Manners asked.

'I don't think so.'

'I don't ordinarily forget a face. Used to be a lad up at Cumver Hall looked a lot like you. Name of Gray. Wouldn't be a relative, would you, sir? If you don't mind my asking, that is.'

'No.' Frank got to his feet, hoping to shake the man off. 'I've never been here before.'

'My mistake, then.' Mr Manners chuckled. 'Just as well, really. The lad I had in mind was no better than he ought to be. Used to be sweet on Miss Grace, the daughter of the house. And him nothing but a stable hand. Her father had to send her away once, and they said even that didn't keep them apart.'

Frank stood with one hand against the wall, supporting himself, trying not to listen.

'Ah, but if these things are meant to be,' Mr Manners said, 'they're meant to be, don't you agree, sir? And young Miss Grace has found herself a diamond of a man to wed, just this last week, in fact. So she made the right choice in the end, eh?'

Around the bend of the road a red motor car came clattering, blowing a little blue smoke but running strongly, with water spraying from its big wheels. Frank caught a glimpse of a white scarf and the flash of reflected light from a pair of goggles. In a moment the car was gone, but behind him a train pulled into the platform, the thumping of its engine smothering the sound of his own harsh breathing. Doors clumped. Smoke and steam flattened against the wooden roof and came mushrooming down.

'Just one minute, sir, if you'll excuse me.' Mr Manners stepped onto the platform, looked down the length of the train. He put a silver whistle in his mouth and raised a green flag.

The engine's beat lifted again, pistons banging, and the train began to move. Frank stepped past Manners and swung himself up onto the running board, hauling at a door handle.

'Wait, sir! This ain't your train! 'Tis the wrong direction entirely!'

Frank wrenched the door open and half-fell into a compartment raw with tobacco smoke and the smell of wet clothes. Someone grabbed his arm and dragged him into a seat; someone else shut the swinging door. People were speaking to him, anxious or admonishing. Someone asked what he thought he was doing.

He didn't answer. He crouched in the corner, hunched over his pain, until the voices were quiet again. When he opened his eyes, his face was close to the window, and wet winter fields were gathering pace as they slid past.

Epilogue

31 December 1898

Frank walked down the drive between the poplars. The sky was like wet canvas and the trunks as black as iron. The house looked dark and shuttered. He wondered if the place could be empty, until he remembered that the household would be in mourning. He paused at the bend in the track and leaned on his stick. With his head down he did not at first see the woman in the black dress who had come out of the house and now stood in the middle of the drive, observing him.

'Good afternoon, Corporal,' she said.

He looked up, straightened his shoulders. 'Mrs Freeman.'

She stood a moment longer, as if absorbing the changes in him. 'Oh, young Achilles. How are the mighty fallen.' She walked quickly over and took his arm, and when she spoke it was with a throb in her voice. 'Come along, Corporal. Come along, now.'

She led him in through the hall, half-supporting him, barking orders at the servants as she went. Her strength and authority seemed to take away what was left of his own, and Frank allowed himself to be helped, hearing a gasp or two of sympathy from the maids as they passed. He guessed they were remembering the healthy young soldier of last year. He wondered what he must look like now, and was glad there were no mirrors in the hallway.

Mrs Freeman guided him down the corridor and into Cavendish's study. A fire blazed in the hearth. She ushered him to the armchair he had last occupied almost twelve months earlier and he sank into it. He looked around him. Cavendish's books crowded the shelves and his Indian and Arab curios filled the mahogany cabinets. His vivid map of Egypt and the Sudan was still pinned to the easel.

'I've had the fire lit in here every day this winter,' Mrs Freeman said. 'It comforted me somehow, as if I were preparing for Freddie to come home.' She poured two brandies at the sideboard, freshened them with soda from a siphon, and handed one to him. She sat down in the chair on the far side of the fireplace. 'Foolish, isn't it? Since we were children

I only ever saw him for a matter of weeks every few years, and then he couldn't wait to leave. But now . . .'

Frank found that he was sweating; his hand trembled as he held the glass. She sat watching him quietly.

She said. 'You were together, were you not? At the end?'

He lifted his eyes to her. 'Mrs Freeman, there's not a day goes by—'

She held up her hand. 'Corporal, I haven't a shadow of doubt that you did everything you could for Freddie. How could you not? You loved him.'

Frank stared into the fire.

Mrs Freeman nursed her drink. 'They told me that you had died at Omdurman and that Freddie was missing. I was . . . prostrated with grief for some little while, I have to confess. Probably you find that hard to imagine.'

'No, ma'am. I don't.'

'It is such a balm to me that you at least survived.' She took a deep breath. 'Well, and shall you make a full recovery, Corporal? You look shockingly reduced at present, I must say.'

'I'm stronger every day, ma'am. Though at present that's not saying a great deal.'

'You must of course stay here as long as you wish. I should like you to regard Faldonside as your home. You have been through a great deal, I can see that.' She looked steadily at him. 'And are you altered by your experiences, Corporal?'

He held her gaze. 'I believe I am, ma'am.'

She nodded. 'I believe so too.'

She got up, took both their drinks and topped them up, returned to her chair. She brought back with her a large white envelope which she held in her lap, stroking the thick paper with her thumb. Frank could see his own name written across it in blue ink. The handwriting was Cavendish's.

'Freddie left this with me last year, before the two of you went to the Sudan.' She handed it to him. 'Open it, Corporal. I already know more or less what it contains.'

He tore open the thick envelope and pulled out a sheet of cream notepaper.

My dear Frank:

I have a sense that I shall not survive this campaign. If you are reading this, then I am proven right. But by the same token, you at least must have come through, I hope unscathed. Strange, but I felt that you would.

Harriet will explain what these documents mean. In brief, I have settled a considerable sum of money on you from my estate. It will not make you rich, but it will be sufficient for the purpose I have in mind. I hope you will use it to further your career in the Army, as an officer in a respectable regiment, where I believe your talents will be put to best use.

But however you choose to employ this money, it is my dearest wish that you enter the service of this grand, brutal, ramshackle, tottering Empire of ours. It will need you, Frank. It will need every decent and courageous man our old country can produce, to tip the scales against the greed and bigotry of the other kind of Englishman we spawn in such numbers.

But there is more between us than this, Frank, is there not? And if you are reading this, then you will have learned at last where we met so long ago. What am I to say to you? I was a different man then. That is not an excuse – there can be no excuses. But perhaps it shows that a man can change himself, and can turn away from the path of disappointment and destruction, and build something from his life after all. If I have been able to persuade you of this much, then I shall sleep peacefully.

God bless you, Frank. As I said to you last night by the study fire, I never had a son of my own. If I had, I could not have hoped for a finer one.

Frederick John Cavendish

Frank folded the letter carefully. The fire blazed up, flashing on his brandy glass and on the brass fire irons. A branch scratched on the window and he looked up. Outside, the last day of the old year was fading into evening.

About the Author

T. D. Griggs was born in London and has lived and worked on four continents. He holds British and Australian nationality. A professional business writer with an international client base, his first novel was published ten years ago. His most recent work includes *The Warning Bell*, written under the pseudonym Tom Macaulay. He has degrees in English and archaeology, and now lives with his wife Jenny in Oxford, UK. To find out more, visit www.tdgriggs.co.uk.